The Ravanmark Saga
Book Four

I0630645

Acts
of the
Redeemer

Sandra Miller

Acts

of the

Redeemer

Acts of the Redeemer

Published by Onda Mountain Books

Cover Design
By Karri Klawiter, www.artbykarri.com

Cover Art
© Angela Harburn | Dreamstime.com
© Simone Gatterwe | Dreamstime.com
© Lane Erickson | Dreamstime.com

Discover other titles by Sandra Miller at
www.sandra-miller.com

Sandra Miller

Chapter One
THE END OF THE DARK ALLIANCE

wenty-five years ago, Archford Estate had been a wondrous place, glistening like the jewel it was — the pride of the holding that was the reigning couple's favorite. Baron Prubard had never understood the reasons for the favoritism — if reasons actually existed, and he was spitefully sure that they did not — but the favoritism itself was obvious and undeniable. Prubard himself had been there all those years ago, celebrating the occasion of the birth of the duke's son, forcing a smile in a room full of people that he assumed, like himself, had better things to do. He had excused himself to the sumptuously flowering courtyard, seeking escape from the false smiles of nobility in the misty moonlight air, heavy with the scents of roses. He remembered it well.

But now, that same courtyard was unrecognizable in the brief glance that he raked across it. He moved his bulk across the remnants of the place uncomfortably — nothing felt familiar here. The raging fire that had burned through fifteen years ago had left devastation behind, and two months of use as a test site for Lord Malrec's miracle bombs had destroyed most of what was left. Blackened, jagged walls that were only half standing surrounded the yard, and where anything grew in the courtyard itself, it was only scrubby weeds. The place felt dark and solemn, almost sacred, like a mausoleum. It was unnerving, even for a man of Prubard's stalwart constitution, to see how utterly the mighty had fallen. He was tempted to an

7

unkind, jealous pleasure — and yet, he could not silence the niggling voice in the back of his mind, the voice that said this barren desolation was more than justice.

It was an omen.

He tried again to push the voice aside, and strode deeper into the ruined courtyard. He had no time for ridiculous notions like omens tonight. Tonight the ruins bustled with activity; tonight Archford Estate held more people than it had seen since the duke and duchess died. Tonight Baron Prubard and his forces launched their final assault on the Great Palace, and the courtyard of Archford Estate was their staging area. It amused Prubard that the place the Crown had once so favored would now play such a part in its ultimate downfall. He chuckled, but kept moving. He had no time for amusement either. Important things were already afoot.

In the southern half of the courtyard his men readied themselves for war, sharpening weapons and donning armor. Near them stood two giant paintings, held on low, stable easels specially built for this occasion — when dozens of men charged through the paintings in rapid succession, there could be no mistakes, no slipping canvases or collapsing easels. The paintings were open, just like every other painting in the courtyard; thanks to Princess Delline's new everlasting gloss, they did not need an artist with them to keep the portals active.

Prubard studied the paintings, trying to gauge the situation at the Great Palace, but had to abandon the effort as futile. It was too dark — one painting looked out into the inner ward, where the light of a single, partial moon did little to lift the gloom. The other depicted the antechamber behind the Great Hall, where the situation was scarcely better. The single torch burned as always — the king's emergency escape couldn't be left in utter blackness, after all — but it carved little more than a flickering fraction from the darkness of the old stone room. It felt like looking into a tomb.

Baron Prubard sighed. Again with the omens. This he did not need.

Lieutenant Dann hovered at Prubard's meaty shoulder, staring intently at the paintings as though he could discern some hidden meaning there through sheer force of will. The baron turned on him in frustration—if he himself could make nothing out in the darkness, what made Dann think he would fare better?

"Are the men clear on their orders? There can be no mistakes tonight."

Some of his frustration must have spilled into his tone. The lieutenant took a step back, clearing his throat. "Yes, my Lord. The main force prepares here for their assault upon the Great Hall. They will travel through the painting to the inner ward, and attack the hall once they have all assembled." He waved an arm at the milling horde of men closest to them. "Would my Lord care to address them?"

"What? Why in the world should I do that?"

Something shifted behind Dann's eyes, something that made Prubard think his lieutenant had expected just that sort of response. "They are your men, my Lord. It is customary for a commander to address his troops before leading them into battle."

"Leading them into...now see here, Dann, I have no intention of doing any such thing, and I'm frankly shocked you would even suggest it. Are you that eager to be rid of me?"

"My Lord!" Lieutenant Dann sounded scandalized. He glanced over his shoulder, as if making sure the men hadn't overheard. "You must not say such things. You will upset your men."

"Are my men such frightened rabbits as that? They know their duty; they should be quite capable of executing it."

"That isn't how things work." Dann hissed the words between gritted teeth. "My Lord knows it isn't. You cannot ask these men to do something you won't do yourself."

"I should bloody well say I can," Prubard said. "What's the point of being a baron otherwise?"

"Technically, my Lord is not a baron any longer," Dann said cheekily, then barreled on before Prubard could respond. "But that isn't even the point. You are their leader, and they need you. It is your duty to lead them."

"Duty," Prubard snorted. He wore his most fearsome scowl, but he knew this battle was already lost. He would rather have done anything else, but he couldn't risk losing the palace simply because he wasn't there to take it. "I don't suppose you've forgotten your part in this, in your haste to see me do mine?"

"Of course not, my Lord." Dann's offense was barely detectable in his tone, but Prubard *did* detect it, and hearing it gave him a mean sort of satisfaction. "I have separated fifty men into a strike force. They are preparing to use the painting into the antechamber. I have instructed them not to begin until after your force begins their attack. I will lead them through the antechamber into the Great Hall, and we will attack the defenders from behind."

"Splendid," Prubard said with real satisfaction. "They will never expect it. Be sure that the strike force carries bows, Lieutenant, and bring the flaming arrows. There will be archers up in the balconies that must be handled."

"Yes, my Lord."

Prubard turned his back on Lieutenant Dann and stomped his massive bulk over to the north end of the courtyard, trusting the lieutenant to follow with his armor. Prubard hated armor. He felt overheated and uncomfortable at the best of times, but when he strapped his fleshy folds into layers of unyielding, confining leather and metal armor, he could hardly breathe.

Still, he hated the idea of dying in battle even more than he hated armor, so he held out his arms and allowed Dann to squash him into it, away from the men where at least he wouldn't be seen.

"What else?" Prubard demanded, eager to distract himself from his discomfort. "How are things progressing for the others tonight?"

"As well as can be expected so far, my Lord. All's quiet in Castle Glennayre. Lord Diabon gathers his men in Westmore Forest as we speak."

Prubard scowled into the paintings, displayed in a neat line on their easels. It was true, Castle Glennayre was quiet — *too* quiet to suit the baron. Lord Malrec had been so sure the king and his friends would go to the castle. What if he was wrong? What if the Great Hall was the real trap? He muttered unpleasantly under his breath, scanning the paintings for some clue. Of course the tower bedroom was Talent-proofed, so they couldn't observe there — and that was the very location where Malrec and the others would be, if they were in the castle at all. The study sat empty, polished furniture gleaming smugly in the flickering firelight, and nothing moved in the near-darkness of the cavernous library.

"Does something trouble my Lord?" the lieutenant inquired mildly.

"It's too quiet," Prubard snapped, annoyed to realize he had just been thinking it was silent as death, "and too dark. How can we be sure they are even in there?"

He knew he spoke too soon — he'd seen Arch-Prince Raman charging into the room as the words formed on his lips, watched the silly boy hacking into the dummies gathered there with a ferocity that clearly demonstrated he'd bought the ruse. Prubard knew where all of this must lead, hadn't he played his part in planning it?

Scarcely had the thought formed in his mind than the library exploded into a great rolling ball of flame. Prubard had known this was supposed to happen — expected it, even — and still he couldn't quite suppress a gasp of surprise.

"There," Lieutenant Dann said, holding up his hand to shield his eyes. The conflagration rumbled in their ears like thunder; he had to raise his voice to be heard. "Exactly as my Lord predicted all along."

Prubard smothered a curse, chewing on the inside of his cheek. *He* had predicted no such thing—Lord Malrec had, and it was a bit galling to see everything going off exactly as the arrogant prig had said it would. He should have been happy to see it; they all stood to gain immensely from this night. But he couldn't rid himself of the nagging certainty that something was wrong.

He looked at the other paintings—the broad, sweeping views of the field at the foot of the ridge where the Great Palace's army kept watch. The men there were casual and relaxed, joking as they tended to their camp, apparently unaware of anything untoward in the forest.

As they should be, he thought, frowning. It didn't mean anything was wrong. It certainly didn't suggest that Lord Diabon's force was not there at all. They would attack, and they would carry the advantage of surprise when they did.

He didn't know whether he felt better or worse when he saw Lord Diabon and his men ride out of Westmore Forest. It was clear Lord Diabon had not expected such a large force, which Prubard found curious. Everyone knew the army defending the Great Palace was enormous. He'd privately thought Diabon quite brave for accepting the mission to engage them—foolish, no doubt, a sobering reminder of the dangers of taking one's duty too seriously —but brave.

Diabon directed his men, sitting straight and tall in the saddle, his black hair and beard shining in the moonlight, and for one brief, glorious moment Prubard believed they might actually stand a chance. Their sole purpose was distraction anyway; Lord Malrec seemed to believe the palace army might otherwise help defend the Great Hall. Prubard didn't see how that would even be logistically possible, but he didn't make a habit of arguing with Malrec when he was sending other men on perilous missions with little hope of success.

Then Lord Diabon bailed off the horse and ran from the field of battle, alone and on foot. Prubard swore under his breath, trying to figure out how this cowardly desertion might affect his own campaign.

"My Lord! My Lord, you must see this at once — things go badly for Lord Malrec, I fear."

Prubard spun to face Lieutenant Dann, who was standing horrified in front of the painting of the art room in Castle Glennayre. They'd had high hopes for this painting — Prubard hoped to carry news of the death of the King of Ravanmark into the Great Hall to demoralize their opponents, and he hoped to see that death here.

But he could already tell there would be no victory for them at Castle Glennayre. The only one in the room with a sword drawn was Arch-Prince Raman — how in the Seven Hells had he even survived the library? — and it was clear that Lord Malrec was on the run. Never, not once in all the months he'd spent at Castle Glennayre, had Prubard seen fear in Malrec's eyes. And yet it shone clearly there now, as bright as the flames still burning in the library.

Watching the scene that unfolded in the art room felt like watching the world crumble around him. Lord Malrec fell, gutted like an animal on Raman's blade, and the others had the key to the Collar of Silence.

Even Lord Malrec's damned apprentice had betrayed them, in the end.

Prubard wasn't sure what to make of that. Creft had to know that he and his forces were in the courtyard, that he was watching — why didn't the boy fear retribution? And what should Prubard do with those forces now?

Creft was watching the same locations as Prubard. He must have known about Diabon's desertion. And now, allowing Malrec to die — clearly Creft did not feel that Lord Malrec was the leader they needed. He had left Diabon to die, or to run like a rabbit until death found him.

But he hadn't turned on Prubard.

Fine, then — if Creft felt that Prubard was the best shot they had to win this thing, who was he to disagree? He had not been used to good advantage during this entire fiasco, and he could not deny that he would make a better king than Lord Malrec and Lord Diabon put together.

So be it, then. They could still pull this thing out of the fire, and when they did, he would be Prubard, King of Ravanmark.

And his first royal act would be to appoint Creft as grand chancellor.

♫

Baron Prubard turned his back on the failures in the paintings, drew his impressive bulk to its full height, and strode to the other end of the courtyard with every shred of dignity he possessed. These were only failures, after all, when viewed through the lens of expectation. In the eyes of history, these would be the events necessary to clear the way for Ravanmark's most celebrated king, Prubard. He still dreaded this attack, would have rather done nearly anything else but actually fight. But it was plain to him that an opening had been created this night, and the crown would fall to the man who won the Great Hall.

He would not allow that man to be anyone but himself.

"The time is at hand," he said, conscious of the gravity of the moment. "We attack!"

No one cheered, which annoyed him. The moment would have been so much grander if the men had applauded.

Ah, well, he would add that in when he told the story later. For now, he joined the main force of his men, moving through the painting into the quiet darkness of the inner ward. He held his breath, hoping against hope that he would be all in one working piece when he made it to the other side.

There was not a person in sight. Not a single sound broke the stillness outside the Great Hall, which suited him perfectly. The men moved quickly and quietly into a narrow formation to charge the big double doors.

That, Prubard had to admit, was idiocy. Had this been left to him, he would simply have used a bomb to destroy the wall and any of the king's men who happened to be too close to it, and let his forces deal with whoever was left. But Malrec had forbidden it—he intended to be crowned in the Great Hall just as generations of kings had before him, and he would not hear of any damage there. It was sentimental rot, and Prubard had told him so, but Malrec was obstinate, and he was the only one who knew how to make the bombs. So here they were, stuck with the plans of a dead man, squeezing into tight line formations to get them through the doors as quickly as possible.

Prubard pushed the annoying thoughts aside and rushed with his men in the main charge through the doors. He didn't hold with leading charges—what possible sense could there be in putting the most valuable man of them all right in the front, where he could easily be skewered by their enemies? No, Prubard came in at the back of the formation, well-insulated from the opposing forces, and it looked to him like that was a good thing. The Great Palace had clearly expected an attack like this, and the Great Hall was heavily defended.

Even so, it looked like his men were having some success. They were fresh, eager to attack, and going strong. He couldn't guess how long the defenders might have been in position, waiting for invaders without any real idea when they might arrive. The Dark Alliance forces cut a swath of destruction into the hall, and Prubard smiled grimly to himself, imagining the ambush soon to come from the antechamber on the far side of the room. The Great Hall would be his before sunrise. He drew his own sword and waddled into the fray, moving toward the clear target presented by an unsuspecting man's back.

"Watch yourselves!" The high shout came from the same door he had just come through, and it shouldn't have had a hope of being heard over the sounds of battle filling the room. But somehow it carried clearly across the hall, and he knew that had to mean Talent. All at once he felt a good deal less confident. "There are more men about to attack from behind you!"

Blistering anger choked Prubard, and he spun to face the door. Lady Alannys stood there, wearing a brigandine and carrying her cursed sword, as if she actually intended to fight. Her hair, still too short to be ladylike, barely cleared the bottom of her helmet, and her boots were clearly too big. She looked more like a squire who had wandered in by mistake than a soldier, but she was there, and she showed no inclination to leave.

And the damned woman was trumpeting his plans to the enemy, ruining his best chance for success.

King Dorramon charged in behind her, sword drawn, looking insufferably noble in his royal armor. Eyes ablaze, he barreled straight into the hall to take up the fight, slashing grimly without a glance to the left or the right. Arch-Prince Raman was scarcely more than a blur behind him, fiercely wielding a blade Prubard knew had already tasted blood that night. How much more blood would it carry, before this was over? Their determination was exactly the sort of thing the baron did not want the palace forces to see.

Incandescent fury clouded his vision, white-hot and brilliant. The woman's timing could not have been worse; the palace forces on the dais turned just as his men began their charge from the antechamber. Like a blighted idiot, Lieutenant Dann led the advance, with a raised sword and a war cry that started out fearsome, but ended in a pitiful gurgle as he slumped to the ground, gutted on Captain Grayble's blade. Before their ill-fated ambush even had a chance to begin, the strike force was gone, slaughtered like animals, bleeding and dying on the big dais.

Damn her, damn her, *damn her!* Prubard had not even managed to come to terms with the sudden, brutal loss of his strike force before he heard a new, chilling, sound — the sound he dreaded above all others in the world.

The sound of singing.

But it wasn't just one voice, or even two — there were tens of voices, ringing high through the vaulted ceilings. All around him, men began to panic, to clutch at their ears. One by one, they began to fall.

Only his men, though. The palace forces, he realized with ire, wore helmets with padding in the ears. Seven Hells! Why hadn't they *foreseen* this?

He pulled his own leather helmet down low over his ears, muffling the diabolical sound as much as he could. The woman wasn't singing — this time — but he knew somehow, some way, she was responsible for the abomination dropping his men like flies. He wouldn't live to leave this place, none of his men would.

But he would by the demented song of Soth himself make it long enough to take that damned woman with him when he went.

♬

Alannys had been in a fight or two since coming to Ravanmark; she knew how it could mess with her sense of time.

And yet she wasn't at all prepared for the sensory overload of battle — everything seemed to speed up, and slow down, all at once. She moved in a numb sort of slow motion, and there was so much to hear around her that her ears went into overdrive. She heard everything, but none of it made sense to her. She fought in a dazed delirium, focusing only on the man in front of her at each moment, concentrating only on surviving until the next moment, the next attacker. She wasn't dead yet, and she was aware of other palace forces continuing to fight around her, and she supposed for the moment, that was enough.

But then the Singari began to sing, and that was the moment the tide of battle really began to turn. Of course warning Grayble's men of the ambush had been a big help —Creft's treachery had served them well, in the end. But when the singers started, rapidly opening up into a three-part harmony that gave her goosebumps—*that* was the moment she could look around the hall and see that the palace forces really were going to win this thing.

She pulled her helmet down to better cover her ears, looking frantically around the hall-turned-battlefield. Dorramon and Raman had known about the singers, of course, but she was pretty sure they hadn't thought about that before charging into the fray. There was too much to see—she scanned the hall with a sort of tunnel vision, catching glimpses of clarity here and there, aware that she was missing almost everything in the vast blur of motion around her.

And that was how Baron Prubard nearly took her head off before she even knew he was there.

♬

Baron Prubard bore down on Alannys, his face red and his eyes glinting in the torchlight. He wielded a short sword with a lot more competence than she would have expected. He was no cloaked swordsman, but he looked utterly mad, and belatedly she realized her danger.

Alannys jerked Songstrike up and managed to turn his blade, narrowly avoiding being skewered. The ancient blade glowed in her grasp, soaking up her fears and radiating them back out in a bright blue light that she might have expected to give the baron pause. It didn't stop him, though, or slow him down; Prubard kept right on advancing, slashing furiously at her faster than she could follow; she dodged and parried more from instinct than thought. Every blow she blocked jarred deep in her wrists and shoulders, and still he kept advancing, driving her back against the stone wall.

"Just one scratch," he muttered, over and over. "Any tiny scratch."

There were battles all over the enormous hall; Alannys

could see a surprising number of them from her spot against the wall. She could see archers on the main floor, sending arrows high into the balconies. All around her men fought for their lives, just as she did. This battle was no more important than any of those, she knew that. It was hard to remember it, though, at a time like this.

"Baron Prubard!" she cried. "Stop this madness. You can't win this!"

"Perhaps not," he said, sounding so calm that she thought he really must be insane. "But if I go to the Seven Hells tonight, I can take you with me, *my Lady.*"

Alannys held Songstrike out in front of her, in a posture as close to Ready position as she could manage, crammed up against the wall. The blade flared brilliant, bright blue, but the baron still didn't seem to notice. "I wouldn't be too sure of that," she said, and drew breath to sing.

Baron Prubard swung his sword back as though he intended to lop off her head, when suddenly his eyes bulged and the blade dropped from his hands. Alannys held her position, eyeing him warily, trying to figure out what had just happened.

"Why is it," came a familiar voice from behind Prubard's great bulk, "that someone is always trying to kill you?"

Alannys blew out a great sigh of relief, and wondered, why *was* it that someone was always trying to kill her? It was an interesting question, for reasons she was not prepared to ponder while the fighting continued around her.

She peeked around Prubard to find black hair, damp with exertion, caramel skin smeared with blood, and dark eyes that sparkled at her as if the rest didn't matter. Chen had the baron's arm twisted up high behind his back, and he was keeping it there despite the bigger man's struggles.

"Bless you, Chen," she said, and her voice broke as though she might cry.

"Yes," Baron Prubard sneered, shattering the moment, "bless you, boy. You are going to need it. Unhand me, you miserable Singari mutt, so I can run you through!"

"Ah, how can I refuse such a polite request?" Chen said, winking at Alannys.

Alannys took Songstrike's grip in both hands, raised it high over her head, and clubbed the butt end of the sword into Prubard's leather helmet.

The baron collapsed to the floor in an unconscious heap of fleshy folds and strained armor. Chen backed up, brushing his hands together, shaking his head. "That man is disgusting."

"Tell me about it." Alannys jammed Songstrike back into its sheath, turning when she heard shouts behind her.

Singari shouts.

Her blood suddenly ran cold with a kind of fear she hadn't felt during the entire battle, not even when Prubard had nearly decapitated her. Three Singari were running toward them through the wreckage littering the hall-turned-battlefield, but her eyes locked onto the bulky form of Tor. And in that moment everything else faded; the shouts of the Singari, the celebrations of the palace army, Chen grasping at her arm. Everything she could see or hear, all of her perceptions narrowed to the bleeding form sprawled in Tor's arms, a whittled flute dangling from limp fingers.

It was Eleana.

♫

"...and she hasn't moved since."

"Is she still breathing?"

"Shut it, you! Of course she is. Could've been worse. Least it wasn't a flaming arrow."

"But what do we do now? She should never have been allowed here, girl's too young!"

The voices fretted and bickered around Alannys where she knelt on the floor, gripping Eleana's cool hand in her own. She didn't know or care who spoke, and she couldn't make herself care what they said. The voices carried on, oblivious, some looking to Chen, others to her, all wanting guidance.

Alannys couldn't guide them, not now. What could she tell them, what could she do, that could possibly matter next to this? She and her friends had dumped the songs in her room, and come to head off the ambush...they believed they had saved the day. She had nothing left for them now, no words, no feeling at all except despair.

Chen didn't look much better, sitting across from her, clutching Eleana's other hand as if he could will her better by the force of his grip. The rest of them could have ceased to exist for all the notice he gave them—indeed, Alannys realized suddenly, he might actually *be* completely unaware of them. Chen had always been singularly bad at handling emergencies.

It was on her, then—the others couldn't save Eleana, and Chen wasn't in control enough to try. She steadied herself and pulled in a deep breath, preparing to sing.

"Not here." The heavy hand that fell on her shoulder startled her, and she jumped even as she recognized the voice as Captain Grayble's. "Not now."

She craned her head around to look at him, and found him watching her with such sympathy in his eyes, she nearly lost it and burst into tears right there. "But Captain, I have to...she can't..."

"I know." His gruff voice was unusually gentle, as if he spoke only for her, but his eyes roamed the big hall, aware of everyone who was watching. "We will do everything we can for her. But you must not sing—not here, not now. I swear to you one of the king's own master healers will tend to her. And you may all sing all you want—once she is safely away from here." He stepped nimbly around Alannys and scooped Eleana off the stone floor into his arms.

That got Chen's attention. "What are you doing?" he demanded, looking at them like he had just realized there were other people around. "Where do you think you're taking her?"

"To the keep." Grayble's tone was utterly devoid of impatience, or hostility; he seemed to understand their shock. "We're summoning a healer for her now."

"A healer," Chen echoed, glancing at the fretting Singari gathered around them. "But we have a healer. Nashara…"

The captain was already shaking his head. "Your healer isn't here, Chen. And you don't have time to bring someone from camp. She won't make it that long."

Alannys swallowed hard and grabbed Chen's arm convulsively. "Chen—let him take her. You've got to let the healers get started. You can't risk…" She choked on what she knew should come next, and fell silent.

Chen bit his lip, and nodded. "All right. But I'm going with her."

"Of course," Grayble said at once. "Follow me."

Chen threw one last indecipherable glance at Alannys, then turned to follow the captain's departing back.

Alannys floundered for a moment, trying to think of something appropriate to say to the Singari around her. Finally she concluded that there *was* nothing she could say, so she ducked her head and turned to follow Grayble as well. She couldn't imagine being anywhere else, not now.

Strong hands caught Alannys by the shoulders and spun her around. She found herself looking into Dorramon's pale, anxious face. "Alannys, are you all right? They told me Prubard attacked you. Did he harm you?"

"No—no, I'm fine."

Raman stepped out from behind him, pushing at Prubard's unconscious bulk with his boot, and sheathed his sword. "Chen did this?"

Alannys smiled awkwardly. "Well…he had some help."

His glance flicked across her face, then back to the ex-baron. "Still...I wouldn't have guessed he had it in him. Then again..." He looked at her again, frowning. "He bears watching, I think. One day he may surprise us all. Don't you think, Dorr?"

"Absolutely," Dorramon said immediately.

Alannys frowned at him. "You have no idea what we're talking about, do you? Are you all right?"

"Of course. It's you we should worry about—when I saw that group of Singari around you I thought...thank the Muses you are unharmed." He wobbled on his feet. Just as she grabbed his arm to steady him, he turned away, making a visible effort to stand straighter and raising his voice. "Raman! Help me restrain the ex-baron."

Alannys frowned at his back, unconvinced. He still looked unsteady to her, and his skin stood out stark and white in the light of the hall. Looking at him reminded her of the too-cool feeling of Eleana's hand in her own, and she shivered.

Then she looked down, and saw blood smearing her hand where she'd held his arm.

It wasn't her blood.

"Dorramon!" She looked up just in time to catch him when he fell backwards towards her, unconscious.

♪

Everything became a sheer blur of terror after that. Alannys couldn't separate her tangled impressions into anything that made sense—there were too many voices, shrieking with fear or shouting advice she couldn't decipher, too many people grabbing for her attention. They couldn't reach her; her panic was a wall around her, isolating her.

And yet she was aware of the seconds flying past her— her frazzled mind made note of each one as she stood there, running in frantic mental circles, trying to come to grips with a reality she did not wish to face.

"Clear out, you lot!" Raman's furious roar was the first thing to breach the wall around her, the first thing to pierce the curious numbness that insulated her. "The king needs space!"

He did, Alannys realized, and he needed a lot more than that. He was sagging in her arms, but she had somehow kept him off of the floor. She straightened, securing her hold under his arms, and nodded to Raman. "Help me—I can't lift him alone."

If Raman hesitated, she never saw it. He hefted Dorramon's legs at the knees, and between the two of them they carried the unconscious king out of the Great Hall, leaving the Royal Guards to restore some sense of order there.

She shuffled backwards across the dark inner ward, struggling to keep the head of the country aloft, her soft soled boots scuffing along the ground. With all of his armor, he was surprisingly heavy, and the work was harder than she would have expected. The sounds of battle from the palace gate encouraged her to hurry, as much as she was able. Dorramon never twitched, never moved a muscle. Worry gnawed at her like a live thing, sinking icy teeth deep into her bones.

"What's...wrong with him?" she panted. "What happened?"

Raman shook his head, his own worry putting lines in his face that hadn't been there before. "I don't know. He can't have been hurt that badly—I don't know."

The keep was only across the courtyard of the inner ward—not that far, Alannys knew, but she was beginning to wonder all the same if she would make it there, when movement at the corner of her vision caught her attention. A man ran from the barracks of the Royal Guard, headed for the Great Hall with scarcely a glance in their direction.

"Guard!" Raman barked. "A little help, if you please."

The guard veered their direction. "Certainly, my Lord." He pulled open the door to the vestibule of the keep and held it while they shuffled inside.

"Thank you," Raman said, "Ensign...?"

"Wermal," the guard replied, keeping pace with them but moving briskly, as though they went too slowly to suit him. "Ensign Wermal, at your service. It's my pleasure to assist you however I can."

Alannys noticed that despite his words, he never moved to help her. She hoped that meant maybe she was hiding her struggle better than she had thought.

"Thank you," Raman said again. "Perhaps you could give Lady Alannys a hand—she seems to be having some trouble."

So much for that idea. The only thing more embarrassing than having her weakness called out was the way Wermal completely ignored the arch-prince's request —he might as well have not spoken at all. The guard hurried ahead to get the next door without acknowledging her in the slightest.

Alannys supposed she should just thank her lucky stars that the king's chambers were on the first floor of the keep. She didn't know how she managed to stand there, gasping and heaving, while Wermal opened the room for them. Still he ignored her, but between Raman and herself, they somehow got Dorramon stretched out on his own bed.

"Imagine that." Wermal's voice came from somewhere behind them, snickering and unpleasant. "His Majesty will be upset indeed, to find that he missed a personal bedchamber visit from the king's whore. Perhaps you could be troubled to wait for him to wake up? I could bring round a few of my mates, to pass your time."

Before Alannys could blink, the Royal Guard was pinned against the wall, with Raman's sword at his throat. "Would you care to repeat that, Ensign?"

Wermal swallowed hard, his Adam's apple bobbing visibly, pressing against the blade. "N—no, sir. Your Highness."

Raman's expression could have wilted flowers. "No, I daresay you wouldn't. You're just lucky the captain wasn't here to witness this. Would you like me to pass your remarks along to him?"

"No! No, your Highness, I—I won't say anything like that again."

"See that you don't. Look, Wermal, I don't care what you heard or where you heard it. That term is never used in this palace. Use it again and your service here will no longer be required. And if you ever proposition the Lady Alannys in that manner again, I will gut you where you stand. Do I make myself clear?"

Wermal closed his eyes and scrunched up his face, forcing himself to swallow again. "Crystal, my Lord."

"Then get out of here." Raman lifted the sword, and the guard squirmed away from the wall and skittered out of the room, not even pausing to look back.

They heard the sitting room door slam behind him.

♫

Raman turned back to Alannys with a muttered oath, sheathing his sword. "I'm sorry, my Lady."

Alannys laughed, but it sounded harsh. "You? What on earth do you have to be sorry for?" She fumbled with the fasteners on Dorramon's armor. What call did she have to be upset? There were bigger problems here, as his limp form and ashen complexion reminded her.

Raman didn't answer, turning to pull a silken cord hanging from the ceiling near the bed—a call for a servant, she assumed. He turned back to her, and frowned. "What are you doing?"

Alannys couldn't see her fingers clearly through the sudden tears that clouded her eyes, but she could tell the fasteners were still tight. She pulled her hands back into her lap. "Messing things up, as usual." The bitterness in her own words surprised her. "I thought…"

Raman flashed an unreadable look in her direction, then stepped up beside her to finish unfastening the king's leather armor. "You thought what?"

"I—I—" She swallowed a hard lump in her throat. This

was a ridiculous time to be on the verge on a full-on bawl-fest; she had so much else she should be worried about! "After all I've been through...after all the dangerous situations and the hostile places...I guess I had come to think of the Great Palace as my refuge from all the anger and the hate. My safe harbor, you know? Our safe harbor." She saw again Dorramon's broken form sprawled on his royal purple bedclothes and tried to force down the sob that threatened to undo her. "But it isn't really, is it?"

Raman hauled the heavy leather chestplate off of Dorramon and turned away from her, sighing. "I'm sorry, Alannys. You know you mean the world to his Majesty, and Grayble and I would do anything for you. But—no, I'm sorry. If you are looking for refuge, I don't think you will find it here."

Alannys helped hold Dorramon up off the bed so that Raman could pull off his chain mail shirt, and the quilted wool shirt under it. Raman's words weren't particularly cold, but something about the matter-of-fact way he said them...they hit her like a bucket of water dashed in her face. "What is it?" she said. "There's something you aren't telling me. What happened?"

Raman sat down on the foot of the bed, opening his mouth to speak, and she suddenly held up a hand, cutting him off.

"Wait," she said, "strike that. Tell me in a minute. First we need water, and washcloths. This doesn't look right." She dragged a chair up to the beside and sank into it, pulling Dorramon's arm into her lap, probing with gentle fingers at the angry gash in his bicep. The usual electricity *felt* wrong here, like it had soured, somehow. "How did he get something like this through chain mail?"

Raman shook his head, and went into the bath chamber. "No armor can stop everything," his voice floated out to her. "But that isn't very deep at all. It shouldn't be bleeding like that."

"I agree," she said, raising her voice. "But did you see

how his skin is green around the edges of the cut? I think the weapon was treated with something to make him bleed."

Raman hurried back to her, carrying a basin of water with a couple cloths floating in it. "Something to make him bleed?" He sounded shaken. "There are things like that out there?"

"There are." She couldn't look at him. She fished one of the cloths from the water and wrung it out, avoiding his gaze. "I have...experienced something of that nature before."

Raman folded his arms and watched her, saying nothing. She could feel her face burning. How much did he know? She couldn't guess, and she would never ask.

Alannys swabbed at Dorramon's arm with the damp cloth, doing her best to ignore the anxiety that gnawed at her insides. Whoever had done this had done it deliberately, planning for this to happen. What if...what if they succeeded? She couldn't even consider it. Sheer, black panic opened in her mind at simply verbalizing the thought to herself. The room felt close and crowded, even with just the three of them in it. The very air around her hung heavy with her fear.

"Didn't you call for a servant?" she finally said, more to break the oppressive silence than anything.

"I did." A frown creased his forehead as he remembered. "I'd better check on that."

She didn't answer, didn't look up as he stomped over and threw the door open, then disappeared down the dark corridor behind it. She rinsed her cloth, and swabbed at the wound, rinsed and swabbed, over and over, trying to keep her mind on her work. She kept her movements mechanical, tried to *be* a machine, a machine that couldn't eat itself up with worry, a machine that wouldn't keep sneaking glances at Dorramon's handsome face and asking her if somehow, this wasn't all her fault.

It didn't work.

Raman's words echoed in the silence, tormenting her further. *If you are looking for refuge, I don't think you will find it here.* At last she could see the truth, and she couldn't pretend to like what she saw.

There was no refuge, for her or for Dorramon. Not out there, not in here.

Not anywhere.

♬

"We're on our own," Raman said shortly when he came back into the king's chambers, startling Alannys from her dismal reverie. "No servants are getting in here tonight."

"Servants I can do without," Alannys said, finally dropping the cloth back into the basin. "I don't mind tending to him, Raman. I'll do whatever needs doing. But I had hoped to get a healer to look at that arm. I've done everything I can for him, but I don't know if it's enough."

"Not going to happen." Raman's tone was firm, but not unkind. "They've evacuated the inner ward — the only people left here are the ones fighting to defend the Great Hall. And the outer ward is in a panic, and it's such a mess — no one's getting through that tonight. Didn't you say you'd seen this before? What does your experience tell you?"

Alannys ran her fingertips over the gash in Dorramon's arm and sighed. His arm felt normal to her again, and she supposed that was something. "He should be fine. Washing the stuff away was all it took before. But he's the king. And I — what about the royal healers?"

"Royal healers?"

"Yes. Grayble said he would have one of them see Eleana."

For just a moment, Raman looked totally flummoxed. Then understanding dawned in his eyes, and he snapped his fingers. "Of course! Master Rhayred! I remember hearing about that." His expression sobered, and the way he looked from her to Dorramon did not inspire confidence. "But Alannys, from what I understand, the Singari girl was in much worse shape than Dorramon. His color is already back, and he would say that cut is only a scratch. I'll tell Rhayred to check in when he's free, but I'll also tell him it isn't urgent."

"Fair enough." Alannys knew she didn't sound convinced, but she couldn't help it. Dorramon, or Eleana? The man she loved more than life, or the teenager who had relied on her as a teacher, a leader, a savior? How could she possibly choose?

She couldn't, and she deeply resented the position she was in right now. Nothing she could say or do would make it better, though, so she did her best to push it all out of her mind, scooped up the basin with its dirty water and soiled washcloths, and headed into the royal bath chamber.

Too late she heard Raman behind her, shouting "Alannys, wait!" Too late he dashed around in front of her, blocking her view, lifting the basin from her arms and shooing her back out into the bedroom.

Too late. She had already seen it, and as she tottered back over to Dorramon's bedside, she couldn't unsee it. It was still there, floating in front of her, scorched onto her retinas. She doubled over and scrubbed at her eyes with the heels of her hands, but still it hovered there, right in front of her but completely out of her reach.

It was a note, scrawled in a heavy, unskilled hand on jagged parchment, stuck to the wall of the king's bath chamber. Its missive was simple:

BURN THE WITCH

and the point was driven home by a scribble of a stick figure in a cloak, consumed by flames.

To call the drawing crude would have been an understatement—maybe even a compliment. She had heard what trying to force Talent sounded like in Tralice's gravelly voice; now she saw what it looked like splattered across a page, and it wasn't pretty. But it made it worse, in a way; it conveyed the ugliness of the intent almost too well. She shuddered to think how much effort that abomination had taken to create.

Raman came back out of the bath chamber, carrying a dry towel. His face fell as soon as he saw her—clearly he could tell that she knew. "Seven Hells—my Lady, I'm sorry. I should have been paying better attention. I had hoped you wouldn't have to see any of those."

"Any of those?" The way her voice shook made her want to swear, too. "You mean that wasn't the only one? There have been others?"

"There have," he said grimly. "This wasn't the first, and it won't be the last."

"But if you didn't want me to see it, why didn't you just get rid of it? You were in there earlier."

Raman sighed. He sounded exasperated, which Alannys felt was just a little unfair—she certainly hadn't *planned* to walk in on the threatening note. "I didn't want *you* to see it, Alannys. Dorramon—that's a different story. More needs to be done, and he's not doing it."

"You aren't talking about the Dark Alliance, are you?" she asked, suddenly on edge again. "What's this about, Cadenda? What's happened?"

"Sit down, Alannys." He parked himself on the foot of the bed again and gave her the towel, and she sank back down into her chair. While she wrapped the towel around the king's arm and kept her face carefully neutral, Raman tried to answer her question. "Look, I know things seemed pretty stable here when you left. But in the time since..." He shook his head. "These notes have been showing up for a while. And it's disturbing—clearly this is someone with unfettered access to the keep, someone whose true feelings are pretty dark. And nothing we've done has slowed him down."

"Then there must be some way to find out who this

person is. And then he could be expelled from the palace, kept away from the king."

"I'm sure you're right. But I don't think Dorramon is willing to do that. If he drives this person out, then he'll have no idea what they're getting up to. I think he's content being your shield."

Alannys swore under her breath. She didn't know why she was so surprised—Dorramon had been protecting her with his position in various ways for months; he probably didn't see any reason why this should be different. Brave and foolhardy could sometimes be two sides of the same coin.

"But that's not the worst of it. There have been protests, Alannys. That is something that never happens, not here at the palace. These notes are the work of a single disgruntled individual, but these protests...they show that there's a whole mass of disgruntled people out there."

"Protests," Alannys echoed numbly. "Protests against what?" She figured she already knew the answer to that. She had to be sure, but at the same time she wasn't sure she could handle hearing it said. She reached out and took Dorramon's hand in her own, lacing her fingers between his and holding tight for courage.

"Against you. I'm sorry. I know you have friends here, but that doesn't mean everyone here is friendly. There are those who blame you for the Dark Alliance, and for the threat of war with Cadenda. There have been demonstrations in support of Princess Varilyn. The Royal Guard suppress these things, and the agitators are jailed...and then mysteriously escape."

"Just like Haltred," she said.

"Yes. Just like Haltred. There is no way all of these jailbreaks have happened independently. Grayble keeps as tight a hold on his men as any captain can, but there are those in the Royal Guard who are working against you. And it probably goes deeper than that."

"Protests," she said dully. "Demonstrations."

"I can't count the number of emergency midnight meetings the grand chancellor has had with Dorramon, begging him to reconsider his stance."

"Midnight meeting?" She looked from Raman to Dorramon's slack face, and back again. "Why midnight? The court looked like a ghost town when I was in there."

Raman chuckled, but it was a tense sound. "I suppose Dorramon didn't want me to know about it. I'm enough of a thorn in his side already. Look, Alannys, I don't know if you are aware of it, but there is a very active rumor mill out there that takes everything you do — everything Dorramon does — and exaggerates it all out of proportion, spreading it across the entire country. I know Lord Malrec started it, but I don't think it's going to die with him. That's not even to mention Ambassador Thell and his compatriots from Cadenda, doing everything they can to put even more pressure on us. Things are strung out so tight...Ravanmark is a tinderbox. And anything you or Dorramon do — even something that seems small, taken by itself — could be the spark that sends everything up in flames."

Alannys sat there in the cold, quiet room, her palms slicked with sudden sweat. She could see the precipice looming before them, could see danger yawning at her feet like an abyss. How had she never realized before the desperate, terrible line that Dorramon was walking — or the truly horrible consequences if he should miss a step?

Was he doing this somehow for *her?* Was that her legacy here — the crazy outsider who took an honorable, dutiful king and so twisted him that he risked his entire country in an effort to please her? An effort that could only be futile, in the end?

The enormity of it descended on her like a physical object, crushed her so she couldn't breathe. A wave of nausea washed over her, violent and intense. She jerked her hand away from Dorramon's, and pressed it against her own hot forehead, fighting with sudden, visceral horror. "This...this is terrible."

"I know. That's what I've been trying to tell him for weeks, but—well, I guess you know how stubborn he is. Don't get me wrong, I would love for him to be happy. But at what price?"

She turned to look at Dorramon, lying wounded and unconscious on the big bed. At what price indeed?

She heard steps behind her, and Raman's hand fell heavily on her shoulder. She couldn't look at him. She reached up and patted his hand weakly with her own.

"Go on," she told him. Her voice shook. "Don't worry about me."

He squeezed her shoulder, then quietly let himself out without another word.

Alannys sat in the chair, staring at Dorramon in a kind of shock. She wanted to hold his hand again, but she was afraid, at that moment, to touch him. She thought about him, and about his engagement with Princess Varilyn, and about all the untold number of lives that hung on the decisions he was making now.

The room was cold, and poor Dorramon was lying there shirtless and uncovered. There was a heavy quilt folded at the foot of the bed—she got up and shook it out, drawing it up under his chin.

He stirred suddenly, his head thrashing on the pillow, but his eyes stayed shut. "Alannys," he muttered.

She held very still. Obviously she had disturbed him; perhaps if she didn't bother him any more he would sleep soundly again.

It didn't seem to be working. "Alannys," he said again, louder this time, his hand reaching for the edge of the bed under his quilt.

She sat back down in her chair, reaching under the quilt to take his hand in hers. "It's okay. I'm here."

His hand squeezed hers so tightly it almost hurt, then went limp in her grasp. "Don't...don't leave me."

"Shh. I won't leave."

"Don't leave me," he said again, his voice fading as he succumbed once again to sleep. "Don't leave me with Varilyn."

Alannys sat frozen to the spot, holding Dorramon's hand in her suddenly cold fingers. What could she do for him now? It was too late; too late for him, for her, for all of them. She wasn't safe here, she knew that—she wasn't safe anywhere. She wasn't safe here and neither was he—because he was with her.

Only without her would he be safe.

It was the rose that did it, Chen's voice echoed in her mind. *He means to marry you, Alannys...he's decided, mark my words.*

Chen may have been right. But she realized in that moment what she should have known all along—it wasn't his decision to make; he *couldn't* decide. He didn't have any choice, and he never had.

Neither of them had.

Alannys crumpled forward, burying her face in the heavy quilt, and cried, clutching Dorramon's hand like a lifeline.

♫

Alannys woke up warm and comfortable, and dead tired. It couldn't have been more than two or three o'clock in the morning, and her whole body felt rusty. She stretched out under the covers, not much inclined to get out of bed, or even to open her eyes.

Until she realized her pillow was someone's arm.

She sat bolt upright in the bed, shocked to realize she was not in her familiar room. The various pieces of armor she had worn the night before were scattered on the floor beside the bed, leaving her in her linen shirt and leather pants. Belatedly she remembered the mission to Castle Glennayre, the defense of the Great Hall, and Dorramon's injury. This was the king's bed.

And the king was still in it.

She found Dorramon watching her with twinkling

eyes, a faint smile on his face. How could he look so lively, after the night he'd had? His complexion was still pale.

The only saving grace she could see was that at least she had not been lying on his injured arm.

"Good morning, my Lady." The same humor that touched his face laced his tone. "You look surprised."

"Yes." She glanced at the chair behind him. "I remember sitting in that chair last night, your Highness. I distinctly do *not* remember climbing into your bed."

Dorramon laughed, but it sounded somehow hollow, and his blue eyes clouded with consternation. "Going formal, are we? We're not at court, Alannys—you can call me by my name."

Only she couldn't—not after her conversation with Raman the night before. And she didn't think she could explain that right now. She averted her eyes and bit her lip, searching for some way to answer him that wouldn't hurt his feelings.

He watched her for an uncomfortable moment, then arranged a pleasant smile on his face. "I'm sorry for distressing you. I woke up in the night and found you slumped over against the bed in the cold—even your hand holding mine was like ice. So I moved you."

"You moved me?" She couldn't quite keep the shock out of her voice. "But you're hurt! Do you have any idea how much blood you lost? You shouldn't have even gotten up, let alone carried me!"

"I wasn't trying to upset you. But I'm fine, as you can see, and I couldn't just leave you there in the cold."

His calm demeanor shamed her. "I'm sorry. You're right—you've only done something nice for me, and here I am jumping all over you." She laid back—against the actual pillow this time—trying to ease some of the discomfort she'd built between them. "Thank you. This may be a pretty poor way to show it, but I am grateful."

"Think nothing of it. You can jump all over me anytime."

She heard his low chuckle, and before she could react he'd rolled over on top of her, pinning her to the bed.

"Your Highness! What are you—" She reached for his shoulders to push him away, but he caught her hands and pulled them up over her head. Her heart hammered in her chest and she stared up at him wide-eyed, trying to think past the rush of blood in her ears and the sudden warmth in her skin.

Dorramon trailed hot, biting kisses down the side of her neck, leaving tingling electricity in his wake and not making it any easier for her to think at all. "Now then," he murmured against her skin, "here we are, all alone in bed, and nobody expects us anywhere until sunrise. However shall we pass the time…?"

Alannys stiffened, fighting for control of her heightened senses and raging emotions. "No—Dorramon, stop. We can't do this."

"What?" He raised his head and looked at her in surprise. "Says who?"

"Says me!" Alannys hadn't meant to snap. Her frustration was with herself, not with him—everything had changed, but only for her. How could she make him understand? She squirmed, finally pulling her hands loose. "Let me up!"

He did. He rolled over onto his side as she bounded from the bed, regarding her in frank shock. "Alannys? What's wrong?"

She shook her head, but kept her back to him. "Nothing. Everything. We can't do this, Dorramon, it isn't right. You're engaged to marry somebody else." It was a weak attempt at distraction, at avoiding the real issues eating at her, the things she didn't even want to say out loud.

It was also a mistake. She could feel his somber eyes on her back. She had surprised him, she knew—but she'd also hurt him. She could feel it, and she didn't know how to face him. "For the moment," he said. "It doesn't change anything. I love you, Alannys, and I thought you loved me. You're just...giving up?"

She rounded on him. "What else *can* I do? This isn't up to me, Dorramon, and it isn't up to you."

He made no response, just watched her pace. A curtain had dropped behind his eyes; he looked at her the way he might have looked at a stranger, and that wounded her more deeply than anything else that had happened to her in Ravanmark. She couldn't leave it like that—she had to make some attempt to tell him the truth.

No matter how much it hurt.

"This whole thing was arranged with no consent from either of us, you know that. But it's done now, and to try to change it is to risk not just Ravanmark's citizens, but Cadenda's as well, in a war nobody really wants. People want me dead, and now they're threatening you, too—because of me. Because of me, you are in danger. You'll never be safe, as long as I am with you. How can I be happy with you knowing that? How can you be happy with me?"

He didn't answer. He just kept watching her, silent and still.

"I'm sorry," she said, and her voice cracked. She was hurting them both and she knew it—her soul was bleeding out, right there on the floor. "I should have known—I wasn't using my head. Having your attention..." She swallowed hard. "...loving you and being loved by you...it was all like a beautiful dream."

Still no response. She got a sudden chill—why wasn't he saying anything? His silence was harder to bear than his anger or condemnation would have been.

"But it was all just fantasy." She could hardly force the words out; her voice was not much more than a whisper. She drew a deep, shuddering breath and made herself say the words she dreaded, the last words she would ever have believed she'd say. "It's time for me to give it up. Dreams like that can't come true. It's impossible."

She turned and quietly left the room, with Dorramon's ominous frown on her back.

"It's impossible," she whispered again, more for herself than for him, and the door fell shut behind her, as if to emphasize the point, to stab it deep into her heart, where she could never forget it.

♫

The king's chambers were not really that far from Alannys's own rooms. She knew that, but walking down the corridor alone at three o'clock in the morning, after the most painful conversation she had ever had with him...it felt like a very long way indeed.

She was so deep in her own misery she had almost made it to her door before she heard the slight sounds of someone walking in the inner garden. She wondered who would be out in the courtyard so late on such a night, and she veered that direction to find out.

No sooner could she make out a vague silhouette than she realized she was looking at Chen. Her heart wrenched, taking in his slumped posture and down-turned face. He paced slowly, almost aimlessly, barely lifting his feet, dragging himself across the ground in a manner than could hardly be called walking. He looked utterly broken, and it pained her to see it. "Are you all right?"

She had made no effort to move quietly, or hide her approach, but he jumped anyway. "Alannys! I'm sorry, I—I thought I was alone out here."

"I see that." She settled herself onto one of the wooden benches, looking out over the water garden. The flowering bushes around them were just beginning to bloom, and the air was heavy with their scent. It would have been a very pleasant moment, under other circumstances. "What are you up to, out here all alone? How is Eleana?"

He shot a glance in her direction, and the darkness in his expression told her she had found her answer before he even spoke. "Not so well."

"I'm sorry I disappeared...Dorramon collapsed. He

only had a small wound, but we think they used something to make him bleed. He lost so much blood...I had my hands full for a while."

"I heard. Don't worry, I'm not mad." He seemed to be telling the truth. He certainly didn't *sound* angry; his words were flat, drained of any emotion at all.

"Is there really no improvement at all?"

"*Improvement?* No. No, not at all. That's why I left, I —" He stopped abruptly and took a long breath. "I couldn't take being in there. Master Rhayred thinks the arrow that hit her was treated with some kind of poison. But he can't —he can't find anything that works on it, and she's burning up. He and his two apprentices have been in there all night, but she just keeps getting worse." He sank down on the bench next to her. "I'm afraid...I'm afraid that..."

He couldn't seem to get the words out, and she didn't think she could stand to hear them said. "I'm sorry," she said again. "I should have been here. You shouldn't have had to do this alone."

Chen shook his head. "How is the king?"

"He'll be fine." Alannys tried hard to keep her tone neutral, not to let any hint of the unpleasantness between them seep into her words.

She could tell she'd failed when Chen turned his head, looking at her sharply. All at once she wished she had just minded her own business and gone back to her room— this was a conversation she most distinctly did not wish to have.

The door to the guest chambers across from them opened, and both of them forgot the conversation as Master Rhayred shuffled over to them.

Even in the dark, Alannys could see enough of his expression to guess the news he brought wasn't good.

"I'm sorry," he said simply. "She is gone."

For one brief moment the world seemed to stand still. Master Rhayred shuffled back the way he came, but

Alannys never saw him go. She felt like she had been kicked in the stomach, like she couldn't even breathe.

Chen slumped forward, burying his face in his hands. "What have I done?"

She reached out and put her hand on his back. "Nothing. You didn't do anything wrong, Chen. This was not your fault."

He turned to her in a blur of sudden motion, gathering her into a crushing hug. "Thank you, Alannys. I don't know what I would do without you."

Chen meant absolutely nothing hurtful by his words, she was certain of that. And yet they did hurt, they burned like a slug of strong whiskey, making her eyes water. How had she made such a mess of everything? Chen needed her. She needed Dorramon—she couldn't have him, but she couldn't let him go.

She was doomed to misery, it seemed, and doomed to drag everyone around her down with her.

♬

Alannys didn't know whether to be disappointed or relieved when Dorramon did not show up to escort her to Princess Delline's funeral. She knew she had left things badly between them, and she knew it should worry her that he was avoiding her.

Or maybe he was just giving her some space. She was dreading their next, awkward meeting, and he had to be feeling much the same. She had to put some distance between them—for Ravanmark's sake, for his sake.

But she didn't have to like it.

So just before sunrise, she put herself into a somber black dress and a black velvet cloak she plumbed from the depths of her closet, and started the long walk to the west side of the palace. It gave her a cold shiver to realize nearly everything she had in her sizable closet had once belonged to Delline...even the clothes she was wearing now.

Alannys hadn't been to this cemetery since the mass of

burials following Lord Malrec's bomb attack on the palace. In the far back of the cemetery, a tree-lined field had been gated off from the rest. Looking at the finely crafted headstones, the carved marble sculptures, and even the mausoleums that dotted the gently rolling field, Alannys could tell that this part of the cemetery was where the nobles buried their dead. The princess had forfeited her right to an interment in the royal catacombs when she married the head of the Dark Alliance and participated in the coup against the Great Palace. It seemed sad to Alannys that she would forever be so far from her family, but as she crossed the verdant field and saw Dorramon waiting at the burial site, staring wistfully into the trees, she thought maybe he saw it differently. She remembered his self-professed hatred of the catacombs and wondered if he would trade his royal interment for something like this, given the chance.

It was the kind of question she had no business asking — the kind of thought she had no business thinking, really. How could she hope to put any distance between them when she still identified with him so strongly?

She sighed, pushing that whole depressing train of thought aside as she approached the place where Delline would eternally rest. The last thing she wanted, personally, was distance between them — even thinking about it hurt, like twisting the knife that pierced her heart — but there were bigger concerns here than what she wanted, as the open grave near Dorramon's feet reminded her well enough.

This was to be a small service, nothing on the scale of the state funeral she had witnessed before. There weren't many people in attendance, and a quick glance showed many of them to be people she knew. She could see Queen Mother Farrine, standing under a big oak tree as though she feared she might need to lean on it, her face obscured by a long black veil. Captain Grayble stood nearby, with the same deferent bearing as the other guests, but the way he kept his hand on his sword and scanned the surroundings made Alannys wonder if he was there as a mourner or a keeper of the peace. Grand Chancellor Ebrad appeared to be offering his condolences to the queen mother. Farther on she could see Raman and Kalyn, absorbed in a quiet conversation. She gave them a wide berth as she passed, preferring not to intrude, and went to stand at the far end of the group of mourners, removed from all of them. She felt more like an outsider here than she had in a very long time. The crowd was small, but even so half the people in it probably wished she was somewhere else — and Dorramon may well have been among them. It took everything she had to keep her head up and stand among them, fully aware of how vehemently she was despised here.

She had to do it; there was a chance that Dorramon still wanted her here, that her presence would make this horrible thing a tiny bit easier for him. As long as that chance existed, she would stay.

She could have asked him, of course, and she knew she didn't even have to approach him to do it. The mindlink was there, as always, glowing like a live wire between them. She wasn't sure how to reconcile its intimate connection with her resolution to distance herself, and so she did the best thing she could come up with, which was just not to touch it.

A chilly breeze blew through the cemetery, fluttering her cloak around her. As if it was a sign he had awaited, Dorramon straightened, faced them all, and began to speak.

"First of all I want to say thank you to each and every one of you here this morning. So many things have been difficult about my sister's death, but this perhaps most of all. This funeral is happening much too soon. I can't be the only one here who still feels this can't actually be real." The early morning sunlight angled sharply across his face, and in its harsh light he looked more haggard than she had ever seen him. How had she not realized what the loss of his twin was doing to him? How had she managed to offer him no support whatsoever?

"But all of that aside, this isn't the service we ever expected to be holding for my sister. It isn't even in the right place—Delline had a spot reserved for her in the royal catacombs. Surely a cemetery burial must be a step down, or so it would seem."

Because it wasn't her place, that was how. Alannys balled her hands into fists under her cloak, digging her nails into her palms, battling an almost physical urge to stray from the path she had set for herself. She couldn't support him. She was bad for his kingdom, bad for his safety, bad for him.

"And yet I would ask you to look deeper. Delline had many things to teach us in her short life, and in her sudden death. I do not think she would look upon it as punishment, to be laid to rest here, under green trees and blue skies and bright flowers. Delline was a person, most of all, of love. Love drove her every action. She left her home and her family for love of Lord Malrec, and supported the Dark Alliance out of a love for her country that was real, if also misguided. In the end, it was her love that saved us when she chose to sacrifice herself rather than harm me. This was her most important legacy, I think. Love," he said somberly, his eyes touching sadly on Alannys, "may yet be the saving of us all."

It was a brief moment, a tiny moment, but it tore through Alannys like sheet lightning, taking her breath away. For just a moment she could see the world in the same rosy hues Dorramon so often seemed to see, and it really was beautiful. For a moment Delline's whole life really had been driven by love, and all things were possible.

Then she tore her eyes away from his and reality descended around her again like the fog floating around her feet in the cemetery, cold and uncaring. She remembered Princess Delline as she had known her — a deeply, unapologetically bitter woman, so jealous she could hardly see straight. *That* was reality, and that was the world in which she had to live, and in it there were many things which were impossible.

Including a few things she dearly wished could be possible.

The gravediggers moved into position around Delline's closed coffin, hefting the ends of the several thick ropes they had run underneath it. The mourners began to shift uncomfortably around Alannys, and she wondered if this might be a good opportunity to make a quick exit.

Before she even had time to consider the question, Kalyn appeared at her side, her red hair pulled into an elegant twist, her eyes puffy and swollen. "Thank you for coming, Lady Alannys. You certainly didn't have to."

"I could say the same for you," Alannys replied, trying to sound brighter than she felt. "Are you all right?"

Kalyn nodded, wiping at her eyes. "Yes — yes, I'm fine. I never knew the princess that well...I wouldn't say we got along very well...but I never wanted something like this to happen."

"I know what you mean," Alannys said.

Kalyn peered at her. "That's right, she didn't like you at all, did she, my Lady?"

Alannys shook her head and bit her tongue. She wouldn't have said Delline disliked her; she would have said Delline *hated* her, from the very moment they met. But such things were not to be said at funerals.

"All the more reason why it's a noble thing, you coming here."

"I didn't come for her," Alannys finally said, her voice low. "I came for Dorramon. He shouldn't have to do this alone."

"Oh, I see." Kalyn sounded surprised, looking from Alannys to Dorramon, across the distance that separated them. It seemed even wider, reflected in Kalyn's green eyes. "But...he is rather doing it alone, isn't he?"

There it was, another casual remark that cut Alannys to the quick. Her face flushed, and she looked away. "I can't help that. I don't...I don't have the status to be up there with him." That wasn't exactly a lie—it dodged the entire issue of their falling out, and it might even have been true, if she hadn't been well aware that Dorramon didn't give a tinker's damn about her status, or lack thereof.

Kalyn's expression said she knew this as well as Alannys. "I...well, I see. It's a difficult thing all around. I didn't come to make you uncomfortable. I only wanted to make sure you plan to come to the wedding this afternoon?"

"Wild horses couldn't keep me away," Alannys said immediately. "But will the Great Hall be ready in time?"

"I think it will. There is a whole crowd of maids in there right now, cleaning it up. I'm actually on my way back to help them, now that this is over."

"I'll walk part of the way with you," Alannys said. "I wish I could help, but I have another funeral to attend."

Kalyn's smile sobered. "I'm sorry. I heard what happened. It sounds just awful...and she was so brave, a teenager helping to fight for the palace. Did you know her well? I know you spent a lot of time with them, but I can't imagine what it must have been like."

"I knew her." Alannys swallowed a big, hard lump in her throat, and tried to blink away the wetness in her eyes. "I know from outside they can seem very much alike, but the Singari are a big, diverse group...too big, really, for me to know everyone well. But I had...a group of musicians that I was teaching..." She had to stop and force down another lump—she'd never dreamed how hard it would be to talk about this! "Students. Music students. Eleana was one of them. She played a wooden flute, and I taught her. If...if I hadn't taught her..."

"No." Kalyn laid a hand on Alannys's arm, her eyes full of sympathy. "This was not your fault, Lady Alannys.

You shouldn't feel responsible. There was nothing you could have done."

Alannys managed a sickly smile. She had never realized how hollow those reassurances sounded—had she sounded the same, to Chen? "I know. I'm fine, really."

Kalyn didn't look convinced. But she smiled back and turned to start the long walk back to the palace. Raman fell into step at her side, looking shell-shocked. Alannys followed a few steps behind, feeling out of place again. Nothing she did today felt right.

She glanced back over her shoulder, and saw Dorramon, sad and alone, watching as his sister was slowly lowered into the cold ground. It haunted her—even when she turned back around, she could not unsee his pale, strained face. She needed everything she had to keep going, to continue putting one foot in front of the other. She couldn't keep endangering him with her presence. What if next time it was his coffin she mourned over? What if his death was her fault, because she had stayed, and by doing so put him in danger? She would do anything to avoid that.

Even this.

She could hear Tryn's gritty voice in her mind, from all those months ago. *Unless I'm very much mistaken, people are going to die for you. You're going to have to find a way to live with it.* The words had seemed to come so easily to him at the time, but now she suspected there was hard experience behind them—experience he had been trying to spare her with his teachings. Some student she was. He'd been right; it had happened, over and over. She never had learned to be okay with it. Maybe if she had, she wouldn't be walking away right now.

She wrapped her arms around herself and walked on, knowing that no matter what, she would never be okay with it.

♫

Alannys's dour mood hung over her like a thundercloud at Eleana's funeral. Chen met her as she approached the camp, and he looked about as glum as she felt. Neither of them were much in the mood to talk, so they stood silently side by side, watching as Eleana's family carried her to her funeral pyre. Alannys pulled the hood of her black cloak farther over her head, using its shadow to hide her face. She didn't think she could stand to make eye contact with anyone right then.

The wailing and tearing of hair commenced as Alannys remembered, followed by the ritual speech of the elders and the lighting of the pyre. As they had in the only other Singari funeral Alannys had ever attended, the people broke into song and dance, celebrating Eleana's passage to the Valley of the Muses. It made her just as uncomfortable as it had at Alara's funeral, and she turned away.

"Alannys." Chen touched her arm, startling her from her dismal thoughts. "Come with me."

She followed him away from the camp, to the shade of a big tree where they both sank down to sit on the grass as if they couldn't stand a moment longer.

"I'm sorry," Chen said. "I don't know what's got into me. I've been to so many of these over the years...I've never had a problem joining in, until now."

"Don't sit out because of me," Alannys said. "My customs are different, but I understand."

"It isn't that," Chen said, staring up into the sky, watching the billows of smoke rise, and slowly dissipate. "It's just...different. It's the first time a Singari has died since I became *kortha*. We lost Eleana on my watch, you know."

"It wasn't your fault," Alannys said immediately.

"Ah, and how can you say that? Because you think it was yours. We are alike that way." Chen laughed darkly. "I said before I'm not cut out to be a leader—pity nobody listened to me."

"You're wrong again. You're a fine leader."

"Do you think so? Because I don't see it. If I hadn't let this happen, she would be home right now, with her friends and family. And the rest would still be the same — her death didn't even matter."

"I disagree. Eleana died doing something she thought was important. She died fighting against evil, Chen — that's always important. For all we know, she may have landed the blow that turned the battle in our favor."

"I'm not going to quibble with you over something nobody can prove." He heaved a sigh so big she could see his shoulders rise and fall, and finally pulled his gaze away from the smoke, floating gently away from them as though this world's troubles were of no concern at all. "I'm not the only one who thinks that way. I've heard others say the same things. Maybe they're right. Maybe I let my personal feelings interfere with my duty to protect my people."

"Maybe." Alannys brushed grass off of her cloak; the pile of the velvet seemed to attract everything it touched. She pushed the hood back and tipped her face to the sky, enjoying the feel of the morning sun. "Or maybe you took a stand for what you thought was right, and allowed others to do the same. It's not as though you shoved a sword into every Singari hand and forced them into the Great Hall. Most of them weren't affected by the war at all."

"No," he said finally, "I suppose not. I still wonder about that line, though, between me and my duty. How do I know I've got it in the right place?"

Alannys snorted. "You're asking *me*? I'm no expert — hell, half the time I forget to draw the line at all."

"Now who's being too hard on themselves? You're doing just fine, Alannys, and don't let anyone tell you different." He reached out and ruffled her hair.

His unfailing good humor choked her up. How could he do that, how did he stay so kind to her after everything she had put him through? She scrubbed at the tears that sprang unbidden to her eyes.

"What?" he said, dropping his hand back into his lap. "What did I say?"

"Nothing." His direct gaze was unsettling; she fixed her eyes on a point somewhere behind his left shoulder. "How do you do it, Chen? You were serious about me — as serious as I've ever seen one person about another. How do you stay near me when there's no hope left? How can you still be my friend?"

For a long, long moment, Chen didn't answer. The silence stretched on and on, tense and heavy. Finally, she forced herself to look at his face, and found him frowning at her. "Why are you asking me that?"

Alannys shrugged uncomfortably, but said nothing. Her current muddle wasn't really something she wanted to discuss.

Chen sighed, and swept a glance around them, almost as if he expected the Singari to be eavesdropping. "Look, Alannys, there's no easy answer to that question. I think — I think being around you is one big learning experience for me. I told you before that you taught me there was something I feared more than losing you to the king — losing you permanently and forever, gone from this world. Do you remember?"

Alannys swallowed hard. "Yes, I remember."

"Well. I did plan on leaving here with the Singari, and trying to get back to normal — at least as normal as life ever gets for me. But after last night...fighting here without you while you were in danger somewhere else...not knowing if you lived or died, if you got hurt or captured or worse..." He shook his head. "You taught me something else. I don't think I *can* leave, not if I want to stay sane. I have to stay nearby. I have to know you are all right."

She stared at him, stricken. What could she say? He buried his own pain and grief so deeply, just to be able to stay near her. She'd missed his suffering, just as completely as she had missed Dorramon's. "Thank you,

Chen." Her voice broke oddly, but she ignored it and went on. "I don't know how you do it, but thank you."

"Well, I...you're welcome, I suppose," he said, flustered and embarrassed. "But really, what's wrong? Or don't you want to talk about it?"

Alannys hesitated, biting her lip. On the one hand, she couldn't say she did want to talk about it, not really. And yet everything she felt and couldn't act on, everything she wanted but could never have—they threatened to overwhelm her if she didn't let it out somehow. But she had been so horrible to Chen, how could she impose on him yet again? She just didn't have the right.

"No," she said finally. "I don't guess I do. It's—it's pointless, don't you see? It won't change anything. Nothing can be changed."

"Don't give up, Alannys. Anything can be changed." He grabbed her hand, squeezed it, and released it again. "Anything."

♫

Chen walked Alannys back to the Great Palace when the billows of smoke from camp started to fade. The sun had burned off the fog from early that morning, and the sky glowed bright blue and beautiful over their heads. It should have been a pleasant walk, but neither of them were in the mood to appreciate it. She walked mechanically, in a numb haze, and they had crossed the drawbridge into the outer ward before she realized how far she was dragging Chen out of his way.

"I'm sorry," she said, suddenly feeling selfish and awful. "You didn't have to come all this way—I can find my own way back."

"I don't doubt it," Chen said, "but I'm not leaving you alone. You don't even seem to realize it, but you're in danger everywhere you go, Alannys, even here." He cast a furtive glance around, though as far as she could tell no one was paying them any particular mind. "Maybe especially here."

"You, too?" Alannys said. The market buzzed with people and activity, and as always the mouth-watering smell of roasting meat wafted over all of it. Everything felt so alive, so normal, it was difficult to credit the things she'd been told. "Has everyone heard about this civil unrest but me?"

Chen didn't answer immediately. "I think life in the inner ward does kind of keep you isolated, yes. It's no one's fault, really, but you are very sheltered here."

"Damn straight," said a rough voice from behind them, "only it is someone's fault, and I can tell you who in three words — our exalted king."

The heavy sarcasm in the words took Alannys's breath away — who would dare to speak so of the king, in his own palace? She whirled around to find an unfamiliar man watching her with hard eyes, good-looking but rough. Worse than that were the others she could see gathering behind him — too many others for her to count at a glance. She took an instinctive step backwards.

"The king protects you," the man continued, matching her step with one of his own, "even though anybody can see you aren't doing us any good. Nobody wants to go to war for you, nobody wants to fight Cadenda for you."

There were grumbles of assent behind him. Carrying Songstrike to a funeral would have been atrociously bad manners, but Alannys wished she had done it anyway. Standing here completely unarmed facing this hostile crowd — it brought back every flashback, every nightmare she'd had since her ill-fated confrontation with Trago all those weeks ago. She should have spoken up, should have tried to rein in the situation, but she couldn't find the words. She just watched, wide-eyed, as everything spun out of control.

"Your Singari friend is right. You're destroying Ravanmark and you're too out of touch to even see it. Seems there's only one way our king is going to do what's right, and that's if we take you out of the picture."

"Stone the witch!" someone shouted from the gathering crowd behind him.

"Drown her in the moat!"

"Burn her!"

The man in front of her smiled a toothy smile, as though that had been his intent all along.

"No," Alannys said, scarcely more than a breath. "You can't do this. The Royal Guard..."

"The Royal Guard?" His laughter mocked her. "You really *are* out of touch, aren't you?"

"Alannys," Chen said from beside her, *"run!"*

She didn't wait to be told twice. Odds were good none of these people, on their own, would be capable of the kind of violence they were clamoring for, but in a group, as part of a mindless mob...

She wasn't waiting around to find out. She lifted the hem of her black gown halfway to her knees and ran as though Soth himself pursued, weaving past people and wagons, ducking under ill-placed clotheslines, and leaving more than one person in her wake swearing and rubbing whatever body part she had bumped in her haste to get by. It was a mad, breathless flight, without even the time it would take to look behind her and gauge her pursuit. She could never outfight all of those people. But she could by every one of the Muses and all of their songs outrun them, and she spared no effort, held nothing back.

Her chest heaved like an old bellows and her lungs were on fire by the time she flew through the inner ward gate and nearly barreled right into Baroness Lae. She doubled over, bracing her hands on her knees and sucking great gasping breaths, while the baroness watched in apparent astonishment.

"Sorry," she panted, tilting her head back to regard the baroness. "Ran into...a bit of trouble...in the outer ward."

"It looks to me," Lae said, "as though you ran *out* of some trouble in the outer ward."

Alannys laughed out loud before realizing how badly

that would hurt. "I suppose you're right, at that. What are you doing here, if you don't mind me asking?"

"Waiting for you. I never go into the outer ward myself...I guess I don't run fast enough. I am sorry to trouble you, but I need to ask a favor."

"Anything."

The baroness laughed like the tinkling of bells. "You may not find it wise to agree too quickly, my Lady! Perhaps you would prefer to hear what I'm asking of you before you consent."

Privately, Alannys couldn't imagine refusing Lae anything. The baroness was unfailingly kind and generous, and she had never been anything but helpful to Alannys. And she always gave an impression of such fragility. How could Alannys possibly turn her down? "Perhaps," she said aloud. "What do you need?"

Lae's smile suddenly faded. "I need you to come with me to the dungeon."

Alannys blinked at her in dumb surprise. "The dungeon? But why on earth would you go there?"

"My husband has asked me to visit him."

"Oh." For a moment, Alannys couldn't think of anything else to say. Of course she knew that Prubard had been imprisoned after his ill-fated attack on the Great Hall. But it had never occurred to her that Baroness Lae would have anything more to do with him. "And you, you would like to see him?"

"Oh, no. No." Lae's brow furrowed; her translucent eyes couldn't seem to meet Alannys's gaze. People passing by gave them a wide berth, and Alannys couldn't help wondering what they made of this oddly intense conversation between the stately baroness and a disheveled woman who didn't even look like she belonged here. "I would prefer not to see him. And I am afraid to go alone. For myself, I would not trouble you, my Lady, but one of the Royal Guard asked me this morning if I would make the visit. It seems my husband has been making something of a nuisance of himself, and it is making things difficult for the guards."

"One of the Royal Guards asked you that?" Alannys's tone was sharper than she had intended. "I don't think they're supposed to do that."

"No. From what he told me...it sounds as though Captain Grayble specifically forbade them from telling me of Prubard's request. He wished me to visit my husband only if it was my desire to go."

"I think Grayble has it right," Alannys said. "Which guard was this? Did you get his name? I think we should report him to Captain Grayble."

"No!" Baroness Lae held her hands out in front of her. "No, I couldn't do that. These men are doing their best. It isn't their fault my husband is such an unreasonable man. I'm sure he's pushed them far past what they could be expected to endure."

"Perhaps," Alannys muttered. "Or perhaps the Royal Guard harbors some Dark Alliance sympathizers."

"Oh no, certainly not!" Lae sounded honestly shocked. "No, I will not entertain any such notion as that. All I need to do is go listen to whatever Prubard has to say, and this will settle down. Then these poor men can go back to doing their jobs in peace."

Alannys sighed, raking her hand through her windblown hair. Her only plan had been to help prepare the Great Hall for Raman and Kalyn's wedding. And she had to admit that decorating for a wedding was about the last thing she felt like doing at that moment. "Okay," she finally said. "If you're determined to go, I can't let you go alone. But I've been at funerals all morning. Do I need to change clothes?"

"What for?" Lae said mildly. "My husband would not put forth such effort for either of us."

"I—I suppose you're right. Shall we go, then?"

Baroness Lae turned and started across the inner ward. Alannys moved to follow her, but before she could take a step, someone caught her by the arm, stopping her heart. "Wait."

She turned to see Chen frowning at her, his dark eyes full of worry. "Chen? How long have you been standing there?"

"Long enough." He didn't seem nearly as out of breath as she was. He looked at her a moment, then looked away. "Are you sure you should do this? You really think it's a good idea to go visit Baron Prubard?"

Alannys glanced over her shoulder. "What should I do, Chen?" she hissed. "Let her go alone?"

"Of course not. I don't think either of you should go at all. What possible good can come of it?"

"Unfortunately I don't think not going is an option. She's going, with or without me. I can't send her in there alone."

"Well." He sighed, looking at the people pretending to ignore them while actually keeping a close watch on them. "I can't let the two of you go alone. So I guess I'm coming with you."

"Oh! Chen, you don't have to do that. In fact, you probably don't *want* to do that. Baron Prubard is one of the world's least pleasant people."

"I know. I've met him, remember? It's pretty evident where Trago gets his sparkling personality."

Alannys laughed, then tried to smother it and ended up making an awkward snorting sound. "I guess you're right. But really, Chen, you don't have to do this. You already do way too much for me."

"Stop that." He wouldn't look her in the eye, just grabbed her arm and threaded it through his. "You know saying that won't change anything. Let's just go."

"Okay." She walked with him after Baroness Lae, aware of the many eyes following their progress across the inner ward. She knew he wanted her to drop it, but... "Thank you," she whispered, her voice barely audible.

She might have thought he hadn't heard her. But his

step suddenly faltered. He never said a word, just covered her hand on his arm with his own.

♫

"I am sorry to trouble you both," Baroness Lae said, as Alannys and Chen fell into step beside her in the inner ward. "I hope it's not too much bother for you."

"It's no bother at all," Alannys said smoothly, even though everybody knew it was. "I understand you feel obligated."

Lae looked at her sidelong. "The mystery is why, am I right?"

"Well..." Alannys waffled, uncomfortable with such a direct acknowledgement of someone else's personal matters. "If I'm being frank, then yes — but if I'm being frank, it's also none of my business. I'm here to help you. There is not a single thing about this situation that I'm really entitled to say."

"That isn't true," Lae said. "You are my friend, Alannys. You are entitled to say anything you think. You're too polite, that's all." The inner ward was relatively quiet; many of the courtiers had not yet returned and fewer people than usual moved in the castle's inner sanctum that morning. Still, the three of them moved slowly toward the barracks of the Royal Guard, in no hurry to reach their destination. "You must have wondered. I know I would. I can scarcely conceive of a stranger couple than Baron Prubard and myself."

Alannys cleared her throat awkwardly. She couldn't imagine a suitable response to that remark, but the baroness watched her, eyes twinkling, clearly waiting for one. "I am certain," she finally said, "that the baron must have...his own...appeal."

Baroness Lae burst out laughing. "Lady Alannys, you've missed your calling. That is the most diplomatic answer I have ever heard. It's plain you should have been an ambassador."

Was that a compliment? Alannys knew the baroness

wasn't mean-spirited. And yet she couldn't help wrinkling her nose, thinking of Ambassador Thell. "I think that must be the first time anyone has said that to me. I don't think I would be very good at it, myself—everything would be fine until the first time I got irritated and spoke my mind, and then we'd find ourselves in a war because I can't keep my mouth shut."

Chen laughed out loud, pulling open the door to the barracks for them. "That's the truth. You must show a nicer face here at the palace than you do with us, Alannys."

Alannys didn't know how to answer that. She felt her face burn red.

Baroness Lae chuckled quietly, leading them into the building. "And now I've embarrassed you. It wasn't my intent, I assure you." Her lips thinned, and she took a few steps in pensive silence. "I married Baron Prubard because I had no other choice. To refuse him would have ruined my entire family."

"Really?" Alannys didn't want to pry, but she couldn't stop her reaction. "I had no idea refusing could cause that kind of scandal."

"No..." Lae sounded uncomfortable, but she wasn't blushing. In fact, her face looked unnaturally pale, and Alannys wondered if it really was a good idea for her to talk about this. But before she could say anything, the baroness spoke again. "The scandal happened many years before that. Before I was born, actually. But Prubard...knew about it. He even had proof...and he would have exposed them."

"I see. Basically you were blackmailed." Alannys could hear the darkness in her own voice. "That doesn't raise my opinion of your husband any at all, you know."

Baroness Lae smiled, but it looked a little shaky. "I'm not familiar with that term. But I doubt there is anything I could tell you about my husband that would raise your opinion of him. Nothing true, that is. I know what kind of man I married, Lady Alannys. It has been my challenge to live with that. In many ways, Prubard's defection to the Dark Alliance was the best thing that could have happened for me and my girls."

Alannys couldn't think of any response that wouldn't make her feel worse, so she kept her mouth shut and walked. They stopped at the end of the corridor past the training rooms. A staircase in the floor descended into a dark, stone passageway. A heavy wooden door reinforced with iron bars lay across the opening. The brass padlock that secured the door to the iron ring in the floor was open, but it didn't really matter.

Standing in front of the door, watching them suspiciously with one hand on the grip of his sword, was Wermal. His narrow eyes flitted from her, to the fearful face of the baroness, to Chen. Nothing he saw seemed to improve his mood.

Alannys tried to smile like she meant it. "Good morning, Wermal."

He said nothing, but remained planted in their path.

"I'm afraid we may have gotten off on the wrong foot," she continued, as pleasantly as she could. "I'm sorry for all that business in the king's chambers."

Wermal stiffened. "What do you want?"

"The baroness has come to visit her husband. Can we take her into the dungeon, or will we need Captain Grayble's permission to do that?"

Something moved behind Wermal's eyes then, something hard and calculating, gone before Alannys could get a good look at it. In its place she found a friendly smile that she guessed he very much wanted her to believe was genuine. "No, no, it's no problem at all. Of course the baroness and our dear Redeemer may go wherever they please." He turned and heaved open the heavy door, then stood back to let them pass.

Alannys followed Baroness Lac down the slick, dank, chiseled stone staircase. The air hung thick around them, and the narrow corridor flickered with a barely sufficient light. Shadows reached for her like spindly fingers. It felt like descending into the bowels of the planet.

But that wasn't the worst part.

The worst part was feeling Wermal's eyes boring into her back every step of the way, and no matter what his smile said, that did not feel friendly.

Not at all.

♫

The dungeon of the Great Palace gave Alannys cold chills. The ragged ceiling hung low over her head, with things hanging from it that could have been the roots of living plants, or could have been the dried corpses of things long dead. Small, dark cells lined the corridor, chilly and stale, with a smell hanging in the air that implied long dead corpses were no oddity here. Dampness surrounded her, and moss grew on the lumpy walls and the jagged, uneven floor. Two small torches flickered on the wall, casting a faint and altogether insufficient light partway through the darkness. It was hard for her to believe the palace she loved concealed something like this — like admiring a perfect, rosy apple, only to find it rotten beneath the skin. The whole thing gave her a claustrophobic feeling that reminded her unpleasantly of the royal catacombs and all that had happened there. She shivered and clung tightly to Chen's arm.

Ahead of them, the baroness slowed, finally stopping before a cell all the way at the end of the corridor. Alannys hung back. She knew she needed to be there to support Baroness Lae, but she had to admit she really, *really* dreaded seeing Prubard again.

"Lae. You have certainly taken your time." The voice oiled from the dark recesses of the cell, slithered between the iron bars and wormed its way into their ears. He clearly wanted the lines to be charming, as Lord Malrec might have delivered them, but frustration was plain in his tone and it spoiled his effort.

Baroness Lae regarded him silently a moment. She appeared calm, but her hands trembled. She clasped them tightly together, perhaps attempting to hide the sign of weakness. "I'm surprised they let me in at all. I've heard you've been making quite a nuisance of yourself."

"Great Muses, woman, can you blame me?" Shock and outrage colored Prubard's tone. "I've been locked in this tiny, filthy cell; I've been treated most terribly and called the most atrocious names; I've been beaten and I've been starved. Is that any way for a man of my station to be treated?"

"I don't know what you expected, when you took up arms against the palace." Alannys hadn't planned to speak, and the cutting, sarcastic sound of her own voice surprised her. "These men have had to clean up the mess you made, Prubard. They've lost...we've lost friends in your stupid rebellion. You're lucky you're still alive."

Prubard stiffened, clutching at the iron bars in front of him. "You!" His tone had lost all civility, and the single word was nearly a shriek. "Lae, explain yourself. Why have you brought this woman here? And the wretched Singari dog as well, I see?"

"They are here because they are my friends, my Lord." Lae spoke quietly, but she held her head high. Alannys breathed a sigh of relief to see it—perhaps they would make it through this after all. Whatever the reason Prubard had summoned them, she didn't imagine it would be good. "What could my Lord possibly have to say to me that he could not say in front of them?"

"Are you...are you jesting? Is this a *joke?*" Prubard looked back and forth between them all before settling on Lae again. "I know it is clear the dire situation I am in; I know you can see how far I have fallen. I did not expect you would bring others to mock me in my misery."

Alannys frowned. Prubard didn't sound like himself— she had never heard him adopt such a formal tone, not even at court, where it would have been appropriate.

Prubard was a blunt, plain-spoken man—often to the point of rudeness. What could be so important that he would behave this way now?

"Of course not, my Lord," Baroness Lae said calmly, seeming as though she noticed nothing wrong. "They have simply accompanied me here to support me in this difficult time. No one here is mocking you."

"I see." Baron Prubard's eyes flicked to Alannys, then back to his wife, unconvinced. "Perhaps it is as you say. In the end it does not matter to me. You have come, and that is the only thing that is important to me."

Lae didn't seem to know how to respond to that. "I—I see."

"So you called her here just so you could stare at her pretty face?" Chen sounded amused. "I didn't figure you for that sort of man, Prubard."

The baron's eyes narrowed, dark and unreadable behind the folds of flesh that framed them. "You insolent cur. How dare you address me, and by name? When I am free of this place I will have you whipped like the dog you are."

"There's only one dog in this room, Prubard," Alannys said sharply, "and it isn't Chen. His point is valid. You must have had some reason for troubling the baroness to come see you. Why don't you just get to the point and tell us what you want?"

"Isn't it obvious?" he snapped. "I want out of this place. Lae, you seem to have made yourself quite cozy at the Great Palace. Exert some of your influence and get me out of here. For a man of my stature to be held in such a place as this...forced to speak to such people as these...it is unthinkable!"

"That's certainly one word for it," Alannys muttered. She glanced over at Lae, but the baroness seemed deep in thought, staring at her feet and acknowledging none of them. "Tell me, Prubard, exactly what stature do you imagine you have?"

His fleshy face conveyed nothing but confusion. "What is wrong with you, woman? I am a baron. The Baron of Orinthal! I do not belong imprisoned in a dungeon like a common criminal! Nobles guard their own...this is not how a man of my position should be treated."

Alannys shook her head. "I am sorry to disillusion you, Prubard, but you are not the Baron of Orinthal. That dubious honor falls to your son Trago, at the appointment of the king himself."

"What?" The color drained from Prubard's face in a sudden rush, and he crumpled to sit in a disheveled heap on the dirty stone floor. "This cannot be. You—you are lying to me! I will be free of this place, and I will take back what is rightfully mine and I will have my revenge, woman, on you and all the others!"

"No." The voice that cut across Prubard's half-insane ranting was calm and firm, and it did not come from Alannys. She turned in surprise to see Baroness Lae, standing tall and looking down dispassionately at the fallen lump of flesh that used to be her husband. "You can't seriously have thought you could rebel against the throne with no consequence at all? You are not a baron of anything now, and Orinthal has a ruler who will handle it much better than you ever did. You will not leave this place. The king will make certain of that."

"But..." Prubard stammered. "But, but you—you have a *duty* to me, Lae!"

"No more. I will not help you, Prubard," Lae said. "You are a small and despicable man, and you have pushed me around for too long. This time, you'll face your own consequences. I will not save you."

"You—you ungrateful *bitch!*" Prubard howled. "How dare you defy me! Do you have any idea where you would be without me?"

"Does it matter?" Lae said mildly. "Anywhere would be better than with you."

She turned and walked out of the dungeon, head held

high.

"Alannys," Prubard croaked, as she was turning to follow Lae. "Alannys, wait. Please."

Against her better judgment, Alannys turned back to face him. She felt Chen's hand fall on her arm; a warning. "What?"

Prubard reached out toward her through the bars, still sprawled pitifully on the floor. "You know I've always liked you, Alannys. Whatever you may think of me, you must know that I don't deserve this. Help me. Please."

"*Liked* me?" Alannys snorted. "Is that what you call your vile proposition to the king the first time we met? I'm sorry, I can't agree with that assessment. Any of it. I do think you deserve this, Prubard. You cast your lot against Dorramon months ago, and have spent every minute since working to destroy everything he fights for. There is justice in reaping what you sow. And you have sown this for a long time."

Prubard pulled his hand back inside the cell. "You'll regret that. Do you seriously think you and your precious king can get rid of me this easily? I will be free, and when I am I will exact my revenge. You will get no mercy from me."

Alannys took a step closer to the cell, staring dead into Prubard's flat black eyes. "Bring it on. You're a pathetic man, Prubard, and I'm not afraid of you. If you manage to find your way clear of here, I'll be waiting. Do your worst."

She turned her back on the ex-Baron of Orinthal, and stormed out of the dungeon with Chen at her side. She never looked back, never slowed down, just stomped up the slick stairs as if her fury made her immune to injury.

Only, as it turned out, it didn't. She emerged from the dungeon and started back down the corridor with nothing more than a perfunctory "thanks" over her shoulder to Wermal. But before she had taken three steps, an almighty blow knocked the entire world sideways. For a moment that seemed much too long, she couldn't seem to understand what had happened. She stumbled, seeing spreading black splotches, feeling lightning streak across her brain, hearing Chen frantically calling her name. Every thump of her heartbeat resonated like painful, pounding thunder in the side of her head. She managed to put her hand against the thundering spot, and it came away wet.

Wet with blood.

Then she understood—too late, the world was slipping away from her like grains of sand through her fingers. The black splotches spread to consume her entire field of vision, Chen's voice faded to nothing, and she knew no more.

♫

The world was slow to focus when Alannys cracked open her eyes—fuzzy, like she was looking out of cloudy glass. Her neck felt stiff and creaky. She had a pounding whopper of a headache, and she couldn't remember why. She felt certain she should be much worse off, but she couldn't remember the reason for that, either.

Her hand tingled with electricity.

She blinked a few times, squeezing her eyes shut, trying to clear her vision. She was somewhere in the keep of the palace, she was pretty sure of that much. But beyond that...

"Are you awake?" The voice was Dorramon's, and he sounded concerned. That explained the tingling in her hand, anyway.

Too bad nothing else made sense.

"Alannys? Are you all right?"

She forced her complaining neck to turn her head toward the voice. Her vision cleared, like fog burning off in the sun, and she could see him at last, kneeling in front of the sofa in her sitting room, on which she was apparently sprawled. His blue eyes were cloudy with worry and fatigue, and his face looked drawn and haggard. "I'm fine," she said finally. It felt like her voice came from somewhere else; it didn't even sound right in her ears. "You look awful."

He laughed, but it was a tense, preoccupied sound, with none of its usual sparkle. "Do I? I guess it's to be expected — I've been singing."

"Singing?" she echoed in sudden alarm. "Why? What's happened?" The world danced around her when she sat up, and she swayed, putting a hand to her forehead.

"You happened, as usual." The remark was obviously meant to be teasing, but there was no humor in the way he said it, and he was still inspecting her face as though he was looking for something. "Dizzy?"

"No, not at all." She faked a smile and forced her hand to her side. She couldn't have said why she was lying — it was embarrassing to be seen as weak, maybe.

A frown flickered across his face, and she knew he'd caught her — it was very difficult to lie with a mindlink, especially when she wasn't feeling so red hot anyway. "If you say so. Maybe you should lie down a bit longer."

"Nonsense." She stood up on feet that felt strangely uncoordinated, and attempted to weave her way into the bedroom. "I have to go get ready for the wedding."

"The wedding." He caught her arm as she stumbled, and steadied her. "Are you sure that's a good idea?"

Something about his face felt unfamiliar to her. Or maybe it was something about the room...her impressions were scattered and difficult to pin down. "Of course. They're a couple of my best friends. How could I miss it?"

"Under the circumstances, I think you might be forgiven," he muttered. "Tell me, Alannys, how much do you remember about what happened today?"

This question didn't make sense to her. She frowned, wondering if that could be what felt different about his face.

Did that even make sense?

"Do you mean the funerals?" she said finally. "I'd rather not remember any more than I have to, honestly."

"No. I'm not talking about the funerals. What happened right before you woke up in here?"

"I—" It felt like her brain missed a shift. Where there should have been a memory, as clear as any of her others, her brain served up...nothing. "I don't remember. I remember coming back from camp, and...Baron Prubard? Wait, that doesn't make sense. I haven't seen him since the fighting last night. Why would I remember seeing him today?"

She *did* remember seeing him, there was no question of that. She had brief, fuzzy recollections...he had threatened her, hadn't he? And he'd called Lae an ungrateful bitch. But none of it made sense—it was as if someone had taken a proper memory and chopped it up, then shuffled the pieces.

Dorramon sighed, still holding onto her arm. "You remember seeing Prubard today because you did see Prubard today. But you don't remember it clearly, and you don't remember what happened next, because you have a concussion. I don't think it's very bad—I hope it isn't bad —because I've been singing for close to an hour."

"A concussion." Did that explain how strange everything had felt since she woke up? Even the word felt strange, at least applied to her. "How on earth did I...wait. Wait, it's coming back to me...bits and pieces. It was a royal guard—Wermal! That bastard hit me!"

"Yes. And he nearly killed you. So I think, all things considered, it might be best if you give the ceremony a miss."

"But—"

"I'll stay with you," he said, suddenly averting his eyes. "You don't need to feel left out."

Alannys studied his face a moment, trying to figure his angle. He still refused to look at her. "Dorramon," she finally said, "I'm sorry."

"Sorry?" He wouldn't look at her but he sounded disinterested, as though they were discussing the weather.

"Whatever do you have to be sorry for?"

"About this morning." The words came hard, and they sounded stiff. "I know you weren't expecting that. I just…"

"Just what?" Dorramon abruptly *did* look at her, and now that she had his attention, she didn't know what to do with it. "I don't know what you must think of me, helpless and chained to the Great Palace while you travel the country doing the dangerous work. I know well enough about the rumors that would make me your abuser, or your pet. But I'm not a hero, Alannys, or a villain. I'm not a noble, perfect king. I'm just a man."

"I know that," she said haltingly. "I didn't mean to hurt your feelings. I'm sorry."

Dorramon stared at her a moment, then dragged his hand down his face as though he was scrubbing away something unpleasant. "Look at me. I swear I did not come here intending to shout at you. You don't need to apologize to me, Alannys. I should apologize to you. I know your situation is impossible, yet I continually ask too much of you."

"No, I—"

Dorramon held up a hand, cutting her off. "It's not necessary. I know you are only trying to do what you believe to be right. So am I. That should be enough for both of us, I think, and it isn't why I'm suggesting you stay here. I just think you aren't up to it—you need to rest."

"Nonsense. I have to go, you know that. You won't go without me, and they won't have the wedding without you. I'm not willing to ruin their big day over this, are you?"

"No," he said begrudgingly. "But I'm still not sure this is a good idea."

"Me either. But have you got a better one? We can't ruin their wedding."

All that got her was a grunt, which at this point was

probably as close to assent as she would get. To her surprise, he disappeared into her big closet, and returned a few moments later, holding the same red gown she had worn to his coronation, what felt like forever ago. He thrust it into her arms without preamble or explanation, and she looked from it to him in confusion.

"I think you should wear that today. A bit of a statement, if you will. People will remember it, and it seems they need to be reminded."

She didn't know what to say to that, so she didn't say anything, just took the gown with her into the bath chamber. She washed the dried blood out of her hair with unfortunately cold water, grimacing at how sensitive the side of her head was. She almost expected to feel a dent in her skull.

So Dorramon thought a statement needed to be made. It was hardly surprising, given everything that had happened, but it was concerning. She had brought more than chaos to the palace, she had brought danger, and if she stayed here, it would eventually reach him as well. But what, at this point, could she do? She couldn't stay here and endanger him further, but how could she leave him? What would she even do? Chen had said the Singari would always take her back, but she knew he was overstating his case. Too many of the Singari had never wanted her there in the first place—too many of them would be glad now that she was gone. And what could she do for them now anyway? They had accompanied her on her mission—a mission that was now over, any way she looked at it. Where should she go from here? Where *could* she go from here?

She could only think of one real answer to that question, and she wasn't sure she liked it. To be honest, it scared her. A lot.

All of which meant Dorramon wasn't likely at all to go along with it. But she didn't have much choice, not if she wanted to do the right thing.

She pulled her towel-dried hair into a short, messy French braid, and tied the end with a ribbon. She fastened her royal bracelet around her wrist, did her best to make herself presentable, and went back out to meet Dorramon again.

Apparently he had ducked out to change while she cleaned up, because she found him waiting in her sitting room, resplendent in his coronation clothes, his crown glittering atop his head.

It seemed she wasn't the only one making a statement today.

He made no comment, just stepped up to her and slipped her royal medallion over her head. She watched it glitter against the front of her gown, and choked up, hearing Raman's voice in her mind again. *I think he's content being your shield.* He obviously wasn't ready to quit just yet. But how could she let him continue?

Dorramon offered his arm, and together they left her rooms and started down the corridor, while she tried to figure out some way to approach what she had to say.

"Aren't you and Raman worried about any push-back," she finally said, deciding to come at it sideways, "for Kalyn marrying so far above her station? Or for Raman marrying so far below?"

For a long moment there was no reply. Alannys though perhaps she had offended him, or touched on a topic she shouldn't have. She sneaked a glance in his direction, and found him staring straight ahead with his lips pressed into a tight line, wearing a contemplative expression that made her wonder exactly what he was reading into the question.

"No," he said finally. "Most of the people who would be likely to make a fuss about something like that left the Great Palace months ago."

"Oh," she said, "that makes sense—"

He cut her off, almost as if he hadn't even heard her. "But really, it doesn't matter."

"It...doesn't?"

Dorramon smiled gently at her. "Neither Raman's happiness nor Kalyn's should depend on what other people think. Don't you agree?"

She started to answer, then hesitated, biting her lip.

He pushed open the door to the keep and stepped aside, holding it for her. The sun streaking across the vestibule floor looked impossibly bright and cheerful, part of a world where she could never truly belong. "Alannys?"

She wanted to give it her blessing. Of course she wanted her friends to be happy. But she was well aware that Dorramon was probably drawing a parallel here, a parallel that she felt was inappropriate. "No one will go to war for Raman and Kalyn's happiness," she said quietly, her eyes on her feet as she walked out into the inner ward. The sunlight seemed to fade as soon as it touched her. "No one will die for it."

Dorramon sighed, a sound so faint she could almost believe she had imagined it. "Raman should never have told you those things, Alannys. It was no accident that he waited until I was indisposed to speak of it."

"You didn't want me to know?" She could hear aggravation in her rising tone. "How would that help? How long did you think you could hide the fact that things are falling apart around you?"

For a moment, Dorramon stopped dead in his tracks. Alannys stopped too, but she feared she had finally crossed a line. She couldn't speak to him, much less look at him. Maybe she didn't have to worry about leaving — maybe she was about to be summarily banished. She stared uncomfortably at her feet, holding her breath, until he started walking again.

She fell in beside him, sneaking a peek at his face as she did. He was frowning.

"You won't believe me," he finally said, "if I tell you that you've got it wrong. I can't pretend to know exactly what Raman told you. But you should both know better than to think I would let Ravanmark fall down around my ears."

His words shamed her. She felt bad for hurting him before, and she knew her doubt was only adding to it. But she also knew what she had to do. "And Wermal?" she said. "How does that sort of thing fit in? How do you stop him?"

"We don't have to," Dorramon said flatly. "He's dead."

"D—dead?" She hadn't been ready for that. "You had him executed?"

"I did not touch him, nor did any member of my guard. But the man is dead, and nothing remains for you to worry about. Will that suffice?"

His formal tone stung. She pulled in a deep breath and pressed on. "No. I'm sorry—I don't think Wermal left those notes in your room, and I don't think there is nothing left to worry about. It's plain my presence is causing problems." There was nothing else for it, an indirect approach only gave her time to stall. "After the wedding, I'm going to be packing. I'll be leaving tomorrow to attempt the acts of the Redeemer. I'd like you to announce it after I'm gone—maybe it will buy you some peace."

"No."

"Look, Dorramon, I know you aren't crazy about the idea, but—"

"No, you look, Alannys. I know you think I'm biased and you're probably right, but I am telling you as objectively as I can that now is not a good time for the acts. It isn't a good time for you to leave at all. Big things are about to happen here...things that you are very much a part of. You can do the acts after this is all settled...in fact, I'll go with you when you do. But for now, I need you here."

Alannys didn't know how to respond to a speech like that, didn't know what she should do. She had expected resistance, sure, but she hadn't expected to be shut down so completely. And she wasn't wild about the idea of taking off on her own again, when everything she really wanted was right here. But it felt like defeat to say so.

Side by side, they walked on toward the Great Hall in a silence that felt heavy and strained.

After a few steps, Dorramon reached out and took her hand in his, lacing his fingers between hers. His hand was warm and gentle, and the gesture seemed to say everything that neither of them could voice.

Tears welled up in her eyes, and she didn't trust herself to speak. She just squeezed his hand. After a moment, he squeezed back.

Alannys loved Dorramon from the bottom of her soul —she was more certain of that than she'd ever been of anything in her life. She didn't want to upset him, or hurt him, or make him unhappy.

So why did that seem to be all she could do lately?

♫

They ended up arriving late for the wedding. Of course the ceremony wouldn't begin without the king, so when they walked into the Great Hall they found the assembled audience waiting quietly, if impatiently.

Alannys immediately flushed bright red. Her first instinct was to apologize to everything and everybody in the room. She knew that, given everything that had happened, it was lucky they had made it at all. Somehow, though, that failed to make her feel any better. But Dorramon started up the center aisle as though nothing was amiss. She held her tongue and walked beside him, headed for the seats reserved for them in the front, surrounded by Royal Guards and apart from the rest of the crowd. She could feel all of the many eyes following their progress, and she knew not all of them were friendly. It bothered her, in a way it never had before, to know this.

Alannys loved weddings, especially when they were for friends. And she had never seen a wedding in Ravanmark. She took her seat next to Dorramon with every intention of watching closely and enjoying the ceremony.

But almost immediately, she knew something was wrong, almost as soon as she sat down she started receiving short, uncontrolled bursts through the mindlink, so brief she had a hard time even processing what was happening.

Dorramon slumped forward oddly in his chair, almost as though he suddenly lacked the strength to hold himself upright, drawing strange, surreptitious glances from the guards.

"Dorramon." She leaned close and delivered the word —barely a whisper—right into his ear. The way things were, she didn't trust the mindlink. "Are you all right?"

His head twitched convulsively in something that might have been a nod. "Muse's Fever. It will pass."

"Muse's Fever?" Alannys couldn't keep the horror out of her tone, even at a whisper.

"Don't worry—I had some Muse's tea. I'll be fine."

"Muse's tea isn't a cure, you know that. You shouldn't even be here!"

Dorramon didn't say anything, and Alannys realized, with a renewed rush of horror, that he was keeping his silence because he couldn't say anything *nice*. It was her fault he was here—he had tried to talk her out of coming altogether, and she had insisted.

"You might have mentioned you were sick," she muttered under her breath, but the words carried no sting. That was her fault too, for it was her life he had been singing to save.

That didn't really make her feel any better.

She caught him as he slumped even more, and ended up supporting him. He leaned against her, burning up, his head on her shoulder. She didn't even think he was conscious.

The wedding was happening right in front of her—she knew that, and yet she wasn't even aware of the proceedings. As though a dam had burst, the mindlink rushed with a torrent of images, feelings, recollections, and experiences, threatening to overload her brain. She felt she might drown, swept mercilessly along on a tidal wave of sensations that weren't her own. The sumptuously decorated Great Hall, Brale's droning oration, even Raman and Kalyn on the dais in their finest attire faded from her awareness. She felt completely cut adrift in the deluge.

Occasionally a clear impression would make it through, like breaking the surface of rushing waters to see the sun.

She saw a grassy, tree-lined field dotted with tombstones and mausoleums. She could feel the clammy fog brushing her skin, could hear the muted conversations of the mourners around Delline's gravesite. She could see Queen Farrine, her pale face looking stark and strained as she leaned heavily on Grand Chancellor Ebrad for support. A few feet away, Kalyn sobbed quietly into a handkerchief. Raman had his arm around her, shielding her as she grieved. And the thought appeared, from someone else's mind, that this was as it should be.

Then she saw herself, starkly cold and alone in the foggy morning, accepting neither support nor shelter, and looking as though she never would. It was the first time Alannys had ever seen herself through someone else's eyes, and she didn't like the picture of her it presented — cold and aloof, holding herself away from everyone who cared about her.

Because Dorramon *did* care about her, there was no doubting that, it was loud and clear in his memories, and she could feel his emotions as clearly as her own — he loved her with a depth and breadth that was only matched by her feelings for him. It nearly overwhelmed her, all that intensity — all Dorramon had wanted, in that moment, was to give her that support and shelter he knew she would not accept.

She scarcely had time to acknowledge all of this — let

alone process it—when the tide swelled up around her and swept her away. The next time she found her feet she was somewhere else entirely; inside, with stone walls and smooth floors, nearly deserted, quiet in that shocked manner that falls when something awful has happened.

It was the corridor in the barracks of the Royal Guard leading to the dungeon—the heavy grate stood open, leaning against the wall. She was standing stone still, overcome by someone else's shock and horror. Dorramon's emotions flooded her so intensely, so viscerally, that for a moment her frazzled brain couldn't even make sense of what she was seeing.

She could see herself, sprawled gracelessly on the hard floor, her frighteningly pale face resting in a slick pool of her own blood. A sticky mess caked the side of her head, and she couldn't blame Dorramon for wondering, in that first frantic moment, if he had already lost her.

But she wasn't the only person there lying in a pool of blood.

Wermal lay lifeless on the floor a few feet away, his fingers still clutching the wooden baton he had evidently used on her, an expression of pole-axed surprise fixed forever on his dead face. He had been stabbed—over and over, so many times she had to wonder if someone had continued attacking him well after they knew he was dead.

That thought sent a cold chill creeping down her spine, or Dorramon's—it was difficult to tell her reactions from his at this point.

Someone stood over Wermal's corpse even now, a man with blood-slicked hands clutching a dagger, a man with the dead guard's blood spattering his face and clothes. Slowly her gaze dragged up to regard him, her heart pounding and her dread growing as realization dawned...

The man was Chen.

♫

Raman and Kalyn ran down the center aisle of the

Great Hall, hand in hand, their heads ducked as their guests tossed rose petals and thyme over them. Alannys came back to herself in time to watch, but not in time to grab her own pouch and participate. She figured Dorramon had to be doing better though, for her to even be aware enough to witness the end of the ceremony. It was a joyous scene and she couldn't explain why it should give her a pang to see it. But it did, and her mood was worse after the wedding than it had been before.

All at once Dorramon leaned over to her. "Do you see?" he whispered. His lips were so close, they brushed her skin when he spoke, and his breath was hot in her ear. Her heart gave an almighty thump, then beat double-time. She tried to focus.

"Truly," he said, "anything is possible."

She knew he meant it. She didn't see how he stayed so positive in his position, but she had been inside his head and she could vouch that to him all things really *were* possible, and to him this unlikely wedding was proof. Perhaps, to him, it was even a precedent. Anything was possible.

To him.

She just wished she could believe it too.

Dorramon took her arm and led her back down the aisle, toward the big double doors where Raman and Kalyn waited with beaming faces to greet their guests. He strode confidently beside her, moving not at all like a man who was ill, and a surreptitious glance at his face revealed none of the strain she would have expected to see. The Muse's tea must have been more effective than she had expected, or he was better at hiding it than she imagined.

Or both.

Dorramon grinned broadly at his friends, clasping their hands tightly. "Congratulations, you two. I'm so happy for you, I don't even have the words. Good luck, Kalyn. I don't know how you put up with him."

Kalyn's face colored, and Dorramon and Raman

laughed out loud. Alannys felt like a raincloud hanging over their happiness, and she attempted to put herself in a better mood, to offer them a smile that felt a bit less forced. "Double congratulations from me," she said. "This was such an amazing wedding. I know you will both be very happy."

She reached for Raman's hand, but he grabbed her and pulled her into a crushing hug instead. The gesture caught her off guard, but she hugged him back. She didn't have many friends as true as Raman, and she really did wish him the best.

"I know this had to be hard for you," he said, low and right into her ear. "Are you all right?"

Abruptly her throat closed up, and for a moment she couldn't speak. She nodded her head, and finally forced out the words. "I'm fine. Really. You shouldn't worry about me."

"You know I do. If you need anything, you tell me. Any time." He held her at arm's length, studying her face. She wondered if he could see the tears that suddenly threatened to overwhelm her. If so, he gave no sign of it as he clapped her on the shoulder and turned to the next person in line.

"He really is fond of you, my Lady," Kalyn said, looking into her face anxiously. Alannys wondered how much of her inner turmoil they sensed, how much of her impossible situation they had discussed, and felt very exposed.

"And I am of him too," Alannys answered automatically. "You picked a good one, Kalyn. I really do think you two are going to be so happy together."

"Thank you." Kalyn smiled, but then she bit her lip, looking at Alannys again. "Please do let us know if there is anything we can do for you. I'm afraid I won't be able to come help you anymore...with the change in my station...and my married duties..."

"Oh, don't worry about that! Really, Kalyn, I'm fine. I

want both of you to stop fretting over me, especially at a time like this."

Kalyn didn't look convinced. "Thank you, my Lady." She turned to Raman and the guests in line, but she glanced back at Alannys and Dorramon, and bit her lip again.

"I should never have come here," Alannys muttered. "I'm just spoiling everyone's fun." She turned away, feeling like a great big wet blanket, planning to sneak away from the party in the inner ward and hide alone in her room for a while.

"Nonsense." Dorramon's voice was unruffled and his face was smooth — she couldn't tell what he was thinking. But he caught her arm in a firm grip that left no possibility of sneaking anywhere. "They would miss you if you weren't here, you know that. They only worry about you because they are your friends."

"I know. But Dorramon, I really don't feel much like celebrating right now. I've just been knocked halfway to next week. And you've just had Muse's Fever."

"That's all the more reason to celebrate." His tone brooked no opposition. The inner ward had been decorated for the reception, with colored candles and tables of food and drink. Dorramon handed her a silver goblet of strong red wine, and took one for himself. "You're still here, and so am I. Everything is fine. Relax. You've had a lot on your mind lately."

A lot on her mind. Well, she supposed that was one way of putting it. She drank deeply of the wine to cover her discomfort, surprised to find that it was actually quite good. It had been warmed against the chill of the evening, and it seemed to warm her when she drank it.

Alannys knew there was a lot they needed to talk about. But she also knew none of it was suitable for public discussion, so she stood silent and awkward next to Dorramon, watching him but pretending not to, as the remaining light faded around them. How much longer would she be able to stay near him? She didn't have a good answer for that, and even asking the question made something crack inside her heart.

She didn't know how long they stood there together in that uncomfortable silence. She finished her first goblet of wine, and a second, and had made a good start on a third, when Dorramon glanced at her, eyebrows raised. "Are you sure you're not drinking too much of that? It might not be a good idea—perhaps something to eat would be wise."

"I'm fine." Wine always made her feel warm. On a cool night like this one, that seemed like a blessing. She could feel the color rise in her cheeks under his gaze, and that felt a bit less like a blessing. She averted her eyes. "I think it cuts the chill. Besides, it might improve my mood."

Dorramon sighed, and turned suddenly to face her. The look on his face was serious, and the shadows falling across his handsome features imparted a resoluteness she had never seen there before. She felt herself tense. "Look, Alannys, I know things haven't been easy for you. You went through so much in your travels—and it hasn't exactly been smooth sailing since you came back. I understand your worries, but..." He trailed off, searching her face as if the words he wanted might be found there. "But I don't think—"

"Toast!" She didn't know who had raised the shout, but it was close enough it made her jump. Others immediately took up the cry, and it became a loud, incessant chant. "Toast, toast, toast, toast!"

"Ach." Dorramon ran a hand through his hair, clearly frustrated. "That's my cue, I'm afraid. Don't go anywhere, all right? We'll continue this conversation when I get back."

"But..." She felt claustrophobic, cornered by his concern and well-meaning. She hadn't yet worked out what her path should be from here, and she feared she might be pushed into making a premature choice. "But I should really—"

"Alannys, please. This is important. Just—just wait for me." He carried his goblet into the center of the open inner ward, where the torchlight was strongest. The crowd fell silent, and he addressed them, his ringing tenor carrying easily through the space. "Tonight we celebrate the marriage of two of the finest people in all of Ravanmark. Our dear Kalyn, whose freedom from the tyranny of Lord Malrec has now been echoed in the freedom we all so recently gained, and the Arch-Prince Raman, whose winding path has led him up many hills and around many bends, but never seemed to be leading him here. It is a miracle of sorts that these two have come together at all. It seems to me that our dear friends have taught us a valuable lesson this night, and that lesson is that miracles are not only possible but perhaps more likely than we think."

His eyes found hers on those last words, and gave her a start. It made her uncomfortable—how many people listening to him now knew what he really meant when he spoke to them of miracles? As soon as his eyes left her, she turned and hurried toward the keep. Maybe her room was the best place for her after all. Dorramon's hopeful words were meant to be uplifting, she knew that. But in her mind's eye she could see the Great Hall as she had seen it the night before, smeared with blood and littered with bodies of dead and dying men...and she knew she couldn't stand there any longer. She couldn't condone any more bloodshed on her account. Her guilt spurred her on and she moved quickly, seeking the cover of the shadows at the edges of the reception.

"Sneaking off?" The low voice from the shadows sounded darkly amused, and it froze her in place.

"Ch—Chen?" She stopped cold in shock, and saw him again in her mind, as blood-smeared as the hall she'd just been remembering. "What are you doing hiding over here in the dark?"

"Staying out of the way. I don't—I don't quite feel as though I belong here." His gaze flitted out, over the reception and away again, never touching on her, and she thought perhaps she wasn't the only one nursing a guilty conscience that evening. "I have no place in decent society."

She frowned at him. "Ballocks. I don't agree with that."

"That's only because you don't understand. I'm not—I don't mean because I'm Singari. Because I'm a murderer. I'm a killer, Alannys."

"I already know that. And I still say I'm right. Why did you kill him?"

"What?"

"Wermal. You had a reason, right? What was it?"

"He was trying to kill you!" Chen's reticence was gone now; his dark eyes flashed with outrage. "He hit you—you were lying there bleeding—but Alannys, he wasn't stopping! He seriously meant to kill you—I had to stop him. I had to."

Alannys tried to give no indication of how deeply that upset her. She'd known Wermal didn't like her—but he had seriously wanted her dead? Enough to do it himself? "Well, don't you think that matters? You had a good reason for what you did. You didn't just take a random notion to kill someone, like he did."

Chen didn't argue, but he didn't agree either. And he still wouldn't look at her.

Alannys sighed. "Look, Chen, what you did is killing in defense of someone else. It's no different than what Trago did in the Cavern of the Damned. Hell, I'd have done it myself for you in Shadowkeep if you hadn't been so bad off at the time. Even Dorramon has done that before. If you're a monster, you're only as much as he is, and you've every bit as much right to be here. Unless you want to argue that the King of Ravanmark is an uncivilized monster who isn't fit for decent society?"

"I don't guess I'd care to make that argument, no."

Chen's tone was sour. "But it doesn't really make me feel any better. I just...I don't think I ever realized I carried something so...dark...inside me. *Part* of me."

"All humans have the ability to kill, Chen. It's when and why they choose to use it that makes the difference — not having the ability at all."

"I hope you're right. It's going to take some getting used to, that's for sure." He heaved a massive sigh, as though he was expelling something unpleasant. "None of that explains what you're doing over here, though. Or am I wrong that you're running away?"

"Sorry," Alannys mumbled, not quite meeting his gaze. All of the sudden it was her turn to be evasive. The light really was bad over here; his dark hair and dark clothes seemed to fade into the darkness around them. "I'm not much in the mood for a party, I suppose."

"Party?" Chen echoed. Her eyes were finally adjusting; she could see him holding a silver goblet full of red wine as though he wasn't sure what to do with it. He looked at the gleaming goblet, and out at the crowd of people scattered into little groups across the inner ward. "Can you even *use* that word to describe this? It would certainly be the dullest party I've ever seen."

Alannys laughed, remembering wild revels around blazing bonfires. "I suppose it would be. What are Singari weddings like, Chen?"

"Oh, that's right, you never got to see one." He sounded surprised. "I'm not even sure how to compare them, we do so many things that would never fit in here. Money dancing, for instance, and jumping the broomstick — I'm sure everyone here would be horrified."

"Dancing." Alannys realized with some surprise that her goblet was empty again; she held it up anyway as the crowd toasted Dorramon's apparently finished speech. Was it the wine that had made her mood so dark? "You're probably right, they probably wouldn't know how to handle it."

"Outsiders," Chen said, as if that explained everything, and slugged back the rest of his wine in one pull.

"When I get married," Alannys said decisively, "I'm having dancing at my reception. With music."

Chen stared at her, his shock plain even in the low light. Alannys was surprised at herself, too—where had that blunt declaration come from? Was the wine really that strong?

But she couldn't deny that what she had said was true.

Belatedly, she noticed Chen's knuckles were strained and white on the hand clenched around his goblet. That made her feel bad—knowing that she had hurt him. "Is it —is it official, then? We're to the point of planning weddings?"

"No." Her response was as blunt as it was painful. She knew her reaction was unreasonable—how could Chen have expected the simple question to hit a nerve? But she couldn't help it; on this particular issue she was still raw and bleeding. "Forgive me—I don't know what I'm on about, talking about weddings. I'll never have one. I will never marry."

Chen couldn't seem to summon a response. Alannys turned away to put her empty goblet on a table...

...and found Dorramon standing right behind her, frozen to the spot, a stricken expression on his face that pierced her to her core.

For a split second she stood there in mute shock, unable to do anything but stare. She'd had *no idea* he was so close—what had possessed her to shoot off her mouth in the first place?

And how in the world could she fix it now? She had hurt him worse than she'd hurt Chen—and she hadn't meant to, either time. But she couldn't make it better and she didn't think she even had the right to try.

Alannys turned and ran headlong to the keep. She didn't slow down for her own guilt, or for the anguished voice that called her name behind her. She didn't stop running until she was safely inside her own room.

Then she leaned back against the door behind her and cried as though her heart had broken.

♪

Alannys spent the rest of that night locked in her room, huddled in a ball on the bed with her knees pulled up against her chest. Sometimes she thought, sometimes she cried, but she didn't sleep at all. Three or four different times people knocked at her door, but she never answered and they all eventually went away.

Dorramon had tried to contact her through the mindlink, so she held it shut. What could he say that would make any difference now? What could she say? She understood the situation well enough, and if she was having trouble accepting it, that was her own lookout. Dorramon's kind consideration toward her feelings was only slowing everybody down, and in the long run it probably wasn't doing either of them any good. She didn't pack, but she knew she should.

Eventually a faint light began to glow in the window, gradually gaining strength. Dawn had broken, but what did it mean to her? She had spent all night trying to figure out what place there was for her in Ravanmark, and she was no closer to an answer than she had been when she ran from the reception the night before. Once upon a time she'd told Chen she had to come back here, that she had to stay at the Great Palace even if all she could do for Dorramon was stand on the sidelines and watch him live his life without her. She shook her head, remembering her confidence back then. Had she had any *idea* of the sheer magnitude of pain involved in what she had sworn to do?

She watched the new sunbeams streak across the floor of her bedroom, but felt nothing. The bright light didn't lift her spirits, it didn't even feel cheerful — it felt harsh and demanding, and she tired of looking at it almost as soon as she saw it.

It was a measure of a person's mood, she thought,

when something as warm and good as sunlight could rub them the wrong way.

She pulled on her leather boots and wandered out into the courtyard, in the same rumpled linen shirt and work pants she'd spent the night in. She needed some distraction, even if it was just a change of scenery, and she figured there wasn't much chance of running into anyone in the courtyard this early.

A morose sigh from the garden was her first clue that she was wrong.

She froze in mid-step, squinting out into the courtyard, poorly lit by the oblique angle of the morning sun. She probably should have turned and gone right back into her room, but after a breath a fresh air, she dreaded going back.

So she went quietly on out toward the garden, wondering who else in the keep had been driven from their chambers this early by demons that they could not quite slay.

Then she saw the figure slumped on one of the benches near the water garden, the forehead buried in caramel-colored hands, the shiny, longish black hair obscuring the face, and she knew. Of course. There were enough demons to go around, and not just for palace residents.

"Chen." She stopped near the bench, unsure how she should proceed. He must have heard her approach—he must have. No one moved that quietly, least of all her. And yet he hadn't moved, in fact he was so completely still she might have thought he was asleep, if his position hadn't made that impossible. "Are you all right?"

"Alannys." He still didn't move, but his voice told her pretty well how he would look—the single word had no inflection at all. He sounded ragged, and utterly exhausted. "We've got to stop meeting like this."

No joking laced the words; they were flat, completely deadpan, and yet they reminded her of something she had sensed through the open rush of the mindlink during

Dorramon's Muse's Fever: jealousy. Dorramon was torn, driven to distraction by his own conflicting emotions — she knew this because she had felt them herself. On the one hand he was jealous — madly, bitterly jealous of Chen, of the time he had spent with her, of the casual familiarity they shared, of the feelings still hanging there between them. But on the other, he knew no one had forced her to come back, he knew that he could trust her, and he did. He knew she loved him, and he buried it all so deeply no trace could be seen. Alannys didn't know how he managed, and the sudden reminder made her feel guilty again. She shifted uncomfortably from foot to foot. "I can't argue that. And yet I notice you've managed to completely sidestep the question. *Are* you all right?"

"I am perfectly fine," he said, "at least as fine as it is possible for any of us to be. I've just been thinking." He raised his head and regarded her wanly, from a face that looked gaunter than the last time she'd seen it. "Worrying doesn't suit me — I'm not used to it. But what about you — are you all right, Alannys? You really look terrible."

"Blunt as always," Alannys said wryly. "I could say the same for you, but I was trying to be nice. I didn't get much sleep, I'm afraid — I was up all last night."

"All night." Chen leaned back against the bench, folding his hands behind his head. "Doing what? Stewing?"

She glanced at him in sharp surprise. "I guess that's accurate enough. I was thinking, and it wasn't very pleasant."

"Thinking all night? It doesn't *sound* very pleasant. What were you thinking about, if you don't mind my asking?"

Alannys stalled, wandering toward the water garden. When she sat down on the edge and found him still watching her expectantly, she figured she'd have to answer him somehow. "Myself, I suppose. Why I even came here. I was so busy for a while, but...now I can't really see any place in Ravanmark for me at all."

"Now hold on." Chen sat up suddenly. "I don't think I like the way you're talking. No place in Ravanmark for you? Have you forgotten everything you've done here? I wasn't with you for all of it, but even I have heard the rumors of Garrant. There's a whole big seaboard town of people that wouldn't even be here if it wasn't for you. If you had never come here, Ethal would still be running free slaughtering people, and Orinthal Holding would still be falling apart with no leader—Seven Hells, even our own people would still be suffering under Brutagar. You've taught people, and saved people, and changed everything around you, and now you want to toss all that out? Now it doesn't matter anymore?"

She tried to grin at him, but it came out a little crooked. He was serious—she could see it on his face, could hear it in his voice. And his words hit too close to home for comfort—everything he spoke of came to life again in her mind, and each memory felt like a wound, open and bleeding. She had been so focused then, so full of purpose. It had all seemed so clear at the time.

"Can I run off with you and the Singari again?" She didn't know why she had blurted the question out like that—a rush of nostalgia, maybe—but she couldn't deny that when she thought about their time together, she desperately wanted to feel that way again...that sure, that happy, that *alive*. She held her breath, waiting to hear how he would answer. If he said yes...she would go.

For a long moment, he didn't answer. He just stared at her, his mouth moving, but making no sound. "Why— why are you asking me that?"

"I don't see how I can stay here, Chen. Dorramon doesn't want me to do the acts yet, but I can't stay at the palace—this place is tearing itself apart because of me. I just keep making things worse—I need to leave."

Chen bit his lip, and looked away. "Ah, Alannys. If you had asked me that when you first got back to the Great

Palace...I would have had an altogether different answer for you."

"I thought you said I would always have a place with you." Her voice sounded dull. Was she disappointed? Did she want to go, or to stay? She didn't know for sure, and she supposed that was the whole problem.

Chen winced. "You do. You know you do. But this, now..." He shook his head. "Everyone is entitled to a crisis of faith, I guess. But you really have picked the worst time of all to have yours."

"I...don't understand."

"I don't think you do." Chen's smile was gentle, but she couldn't shake a feeling of foreboding. "I think you mean to go through with this, do you know that? If I pressed my case to you now...I think this time, you would leave with me. And eventually—not today, not tomorrow, but sometime in the not-too-distant future—you would be ready to marry me."

She couldn't look at him, but she shook her head, forcing words out past her burning embarrassment. "No. Don't mistake me, Chen—that isn't what I'm after. I meant it when I told you I will never have a wedding. If I can't marry Dorramon, I won't marry anyone. I'm sorry, Chen. But this...once you have it, you can't just substitute for it. Maybe...maybe if I had never met him, things would be different. But now...now all I am looking for is escape from a situation that feels intolerable."

His laugh was harsh. "Do you think so? I suppose I can see that. But I still think you should stay here, at the palace. It comes down to this, Alannys—I would rather see you happy with someone else than unhappy with me."

"*Happy? Is that a joke?*"

"You've fought awfully hard to get back here, even knowing that he was engaged to marry somebody else. You knew what you were getting into, and you can't have expected it to be easy. What has changed?"

"Everything!" She stomped away from the water

89

garden, pacing in short, agitated strides. "I wanted to come back because I thought he needed me. I thought I could support him, and help him. But all I do is make things worse! My being here is making everything harder on him, and it's putting him in danger. I can't make either one of us happy!"

Chen watched from the bench, chewing on the inside of his lip. "You can't have thought things were going to be easy. You *knew* what you were getting into. Alannys, I told you back at Danningham Manor that I believe he intends to marry you. I haven't seen anything here that changes my mind. I think he's only waited this long because he worried that you might have wanted me instead."

"He *can't* marry me, Chen! It isn't up to him!"

All of the sudden Chen was right in front of her, and he grabbed her hands. She hadn't realized they were balled into fists until he held them up in front of her. "Look at you. Now do you see what I mean by a crisis of faith? I've just told you the man intends to marry you. And your response is to tell me what he can't do?"

"There's more to consider here than just me." She jerked her hands away from him. "There's more to consider here than just *him.*"

Chen's sigh sounded impatient. "Do you think you are the only person who ever thinks about Ravanmark? Look, Alannys, just exactly how much of your own happiness are you expected to give up, because you are the Redeemer? How much is King Dorramon expected to give up, just because he happened to be born a prince? Aren't you both still people? Don't you both still deserve what all people deserve?"

She stared at him, stricken by questions she had never considered before.

"Calm down. This is King Dorramon we are talking about. You know him better than probably anyone else in the world. Now forget about everything else—forget for a minute this is you we're talking about. If I told you he had made up his mind to do something everyone said was impossible—fully intended from the bottom of his soul to do this thing everyone says he can't do—what would you say? Would you believe he could do it? Or would you become another naysayer telling him he's wasting his time?"

She didn't answer at first. She stood there staring into Chen's resolute face, and finally she understood—finally it *hit* her—what Chen was talking about. She'd thought she was having a bad morning, after a bad night, but something pivotal was happening here. This was a turning point that would define the rest of her life, and it took a chance meeting in the garden to make her realize it. She swallowed hard, her throat suddenly dry.

Because she finally saw clearly what she had done yesterday. She had, in Chen's words, become just another naysayer. And then she had refused to even hear anybody out. But when Chen posed the question to her that way, there was only one answer she could honestly give. And they both knew it.

"I'd believe it," she said, and her hands fell limp at her sides. "I know what it looks like, I know how I've behaved, but I don't doubt him. I can't doubt him. I have more faith in him than anyone I've ever met in my whole life. If he's made up his mind, he'll make it happen. But...but I can't forget about the cost."

Chen reached for her face, wiping away tears she hadn't realized were there. "Now, that's what I'm talking about. He's the King of Ravanmark, Alannys—the cost isn't yours to worry about, but his. And if you have faith in him, you have to believe that he will work that out. Do you think he cares that little for his kingdom?"

"No. You're right. Good heavens, what must he think of me right now? I have to go talk to him!"

"Yes. I don't think you should wait much longer."

Something about his tone brought her up short. "What is it? What's happened?"

All at once he seemed to be looking everywhere in the courtyard except at her. "You probably already know there are two Cadendan warships anchored just outside the harbor, near the diplomatic ship that brought the ambassador. Two days ago, the royal ship anchored as well."

"The royal ship?" She remember in a sudden rush what Raman had told her days before. "They say the King of Cadenda is on that ship…"

"Right. He hasn't shown himself, though, not yet. But a party of three men was offloaded at the docks, and they are supposed to arrive at the Great Palace this morning. Whatever King Dorramon does now is likely to determine our future with Cadenda."

"Oh, what a time for me to be in a snit!" Alannys cried. "I have to go find him, right now!"

"As if your snits are ever particularly well timed," Chen snickered.

She look up in surprise, and found him smiling at her in a way that took the sting out of his remark. Her throat closed up, and her vision blurred. "Thank you, Chen. Thank you for everything. I don't know what would have become of me without you."

"Don't think you've got rid of me just yet," Chen grumbled, but he couldn't seem to look her in the eye. "I'm coming with you."

She stopped short on her way to the corridor, looking at him with complete incomprehension. "Coming…with me? To see Dorramon?"

He cleared his throat, still not quite managing to look at her. "Well, I will certainly escort you that far, anyway. You can't judge the state of the outer ward by the inner ward, Alannys. You can't imagine the rumors that are spreading out there — people are scared, and angry — the whole place is a mess. I don't think you would be safe wandering around out there alone right now."

Alannys swallowed hard. It pained her to think of the

outer ward of the Great Palace reduced to such a state because, essentially, of her. "Thank you, Chen." She didn't know what else to say. She started walking again, her eyes on the ground.

Chen fell into step beside her, and put her arm through his. It seemed he didn't really know what to say, either.

But between the two of them, as always, no words were necessary.

♫

Alannys knew that Chen had meant what he told her about the state of the Great Palace. She knew he'd been out there; he would know what it was like. And yet she couldn't really believe it; she couldn't quite accept any of what he had described as *real*. Some part of her mind doggedly held on to her vision of the palace as she had first seen it—a gleaming castle from a fairy tale, prosperous and peaceful, filled with happy, content people.

But as they crossed the quiet inner ward she could hear ominous sounds—faraway shouts, the ringing of distant swords, crashes and thuds—that got her heart pounding. It sounded as though perhaps the outer ward really *was* as bad as Chen said. The thought tormented her, filled her with a restless, gnawing guilt she could not quell— because she knew this was fundamentally her fault. What she hadn't figured out yet was how to live with it.

The gate between the wards was shut. Alannys had never seen that gate closed in all her time at the Great Palace. She knew the Royal Guard kept a close eye on who came and went, and refused admittance to some, but...to see that massive iron gate blocking any passage between the two wards...she tried to imagine how bad things must be out there, to cause that. Even in the aftermath of Lord Malrec's horrific bomb attack, that gate had stayed open. To see it closed now...it gave her a very bad feeling about going out there at all. But she remembered what Chen had told her, and she knew she didn't have time to wait.

The uniformed Royal Guard standing watch at the gate frowned at her severely, from a face that looked too young to bear such an expression, and she figured this too was her fault—Ravanmark's young growing prematurely old and humorless. She felt older than her years these days too. "I hope," the guard said archly, "that my Lady and her companion are not considering going out there."

"I hate to disappoint you," she said, her eyes scanning what little she could see of the outer ward on the other side of the gate, "but we are." Was that *smoke* she could smell on the air?

The guard's frown deepened, carving dark lines into that too-young-looking face. He didn't look made for such a scowl. "Please, my Lady. You can't expect us to raise this enormous gate for a person or two to pass. That's not reasonable."

"Not reasonable?" Chen sounded entirely calm—they might have been discussing the weather. "Isn't that what you do when the king goes in and out?"

This observation did nothing to improve the Royal Guard's mood or expression. His pale face flushed, making his red hair seem orange and almost completely hiding his freckles. "As a matter of fact, it is. But—and I realize this may be a tricky distinction for a Singari like yourself—this woman is not, in fact, the King of Ravanmark."

"No, it's pretty clear she isn't. I daresay even a Singari like myself could work that out." Chen was still unruffled —Alannys was ready to spit nails, herself, and she wondered how he could keep such a civilized tone in the face of such outright, deliberate rudeness. But he had always been like that. Perhaps she wasn't the only one who had missed a diplomatic calling. "But then, she is the Redeemer of the Realm, invested as such by the King of Ravanmark himself. She's been at every major palace function for the last six months. *I* would certainly hate to be the one who turned her away, if he should find out about it later."

"Tch." The guard clicked his tongue and turned away in apparent aggravation, but not before Alannys saw his red face go suddenly pale. "Stand here, you two."

Chen and Alannys moved to the spot he indicated, right in front of the center of the gate. It made her feel uncomfortably small, standing in front of the massive iron grid. She could see rust in the corners of the frame, but it implied only age, not weakness—this gate could easily keep out her and every person she had ever known in the relatively short span of her life. It felt like the gate knew that too, somehow, and she fidgeted, waiting.

The red-haired guard snapped to attention, crossing his arm over his chest in stiff salute, and raised his voice. "Guards of the ward! Assemble at the gate!"

Every guard patrolling the inner ward left his post, and formed lines to the left and the right of Chen and Alannys, completely covering the gate except the spot where they would pass when it opened. Standing in that line of fighting men intimidated Alannys—she knew well enough they weren't there for her protection going out, but to keep any of the trouble in the outer ward from finding its way in. She couldn't stop herself from wondering how many of these men shared the red-haired guard's hostility, and that made her fidget even more.

"Guards of the tower! Raise the gate!"

With the heavy clink of thick chains, and the low groan of iron under massive pressure, the big gate began slowly to raise, in stilted fits and starts, inch by precarious inch. How many guards did it take to work the enormous winches that moved the gate? Small wonder they didn't want to go to the effort for just anybody.

As soon as the gate began to move, Alannys could see the shapes of people, appearing like ghosts out of the smoky air of the outer ward, pressing up against the iron. Old and young, dressed well and in dirty rags, they clamored together, reaching through the bars and begging for passage.

"Jomain!" cried a sudden voice from the far side of the gate, shaking with age and yet surprisingly strong. Alannys could see her wrinkled, weathered face, surrounded by a fuzzy cloud of white hair, clinging to the bars with pale hands in which blue veins were clearly visible. "Jomain, you must bring me in there with you. You can't leave me out here!"

The redheaded guard flinched. "Sorry, Granny," he muttered. The old woman reached through the bars and caught his arm, but he shook her off, turning to face Alannys evenly. "Look, my Lady, as soon as you can get under this gate you must go. Don't wait, and don't hesitate. As soon as you are through they will lower it again, and fast."

Alannys stared at him, not sure whether she was impressed by his composure or horrified by it. "That's your grandmother?" she said, and her eyes flicked of their own accord to the withered old woman still calling out to his back. "She's your grandmother and you're just going to leave her out there in all of that? Doesn't that bother you?"

"As a matter of fact it does." Jomain's eyes flared anger so strongly she couldn't hold his gaze. "It bothers me more than I imagine you know. But I don't have any choice — we are under very specific orders about who may enter the inner ward right now. And we don't all have the luxury of breaking the rules because of personal friendships with the king."

She wanted to snap back at him, but how could she? There was nothing she could say, not to the boy, not to his grandmother. Whether she wanted to hear it or not, he had a point. She bowed her head, listening to the creaking and clanking of the big gate as it inched higher, willing it to move faster.

"You're tossing aside what they want most," Jomain said. She didn't look at him; his voice was hard as flint and she knew she wouldn't like what she would see. "I wish you much luck with it. It isn't fit out there for man nor beast, and least of all for a woman."

She felt Chen's hand on her arm in the same moment that she heard his voice, low and right in her ear. "Come on, Alannys. We can make it under now."

She ducked down and crawled under the gate behind him, keeping her eyes fast to his back. She heard the sounds of struggle around her, and she didn't want to see the Royal Guards fighting to keep their friends and relatives on the wrong side of the gate. She didn't think she could live with the sight.

♫

As soon as more of Alannys was in the outer ward than the inner ward, the massive gate came crashing back down. She pulled her knees up to her chin and rolled clear, narrowly avoiding the loss of body parts to its mad rush. The finality of the heavy crash made her shiver. She tried not to hear the heartrending wails of the people who had wanted so desperately to get through, tried not to think what they might be consigned to out here.

What she and Chen might now be consigned to, as well.

Chen hauled her to her feet, and helped her brush the dirt off of her clothes. "We should get moving."

Before he even let go of her, she heard another sound, one that convinced her that he was right. They had much more to worry about than whether the guards of the gate had hurt anybody's feelings.

"They open the gate for that woman and her pet Singari, but not for us." The resentful mutter sounded a world away from the pleading grandmother, but there she was, her bony hands clenched into fists, her wrinkled face twisted with rage. "My own grandson—the man I raised like he was my own—he opens the gate for her and not for me. Guess it pays to be the king's whore, even in times like these."

Alannys took a hesitant step backward, her skin prickling. The old woman might not have been much of a threat, but there were at least a dozen people behind her, and Alannys had to assume they all felt more of less the same.

"This whole country has gone in the moat, and it all goes back to her. Why should we all be put in danger—for her? Why should our sons, our grandsons, our husbands and fathers go to fight Cadenda—for her? If the king will not hear us, there's but one thing to do—get rid of the woman ourselves!"

Shouts of assent surrounded the old woman, chilling Alannys to her core.

Chen grabbed her hand and tugged at her. "Come *on*, Alannys!"

Alannys turned away, running behind him, away from the gate, wondering what she had gotten herself into. She remembered all the times during her travels that she had fervently wished to be back at the Great Palace. She could never have imagined it like this! Maybe the old woman was right. It seemed she brought trouble wherever she went.

She grabbed Chen's arm and veered toward the royal stables, where the crowd wouldn't be able to follow. She flashed her royal medallion at the two startled Royal Guards on duty as she raced past, but didn't slow down until they were inside the stable and out of sight.

"That..." Chen gasped, "was good thinking."

They stood in the wide center aisle, flanked with stalls, breathing deep the warm scents of hay and horses, trying to catch their breath. Their sudden entrance had disturbed the building's equine occupants; Alannys could see twitching ears, could hear snorts and the stomping of hooves.

"You ever notice," she said, aware that she was coming at him out of left field, "the Royal Guard?"

Chen looked at her in surprise. "Of course—I'm

Singari. I keep an eye on people who look at me like that, especially people with authority. Those guys are everywhere."

"They are, aren't they? They're everywhere around the palace, so much that we take them for granted. We don't even notice them — unless we have a reason to."

Chen straightened up, watching her closely. "What are you getting at?"

"I guess...I guess I have a reason now. I've been attacked by a royal guard, and whether I mean to or not, I notice them now. And it makes me think, Chen. It feels threatening. When a group of people is everywhere...when they are completely ubiquitous...what happens when you can't trust them anymore?"

"You don't," Chen sighed. He untied the red scarf he wore about his waist, and pulled it over her head. "You can't. You watch, and you wait, and you always try to be ready. Because even though you hope you're wrong, Alannys — if you feel that way, you're probably right."

He knotted the ends of the scarf under her chin, and she frowned at him. "What are you doing?"

"Trying to give you a bit of a disguise," he said, as if that should have been obvious. "I think it would be better right now if people don't know who you are, especially after that mess at the gate. Wearing a headscarf, walking with me..."

"People will assume I'm Singari?"

"At least they will if they don't look any closer." He pulled the edge of the scarf down over her forehead and gave her a crooked smile. "It isn't fit out for man nor beast, but for Singari, who are some of both and all of neither...we may get on just fine."

"Chen!" Alannys gasped, scandalized, and then she started to laugh with him. "I suppose we might, at that. I suppose we might."

♩

The outer ward loomed dark and unfamiliar around

them, the same and yet not the same, like something out of a nightmare. Smoke laced the air, thick and unpleasant, making their eyes water. Alannys pulled the edges of Chen's scarf over her nose and mouth, remembering the times she had walked through here delighting to the scent of meat roasting over open flames. Now darker smells hung in the air—homes and businesses burning to the ground. They saw merchant tents torn down and trampled into the mud, peasant cottages burned to nearly nothing, their blackened, burnt-out frames jutting from the ground like old bones. In the places that still stood, families huddled in the dark, afraid to venture into the madness that infected the streets. In her mind she could see a similar scene, on the other side of the palace—the outer ward a crumbling, rubble-filled, smoking ruin in the aftermath of Lord Malrec's bomb. In a way, this was worse —what surrounded her now was not the result of any attack from outside. This came from within. It felt like it negated everything she had accomplished there.

Alannys and Chen crept through the mostly-abandoned streets, keeping to the alleys and avoiding any sign of people. Twice they passed gangs of thieves and vandals, destroying shops and looting the goods that stocked them. Alannys turned unthinkingly toward them, her fists balled, and Chen's hand tightened on her elbow.

"No." The whisper was low and intense, right next to her ear. "You stay out of that. You aren't even armed. Do you fancy getting yourself killed here?"

"Chen!" She jerked her arm free. "This isn't right. We can't just ignore this!"

"We can, and we'd better. Look at those guys—those are no kids, Alannys, acting out because nobody's watching. They know what they're doing. Do you really think they're going to be afraid of a woman who isn't even carrying a sword?"

Alannys looked at him, and back at the looters. She knew what was right—how could she convince her conscience she had to do something else?

"Alannys," he hissed, pulling at her arm again. "There is nothing you can say or do here—you of all people!—that will make this any better. Listen to me! If you're going to help at all, you're going to have to do it higher up."

"Higher up," she whispered.

He shook her arm, smiling like he had just seen the sun. "Yes, Alannys. Yes! Right at the very top. I know it's crazy out here, but look at it this way: every minute we delay is another minute that King Dorramon is out in this too. It's not just our safety, but his—we have to keep moving."

He was right. Damn him, he was *right.* She didn't like it, but she could see it. Her heart dropped and she ducked her head, hurrying away next to Chen. It went against every moral she had to walk away from something like that. But he was right—to help any of these people, she was going to have to go right to the top.

Assuming, of course, that she could keep herself alive long enough to make it to the top.

Thinking in that line brought her uncomfortably close to the realization Chen had spelled out for her, a realization she'd been trying hard to avoid—Dorramon was *out here,* somewhere in this same madness that threatened her. She couldn't imagine it, she didn't want to. What if something happened to him?

Alannys abruptly realized their places had reversed—all at once she was dragging Chen along with her, moving too fast for stealth. "Sorry," she muttered, averting her eyes.

"No worries," Chen said, with a fleeting smile that made her think he knew exactly what was behind her sudden burst of speed.

No worries. The phrase echoed in her mind as they ran through the deserted and half-destroyed lower market, an odd and incongruent choice of words. Her mind was nothing but worries, and her worries drove her on, faster and faster still, with no regard for the danger surrounding her.

They finally cleared the ghost of the market, and the massive main gate came into sight. Even from that distance Alannys could see that the drawbridge was open — but the gate was closed. The scene before her was so unexpected it stopped her in her tracks, and it took her befuddled brain a moment to sort through what was happening in front of her.

There in front of the guard tower was King Dorramon, next to Grand Chancellor Ebrad, both surrounded by two rows of Royal Guards in a defensive double-circle. Even Captain Grayble was on guard. With so many people around them it was difficult to be sure, but to Alannys it looked as though they were arguing.

Or rather, Ebrad was arguing, waving his arms, his broad face twisted into a scowl that made his sharply hooked nose appear even more beak-like than usual. In his loose robes, the histrionic spasms of his rage made him look like nothing so much as a great, flapping bird in the midst of all those people. Dorramon watched his antics impassively, with Grayble standing just behind him, wearing the peculiar stone-faced expression that meant he was actively concealing his dislike.

What was the chancellor on about? Given the closed gate, the answer was clear — Dorramon had refused, for the final time, to receive Cadenda's emissaries, and Ebrad looked as though he might have a conniption fit because of it.

Farther back, at the enormous gate, she could see Raman, talking equally animatedly through the iron bars with Ambassador Thell.

Ambassador Thell! She hadn't seen him in months, but that did nothing to quell the wave of intense dislike that washed over her when she recognized the man himself at the gate, wearing his flowing silk robes and his customary sneer. He had his arm pushed between the bars, waving around a large, thick envelope bearing a gold gilt crest—an envelope nobody inside seemed willing to take.

"Your Majesty!" Thell's reedy voice, made for sneering, sounded just as she remembered, and hearing it again gave her stomach a sour twist. "You must reconsider! Are you really prepared to commit both of our kingdoms to war, over that whore?"

Dorramon spun to face the gate, wearing an expression of such extreme fury, such absolute hatred, it might have been a mask. Captain Grayble caught his arm and held him back, but Thell stepped back from the gate anyway, his composure finally rattled.

It didn't matter. His remark had served its purpose—the damage was done. It was as if someone had dropped a lit match on a pile of dry kindling—the outer ward exploded into furious activity. Everywhere she looked she saw red faces, and in the clamor of angry voices it was impossible to make out individual words. And behind her was the burning wreckage from the violence that had nearly consumed the market.

...you should both know better than to think I would let Ravanmark fall down around my ears. She could hear his voice then, as clearly as if he stood beside her, his words ringing with the same conviction they'd had when he said them.

But from where she stood, as much as it hurt to admit it, this looked an awful lot like the kingdom falling down around his ears.

And as much as it hurt to admit it, it looked like it was all her fault.

♫

Alannys panicked at her sudden realization. She burst into a dead run toward the Royal Guards surrounding Dorramon, unable to just stand and watch the world go to hell any longer.

"What are you doing?" Until he spoke, she hadn't realized Chen was running with her. She saw Raman turn away from the gate and charge into the knot of guards. The darkness in his expression seemed to confirm her fears.

"I have to get to the king," she said, skidding to a halt in front of the defensive ring of guards. "I have to talk to him!"

"Sorry," said the guard in front of her. His kind tone surprised her, and she looked up into eyes that were green and very clear. "His Majesty can't be disturbed right now. But if you two can be patient for another hour, I imagine we'll have the gate open and you can go back to your camp."

"N—no," she stammered. She *had* been taken for Singari, and she wasn't altogether sure what to do about it. "You don't understand, I—"

"Her fault," muttered the guard next to her green-eyed friend, startling her into silence. This man's eyes were dark, and the expression in them darker still, leaving her cold. She backed up a step in sudden, instinctive fear. "She ain't Singari. This whole mess is *her fault*."

The man was small but fast, moving towards her in a blur, and before she could turn and flee he drove his elbow deep into her stomach, doubling her over. She dropped to her knees, unable to breathe, unable to move, unable to *think* in the onslaught of crippling pain.

Her awareness seemed to cave in on itself, and she had a hard time keeping up with that was happening around her. She felt more than saw Chen jump in front of her, blocking the guard's approach, berating him for attacking her. A third guard dove in from the edge of her vision, bowling Chen over and wrestling him to the ground.

"Barat!" The green-eyed guard sounded honestly horrified, moving into Chen's recently-vacated spot to block her. "What have you done? These Singari have hurt no one!"

"Already told you," the dark-eyed guard—apparently Barat—grunted. "She ain't Singari. Everything that's happening here is down to her, and we got to stop her."

"No," the green-eyed guard said. "Leave her alone."

Barat lifted a hand casually, as if in greeting, and knocked the green-eyed guard sideways. Alannys managed to drag one halting breath past the stabbing pain that flared in her middle, before a boot crashed into her back and sent her sprawling into the dirt. She tried to pull her arms under her, to push herself up off the ground, but it seemed her battered body had quit taking orders from her. She could see her own hand lying next to her face, as limp and unresponsive as if she had never tried to move at all.

"Now," she heard Barat's voice grate above her, "help me haul her out of here. We got to finish her."

"N—no." The green-eyed guard sprawled on the ground near her, nursing a bloodied nose. He sounded completely flabbergasted, but he was resolute. "You're mental, Barat! Leave that woman alone!"

"So that's the way of it." A brown boot crunched down near her face, then another. "Guess I better handle this myself, then, and finish her now." Barat drew his sword, and knelt down in front of her. "Got any last words, woman?"

"Ungh..." It was the only sound she could push past the pain that seemed to have consumed most of her torso.

Barat's laugh was unkind, and the glint in his eyes was positively cruel. He didn't say anything more to her. She was too dazed and pained to save herself. She could hear Chen raising holy hell a few feet away, as Barat and his weapon loomed closer.

Suddenly he froze. His muscles tensed and his eyes bulged—his mouth worked frantically but no sound came out. Before Alannys could make sense of what she was seeing, a big hand pushed Barat out of her field of vision and Captain Grayble knelt down in front of her, peering into her face. "Great Muses, my Lady—are you all right?"

She managed to nod her head—a pathetic gesture,

sprawled on her belly in the dirt as she was. Captain Grayble helped her to her feet, the gentleness of his hands cutting a sharp contrast to the iron in his voice as he barked orders to his men. "Get my sword out of him. You two, hold him up—I have some questions for him. Don't be daft, he isn't dead yet. And for pity's sake, quit fighting with that Singari! Do none of you have any wits at all?"

The world faded as she stood upright, then swam back into focus. She could see the guards hurrying to carry out orders, heads bowed and faces averted. Farther away, she could see the grand chancellor, staring at her with barely concealed fury. And next to him, Dorramon, pale and frantic. Raman held him back, both arms wrapped around his middle.

"Damn it, Raman!" Dorramon's voice carried clearly to Alannys, over every other sound around her, as he shook Raman off. "Let go of me!"

Ignoring the chaos surrounding them, he hurried to her and took her face in his hands, inspecting her closely. The electricity of his fingers tingling against her skin soothed her, but it was hard to hold his gaze—the shock and anger she read there touched her too deeply. "Muses," he breathed, and turned to Grayble in a rush of fury. "What is the meaning of this? Why did your man attack her? Do the guards hate Singari that much?"

"He didn't think she was Singari," Chen said sourly, beating the dust from his clothes. "The other guy did, but not him. Whatever this was about, it wasn't that."

"What?" Dorramon's eyes cut to her. "He knew who she was—and he attacked her anyway?"

"Yes." Captain Grayble glowered at Barat, held up between two of his men. "Explain yourself, dog. Why did you attack Lady Alannys?"

Barat's eyes wandered among them all. Maybe he was avoiding eye contact, or maybe he was having a hard time focusing—it was hard to be sure. "That wasn't Lady Alannys. Just some Singari bitch."

"No." Grayble didn't hesitate. "I heard what you said, Barat. You clearly knew who she was. Who are you working for?"

Barat laughed, a shrill, manic sound. "This is bigger than me, Captain. Bigger than you! The storm is coming, and you can't blow it away with all your bellowing!" His laugh degraded into a hacking, bloody cough.

Captain Grayble grabbed Barat's shirt in his fist, jerking him forward, shouting right into his face. "Damn you! Who are you working for? Who put you up to this?"

Barat's face was waxy and pale. Even his lips, speckled with flecks of his own dark blood, were colorless underneath. His voice was a weak whisper, and yet everyone heard him clearly in the silence blanketing them. "You can't stop this, Captain. The evil will be purged...and the power...held by the few...given to the many."

Grayble let go of Barat's shirt and stepped back, staring at him. "You're raving."

"Power...to the many." Barat slumped against his captors, and moved no more. But his words seemed to echo off the stone of the curtain wall, sending a shiver up Alannys's spine.

The power held by the few, given to the many.

Lord Malrec was dead. The Dark Alliance had been beheaded, the revolt squashed. Where was this rhetoric coming from? If Barat was simply a puppet, who was pulling the strings?

What new menace faced them now?

♫

The massive main gate clanked up inch by arduous inch, slower and with even more noise than the gate to the inner ward, commanding the attention of every person in the vicinity. Alannys watched it raise, leaning heavily on the king, yet feeling her heart lift with it. The raising of the gate heralded the return of something like normal, and Alannys was all for the return of normal.

Or even something like it.

"This is where I must leave you," Chen said, jolting her from her dazed sort of reverie. "In name at least, I'm still *kortha*. I have to check in on the tribe every now and again."

"Thank you," Dorramon said. "I'm not sure why you thought Alannys should be here, but that you for staying with her. I'm not sure how she would have fared out here alone."

"Perhaps she would have fared better," Chen said, but he gave a small bow. "I'm honored that I was of service to both of you. I wish you luck." He aimed a mock-salute in her general direction, then turned and headed for the gate.

Alannys frowned. That seemed like an odd sort of farewell. But if anyone else thought so, they were giving no indication of it.

"We should head back to the inner ward as well," Dorramon said.

"Double circle formation!" Captain Grayble barked to his men. "Protect the king and his lady, no mistakes! Move!"

"Talk to me, Grayble," Dorramon said. "What just happened?"

They were moving fast for a group of such size; evidently nobody liked being in the outer ward just then any more than Alannys did. Dorramon was supporting her, and she was struggling to keep up even so.

Grayble glanced over at them, then looked straight ahead. "I don't know, your Highness. And that is what bothers me. You know that we have suspected for some time that some of the Royal Guard oppose Lady Alannys. But I never seriously imagined they would resort to treason."

"Treason?" Alannys said. "Barat almost committed murder, certainly. But murdering me isn't treason. I'm not the king."

"No," Grayble said. His eyes roved over the ward, scanning every shape and shadow that might conceal an attacker. "This may not technically have been treason. But it's only one short step away. In the minds of the people, my Lady, you and his Majesty are closely connected. It is a small step from taking a stab at you to taking a stab at the king himself. And I am determined to rid the Great Palace of this conspiracy before either of you are harmed."

"That would be easier," Dorramon said, "if we had any idea who was behind it."

"True." Captain Grayble's tone was sour, and his craggy face twisted into a grimace. "I must apologize, your Majesty. This is my fault—I should not have killed Barat."

"You did what you had to do," Dorramon said.

"No. It was an amateur mistake. It was not my intention...I am afraid I let my anger get the best of me."

"Given the situation," Dorramon said, his jaw hard, "I would say you can be forgiven."

A shadow of a smile crossed the captain's face. "Thank you, my Lord King. But nonetheless, my actions have made things hard for us. Without knowing who is involved in this, we must assume anyone could be. We know there are surviving members of the Dark Alliance, your Highness, even one that can paint. I recommend we Talent-proof Prubard's cell. It will not stop anyone who wishes to free him, but it will make it harder for them to work undetected."

"Agreed," Dorramon said. "See to it, as soon as possible."

"A wise plan, your Majesty, I am sure," Ebrad said from behind them, "but does Prubard really merit the effort? Whether on his own or allied with others, the man is hardly capable enough to cause real problems."

"He took an active part in a conspiracy to steal the throne," Dorramon snapped. "That is enough of a problem for me. Any threat to the country must be taken seriously."

"Doubtless my most wise Lord King is correct," Ebrad

said, "but any threat presented by the ex-baron must necessarily be minimal. Undoubtedly the largest threat to the country right now is docked in the Port Grandview harbor, and your Highness has only just now refused to admit their envoys."

"Ebrad," Dorramon said, "this conversation is over."

His tone brooked no opposition. The grand chancellor fell silent. Alannys risked a look back and saw him and Raman wearing almost identical expressions of dissatisfaction.

"Dorramon." Raman's tone carried a warning — Alannys felt her back stiffen when she heard it. "You can't wish this away."

"Raman, listen to me—"

"No. For once in your life, try listening to me. The King of Cadenda isn't going to turn around and sail quietly home because you ignored him. 'Death before dishonor,' remember? They won't back down from this."

"You are welcome to your opinion," Dorramon said shortly. "But you must let me handle this."

"Now that's where you're wrong." Raman smiled, but it was a feral baring of his teeth that did nothing to make Alannys feel better about the situation. "It is certainly your responsibility to handle it, I'll grant you that. But I am in no way obligated to sit idly by and watch you commit Ravanmark to a war no one—not even you—really wants."

Alannys had never heard Raman take such a blatantly disrespectful tone with the king, especially in front of others. But she felt Dorramon's hand tighten on her arm, heard his low oath in her ear, and she knew there was more to this than simple rudeness.

Raman's smile twisted, hardened, and he reached into his vest with a flourishing twitch of his fingers to produce...

...a heavy envelope of fine linen paper, its gold gilt crest glittering in the sun.

♪

The gate to the inner ward was open when they arrived — Alannys didn't know if the outer ward had settled enough to leave it open, or if the Royal Guard had just known they were coming. What she did know was that it didn't really matter either way, and she was distracting herself from greater concerns by considering it at all. Concerns that *did* matter, concerns like—

"I've already told you, Raman, I'm not touching that letter." Dorramon had gone past snapping, past anger, and was now royally pissed off, stomping into the inner ward as if he suspected every person and every thing in it of conspiring against him. "I told Ambassador Thell, I told every single guard in the outer ward, and I told you. The fact that you alone decided the command of a king didn't bind you is neither my fault nor my problem."

"But what am I supposed to do with it?" Raman protested, in a fit of agitation.

"Also not my problem. You made this bed, Raman, I suppose you'll have to lie in it."

Raman veered sharply away from them and stormed off toward the keep, muttering a barrage of curse words that they all heard clearly.

"I'm only going to say this once," Dorramon said with eerie calm, eyeing in turn each of the Royal Guards around them, "in case any of you have a memory as poor as the arch-prince's. None of you are to touch that letter. It has never been officially accepted, and it never will be. Do I make myself clear?"

The guards saluted in unison, with a crisp "Aye!" that seemed to come from all of them as one.

"Very well. You are dismissed."

Grayble herded his men into the barracks, barking orders in such quick succession that Alannys found them unintelligible. Dorramon watched them go with a peculiar look on his face, as though he was mulling over something he didn't like. To her surprise, he didn't release her, and headed for the Great Hall still pulling her along with him.

"D—Dorramon? Shouldn't I go back to my room?" She was acutely aware of her rumpled clothes, of her dirty hair and face. She looked entirely the part of someone who had just had the stuffing beaten out of them—not of someone who belonged in the royal court.

"No. After what just happened, I'm not letting you out of my sight. I won't hear of it."

"I'm sorry. I never meant for any of that to happen, I never meant to worry you. I just…"

He stopped suddenly in the open courtyard of the inner ward, and rounded on her. "What? You just what?"

Alannys swallowed hard, suddenly nervous under his direct gaze. How could she answer that? *I just didn't want you to run off and marry Varilyn? I just worried that this might be the start of an international war? I just couldn't bear the thought of you out there in all that chaos?* All entirely true, and yet she couldn't give voice to any of those answers now, out in the open inner ward, with Dorramon's clear blue eyes steadily on her, challenging her to own her feelings. She cleared her throat, stalling. "I just…wanted to apologize."

"Apologize?" He crossed his arms, watching her squirm. It was clear he hadn't expected her to say that—but it was equally clear he thought she should apologize. "What for, if you don't mind my asking? Trying to sneak away with the Singari without even a goodbye?"

"I—sneaking…what?"

"Isn't that what you were doing? Right up until you found the gate closed?" His blue eyes felt cold, suddenly…hard, like ice. She had never thought of ice as something to fear, but that was before she saw the way he looked at her now…ice could cut after all, could cut very deeply.

"No! No—I told you I was going to pack, Dorramon, and go attempt the acts…but you told me not to, so I didn't."

"That's what I thought, too, until I saw you in a headscarf and realized you don't need to pack—you have everything you need in that camp. And who better to get you where you want to go?"

"No. Just no." People were beginning to stop and stare, but Alannys didn't care and neither, it seemed, did he. She pulled the scarf off her head and held it in front of him. "This is not a *braytha*. This is Chen's, and he put it on me to help me avoid attracting attention, even though that didn't work out so well. I didn't come out here intending to leave. I only came to stop you from doing something rash."

"Something rash." His eyes flicked from the scarf in her hand, dancing like a flame in the slight breeze, back to her face. "That's not very specific, is it? People are always vague when they are trying to hide something. So why don't you get more specific for me, Alannys? Why don't you tell me directly that you don't think me competent to rule my kingdom—that you don't trust me any more than Raman does?"

"What?" She was too shocked to say more. She had known he was upset with her, but she could never have imagined *this*.

"Go ahead, say it! Now is your chance to get it all out without worrying about any retribution from anybody. And once you've said your piece, you should go back to the main gate, and keep right on going to the Singari camp. Because I don't think I can stand to keep you here...to look into your eyes every day, knowing thoughts like that are behind them."

"No!" Alannys never made a conscious decision to move, but she was on her knees, kneeling before Dorramon like a supplicant with her head bowed, while people passing by watched, pretending not to. "No, listen to me, you are reading this all wrong, I swear. I messed up last night and hurt your feelings, and I didn't know how to fix it so I ran away and hid. I came out to the gate this morning because I know how badly I messed up and I was afraid I pushed you into marrying Princess Varilyn. I came back here to try to help you and all I have done is make everything worse and I totally understand if you want me to leave, but I swear to you that's all it was."

The words rushed from her in a frantic torrent, leaving her empty and exhausted and gasping for breath, like something big had just found its way out of her, something she wasn't quite sure she had been ready to let go of just yet. She wasn't ready for that, and she certainly wasn't ready to find out what kind of reaction she'd gotten. She braced her hands on her thighs and leaned forward, panting like she had just run a mile.

Something thrust suddenly into her field of vision, startling her—Dorramon's hand, extended to help her up. She blinked at it in surprise, then reached out to accept it, finally daring to look up as she did. In the bright cool of the morning, his hand wrapped around hers felt like the warmest thing she had ever experienced, until she met his gaze. The ice in his eyes had melted completely. The only thing warmer was the crushing embrace he pulled her into.

The people in the inner ward walked on by, not even pretending they weren't watching.

♫

Dorramon strode through the Great Hall, up the red granite walkway to the dais, ignoring the courtiers scattered through the room, scowling in a manner that encouraged them all to keep their distance. A pageboy awaited them on the dais. "Bring the lady a chair," Dorramon said, and flopped down into the throne in a manner that didn't really seem to suit Alannys's idea of kingly behavior.

The page brought a chair and set it down near the throne, then scuttled away backwards, apparently eager to put some distance between himself and the monarch's bad mood.

Alannys sort of felt the same, but she recognized that this — like so much else affecting Ravanmark — was pretty much her fault. She stood awkwardly on the dais, shifting from foot to foot, looking everywhere but at the throne in front of her, wondering what on earth she could do to get out of this.

"Sit." Dorramon jerked his chin in the direction of the extra chair.

"Thank you." She perched herself on the edge of the chair, as though she expected to have to make a run for it. That assessment probably had more truth to it than she wanted to admit. She might have expected clearing the air between them to raise Dorramon's spirits; she might have expected her emotional — and, truth be told, embarrassing — public confession to put him in a better mood.

She would have been wrong.

It seemed like a good time to tread carefully. "Your Highness, are...are you mad at me?"

"No." He sighed heavily, and she had to admit he didn't sound angry. He sounded world-worn, sad, and very, very tired. It was a mistake, and probably a vain one, to assume his every emotion had to do with her — it was plain he had a lot on his mind. "Please stop using titles when you talk to me. It's bad for morale."

"Bad for morale?" she echoed in confusion. "People expect to see proper respect for the king."

"Not bad for their morale," Dorramon said, waving a hand at the hall. "Bad for *mine*. I hate it when you talk like that. Whatever differences you see between us, Alannys, I don't see them. I don't accept them."

"Still...you must see it wouldn't be wise for me to take too casual a tone with you. Even your parents used titles with each other in public. Your Highness."

"Agh." He rubbed the bridge of his nose between his thumb and forefinger. He looked exhausted, and she felt bad for arguing with him. "I'll have to concede defeat on that point, I suppose. Still, I would appreciate it if you would stop doing that when we're alone. It feels like an insult."

"I'm sorry," she said, and she meant it. "It's never my intent to insult you. I'll do my best to stop."

This minor victory seemed to finally raise his spirits. But before she had time to properly appreciate his warm smile, a knot of people exploded into the Great Hall, led by Captain Grayble and Arch-Prince Raman.

She stood up, peering down the hall, taken aback by the noise and indignity the group brought with them. Raman and Grayble walked with their heads high and their expressions stony, looking straight ahead as though they were somehow unaware of what followed them.

Behind them were four men in flowing white robes with voluminous sleeves and big rounded hoods that draped low over their faces. It was a sight Alannys had not seen in months but recognized immediately, with a cold, clammy tingle, like seeing ghosts.

The warrior monks of Brookeshire Castle had come to the Great Palace.

♫

Captain Grayble and Arch-Prince Raman marched crisply down the center of the Great Hall, each followed by two ghostly warrior monks. The billowing robes covered them so completely they appeared to float across the red granite walkway. Between them they dragged a figure in the tattered remnants of noble garments, now so dirty and bedraggled they were little more than rags. The man's sharply pointed face was overgrown with many day's worth of unkempt whiskers, and his hair hung untrimmed and tangled around him face. Yet for all of that his carriage was proud and tall, his eyes sharp and intelligent, and his voice was strong and imperious as he demanded his immediate release. For all his reduced circumstances, there was no mistaking the person Brookeshire's guards dragged ignominiously into the hall.

"Lord Diabon!" Alannys gasped.

"None other," Raman said, in a tone that seemed far too cheerful for the occasion. "With Lady Etherra's compliments. Apparently he tried to sneak into Brookeshire Castle."

"A man such as myself should never be required to sneak anywhere, least of all into his own home," Diabon announced, as though they had been eagerly awaiting his thoughts on the matter. "Imagine, my people—my very wife—turning against me. Me! It's utterly inconceivable!"

"And yet, here you are." Dorramon's face remained impassive, but he sounded amused. "What are we to make of that?"

"You know well enough." Diabon's chains clanked as he struggled to raise his arms to point at Alannys. "That demon witch of yours has bewitched better minds than Etherra's."

"Ah, I should have known," Dorramon muttered. "There's no point to this. Raman, see that the Royal Guard escort our guest to the dungeon, please. Same cell as ex-Baron Prubard. I imagine Prubard will have some choice words for Diabon about his desertion."

"With pleasure." Raman's grin was alarming; it looked almost—feral.

"You are wasting your time," Diabon declared, pulling himself up as tall as he could manage. It ought to have seemed dignified, but the coarse, unkempt hair covering his hollowed-out cheeks made him seem more like insane. "You and that woman won't be in command much longer. The tide is soon to turn, and when it does, it shall wash you away."

"Whatever are you on about?" Dorramon sounded utterly bored, and Alannys realized at last that he was baiting his prisoner. "Malrec is dead, Prubard is imprisoned, and you are soon to join him. Your little rebellion is over—even you must be able to see that."

Diabon cackled with unkind laughter. "Over. Perhaps. Or perhaps a fallen leader is replaced by one superior, and the rebellion goes on. It all depends, I suppose, on what one is rebelling *against*."

Dorramon's face showed no reaction, but Alannys could see his knuckles whiten on the arm of the throne. "What are you talking about, Diabon? Have you found a superior leader? Are *you* the superior leader?"

Diabon laughed his crazy laugh again. "I have no intention of indulging your curiosity. I am here only to deliver a message."

Dorramon's eyes narrowed. "And what is that message?"

For a long moment, Diabon didn't answer. Silence blanketed the hall, heavy and oppressive, making the very air seem thick around them. The tension grew with every passing second, and Alannys had to wonder how anyone could face a king that uncooperatively. Diabon had not once, she realized, used a single title of courtesy — no *your Highness*, no *your Majesty*, not once.

That seemed like a singularly bad sign.

Lord Diabon savored the silence a moment longer. When he spoke, his sepulchural tone echoed hollowly in the hall. "The winds of great change have begun to blow, and not even the power of a king can turn them back now. The power now held by the few shall soon be given unto the many."

The words hit Alannys like an electric shock. She never saw Dorramon come out of the throne, but suddenly he was standing, glowering like a mighty thundercloud at the prisoner below. Alannys was reminded yet again of what she so often managed to ignore — this man was king of the most powerful nation on the planet, and any person courted his disfavor at their own peril. Lord Diabon must have reached a similar conclusion, judging by the way his face blanched under Dorramon's fearsome scowl.

"Explain yourself," the king commanded.

Lord Diabon drew himself up straighter. "I have nothing more to say. My message has been delivered."

"Get him out of here," Dorramon snapped. "Captain Grayble, a word, if I may."

Captain Grayble approached the dais, as Raman and the warrior monks dragged their prisoner back toward the door, still loudly protesting his treatment to any who would listen. "Yes, your Majesty?"

Dorramon sat slowly back down. When he spoke, his voice was carefully pitched not to carry, even in the acoustically live hall. "Grayble, that man is hiding something. Maybe quite a few somethings."

"Yes, your Highness."

"I want you to find out what." Dorramon's eyes were uncharacteristically hard. "Do you understand? I want you to use any means at your disposal to get answers from your prisoner."

"It shall be as you command. Rest easy, my Lord King, I will have the answers you seek." Grayble bowed low, then turned sharply on his heel and followed the others out of the Great Hall. A cold wind blew in behind him.

♫

Dorramon glanced at Alannys sidelong. "Please, sit. I am sorry you had to witness that." He slumped in the throne as though he could scarcely imagine being more relaxed, and yet it didn't quite feel as though that regal aura had left him. Was it her imagination, or was there the barest edge of a command in his request?

Alannys didn't remember standing, and it came as a bit of a surprise to find that she was. "Don't apologize. That was...enlightening."

"Was it?" Dorramon sounded wry.

She sat carefully back down on her chair, smoothing her pants over her lap. "Why do you think Diabon is hiding something? Perhaps he's just repeating what he's heard from others—trying to make himself seem important, so he has some bargaining power."

Dorramon shook his head, but he didn't look at her, his faraway gaze wandering the lights and shadows of the hall as if he wasn't really seeing any of it. "Under other circumstances, I could believe it—that would certainly be in line with his character. But right now—he isn't acting right, Alannys. Diabon is fundamentally a coward. We know that. We heard just recently how he ran from battle to save himself, remember? Now he's dragged in chains before the very king he tried to overthrow, and the only reasonable expectation he can have is execution. What does he do? He doesn't beg, or apologize, or attempt to placate me in any way. He's arrogant, he plays games and issues veiled threats—he treats me as if I am somehow irrelevant to him. Now here is the puzzle I present to you: what could make a man who values his life behave in such a manner?"

Alannys thought about it. Everything Dorramon had said was true. How could she make that make sense? Could any set of circumstances account for Lord Diabon's seemingly suicidal behavior? "The only way he could act like that," she said slowly, "is if he had the backing of someone else, someone he truly believed to be able to protect him from the consequences."

"Yes. And who is able to protect him, and how, in my own castle? Every answer I can conceive to that question is profoundly disturbing."

"Profoundly disturbing," Alannys echoed. She shivered in a sudden chill. "Is that why you told Captain Grayble to torture him?"

The glance Dorramon directed at her then was difficult to decipher. "Grayble is a very capable Captain of the Guard. I never doubt he will find what he seeks, no matter who withholds it. Do you?"

"No," she admitted. "But it sounded as though you were approving methods—more forceful than usual, shall we say."

"Yes. And you think that was badly done?" His tone carried a defensive edge that reminded her of their recent unpleasantness, and made her feel a touch defensive herself.

Alannys felt her face burn, and looked away. "It isn't my place to question you, your Highness. It's just — don't you think...torture...is a bit...beneath you?" There was no way to keep the question from sounding accusatory, no matter how she tiptoed around it.

"Beneath me." Dorramon sat back in the throne, looking out over the hall. "I suppose you must not think much of me. Believe it or not, I don't get any joy from the thought of causing other people pain, Alannys, even people like Lord Diabon. Under normal conditions, I would never advocate treating a prisoner that way. But these are not normal conditions. Those kinds of scruples are for people who don't have anything to lose."

"I guess I understand," she said, trying to make it so. "They are trying to take the throne, after all. And we don't even know who they are."

"The throne?" Dorramon looked at her in evident surprise. "The throne has been under attack for months. These people are targeting *you*, Alannys. When they talk about the power held by the few...I really don't think they are referencing the monarchy. Whatever this new conspiracy is, it's dangerous to both of us, but it's *about* you. And I'm not going to let them harm you. I will do whatever I must to protect you. I can't...I can't lose you, Alannys. I just can't."

Alannys stared at him, stricken. Her mouth was suddenly dry; her throat worked painfully but no sound emerged. Dorramon, Captain Grayble, all of them were doing this for her. They wouldn't torture people to save the throne, but they would do it for her. She wasn't sure how to live with that.

"I'm sorry," she said hoarsely. "It isn't my place to question you. I do know that. I'll try to do a better job of showing it."

"I don't believe I said anything like that." Dorramon looked at her in sudden concern. "You look burnt-out —

are you all right? Do you need a nap?"

"A nap? Didn't you tell me I wasn't allowed out of your sight?"

His quiet chuckle barely reached her ears. "And I thought you weren't paying attention. I did say that. But with Cadenda's emissaries headed back to the harbor, and Lord Diabon safely behind bars...I suppose I can turn loose of you long enough for you to take a nap. You really do look like you need it. I'll be busy here for a while, but I'll have Raman take you to your rooms." He nodded to the page, who bowed once and ran down the hall and out the door.

Alannys watched the boy go. Her befuddled brain was having a hard time keeping up. Perhaps Dorramon was right; maybe she really did need a nap. She hoped that was all it was.

She couldn't bear to think about the alternatives.

♫

"So what did you think of your adventure in the outer ward?" Raman's mood seemed greatly improved since Lord Diabon's capture. Alannys didn't think she could ever, in good conscience, refer to that as an adventure. She walked with him across the inner ward, wondering how she could possibly answer such a question.

He must have seen her hesitation in her face, because he chuckled, taking her arm as they walked. "Yes, I quite agree. An adventure like that, I could have done without myself. Who could ever have imagined the outer ward coming to that?"

"Not me," she said glumly. "But I suppose I shouldn't be surprised. I seem to bring nothing but disaster to every part of Ravanmark I touch."

Raman's expression turned abruptly serious. "Now that I can't agree with. You've done a lot of great work here, Alannys. And you know this current mess isn't your fault."

Alannys sighed, looking away. "If you say so. What

happened out there, Raman? At the gate?"

He stopped outside the keep, and held the door open for her. His expression just kept clouding over; he looked downright somber. "Dorramon ordered the main gate closed early this morning, well before the emissaries from Cadenda had even arrived. He really had no intention of acknowledging them at all, I think. Of course the people reacted badly to the closure of the gate, and the fear and uncertainty out there..." He shook his head. "And then the delegation from Cadenda arrived; Ambassador Thell, two advisers, and their guards, all on spent horses. They brought a sealed letter from the King of Cadenda himself."

"And?" Her voice quavered; she was almost afraid to hear what happened next. She had seen the end—she knew it couldn't be good.

"And Dorramon refused to admit them. He wouldn't speak to them, he wouldn't even accept the letter."

She didn't know what to say, so she said nothing, listening to her footsteps in the deserted corridor.

They stopped outside her door, and Raman turned to her suddenly, sighing. She couldn't remember the last time she'd heard him sigh quite like that. It seemed like a warning, and she felt her spirits sink again.

"Look, Alannys, I don't suppose you are very familiar with Cadenda, or what it takes to get from here to there. Cadenda is on the other side of the world from here. Imagine you are looking at a map. Ravanmark would be right in the center. Off to the right of Ravanmark, separated by many kays of ocean, you would find another continent. This continent holds several countries, and it's tall. Passing it on the north gets into icebergs and other unpleasant dangers. To the south are some very dangerous, turbulent waters, infamous the world round, known as the Muse's Cauldron. Father south than that are ice floes."

"That sounds horrible," Alannys ventured, "but why —"

Raman held up a hand. "Hear me out, please. Out to the left of Ravanmark is a vast, open sea. This sea is treacherous — the word 'open' is perhaps a bit misleading here. There are underwater volcanoes and Muses-know-what-else out there. There are few maps of that sea, and they are all inaccurate. You could sail out and draw one this week, and it would be inaccurate by next week. Little volcanic islands appear out there, only to be swallowed up by the sea again a few months later. Underwater lava formations are grown tall enough and sharp enough to gut a sailing ship...and then are swept away again. Terrible storms and killing squalls flare up, rage, and die again."

He stopped, seeming to collect his thoughts. Alannys stared at him in grim silence.

"What I'm telling you," he said finally, "is that sea travel is no small thing. The journey takes many days, and as many people die at sea as make it safely across. Only in the last thirty or forty years have ships advanced enough that safe travel is even really possible. This journey is not lightly taken. King Rathmar's visit is enormous — unprecedented, even. How bad would a situation have to be for a king himself to risk his life in that sea, to deliver a letter? And what would be the consequences of refusing to accept it?"

She couldn't hold his gaze. She averted her eyes, looking awkwardly out into the garden. "I'm sorry, Raman."

His hand fell heavily on her shoulder. "Don't apologize. I know you are doing everything you can to make things right. That's why I wanted to give you this."

He reached into his cloak and pulled out a familiar linen paper packet, sealed on the back with wax, and glittering with a crest she didn't recognize.

It drew her gaze like a magnet; her field of vision seemed to narrow around it. "Is that..."

"The letter itself. Yes. I convinced the ambassador to give it to me at the gate. The advisers weren't happy about it—their orders were to deliver it to Dorramon only—but nobody wants a war, Alannys. I promised Thell I would get it to him, and this way he can tell King Rathmar the letter was delivered. Their national motto is 'death before dishonor.' They aren't going to back down—this must be delivered."

"But I'm not Dorramon." She eyed the letter dubiously, the way she might look at a venomous snake, and made no move to take it.

"No. But you are the next best thing. He'll never take it himself—simple pride would keep him from ever reading it."

"Then you could..."

Raman ran a hand through his hair. "Alannys, I could read this letter and spend the rest of my life nagging him like a fishwife about what it said. And he would spend the rest of his life stubbornly ignoring me. The only one who has a chance of fixing this, the only one who has a chance of making him listen, is you. And that's why I'm giving you this letter." He reached out and took her hand, gently closing her fingers around the paper packet. "This is state information, Alannys. Whatever is in this letter is important, and secret, and you must not let it out of your sight unless the king himself takes it."

"Raman—"

"I know you'll do the right thing." He turned away quickly, obviously expecting further protest, and hurried back toward the vestibule. He stopped just before reaching it and looked at her again. "Just think, Alannys—think of all the lives that might be saved."

Leaving that final thought floating on the air between them, Raman turned away again and disappeared from view.

♫

Alannys looked down at the paper packet in her hand, then let herself into her room. Now that she actually had it, she confronted the problem of what exactly she should do with it.

She wasn't going to read it, of course. She knew Raman was manipulating her, and she knew that Dorramon wouldn't want her to have anything to do with it. Nothing in the world could make her break that seal.

The paper packet made a heavy, solid slap landing on the little table in her sitting room. She turned her back on it and headed through the arch into her bedroom, to the bath chamber to clean herself up. She'd been told, after all, to have a nap.

She ran herself through a bath, into a nightgown, and back out to her bed. She burrowed into the covers, pushed her head down into her pillow, and told herself she was going to fall immediately asleep.

She wasn't fooling anyone, least of all herself. She laid on her back and stared at the ceiling, rolled over on her side and stared at the wall, rolled over on her *other* side and stared at the mid-morning sun through her window, but all she saw was that ivory envelope with its golden crest.

It haunted her, that envelope, called to her like the song of a siren. She couldn't forget it, couldn't ignore it, couldn't stop it consuming her mind like a slow-burning fire.

She found herself in her sitting room, gnawing on the ball of her own thumb and pacing in front of the coffee table, back and forth.

She wasn't going to have any peace. The thing had gotten hold of her now, driven its twisting, spiny roots into her brain, and there was no escape for her now.

Back and forth.

Her own curiosity would drive her mad, push her right over her limit and abandon her there, if she left things as they were.

Back and forth.

Had Raman known? Had he forced that letter into her hands knowing how it would torment her, knowing how she would suffer until she gave in and did as he had wanted all along?

"Bastard," she muttered, and snatched up the letter.

She didn't even sit down. She broke the seal, and began to read, pacing her sitting room as she did.

To my Most Noble Cousin,

King of the Land of Ravanmark,

It is my sincere wish that this humble Correspondence should find you well. All talk of Ravanmark these days is talk of Trouble, it seems, and this grieves me greatly. The future of one of our Kingdoms will undoubtedly become the future of both, and I would like to see both of them Bright.

In that vein I must admit my great disappointment upon hearing of the delay in the consummation of the Royal Engagement between yourself and my dearest Daughter, Varilyn. Rumors of the most distressing nature surround this delicate Topic, and I suppose I need not tell you how discouraging it is to me to hear these — to say nothing of my lovely Varilyn, whose Merry Disposition has faded to a mere ghost of its former self, and whose pleasing figure begins to wither from the enormity of her Troubles.

Naturally I do not intend to make light of your own feelings on the matter, my young Cousin, for as you are a Man of great honor and impeccable character (as I repeatedly remind all of those around me) I know that this untenable situation aggrieves you as well. Heavy indeed must be the Burden that forces you to neglect your Betrothed in this despicable fashion. Well do I remember my exchanges with your dear Parents, arranging the Wedding we all now soon hope to celebrate. Great was the joy and high was the excitement that surrounded all of these tedious tasks, made wonderful by the knowledge we all had of the Happiness that these arrangements would one day bring to you and to my beloved Daughter. It pains me inhumanly to think of the sorrow that would assail my sainted Uncle, should he chance to look upon us from his rest and see the ruinous Delays which have beset his cherished Wish.

Of course I do not mean to overlook your own Regret, which I know must be very great, because undoing your departed Father's plans is a grave Dishonor none of us would willingly bring upon ourselves. It pains us all to see the closer ties we had all wished between our two Nations jeopardized by this distressing Delay.

You may read the depth of my concern in the Journey I have undertaken, in order to deliver this most Humble, and most Important, correspondence into your Hands. Such a perilous voyage I would not risk for any other matter in the world; but for the Happiness of yourself and my beautiful Daughter, as well as the continued peace, prosperity, and safety of our combined Kingdoms, we all must do whatever we can. I know that you share my Sentiment, and I eagerly await your favorable Reply so that we may begin the formal arrangements for the Day that will make you the happiest man in Ravanmark and Cadenda combined. Until that Time I shall remain

Your doting Cousin,
and most forbearing Friend,
King Rathmar II of Cadenda

♪

Alannys stood motionless in the middle of the sitting room, surrounded by the litter of pages she had already read and dropped to the floor, staring at the signature scrawled across the page she still held in her hand.

Heavy indeed must be the burden that forces you to neglect your betrothed...

Was that how the rest of the world saw them? The noble, dutiful monarch, and the selfish, headstrong woman who led him astray? The entire letter sounded too much like Ambassador Thell to her, and she wondered what plans and emotions were concealed behind the flowery language and reassurances.

What was she supposed to do about this now? She had never felt quite so lost in Ravanmark as she did these days —it seemed like every course of action before her was wrong, like nothing she could ever do could please all the people who were counting on her. Dorramon hadn't even wanted her to read that letter. She remembered swearing her oath to him in full view of the inner ward, and guilt burned her like a red-hot coal.

Have faith in him, Chen had told her. *Don't be just another naysayer telling him his dreams are impossible.* But Dorramon needed more than just faith—he needed someone who could stand beside him, support him, be worthy of him. How could that be her? And these dreams—they were her dreams, too. Did anyone care about that?

Do what's right. She could hear Raman now, as clearly as if he stood with her in the room. *He has a duty, and so do you. You must get this through to him.* They *did* have duties—more than one, and to so many different people. But they also had duties to themselves. How much of himself was Dorramon required to give up, in service to the people he ruled? Where was the line? Who decided what was right? Raman? Dorramon? *Her?*

The letter in her hand caught her eye again, certain words jumping from the page as though they were meant for her alone. *...for the continued peace, prosperity, and safety...*

Safety...

That was a threat. Leaving aside everything else in the letter, that line contained a very real, if somewhat veiled, threat. The danger was clear, but it seemed that no one could tell her what she should do about it.

Alannys sank to the floor amid the various pages of the letter, regarding with fear and hostility King Rathmar's signature scrawled across the paper in her hand. The bold, black slashes that made up the name seemed like a bad omen for them all.

♫

"Merciful Muses!" The voice was female, shocked, and full of familiar gravel.

Alannys hadn't even heard anyone come into the sitting room. She looked up through blurry eyes to find Tralice standing there, looking down at her with surprise written all over a face that carried more lines than Alannys remembered. Her dark eyes wandered across the papers littering the floor, and she frowned. "My Lady, are you all right?"

Alannys didn't know how to answer that, so she just looked back down at her lap, where King Rathmar's signature was faring badly against the tears that had fallen on it. She didn't know when exactly she had started to cry, or how long she had sat here since, and she didn't really care.

"Oh, dear. This won't do, my Lady, this won't do at all. You'll catch your death sitting on that cold floor." Tralice grabbed Alannys by the arm, attempting to haul her off of the floor.

Alannys wasn't much in the mood to be hauled anywhere, especially by someone she could be only half sure wasn't imaginary anyway. She jerked her arm free and returned her attention to the last page of Rathmar's letter, staring at the tear-stained signature. Yet another thing she'd messed up, and didn't know how to fix.

The thought didn't make her feel any better, and she sobbed out loud, a choking, hiccuping sound.

"Now, now," Tralice said, "nothing's as bad as all that. Come, now, my Lady — up with you."

It turned out Alannys was also not in the mood to be bossed around. She remained stubbornly where she was, regarding Tralice balefully. What call did the woman have to barge in after all this time and start issuing orders like nothing had changed?

"Oho, so that's how it is, is it?" Tralice folded her arms and regarded her obstinate charge.

Tralice, Alannys suddenly remembered, could be pretty obstinate herself.

"What are you doing here?" Alannys tried to keep her bad mood out of her tone, but she was only partly successful. She sounded sullen, like a pouting child. She probably looked like one too, parked on the floor like she was.

"That is a fine how-do-you-do. I am here, my Lady, to take care of you—a good thing, too, because it looks like you need it. I was a bit surprised to find you here, actually —I had rather expected you would already be out attempting the acts of the Redeemer. I heard you found the songs."

Alannys said nothing. She was duly chastised, but she also felt this was an odd thing for Tralice to have heard, and she wasn't quite sure what she should do about it.

Tralice studied her a moment, then shrugged. "Not in a talkative mood today, are we? Have it your way, I suppose." She bent down and reached for the papers Alannys had left scattered on the floor.

"No! Don't touch those!" Alannys scrambled over on her hands and knees and gathered the pages to her chest with both arms. Hands shaking, she tamped them into a neat stack and attempted to fit them back into the envelope.

Tralice watched Alannys's efforts with her hands on her hips, eyebrows raised. The gold gilt flashed in the light, and something in the maid's eyes shifted. "My Lady, really. This is an embarrassment. You must get yourself up off the floor! Give me that letter."

"No!" In a fit of pique, Alannys crushed the whole packet to her chest. She couldn't pass it on the king now even if she wanted to—between the crumpling and the tear stains, it wasn't suitable any more. This did little to help cool her temper. "No, I'm keeping this, and I'm not getting up! I'll wallow here the rest of my *life* if I want to. I'd like to know just who in the hell you think you are, to come waltzing back in here after all this *time,* telling me what to do, telling me I'm not *good* enough, I'm only making things *worse…*"

Tralice stared at her in utter shock, and something Alannys hadn't even known she was holding on to abruptly broke loose.

She buried her face in her hands. She wasn't even sure when she had started crying again. "I'm sorry, Tralice. I'm sorry. I just...I've been having a rough time lately. I didn't mean to take it out on you. Things have been going from bad to worse, and there's nothing I can do to stop it, and...oh, Tralice, I've missed you."

"Ach, my Lady, I can see that." Tralice had some of her usual humor in her tone, and when Alannys dared to look at her, her gaze had softened. She took Alannys's arm and helped her up. "There, there, my Lady. Let's get you to the sofa. That's right. Lie down, my Lady, and dry your tears. I'll be back directly." She pressed a handkerchief into Alannys's hand and disappeared into the bedroom.

Alannys laid the paper packet on her chest and dried her face, staring up at the ceiling with gritty, sore eyes. Nothing was making sense, but that seemed very much like the way of things lately. She tried not to think too much about it, lying on her back on the couch and drawing shuddering breaths that did little to improve her mood.

Tralice returned from the bedroom carrying a damp cloth. "Just close your eyes, my Lady, and calm yourself. Nothing is as bad as it seems." She spread the cool cloth over Alannys's forehead, murmuring soothing sounds. "Now you just rest yourself. I'll run and bring you some tea. Everything will look better after a nice, hot cup of tea, you'll see."

She bustled around the room a moment longer, before disappearing out the door. It all seemed so familiar, Alannys could almost believe that she had never left at all.

But Tralice *had* gone, Alannys knew that, and she had been gone for quite a little while. And just now everything felt so bizarre that Alannys was quite prepared to believe that King Rathmar's royal missive had pushed her right over the edge, and this was all nothing more than a hallucination.

As far as hallucinations went, though, this one was, at

the moment, uncommonly comfortable. She lay in the quiet, with the cool cloth against the hot skin of her forehead, listening to her own breathing slowly return to normal. She felt better in that moment than she had all morning — like a weight had been lifted from her.

It was only then that she realized — Tralice had taken King Rathmar's letter with her when she left.

♫

When Alannys awoke, the first thing that she noticed wasn't that she was still sprawled out on her sofa, or that her wet cloth had fallen off onto the floor. The first thing that she realized was that she was not alone. Someone sat next to her; a familiar presence perched between her and the edge of the couch.

But before she could even put a name to that familiar presence in her mind, before she could even open her eyes, warm lips moved against hers in a gentle kiss. She had been holding him at arm's length ever since they came back from Castle Glennayre, but she just didn't have it in her to push Dorramon away anymore. Alannys threw her arms around him and kissed him back, forgetting for the moment all the troubles that had clouded their interactions lately, surrendering herself to the music and the electricity that swirled around them as him lips pressed against hers, as his fingers tangled into her hair, as his velvet doublet pressed against her.

Finally he sat back and looked at her, his eyes sparkling. "Well, now. Tralice told me you were upset, but your mood actually seems much better now."

She felt a tingling blush creeping up her face. "Yes, well...I suppose you were right, what I really needed was a nap."

"Is that so?" Dorramon didn't laugh, but he sounded as though he might have liked to. "Well, then, I'm glad I suggested it. Here, sit up and I'll pour you some of this tea Tralice kindly brought for you."

She pushed herself upright on the sofa. "Thank you.

But, Dorramon—didn't you say you had to be in court?"

He looked away, busying himself with the silver tea service laid out on the coffee table. "That was the plan, yes. But Tralice told me how she found you...I couldn't ignore that."

It might have been only her imagination, but it looked to her as though his hands trembled when he passed her a teacup on a saucer. "Thank you," she said again.

Then her gaze landed on the stack of papers next to the tea service, and the tea cup clattered against the saucer in her hands. She snatched up the cup and drank deeply to cover her surprise, grateful that the tea had cooled somewhat while she slept. "I...see she brought you the letter," she said lamely. "Did you read it?"

"How could I not?" Dorramon leaned back against the cushions, rubbing at his face. "I had to know what had upset you so badly, didn't I? Look, Alannys, that letter never should have been here. Curse Raman for giving it to you in the first place. What was he thinking, saddling you with something like that?"

She leaned forward, carefully placing her cup and saucer on the table. "He was thinking it was the only way he might get you to read it. And it looks like he may have been right."

"I don't like being manipulated," Dorramon grumbled, "even by him. And I like it even less when he uses you to do it. This changes nothing. What has he accomplished here, beyond making you cry?"

"You—you aren't going to answer the letter?"

"Answer it? I should think not. I want you to forget about that letter. It's not important."

"Not important? How can you even say that? King Rathmar obviously went to a lot of trouble to get this to you. Don't you think you should—"

"No. I told them I would not accept any correspondence from them, and I meant it. Whatever he wrote in this letter, Rathmar obviously expected as much. I have heard that he and his entourage set out for the Great Palace the day after Ambassador Thell left to bring this letter."

"The day after…?" She stared at him. "Then he will be here — tomorrow?"

"Yes." Dorramon looked at her, then looked away. "They tell me Prince Cardoth and Princess Varilyn ride with him."

"What?" The word sounded weak. "I thought there was no way she would come here right now."

"So did I. It would seem they are serious about this wedding — or this war."

Alannys buried her face in her hands. His decision was being forced, then — and they had never even talked about it.

"Alannys? Are you all right?"

"No." Her voice was muffled by her hands. She folded them in her lap and regarded them morosely. "I'm sorry, Dorramon. I know you're in an impossible position, and I haven't been making things any better for you. What are you going to do?"

He watched her for a long moment without answering. When he finally did speak, his voice was very low. "What do you want me to do?"

"What?" She looked at the letter on the table, then looked away again. "It doesn't matter what I want, you know that. There are bigger concerns here than that."

"No." He grabbed her shoulders and turned her to face him, forcing her to look at him. "Listen to me — I want you to forget all of that. King Rathmar isn't your concern. You've done everything you can for Ravanmark, and now I want you to forget about it. There's nothing here but me, and you. What do *you* want?"

Facing him directly, with such a simple question, she couldn't hide any more. "I want you," she said simply, and the truth of it washed over her like a physical force, cracking her voice and burning her eyes with unshed tears. "I know it's selfish and I know it's wrong and I've spent I-don't-know-how-many hours trying to find a place for myself in Ravanmark that doesn't involve dragging you away from your duty. But I can't do it—I don't want to see Ravanmark go to war, but if I have to stand by and watch you marry another woman, I think I'll go mad. I think it'll kill me, Dorramon. I love you too much."

For a moment he just stared at her, motionless, and she wondered fleetingly if she had gone too far, said too much.

Then he grabbed her into the warmest embrace she'd ever felt, pulling her face into his chest and burying his face in her hair. "Oh, Alannys. You can't imagine how happy I am to hear you say that."

"I don't know why," she said. "It doesn't change anything."

"It changes everything." He squeezed her tighter. She could hear his heartbeat, steady and strong, and all she wanted right then was a way to make that moment last forever. "You've just given me the only chance at real happiness I think I've ever had. When you left this morning..." He held her at arm's length, studying her face. "I learned something today. All my life I've been raised to be king—it's all I thought I was here for, the only reason I existed at all. The measures of a good ruler are the only way I know to judge my worth, and my duty is all I've ever had. For most of my life it was all I cared about.

"But today I discovered there are other measures, and the yardstick of a good ruler doesn't measure some of the things that matter most. Duty isn't everything. I can't stay here and watch you leave again. If being King of Ravanmark means letting you go, then I'd rather throw my crown in the moat and start a farm somewhere. I love you, Alannys, and I want to stay beside you. I want you to stay beside me, forever. Will you marry me?"

"What? But...but...Cadenda, and—"

"Forget about that! I don't care what happens, we will

figure out a way to handle it. No one is going to force me to marry anyone else, not while the woman I love more than anything in the entire world is right here and she loves me, too." His blue eyes were intense, and dead serious.

She stared at him for a moment. Could she really keep arguing with him...arguing against what she wanted more than she had ever wanted anything before? She swallowed hard. "Are you—are you sure that's what you want? I don't think this is going to be easy, or safe."

"Nothing worth doing is ever easy." There was something wry about the smile he gave her. "How often does the easiest, safest path prove to be the best path?"

She recognized the very words she had once said to him, all those many months ago, and she laughed out loud. Her heart might have sprouted wings, for the sudden lightness in her chest. "I suppose I can't argue with that. Oh, Dorramon, I wish I had words to tell you how happy I feel right now."

"Hold on to it, because tomorrow things are going to get rough."

"I don't care. I think with you beside me I could stand anything."

He chuckled, a low and inviting sound, and pulled her close. "Well, then, we should be nigh onto invincible, because I feel the same way with you."

Alannys took his face in her hands and kissed him, savoring the play of electricity between his skin and her hands, between their lips. Dorramon groaned against her mouth, pulling her tight up against him, and she flushed with sudden heat. She knew she should probably feel bad —who knew what ramifications their decision would yet have?—but at that moment, she couldn't seem to do it. Let the world cast whatever slings and arrows it could muster. She would never again leave the side of the man beside her now.

♪

The sitting room door suddenly opened. "Your Highness? Oh, your Highness, I am sorry to interrupt!"

Alannys recognized Tralice's flustered voice and sighed, slumping back into the sofa in resignation. She raked her hands through her unkempt hair and straightened her rumpled nightgown, even though part of her had to wonder what it really mattered anymore.

"Again." Dorramon released her grudgingly, and she couldn't help but think his tone as he turned to the maid was a bit short—evidently she wasn't the only one getting frustrated.

"What?" Tralice sounded confused.

"You're sorry to interrupt *again*. This is hardly the first time this has happened, wouldn't you say?" Something like humor twinkled in his eyes.

"But this time it isn't my fault! Captain Grayble begs your presence at the dungeon, right away, your Majesty!"

"The dungeon? What's this?" Dorramon was abruptly serious.

Tralice shook her head. "I don't know all the details, my Lord King, but he says that Lord Diabon and Baron Prubard have escaped."

Dorramon swore, a blistering oath Alannys had never heard from the royal lips before. "Why in the Seven Hells didn't they Talent-proof that cell?"

Tralice fidgeted, her eyes wide and round in a face that suddenly looked strained. "Begging your pardon, my Lord King, but—they did. The prisoners, they escaped anyway."

A thundering silence enveloped the room, full of the shock that Alannys was sure they all had to be feeling. It was chillingly obvious what this revelation meant—the prisoners must have had help from the inside. There was just no other way both escaped from a Talent-proofed cell.

Dorramon's jaw hardened, and he stomped off toward the door. He was halfway there before he stopped and looked back at her. "Stay here. Don't worry about this—

I'm going to take care of it. And don't forget your promise. We'll get through all of this, one way or another, and I'm going to hold you to it."

She was too stunned to do anything more than nod. Diabon and Prubard — escaped? *There is no way all of these jailbreaks happened independently.* When had Raman said that to her? She couldn't remember, but whenever it was, he had been right.

Dorramon was going to take care of this — how? How could any of them battle a force they couldn't even contain?

♪

When Alannys finally recovered from her shock and looked around her sitting room, Tralice was standing there alone, watching her. "Is my Lady all right?"

"I am. I'm sorry, Tralice. What about you? Are you all right? I didn't expect to see you back at the palace."

"I gathered as much." Tralice turned away and started cleaning up the remains of the tea. Her voice sounded strained, but she kept her back to Alannys. "A girl has to get her money from somewhere, right? And you were bound to run out of dresses you could put on by yourself eventually."

Alannys brushed aside this odd attempt at a joke. There wasn't a trace of humor in Tralice's tone, and the words rang flat. A peculiar distance had opened up between them, a distance Alannys had never sensed there before and did not know how to close. "I wasn't asking about the job, Tralice. I was asking about *you*. I thought we were friends."

"Of course, my Lady," Tralice said stiffly. "You need not worry over me. I returned to my work because it was time for me to return to my work, that's all. I am living my life now for my husband, and my boys."

Alannys didn't know what to say to that. She wasn't even sure what most of that was supposed to mean. Tralice *said* they were friends, but she didn't *feel* very friendly. All Alannys was certain of was that there was a darkness about Tralice now, an ominous aura that had never been there before.

"But you, my Lady," Tralice said suddenly, "I am happy to find you doing so well. And still so close to his Majesty, it seems."

Alannys frowned. How was she even expected to respond to that? She couldn't tell if it was her imagination, or if something more than idle conversation lurked behind the observation. "Yes, well...we've had a bumpy time of it lately, but—"

"It makes me happy to see you've both come through it so well." Tralice deposited the tray holding the dirty tea service on the table and turned back to Alannys, wiping her hands on her apron. "It's a bit of too bad it'll all change, now Princess Varilyn has come to claim what's hers."

Alannys was immediately on the defensive. "I don't think so."

Tralice glanced at her face and then away. She moved to the far wall and made a show of straightening the royal tapestry. "I do admire your courage, my Lady, and I can't fault your ambition. But...well, most kings keep concubines, as I suppose you know well enough, but not as they are getting married! There is a way to these things, after all, and proper decorum must be observed. You'll have to make yourself scarce, my Lady, at least until Princess Varilyn's first child is born."

Alannys closed her eyes and tried to collect herself, pushing the unwanted mental images Tralice had given her aside. "No, Tralice, I don't think you're understanding me. Dorramon doesn't have any intention of marrying Princess Varilyn. I haven't told anyone yet, but he proposed to me, today, just before you came in."

Alannys could remember all the time she had spent with Tralice since she came to Ravanmark, all the laughs they had shared, the secret scandalous jokes. In her mind,

Tralice would be thrilled by this news, grabbing her hands and squealing like a schoolgirl.

In actuality, Tralice didn't react at all for a long, long moment. She stood stock still, her hands frozen on the big tapestry. She didn't even seem to be breathing.

Then she turned around to face Alannys, folded her hands primly in front of her, and said quite calmly, "I believe I must have misheard you, my Lady."

Alannys frowned. "I would be very surprised if you did. It was pretty clear."

"Then you must have misspoken! What you just said is impossible!"

Alannys wanted to snap back, but her maid's reaction worried her more than it angered her. "Tralice, I don't understand. This is not impossible. Dorramon sat right here on this sofa and proposed to me, not ten minutes ago. It was the happiest moment of my life, and I frankly expected a completely different reaction from you. You've known about Dorramon and I since the beginning, and you've always been supportive."

"I support him having some fun, not overturning the whole social order!"

"Calm down." Alannys sat down on the sofa, trying to look more in control of the situation than she felt. "No one is overturning the social order."

"Aren't you? You can't marry a king on the strength of a courtesy title, my Lady!" Tralice wasn't backing down, and her eyes blasted Alannys with hard accusation.

"What about the title of Redeemer of the Realm?"

"Now you're just trying to confuse the issue. This was supposed to be a bit of harmless fun for you both, not *marriage!* There are *rules* for these things, Lady Alannys, these things are *serious,* and the rules don't include kings marrying commoners. Especially *alien* commoners!"

"I'm sorry you feel that way, Tralice. I assure you I love Dorramon just as much as you loved your husband. Is it fair to tell us we can't be together because of my position, or his?"

"Fair?" Tralice demanded, balling her hands into white-knuckled, tendon-corded fists. "*Fair?* You dare to even *speak* to me of fair?" She stopped suddenly, pulling in a shuddering breath. "It doesn't matter. It's *just not done.* You are overstepping your boundaries, my Lady."

There was no point to this. Alannys stood up, staring evenly into Tralice's flushed face. "I acknowledge no boundaries."

She walked stiffly into her bedroom, doing her best not to slow or stumble under Tralice's stony glare.

♫

Alannys sat on her sofa bright and early the next morning, with her face buried in her hands, trying to tune out some of the noise and confusion raging around her.

"Lady Alannys, about bread—"

"No! No, no, no—Lady Alannys was talking to me! You must wait your turn!" The tailor stepped in front of the baker when he interrupted him, using his portly frame to physically separate him from her. He was but one person in quite a vocal group of people crowding her sitting room, all vying for her attention and each looking for answers. She wasn't much in the mood for it and probably would have sent them away, only they were all evidently there at the request of the king.

"My Lady!" the agitated tailor continued, turning back to her. "You simply must pick a color. I can have trunks of samples brought for your review, but I must have the color first!" He sounded almost apoplectic.

Alannys had to wonder how much pressure Dorramon had put on these people. "You mean you don't use white wedding gowns here?"

"White? No. I can't think of a single queen who wore white to her wedding. It's rather...drab, wouldn't you say? It seems like a common choice, if my Lady will forgive me for saying so—not really suited to the woman marrying the King of Ravanmark."

"Well—all right." Alannys had no desire to argue it. If traditions weren't the same here, then so be it. "What color do queens wear to the weddings?"

"Ach, my Lady, if there was a simple answer to that question I would not be asking you! It can be anything you want—even white, although I would not recommend it, myself. You could choose royal purple, for obvious reasons. Or maybe blue, it's quite feminine…"

"Red," she said.

"Red?" The tailor considered it, staring at the ceiling and rubbing his chins. "That will be quite...striking, my Lady."

"Yes...I want the same color his Majesty wore to his coronation."

"Ah! I see your meaning. A fine choice, my Lady. Very striking. Give me two days and I will return with fabric samples for you to inspect. Then we can begin to discuss the styling of your gown."

"I'll look forward to it," she said, happy and relieved that her choices finally met with his approval.

"Do that. Do that! I will too." He grabbed her hand and pumped it enthusiastically.

Her joy was short-lived. The tailor had barely released her hand before the baker, a wiry little man, pushed him out of the way. "Rye, pumpernickel, or sourdough?"

She blinked at him. "Pumpernickel. What am I choosing?" A knock sounded at her door.

The baker probably didn't even hear her question; he was snorting in poorly concealed distaste before she even finished her answer. As soon as she named the bread, he spoke again. "Apple, strawberry, or blueberry?"

"Strawberry. But what—"

"Veal, venison, or pheasant?" The knocking continued.

"Veal." She gave up trying to understand the choices she was being offered and just made decisions.

The baker marked her answer on a parchment sheet, and looked at her out of the tops of his eyes, his face still turned down. "Look, you do understand this is for the royalty and nobility attending your wedding, right? Not the peasant rabble?"

"What, have you got something against veal?"

"Love it, myself." He quirked a sardonic grin at her. "But then, I'm only one small step above the peasant rabble. Nobles don't—"

"If my selections are unsuitable, how about you just make some suitable ones for me and save us all some aggravation?" The knocking at her door had become a thundering, incessant pounding, and it felt like it was driving her mad. "Tralice! Would you very much mind getting the door?"

"As it happens," Tralice said airily from behind her, "I would mind."

"What?" Alannys spun to face her, surprised by the defiance in her tone, only to find it reflected in her expression as well. "What are you talking about?"

"I don't think it's appropriate." Tralice planted her feet and crossed her arms, the very picture of obstinance. "It isn't right for the king's betrothed to receive unmarried men in her rooms—especially Singari men; they cause enough scandals all on their own."

"That's Chen out there? And you didn't let him in?" Alannys was already halfway to the door, ignoring the questions that continued to fly at her back. *What's your favorite flower? Red wine, or white? Do you prefer your hair up, or down?*

"My Lady." Tralice sounded like she was gritting her teeth. "This is *not appropriate!*"

"I don't give a single damn about what is appropriate. My friends are my friends, and they are always welcome here, regardless of their rank." She threw the door open, relieved to see a friendly face in the whirlwind of frenetic activity that her sitting room had become.

He smiled at her, but it seemed like a half-hearted smile. He shot a wary glance around the busy room.

"Muses, Alannys, I didn't think you were going to answer! Is this a bad time?"

"Maybe, if you ask them. What's going on?"

"It's the King of Cadenda." His voice was low and flat. "I don't know if anyone's told you, but he's here."

"What? Now?" The world lurched sideways, and she grabbed the doorframe to steady herself.

"Almost. You know we're camped near the main road. I could see the royal party approaching, so I figured I'd better get over here and tell you, because I didn't know if anyone else would."

"Mercy. I've got to get to the Great Hall." She looked down at herself, surveying her clothes. Tralice had helped her dress that morning, and though her gray brocade gown was simple, it was a good deal nicer than anything she would have worn on her own. But she didn't have Songstrike, or even her dagger, and she didn't have time to get either of them.

"Alannys?" Chen was already turning away from the door, and he looked back at her over his shoulder. "Are you coming?"

She pushed away her doubts. "Everybody out!" she shouted. "I'm sorry, but I have to attend an audience. We'll have to continue this later."

She didn't wait for them to comply. She walked out the door with Chen, heading for the Great Hall as fast as her legs would carry her.

"So," Chen said, staring straight ahead, "last time I asked you, things were not official. I'm guessing that now they are."

His tone was carefully neutral. She glanced at his face, and had to look away. "Yes. I'm sorry, Chen."

"I don't think you should be sorry. I wouldn't have taken you to the outer ward if I had expected any less. Judging from the state of your room, it doesn't look like the king is in any mood to wait, and the Singari just happen to be here. If you were serious about music at your reception, I hope you'll consider letting us provide it."

"Are you — are you sure?"

He shot a crooked smile at her, then looked away. "We're tired of singing for battles. I don't think we've played for entertainment since Pinevale."

"There is that. I would be honored, Chen, really."

"Good." He held the vestibule door open, and they walked out into the bright, chilly morning. "I'm happy for you, Alannys. I really am."

"Then why do you sound so gloomy?"

He sighed. "I'm glad you two finally cleared the air between you. The king and the Redeemer...it's like something out of a fairy tale, with a dark, scary forest and a shining castle, and everybody lives happily ever after at the end."

She didn't say anything, just looked at him expectantly.

"Be strong, Alannys, because I think you've got a bit more time in the dark, scary forest before you get your happily ever after." He kissed her hand in a gesture that seemed quite courtly, then turned and headed for the gate to the outer ward.

She stared after him, wondering how much of his assessment was true. She wanted to blow it off entirely, but she had a sensation she couldn't shake, a sensation her grandmother would have had a quick explanation for.

Someone, somewhere was walking on her grave.

Chapter Two

THE EMISSARIES

*T*ension gripped the Great Hall like a white-knuckled fist. The very air felt brittle and hard. More people crowded the hall than Alannys had seen in there since before she left three months ago, clutching papers and engaging in earnest conversations, all the while keeping one eye toward the door. They waited expectantly, eagerly, like carrion waiting for the kill.

The thought did not improve her mood. She hurried up the red granite walkway, feeling the anxiety in the room seep into her bones like a crippling disease. She saw some familiar faces in the crowds—Raman was there, and Captain Grayble patrolled the outer edges of the room, along with several of his men—but she didn't have the time or the inclination to stop and greet them.

Dorramon did not look entirely happy to see her there, but he did his best to smile. She knelt at the foot of the dais while the page recognized her and bade her approach.

"Well, now," Dorramon said, as she walked up the stairs, "it seems the walls really do have ears. Especially when one is in with the Singari. I had half hoped you wouldn't find out about this."

She looked down at her feet. "If you want me to leave, your Highness, just say the word."

"No." He nodded at the page, who quickly retrieved her usual chair. "I said half hoped. This concerns you as well. You have a right to be here. But I'm afraid it won't be pleasant."

"All the more reason for me to be here. Why should you face this alone?"

"Please, sit. I admire your bravery. But I hope you're holding on, because the waters could get rough."

No sooner had he finished speaking than two heralds strode into the Great Hall, uniformed in black and gold. Each carried a large red flag, bearing the royal crest of Cadenda, the same crest she had seen in gold on the king's letter: a black snake, poised to strike, silhouetted against a bright yellow sun. The crest felt threatening, and it gave her a chill — a sensation that was only compounded by the long sword hanging at each herald's side. They marched halfway up the granite walkway with crisp, sharp strides, then stopped and recited in perfect unison.

"Announcing the entrance of the Lord High Priest of the Temple of the Most Holy Sun, the King of the Great and Noble Land of Cadenda, his Imperial Majesty Rathmar the Second."

At this speech, all eyes turned toward the doors, awaiting the arrival of the announced king.

Through the door came a young man — noticeably younger than the heralds — dressed in the same black and gold uniform. He proceeded solemnly up the granite walkway, scattering sunflower petals with great concentration, as if walking on the floor of Ravanmark's palace might soil his king.

Alannys looked at Dorramon, and raised an eyebrow. He met her gaze, and gave a minute shrug.

At last the king himself strode through the door. Tall and stately, with broad shoulders and black hair greased back from his face, King Rathmar II easily commanded the attention of every person in the room. His dark complexion and athletic build spoke of many hours in the sun. He wore a yellow silk tunic and pants, and a long black fur cape that required two more of his peculiar herald-guards to hold up off of the ground behind him. A tall, golden crown bearing a single, carefully faceted yellow stone gleamed on top of his head. He came purposefully down the center aisle, spreading his gleaming smile in every direction throughout the hall.

Behind him, unannounced, followed two elegant people Alannys could only assume were Prince Cardoth and Princess Varilyn. The prince was a younger, slightly less ostentatious version of his father—the same deep tan, dark eyes, and greased back hair, in a nicely tailored red doublet that made apparent how fit he was. No sooner had he stepped into the room than his gaze locked onto Alannys, his dark eyes burning into hers like two smoldering coals. It made her acutely uncomfortable and she shifted in her chair, turning her attention to his sister instead.

Princess Varilyn wore her chestnut hair pulled back into an elegant braid. Her open-backed, rose-colored gown put Alannys's demure one to shame, and her pale skin glowed as though it had been carefully protected from the sun.

Alannys swallowed hard, suddenly wishing Chen had been a little less thoughtful. She was up against *these* gorgeous people? *This* graceful, beautiful woman was her rival? All at once it was a lot harder to blame the people for demonstrating—even she knew she didn't hold a candle to Princess Varilyn. Prince Cardoth's eyes had never left Alannys, and she was sure that he, along with everyone else in the room, was finding fault with everything about her. She sat up straighter in her chair, twisting her fingers together in her lap so her hands couldn't shake and betray her nerves.

Even the usually self-important pageboy faded silently into the background behind the royal throne as King Rathmar approached. Dorramon stood to greet him, his own crown glittering in the torchlight with his every move, his royal purple velvet cloak draping elegantly from his broad shoulders as he bowed formally. "King Rathmar, allow me to welcome you to Ravanmark."

King Rathmar bowed in return, somehow making the gesture seem dashing and sophisticated. "Many thanks, your Highness, for your gracious greeting. Might I make so bold as to inquire after the letter I recently sent to your Majesty?"

Rathmar's voice was deep and sonorous. Alannys was glad she was only watching the exchange—the King of Cadenda was overwhelming in every way.

Dorramon's smile never changed, but his tone cooled noticeably. "I did have the pleasure of reading it. However I received word of your approach before I had composed a response."

King Rathmar laughed out loud, and waved a magnanimous, bejeweled hand. "Think nothing of it. Letters are too pretentious for such as we—much better to talk face to face."

Dorramon inclined his head but said nothing.

"I would like to introduce my son, Prince Cardoth. Regrettably Crown Prince Vox could not join us on this journey. And of course you remember my beautiful daughter, Cadenda's most precious flower, future queen of Ravanmark and your wife-to-be, Princess Varilyn." Rathmar turned back to Dorramon expectantly, with a pointed glance at Alannys.

Dorramon took the hint. He took Alannys's hand and drew her forward to stand next to him. "Allow me to introduce to you our national hero, the Redeemer of the Realm, Ravanmark's beautiful Lady Alannys of Gale."

Of course Alannys understood what he was doing. These bragging introductions were a contest of sorts, and Dorramon had to match Rathmar's efforts. She would have liked to stand as proud and unaffected as Princess Varilyn, but Dorramon's praise made her blush, and she couldn't pull it off. He glanced at her flaming cheeks and grinned, placing his hand on her arm.

Rathmar's expression froze. His eyes seemed to frost over as he looked at her. "I must confess myself disappointed." Even his warm, rich voice had gone cold and hard. "I had hoped this was merely a case of youthful indiscretion—regrettable, certainly, but forgivable in the end. The woman does appear to have some features to recommend her for such pastimes, after all, and you are yet so new upon the throne…" He shrugged. "But to have her here with you, now—it is intolerable. Unforgivable. This woman's very presence here is a grave insult to my daughter."

"This woman has a name," Dorramon shot back roughly, "and everything you just said is a grave insult to her. I apologize to your daughter, Rathmar. I meant her no offense. Can you honestly say the same to the Lady Alannys?"

Rathmar's face darkened with anger. His eyes narrowed, and Alannys tensed, bracing herself for his verbal onslaught.

But it never came. King Rathmar glanced around the room, and seemed to remember all of the courtiers watching. Gradually his demeanor calmed, and he served up a carefully polished smile. "Of course, of course." His tone was smooth as silk again; warmth spread through his voice like melted butter. "You know it is never my intention to upset you, your Highness, or any that you call friend." He inclined his head to Alannys. It was a very gracious gesture, but it felt dangerous, and her hand clenched involuntarily on Dorramon's arm. "I apologize if I have gotten us off to a poor start. I want only a reasonable, peaceful solution to our present difficulties, for both of our lands. Perhaps we should adjourn for now, that cooler heads might later prevail. I believe it is customary, when receiving guests of state, to hold a welcoming banquet. Perhaps we could continue this discussion there."

Dorramon frowned. They all knew he was being manipulated, but how could he refuse? Even Alannys could see that Rathmar's primary objective was to make sure he seemed in the right to the onlookers. To refuse this would only make Dorramon look worse—by asking,

Rathmar had already made Dorramon look rude for not inviting them first. "Of course. I'm afraid we don't have accommodations to offer you in the keep, but I will arrange rooms for you at the Raven's Nest. Our nobility stay there as well, when they visit the Great Palace."

A delicate frown skittered across Rathmar's handsome face, smoothed over before it could even settle properly. "Of course. Please don't put yourself to any trouble for us."

Alannys's free hand clenched into a fist at her side. She was well aware that last remark was delivered just to make sure everyone in the room knew that the noble Rathmar felt the inn was not suitable for a king, but was too much of a gentleman to say so.

King Rathmar dropped a stiff little half-bow. "Come, children," he intoned, and turned to leave, his entourage falling into position around him. Prince Cardoth turned smartly to follow, but Princess Varilyn hesitated, looking back at the dais, her eyes wide and round.

"Please, my Lord King!" she cried. Her voice was high and querulous—she sounded panicked. "Am I to leave without a word to my betrothed?"

Rathmar turned and glowered at her in earnest, and it was a fearsome sight. "Don't make a spectacle of yourself, girl. I have said we are leaving."

"But Father, please!" Her eyes glimmered with unshed tears. "I have not seen him in so long. Please, allow me to greet him before I must leave him again."

King Rathmar raked a glance around the big room. He must not have liked what he saw, because he sighed dramatically. "Very well. But be quick."

Princess Varilyn dropped a quick curtsy and turned away, hurrying to the foot of the dais. She crumpled there in an abject kneel while the flustered page gawped, wondering what he should do.

"The Crown of Ravanmark," he finally croaked, "recognizes Varilyn, Princess of Cadenda. His Majesty bids you approach."

She rose, and slowly ascended the steps to the dais. Alannys shifted uncomfortably and moved back. This was a level of awkward beyond anything she had ever experienced.

Almost as if he hoped to hurry things along, Dorramon took a step forward, offering his hand. "It is a pleasure to welcome you to the Great Palace," he said, his manner stiff and formal. "It has been too long."

Princess Varilyn looked from his extended hand back to his face. Alannys watched with a palpable sense of dread, feeling everything happen in slow motion. Varilyn reached out as if to take his hand, and then suddenly threw herself against him, wrapping her arms around his neck. Dorramon stood there motionless, plainly stunned, and in full view of the entire court Varilyn planted a big kiss on the side of his face.

"Varilyn!" Rathmar's shocked gasp could be clearly heard through the silent hall.

She stepped back from Dorramon, dropping into a deep curtsy. "I beg your forgiveness, your Majesty. I was overcome with emotion." She turned and walked back to her father in a stately, measured stride, her head held high.

Alannys couldn't help thinking that she certainly didn't *look* overcome with emotion.

King Rathmar cast one more appraising look around the Great Hall, and smiled broadly, clapping a hand on his daughter's shoulder. "We shall take our leave of you, then. I do look forward to our dinner, your Majesty." He turned and swept out of the hall, his entourage in tow.

Dorramon watched them leave, unmoving, his face dark.

The Great Hall was silent in their wake. Alannys stepped tentatively up next to Dorramon. "Are you all right?"

He jumped, startled. "What? Of course. I am sorry you

had to witness that."

She laughed, surprised at the bitter edge on her voice. "That was certainly unexpected. I had no idea Princess Varilyn was so—attached to you."

"She isn't." Dorramon looked at her and tried to smile, but it was plain he was still brooding. He took her arm and escorted her back to her chair. She sat down, and he stood looking at her seriously, his back to the hall. "That was not a kiss."

"It—wasn't? It certainly looked like a kiss."

His face suddenly flushed bright red. "That was deliberate. People are easily fooled. I'll show you what a real kiss looks like later." He ruffled her hair and sat down in the throne.

"Wait," she said, keeping her voice quiet, barely more than a whisper, aware of all the listening ears. "If she wasn't kissing you, what was she doing?"

"Whispering," he said, his voice every bit as quiet as hers. "That wasn't a greeting, Alannys.

"It was a warning."

♫

The Great Hall had never felt quite so small to Alannys as it did in the moments after King Rathmar's eventful audience. The entire massive room seemed to close in on her. It didn't help that everyone in the room kept one eye on the dais. She felt positively squeezed.

She looked away from the throne, frowning. A warning, Dorramon said. But a warning of what? To what purpose? She couldn't seem to follow half of what went on around here. She sighed, wondering if Chen had really done her any favors by sending her here.

"Alannys?" Dorramon said, his voice barely audible. "Are you all right?"

She turned back to him, doing her best to present a smile. "I'm fine. It's just a lot to think about. I don't know how you handle such things so calmly. Watching you, it's like all of this is no big deal at all."

Dorramon laughed, and conversation in the room finally began to pick up and return to normal. "Trust me, it's not that easy. I've been taught all my life to show no weakness, to keep my composure under pressure, but...King Rathmar has a way of getting under my skin. If you hadn't been there to keep me steady, I really don't know what might have happened."

Alannys remembered Varilyn, and felt her ears get suddenly hot. "I don't know, it seems like plenty enough happened while I *was* here." The quip was out before she knew she was going to say it, before she had a chance to censor her feelings. It wasn't wise, but it was honest. Everywhere she looked she saw groups of courtiers talking animatedly. She wondered if they were all discussing the princess's sudden public display of affection.

For just a second, Dorramon's blue eyes widened with shock, and then he frowned. "That didn't mean anything, Alannys. I told you Varilyn was only delivering a message, nothing more. Don't you believe me?"

"Of course I do. I just...I'm hopelessly out of my depth here, and I don't know what I can do about it. Maybe nothing. I can't compete with those people, not any of them. I had no idea you were engaged to someone like that." She folded her hands in her lap, focusing on them instead of the courtiers eagerly watching her and Dorramon for any clues to their reaction to the audience.

Dorramon looked out over the hall, still frowning, as if he too was acutely aware of the scrutiny they were receiving. "Things seem to have settled down in here. If it's all right with you, I'd like to adjourn for a bit."

"Of course." She was surprised by the suggestion, but she wasn't going to turn down the chance to leave that crowd behind. But his expression worried her, and she wondered if it had been wise to share so much of what she was really feeling. "I'm sorry if I did anything improper."

"What?" He stood up, taking her hand and pulling her

to her feet as well. The page scurried up to announce their exit, but Dorramon waved him off. "No, no, I'd rather not make a production of this. There's been enough of that in here today. Go and find Arch-Prince Raman and Captain Grayble, please, and send them to the Lesser Hall. There's a good lad." The page ran down the steps and into the throngs of people in the hall, and Dorramon turned back to Alannys. "I think you did just fine. The only bad behavior here was Rathmar's. And possibly mine. But I couldn't just stand there and let him denigrate you like that."

"Thank you," Alannys said, humbled. She didn't know what else to say, and she was glad they were walking toward the royal antechamber—judging by the looks the two Royal Guards by the door gave her, her expression was strange.

The antechamber was just as she remembered it: small, chilly, and rather dark. The single torch that always burned in the chamber provided just enough light to get safely through it, but the shadows stretched long and deep from the untouched corners of the little room. It felt stale, somehow, and very, very old.

No sooner had the heavy door blocked them from sight than Dorramon caught her by the shoulders and pulled her into a long, gentle kiss, warming her to her toes.

Then he hugged her tight against him, cradling her head against his chest. "Alannys, you've got nothing to be jealous of. And you've got nothing to worry about. I won't let anyone harm you, and I won't let Rathmar succeed in any of his goals here."

Alannys could hear his voice resonate in his chest, and the steady cadence of his heart beating. He always looked out for her, always put her first, even after the way she'd acted. She thought about how he handled his jealousy of Chen and how she'd handled her jealousy of Varilyn, and that shamed her, but she clung to him anyway. His arms around her felt strong and sure, and the velvet of his doublet was soft against her skin. In that quiet, perfect moment, all she wanted was to stay like that forever.

But she was aware of the time passing them by, and all too soon Dorramon released her and stepped back, sighing. "I suppose we had better get moving. It wouldn't do to summon Raman and Grayble to the Lesser Hall and keep them waiting."

"No, I—I suppose not." She reached out and took his hand, unwilling to break the connection between them entirely.

Dorramon gave her hand a squeeze, and together they walked into the almost-completely-dark passage under the inner ward.

It was only then, in the ominous underground blackness that felt close and threatening, that she remembered Dorramon's oddly worded statement, and wondered what he meant when he said *any* of King Rathmar's goals here.

♫

As it turned out, they had kept their friends waiting, and Raman was not doing it very patiently. He paced the Lesser Hall like something wild that had been caged, peering into all of the tunneling alcoves suspiciously, casting sullen glances across the ornate dais, and constantly checking his sword in its scabbard. He spun to face the dais when Alannys and Dorramon appeared from the hidden door, taking in their linked hands with a dark expression. "Are you sure, with everything going on, that is wise? Are you *trying* to provoke them?"

Dorramon regarded him placidly. "I'm sure I don't know what you could mean, Raman. Do you find some wrong in a man walking hand in hand with his betrothed?"

Raman buried his face into his hand, dragging his fingers roughly down his cheeks. "Is this—is this a *joke?* Are you trying to be *funny?*"

"Do I look like I'm joking?"

"Seven Hells!" Raman exploded, throwing out his arms in a dramatic display of anger. "I counted on you to talk *sense* to him, Alannys, not drag him even further off course! I thought you wanted to *help* Ravanmark!"

She stiffened, but Dorramon stepped around in front of her, blocking Raman from her view before she could respond. "Now that's uncalled for," he said sternly, "and I'm not going to stand for it. Calm down. You know I'm always interested in your opinion, Raman. But I'm not interested in hearing you malign Lady Alannys."

"Dorr! How can you defend this? Do *either* of you have any idea what you have done?"

"Calm yourself, my Lord." Grayble's voice cut across their squabble, calm and firm. He was leaned sharply back against the far wall, half hidden in an alcove, his boot against the wall to support him. He regarded them all over folded arms, then pushed himself upright and came forward. "You must have been aware this was the direction his Majesty has been leaning since — well, since before Lady Alannys ever left the Great Palace."

Raman raked a hand through his blond hair, leaving it looking as frazzled as he seemed to be. "I knew well enough which direction he wanted to go, Captain. I never really thought he would *commit* to gutting his kingdom over a woman!"

"Stop right there." Grayble's tone had an edge of iron, and his hand gripped the handle of his sword. "I know you and your Highness are like brothers, but this is pushing it too far. If you insist on speaking to him in such a treasonous manner, I will escort you to the dungeon myself. I would have taken you there after your actions in the outer ward if it had been left to me, but the king stayed my hand. Whatever your feelings on this matter, he is your king. Do you support him, or are you a traitor?"

♫

For a long moment Captain Grayble and Arch-Prince Raman stood there, glaring fiercely at each other. Alannys didn't even dare to breathe. This was it, she knew — the outcome of this moment would define everything between the group of them from here on to forever. The moment hung there, frozen, balanced impossibly on the edge of a knife, waiting for the slightest touch to make it fall.

Raman puffed out his cheeks and blew out a heavy sigh. "Of course I support him. If you're looking for treason, you'll have to look somewhere else, Captain. I will stand behind any decision he makes. But...I don't like where this is headed."

"You don't like where *you think* this is headed," Dorramon put in. He sat down on the edge of the gold-trimmed dais, looking surprisingly informal. "The bad news is that I don't really know where this is all headed. The good news is that you don't either — certain war exists only in your mind."

"At this rate it will exist all around us before long," Raman muttered.

"You don't know that." Dorramon was gentle, but insistent. "Relations between countries are a lot like relations between people — fluid, changeable. What is certain now may become impossible tomorrow. I can't guarantee a storybook ending, Raman. What I can tell you is that I am doing my best to navigate this situation in a way that will not lead to war, without giving up the woman I love. Is that fair enough for you?"

Raman shook his head and turned away.

"You'll never get that one to admit defeat, my Lord King," Grayble said, with some humor. "But he'll come around. Give him some time."

"Time," Raman snorted. "Cadenda is here. Time is the one thing we do not have. Look, Dorramon, is this engagement of yours official?"

"Official...no," Dorramon said. "It won't be official for about two more hours — which reminds me, your presence is required in the Palace Chapel, two hours from now."

"I swear by the Sacred Song I don't understand how

you can be so flippant about this. If it isn't official then there is still a chance. Varilyn is here, maybe you should require her presence in the Palace Chapel in two hours. I'll gladly witness that for you."

"Now you're being rude to Alannys again, and I've already told you I won't accept it. I never had an engagement ceremony with Varilyn, and I never will."

"Never had it because you begged off of it," Raman accused. "This should have happened nearly ten years ago. I'll never understand why King Caleb supported you in shirking your duty."

"My father's actions, and the reasons behind them, are neither your concern nor your problem. I understand that this audience has left us all a bit tense, but you need to take a step back and rethink your attitude. I've asked Alannys, and she has accepted, and that is official enough for me." Dorramon waved Alannys over, and pulled her down to sit next to him. "What did you make of the audience, Grayble?"

Grayble stroked his chin thoughtfully. "Well, I suppose that depends on what Princess Varilyn said to you."

Alannys had the disconcerting sensation of feeling her own eyes widen without any conscious intent on her part. "You knew that kiss was fake? Am I the only one she fooled with that?"

Captain Grayble laughed out loud. "No, I very much doubt you were the only one fooled, my Lady. At the very least I am certain her father and brother did not suspect."

"Neither did I," Raman grumbled, coming back to join the conversation again. "What did she tell you, Dorramon?"

"Only a few words. She said, 'This is a trap. And not just for you.'"

"That's it?" Raman said. "She made all that fuss just to tell you that?"

"It isn't like she had a lot of time," Alannys said. "Maybe the more important question is, what do we do about it?"

"There's precious little we *can* do," Grayble said, "without knowing anything more specific than that. We certainly suspected as much before she said so. And there's always the possibility that she is lying, or that her sudden confession was also part of their plan all along."

"My head hurts," Alannys complained.

Dorramon laughed and put his arm around her shoulders. "Mine, too."

Captain Grayble watched them both, but his expression seemed as though he wasn't really seeing them at all. "I'm afraid the only conclusion we can draw from this...is that we can draw no conclusion until we have more information."

"I disagree," Dorramon said. "It seems obvious there is more going on here than meets the eye. We may have suspected as much before, but we couldn't be sure. In light of that, Captain, I'd like your men to keep a close eye on our visitors. I want to be informed of everything they do."

Grayble crossed his arm over his chest in salute. "It shall be as you command, my Lord King."

"And for the rest of us," Dorramon continued, "we must watch ourselves. If King Rathmar is here for evil ends, any of us might find ourselves in danger."

Raman shook his head. "Don't be too quick to trust Varilyn. You know what she's like. The worst danger we'll face is further abuse from King Rathmar's sharp tongue. You should invite your mother to the dinner, Dorramon. He obviously has no real respect for any of us."

"My mother has to attend. This is a state occasion — it would be unthinkably rude if she did not. Rathmar strikes me as a man who cares a great deal about what other people think of him — he would notice a slight like that. She must attend, as must you and I."

"Where are you planning to have this dinner?" Raman asked, sounding as though something unpleasant had just occurred to him. "Surely not in the royal dining hall?"

"I don't have any choice about that either," Dorramon said, "not for a state occasion of this magnitude. Protocol demands a state dinner in the royal dining room. A private dinner in any other venue could be seen as a grave insult."

"Your Majesty, you can't!" Captain Grayble sounded appalled. "It would be a very bad idea to permit these people any closer than they need to be."

"It can't be helped," Dorramon said.

"Just hold the dinner in the Great Hall," Raman said. "They are here to seek peace; they won't be looking for offense."

"The Great Hall," Dorramon said dubiously, obviously unconvinced.

"A most wise suggestion, my Lord. The Great Hall is much easier for us to secure, offers better escape, and is still quite suitable." Relief was plainly evident in Grayble's tone, and Alannys wondered about that. She knew she didn't like these people, for reasons she largely attributed to personal bias—what was the battle-hardened captain sensing from them that had him so worked up?

Alannys shivered in a sudden chill. "Should I stay in my rooms for dinner tonight?"

Dorramon squeezed her shoulders. "Of course not. I won't hear of it—there is no way I am attending without you. Besides, anyone would make a better target alone than in a group."

True, but she wasn't sure she liked the sound of that any better. "Well, then—should I wear Songstrike? Or at least my dagger?"

"No," Raman said quickly. "I'm sorry, but I think showing up armed to a state dinner is likely to offend our guests."

"Uninvited guests," Dorramon muttered. "Unwelcome guests."

"Well, be that as it may, I should think if we are trying to get through this without igniting a war, offending them directly would be a bad idea."

Grayble moved to stand near her. "Don't worry yourself, my Lady." His voice was low. "I will be there tonight, and I *will* be armed. No harm will come to you while I stand."

She took in the serious expression on his face, and shivered again.

♫

Alannys approached the Palace Chapel two hours later to find Arch-Prince Raman leaning against the wall next to the door, his arms crossed and his face arranged in a hard scowl she was learning to dread.

Inside she cowered; inside, she burst into unhappy tears and ran the other direction. Outwardly she put on a faltering smile and a pleasant tone. "Good afternoon, Raman."

"Don't look at me like that. I'm not here to drown your puppy."

"No...no, I think you're here to do something even worse. Otherwise, you would already be inside."

Raman sighed, pushing himself off of the wall, but not quite looking her in the eye. "Look, Alannys, I know you don't want to hear anything I have to say. But just hear me out, will you? Nothing is official yet. You haven't done anything that can't be taken back."

"Taken back? Why would I—"

"Yet. Once you step through that door, things will be set into motion, things that can't be undone. Dorramon will get what he wants, but...Alannys, it's not too late to do the right thing."

"Do the right thing." Alannys folded her arms, finally resigning herself to the conversation. "You seem to think Dorramon's pushing me into this. This is my choice too—I want this. Am I somehow giving a different impression?"

Raman shook his head, shooting a dirty look at the door to the chapel, like he begrudged its very existence. "No, I know what you want well enough...but I also know you share the same concerns I do, concerns that Dorramon seems determined to push aside. You don't have to let him. You don't have to go along with this."

"Go along with…" She caught herself right at the last moment, just before she raked her hand through her hair in frustration and ruined a careful hairstyle that had taken Tralice twenty minutes and a whole handful of ribbons to create. She lowered her hand and resolved to keep her temper on a tighter leash. "I can't pretend to know what you're thinking. But I assure you that Dorramon is not pushing me into this. In fact, for the first time in a long time, *no one* is pushing me into *anything*."

The emphasis of her remark was not lost on Raman—he squirmed uncomfortably, but said nothing.

"The concerns you mentioned are just that; concerns, and they are his as well. But at some point, Raman, you have to ask yourself whose side you are really on. I decided I'm on his side, and I decided to start acting like it. Whose side are you on?"

Raman frowned. "That's a bit of a false dichotomy, isn't it? This is an engagement—Ravanmark and Cadenda are on the same side here."

"Do you think so? I was there too, and from where I was standing…" Alannys pulled open the chapel door. "It didn't look like King Rathmar was on our side at all." She disappeared inside before Raman could respond, leaving her ominous remark hanging on the air beside him.

♬

The light, open interior of the chapel felt like a breath of cool air to Alannys, after the claustrophobic scrutiny of her conversation with Raman. Walking into the chapel always felt like shedding a burden she wasn't even aware she carried.

Brale stood near the pedestal in the middle of the room, wearing the same white woolen tunic and white linen robe she remembered from the last time she had seen him, months ago. His white hair was combed neatly over to one side, and he was the first person she had seen who looked genuinely happy to see her and Dorramon together. "Lady Alannys! Come here, my dear, and let me get a look at you. It is such a treat to see you both together and looking so well, and on such a happy occasion!" He took one of her hands in his, and one of Dorramon's in his other, and squeezed them both. He looked like nothing so much as a proud grandfather, beaming back and forth between them. "And you, dear boy, I haven't seen you around much as of late. Frightfully busy, I'm sure. May I inquire after your...understanding with Cadenda? Do they know about this?"

"Not yet," Dorramon said, with an apologetic look in Alannys's direction. "I know this would usually be done in the Great Hall, before as many witnesses as it can hold...but that understanding you mentioned is still being dissolved. I have no intention of marrying Princess Varilyn, but until that business is settled, I thought it would be wise to keep this quiet, and the ceremony small."

"Quite right, your Majesty, quite right. Most wise." Brale did not seem perturbed at all by this news, continuing to beam at both of them. "I'm sure Cadenda will give you enough trouble — it should be comforting to know that in the eyes of the Muses, the betrothal we shall sanctify today is the only one you have ever had. Without this ceremony, it isn't official; without the ceremony, it's nothing but words."

"Nothing but words," Dorramon echoed. "That's fitting — if there is one thing King Rathmar is good at, it's producing words."

"Lots and lots of words," Alannys said, and they both giggled like a couple of schoolkids.

The chapel door opened and Raman came in with Kalyn on his arm, looking more like he was there to face a firing squad than to witness an engagement. The laughter dried up pretty quickly.

"Well, then." Even Brale seemed put off by Raman's sullen demeanor, and he moved to stand at the pedestal. Alannys could just see the water over the lip of the alabaster basin, with rose petals and thyme leaves already floating in it. "Let us begin, shall we?"

Dorramon turned solemnly to face Alannys, and she stood looking back at him with her heart in her throat, suddenly, inexplicably nervous. Brale cleared his throat and began to speak.

"Let us take a moment, here among our friends, to consider engagement. Like many things in the sight of the Muses, engagement is both a beginning and an end. And engagement marks the end of an informal relationship between two people, the last chance for either to walk away owing nothing to the other.

"But it is also a beginning, a momentous one. Engagement marks the beginning of a journey of deep discovery about each other that will last, in some ways, the rest of your lives. It is the start of a long process of taking two lives, two hearts, two very souls, and mingling them to form one. It is in this journey that we most delight the Muses we serve, and we most please them when we observe the ceremonies that sanctify this journey."

Brale paused, letting his words sink in to everyone in attendance. "Dorramon, King of Ravanmark, and Alannys, Redeemer of the Realm, I now address myself directly to you both. Today you stand before me with open hearts and determined minds, ready at last to embark upon your journey to entwine your two souls into one. Today you formally bind your futures, each to the other, and announce your love for each other to the Muses and to the world. I ask you now, do you solemnly pledge to love and support each other as you journey together toward the day you will wed?"

"I do," Dorramon said softly, his blue eyes locked on hers.

"I do," Alannys said. Her voice broke; hearing it made

her cheeks burn. A smile played around the corners of Dorramon's mouth.

Brale smiled kindly. "Now I would like to address myself to our witnesses. Arch-Prince Raman, Lady Kalyn, today you undertake the solemn responsibility of attesting before the Muses to the true nature of the couple we seek to celebrate. Today you offer your commitment to them and their journey. Can you both swear to us now that Dorramon and Alannys are a happy, loving couple, suitable to travel together from here to the end of the Sacred Song, deserving of all the blessings the Muses can bestow?"

"I do so swear," Kalyn said.

"I do so swear," Raman said, and his response was so immediate, so obviously heartfelt, that it took Alannys completely by surprise. "I have never in my life known two more deserving people."

Her vision suddenly blurred, and she found herself blinking fast.

"And do you both," Brale continued, "give your solemn pledge to support and aid Dorramon and Alannys on their journey to wedlock, and beyond?"

"I do." This time Raman and Kalyn spoke so close to simultaneously, Alannys couldn't tell who answered first.

"Now," Brale continued, "I would ask the grand chancellor to bring forward the rings."

Alannys couldn't help a small start as Grand Chancellor Ebrad emerged from an alcove in the back of the room, his long face set into an expression of intense displeasure. His nose hooked out over a mouth twisted so sharply downward, he looked more like a man who had just bitten into a lemon than a man attending a royal engagement ceremony. He carried an aged wooden chest, polished to a soft, oily sheen—beautiful, but clearly very, very old.

She pulled her gaze away from Ebrad to find Brale watching her. She couldn't tell if his next words were usually part of the ceremony, or if he spoke them purely for her benefit. "Two golden rings, royal relics, have been passed down to us from the time many hundreds of years ago when Ravan, as Queen of the new land of Ravanmark, participated in the first royal engagement ceremony with the man who would later become her king. Since that time, every crown couple of Ravanmark have worn these same rings during their engagement, as a physical symbol of the continuity of the royal line of Ravanmark. Now you, Dorramon and Alannys, are this day becoming the latest couple in that esteemed line, and so the grand chancellor has brought us these rings from their resting place in the royal vault, that they may once again bless and keep a sacred vow of royal betrothal."

Brale nodded, and Ebrad opened the chest in his arms. It was small, no bigger than a candy box, and in its velvet-lined interior two matching golden rings glimmered from custom holders, one slightly bigger and thicker than the other.

Dorramon pulled the smaller ring from the box and faced Alannys, taking her left hand in his free one. "On this day of our choosing, in front of these witnesses and in front of our friends, before the Muses and before the government of Ravanmark, I present you with this ring as my token and take upon myself a solemn vow to marry you." He slipped the ring onto the third finger of her hand, and its cool touch felt final somehow, sealing.

She reached into the chest in turn and lifted out the larger ring. Its weight was slight in her hand but solid — it felt heavier than it was, as though it carried all the weight of its own import. The gold shone softly in the light but did not carry the mirror-like sheen of a newly-forged ring — this ring bore more surface scratches than she could count, buffed over and scratched again, from long years of wear on royal fingers. It was like holding history, and it made her mouth go suddenly dry. How many women had held this ring before her, vowing their eternal love to men who were now nothing more than bones in the royal catacombs? She pushed aside the ghosts of the past and began to speak. "On this day of our choosing, in front of these witnesses and in front of our friends, before the Muses and before the government of Ravanmark, I present you with this ring as my token and take upon myself a solemn vow to marry you." She pushed the ring onto his finger, surprised to find that it looked as though it belonged there.

She beamed up at Dorramon, heartened by this thought, and he smiled back at her.

"Then we have but one ritual left to perform," Brale said, producing a long, white ribbon. "Dorramon, Alannys, I ask you now to clasp your hands bearing your rings."

Alannys raised her left hand in front of her and laced her fingers with Dorramon's wrapping her thumb around to the back of his hand. It was an awkward clasp, and yet it felt important.

Brale solemnly wound the ribbon around their clasped hands, and tied the ends in an ornate bow, with lots of decorative loops, almost like he was wrapping a gift. He sprinkled a few drops of the rose and thyme infused water onto the ribbon and onto their hands, and broke into his grandfatherly smile once again as he lifted the ribbon up and off of their joined hands. "Let me be the first to congratulate you both," he said. "On this day your intent to marry has been accepted and made official, blessed by your friends and your Muses. You have begun a momentous journey today. This is your handfasting ribbon." He laid the knotted ribbon reverently into Alannys's hands. "It represents the bond between you both and as long as this knot remains, your love shall grow deeper and closer, for all eternity. So we have said, so the Muses have heard; if it is their will, so shall it be."

"So shall it be," the rest of them said together.

♫

Kalyn was at Alannys's side immediately after the ceremony, before anyone else could say a word. "Oh, my Lady, I am so happy for you!" She threw her arms around Alannys in an exuberant hug.

"Thanks," Alannys said, abashed.

Kalyn grinned at her, then grew abruptly serious. "I wanted to talk to you, though. I know this has all got to be new to you, and I wondered if you're ready for the massive amount of preparation a royal wedding takes."

"Not really," Alannys said, thinking back to the circus in her sitting room that morning.

"Ah. I thought that might be the way of it. I know you're going to be insanely busy, with all of the business with Cadenda, and I wanted to offer to help with the wedding preparations. I could be your go-between, and handle all of the people who work on the wedding, and only trouble you for the necessary things."

"That sounds fantastic," Alannys said. "But are you sure? You just got married yourself."

"Something tells me I will still have more time to devote to this than you will." Kalyn's words were light, almost teasing.

"Listen to the lady; she speaks the truth." In contrast, Raman was blunt and matter-of-fact. "This was a beautiful ceremony, but the timing could hardly have been worse. Why didn't you just wait until Cadenda is dealt with and our guests have departed, and have it then?"

Dorramon cut a glance to Alannys before answering. "It isn't that simple, Raman—at least not to me. If we've learned nothing else today, we've learned that we are all in danger. Some of us more than others. And if...and if the worst should happen, we would rather be formally engaged than not. Perhaps it's sentimental rot, but I would feel better going to my death knowing I leave behind official recognition of the only real love I've known in my life."

Alannys couldn't speak; she was too choked up. But

she took his arm and nodded alongside him. She knew what he was talking about and it gave her an awful, sinking feeling to think about it too closely.

But she still had to agree.

♪

Tralice was waiting in the sitting room when Alannys returned, waiting to inspect her hair and gown before she left for the state dinner.

"Your hair has held up surprisingly well." Tralice sounded happy, maybe for the first time since she had returned. "Just let me redo this right here..." She lifted the braid hanging at Alannys's right temple, pulled it loose, and began to re-plait it.

Alannys turned the handfasting ribbon over in her hands, watching the sheen of the light track across the surface of the satin. "Tralice, what do women usually do with their handfasting ribbons?"

"Do with them, Lady Alannys? I suppose it depends on the woman...whatever they want, really. My wedding was a bit of a last-minute affair, so we didn't have an engagement ceremony. My sister — well, Helva always had a practical streak. She said the whole thing was superstitious rot. She untied hers and used it as trim on a bonnet before she and Petras even married."

"Hmm. I see." Neither of those answers really shed any light on the question of what she should do with hers.

"Why do you ask?" Tralice finished with Alannys's hair and finally noticed what she held in her hands. "What are you — my Lady, you should not have that!"

"What? Whyever not? It's from my engagement ceremony."

"Of course it is — that is exactly why you shouldn't have it. Your handfasting ribbon is a royal relic, my Lady, and it should be packed away in the royal vault, with all of the others."

Alannys's fingers tightened around the ribbon, and she pulled it close to her chest. "No, this is mine. Brale gave it

171

to me."

Tralice sat abruptly down on the sofa. "Brale is a sentimental old fool. I can't believe the grand chancellor let you walk out with that. He'll come here looking for it, you can be sure of that."

"Well, he can't have it."

"My Lady." Tralice stood up again, apparently recovered from her shock and ready to fight. "My Lady, this is a serious matter! Royal relics are important; they are *symbols*. They must be properly protected, preserved for the people. Give me the ribbon, my Lady. I'll see it gets to the chancellor and this whole problem will go away."

"No." Alannys looked at her maid's stern expression and outstretched hand, and took a step back. "No, I've already said he can't have it, and neither can you."

"My Lady! You must be reasonable. What are you even going to do with it?"

"Does it matter? It's mine!" Alannys took a deep, steadying breath. Of all the things she never thought she would have to fight over! "Look, Tralice, I get what you're saying about royal relics, I do. I've been to see collections of them myself, before I came to Ravanmark. But it's different from where I'm standing. This..." She held the ribbon in its elegant bow up in the light, and both of them watched the glowing, glimmering white satin. "When I look at this, I remember the feel of an ancient ring in my hand, the whole history of Ravanmark weighing on me as I put it on the finger of the man I love. I remember the conviction in Raman's eyes when he swore before the Muses that Dorramon and I deserved to be together. I remember the look in Dorramon's eyes when he slipped this ring on my hand, the feeling of his skin warm against mine when Brale tied this... To everyone else, it's just a royal relic. Just a pretty ribbon. No one else has those connections to it. Do you really think it's right to take it from me?"

A sharp knock at the door curtailed any response

Tralice might have planned. Alannys turned away from her and threw it open. "Yes?"

A young pageboy stood there, eyes like saucers. Alannys felt sorry for him—he'd probably never expected to be greeted in such a fashion. He gripped a blown glass vase full of flowers as though he feared he might drop it.

That was probably more of a possibility than she wanted to admit, after the fright she had given him.

"I—I beg your pardon, my Lady. His Royal Majesty bids you accept these flowers, with his...with his compliments." The boy's cheeks blazed red, right up to his ears, and Alannys had to wonder what his Royal Majesty actually had said.

"Thank you," she said seriously, trying very hard not to give any sign of her amusement. She accepted the vase, and watched as the page ran back down the corridor.

The vase she held was a piece of art, blue blown glass, narrow at its base. Near the top, though, it suddenly opened out, blossoming like one of the flowers it was meant to showcase. It was full to bursting with an enormous bouquet of blooming pink primroses.

Pink primroses. She blinked back sudden tears—her little speech earlier had topped out her tolerance for sentimentality in front of her maid. She placed the vase on the coffee table, running her fingers over the soft pink petals.

Inspiration struck and she lifted the vase again, sliding the handfasting ribbon over its base and halfway up its length.

It fit like it was made to sit there. Had he somehow known? Alannys smiled, regarding the white bow against the deep blue glass. Dorramon to the rescue, again.

"Quite lovely, my Lady. But it is, after all, just a ribbon." Tralice's tone was flat, unimpressed—a warning.

"Tralice..." Alannys turned back to her with a sigh. "I know your sister thinks this is sentimental rot. Maybe you do, too. I'm not asking you to believe any differently. But that ribbon is important to me, and deeply symbolic. As long as there is a single chance that it means anything at all, I want it here with me, where I know it will never be untied. Don't take it from me — don't let Ebrad take it from me. Please. I'm asking you, as my friend."

Tralice looked from Alannys to the ribbon, and back again. Her shoulders slumped in resignation. "All right," she finally said, "you win. I can't take it from you — as your friend."

They both stood for a moment and looked at the luminous white ribbon, tied around its blue glass vase overflowing with pink primroses. It seemed to brighten the whole room.

♫

The dying sunbeams streaking into the palace that evening found Alannys standing in the Great Hall, holding a goblet of mulled wine and trying to pretend she didn't feel entirely out of place. She was wearing exactly the same gown she had worn for the audience, but now she felt oddly exposed, standing there without either of her blades, preparing to face powerful people she knew to be hostile. She wasn't cut out for this sort of thing.

She just hoped that wasn't as obvious to their enemies as it was to her.

Dorramon stood next to her, pretending to have a conversation with Raman while he kept one eye on the door. Captain Grayble listened politely to the queen mother, while watching his men secure the room. All of them ignored the long, polished banquet table set up in the middle of the hall, gleaming with silver tableware. If the others felt anything like her, they were too nervous to sit still anyway.

With none of the ostentatious fanfare that had preceded them earlier, the party from Cadenda filed into the Great Hall. They looked as though they were also pretending to be in fine spirits. King Rathmar came in with Princess Varilyn on his arm. Behind them came

Prince Cardoth, and behind him — Ambassador Thell?

Alannys stiffened. It took a nerve to bring the man who had been banned from court over five months ago and never readmitted. His long face carried an unpleasant smile, a smile that made Alannys think of dark alleys and long, pointy knives.

It broadened when his glance met hers.

Dorramon turned to face King Rathmar with a smile of his own, a smile that looked only mostly forced. Alannys took the opportunity to edge over a little, so that he nearly concealed her from view. "King Rathmar, welcome. It is a pleasure to see you and your family this evening."

"The pleasure," Rathmar boomed in his deep voice, "is all ours."

"I'd like to present, if I may, Queen Mother Farrine."

Alannys had never seen the queen mother wear anything but black since King Caleb died. Tonight was no exception; she stepped past Dorramon like the cold wind of death shrouded in a forbidding black gown, her graying blond hair pulled back into a bun so severe her face looked positively skeletal.

Rathmar started visibly, and Queen Mother Farrine smiled a tight, humorless smile, extending her hand. Rathmar moved quickly to kiss her fingers. "Queen Farrine! What a pleasant surprise. It has been too long."

"Indeed," she said coolly. "I am quite sorry I missed your visit to court earlier. It sounds as though you made quite a spectacle of yourself, Rathmar."

He had the good grace to look uncomfortable at that, but he summoned a smile from somewhere. Alannys was well aware of how acerbic the queen mother could be, but even so it was surprising just how ably she handled King Rathmar.

Dorramon glanced around and finally found Alannys, more or less hiding behind him. He turned to her with a wry smile and a look that warmed her to her toes, taking her arm and pulling her up to stand next to him.

The mood in the room instantly congealed. King Rathmar's face hardened, and there was no kindness at all in the glare he aimed at her. Ripples spread across the surface of her wine as the heavy goblet trembled in her grasp. "Again you bring that vile woman before us? I'm most appalled, Queen Farrine. Have you taught your son no better than this?"

Farrine eyed him coldly, unmoved. "Strong words, from the one who has brought with him a man who was officially ejected from this court some time ago, and never reinstated."

Rathmar's face turned dark purple with rage. "That is in no way similar! My ambassador has a job here, an official position that permits his presence. What position does that woman hold that requires us to suffer her company?"

"Redeemer of the Realm," Farrine said shortly. "I have no love for the woman either, but her position, such as it is, is official. Perhaps you should show a bit more respect when you speak to her."

"Redeemer," Rathmar snorted. "Stuff and nonsense! We do not acknowledge the existence of such a person. Respect, indeed! This is an insult, I tell you, a grave insult! Why, I've half a mind to—"

"My Lord King," Varilyn interrupted, tugging on his arm, looking around at all of them with eyes so round and innocent Alannys felt she had to be up to something. "I think she should stay."

♪

Every person in the Great Hall stared at Princess Varilyn. She was the last person Alannys had expected to come to her defense. She recognized that Varilyn was probably simply trying to defuse the tense situation before it got any more hostile, but that didn't do much to lessen her shock.

Princess Varilyn, she was learning, was full of surprises.

Rathmar's mouth worked silently for a moment before any sound emerged. "You interfere too much, girl." He sighed. "Very well. I suppose if it means that much to you, she may remain. Honestly, you are too forgiving of those who have slighted you this way."

"The Lady Alannys is a paragon of consistency," Ambassador Thell said with a sneer. "She is exactly as she was when I met her: graceless, and thoughtless to boot."

"One more comment like that and you will take your dinner in the dungeon, Ambassador." Dorramon cast a hard look across his visitors. "Lady Alannys's presence is a constant in my court, and I encourage you all to set about getting used to it. Now then, shall we take our seats?"

"Of course, of course," Rathmar said, grabbing Varilyn's arm and dragging her towards the table. "Varilyn, dear, you should sit next to your betrothed, of course, it's only proper—and I had a few questions for his young Highness myself, so I'll take his other side..."

With a precision that Alannys uncharitably suspected was planned, the group from Cadenda guided them into a seating arrangement that none of them would ever have chosen on their own. Dorramon sat at the head of the table, with Varilyn on his left and Rathmar on his right. Alannys found herself sandwiched between King Rathmar and Ambassador Thell. Directly across from her was Prince Cardoth. Farrine sat at the foot of the table, and Raman was on her right, across from Thell.

Looking around the table gave Alannys an odd feeling —the way Rathmar had worked things, she and Dorramon were the only two people at the table surrounded on every side by people who felt like enemies. She knew that Captain Grayble had his Royal Guards posted in all corners of the room, but that did little to relieve her discomfort.

"That is a lovely ring, my Lord King," Varilyn said, watching Dorramon's hands as he unfolded his napkin.

She was either genuinely interested or giving a really good impression. "I don't recall seeing it before."

"Thank you," Dorramon said, suddenly finding himself the subject of the unwelcome attention of every other person at the table. "I actually just acquired it, but it's been in the family for generations." His smile was enigmatic.

Servants filed in and placed covered silver platters in front of them. Alannys followed everyone else and uncovered hers. She even ate from it, but she could not have said what it was. She fervently wished that she had stayed in her room after all. She could have faked a headache, could have pleaded illness. Anything would have been better than this.

King Rathmar watched his daughter engage Dorramon in polite conversation with a satisfied smile, and then turned to Alannys. "Well, and what do you think of the dinner?"

"It's—it's delicious," she said, flustered. In truth she had not tasted a single bite; her nerves were too acute.

He laughed, but it felt sharp, somehow, and unkind. "I imagine so! Quite a step up from anything you are accustomed to, I should say."

She froze, holding her goblet in midair. Was he trying to insult her? Again? "I beg your pardon?"

Too late she realized her mistake; too late she saw his eyes narrow on her ring. Clumsy with haste, she thumped the goblet back down on the table and hid her left hand in her lap again. He followed the motion with an unpleasant look on his face. "You don't belong here. You're fortunate, really, that my daughter was generous enough to allow you to stay." He gestured across the table with his fork, and his tone turned downright nasty. "She's too kind for her own good. You aren't fooling anybody. The whole world knows that you are but a low-born strumpet that King Dorramon is trying to render acceptable with an undeserved title."

Alannys stiffened, staring down at her plate without seeing it. Her left hand clenched in her lap. He wasn't trying to insult her, he was trying to *humiliate* her. Perhaps he felt he could chase her out that way.

She sat up straighter, and turned to him with a smile. "Thank you for sharing your opinion, your Majesty. It seems to be good enough for you, and that's all that really matters, don't you think?"

Rathmar's eyes narrowed and his mouth twisted. He was such a handsome man, and yet when he looked at her like this...all of his attractiveness seemed to disappear. "Don't try to play games with me, young lady. You don't stand a chance."

She turned away, back to her own plate. "I'm sorry, your Highness, but you started it."

He snorted and looked away from her.

She sat still for a moment, regaining her composure. She hated this sort of thing. Outright, open hostility was easier to bear than this bitter dislike concealed behind layers of superficial politeness and respectability. She remembered fighting the gang who had attacked Chen, and thought that she probably preferred that to sitting here surrounded by these elegant, two-faced people.

Finally she recovered herself, and looked up.

Prince Cardoth was staring at her across the table. Eyes the color of dark chocolate reflected the flickering torchlight around them, and his black hair gleamed, greased back from his face. He was a smoother, even more handsome version of his father, and his direct attention was acutely disconcerting. She gave an involuntary start, then smiled weakly and averted her eyes, blushing right to her ears.

When she risked glancing back in his direction, he was still watching her intently. It unnerved her—Cardoth was undeniably handsome, but it seemed to her that he was handsome in a dangerous, scary way. Looking into his eyes was like looking into Lord Malrec's, and she looked uncomfortably away.

Cardoth chuckled. It was a low, intimate sound, and yet it reached her clearly, making her skin crawl. He spoke up suddenly, interrupting every other conversation at the table. "Is it true, King Dorramon, that Talented people are still born in Ravanmark?"

An unpleasant jolt stabbed through Alannys's middle. Cardoth was ostensibly speaking to Dorramon, but he had never taken his eyes off of her. And his *voice*—low and rich, dark and decadent—and familiar. The sound touched some memory, but she couldn't bring it into focus—as though it was buried too deep for her to pull up now.

Then she realized that just as much as Cardoth looked like his father, with his jet black hair and suntanned skin, he sounded like him as well. So much so that it probably shouldn't have surprised her that he sounded familiar.

Dorramon looked taken aback, his eyes flashing to hers in a worried glance that was probably involuntary. "Well, yes. Yes, of course. I imagine the stories have probably even made it as far as Cadenda."

"Yes," Cardoth mused, stroking his chin and eyeing Alannys speculatively, "but one never knows whether to believe such things. Talents—still, after all these many centuries, when the rest of the world has none?"

"It may be hard to believe," Dorramon said, frowning, "but it is true. Now, perhaps we should—"

"Fascinating," Cardoth cut him off. "Then may I request a demonstration?"

Alannys felt suddenly cold. She realized her legs were tensed, as though she expected to jump up from the table and run.

"A...demonstration?" Dorramon said warily.

"Certainly. That is, the stories you have mentioned also indicated that Lady Alannys is Talented. Surely we would all appreciate the opportunity to witness the singing of such a beautiful woman." The torchlight reflected in Cardoth's dark eyes suddenly flared, giving Alannys the impression of something predatory.

She felt the pressure of the request, and of the delicate diplomatic situation. Why was he asking for that? She didn't know, but her every instinct screamed that she should refuse. But how could she? "Well," she began slowly, "I suppose I could —"

"No." Dorramon's voice cut across hers, absolutely unyielding. "No. I am sorry, but there is no way I can allow that."

Rathmar sat back in his chair. "How disappointing. My son seems quite taken with her; I am certain he would have enjoyed the performance. May I ask why you will not permit it?"

Dorramon's face darkened. Whatever had set Alannys off about the situation was obviously bothering him as well.

"I am afraid that music is not considered appropriate for polite company," Farrine intervened, smooth and calm, completely at odds with her usual manner. "It would not do for us to insult our honored guests, even inadvertently."

Prince Cardoth inclined his head, perfectly gracious. "I see. It is of course my pleasure to bow to the wishes of the queen mother, though I do hope Lady Alannys is aware that nothing she could possibly do could offend me. I would relish any time spent in the company of so captivating a woman, the more...*inappropriate*...the better." Cardoth chuckled again, watching her face redden. "I have heard, my Lady, that the Singari here are exceptionally...well-endowed...in many respects, including the Talents. Is this true as well?"

If he was trying to make her touchy and defensive, he was doing a fine job of it. "That...seems an odd change of subject, my Lord Prince."

He regarded her with a roguish smirk, and she had the fleeting impression that by dodging the question, she had told him what he wanted to know. "Perhaps. I apologize if the subject was poorly chosen. My Lady has a reputation as something of an expert in matters of Singari endowment."

Her face burned, flaring with sudden, embarrassed heat, and she looked hastily down to hide it. She could hear Rathmar's snort of unkind laughter beside her, could hear Dorramon's sharp reprimand a bit further away. She fought to control her emotions, determined that this dinner would not fail because of her. But what was Cardoth trying to do? He had seemed so flattering, and now this — she couldn't get a handle on him.

"Now, now, young lady, nothing to get your petticoats twisted over." Rathmar elbowed her in the ribs, hard. "Singari are wonderful creatures, fabulous companions for a commoner of your years. Even back home, their appetites are quite — voracious."

Appetites? Her stomach lurched sideways, and she turned away from his suggestive leer, only to find Cardoth's eyes boring into her, a sly, speculative smile on his face.

All at once she felt as though she might really be sick, all over the banquet table and everyone seated there. "I beg you all to pardon me," she croaked, and stumbled to her feet.

"Alannys!" Dorramon stood up too, with Varilyn's hand still on his arm. He didn't even seem to notice; his face showed nothing but worry. "Wait! Let me —"

"I am sorry; I'm not well. Please — please forgive me." She turned and fled the room. She didn't slow down, didn't look back, didn't acknowledge calling voices — she couldn't handle talking to anyone at all right then.

She had been right all along. She would far rather face ten enemies with swords than two at a dinner table with insincere smiles.

♪

Alannys ran headlong across the dark inner ward, heedless of the risks she was taking with her health and safety, completely uncaring about how foolish she must have appeared in mid-flight. She didn't look back, didn't slow down until she reached the keep. She jerked the door open and hurried inside the vestibule.

Just being in the peaceful, quiet keep made her feel a bit better. It felt like a safe haven—ridiculous, she knew, since that haven had been violated on several occasions before—but she couldn't deny that just being there helped her to calm down. She had planned to go straight to her room and hide there, maybe forever. But as she walked alone through the dimly-lit corridor, she began to feel bad for running away the way she had. And after all her talk about supporting Dorramon—all it took were a few off-color comments to drive her away!

She owed him an apology, a big one. She couldn't imagine the delegation from Cadenda would care that she had left—in fact that seemed to have been King Rathmar's goal from the start—but she had worried Dorramon, and that wasn't right. She couldn't use the mindlink and interrupt him during that tricky, tense dinner, but she thought she could wait in the courtyard until he returned.

So she turned sharply out toward the garden in the center of the courtyard, thinking to seek solace among the trees and flowers. No sooner had she set foot inside the ring of wooden benches than she heard running footsteps behind her, closing fast.

She whirled around, wondering if perhaps one of her friends had followed her, only to find Prince Cardoth, out of breath and disheveled. Even in his state, he was ridiculously handsome, and the pale moonlight and deep shadows were kinder to him than they needed to be, doing things to the contours of his face that made him look dramatic and fantastic, like some other-worldly creature from an ancient myth, a god walking among mortals.

Every muscle in her body tensed—he was about the last person she had expected to see. What new trouble was this?

"Prince — Prince Cardoth?" She desperately wanted to show no weakness in front of this strange man, but the nervous tremor in her voice gave her away. "What are you doing here?"

"Following you," he said shortly, smoothing his clothes. "I had to make sure you were all right."

This response surprised her, and humbled her. She wondered if perhaps she had him pegged wrong. Maybe she had judged him too much by his resemblance to his father. "Thank you, but you didn't have to do that. I'm not really your concern."

"I disagree. Maybe it's my natural arrogance showing, but I'm afraid I might be the reason you left in such a hurry."

She laughed, hoping it didn't sound as false to him as it did to her. "Of course not, your Highness. I just — I suppose I needed some fresh air. I'm sorry I ran off like that."

Cardoth took a step toward her. She couldn't help it; in spite of her resolution to show no fear, she took a reflexive step back. The prince chuckled. "Don't apologize, please. I'm very sorry I upset you, but — at the same time, I must admit it's much nicer being here with you, alone."

He leaned on his last word. Alannys took another step back, alarmed, and bumped into the water garden. She sat down on the edge of it to cover her surprise, but she didn't have any idea how to respond. Prince Cardoth had an unsettling knack for making her feel cornered. "Are...are you sure you shouldn't go back to the dinner? I don't want to spoil your good time."

His eyes glinted in the moonlight. "I'm certain you could never do that." He cast a glance around them, taking in the arcades bordering the corridors. "Is one of these rooms yours, then?"

"What?"

He chuckled again, evidently amused at her discomfort. "I'm sorry, I don't mean to upset you again. It seemed a harmless question. The information may prove useful later, you know, should we get lonely."

She blinked at him. So bluntly forward, and yet not a single thing he said or did seemed to make sense. He didn't wait for a response, just stepped over and sat down next to her.

Alannys scooted away.

Prince Cardoth sighed. "I really am sorry, my Lady. Do you believe me?"

She wasn't sure — but she also wasn't sure it would be a good idea to say so. "Of course, my Lord Prince."

He quirked a strange, crooked smile at her, and all at once she could *feel* the danger around her. "Then please...sing for me."

♫

Alannys felt as though her heart had stopped, sitting on the edge of the water garden in the dark, staring into Prince Cardoth's hypnotizing eyes, hearing his absolutely impossible request echo in her ears. "What did you just ask me? You must know I cannot do that."

"Please." He slid a little closer to her, turning to face her. "I don't know if anyone ever told you, but we don't have Talents in Cadenda. Talented people are only born in Ravanmark, and those people don't ever come to Cadenda. I've never heard music in my life. Is it really as wonderful as they say? Does it really hold such power?"

His rich voice was pleading, and his handsome face exuded such wistfulness, it almost hurt to look at him. "Yes," she said, unable to refuse him the answer. "Yes, it does."

"And you are Talented? You can sing?"

How much should she tell him? She didn't want to talk to him at all, but if there was any way to salvage relations between their two countries, she would ruin it if she angered him. "I can."

"Then sing for me, my Lady. Please. Let the first song I hear be yours."

Prince Cardoth was really laying it on thick, but why? Why did he want her to sing so badly? He was unleashing his considerable charm on her, and it was dizzying, but she didn't think he even really liked her.

"I can't," she said, and looked away, drawing a shuddering breath, trying to rein in her overloaded senses.

His hands clenched suddenly into fists. "Why not? You sing for *him*, don't you? King Dorramon?"

Every instinct she had shrieked at her not to answer that question. She stared at him, wide-eyed, wondering how far she would make it if she ran, but she said nothing.

"He isn't here now." Cardoth's eyes were dark and intense, pinning her to the spot. "He didn't come for you, Alannys. I did. Sing for me."

"No." She shook her head. "I can't. I'm sorry, your Highness, but—you're putting me in a very bad position."

"Me? *I'm* putting *you* in a bad position?" In a flash Prince Cardoth was on his feet. He grabbed her by her upper arms, his fingers digging into her flesh. "Do you have any *idea* what you've done to my family? And my sister—can you be unaware of the dishonor you've brought upon her?" He leaned menacingly over her, tipping her back toward the surface of the water. Her feet pulled up off the ground.

Death before dishonor. Alannys swallowed a hard lump of sudden, cold fear, and held very still. She knew she couldn't fight him off. And her angle now was too steep for her to support herself—he was holding her up, and if he released her, she would be flat on her back in the water, with no leverage to pull herself up. "And you seemed so charming before. Are you going to drown me, then?" She was going for humor, but her voice shook, betraying her fear.

"I should." His fingers ground painfully into her arms and he pushed his face right up in front of hers, filling her vision. Handsome but scary—she had been right all along. "Damn me, I *should*. It would make things easier, for certain." Prince Cardoth pushed her back even further toward the water. If her hair hadn't been so short, it would have been hanging in the water with the roots of the plants and the fish.

She reached up and grabbed hold of his biceps. "Easier for you, perhaps, but I would just as soon you didn't." She wanted to talk him down with humor, but her nervous laugh sounded more like a sob.

Cardoth bit his lip. He leaned over her, peering into her face, his dark eyes boring into hers. He might have been about to kiss her.

Or he might have been about to murder her. From where she was sitting, it was exceedingly difficult to tell the difference.

"Why?" he demanded, his voice hoarse. "Why does King Dorramon protect you? Why does he forbid us to hear you sing? Why does he risk open war with us—for you?"

Alannys couldn't think of any response to that question that would be likely to improve her situation. She held onto his arms, and tried not to move or panic.

"Cardoth!" The angry voice shouting from across the courtyard was undoubtedly Raman's, and she heard running footsteps approaching fast. "Cardoth, what in the Seven Hells do you think you are doing?"

Prince Cardoth ground an oath through gritted teeth, and jerked her up to stand next to him. "Speaking with Lady Alannys, of couuse." He sounded completely calm, but he still had one hand wrapped in a crushing grip around her arm, encouraging her to keep her silence. "Isn't that right, my Lady?" His fingers clawed into her bicep.

Alannys mustered up a weak smile from somewhere, and kept her mouth shut.

Raman frowned at her, then at Prince Cardoth. "I think it's time you should be leaving. The keep is no place to wander uninvited."

"Perhaps you are right. But I do think I've had my fill of dinner. I shall return to my room." He released her suddenly, presented her with her freedom like a gift, and gave her a cordial bow. "Might I convince you to join me, my Lady? I would consider it quite an honor. I have found our conversation to be most—stimulating."

Alannys stared at him in complete and utter shock. "I —I agree, of course, your Highness, but I must decline."

"Ah, but my Lady, I won't take no for an answer." Prince Cardoth reached for her arm again, and she shrank away from him.

Arch-Prince Raman stepped forcefully between them, pushing her behind him. "Are you disrespecting the lady, Prince Cardoth? Or is it your intent to insult King Dorramon himself?"

"King Dorramon," Cardoth spat, his eyes flashing dangerously. "What complaint could he possibly have, while he is honorably engaged to my sister? What could he say of it?"

"It might surprise you," Raman said wryly. "Regardless of your view on the situation, she is here as the king's guest and under his protection. He takes a...personal interest in her well-being. I doubt your unwelcome advances would please him."

"You assume that I have made advances. As for whether or not those advances would be unwelcome— well, we shall see about that, won't we?" He gave a curt little bow. "I shall take my leave of you now, my Lady—I can see that you are tired, and you did say you felt unwell. But I have no doubt we will see each other again soon."

He turned and walked stiffly away without further comment, and finally some of the dreadful tension left her. "Thank you so much," she said to Raman. Now that the adrenaline was finally subsiding, she was shaking like a leaf. "How did you know?"

"I didn't. Steady, there." He reached out and took her arm. "I only thought it was odd that he excused himself and left in such a blazing hurry, right after you did. I thought I had better find out what he was up to."

"I'm awfully glad you did. Thank you." She shivered in a sudden chill.

Raman raked a hand through his hair. "Don't mention it. I certainly never imagined anything like that could happen. I'll have to ask Grayble to post guards at the keep."

"That's a good idea. I wonder why we didn't think of it earlier."

Raman shook his head, looking around the courtyard as though nothing he saw pleased him. "What reason did we have to think they would try to come here? Nobody foresaw Cardoth's obsession with you."

Obsession. She turned the word over in her mind, and shivered again.

"Let's get you back to your chambers." They started walking back across the courtyard. After a few steps of silence, Raman glanced over at her—a little sharply, it seemed to her. "Alannys, what was going on back there? I couldn't tell if he was trying to kiss you or kill you."

"Honestly, I couldn't tell either." She laughed, but it was a barking, unhappy laugh. "I'm not sure *he* knew." They stopped outside her door, and she frowned, thinking back over all of it. "He followed me out there—he drove me deliberately from dinner, and then followed me—and I don't know why. The only thing I'm sure of is that there is more going on here than any of us can see."

Raman looked at her bleakly. She wanted him to deny it, to assure her that everything was well in hand, but he just nodded. In a way that made her feel worse, because it proved her words had been true.

It proved that the danger surrounding them all was frightfully real.

♫

Raman left the keep at a dead run before Alannys even opened the door to her rooms. She assumed he was going

189

back to dinner, or perhaps to ensure that Prince Cardoth kept his promise to leave the inner ward. How long could things keep moving so fast, and making so little sense?

She shook her head, and stepped into her sitting room. She found Tralice there, staring at her with wide eyes, hastily folding a paper and stuffing it into her apron. "My Lady! I—I did not expect you back so soon."

"Sorry," Alannys said, though it struck her as just a little ridiculous to be apologizing for entering her own rooms. "I wasn't planning on it—I'm sort of running away."

"Running away?" Tralice sounded only marginally interested. "From who, my Lady?"

"Prince Cardoth," Alannys said shortly. She distinctly did not want to get into a conversation about it, especially the kind of conversation Tralice usually favored about men.

"Ah, Prince Cardoth. A right handsome man, or so I've heard." Tralice did not clamor for more details. She did not extoll his physical virtues or offer her opinions on his charms. Alannys had never heard her speak of any man in so flat a tone, especially a handsome man.

"Are you all right, Tralice?"

"All right, my Lady?"

"Well, yes." Alannys felt her cheeks burn. Why should she feel silly for inquiring after someone else's well-being—and why was Tralice making her feel that way? "You don't seem yourself. And you looked startled when I came in."

"Ach, it was nothing, my Lady. I was just reading a letter."

Alannys wondered what kind of letter it would take to provoke such a dismal tone. "Not bad news, I hope?"

"No. No, not at all. It was from a friend, I suppose. A friend who is concerned for my well-being."

"You have many friends who are concerned for your well-being, Tralice," Alannys said pointedly.

Tralice looked away. "Yes. Shall I help you change, my Lady? Or would you prefer a hot bath? You look as though you might like to relax."

Alannys sighed. There was just no talking, it seemed, about subjects that Tralice was determined to avoid. She didn't like being held at arm's length, but what could she do? "I'd be very much obliged if you could help me out of this dratted gown. I've had rather my fill of high society for one day. I think my plain shirt and leather pants will suit me well enough for now."

"Of course, my Lady," Tralice said, but her eyes were round. Evidently a king's formal betrothed did not lounge around wearing workshirts and riding pants.

Alannys didn't care. It was her own little act of rebellion, against King Rathmar II, his graceful daughter, and his too-handsome-to-be-real son; against the polite conventions which required her to be civil to all of them; against everyone and everything inside the Great Palace that seemed to be sitting in judgement of her just then. Besides, she could put these clothes on herself, and she had forgotten just how wonderful that felt. She stretched gratefully, feeling truly comfortable for the first time in days.

"My Lady," Tralice began, eyeing her doubtfully, "I don't think that attire quite suits—"

A sudden, harsh knock at the door interrupted her.

"It's—it's Dorramon," Alannys said, frowning as she pulled open the door, wondering how on earth he could be there so fast.

"Alannys," he gasped, his chest heaving visibly. "Are you all right?" His black hair looked disheveled, and his face was flushed and damp.

"Yes," she said, alarmed by his appearance, "of course, but why…"

Before she could even finish the question, Dorramon grabbed her up in a bone-crushing hug. His arms squeezed around her so tight she almost couldn't breathe, and she realized just how worried he must have been. "Raman told me that Prince Cardoth followed you."

"He did. I still can't figure out why, though."

Dorramon stepped back, looking at her face incredulously. "You don't think that's obvious? He stared at you all the way through dinner, Alannys—I think he's quite taken with you."

She couldn't seem to find any words to say. She stared at him, her mouth working silently, feeling something like a fish. "No," she finally managed.

"What? You honestly couldn't tell?" He puffed out his cheeks and looked away. "I was rather harsh with King Rathmar, after Raman told me what happened. We are not tolerant of trespass into the keep—the Royal Guard would have been completely within rights to cut him down where he stood, if they had seen him. And all I got from him was a shrug. He said that the fire of love burns too bright for logic."

"I'm telling you, that's not how it is."

"Muses, Alannys, you can't be that oblivious! Look, you need to accept this right now. Cardoth is powerful, and accustomed to getting what he wants, no questions. When someone like that takes an immediate, overwhelming obsession with you...it can't lead to anywhere good. The more you deny this, the worse your situation will be."

"Dorramon—"

"Alannys! Can't you just trust me on this?"

"No." She had to look away. "I'm sorry, I'm not trying to upset you. I'm not trying to be stubborn, or falsely modest. Prince Cardoth is dangerous."

"Now that we can agree on." Dorramon puffed out his cheeks. "If he's fixated on you, don't you see that it makes him *more* dangerous?"

"It does," she said. "But I don't get the feeling he really likes me at all. He wanted me to think so, though."

Dorramon glanced around them, taking a moment to

consider her words. "That might be even worse. I don't believe he's pretending; I can't imagine what motive a man could have to feign such an intense attraction to someone...but if he is..." He shook his head. "If he is, it can't be leading to anything good. It just can't."

"I don't know what's really going on here. Nothing makes sense. He did try to get me to sing."

Dorramon frowned, raking his hand through his hair. "I don't like that. I'm absolutely certain it's a bad idea for him to hear any kind of music. Why is he so hell-bent on finding out what it can do?"

Before either of them could venture an answer to that question, a guard ran up behind Dorramon. Alannys saw the orange flash of red hair in the torchlight and recognized Jomain with a twinge of discomfort. He stood at a ragged attention, disheveled and out of breath. "A thousand pardons for the interruption, your Majesty! But King Rathmar just left through the main gate with Prince Cardoth and Princess Varilyn. Captain Grayble said you would want to know."

"Left? Where are they going?" Dorramon's voice dripped with the same dread that Alannys felt gripping her stomach.

Was it only her imagination, or was the quick glance Jomain shot in her direction full of accusation? "A thousand apologies, your Majesty! We were not given orders to stop them, or question them. I did overhear some of their conversation, though, and from what I heard— well, it sounded as though they were headed for the Singari encampment, your Majesty."

Singari encampment! The words sizzled through Alannys's brain, triggering a protective instinct she hadn't known she possessed. She clutched at Dorramon's arm, and in the flash of his eyes as they locked on hers, she understood that her concerns were also his.

"Thank you," he said, already turning to lead her to the door. "I think we shall pay our visitors a visit, as it were.

Make sure the gate stays open until we return."

"Yes, your Majesty," Jomain said, with a deep bow.

Before he had even stood upright again, Dorramon and Alannys were gone, barreling down the corridor at a full-on run.

♪

Dorramon and Alannys kept right on running, straight out into the outer ward. A quick stop by the royal stables to pick up their horses, and they rode as fast as they dared through the dark streets. When exactly had Rathmar and the others left? How much of a head start did they have?

What could they possibly want from the Singari?

Alannys could only come up with one answer to that question, and she didn't like it. She rode alongside Dorramon, with the clatter of hoofbeats on cobblestone in her ears and the jarring of a running horse in her bones, but her entire awareness was consumed with worry. Once they crossed the big drawbridge, they gave the horses their heads, letting them run harder and stretch their legs. They were down the ridge in a matter of minutes that felt like hours.

They dismounted and walked the horses toward the encampment. Even from a distance Alannys could see the beginnings of a bonfire in the center of the camp, puffing out clouds of white smoke as the kindling started to burn.

Inside the wide circle of outer wagons, they found a ring of logs arranged as seating around the great bonfire. King Rathmar sprawled across one of these as if it was the most comfortable seat he had ever had, cradling a mug of warm wine and smiling broadly at everyone and everything around him. Princess Varilyn huddled next to him, ducking her head, making no eye contact whatsoever. Prince Cardoth sat over on the other side of the log circle, watching her intently from his seat cozied up to —

Pesia?

Alannys gave a violent start, watching her old nemesis

batting her eyelashes and chatting up her new one. What could the mother of Drigo and Brutagar, the woman who was her most devoted hater in the Singari, possibly have to say that would interest Prince Cardoth? She couldn't even imagine.

Cardoth noticed her discomfort and dropped her a broad wink before turning back to Pesia.

"Why, if it isn't King Dorramon!" Rathmar's eyes looked unnaturally bright, and his words slurred. Alannys eyed the cup in his hand, wondering just how many he'd had. Had he really been out here that long? "Come, King Dorramon, join us!"

Dorramon folded his arms, taking in the entire scene. "Why do you trouble these people, Rathmar? What goes on here?"

"Nothing," Rathmar said jovially, "that is, nothing that need concern you. We've heard how important the Singari are to certain...people who are important to your Majesty. For that reason, if no other, we considered it a grave offense not to greet them during our visit."

"But the bonfire?" Alannys said. "Bonfires are no ordinary occurrence in camp."

King Rathmar's glance touched on her briefly, burning with unpleasantness, then slid past. "There is to be a party. Surely that can be no concern of yours."

As it happened, *concern* summed up her reaction pretty well. "Dorramon," she said, suddenly urgent, "perhaps we should go tend to our horses."

Rathmar lurched to his feet, catching Dorramon by the sleeve. "Look, woman, surely you can see to the damned horses yourself. I don't see why else you should have tagged along, honestly, and I'm getting damned tired of your interfering presence. Even someone with your lack of station must see how unseemly it is for him to deal with horses himself. You do him a disservice, putting him in that position." He pulled Bryndel's reins from Dorramon's hands, and pushed them into hers.

Alannys wanted to lash out at him. She planted her feet, balled her fists, and opened her mouth to give him a piece of her mind — only to realize at the last moment, in a sudden flash of embarrassment, that he had a point. She turned away, smothering her anger, as Rathmar pushed a mug into Dorramon's hands and dragged him down onto the log.

"Alannys…" She could tell from Dorramon's ominous tone that he didn't agree with Rathmar's assessment.

She turned to give him a bright smile. He didn't look much like smiling himself, sandwiched between the King of Cadenda and his daughter. "Please don't give it another thought, your Majesty. King Rathmar is correct; it is of course my pleasure to serve in whatever manner I can."

Dorramon frowned at her, unamused. "Perhaps King Rathmar spoke out of turn."

Rathmar laughed uproariously.

"No, no," she said, "he was exactly right. I'll be back in a bit." Through the mindlink, she said, *He won't talk with me around — maybe you can find out more about what they're up to out here.*

All right. Dorramon sounded resigned — pretty much as enthusiastic as she felt about all of this. *But for the love of the Muses, be careful, Alannys. This visit isn't coincidental, and it isn't well-meant. I don't like this.*

What could she say? She didn't like it either.

♫

The bonfire really began to burn, tendrils of flame climbing into the night like ghostly, flickering fingers, throwing the occasional spark up high to float back down, and die. Bryndel and Quicksilver were both good horses, well-trained horses, but neither of them were anything like comfortable being that close to that much fire. They snorted and shied, dancing sideways and communicating clearly to Alannys that if she thought she was going with them, she had better get going *now*.

"All right, all right," she sighed, and led them off.

The Singari horses who owners didn't have wagons were tethered in a small copse of trees off to the side of the camp. It wasn't too far from camp, and it gave the horses just enough cover. She led Bryndel and Quicksilver in that direction. She had only gone a few steps into the darkness when someone fell into step beside her. "Fancy meeting you here. And not even wearing a dress, at that."

"Don't lecture me, Chen." Her tone was as sharp as the sidelong glance she threw in his direction. He looked the same as ever, with the same carefree swagger, but something about his expression put her on guard. "Tralice already gave me an earful."

"Well, now, that's a nice hello. And with me going to such trouble to entertain your guests, too."

"They certainly aren't *my* guests. If they were, I wouldn't be out tending to horses."

"Funny you should say that." He leaned back against one of the trees and folded his arms, looking back out across the camp as she tied the horses. "Since all they've talked about since they got here is you."

"What?" Alannys froze, looking up at him in unpleasant surprise. "Prince Cardoth is talking to Pesia...about *me?*"

"Aye. Knows right where to go for the good dirt, doesn't he? She's flirting like she doesn't have a *braytha* on her head—Drigo is mortified."

She waved aside his laughter, finishing with Bryndel and moving to tie Quicksilver. "Who cares what Pesia thinks? Who cares what she tells him? None of that matters. Cardoth is just a distraction. King Rathmar is out there drinking with Dorramon right now, and I'm back here playing with *horses*." Quicksilver snorted and shook his mane, unhappy with her tone.

"So?" Chen sounded confused. "He's the king—who better to handle another king?"

"It isn't that simple!" She was snapping again, and she forced herself to take a deep breath. "Cardoth and

Rathmar...I don't know what they're up to, but they aren't being straight with us. They're manipulative, Chen, and he's out there alone. I can't help but think that was Rathmar's real intent." She kicked savagely at a tree, and only succeeded in hurting her foot. "I should *be* there!"

"Alannys!" Chen grabbed her by the shoulders. "You have got to calm down."

"But Chen, I—"

"You don't have to tell me. It's awful, being stuck on the *sidelines* while someone you care about is off doing dangerous things. I understand, all right? And I reckon he does too. But here's the thing you have to understand: Dorramon is the king. He's a big boy, and he can take care of himself, and right now you're going to have to let him. This is his job, Alannys. You have got to let him do it."

"I know." She blew out a frustrated sigh. "I *know*. It's just...King Rathmar is tricky. What's he really doing? What's really going on here, Chen?"

He sighed, releasing her. "Actually I had been hoping you could tell me. King Rathmar just showed up out of the blue, demanding a party to celebrate the 'momentous occasion.' He's done nothing so far but ask a bunch of questions about you and throw himself loopy on too much wine, though. It's odd, don't you think? The Singari have gone for centuries without a visit from a king, and now in the space of a month we've had two. I know it's about you, somehow, but...I don't know what to make of it."

"I'm don't either," Alannys said. "The one thing I'm certain of is this—whatever Rathmar's plans are, we want no part of them. I don't know what particular use he has for you, Chen, but the Singari aren't even people to him. If he's interested in you, it's because he thinks you'll make good pawns."

"What a surprise." Chen's tone was cutting, but she couldn't blame him for it.

"I know," she said, "but I'm serious about this. I don't know what he's up to, but I know it stinks. Whatever happens tonight, you absolutely must not let them hear any music. No matter what!"

His hand fell gently on her shoulder. "Don't *worry*, Alannys. It's going to take a better man than King Rathmar to make pawns out of the Singari. And we are well accustomed to dancing without music."

"Thank you." She tried to swallow her unease — everything about this situation felt wrong. Rathmar should never have come out here, the Singari should not be celebrating, and she of all people should not be trying to hide music. Hadn't she just spent the last three months of her life fighting to bring it back? She sighed, and walked with Chen back toward camp.

The bonfire crackled merrily now, its flames casting dancing shadows through the middle of camp. Heat rolled off of it in intense waves that felt marvelous in the chilly night air. Around the fire, many of the married Singari *stortha* had begun to dance to the rhythmic clapping of the onlookers.

"I really am sorry about this," Alannys said under her breath.

Chen laughed shortly, and patted her shoulder again. "Not your fault, Alannys. Besides, things have been so grim lately...we could all use the break. There's nothing like a good party."

"Yeah," she said, "and this is nothing like a good party."

That made him laugh out loud. "Maybe you just need more wine. Any party is a good party with enough wine."

She couldn't really argue with that, and she didn't want to be the rain cloud over everyone's parade, so she kept her mouth shut. But she couldn't shake a bad feeling about the whole thing. Nothing felt right about any of this.

♫

As soon as Alannys and Chen stepped into the warm, dancing light of the bonfire, King Rathmar's eyes narrowed. "You, there. Singari. Over here."

Alannys stopped short, staring at the king in disbelief. Every time she thought she had a handle on him, he went and did something even lower. Her hands balled into angry, tendon-corded fists, and before she knew what she was going to do, she found herself stomping toward King Rathmar. "Now you listen here, Rathmar."

"Alannys..." Dorramon's tone was a warning, but in her blazing, incandescent fury, it couldn't reach her.

"People could like you, do you know that?" she demanded. "*I* could like you. You have everything going for you — looks, charm, even that dramatic flair of yours."

Rathmar guffawed, elbowing Dorramon in an exaggerated display of humor. "I see why you keep this one around, boy! She's got taste!"

Dorramon's tight smile, in contrast, contained no humor at all. "Alannys, please —"

"But it's all worthless! None of it means a thing because all of that is just appearances, it's just superficial. Underneath that shiny skin, the fruit is rotten — underneath you are egotistical and arrogant, narcissistic and shallow, and you believe yourself to be superior to every other living creature you encounter. This Singari has a name, and he is twice the man you are."

Rathmar watched her rant with a smug smile, then turned to Dorramon without even acknowledging her. "She really is most amusing. You want to train her better, though — that sort of performance could get you in trouble with someone who mistook her silly prattling for anything of importance."

Alannys was completely flabbergasted. She would happily have called him out on this condescending nonsense as well, but it seemed for the moment that standing there with her mouth agape was the best she could manage.

Chen chuckled, and pushed her mouth closed with a finger hooked under her chin. "Don't worry; I'm used to this. You don't want to let him pick a fight that easy, do you?"

He was right, and she knew he was right, but it still burned her. She bit down on her tongue to keep herself quiet. Chen turned to King Rathmar, looking surprisingly calm. "Yes, your Majesty?"

King Rathmar still had Dorramon neatly trapped, leaning against him as though he would fall without the support, an arm slung around his shoulders as though they were the best of friends. Dorramon, for his part, looked to be having about as much fun as she was. Rathmar looked up at Chen, blinking as though we was having trouble focusing, and gestured at Princess Varilyn, perching uncomfortably on Dorramon's other side. "My daughter is quite interested in this dance of yours. Teach her."

"You want me to dance with her?" Chen threw a troubled glance at Alannys. "In front of outsiders, unmarried Singari don't..."

"Are you refusing me, boy?" The temper Rathmar had been keeping so carefully in check suddenly flared; Alannys couldn't tell if his face was red from anger or from drink. Varilyn flushed with embarrassment. She couldn't have looked less interested in the dance if she tried. The situation felt dangerous, and Alannys found herself holding her breath.

"Rathmar." Dorramon sounded unutterably tired. "Let's just end this farce, shall we, and go home? You're abusing people I care about, and for what? You can't still imagine I have any intention of marrying—"

"I don't advise you to say any more, your Majesty." Rathmar still sat right next to Dorramon, with an arm around his shoulders, sloshing wine around as though they were great friends—but his tone chilled Alannys. His voice crackled with danger like ice under pressure, and his next words hit her like a bucket of cold water dashed into her face. "Do you imagine Ravanmark is the only country with a navy capable of making war?"

♫

It felt like the entire camp froze, even though Alannys knew no one else was paying attention to the conversation. She stood stone still, watching the situation unfold with horror she couldn't completely disguise. King Rathmar had come right out and said the dreaded W-word — the one word they had all danced around and lost sleep over for weeks. *Dorramon...*

I know. Dorramon straightened up, carefully extricating himself from Rathmar's drunken grasp. "Is this your true purpose here, then?"

King Rathmar laughed out loud. Alannys couldn't tell if he was attempting to defuse the situation with his boisterous laughter, or if he'd simply had too much to drink, but either way it only added to her acute discomfort. "Why, my dear boy, I don't know what you could mean. Our only purpose here is to resolve an apparent misunderstanding between our two countries. It simply seems to me that such purposes are not well served by flat declarations from either side about what they have no intention of doing. Come now, civil discussion should not be beyond us."

"No," Dorramon sighed, "of course not."

"Young lady," Rathmar snapped, tossing her a distasteful glance, "you have no business here. Kindly remove yourself. And as for you, young man, I would be most pleased if you would just dance with my daughter. King Dorramon and I have much to discuss, and we do not wish to be disturbed."

Alannys and Chen exchanged a look of mutual exasperation, then turned to do as they were told. What else was there for them to do? The swiftly deteriorating situation was Dorramon's to handle, and any interference they offered would only aggravate it further.

So Alannys turned away from Chen's awkward attempt to dance with Princess Varilyn — who looked, if it was possible, even more awkward than he did — and tried her best to ignore the quiet but hostile conversation Dorramon and Rathmar were getting into. She turned pointedly away from Prince Cardoth, still deep in conversation with Pesia, who was smiling and twirling her hair around her fingers in a manner she evidently considered quite becoming. It probably would have been a good time to escape back to the Great Palace, but she couldn't stomach the idea of leaving Dorramon out here by himself. She didn't think she would have been able to handle it if he did that to her.

So she gritted her teeth and forced herself to walk around the far side of the bonfire, giving the whirling dancers a wide berth. They wore expressions of grim concentration better suited to unpleasant labor than to a party.

Alannys understood. The campfire circle was usually such a warm, welcoming place — the heart of camp — she could still remember her own wild dance around one with Chen, months behind her now. But tonight, it was a relief to leave the fire behind. Here in the back of the camp a few smaller fires burned, hissing and popping as fat dripped from the meat cooking over them. On the other side of the cooking fires, as far as they could get from the royalty surrounding the bonfire, a dozen or so Singari children played, running through the dark with a complete disregard for life and limb that made Alannys want to scold them, even as she envied them.

She passed them by without giving voice to her thoughts, and went farther back. Past the cooking fires and the children, past even the groups of tents huddled together in the darkness, there was nothing but a couple of unused wagons: a storage wagon and the *prathamol,* sitting alone in the night at odd angles to each other, looking abandoned and somehow forlorn.

It suited her at that moment, so she wandered over to them, leaving behind the flickering light of the fires and the scent of wood smoke and roasting meat. The *prathamol* brought back too many uncomfortable memories, so she sat down on the steps of the storage wagon, her back to the so-called festivities. How long had it been since she stood outside of the *prathamol* in the rain, trying to talk sense to a man who had once tried to kill her? It was hard to believe that man was now a baron. What would he do, she wondered, in the situation they faced now?

She snorted and pushed that line of thought aside. Trago was unfailingly brash and aggressive, and looking to his example would not benefit her now. Nothing he would do could be of any help to them. Whatever was going on here, it was far from obvious. She thought about King Rathmar, with his evident concern for public opinion, pushing Princess Varilyn to dance. He didn't even like the Singari, and he had to be aware of the scandal such a dance would cause for his daughter, should word of it get out. Why would he do that? For that matter, why would he do anything he had done this evening? If negotiation was his goal, the Great Palace was far better suited to the purpose than a log at a bonfire in a Singari camp. And what of his strange obsession with music? Every instinct she had said she was missing the bigger picture here.

"Such a serious frown for such a beautiful lady." The voice was low and right in her ear, resonant and somehow decadent.

Alannys jumped and threw herself to the other side of the step, sucking in a reflexive gasp. How had anybody gotten so close without her realizing it—least of all *him?* She must have been deeper in thought than she'd realized.

Prince Cardoth laughed, and pushed a warm mug of spiced wind into her hands. "Sorry, sorry, I didn't mean to frighten you. Aren't you cold, back here all alone?"

"No." She stared into the dark wine, debating what she should do. In truth she *was* chilly, but she would never have admitted it to him. She thought about getting up and leaving, but where would she go? There was no way

Dorramon and Rathmar were done already. "No, I'm fine. What are you doing here?"

If her manner offended him, he gave no sign of it. Cardoth sat down next to her on the step. "Looking for you, of course. You disappeared."

"You don't need to worry about me." She sipped cautiously at the wine, looking for something to do that didn't involve him. To her surprise, it was sweet — very sweet, sweeter than any wine she'd ever had, and it warmed her whole torso. "I'm afraid it takes more than a little dark and a little cold to do me in."

Prince Cardoth chuckled darkly. The hair on the back of her neck suddenly stood on end, and she whipped around to regard him.

He waved off her concern. "I've heard the stories, my Lady. I suppose if a tidal wave wasn't enough for you, I've got very little to worry about. But you should take more care. Someone who meant you harm would have very little trouble inflicting it right now."

"The only people around here who seem to mean me harm are you and your father," she said pointedly, choosing to ignore the issue of resistance within the Great Palace. "And possibly your new Singari friend."

"What is this, now?" Cardoth sounded amused — and engaged, as though the conversation had just gotten interesting. "Are you jealous?"

"Jealous? I should say not." Alannys snorted and turned away from him, as much as she was able in the confined space.

"You needn't worry, my dear. All we spoke about was you."

"Me?" Alannys turned back around in a hurry; as it happened, that *did* worry her.

"Indeed. She seems quite impressed with you."

"Hmph. I think you mean she was quite impressed with *you*. Pesia has never been what you would call a supporter of mine."

"Ah, Alannys," Cardoth laughed, "you are too hard on yourself. I assure you, she had nothing but good words for you."

"She must not have said very many, then."

Cardoth laughed again. "That much is true...her son came and fairly dragged her away." He gave her a speculative look, as though he was sizing her up. "They are very loyal to you, these people. I quite wonder why." He lifted a lock of her hair and twisted it around his finger, in a manner *he* evidently considered quite becoming.

Alannys had to admit, the gesture was much more...compelling this way. Her ears burned, and she leaned away from him. "Singari camps are not open to outsiders, your Highness," she said shortly. "You must know you and your father don't have the right to just barge in here and impose on their hospitality like this."

"What?" Cardoth sounded less amused now, and he pulled his hand back from her. "Who's imposing? Singari are notorious party animals—everything that's happening here is just what they would do anyway, left to their own devices. You should know their wild nature well enough...I've heard about your Singari boyfriend."

"You don't know what you're talking about," she spat. "I'm not going to sit here and listen to this."

She made to push herself up from the steps, to stomp away, but Cardoth thumped her back down onto her seat with a hand on her shoulder. "I wouldn't recommend that, my Lady. These are delicate negotiations. Do you really want to risk the future of this whole country, just to offend me?"

Alannys looked at him in sharp surprise. "Is Dorramon right, then? Is that your true purpose here—to instigate a war?"

For a moment Prince Cardoth stared off into the darkness. "It disturbs me that you refer so casually to the King of Ravanmark. You must remember he is engaged to another—it hardly seems appropriate that you should feel yourself on a first-name basis."

Her fingers clenched around her cup and she drank the rest of her wine in one go, stalling while she controlled her initial impulse to lash back at him. The sweet wine seemed to soothe her, and when she did speak she was controlled and calm. "That seems an admirable way to dodge the question. Is that your intent? To subdue us with the club of war if we refuse to submit to your demands?"

"Demands?" Cardoth looked at her incredulously. "We are only asking that King Dorramon honor a previously negotiated engagement. What exactly do you feel we are wrongly demanding?"

His direct gaze flustered her. Her mouth felt impossibly dry, and she tried to drink more of the wine. Her cup was empty—she was inexplicably upset to discover she no longer had that particular diversionary tactic available. "I—I'm not sure, my Lord Prince." She was surprised to find it suddenly true—her mind felt fuzzy, and her thoughts were indistinct. She quite simply couldn't remember what reason she'd had for being so upset with him a moment ago.

Cardoth reached out and lifted the cup from her grasp, setting it gently on the landing above them, taking her hand in his own. The gesture startled her, but she couldn't seem to work out what she should do about it. "Now I do like the way you say that."

"Say...what? My Lord Prince?"

"Yes, exactly."

"But...it's just a title, a courtesy." She thought about it, but she couldn't seem to make it mean anything more. Her inability to follow the conversation troubled her. Was this right, this curious disconnect she seemed to have from the world around her? She couldn't remember.

"Certainly. But when you say it, it seems like something more."

"It...does? I'm sorry, then—I meant no offense."

"Please don't apologize." He ran his free hand over her hair. "It's a good thing."

Alannys shied away from the touch. Her brain didn't seem to be firing on all cylinders, but she remembered him laying on the charm like this before. She hadn't thought it was genuine at the time, and she didn't think it was genuine now. But the motion unbalanced her, and she tightened her grip on his hand convulsively, afraid of falling.

Prince Cardoth chuckled again, a low and strangely threatening sound. "Steady, there. I think perhaps you've had too much to drink, my Lady."

"Yes," she said, but she frowned. How could that be, when she'd only had the one cup? She had never seen a wine *that* strong.

Cardoth stood up, pulling her to her feet with him. "We had better get you back to the palace, I think. It wouldn't do for you to wander out here alone in this state."

"But...Dorramon...I don't think he's finished yet."

A frown flickered across the prince's handsome visage. "Yes, that's probably true. But I assure you I can see you safely back to your room. Do you think I would let anything happen to you?"

He regarded her quite seriously, and in the faint light his dark eyes seemed as deep as the night that surrounded them. She stared into those eyes, and felt a memory of something, pulling at the back of her befuddled brain, something she couldn't quite get a hold of and pull into focus.

He lifted an eyebrow. "Well?"

"No. No, of course not, your Highness."

"Just so." He threaded her arm through his. "Stay close to me. I can protect you, my Lady, but you're going to have to trust me."

There was something flat about his tone, something that made her wonder, even then, if he was talking about a whole lot more than the ride back to the Great Palace.

♫

Prince Cardoth set off at a brisk pace, and Alannys could do little more than stumble along beside him, clinging to his arm and trying hopelessly to keep up. He led her around the back of the camp, behind the cooking fires, and she realized with a kind of delayed shock that he intended to take her away without saying anything to Dorramon at all. She pulled Cardoth's arm, hoping to guide him that direction, but it didn't take long to see she didn't have a chance of swaying him in her state.

They were out behind the line of wagons, halfway to the horses, when a figure suddenly stepped right out in front of her. "Alannys! There you are!" Chen looked from her to Prince Cardoth, and frowned. "What are you up to?"

"Leaving," Cardoth said shortly. He attempted to step around Chen.

Chen stepped over to block him. "I see. In that case, perhaps you should stop by to bid King Dorramon good night. It would be ill manners to just leave, don't you think?"

"As you say, Singari, though I fail to see where my ill manners are any concern of yours." Prince Cardoth's voice was clipped and controlled, but Alannys could feel the fury boiling underneath. He turned sharply and stalked out into the camp, dragging her out into the light on the bonfire.

Chen grabbed her other arm, holding her up. "Muses, Alannys, what's wrong with you?"

Alannys couldn't answer. She was too busy trying to make sure her legs stayed under her. The world lurched violently at unpredictable moments, making it difficult to navigate the rocky, uneven ground, even with two people supporting her.

"Great Muses!" Dorramon stood up from the log as soon as he saw her, ignoring Rathmar, who continued to talk beside him. She must have looked even worse than she felt. "Alannys, what happened to you?"

"I fear that Lady Alannys has indulged too heavily in the wine," Prince Cardoth said smoothly, holding her arm tight against him. "I am...escorting her back to her chambers; we merely came to take our leave."

Dorramon's expression hardened; his features might have been cut in granite. "No." There was no kindness in the gaze he turned upon Cardoth, no civility in the single, clipped word. Rathmar reached out to stop him; Dorramon shook him off, irritated, and stomped over to them. "No, I absolutely forbid it. I'll take her back myself."

Prince Cardoth took a wary step backward. "But your Highness is in the middle of important discussions with my father. Please, allow me to see her safely home. I will keep a close watch on her...I personally guarantee she will not lack for...attentive company."

"I said no, and by the Sacred Song I meant it!" Dorramon snatched her arm away and she tottered over to him, wondering what she was missing here. Things were moving too fast for her to keep up, but she honestly couldn't imagine how much they would have to slow down for her to catch up. She couldn't remember the last time she'd felt so awful. "Your father is done here, and so are you. These talks are over. Your party will leave the Great Palace first thing tomorrow morning."

Nobody spoke; nobody moved. Even Alannys could tell that a line had been drawn here—the fates of them all hung on King Rathmar's reaction to what Dorramon had just declared.

But Dorramon wasn't waiting around to find out what that reaction would be. He stormed out of the camp to the horses, dragging her along with him, leaving them all staring after him in undisguised shock.

♫

Alannys didn't remember much about the ride back to the Great Palace. Her mouth and throat were so intensely

Sandra Miller

dry they burned, but she couldn't really feel her tongue or lips, which made it nearly impossible to talk. Her feet seemed to float in and out of her awareness, and she missed as many steps as she landed. Without Dorramon, she would have had to crawl from the camp to the horses — maybe all the way back to the palace.

As it was, she had a vague recollection of riding on Bryndel, with Dorramon behind her, keeping her in the saddle with his legs and supporting her with his arms wrapped around her.

"I've never seen anybody so drunk. What did he do to you?"

She remembered Dorramon muttering that, the words resonating in his chest, right up against her ear as she bounced down the corridor in his arms.

That must have been how she wound up alone in her room, lying on her back on the bed, staring up at the ceiling. It hung there ominously, staring back, and she had the impression it was trying to tell her something important. So she stared at it, stared hard with eyes that couldn't seem to focus on anything. But no matter how hard she stared, she couldn't quite hear what it said.

So she tried to talk instead, to tell the ceiling that if it expected her to hear what it said, it had better speak up. All she produced was a kind of croak as the dry, gritty sides of her throat grated together.

Alannys hauled herself off of the bed and lurched into the bathroom. It seemed to take a very long time to get there, and when she finally did, she wasn't at all sure she'd made it to the right room. The bathtub, for instance — she was pretty sure the bathtub was usually empty when she wasn't using it, but right now it seemed to be brimming with dark red wine. Overflowing, really — wine poured over the edges of the tub and splashed across the stone floor, but the tub just kept filling, like magic. Where was it all coming from?

She watched it a moment, trying to figure it out, but

then she decided it didn't really matter. She was thirsty, wasn't she? She remembered something about beggars not looking choosy horses in the teeth, and besides, if she stood here very much longer she would be swimming in wine. It was already up to her ankles. And she didn't think she remembered how to swim.

Alannys cupped her hands together and scooped them through the wine rippling in the tub. But when she brought them to her lips, they were empty. It didn't matter how many times she tried, she couldn't seem to catch a drop of the wine. Her hands weren't even damp. Or stained.

She grabbed the edge of the tub and leaned in, dipping her face in the wine and slurping—only to discover that slurping air on a bone-dry throat was not just futile, but painful. And in her unsteady state, she feared that if she kept leaning over the tub, she would fall in headfirst. Could she drown in wine she couldn't drink? She didn't think she wanted to find out.

So she turned her back on the tub and its crazy undrinkable wine, and turned the faucet on the sink instead. The water was cold, and it tasted metallic. Or maybe the water was fine, and her mouth tasted metallic. Either way, the water felt wonderful, and she stood there drinking it for what seemed like nigh onto forever. Each time she stopped, her mouth and throat felt instantly parched.

Finally she couldn't handle any more water, and she turned to leave the bath chamber. On her way out, she caught sight of the bathtub—completely empty and perfectly dry. There was no wine in the tub or on the floor, nor any indication that there ever had been.

For the first time, she seriously doubted her own senses. Had the business with the wine really even happened? Had she just spent her time and effort trying to drink wine that *wasn't even there?* What was wrong with her? For a fleeting moment she felt almost coherent, and she thought that what was happening to her went way beyond being drunk.

Bed was the safest place for her. She stepped out of the bath chamber, intent on getting back into bed, and tripped on the uneven ground. It wasn't her fault; the moonlight was faint to begin with and the trees blocked quite a bit of it. She almost fell into the water garden before realizing it was there.

"Steady, there." The voice was rich and resonant in her ears, decadent, like fine chocolate. She turned toward it and looked into the dark eyes of Prince Cardoth. He had his hands on her shoulders as if to steady her, but he was holding her out over the surface of the water garden.

She remembered this! She heard footsteps running toward them, and she knew it was Raman.

"No!"

The voice that ripped through the air between them was not Raman's. She whipped her head around and saw Chen, riding Nightfire across the ridge, sihouetted against the sky. And Cardoth wasn't holding her over the water, he was holding her down in the snow, and as she looked up into his dark eyes, the avalanche roared down over them and everything went black.

Alannys screamed and pushed herself up...on the bed in her chambers? How had she gotten in here? Nothing made sense. Had that all been a dream? If so, it was like no dream she'd ever had. She was flopped face down over the side of the bed — more like she'd tripped over it than like she'd been sleeping in it. And she still couldn't hear whatever the ceiling was saying.

But whatever it was, dream, hallucination — it was right. She knew with dead certainty, even through the fog currently shrouding her brain, that Prince Cardoth and the cloaked swordsman who had stalked her across all of Ravanmark were one and the same.

♫

The realization sank into her bones, chilled her like ice

in her veins. And with that realization, there was only one thing to be done. She had to tell Dorramon, had to tell him *right away*. This changed everything, this made their entire situation so mind-bogglingly much more dangerous that she couldn't even work through all the ramifications, standing there dazed in her bedroom, with a curious numbness in her limbs and a heavy fog clouding her brain. So she opened the mindlink.

Or rather, she tried to open the mindlink. The mindlink would not open. She had never felt anything like it—the connection was there, she was just utterly unable to use it. It was like the feeling she got in dreams sometimes, when she would try with all her might to run, but remained steadfastly rooted to the spot.

What was *happening* to her? She didn't have time to worry about it. She had to find Dorramon, now. She stumbled out into her sitting room, doing her best to run, but managing only a clumsy, lurching sort of stagger on feet that felt like they weren't quite reaching the floor.

Alannys grabbed the door and threw it open, ready to take her staggering, lurching run out across the keep to the king's chambers.

A pair of dark eyes waited just outside her door, regarding her narrowly over a black scarf pulled up high over the rest of his face. A shadowy man in amorphous robes hovered behind the black-cloaked, dark-eyed specter facing her, but she had no notice to spare for him.

"You!" Her voice was rough from the dryness of her throat, and her numb mouth made speaking clearly difficult. She tried her best to scream anyway. "Help!"

The cloaked swordsman pushed her back inside her room, stepping quickly in after her. His man followed, closing the door behind them.

Alannys stumbled backwards and fell onto her backside. She could feel her enchanted dagger burning against her leg, which was pretty strange since she knew she wasn't wearing the dagger. "Prince Cardoth. Are you here to kill me?"

"So you've figured me out. And here I thought I gave such a wonderful performance as the avid suitor." He pulled the scarf down off of his face, and jerked his chin sharply in the direction of her bedroom. "In there," he said to his man. "There is a sword, and a dagger. Make sure you bring them both. And she has a royal medallion. Find it." He turned back to her. "I'm impressed. No, I mean that. I didn't expect to find you conscious right now, let alone solving puzzles. You truly are a woman of many surprises. What gave me away?"

She tried to scoot backwards, away from him, but her soft boots slipped ineffectually on the smooth stone floor. "It was the snow," she said, "in the courtyard."

Cardoth stared at her a moment, then laughed. "Ah, I see. It seems you are perhaps not as coherent as I had imagined. Good, then. This should make things much easier." He pulled out his black scarf, and folded it down to a long, narrow strip.

When he stepped toward her, his black cloak and flowing robes billowed out behind him. It reminded her of wings, and for a moment she could *see* big, black wings unfolding behind him, reaching toward the ceiling and casting long shadows across her room. He looked like an angel of death.

"I don't want to die," she muttered, staring up at those wings. They melted away, even as she watched, and she shook her head roughly, trying to keep her wandering mind in check. It was hard to be sure of anything she saw or heard when her senses kept playing tricks on her.

"I'm not here to kill you," Prince Cardoth said, but he gagged her anyway, pulling the scarf tight around the back of her head and knotting it. "I'm sorry, Alannys."

The words were just barely loud enough for her to hear, and she wondered if she had imagined them, hallucinated them as she'd evidently hallucinated so much else this night. It was possible, she had to admit, that none of this was even really happening at all.

That thought was actually comforting.

Cardoth hauled her to her feet and pulled on her arm, reaching for the clasp on her royal bracelet. Alannys jerked her arm back, trying to force words past the gag in her dry mouth, trying to demand to know what exactly he thought he was doing.

"Sorry," Cardoth said again, not quite looking her in the eye. "But everyone knows you would never leave this, if you were coming back."

Alannys knew something was dreadfully wrong with her, of course—but even allowing for that, his words didn't seem to make any sense. She fought him anyway, but it was a losing battle—in a matter of moments, he wrenched her arm from her chest and took her bracelet, then pried her fingers one by one from her clenched fist and took her engagement ring.

Then he dumped them both on her coffee table without a second glance and left them there.

She watched him in sullen silence, angry tears burning down her cheeks. Why take her things from her, things that didn't matter to anyone in the world but her, just to treat them like that?

Cardoth wasn't giving any clues. He grabbed her arm and hauled her through the archway into her bedroom, glowering at the man there rifling through her belongings. The man held her dagger in one hand, Songstrike in the other, and her royal medallion hung glittering from his neck. The hits, it seemed, just kept on coming. She hadn't felt this belittled, this violated, since Archford prison, and she hated these men for bringing that horrible, helpless feeling back to her. She mustered up her most ferocious glare and directed it full-on into the man's face—only to stumble in surprise. She *knew* this man standing in her chambers, casually draped in her most precious possessions, regarding her with a smug smirk.

Ambassador Thell!

"You've found them," Cardoth said, pulling her to her feet as an afterthought. "Good. She has a cloak, a heavy leather one for riding. Find it. We need to get out of here."

"Of *course,* my Lord Prince," Thell said, his reedy, sneering voice heavy with sarcasm. "I *live* to serve." He disappeared into her closet.

A moment later, Chen emerged, carrying her old leather cloak. He walked right up to her, not seeming to even notice anything amiss around them.

"Alannys," he said, and his voice was as kind and warm as ever. His eyes were soft with sympathy. "Things are about to get rough. Be strong." He held the cloak out to her.

Alannys grabbed his wrists, sobbing. She wished she could talk to him, but the scarf made that impossible. It seemed strange, even to her, that Chen didn't seem to notice or care that she was gagged.

"Are you certain about this, my Lord Prince?" The voice came from right in front of her, but it was harsh and nasal, dripping with disdain. "The woman has never been what I would call clever, but now — she doesn't seem right in the head."

Prince Cardoth sighed heavily. "Perhaps you could extend her a bit of understanding. She isn't quite herself." Alannys looked at Cardoth in confusion, then back at Chen.

Only it wasn't Chen who stood in front of her. When she looked back, she found a tall man there, dressed entirely in black, regarding her with a familiar sneer on his long face. Ambassador Thell — again!

And she was holding him by the wrists.

She released him and jumped back with a squeak. He barked with unkind laughter, and Prince Cardoth shushed him.

"This isn't easy on her," he said, and his sharp tone silenced Thell's laughter. "I can't imagine what's going on in her head right now. But she'll be all right." He peered into her face, his brow knit with worry. "At least, I think she will. It's hard to tell with these things." He waved his hand in front of her face. She tried to track the motion with her eyes, but everything went blurry and she gave up.

Prince Cardoth shook his head and turned away, grabbing the cloak. He slung it around her shoulders and fastened it, then scooped her up and tossed her over his shoulder. For the second time that night, Alannys traveled through the corridor of the keep under someone else's steam.

She bounced along on Cardoth's back, unsettled and nauseous, wishing *something* would happen that made sense. Prince Cardoth had tried for months to kill her — once in the very same room they had just left. Why suddenly drag her away, when he finally had her dead to rights? Why bring along her things?

Alannys could only come up with one answer to that question, and it made as little sense as anything else that had happened that night. It also scared her to death.

Cardoth was abducting her.

♫

Cardoth carried Alannys through the outer ward for what felt like forever, sometimes moving fast, and sometimes slowly with great care. She quickly lost her bearings, bouncing around over his shoulder like a bag of potatoes, and she had no idea where he might be taking her. They traveled silently through many quiet back alleys, winding through the ward and studiously avoiding any place where they might encounter others. He carried her up a long, spiraling staircase, and finally stopped and set her on her feet. She wobbled, dizzy at suddenly being right-side-up after so long upside-down.

"I cannot express to you," said a cutting voice, "what a terrible idea this is."

Rathmar? Was that *King Rathmar* addressing them sarcastically in the darkness? As best as she could tell, they were up on the parapets of the outer curtain wall, at the top of the guard tower next to the drawbridge. What on earth could King Rathmar be doing up here? Why would the Royal Guard even allow him access? It made no sense. She had to be hallucinating again.

"I believe you have already expressed exactly that," Cardoth said, "several times."

"I clearly have not expressed it *enough,* if you brought her here anyway. You were tasked with killing her, Cardoth, and that is precisely what you should have done. She would be far less dangerous dead."

"Undoubtedly," Cardoth said. "She'd also be far less useful."

"Useful," Rathmar snorted, as if he had never heard a more ridiculous notion. "Precious little to be done about it now, though. Come, our guide is waiting."

She could hear his footsteps, receding into the darkness before them. Prince Cardoth sighed next to her in evident exasperation, and took hold of her arm. "Come, my Lady. Just a little longer, and you can rest."

She jerked her arm free, stumbling a little from the force of the motion, teetering away from him. She didn't think she could get herself safely down from the parapets in her state—but she also didn't care. She didn't know what could prompt Cardoth to call her 'useful,' and she sure as anything didn't want to find out.

Ambassador Thell put his hands on her back and shoved her in Cardoth's direction. "I swear I do not see why your Majesty puts up with this."

"Hush, Thell." Cardoth grabbed her arm again and started after his father, and she staggered along beside him. She felt more like she was on a tightrope than in the parapets. Footing was hard for her to find, and her extremities still felt oddly numb. She felt rain falling on her—she could hear it pattering wetly around them—but she remained completely dry. She couldn't see any rain anywhere. Lightning forked down from the sky, close enough to stand her hair on end, but she didn't hear the crackling rip it should have made. No thunder sundered the air in its wake.

And nobody seemed to notice any of this but her.

Cardoth did, however, notice her flinching and starting as they attempted to make their way down the narrow parapets in the faint moonlight that managed to trickle through the heavy cloud cover. He watched her with a worried frown, then hissed ahead at his father. "Can we hurry this up, please? I don't know how much longer she's going to make it."

"*That* is entirely your lookout for bringing her in the first place," Rathmar snapped back. "Don't forget we were waiting on you. This whole thing has to be timed around the guard rounds; there isn't much anybody can do about it."

The tense set of Cardoth's jaw gave Alannys the impression he was gritting his teeth. He tightened his grip on her arm, and pulled her along toward the midpoint of the curtain wall. "What a farce."

Rathmar waited for them in the near-darkness, with Princess Varilyn cowering in his shadow, under a cloak that concealed her face completely. Behind them a thick rope had been secured to one of the crenelations, and it dropped over the outside of the wall and down out of sight.

Beside Rathmar, a Royal Guard in uniform tested the knot in the heavy rope, pulling it tighter. His back was to Alannys, but she saw his tousled mess of red hair, reached up to pull the gag from her mouth, and his name was out before she could stop it, in a pitiful croak.

"Jomain!"

He spun to face her in apparent shock, his freckles stark on his pale, strained face. His eyes went wide, and his skin glowed like candle-wax in the night. "Your Majesty! What goes on here? That's—that's Lady Alannys!"

King Rathmar arched an eyebrow. "Yes. She and my son are madly in love, as you can see. They are eloping. I don't see what possible difference it can make to you."

Jomain shook his head, holding his hands in front of him as if to ward off evil spirits. "No, no! I am sorry, your Highness—you said you only needed Prince Cardoth and Princess Varilyn removed! You told me your children are in danger here, and I'm more than happy to help you get them to safety. But I can't let you take her; King Dorramon would have my head! It would be the death of me!"

"My dear boy," King Rathmar said, "it already is."

Moving quicker than Alannys could follow in her state, so fast that the motion seemed to blur, he drew his sword and jammed it straight through Jomain's middle.

♫

Rathmar turned away before Jomain's body even hit the ground, completely unfazed. Alannys watched the guard slump to the ground, his wide, glassy eyes locked on her, and she hoped against all hope that this was another hallucination. Another death, down to her account. The debt just kept growing, and Alannys couldn't shake the feeling that she'd have to pay up, when that marker came due. Pay up in blood.

"Varilyn," Rathmar snapped, "get down that rope. Quickly, now! Cardoth, you get that woman down right after your sister. She must not be seen here." He pushed past her to stand in front of his ambassador. "You wait here until they are all down. Then take care of that rope. I'm going back to show my face around the Raven's Nest —I must not be seen here either. Come find me when you are finished." He jerked his chin toward Jomain's corpse, cooling on the battlements. "And bring that with you. We'll need it later."

With a swirl of cloak, he was gone.

"Tsk." Cardoth shook his head, and helped his sister over the wall, presumably to scale down the rope. "Hold on tight, Varilyn, and move quickly. This is a nasty business. Thell, give me the sword and the dagger." He strapped on Songstrike, and secreted her dagger away in some hidden pocket in her cloak.

"I hope you appreciate the risks I am taking," Thell complained. He was still wearing Alannys's royal medallion, and it irked her to see it. She could still feel Dorramon lowering it over her head and kissing her — to think it would end up on this loathsome man! "I have placed myself in quite a perilous position, for you and for your father. I do hope you will both remember it."

Cardoth regarded him evenly. "Go find my father when you've finished here, Thell. You'll get what is coming to you."

Thell stepped back and grinned broadly, bowing with a sweeping gesture toward the curtain wall.

Cardoth shook his head and turned to Alannys. "Now listen to me, Alannys. You're in no shape to climb this rope yourself." He ran a hand over his shiny hair, watching the way she kept wheeling around to see things that weren't there. "Truth be told, you're in no shape to go down this rope with anyone else, either. But we don't have a lot of choice at this point. There is a raft at the bottom of this rope. If you hang on tight to me, I will get you to the raft, and safely to the shore. If you don't, you're going to fall into the moat and drown. Do you understand?"

"I *understand*, Cardoth." Alannys tried to push aside the ghost rain and silent thunder, the colors in the sky and the voices in her head, and pulled together every thread of coherence she had left. Maybe he would throw her over the wall when she finished, and maybe that wouldn't be so bad. "I understand perfectly well. Understand me when I tell you this — if you take me over that wall, I am letting go anyway. I will *never* go *anywhere* with you."

Cardoth stared at her a moment in silence, his dark eyes hard and the muscles of his jaw working. "Perhaps it was too much to expect that you'd show the common decency of gratitude. You were supposed to be dead right now. No matter." He made a sharp gesture, and Thell suddenly caught her arms from behind, holding them to her sides while Cardoth reapplied the gag. Then he turned his back to her and pulled her arms around him, one over his shoulder, and one under the other shoulder. Thell bound her wrists securely together, using some of the same heavy twine that hung over the wall. Cardoth tugged at the knot, testing his ambassador's handiwork. "There, now. I'm serious about this. My intent is not to kill you. I respect your guts, Alannys, but you had better just accept that you have no choice now."

Alannys lurched down the side of the wall, her eyes shut tight and her arms clamped around Prince Cardoth, Thell's rope rubbing her wrists raw. She didn't understand why Cardoth was abducting her, or what was going to happen to her when they left the Great Palace. She didn't know why someone who had spent three months trying to assassinate her would suddenly go to all this trouble to get her out alive.

She did understand how treacherous scaling the curtain wall could be, and she understood what would have happened if Prince Cardoth had tossed her over.

But she had to admit that just for a moment, she wished he had done it anyway.

She had a sneaking suspicion that the moat might turn out to be more pleasant than whatever Cardoth had planned for her now.

♬

The sun blazed high in the sky, stark and distant, casting bright golden light and bringing the temperature just where one would expect on a clear early spring day. It was the first thing Alannys became aware of, shining straight down into her eyes. She flinched away from it.

"I'm very sorry. I've tried to shade you with your cloak, but it keeps falling."

A few other things became immediately apparent to Alannys. She was lying flat on her back, bouncing uncomfortably along on something hard that produced constant, annoying squeaks. She couldn't move, and her head was pounding. Her surroundings smelled of moldy hay, and yet she was ravenously hungry. And she had no idea who was talking to her.

The blinding sunlight turning the insides of her eyelids flaming red suddenly disappeared. Alannys tentatively opened her eyes and saw her leather cloak stretched out over her head, its edges propped up on...hay bales?

She suddenly had a very bad feeling about this.

Princess Varilyn sat next to her. Smears of dirt and even a ragged tear marred her once-beautiful gown, and bits of hay clung to her hair. Purple bags under her eyes spoke of a night passed with far too little sleep, but she somehow managed to smile at Alannys. "I really am sorry, my Lady. I've tried to get him to let me untie your arms...or at least remove that horrible gag...but he isn't listening to me at all."

He. All at once Alannys remembered why she was here, and why Varilyn looked so rough, and why no one had slept last night. And she knew she had to get out of here, whatever it took, before another moment passed — *right now.* Whatever it took.

She pitched a regular fit — kicking her legs, twisting her torso, thrashing her head, all the while hearing Varilyn's agitated voice in her ears, begging her to calm down.

And in the end, it didn't even do her any good. Her ankles were tied tight, her arms bound behind her back, her mouth still gagged so she couldn't speak. She crumpled back against the floorboards, trying to suck air past the black scarf. Varilyn took her arm and helped her to sit up, propping her back against another hay bale. They were, as it turned out, surrounded by hay bales. Alannys looked at them, then looked at Varilyn, her eyes wide. Why was she bound here, traveling with a princess, in a *hay cart?*

Princess Varilyn patted her shoulder sympathetically,

breathing a sigh of relief. "Thank you. You must try to remain calm, my Lady. My brother was right. This is a nasty business, and it isn't of your doing, or mine. I did try to warn King Dorramon."

"Yes," a deep, rich voice said musingly, "and I still think I should lop your head off for it."

Alannys craned her neck around to see her own personal nemesis, Prince Cardoth of Cadenda, driving the hay cart in his black robes. Songstrike and her dagger lay under the driver's bench he sat upon. Fury coursed through her, and she thought in that moment she could understand pretty well why he wouldn't let Varilyn untie her.

"Cardoth," Varilyn said sharply, "this is dishonorable. For a prince to behave this way—and a brother of mine! How shall I survive the shame?"

"I don't know where you get your high-flown ideals," Cardoth said. He didn't look back at them, and he didn't sound particularly stung. "You must know this was all Father's scheme. If Caleb had done his job when he became King of Ravanmark, none of us would be doing this right now."

"I don't know what's gotten into Father, either," Varilyn cried, "but it doesn't mean we all have to stoop to this level! Uncle Caleb was a good man, Cardoth, and Father usually is, too. But this...I can't believe you've gone along with it." She hesitated a moment, biting her lip. "Vox would never have done this."

"Vox?" Cardoth echoed incredulously. "*Vox? He's* your noble hero?" Alannys could hear the disdain dripping from his voice. "Vox is on his way here right now, with three more warships. Don't delude yourself about him, dear sister. Vox was rabid about this plan. He just wasn't willing to take any of the risk. I came to eliminate the Music Mage—the one powerful opponent we might face outside of the royal family. You and Father came to instigate the war. But our dear brother, precious Crown

Prince Vox...he won't step foot in Ravanmark until the war is over and the throne is won. He has all of my faults, and cowardice besides. Don't pin your hopes on him."

War? King Rathmar really did come here just to start a war? Alannys felt like her world had just lurched sideways. *Dorramon!* What on earth had she left him in? He didn't even know any of this had happened! What must he have thought happened to her? In a fit of panic, she scrambled to open the mindlink.

Nothing happened.

Nothing at all.

♫

Alannys went limp against the hay bales. She had just strained so hard she'd made herself dizzy, trying with everything she had to force open the mindlink. No dice. All she had done was intensify her headache. Whatever had messed her up so badly the night before was still with her enough to keep her from using the mindlink. She thought she might die from sheer panic. War! And she had been gone from the Great Palace for close to twelve hours now. Who knew what was happening there? Who knew what had happened to Dorramon? She thought she might go mad with worry.

Princess Varilyn watched her, taking in the changing expressions on her face. "I never wanted any of this."

Cardoth snorted. "Spare me. Of course you did. Queen of Ravanmark, you're telling me you would turn that down? You'd sure never get to be queen of anywhere else, even a backwater like Cadenda."

The hay cart hit a low spot in the dirt road, with an ominous creak and a sudden lurch that sent Alannys and Varilyn crashing into the hay bales. The cloak came flapping down on top of them.

"Sorry about that," Cardoth called. Alannys couldn't help noticing he didn't sound particularly sorry.

Varilyn helped Alannys sit up, then righted the hay bales. She took up the cloak and with a heavy sigh began to arrange it into a shade again. "Don't put words in my mouth, Cardoth. Queen of Ravanmark? Of course it would be wonderful—what girl would turn down the chance to be queen of the most powerful, most advanced, most prosperous nation on the planet?"

"That's what I thought," Prince Cardoth said. Alannys didn't have to look at him to see the smirk on his face.

"But that isn't everything. It isn't even the most important thing."

"What?" Cardoth clearly hadn't expected that.

"Being happy is the most important thing. Period. Whether you are a queen or a peasant, this is true."

"What are you saying? Varilyn, where did you learn this madness you are spouting? Certainly not from our father!"

"It's Ravanmark." Varilyn's voice was soft, almost reverential. "This place is magical. Spend some time here, as I have. It will change you, make you more human than anyone you've met in Cadenda. And then how will you be happy with yourself, knowing you've killed innocents to get what you have? How will you be happy sitting on a throne you've stolen by force, for no better reason than greed?"

Prince Cardoth said nothing.

Varilyn frowned. "And how will you be happy, sitting on a throne that you will have only because you helped your father to steal another throne that belonged to a good, noble man who had never done you any wrong, a man you allowed to be killed for no better reason than greed?"

"That's enough." Cardoth's words had razor edges.

"But Cardoth..."

"No, I'm serious. I won't tolerate any more. We are about to ride through a town. I need absolute silence back there. People can't know you two are here."

Princess Varilyn's face hardened as Alannys watched. Her lips drew into a thin, tight line, and suddenly there were flecks of steel in her eyes that had not been there before. "I see. I suppose in that case you leave me no choice."

"What are you up to?" Cardoth sounded curious, but not unduly concerned.

Varilyn took a deep breath. Her hands clenched into tight fists in her lap. "Simply this. I am jumping out of this cart. I'm going to find as many people as I can, and I'm going to tell them what's going on, and I'm going to get them to help me."

"You're mad! No one is going to help you—they'll all think you're mad, too."

"Perhaps. Some of them certainly will. But some of them will listen. And some of them will help me. I've put up with this as long as I can. It's *wrong*, Cardoth. So we come to it; you have a choice to make. Either start behaving like a reasonable, noble man—like a prince. Or I'll expose everything."

The cart rolled to a stop. Alannys heard the solid thump of Prince Cardoth's boots hitting the dirt, and she froze, listening for some clue to where he was going, what he was doing. He climbed up into the back of the cart, stepping over hay bales and pushing them out of the way as he approached, rocking the little cart with every step. Every muscle in her body tensed—he did not look pleased.

"I'll give you this much," he said, reaching over their heads to pull a rope out from under the driver's bench. "You've got stones, both of you."

"Cardoth, please," Varilyn said. "There's still time to stop this."

"No. Things are already in motion; we can't go back now. The only way out is through." He pushed Varilyn over and hauled her arms behind her, tying them with the rope.

"Stop this! Cardoth, what's wrong with you?"

"Nothing!" The single word was a blistering shout,

echoing with the sound of a man's last thread of control breaking. He stood there a moment, panting raggedly, regarding his bound sister. Gradually his breathing slowed and his red face cleared. "Nothing is wrong with me. The crazy thing is that your plan might have worked, if you had kept your mouth shut about it. You just had to give me one last chance. But I suppose that's you—so *noble*, so...so Varilyn. I suffer none of your compunctions. I am just a minor prince, doing his duty for his father and his kingdom."

"But you don't have to—"

"Yes, I do. I have to do it." His tone was impassive. He folded another black scarf, and gagged Varilyn with it as easily as he had gagged Alannys, hours before. "But I don't have to like it."

He tossed the cloak over the two of them and turned quickly away, leaving the low, quiet words ringing in the uneasy darkness that surrounded Alannys.

♬

Riding through whatever little town happened to be in their path, tied up and gagged in the back of a hay cart, covered with a leather cloak and piled over with bales of hay, was not the most uncomfortable thing Alannys had ever done.

But it had to be in the top ten. Easy. Lying there in the jostling, squeaking darkness, breathing the same stale air over and over, Alannys discovered claustrophobic tendencies she had never even known she had. She wondered what Varilyn was making of all this. What a way for a princess to travel!

She thought about everything that had happened since she went with Dorramon to the Singari camp. All of her memories after Prince Cardoth brought her the wine were wonky; it was tempting to write it all off as fevered hallucination.

But obviously at least some of what she had witnessed that night was real. Her bathtub may never have overflowed with wine, but Prince Cardoth had certainly abducted her from her rooms. She had a sinking feeling that King Rathmar had been real too, and his ruthless, unnecessary murder. Jomain had never liked her, but he had tried to defend her, and he'd been cut down like an animal for his trouble.

It felt like hours later when the hay cart creaked to a stop. She could hear the slight sounds of Cardoth disembarking, could feel the shifting motions of the cart as he climbed into the back and started moving hay bales.

The cloak suddenly lifted and Alannys found herself blinking in the sudden rush of cool air and bright sunlight. Before her eyes had even adjusted to the sudden change, the prince had turned and untied Varilyn. "Look, I'm sorry," he said. "Do you think I wanted to do that? You were being unreasonable."

Only then did Alannys see the tear tracks staining Varilyn's face.

"I'm serious," Cardoth said. "I'm the only one in the family who actually likes you, you know that. Haven't I always tried to be kind to you? Haven't I always considered your feelings? You would be mad to hold a grudge over something like this. Utterly unreasonable."

"Sure, Cardoth," Varilyn said. "You've got two unwilling women bound in the back of a *hay cart,* hauling them away while you work to put your father on another man's throne. But I'm the unreasonable one." She rubbed her shoulders and turned away.

Cardoth stared at his sister's back, and Alannys thought she had never seen his expression quite so dark. What was he thinking? She had no way to tell. And she found that a bit disconcerting, since her fate hung on whatever was going through his mind. She hadn't forgotten he had spent three months trying to kill her.

He reached down suddenly and grabbed her by the arm, hauling her up to stand next to him. Her feet and legs felt numb and useless, and she stumbled.

"Quit that," Cardoth snapped, apparently operating under the delusion that she was being difficult on purpose. "I'm not going to do anything to you. I only thought you might want to eat with us." He untied the scarf around her head.

"Sorry," she gasped, and then stood there in a dumbfounded kind of disbelief. If her arms had been free, she would have smacked her face into her palm. After everything that had happened to her at this man's hands—she'd been drugged, kidnapped, bound and gagged, and hauled away from her home—the first thing she said was *sorry?* The word had come out of her mouth, but she couldn't believe it. It just didn't make sense.

And yet...Prince Cardoth seemed abashed by it. His face flushed red, and he yanked the ropes roughly off her arms without meeting her gaze. "You don't need to apologize. I know this isn't what you wanted, and it hasn't been easy for you. Get down off this cart and we'll have something to eat."

He turned away and hopped down from the cart, leading Princess Varilyn out into the meadow next to the narrow, worn dirt road. Alannys watched them go, rubbing her sore shoulders and thinking about the first sign of humanity she had possibly ever seen from Prince Cardoth.

♫

Alannys found Prince Cardoth and Princess Varilyn flopped down in the new grass, eating dried meat and fruit. It didn't look like a very tasty meal, but since it was well into the afternoon and none of them had eaten anything all day, nobody was complaining.

"Come, eat," Cardoth said, gesturing to a waxed paper packet on the ground, presumably containing food for her.

"I will," she said. "In a minute." She paced back and forth, stretching out her legs, swinging her arms to loosen up her sore muscles.

The prince watched her thoughtfully. "If I didn't know

better, I'd think you were warming up for a fight."

"What?" She looked at him in surprise, but there was no trace of humor on his face — as far as she could tell, he was entirely serious. "Then it's a good thing you do know better. I'm just sore. I learned ages ago that I'm no match for you in a fight."

Cardoth laughed, but the sound was as humorless as his expression. "Good. This would be a very inconvenient time to battle you again. You make yourself altogether too difficult to kill."

Varilyn flinched as if she had been struck. "How can you speak so casually of attempting to murder a woman? Honestly, you don't even seem like my brother anymore."

Alannys eased herself down onto the ground, and opened up the waxed paper packet. Inside she found dried fruit and meat like the others were eating. Her impressions had been correct — it didn't really taste like much, but she was so hungry it didn't matter.

Prince Cardoth tore off another bite of dried meat with his teeth, making the gesture seem unnecessarily vicious. "That's a hell of a thing to say. I've done nothing wrong. I've done only my duty. Shirking that duty, now that would have been dishonorable."

"Dishonorable?" Varilyn's voice rose in disbelief. "There's no *honor* in this, Cardoth, however you slice it!"

Alannys was inclined to agree. She could see Cardoth closing in on himself, though, and she worried that by attacking him — even though he richly deserved it — Varilyn might be encouraging him to dig into his position. So she swallowed her own blistering urge to lash out, replayed his reaction to her apology like a mantra in her head, and forced herself to address him calmly, avoiding anything that sounded like blame. "You've mentioned your duty several times, my Lord Prince. Do you mean your duty to your father? It sounds like the plans here are his."

Cardoth looked surprised, but he was still willing to

talk, which Alannys took as a win. "Well, yes, there certainly is that. It's dangerous to disobey the King of Cadenda, even if he is your father. But honestly, it goes deeper than that. I have a duty to my country, as a prince and as a man. Tell me, Alannys, what is your impression of Cadenda?"

Now it was Alannys's turn to be surprised. "I...don't know." She thought about it a moment, working her way through a dried perapple slice. "You probably know I've only been here a few months. I know that King Caleb was from Cadenda, and he was well-loved. I know Ambassador Thell comes from Cadenda, and I don't like him at all. But I'm afraid I know nothing about the country itself."

Cardoth laughed harshly. "Actually, that may tell you a lot. People in Ravanmark don't think much about Cadenda, and why should they? They have everything they need, and they've been busy for the last thousand years doing fantastic things with it."

The bitterness in his tone took her aback. "You're upset that Ravanmark has advanced so much? I don't understand. Does Cadenda not have everything its people need?"

"It isn't that. It's more...oh, I don't even have words to describe it."

"I do," Varilyn said suddenly. "The issue my brother is dancing around so adeptly is jealousy, simple as that."

"Now that's not fair," Cardoth objected.

"Fair or not, it's the truth." Varilyn turned to Alannys. "Now look. Ravanmark and Cadenda are the only country-continents in the world. Cadenda is a fair bit smaller than Ravanmark, but aside from that they are very much the same, at least physically."

"We don't have Talented people," the prince grumbled.

Varilyn waved a hand in his direction. "See, that's a fine example of the point I'm trying to make. Cadenda may be smaller in size, but we have more abundant natural resources. But instead of concentrating on using those resources to do amazing things, we prefer to gripe about the amazing things Ravanmark does, and hold grudges over anything they have that we perceive as an advantage." She directed a hard glare at her brother. "Cadenda can never be happy being Cadenda while it wants so badly to be Ravanmark."

"Whatever you say," Prince Cardoth said stiffly, but he wouldn't look at either of them. "It's Ravanmark's fault the world is in this mess anyway. Perhaps it is time for a change of leadership here."

"Ravanmark's fault?" Alannys echoed. "I don't understand."

"Tsk." Varilyn shook her head. "How could you understand? It's completely mental. I'm sorry, Cardoth; I don't mean to offend you or anyone else who thinks that way—I know it's a popular viewpoint. But it just doesn't make sense, and if you were thinking about it rationally you would see that."

"I think I liked you better when you were gagged," Cardoth muttered.

Princess Varilyn laughed. It was a light, silvery sound, like the tinkling of bells. "You see, Lady Alannys, my brother—along with probably the majority of people in the world, outside Ravanmark—holds Ravanmark solely responsible for the Rending of the World."

"The Rending?" Alannys said. "But I thought the Rending was the act of one man."

"Strictly speaking, I suppose it was. But that act didn't occur in a vacuum, you know. It was the culmination of a war. And after the Rending, it isn't as though everyone who fought for Soth wound up in Ravanmark, while every other country was filled with those who opposed him. Ravan herself led the forces against him, and she founded the royal line here! Yet people like my brother can talk about the necessity of a change of leadership. It's just rationalization—what my family wants is to take over

Ravanmark, because they covet it. The rest is nonsense. All the world is descended from those who fought for or against Soth, but only Ravanmark carries the bloodguilt for that. It's ridiculous."

"It's the way of things," Cardoth said. "Why should we carry guilt for the Sothwar? Cadenda didn't even exist at that time."

"Neither did Ravanmark! None of the countries of today existed until after the Rending, so why should only one of them bear the blame for it?"

Varilyn was shouting in frustration, her voice more cutting and shrill than Alannys had ever heard it. Her headache flared in response, and she slumped, pressing her hand to her forehead.

"Oh, I'm sorry!" Varilyn cried, placing a sympathetic hand on Alannys's back. "You must feel awful. Deadly nightshade will do terrible things to a person—you've been managing so well, I quite forgot."

Alannys twisted her head around, peering up at the princess out of one eye. "Deadly nightshade?"

"Yes." Varilyn's gaze was hard and unyielding, and it was directed over Alannys's shoulder. Alannys pushed herself upright, and found Prince Cardoth sitting right next to her, holding out an uncorked leather bottle.

"I am sorry about that," he said, looking everywhere but at her. "I know that was dishonorable. I didn't have a lot of choice—I needed to get you out of the palace without you raising any alarm or causing any fuss. I know that you're quite capable of defending yourself."

"So you put deadly nightshade in the wine you gave me?"

"Well, yes. That was my father's idea, actually—he said the juice from the berries is sweet, so you wouldn't notice. He gave me enough to kill you several times over, though —I put only a tiny fraction of that in your wine."

"Yes." Alannys struggled to sort through the hallucinations and remember what had really happened the night before. "I seem to remember that King Rathmar wasn't too pleased to see me. I don't understand—you hunted me for three months, and attacked me half a dozen different times. What was all that? Did you never intend to kill me at all?"

"Oh, no, I assure you I was quite serious." Cardoth still didn't look at her, but he sent his sister an apologetic look. "At that time, we thought the best way to get King Dorramon to break the engagement would be to kill you — in his mourning, he wouldn't ever have agreed to marry anybody else, and then we would have had our war, and far quicker. We also would have removed the biggest threat Ravanmark had to offer against us—you."

"But that part hasn't changed," Alannys said. "If you thought I was dangerous then, you must realize I'm still dangerous now. So why am I still here?"

"Of course I *know,*" Cardoth said. "Why do you suppose you've been gagged for the last twelve hours? Don't think I let you eat from the goodness of my heart—I would have been happy just to let you sit in the wagon. But I don't need you getting sick—and especially after the nightshade, I'll wager I could gut you before you could sing enough to harm me."

Alannys swallowed hard. She couldn't even argue it— he was right. Her food felt stuck in her throat, and she drank from the bottle, hoping to hide her discomfort.

"But it's a different kind of danger, now," he continued. "We regarded you as a threat then because of your popularity, because of the power you have from the public perception of you as the Redeemer, and because of your proximity to the King of Ravanmark. We were worried more about political power, do you see? Coming from Cadenda, we weren't certain if this music of yours actually held any power at all, or if that was just a legend that pleased the commoners. We surely never would have imagined anything like what you apparently do possess."

Alannys froze. Her mind hung on the word

'apparently.' How much did he know? "You didn't believe in Talent? Wasn't a painter helping you follow me?"

"What?" He looked completely boggled, frowning at her over a strip of dried beef. "Nobody helped me follow you, Alannys. I'm the best at what I do."

"I...I see. What changed your mind, then?"

"What, indeed?" Prince Cardoth gazed off into the distance as though he wasn't really seeing a thing that was there. "I am not quick to change my mind, Alannys. You might even be forgiven for calling me stubborn."

"The truth," Varilyn said sourly, "should never be a crime."

The corner of Cardoth's mouth twitched, the only outward sign that he'd heard her at all. "My opinions change slowly, but they do change. At first I thought the stories of your Talent were tales made up to entertain the populace, but something happened in Garrant, there was no denying that. Something I couldn't explain or ignore. And Pinevale...and your friends have a peculiar penchant for surviving wounds that I know damn well should be mortal. But it was your king who convinced me."

"Dorramon?" Alannys said. "I don't understand. He did everything he could to keep you away from any kind of music."

"Yes, and isn't that odd? He's the first Talented King of Ravanmark ever. But he never mentions it, never uses it to please his friends or threaten his enemies. I could understand his protectiveness of you; after all, he thought I was trying to win you. But for the king himself to ride out to a Singari encampment, just to ensure they did not perform for us..." Cardoth shook his head, staring out over the meadow.

"I see." Her voice grated in her throat, tight and uncomfortable.

"Do you? This is where I disagree with my father. He feels the only thing to do with such a power is destroy it. I feel such a power might be useful, if put to the proper purpose."

"Useful." The word settled into her mind with a click — Cardoth really hadn't spared her from the goodness of his heart. "I'm here because you think I might be useful."

"No, my Lady, you are here because I *know* you'll be useful. Look, suppose this plays out according to my father's plans, and the citizens take arms and support him. He wins the throne of Ravanmark. Then what?"

Alannys bit her lip. What he was describing was her worst nightmare, and she couldn't bear to contemplate it. She shook her head.

Prince Cardoth watched her a moment, rubbing at his jaw as though her stricken expression bothered him. Finally he looked away. "Well. Father isn't going back to Cadenda, obviously. The royal family has been working toward this takeover for generations. Caleb may have been well-loved here, but at home he's a coward and a traitor who failed in the single mission he came here for — establishing Cadenda's rule over Ravanmark once and for all. If my father gets his hands on the throne of Ravanmark, he's keeping it."

Alannys stared at her hands in her lap. Did they always look that pale? She concentrated on them, breathing deeply in and out, trying not to consider the situation Cardoth described. "What has that to do with me?" She almost managed to keep her voice from trembling.

"Can't you guess? If my father takes the throne, the very first thing he's going to do is purge every Talented person in Ravanmark. All those Redeemer's Stewards you've created, all those Singari you've trained — they will all be executed, along with any others he can find. Don't doubt that you would die with them, if you remained."

"I don't."

"The second thing he'll do is move Crown Prince Vox here as well, to get his line firmly entrenched and establish a successor. I'm the second son. Do you see what that means?"

"Yes." She was doing her best to stay neutral, to regard this conversation as though it had nothing to do with her. Cardoth told her all of this as if it was important—and no doubt it was, but if she responded with even a fraction of the anger and outrage she felt, he would tie her up and throw her back in the wagon, and that would be the end of her information-gathering. "You would be the King of Cadenda."

"Just so." He sounded as though he wanted to remain neutral too, and she appreciated the effort. But she couldn't help hearing the tiny glimmer of pride that crept into his voice, and it made her want to strangle him. "But here's the problem, Alannys. I can't imagine any way that would be a smooth transition. The royal family has been after Ravanmark for years, but the people..." He shook his head. "The people aren't going to be happy when their king abdicates and takes the crown prince with him. I'm going to be taking over the rule of Cadenda at a very turbulent time, surrounded by people who would like very much to unseat me for their own ends."

"How very unpleasant for you." Her best efforts couldn't quite keep the sarcasm from bubbling into her tone.

Prince Cardoth looked at her askance. "Cadenda may not be much, but once it's mine, I would like to keep it. That's where you come in."

"A weapon." She didn't know why it surprised her. It was Lord Malrec all over again. In the end, no matter how much she did, no matter how much she changed things, she would never be able to save Talented people from those who sought to use them like tools for their own ends. "You want me to be your weapon."

"Well, yes, of course. It seems to me that I could surmount any opposition with you by my side."

"By your...side?"

"You haven't thought this through very well, have you? I can't have a musician running around Cadenda who isn't allied with me. In Cadenda, my house will become your house, my future your future, my interests your interests. Do you understand what I am saying?"

Alannys thought with cold, creeping horror that she probably did, but she couldn't bring herself to acknowledge it. "No." No, indeed — it was too awful. It really *was* Lord Malrec all over again.

Princess Varilyn rose suddenly to her feet and stalked a few steps away. She looked like she was just trying to stretch her limbs, but her mouth was set in a tight, thin line. Alannys wondered if she found this all pretty horrible, too.

Cardoth drew a deep breath, as if steeling himself. "As Queen of Cadenda, your fate will be tied to mine. In fighting for yourself you will also fight for me, and our paths will be aligned." He paused, letting his words sink in, and she bit down on her tongue, hard, trying to keep herself quiet.

"So that's it." Apparently tongue-biting wasn't an effective means of silencing herself. She hadn't even managed to keep the venom out of her tone. "I don't know why I thought you were any better than your father. This isn't about duty, and it isn't about conscience or less bloodshed or a higher calling. It's about a weapon — it's about nothing more than your convenience."

Prince Cardoth scratched the back of his neck, making a point of not looking at her. "Of course not. There's more to it than that. With you as queen — if we brought you here to conceive and deliver, we could re-introduce Talent to Cadenda — and it would be in the royal line! Think of it, Alannys — the monarchy would be invincible!"

Alannys was thinking of it, all right, and the entire scenario was turning her stomach. "Oh, a weapon *and* a brood mare! That makes everything better. Why did I ever doubt you?"

Cardoth did look at her then, and the anger she saw simmering in his eyes would have given her pause, had she not been so far beyond angry herself. "Don't think this situation appeals much to me, either! What part of this is bad for you? You are getting to bring your precious Talents back, aren't you? You're surviving the fate of your peers in Ravanmark. You will still be a queen."

"That's not the point! I don't care about titles, Cardoth, and I certainly don't want to be *your* queen!"

"Are you mad?" he flared back. "Do you have any idea how many women in Cadenda would give anything to have the chance I'm giving you?"

"I don't care!"

Prince Cardoth was suddenly very still. "What is it about King Dorramon? What is so different about you? I'm handsome, Alannys, and that is enough for most women. I'm royalty, and that is enough for the rest. I've never had a woman reject any offer I cared to make her. But you are refusing to marry me — refusing the one prize they all sought?"

Alannys clenched her hands into fists so tight her nails bit into her palms, drawing ragged, panting breaths and trying to force herself to calm down. She didn't need the reminder that this world wasn't her world, and she could never really fit in. "Yes. This isn't about how you look, Cardoth, and it isn't about being a queen. I can't be happy if I'm married to someone I don't love. If you can't see that, I don't know how to explain it to you."

"Love." Cardoth made the single word a derisive snort. "You're an idiot, Alannys, clinging to a ridiculous fairy-tale notion like love, when I'm offering you real-world position, power, and benefits."

"Is that what you think? Let me tell you what I think. I think it's pathetic that you can't even imagine why I would refuse. I'm sorry, but it is."

"I'm sorry, too." He stood up, and before she could push herself to her feet, the black gag pulled tight into her mouth again. "But you have no choice in this, Alannys. You will come to Cadenda, and you will serve the purpose

I have given you."

He yanked the scarf into a knot behind her head. As soon as he released it, she scrambled to her feet, intending to tackle him and fight with everything she had.

But before she could even get turned around, something blunt thudded into her skull, jarring her entire body. She staggered sideways, and the world went dark.

♫

Alannys came to her senses bouncing and uncomfortable. She knew without looking that she was back in the hay cart. Her hands and feet were bound, and she was gagged, but she finally felt clear-headed. Before she even opened her eyes, holding herself still and keeping her breathing even so her captors would suspect nothing, Alannys opened the mindlink.

Dorramon? Dorramon, are you there?

The answer wasn't immediate. The brief silence — just long enough for her to worry — felt stunned, somehow, disbelieving. *Alannys! Oh, thank the Muses — Alannys, I've been trying to contact you for hours! Why didn't you answer me?*

I couldn't. I'm sorry, Dorramon. Cardoth drugged me — deadly nightshade, he said — and I couldn't use the mindlink. It was there, I just couldn't use it.

Oh. The single word was a sigh, dripping with relief. *Oh, thank the Muses. That's the first good news I've had all day.*

Good news? I just told you Prince Cardoth drugged me. I'm being abducted, and — she stopped suddenly. Maybe the rest of Cardoth's plans for her would be a little upsetting to disclose just yet. *And — what part of that is good news?*

Dorramon laughed. It was a strong laugh, sincere and yet oddly tense. *All of it. Honestly, Alannys, all of it is good news. Do you know what the story is here in the palace? They're saying that you and Prince Cardoth ran away together. That you've eloped.*

E — eloped? She couldn't hide her surprise. But it did

have a certain logic to it, especially in light of what she had heard at lunch. It was almost sort of true.

Oh, yes. King Rathmar himself has put forth the story. And it was noticed how doggedly and openly Cardoth pursued you, and people are talking about that as well.

I am certain that was his intent. The man doesn't have any love in him — I don't think he has any softer emotions at all. He just wanted everyone to believe the story, when the time came.

Well, it worked. They believe, all right. Dorramon's voice in her mind was sour — and oddly sharp.

What about you, Dorramon? she asked, suddenly curious.

Me? I — I knew they were up to no good, of course. But then...your weapons were gone, and you were dressed for riding...and your ring, Alannys. Your ring and your bracelet, and I couldn't imagine you would ever leave those behind, and you wouldn't answer me when I contacted you. I have to admit I was worried. Is Varilyn with you?

Yes. Cardoth is smuggling us through the country in a hay cart. What's going on?

A hay cart! Dorramon paused, swearing. *Well, that explains why none of the riders I sent after you found you. They're searching for people on horses, on main roads.*

We're definitely not using main roads. And no one is going to see Varilyn or me at a glance. But why did you ask about her?

There was a brief, hesitant silence. It felt ominous, and Alannys found herself holding her breath before she remembered she was supposed to be breathing evenly. *I'm afraid things have deteriorated alarmingly in your absence, Alannys. King Rathmar is whipping people into quite a frenzy. He claims that I murdered Princess Varilyn.*

Mur — murdered...

Not personally, mind you. I don't think anyone has gone so far as to suggest that. Yet. But sometime last night, Princess Varilyn went missing. Her room at the inn was found ransacked and bloody this morning. Ambassador Thell was there, dead, and the body of a Royal Guard. Rathmar's story was that Thell died defending Varilyn from the attacking Royal Guards. There was even a royal medallion there.

That was mine, Alannys said at once. *I'm sorry. Cardoth had it taken from my room. Thell didn't kill Jomain – Rathmar did. Jomain – the guard – tried to stop them from taking me.*

Dorramon swore again. *We're being set up, Alannys.*

Yes. Watch yourself, Dorramon. Cardoth told me this war has been their goal here from the start. He says Crown Prince Vox is bringing three more warships right now, and they hope to stir the people to take up arms against you as well.

Alannys, where are you? I'll send Grayble and the guards for you right away.

No, you can't! You must keep Captain Grayble there with you!

But Alannys… Dorramon hesitated. *I really don't know who else to send. Any of the other guards might turn out to be traitors, who would kill you instead of bringing you home. He's the only one I can trust.*

And that's exactly why you must keep him there, don't you see? You can't send Grayble, you absolutely must not send Grayble – you've got to take care of the Great Palace before you do anything else. If you've got Royal Guards you can trust, keep them close, because you're going to need them. Deal with Rathmar.

But – but you…

I'll be fine. Prince Cardoth isn't going to hurt me – he's decided I'll be useful as a weapon. I am not in mortal danger. But Ravanmark – Ravanmark may well be. They intend to take over, Dorramon. Save Ravanmark. Worry about me later.

Alannys – be careful.

Don't worry, she told him, filling her mind with false confidence. *I won't let anything happen to me. I've got a promise to keep, remember?*

As do I. I love you, Alannys.

And I love you, Dorramon.

She lay still and slack in the silent darkness after the mindlink closed, thinking about everything they had said. They were in a very precarious situation – her, Dorramon, even Ravanmark itself. She wondered how they would ever get out of this. She wondered what would be left if they did. But most of all, she wondered if she and Dorramon would ever be able to keep that promise they had made to each other.

♫

Alannys opened her eyes, and right away she sort of wished she hadn't. She was lying on her side in the hay cart. Directly in front of her she could see Princess Varilyn, asleep, curled up in a tight ball under a little shelter she'd made of hay bales, with Alannys's leather cloak as a roof. The sky loomed dark and gray; enormous clouds like something in a watercolor painting spattered light rain over them.

But Alannys was warm. She glanced down at herself and found a heavy black cloak covering her completely, tucked up around her chin.

She frowned at the dark improvised blanket. It was high time the world started making sense again; she'd had about all she could stand of the craziness that seemed to have blown in with the delegation from Cadenda. But whether it made sense or not, she had to admit that she knew where this cloak had come from.

Alannys writhed around on the floor of the hay cart, struggling against the restraints that bound her hands and feet. She managed to push herself upright just enough to see up onto the driver's bench. Prince Cardoth huddled there, cloakless, his arms crossed against the damp chill, his chin tucked down against his chest.

She heard something stir next to her, and looked over to see Princess Varilyn's wide eyes staring back at her from the little cave in the mountain of hay bales.

"Oh, you're awake!" The princess sounded relieved. "Honestly, Lady Alannys, it scared the very devil out of me when he hit you like that. I thought..." She shook her head, and pushed her hair back out of her face. "I suppose I should just be thankful you are stronger than I imagine you to be."

Varilyn helped her to sit up, and arranged the hay bales around them to block most of the rain, stretching the leather cloak across the top. It did help keep them drier, except for the splattering little bursts driven inside by the changing winds. Alannys's hair was already damp, and now that she was sitting up, it wanted to fall right into her eyes. Her shoulders, hips, and knees ached from being held so long immobile in unnatural positions. She squirmed around against the floor and the bales, trying to find a way to sit where something didn't hurt. The effort, it seemed, was wasted. She shook her head, trying to flip her hair out of her eyes.

It fell right back in, and the gusting wind blew water into her face.

"I'm sorry." Varilyn pushed Alannys's hair back out of her eyes, and reached over to dry her face with a handkerchief that was only slightly less damp than their clothes. It surprised Alannys how much better she felt, just having a dry face and hair that wasn't prickling her eyes.

The wind abruptly changed direction, and the cloak came flapping down on top of them. A snort of laughter sounded from the front of the wagon.

"Soth's eye," Varilyn muttered. "Cardoth, would it kill you to procure us a few things to make this journey less miserable?"

"No," he shot back, "but you're barking mad if you think I'll do it. I haven't got a whit of interest in making the passage more comfortable. As soon as your dear friend there is comfortable, she's going to start considering means of escape. And I wouldn't put it past you to help her. I'd rather have you both occupied with concerns of basic comfort, thank you very much."

The glare Varilyn directed at the back of his head seemed to indicate she had many things she would have liked to say. Instead, she sighed noisily and rebuilt the little shelter. "I really am sorry about all of this," she said to Alannys. "I would have happily married King

Dorramon, or not—whatever he wished would have been fine. But I certainly never wished any harm to come to him. I never had very many friends, Lady Alannys, but I always counted him among them."

She settled in beside Alannys, and, casting a quick, nasty glance in Cardoth's direction, she began to speak.

ed ed ed

When Princess Varilyn was six years old, her nanny told her a story. It was an occasion that stuck with her, because Varilyn very rarely got to hear stories. She sat listening, wide-eyed and unblinking, to the very end, hoping to memorize the magical experience so that she could replay it for herself later, alone in her dark room.

It was a story of six princes of six mighty kingdoms, born on the same day. The great sun god stood by each of their cradles, and over each infant he spoke a single word. The story showed how each prince's life was influenced from beginning to end, summarized completely by the word the sun god had given him.

Varilyn thought a lot about the story, lying in her bed long after she should have been asleep. She tried to imagine a world with six mighty nations, but she couldn't get her head around it. Her world had only one powerful kingdom—Ravanmark—and from the way the grownups talked, there wasn't room for anyone else with it around. Ravanmark ruled every thought and action of her parents —and a good deal of her own, too, in the years since she had become engaged to Ravanmark's Crown Prince Dorramon.

Now he, Varilyn imagined, must have been like one of the fine princes in the story. What word, she wondered, would mark his life? Strength? Valor? Wisdom? A word so wonderful she didn't even know it yet?

As for herself, she had no doubt. If the sun god had whispered one word as he leaned over her crib, she knew exactly what that word had been.

Failure.

It had shadowed Varilyn her entire life, enveloping her like a shroud, claiming everything that she did, everything that she was. She had been a failure literally her entire life. As the firstborn, it had been her place to be a noble prince, tall and strong—much like she imagined Prince Dorramon to be. Her duty was the conquering of Ravanmark, the bending of the most powerful nation on the planet to the will of Cadenda. She would drink in the glory of the conquest; she would bathe in it, and she would bestow it like rain across her country and her people. It was her destiny.

Only she'd had the ill courtesy to be born female, and in the single, blistering failure, her entire destiny cracked, splintered around her, and what was left was misshapen and cruel. In her earliest memories, she saw her father, speaking to her in cold dislike.

"You were to be my prince, Varilyn," he said, "my brave, conquering prince who would win Ravanmark and bring honor to our house. But now—now you are only the princess we can offer as bait so that someone else may conquer."

She didn't remember if that had made her cry. She supposed it must have, at some point. She had been very small, after all—somewhere in the black mists of her past it must have shocked her to hear people she looked up to talk about her like that.

Her mother had taken a rather more personal view of the situation—to her, Varilyn was the wedge driven between herself and her previously-adoring husband. Even Varilyn could see that Rathmar blamed the queen for his first child's appalling lack of maleness. If Varilyn had expected any comfort from that corner, she would surely have been disappointed. Her father, her mother, her nannies and guards and tutors—all of them felt the shame of association with the firstborn who was not a boy, and all of them resented her for it. Her only saving grace, her one redeeming factor, was the role she could play in the new plans for conquering Ravanmark. Even Rathmar had to admit, however grudgingly, that success was more likely when they could approach their enemy under the guise of friendship, with a royal engagement rendering them seemingly trustworthy. For this single reason they tolerated her, and the little princess swore to herself to do all that she could to help further their goals, so that they would find no further fault with her, and perhaps one day, even grow to like her.

And then she met Prince Dorramon.

Varilyn was sixteen when her parents sent her to visit Ravanmark. She had heard so much about the place, for so long, that actually getting to go there felt like visiting a magical, fairy-tale land. Her excitement made her buoyant; she could hardly keep herself in her seat while her maids dressed her, and tended to her hair, and packed her things.

"Calm yourself, Varilyn." Her mother stood near the door, watching the proceedings disapprovingly, arms folded. "You seem to have entirely the wrong attitude. This is not a voyage for pleasure, child — it's a chore. You are meeting the man you will subjugate. Royal marriages are never about love, but yours...yours is nothing but conquest and domination. You must not *ever* form any real feelings for this man. Do you understand me? This is of utmost importance. *Never.*"

"Yes, Mother." Varilyn was only paying half attention. Of course she understood — how could she forget? She had heard the same, endless refrain ever since her engagement.

And then she arrived in Ravanmark, and it actually *was* a magical, fairy-tale land, at least for her. People in the streets cheered the processional on her way to the Great Palace, and once she actually got there, it was even better.

King Caleb was not the high point of her visit, but then, she had never expected that he would be. He looked at her unsmilingly, through eyes eerily reminiscent of her father's in a lighter hue, and gave her the unnerving impression that he had a very good idea what she and her family were up to. Given what she knew about him, he probably did. She avoided him when she could. To Queen Farrine, she was just an annoyance; little more than an object labeled 'Dorramon's Betrothed,' that must be kept placated if not entirely happy.

But the palace staff adored her. They catered gladly to whims she hadn't even expressed, eager to curry the favor of the future queen. She had never before been surrounded by so many people so delighted by every move she made, every opinion she expressed.

And fourteen-year-old Dorramon was the cherry on top of her magical experience. He bent low as he kissed her hand, and his bright blue eyes looked directly into hers when he said, "Welcome," and seemed to mean it. She had never had the full, focused attention of such a handsome boy before, and it made her face warm and her skin tingly.

It wasn't just her, of course. Over the coming days she saw him interact with enough people to realize that he exuded warmth and acceptance to every person he spoke to, even servants. But he was the only one who ever talked that way to *her*, and that meant something to her that she could not ignore. Prince Dorramon was the first person ever to look at her and see her not as a burden, or a failure, or a pawn in someone's plans, but as who she was.

And he seemed to like who she was. She had never even imagined such a circumstance could be possible, and she couldn't help seeking out his company. Being with the prince made her happy — giddily happy — and she thought for the first time that she could understand why King Caleb had ultimately abandoned Cadenda's dark purpose, once he came to live here himself.

It wasn't all butterflies and rainbows, of course. Prince Dorramon was not the only person her age in the Great Palace. Varilyn never had to spend more than a few passing moments with Princess Delline, but she couldn't seem to avoid the one they called Arch-Prince Raman. She didn't know what an arch-prince was, but she knew what Raman was: her personal nemesis.

Raman confused her from the outset. She had not heard anything about Queen Farrine having more children, but Dorramon treated this boy as a brother. He was young—younger than Dorramon—and for whatever reason he clung tightly to the prince's company, as tightly as she did herself. Much as Dorramon saw her for herself and liked her for what she was, Raman looked at her for what she was, and disliked her for it.

Even that didn't bother her as much as it probably should have. Even that was better than anything she'd ever had at home.

"You have to give him some leeway," Dorramon told her, as they sat in the dining hall one evening. The king and queen had already excused themselves, and Princess Delline had followed shortly after. Raman stared at the tapestries across from him as though he could not hear their conversation. "He's new to the Great Palace, too. He could probably sympathize with you—I don't think he's quite comfortable here, either."

"I sympathize with nothing," Raman said flatly. His voice was so low they could both easily pretend they hadn't heard him, so they did.

"He is new here?" Varilyn couldn't quite conceal her surprise. She'd thought it was a bit odd that she hadn't heard about the birth of another prince, certainly—but not too odd to believe. Only the crown prince really mattered to Cadenda in the end. She had assumed that arch-prince was a title used in Ravanmark to further differentiate the princes who would not be ascending to the throne.

The smile Dorramon gave her was kind and not at all condescending. "Yes. He has only lived here since his parents passed away—he's a prince by adoption, you see, which is why he holds the title of arch-prince."

"Oh! My sympathies, Raman. I had no idea. I am most

sorry to hear of your loss."

"Stop it." Raman's voice was as hard as his face. "Always have just the right thing to say, don't you, Varilyn? And you, Dorramon—encouraging her the way you do. I've had just about enough of both of you."

Varilyn shrank back in shock. "I'm—I'm sorry if I offended you."

"Offended me? I should bloody well say so! Look, I don't agree with Dorramon. I don't see any similarity between us at all. I don't believe a thing you have done or a word you have said since you arrived has been genuine. You're manipulative, Varilyn, and I don't like that. You're making large of your helpless, unhappy self to cozy up to Dorramon."

She shook her head, fluttering her hands frantically in front of herself. Her heart pounded in her ears. She was used to this sort of denigration at home, but she had not expected it here. "No, no, that's not true! I—"

"My parents have been dead for nine months," he said coldly. "My entire town burned to ashes. But I never acted half as forlorn and needy as you do. You're pathetic."

She stared at him, stricken. His stony expression never wavered, and he turned from her to regard the tapestries again.

Tears stung the backs of Varilyn's eyes. Before she could embarrass herself further, she jumped from her chair and fled from the room.

♪

"Varilyn?" The voice was Dorramon's, and it wasn't very far away. To her surprise, he didn't sound angry. "Princess Varilyn, are you here?"

She didn't answer him. She hadn't stopped running until she'd made it to the courtyard in the middle of the keep. Ignoring the benches and the water garden, she had plowed into the trees. Between the tree trunks, the flowering bushes, and the carefully trimmed hedges, she had found a cave-like hollow, practically hidden from the outside, where she could huddle up and cry undetected. She wouldn't have thought Raman would be able to get to her so easily—back home, what he'd said would hardly have counted as mean. Here, though—she hadn't been prepared for it, she had been completely blind-sided. This place had changed her, she finally saw it clearly. She would feel out of place back home now. She could never really go back, and she realized all at once that she didn't even want to. She didn't want to help her father destroy this magical place, these magical people. Even Raman. She sniffed, wiped at her face, and held her breath, waiting for Dorramon's footsteps to fade.

Instead, the branches in front of her suddenly parted, and before she had come to terms with being discovered, Prince Dorramon had crawled in and sat down next to her.

Varilyn blinked at him in surprise. What should she say? What should she *do*? She wondered how quickly she could make it back out of her curious little hiding spot.

"There's no need to run away." Dorramon's low chuckle made her ears burn. "I'm sorry Raman said those things to you. I don't agree with him."

Varilyn had no idea how to answer him. Nobody had ever apologized to her for anything, not ever in her whole life. And now the Crown Prince of Ravanmark was apologizing to her, for something he didn't even do?

"You're going to do fine here, you know. This has been my favorite hiding spot since I was five years old. I don't know how you found it so quickly." He smiled crookedly at her. She couldn't tell what he made of her awkward silence, but he didn't seem to judge her for it. "Here. I brought you a strawberry tart. I don't know if you like them or not, but they're my favorite. I thought it might make you feel better. Will you eat it?"

She looked from his smiling face to the baked pastry. Did she like strawberry tarts? She didn't know—she had never had one. "If you'll share it with me," she said on a sudden impulse. She couldn't have said what had gotten into her — if he declined she would be too embarrassed to face him ever again.

Dorramon's smile broadened, crinkling the skin around his eyes. "Of course. Thank you."

Princess Varilyn sat in the calm, cool quiet of the courtyard garden, shoulder to shoulder with Dorramon, sharing her very first strawberry tart and fighting to believe her entire world wasn't changing around her. How could such a thing exist, in a world such as she had known? What did this *mean*?

She had known before she came to Ravanmark that Prince Dorramon encompassed her every idea of *noble*, defined the word for her completely. What she hadn't guessed was that the word might have meant something very different from anything she had ever imagined.

It wasn't until later, in the quiet darkness of the guest chambers, replaying the memory for the thousandth time, that she realized she was in even greater trouble than she had imagined.

She was developing real feelings for Prince Dorramon.

Varilyn smiled, lost in her memories, oblivious to the dirt on her face and the bits of hay stuck in her damp, disheveled hair. Between the cool evening air and the heavy mist, it was getting cold, but she didn't seem to notice that either.

Alannys thought she had never looked more like a princess.

"He made quite an impression on me," Varilyn said. Her voice sounded dreamy and far-away — the same way her eyes looked. "I had never met anyone so considerate, so kind. I still haven't."

Alannys couldn't suppress a wistful sigh of her own through the black scarf that gagged her. That was Dorramon, all right. He was still that way, even now, even after everything that had happened.

"What a load of sentimental rot." The voice was sharp

and sour, slicing through the nostalgic mood and leaving a shocked silence in its wake. "Kind, considerate—these are not kingly virtues. You may as well hang a sign on the man, Varilyn, that says 'Not Fit to Rule.'"

"I take exception to that." Varilyn sounded stiff. "There is no one better suited to rule Ravanmark, Cardoth. *No one*. I've never met a more perfect gentleman."

"Ballocks. You're just a manipulator scheming on the throne—and he's just the fool who fell for it."

"You're the fool." Varilyn said nothing beyond those few curt words, but her face was lined with sadness. She plainly believed that Cardoth meant what he said.

But Alannys thought about his words, flatly spoken but with no bite or venom in them. And she looked at the black cloak tucked around her, keeping her warm even in the chilling rain.

And she wondered: how hard would it be to hold to one's duty when one's conscience...and maybe even one's heart, if one actually had a heart...was elsewhere?

♫

The faint, cloud-streaked sun disappeared below the horizon, leaving Alannys alone in the cold night with only her many worries for company. Varilyn slept soundly, curled up in the hay bales nearby. Alannys didn't want to fall asleep; she didn't feel comfortable letting her guard down at all around Prince Cardoth—but it seemed she didn't have much choice. Whether it was the after-effects of being drugged, or the stress of her unwilling journey, Alannys started dozing as soon as it was dark. She napped, and when she woke she watched the misty clouds move in front of the moons, glowing softly in the night, and the distant stars glittering like jewels against the far-off velvet background of the sky. She wondered if Dorramon was seeing these same stars, back at the Great Palace. She wondered what the state of things was back there. Was he even where he could see stars?

That didn't make her feel any better. She pushed all of

that aside, closed her eyes, and thought her way through Princess Varilyn's story one more time.

She was napping when the cart suddenly lurched into the rough, grassy ground by the side of the dirt road, and stopped. She felt the wagon bounce as Cardoth hopped off the driver's bench. Alannys squirmed against the hay bales, trying to sit up.

"Don't move." Cardoth's voice came from the back of the wagon—she couldn't see him, but she could feel the cart jostle and realized he was climbing in. He looked over at Varilyn, sound asleep against the far side of the wagon, and then adjusted the cloak around Alannys. "We're going to stop for a few hours. I can't keep going like this...I was hoping to go straight to the harbor without stopping, but..." He trailed off, looking out into the brush and trees surrounding them almost as though he expected to find something looking back. "I've been going non-stop since the royal ship arrived in Ravanmark. Now that it's dark, I can't keep my eyes open. So I'm going to sleep here for a few hours. You may as well try to rest, too, while the wagon's stopped." He rearranged the hay bales so that neither she nor Varilyn could be seen from the road, then gave her a crooked grin. "Don't worry. We'll still make it to the ship in plenty of time."

He turned and left the wagon, sitting down against the trunk of a nearby tree, a black scarf pulled down over his face to help block the moonlight. She couldn't help noticing the way he seemed to drag himself around—she hadn't thought about it before, but he really must have been exhausted. That seemed like a good thing to know.

If only she had some way to make use of it.

She sighed, twisting her head around, trying her best to get a clear picture of their surroundings, without making enough noise to disturb Cardoth. The road they had been following was little more than a pair of bare-dirt wheel ruts here, with dense forest pushing in on both sides. Under all those trees with their heavy, new-growth tops, and the clouds obscuring the moonlight, she would defy Cardoth or anyone else to find her.

If she could just get to that forest.

Alannys tensed, testing her restraints. If only she had her hands free...or her feet...but sitting here with both trussed up like a roasting turkey didn't give her much in the way of options. Everything was tight against her efforts; the knots were good. What could she do? If only he had left her with something — anything — she could use!

Her desperate gaze landed on the driver's bench, and she realized that maybe, inadvertently, he *had* left her something she could use.

Songstrike was out of the question, of course — it was far too long; she would never even manage to get it out of its scabbard in such tight quarters, with her hands behind her back. But she distinctly remembered Thell holding her dagger as well. There was a chance, if she could get her hands on it, that even with her limited mobility she could manage to cut her bonds without also slicing her own wrists.

Not a very good chance, she had to admit.

But it was a chance, and right now she would take it. She kept her eyes glued to Prince Cardoth, watching for any sign that he was stirring, and she kept her ears alert for any sound that implied wakefulness. Moving as carefully as she could to avoid making the wagon creak — moving only a fraction of an inch at a time — she scooted herself over against the back of the wagon, and leaned forward, straining to push her hands up under the bench. It was an awkward, painful, over-extended position, but she held it, trying to feel her way to her dagger's leather sheath without making any obtrusive sounds. She closed her eyes, focusing on light, silent movements.

"Trying to escape, are we?"

She would have screamed without the gag. The words were a slight whisper, barely audible, but the dark shape of a man knelt in front of her, moonlight glinting off of the knife in his hands.

Then she realized this wasn't Prince Cardoth, come to dispatch her for her treachery. The shape in front of her was Chen, and even as she struggled to get her mind around it, he reached around behind her, pulling her arms out from under the bench so that he could cut them loose. He untied the scarf that was gagging her and freed her legs as well, before she even knew what to say.

"Chen!" Her whisper was barely louder than his, but her relief sounded clearly in it nonetheless. "I—thank you, I—what are you doing here?"

"Shh!" He held a finger to his lips, scanning around them for any sign that they had been overheard. She rubbed at her shoulders, trying to restore circulation to her arms. "I've been following you since you left the palace. These things make a lot of noise, you know, creaking by the camp in the middle of the night. And when I saw our dear cloaked assassin driving it...well, I had to follow, didn't I?"

"No," said a deep, rich voice behind him, not even bothering to whisper, "and I'm going to make you wish you hadn't."

♬

Chen whipped around in the dark hay wagon, his dagger held out in front of him, and Alannys could see Prince Cardoth looming there behind him, his curved blade at the ready.

Cardoth's eyes cut to her, as hard and unpleasant as two flints. "Get out of the wagon, Singari. I'll deal with you later—I can't have her singing at me."

Alannys didn't think she could have sung just then if her life depended on it—and it was certainly possible that it did. She was tired, sore, and shaky from being stuck in one position for hours, and still not entirely over her experience with deadly nightshade. Magic seemed utterly out of her reach just then. Cardoth couldn't know that...but she suspected that Chen might, just by looking at her. And Chen didn't have a chance against Cardoth—even if he'd had a proper sword, he was no match for the prince. He had to know that. But he stayed resolutely where he was, holding his knife out in front of him, shaking his head and swallowing hard. "I'm not moving. If you want her, you're going to have to go through me."

"I'd planned on it," Cardoth shot back. "Did you really think I didn't know you were following us? I've been playing this game a bit longer than you. Come on, then, and let's get this over with."

"No!" Alannys howled, pushing herself to her feet. "Leave him alone!"

"Cardoth!" Varilyn's outraged gasp was the first clue any of them had that she was awake. "Now you intend to cut down an innocent man? This has gone too far! Lady Alannys! Catch this!" She turned and reached under the driver's bench, hauled out the swordbelt with Songstrike still in its sheath, and tossed it to Alannys. Its solid weight slapped into her palm—it felt familiar, like a part of herself, and as soon as it began crooning its familiar songs in her mind, she started to feel like this might all work out after all.

Alannys pulled Songstrike out of the scabbard, dropped the belt where she was standing, and vaulted over the side of the hay wagon. She heard Cardoth swear, saw his dark form disappear over the back of the wagon. She could only dream of being that nimble right now—she thudded into the hard dirt with an impact that seemed to jar every bone in her body.

"What are you doing?" Chen demanded, whirling to face her over the side of the wagon. "Are you crazy? You can't fight him like that!"

"Maybe not, but no one else is going to die for me." She could barely feel her hands, but by the time Cardoth came around the side of the wagon, she had Songstrike in Ready position, doing her best to face him without letting on how sore and shaky she was. "You should stand down,

Cardoth. There's still time to do the right thing." She couldn't win this—she knew she couldn't, Chen was right —but she had to try. The alternative was giving up.

And she refused to give up.

Cardoth snorted unpleasantly, circling around her, eyeing her stance. "I am doing the right thing. I'm doing my duty."

"Your duty to whom? Your abominable father, who thinks faking his daughter's death is an acceptable way to raise public support? To your country, which apparently thinks jealousy is a good enough reason to invade an ally?"

"It doesn't matter! It's my *duty,* and I intend to see it done, no matter how much I may personally dislike it."

Alannys watched him circle, doing her best to follow him on her clumsy, half-asleep feet, and wondered—why wasn't he attacking her? He could have killed her three times over by now, especially in her state. Was he—was he deliberately stalling, giving her a chance to recover? Was he hesitating, because he knew on some level that she was speaking the truth? She pressed on, knowing her behavior might be reckless, knowing that it might yet get her killed. "That's bullshit, Cardoth. You are so good at pointing that out, when it comes from other people—it's a shame you're so insistent on serving it up yourself."

He roared and charged at her, and she barely managed to bring Songstrike up to block. The impact jarred her shoulders, and she dug her boots into the ground, fighting to hold him off. "Empty words, my Lady—easy to say for someone who knows nothing of duty."

"Nothing of duty?" She gathered what little strength she had left, and shoved him backwards with a grunt. "Why do you suppose I spent three months traveling the country, making myself a target, suffering people's fear and hatred? For the pleasure of our warm interludes?"

Cardoth dragged his sleeve across his forehead, and frowned. His long day—and the long night before—must have been telling on him as well...it wasn't like him to tire so easily. And she hadn't seen him spin once. "That hardly seems to count. You chose to do that. Nobody forced you."

"Nobody's forcing you, either," she said pointedly. He swung out with a slashing, spiteful middle attack, and she stumbled backward, narrowly avoiding it. "You choose your duty, Cardoth. It doesn't choose you."

"I don't expect you'd understand." His voice sounded strained, and she wondered if he was fighting against more than just her. He attacked again, forcing her back. Her foot came down on a stone, and she fell backwards, her hands slipping madly in the grass, trying to get away from him. "A man must do his duty, even when it is unpleasant."

She laughed, trying to sound braver than she felt. "You said that before, in House Orinthal. Do you remember the boy you injured there? He says that line is something adults use, to rationalize away their principles when it is convenient."

"*Convenient?* Do you imagine any part of this is convenient for me?"

"I do. I think it's a whole lot easier for you to kill me than take a good, hard look at what you've been doing, realize it's wrong, and try to make it right."

Cardoth took a single step towards her, and the cold, sharp tip of his sword was suddenly at her throat. She was afraid to move, afraid to breathe. He had her this time, had her dead to rights. He was too close even for singing—she would be dead before she got the first word out, if she could even summon up a song.

"No!" Chen stood nearby, dagger in hand, looking as though he was trying to find a way to use it that wouldn't get her killed. It reminded her of the first time she saw him, when he threw himself between her and Brutagar, trying to save her from her own big mouth. So this was how it ended. A shame he had to see her die, after everything he had been through.

"Relax, Singari," Cardoth said. "I'm not going to kill your woman." He turned away, jamming his curved blade back in the sheath.

"I—I..." Chen looked as though this all made about as much sense to him as it did to her. Finally he reached out and helped her to her feet. "She's not my woman. You know that."

Cardoth laughed, a dark and almost bitter sound. "I suppose I did know that. Perhaps I should say 'your queen?'"

Chen was red all the way to the tops of his ears. "Perhaps," he shot back, "if your father doesn't manage to kill the king before we get back."

"Cardoth?" Alannys looked from him to Chen, then back again. Neither of them spoke, but they both seemed to understand what had happened. Varilyn sat silently in the wagon, regarding them all seriously, as though she understood as well.

Great—so the only one lost here was her.

"Less talking, more moving," Prince Cardoth said sharply. "You may not think much of my father, but he's very good at everything he does. *Everything.* We don't have much time." He brushed past her to the front of the wagon, and started loosening the horses's harnesses.

"I don't...I don't understand."

Cardoth shot her a glance she couldn't decipher. "I can see that. Look at it this way." He hesitated, and she waited, listening desperately for something that would make sense out of this. "Perhaps my principles don't rationalize away as easily as you imagine."

Alannys heard the words. She even knew what they meant. But it was only when Varilyn came flying from the wagon into her brother's arms for a teary-eyed hug, that she really accepted it.

Her abduction was finally over. Cardoth had suffered a change of the heart she had never believed he had.

♫

The rest of the night and most of the next day was a nightmarish blur of thumping hooves and rushing scenery, of rhythmic bouncing and the smell of sweaty horses. Prince Cardoth and Princess Varilyn each rode one of the cart horses, and Alannys rode behind Chen on Nightfire. They pushed harder than they knew they should, wearing both horses and people to a frazzle, trying to make up time. They didn't talk much; even their stops were short and mostly silent. They rode with grim determination, hoping against hope to arrive in time to avert the disaster King Rathmar intended to unleash at the Great Palace.

Alannys argued with herself, struggling with the question of what to do about the mindlink. She wanted to let Dorramon know they were coming back, but on the other hand she didn't want to risk distracting him while the situation was so perilous. She knew Rathmar's true intentions here as well as anyone. Any small misstep at this point could give him what he needed. The last thing she needed to be doing was taking Dorramon's attention away from what was happening right in front of him.

So she rode in silence, clinging to Chen's back and fretting.

It was late in the afternoon when they rode back into sight of the Great Palace. Just to see it rising from the ridge, tall and imposing in the yellow-tinted evening light, seemed to give Alannys courage. From this distance it was easy to imagine nothing had changed at all. The Singari camp sprawled at the foot of the ridge looked the same as ever, with its clusters of rag-tag tents and ramshackle wagons, and Alannys could see many a woman by the cookfires giving them hard looks as they rode by.

"Alannys! Stop!"

The high, desperate call assailed them just as they began the climb up the ridge to the palace anteyard. Alannys craned her head around and saw a slight figure running toward them, wearing a long, heavy cloak with a voluminous hood. The hood cast a deep shadow that concealed the figure's entire face. "Lady Alannys! Chen! You must not go that way!"

Abruptly Nightfire stopped, waffling between the path to the palace and the figure in the cloak, sensing Chen's indecision. Alannys couldn't blame him—given everything else that had happened, how could either of them justify trusting a random, cloaked stranger spouting cryptic warnings?

Only this wasn't just some random stranger, Alannys was certain of it. She *knew* that voice. And the breeze that skittered through her own unkempt hair wandered into the figure's hood, fluttering the edge just enough to reveal a glimpse of auburn hair against freckled cheeks.

"Alannys?" Cardoth sounded concerned, but behind that concern was a warning. "What are you doing?"

"Wait, Chen," Alannys said, ignoring the prince entirely.

"Thank the Muses," the figure panted, breathing raggedly. "I didn't think I would catch you in time. You must follow me."

"Why?" Cardoth shot back. "We are here to aid the king, and it seems to me we are unlikely to find him lurking around here. Clear out now—we're headed for the Great Palace!"

"No," Alannys said. "I think we should follow her."

"Have you lost your mind?" Cardoth demanded. "This is ridiculous. There's no way the king is skulking around out here with some hooded stranger. We must get to the palace. She's wasting our time!"

"Quickly, my Lady! You must come—there is no time!" The mysterious cloaked figure who might have been Kalyn turned and ran toward the catacombs, the heavy cloak streaming behind.

"We are following her," Alannys said flatly, "and that's that. She's on our side. We can trust her. She's my friend."

"Friend," Cardoth snorted, as if he had never heard a

more ridiculous piece of nonsense. "Even if she is, that doesn't mean you can trust her."

"I've never been to Cadenda, but if everyone there is like you, it must be horrid. Chen, we're following her."

Cardoth threw his hands up in a gesture of impatience. "As you wish, then. I suppose it's not my kingdom we're throwing away on this insanity."

The look Alannys sent him was positively venomous. It was probably all for the better that Nightfire took off before she could say anything in response, galloping toward the entrance to the royal catacombs.

They left the horses outside, and entered the cave on foot. They were in the mouth of the cave before Kalyn finally lowered her hood and faced them. "I am sorry," she said, "but I couldn't afford to be recognized. We are all in danger right now. Even—even the Royal Guard cannot be trusted." She heaved a sigh, looking around them as though she couldn't quite accept her surroundings. Her green eyes were large and round—and filled with fear. "The Great Palace is no longer safe."

♫

Alannys stared at Kalyn's pale face across a silence that felt electric, prickling with shock and sudden fear. "What —what has happened?"

Kalyn shook her head. "Follow me."

She led them into the catacombs, passing silently through the dark, close caves that had left such an impression on Alannys when she'd traveled through them before. The torches were lit, casting their flickering, jumping pools of light through the uneven passages, but their warmth couldn't lift Alannys's spirits. She found that she hated the royal catacombs, hated being in them, and she understood completely why Dorramon regarded the place with such revulsion.

And that was not even to mention the things that Kalyn had said...the vague but harrowing things that had chilled her down to her feet. She stumbled along behind Kalyn, with Chen holding her arm and giving her worried glances, wondering feverishly if all she had done had been for naught, if after everything they had arrived too late.

"So," said a cold, sarcastic voice, whipping her like a lash, "you have finally decided to come back and see the damage you have wrought."

If it hadn't been for the narrow glare Queen Mother Farrine was aiming at her, Alannys might have thought she was speaking to someone else entirely. "Me? The damage *I* have wrought? Do you think every single thing that goes wrong around here is my fault?"

Farrine sniffed haughtily, still glowering like a royal thundercloud. "Only because so far, everything that has gone wrong *has* been your fault. I don't suppose this is any different."

"I—I don't...how can you even say things like that?"

The queen mother folded her arms, regarding Alannys with undisguised hostility. She stood stiffly in a dimly lit corner of the corridor as they approached, but from her bearing she might have been sitting in the golden throne in the Great Hall. "Truth gives one the power to say a great many unpleasant things. I know my son, Lady Alannys. I don't believe he has done anything so wrong as murder somebody. But you must admit he's done *something* wrong—the state of the country could hardly have come about any other way. Unfortunately, he's become most irrational since meeting you."

Alannys bristled—she could practically feel her back go up. "I think I've finally figured out why you seem so out of touch all the time. It's because you *are*. You really don't have any understanding at all of the pressure he's under—the pressure he's been under since his father died...hell, the pressure he's been under since he was *born*. You're his mother, how can you not see any of that?"

"Now listen here, young lady—"

"No, ma'am. I've got a better idea—*you* listen *here*. Dorramon has so many things pulling him in so many different directions...I never have understood how he handles it all so well. I *still* don't understand. He's stretched past any reasonable limit. And here stands his mother, only too happy to rub salt into open wounds. Where were you during our engagement ceremony, Farrine? Do you have any *idea* the price he pays for his duty? And on top of everything else, how does standing here bitching at me, hiding in the catacombs while your son is in danger, help *anybody,* least of all him?"

The silence that fell after her rant seemed to ring, her angry words echoing off the rock around them. Alannys could feel all of them staring at her in shock—Kalyn, Chen, Varilyn, Cardoth—but most especially the queen mother, watching her wide-eyed, outrage written in every line of her face. All of the sudden it didn't really feel like *that* long ago that Farrine had ordered her head chopped off, and it seemed quite possible that she would issue that order again—at least, as soon as she had Royal Guards around her again to hear it.

Then all at once, while Alannys was still bracing herself for a torrent of righteous royal fury, Farrine's eyes narrowed and she began to applaud. She actually *clapped,* a sharp, obtrusive sound in the cave. "Congratulations, Alannys—you've finally grown into someone worthy of a place in this family. I was beginning to wonder if that would ever happen. So tell me, how do you plan to save my son?"

"Ask again later," Alannys said. "I haven't even figured the situation out yet. Unfortunately you are at least partly right. There is plenty of blame to go around for this, and quite a bit of it is mine." Earning the queen mother's respect, if not approval, didn't do as much to raise her spirits as she might have hoped. It didn't get her any closer to rescuing Dorramon.

And she knew, as she brushed past Farrine and went deeper into the catacombs, if she couldn't do that...nothing else mattered.

Nothing at all.

♫

The cavern Alannys walked into next was the same cavern where they laid King Caleb to rest, all those long months ago.

It was a place she would have been just as happy never to visit again.

She had just enough time to frame that thought, before a sudden, vicious fury of blurred motion and rapid swearing exploded beside her, and all at once Princess Varilyn was pinned against the rocky wall, Raman's blade at her throat.

Quick as thought, Prince Cardoth had his own curved blade against Raman's throat. Alannys drew Songstrike, digging the tip into the black fabric that covered Cardoth's chest. "I advise you," she said, "to put that blade away."

"Him first." Cardoth jerked his head in Raman's direction.

"Well, this is cozy." Chen surveyed them all as if he had awoken from a nice nap to find himself in a madhouse. "Someone want to tell me why we're all about to kill each other?"

"I have a better idea," Raman growled. "Why don't you tell me why you brought these Cadendan dogs here? All of this — everything that's happened — all of the hell that's broken loose in the Great Palace — it's *all her fault*. And you brought her *here*, to the last pocket of support the king has left! Are you all *mad?*"

"Someone here certainly is," Cardoth said pointedly. "Let my sister go. She didn't cause any of this."

"Shut *up*, Cardoth!" Raman wasn't backing down, and his sword didn't waver. "Give me one good reason why I should listen to a single word that comes out of your mouth, you Cadendan snake!"

"How about this one — if you don't release Varilyn *right now*, I'm going to gut you where you stand!"

"Stop!" Alannys shouted over both of them, infusing

the single word with a slight edge of musical command. "Stand down, Raman, he's right. There's plenty of treachery here, but none of it was Varilyn's. She's the only one who didn't do anything wrong. We don't have time for your stupid pissing contest!"

Slowly, as if it cost him great effort, Raman pulled his sword away from the princess and jammed it back into the sheath. He turned his back on Varilyn and pushed right up into the prince's face. "But you listen to me, Cardoth. I've heard talk that you're good with a blade, but if you even think about trying anything on anybody in this room, I will personally separate your head from your body before you can even draw that curved piece of dull metal you call a sword."

Cardoth bared his teeth in a sharp, feral grin. "I invite you to try. *Again.* You may find decapitating me to be difficult, while your own entrails are cooling on the floor in front of you."

"Men and their threats," Queen Mother Farrine sniffed, brushing disdainfully past them. "The lot of you are acting like spoiled children."

"She's right," Alannys said, sheathing Songstrike. "I don't care how much you hate each other. Grow up. We've got work to do."

"Seven Hells," Raman spat. "This is a fine kettle of fish. You're lucky I don't have time to deal with you properly right now, Cardoth." He turned away, blatantly ignoring Cardoth's still-extended sword.

"Maybe it's you who's lucky," Cardoth muttered, sheathing his sword as well.

Alannys shook her head and pushed past him, following Raman deeper into the cavern. There was way too much pride and posturing in this room, when as far as she could see it was none of them who were in danger. "Talk to me, Raman." She could see he was walking toward a painting, but at this distance she couldn't tell what was in it yet. "What's going on here?"

"What's going on here is trouble. While you've been out on holiday with your new boyfriend and his sister, King Rathmar has been rabble-rousing. I think he means to take over. And I think he stands a good chance of succeeding." He stomped over to the easel in the shadows, uncomfortably near the carved stone shelves where the royal deceased rested sleeplessly in their elaborate sarcophagi. Alannys stepped up beside him, and in her first clear view of the painting, as bright as daylight, she understood. There was no need for more words—the lifelike, moving image before them said it all.

The painting showed the Great Hall, where a manacled man was undergoing a spectacle of public shaming, in front of a jeering, angry crowd.

The man in the manacles was Dorramon.

♫

The whole world seemed to tip sideways around Alannys as she stood in a cold stone cavern of the royal catacombs, staring into Raman's open painting of the Great Hall. She could hear shouts and jeers from the throngs of people in the hall, visible beyond the dais that filled the painting's foreground. She could see King Rathmar, pacing up and down the red granite dais, a flaming tower of righteous indignation. Grand Chancellor Ebrad stood nearby, fidgeting nervously, glancing down into the hall as if he had a mind to make a run for it. Captain Grayble was there, his expression boiling over with anger he couldn't conceal. And next to Grayble...

Next to Grayble was a sight that hurt Alannys just to see: Dorramon, stripped of his royal cloak and his velvet doublet, in a plain linen shirt and trousers, with his hands cuffed. A Royal Guard stood on either side of him, though it wasn't clear whether they were there to protect him, or to protect Rathmar from him.

It didn't matter. The cuffs were clear enough.

Alannys stumbled. The King of Ravanmark, in manacles, like a common criminal! How had things

Sandra Miller

degraded so far, so fast? If people were willing to cuff him, to stand him up and heckle him...was Dorramon really safe at all?

How could she rescue him from *this?*

Raman turned and grabbed her arm, holding her steady. "Don't you dare give up. I have no intention of letting this happen, and I know you don't either. Look at him, Alannys—really look at him. Does he look like a man who's given up?"

She didn't know—she couldn't stand to look that close. She had seen as much as she wanted to. But Raman wasn't moving, wasn't releasing her, and she finally realized the question wasn't rhetorical. She took a shaky breath for courage and forced herself to look back into that horrible, horrible painting.

"No," she said, surprised to realize it, but even more surprised to hear herself say it. It was true—Dorramon did not look despondent, or even defeated. He watched the proceedings around him silently but very carefully, standing as tall and proud as if the hall was still his to command.

Alannys supposed it was, in name at least. But not for very much longer.

"Of course he hasn't," Raman said. "No surrender, no defeat. Dorramon will never give up. And we won't, either. Why do you think I'm here, with this? I intend to get him out of there before anyone can harm him."

"But that isn't enough," Cardoth said grimly. Alannys wheeled around to look at him in surprise—she had forgotten, for a moment, that he was even there. "What has happened here will not just fade away—you must know that. This thing will follow him—my father will follow him—until it is done, one way or another."

"Well, then, what do you suggest?" Raman shot back. "You helped start this, after all. What's your magic answer for finishing it?"

Cardoth's expression darkened, and he turned away.

"There is no magic answer. I swear, people in Ravanmark. They think their precious magic can solve anything." Varilyn, standing next to him, looked disappointed, somehow...saddened.

"There's only one thing we can do," Alannys said, squaring her shoulders. "We have to prove his innocence."

"Lovely," Raman said. "And how exactly do you propose to do that?"

"The only way we can," Alannys said. "You're wrong, Cardoth, there is a magic answer. And it's right in front of us."

And before anyone could talk her out of it, before anyone could realize the danger and stop her, she grabbed Varilyn's arm and hauled her straight into the icy void of the painting.

♫

On the other side of the timeless, formless passage of the painting, Alannys tumbled out into a world of light and sound she hadn't really been prepared for. The loud, angry audience filling the Great Hall had been easy to ignore in the painting, but it could hardly be missed inside the hall, nor could the line of armed Royal Guards at the foot of the dais, holding them back. She could hear Rathmar, posturing loudly in his theatrical manner, about the grievous wrongs Dorramon had committed against an innocent woman who came to Ravanmark only to honor an engagement with him. The whole thing was jarring — and frightening.

And then she thought of Varilyn, and wondered what on earth the princess must have made of the journey. Varilyn staggered next to her, leaning heavily on her arm, staring around her as though completely unable to comprehend the sudden change in her surroundings.

Alannys understood. Travel through paintings was disconcerting — even after all this time she couldn't claim to be entirely accustomed to it.

So she kept a firm hold on Varilyn's arm, dragging her

out towards the edge of the dais, shouting at the top of her lungs. "You've all been tricked — King Rathmar is lying to all of you! Princess Varilyn is not dead! King Dorramon has committed no wrong!"

If the hall was crowded and noisy before, it was nothing to the sheer chaos that filled the place now. Not a single person seemed to know what to make of this — including Rathmar and Dorramon, who both stared at her with identical expressions of pole-axed surprise that said clearly she was about the last person they had expected to see there.

"Alannys," Dorramon breathed, and she couldn't tell whether he was happy to see her, or upset at her for charging into danger yet again.

She decided to hope for the best, and gave him her best smile before turning sternly back to face the assemblage. "Grand Chancellor Ebrad," she shouted, "end this circus and unchain your king!"

Left to his own devices, Ebrad might well have complied. He looked every bit as flighty and uneasy in person as he had in the painting, and it was plain he only wanted the whole ordeal over with.

But Rathmar recovered his wits before Ebrad, holding out a single hand to stop the chancellor. "The duplicity in this country never ceases to surprise me. So you are the means by which King Dorramon accomplished his evil ends...I must admit I never expected such treachery from Ravanmark's much-vaunted Redeemer of the Realm! I confess myself shocked — to think that someone my sainted son loved so very much could be capable of such a thing!"

The Great Hall was blanketed in eerie silence, as every person in it waited for some kind of response to this. Rathmar had just escalated this beyond the scope of politics, right into religion. Perhaps he hadn't fully grasped the gravity and the religious nature of the role of Redeemer — it had to be the first mistake she had ever seen him make.

If she had her way, it would also be his last.

"I never did anything to you or to Varilyn," she said, "as you know well enough. Your sainted son was tasked with removing us both from the picture, and he was working at your behest. Any other explanation you offer is simply not true. Since your arrival in Ravanmark, every single thing you have done or said has been geared toward one thing—unseating our king and taking Ravanmark for yourself."

An outburst in the hall greeted this speech. Alannys couldn't tell whether they were shouts of support, or dissent—or both—but it was plain that people were paying close attention to everything that transpired on the dais. The line of Royal Guards at the foot had their hands full, keeping the people back.

"That's ridiculous," Rathmar snorted. "I don't understand why you came here at all, if all you have to offer are these wild accusations. We came here on a peaceful, friendly mission to allow your king a chance to put right the grievous insult he dealt my daughter—indeed, our whole country—by refusing to honor his engagement. But it seems there is no honor in Ravanmark, at least not in those who lead it."

"That's a lie!" The words were heated, impassioned, and the force of them struck the hall silent once again.

And they hadn't come from Alannys.

Alannys turned in shock to find Varilyn, shaking in fury as she confronted her father. "Everything you've just said is a lie. Ravanmark's king has far more honor than you. This engagement was a sham from the beginning—a means to trap Ravanmark in a war they never wanted, a means to supplant their own monarchy with...with *you!* King Dorramon has never done any wrong, towards me or towards Cadenda. You yourself had me taken away from the Great Palace in the dead of the night, and now you would use that deception to force your objectives here. If you are looking for a lack of honor, a look in the mirror should suffice!"

Rathmar seemed as dumbstruck as Alannys, regarding his daughter in undisguised shock. He blinked and gawped as his entire face reddened, but he couldn't seem to get a word out.

It was the wrong reaction. The grumblings in the hall were becoming louder, clearer—and they were grumblings against Cadenda, against the foreign king whose devious manipulation the people were just coming to understand.

Rathmar glared at Varilyn, betrayal burning in his gaze —and then that gaze swung back to Alannys. "Damn your interference, woman! Why couldn't you just stay with Cardoth? Why didn't he follow my orders and kill you? I suppose if you want something done, you must do it yourself."

And before Alannys could react, in a motion so fast her perceptions seemed to blur, Rathmar drew his sword and flew at her.

♪

As far as Alannys could tell, everything on the dais happened at once—in slow motion and yet in the blink of an eye, all at the same time. She felt her fingers wrap around the familiar, comforting solidity of Songstrike's grip in the same instant she saw Dorramon's eyes widen in sudden fear, saw him lunging to protect her—insane, since his hands were manacled and he couldn't even hold a sword. The Royal Guards beside him grabbed him and held him back, but she couldn't tell whether it was to protect him, or to keep him from helping her.

She swung Songstrike up hard to block Rathmar's high, incoming blow, bracing herself for the impact. She saw Captain Grayble draw his own weapon to assist her — only to be attacked by the same guards preventing Dorramon from intervening, the same guards presumably in Grayble's command.

Even the Royal Guard cannot be trusted...

Well. Kalyn had certainly been right—Alannys couldn't say she hadn't been warned.

The impact of the clashing swords jarred her shoulders, sending pain flaring down into her back. The crash of metal on metal left her ears ringing.

Rathmar wasn't waiting for her to recover, however. He was already coming at her with a slashing middle attack, sidestepping with a flourish when she countered. It was apparent where Prince Cardoth got his ungodly skill with a sword.

It was also apparent she wasn't going to survive this for long.

No surrender, no defeat. She didn't know if she quite agreed with that, but she certainly wasn't going to surrender, so she did the only thing she could do—collected herself into a hurried Ready position, and prepared to block Rathmar as he came at her again. He was a formidable opponent, but he lacked Cardoth's agility and finesse. He favored a brute force approach that, big as he was, seemed to work out for him.

Too late, she realized his charging attack was a feint—he had never intended to land the blow she'd scrambled to block. He used the opening to slam into her sideways, sending her sprawling onto the floor. Songstrike slipped from her grasp and skidded to a halt a couple of feet away.

It may as well have been a couple of miles. Rathmar was already closing on her as she rolled onto her back, already preparing to drive his raised sword into her chest. She could hear Dorramon's agonized cry even over the sounds of battle around her, could feel his panic through the mindlink, but there wasn't a thing in the world she could do for him—for either of them.

Alannys braced herself for what she knew was coming and glared defiantly up at Rathmar, refusing, even in this last, desperate moment, to give him the satisfaction of surrender.

Defeat, it seemed, was inevitable anyway.

♫

Nothing Alannys had seen in her life had ever seemed to gleam quite as brightly as King Rathmar's sword did, as he held it high over her in preparation for the final blow, the blow that would dispatch her from Ravanmark for good. She scooted backwards, but she knew she couldn't get far enough away from him to save herself.

A pair of dark, dusty boots stepped over her, and she found herself facing Prince Cardoth's broad back, standing between her and his father, his curved blade at the ready.

"What treachery is this?" Rathmar sounded completely boggled, and at least half insane. "By the sun's light, do none of my children have the sense to simply stay out of my way? You're ruining everything we've worked for!"

"Only because everything we've worked for is wrong," Cardoth retorted. "If you want her, you're going to have to go through me to get her."

"How *dare* you shame me like this, boy! And here — in front of our enemies — why, the dishonor is too much to bear!"

"I'm afraid you and I have different ideas about dishonor these days," Cardoth said coldly.

"Clearly, if you can hold your head up after what you've done. You may not care about your honor, but I will salvage mine — the only way I can!"

For just a moment, Alannys dared to hope that the idea of cutting down his own son would prove to be too much for Rathmar.

Then he charged, with an inarticulate cry of rage, and her hope shattered.

Cardoth met him, blow for blow, pushing him steadily backward. "Alannys," he grunted, never taking his eyes from his father for a second, "get out of here!"

She pushed herself to her feet and scrambled to get Songstrike back into its sheath. The Great Hall was in utter disarray — aside from Cardoth and Rathmar battling in front of her, she could see Captain Grayble and Arch-Prince Raman working together to dispose of the two traitors from the Royal Guard. Ebrad stood as far away from all of it as he could get, his eyes wide and fearful, his back pressed against the stone wall as if he wished he could disappear into it. He clutched a brass key she had not seen in his hand before.

Someone caught her arm and she spun to face them, wishing she had not been quite so quick to put Songstrike away.

Then strong, warm arms wrapped around her in a tight embrace. "I am never going to forgive you," Dorramon said, and she realized what Ebrad had done with that key, "for picking a swordfight while I was chained and guarded."

She could hear his voice rumbling in his chest under her ear, warm and familiar, its soft sound completely belying the words he spoke. She couldn't help it; she hugged him back, even though the rioting Great Hall was probably not the most appropriate place. She knew after everything that had happened, both of them were just lucky to see each other alive again. If they waited for an appropriate time and place...they might wait forever. She knew this, and she squeezed him hard, trying to say everything with her arms that she dared not say aloud just then.

He squeezed back, and for the moment, it was enough.

♫

"A most touching reunion, Dorr," said a voice behind Alannys, amused with just a touch of sarcasm, "but perhaps this is not the place or the time for it."

Alannys let go of Dorramon and spun to find Raman watching them, his bloody sword still in his grasp. Captain Grayble stood nearby, and they were both breathing hard. Alannys assumed they had permanently dispatched the two traitorous guards, until she saw them sitting against the far wall, bound and gagged and guarded by the unlucky grand chancellor. Ebrad looked as though he would far rather have run from them — in fact, he looked as though he still might be considering it, if the nervous way he watched them and stepped backward was any indication.

Grayble followed her line of sight, then looked away. "We need them," he said grimly, "for questioning."

"Questioning?"

"I think we've gone quite beyond any possibility that any of these men were working alone, my Lady. Something goes on here, and we don't have any idea what. That bothers me more than I can adequately express right now. How can I protect you from a threat I can't even see? How can I protect my king?"

"I have every confidence in you, Captain Grayble," Dorramon said.

But the words seemed to offer scant comfort. Grayble nodded, but his frown only deepened.

Alannys turned away from them to find Prince Cardoth still fighting his father. It was hard even to watch; Cardoth was in his usual fine form, whirling like a dervish, his wicked curved blade little more than a glittering blur. She could hardly imagine avoiding the blows coming from that whirlwind of motion, let alone blocking them.

And yet Rathmar somehow still stood, an implacable wall facing Cardoth's sound and fury. He moved with sharp efficiency to precisely block any blow that came within striking distance, and let everything else brush harmlessly by. It was like watching a terrifying machine, built specifically to battle Cardoth.

It was terrifying, too, because it looked like there was a good possibility that Rathmar might win this. And Alannys didn't even want to think about what might happen then.

So she grabbed hold of Songstrike's grip, and started away from her friends to wade into battle and back up

Cardoth. He wasn't what she would call a friend by any means, but she was not about to let Rathmar win this, not if she could help it.

Songstrike hummed in her mind, reminding her that she could. She couldn't risk singing — there were too many innocent bystanders ready to become collateral damage — but she could damn sure swing a sword.

Someone grabbed her by the arm, pulling her backwards, surprisingly insistent. She turned, and found herself looking into the surprised face of —

"Princess Varilyn?" Alannys had to admit the princess was about the last person she would have expected to try to stop her from interfering. Maybe Varilyn was better at holding grudges than she had imagined.

"I'm sorry — I really am sorry, I know it's rude to grab you like that, I just...I thought you were going to try to help Cardoth."

"She was," Raman said shortly, "so thank you for stopping her. Rathmar already knocked her on her backside once, but that one's a slow learner." He hefted his own sword and pushed past her.

"No, wait!" Varilyn called after him. "Please!"

Now it was Raman's turn to stare at her in utter disbelief. "Excuse me? Do you *want* your brother to die out there? I mean, it isn't as though I care much one way or the other — I personally trust the man as far as I can throw him — but it seems like you at least might appreciate the help."

"It isn't that, my Lord, it's just...how can I explain this? This is Cardoth's fight."

Raman shot her an indecipherable glance, then turned back to the fight in front of them. "It doesn't feel right, standing by watching."

"I know. But I'm telling you, this is what Cardoth came back here to do, in the end. It's the decision he made when he turned back toward the Great Palace. Do you think he didn't know it would come to this? Cardoth and I have both dishonored my father beyond what can be forgiven. It was always going to come to this, if we stood against him."

"I suppose it isn't as though Rathmar can really escape, no matter what happens here," Raman said, but he didn't sound convinced. "Even if he defeats his son, he'll still have the rest of us to deal with."

"Unless this is all show and Prince Cardoth has returned to help his father escape," Captain Grayble said darkly.

"No," Varilyn said immediately. "That doesn't even make sense. If he wanted to help our father, he'd have kept doing what he was doing before—getting Lady Alannys and me out of Ravanmark, as fast as possible. Look at my father. There is no way he can forgive Cardoth now."

It was true. A grimace of hate and betrayal twisted the king's face into something gruesome, unrecognizable as the handsome, composed man who had swept into this same hall with such confidence only a few days before. He fought with anger and fierce determination, and he wasn't backing down.

And then, as Alannys and the others watched, one of Rathmar's furious attacks swung just a bit too wide, giving Cardoth the opening he needed to spin in for the kill.

Rathmar slumped to the floor, with a gasp that sounded like a sick parody of the war cry he had charged in with.

Cardoth stood over him, panting raggedly, saying nothing, staring at Alannys with a burning gaze that nailed her to the spot.

♫

Alannys hurried to Prince Cardoth, with Dorramon close behind her. "Cardoth." She laid a hand on his arm, and felt the tension in his posture, saw the way his knotted muscles stood out along his jaw. "I'm sorry. I know that couldn't have been easy for you."

Cardoth watched his father impassively, it seemed, but for his tense attitude. "Honor has many meanings in Cadenda, all of them defined by the state. Things are different here, but I think we can agree there is no dishonor in fighting a dishonorable monarch—even if he happens to be your father."

Something about the way he said that last word tore at her heartstrings. "I'm sorry," she said again. "I don't know if there's anything I can do for him, but I'm willing to try singing if you want me to."

Cardoth shook her hand off. "You're an idiot, Alannys." She stepped back, stung, but there was no real malice in the words. "If you save him, what do you suppose he will do? Turn around and go meekly home, because he owes you? He came here intending to take this place over, intending to dispose of you and the king you support. Do you think he has changed his mind? Do you think he would offer any such mercy to either of you?" He jammed his sword back into its sheath and turned away. "If Ravanmark is to see peace, if things between our countries are to get better...he has to die. You must see that as well as I do."

She watched him walk away, biting her lip, still wishing there was something she could do.

"He's right." Dorramon's hand fell on her shoulder, surprising her almost as much as his words.

"About what? That I'm an idiot?"

He laughed with the first real humor she had heard in a while. "Maybe. I prefer to think of you as noble, Alannys —not many would have made the offer to risk themselves to save a man who came here with the express purpose of destroying them. I see that as selfless on a level I can only dream of matching. I can't help but think it would make me a better ruler. Someone more jaded—or more practical, Cardoth might say—could choose to see that as idiocy. It's his loss, or mine, depending on the view you take."

"*Something* has certainly been lost today." She watched

Rathmar's gray face, strained with the effort of dragging in each ragged, sputtering breath. His eyes looked faraway and glassy. "What happens now?"

Dorramon turned away and looked out over the hall, watching Raman and Grayble help the Royal Guard escort people out, slowly restoring order. "We're not out of the woods yet. Cadendan warships engaged Ravanmark's navy this morning."

"So Crown Prince Vox is still out there. Can he win this?"

"Vox." He looked at her, then away. "I don't underestimate Cadendan ships — they are more advanced than ours, in some ways. But I think our superior numbers leave them little chance of success. Either way, Vox will not succeed. His ship sank around noon today, with him still onboard."

"That...that means..."

Dorramon nodded. "Cardoth is King of Cadenda. Or will be, once he returns. An emissary will leave for Cadenda tonight with the news. We'll send Rathmar's remains back with Cardoth. But not before he and Varilyn officially renounce their engagement claim."

"I — I see." She didn't know what else to say.

His tired smile seemed to say he understood how she felt. "We should probably go. There isn't much we can do here — Grayble and the Royal Guard have things well in hand, and they're going to have their work cut out for them getting the rest of the palace under control. It's probably best if we stay out of the way until they do."

She couldn't argue, so she took his arm and let him lead her toward the door to the antechamber, toward the passage back to the keep. Everything was ending, and she knew she should have felt relieved.

But she didn't, not at all. She felt saddened, but more even than that she was overwhelmed with tension. Because what was going on around her didn't feel like the end. Too much had happened since she had come back to the palace from her travels, far too much for one man to have accomplished — especially a man who had only arrived in Ravanmark a few days ago. Rathmar couldn't have been responsible for the corruption of the Royal Guard, and the creepy rhetoric people were still out there. Rathmar couldn't have been responsible for Lord Diabon and Baron Prubard somehow escaping from the dungeon. A resolution to their troubles with Cadenda was nice, but it didn't feel like the end at all.

It felt like the beginning of a new threat entirely, one none of them really understood.

♫

At the other end of the passage, Dorramon and Alannys stepped into the rich, spicy-smelling darkness of the royal wardrobe, pushing through rows of velvet and satin clothes, navigating through the giant closet by feel and Dorramon's memory, until they finally broke out into the light of the king's chambers.

Dorramon raked a hand through his hair with a sigh that sounded painfully deep. He didn't look exactly royal just then — he looked like a bone-tired man who had been dealing with far too much for far too long. His face had lines and hollows that hadn't been there even a week before. Alannys felt bad just looking at him; she didn't see how he was even staying upright, and she didn't think she was making things any easier.

She turned for the sitting room. "I'll get back to my rooms, then. You look like you need your rest."

Dorramon chuckled, a low and inviting sound. "Running away already? You must really be frightened of me after all."

"It isn't that," Alannys said, turning back to him, "it's just...you really look awful. I feel terrible for imposing on you."

"Don't. If I felt — or smelled — just a little better, I would impose right back. But the last couple of days haven't been very nice to either of us. If a bath and a nap sound half as good to you as they do to me, I can't in good conscience keep you from them."

"A bath," she echoed, "and a nap." She sounded the way most people would have sounded discussing the wonders of the ancient world, perhaps, or paradise.

Dorramon laughed again, with real amusement this time. "That settles it, then. Come, my Lady, and I'll escort you to your chambers. A hot bath, a nap, and some dinner, and we will feel like new people, I'm sure."

The moment seemed to call for a humorous response, but Alannys found herself too burnt-out to think of one. She gave him a tired smile, took his arm, and together they walked down the quiet corridor of the keep, and into her sitting room. Everything looked the same as last time she had been in there. It all felt so...normal, it was almost disconcerting, after everything that had happened.

"I can't believe that's really over," Dorramon said. She saw him looking around the room as well, with an expression that made her think she wasn't the only one having some trouble with the return to normal.

"Me, either." She settled herself onto the sofa, moving a bit stiffly — it felt like everything that had happened in the last few days was catching up with her all at once. "I don't know what I would have done back there without Prince Cardoth."

He glanced at her sharply, then eased down onto the sofa next to her. "You'd have gotten skewered, that's what. I appreciate what you were trying to do, but that was reckless."

She couldn't say anything to that, so she said nothing.

"Still, I can't deny that you saved the day with what you did. How did you manage to get back here?"

"Prince Cardoth changed his mind. Well, Chen followed us, and freed me in the middle of the night. But if Cardoth hadn't changed his mind, I would be on a ship bound for Cadenda right now — I've never been a match for him in a fair fight."

"Not many people are." Dorramon sounded dark, and she wondered if he was brooding. "Why did he want you in Cadenda? I thought he and Rathmar wanted you dead."

"They did. At first. Rathmar never changed, obviously. But Cardoth...somewhere along the way Cardoth decided this whole Talent thing was more than just a fairy tale, and he wanted that kind of power available to him in Cadenda. He thought I would be useful, both as a weapon, and as a means to introduce Talent into Cadenda's royal family."

"Introduce...why, that son of a bitch. I ought to have him drawn and quartered."

Alannys laughed uncomfortably. "I'm afraid that wouldn't help salvage things with Cadenda at all. They've already lost their king and their crown prince over here. *Somebody* needs to be alive to run the place, and I think it's just as well for us if that somebody is halfway friendly. He brought me back, in the end, and fought his own father for us."

"I suppose you're right. Maybe it'll be easier to forgive and forget when he's back in his own country again, and out of our hair." He settled back into the sofa, and put his arm around her shoulders. His warmth was comforting, and she could feel herself relax.

"We can only hope." Alannys leaned back against his arm, resting her head on his shoulder and feeling, for the first time in a long time, as though everything was right where it should be — even her.

The door crashed open and Tralice flapped into the sitting room, all fluster and consternation. "Lady Alannys? My Lord King! Are you —" She stopped short, catching sight of them. "Oh, thank the Muses! I heard you both left the Great Hall through the antechamber, so I went to the king's chambers, but you weren't there...and you left the hall ages ago! I was so worried, I thought...I thought..." She stopped suddenly and made a visible effort to calm herself, smoothing her hair back with both hands.

Alannys frowned, watching her closely. "You thought what?"

Tralice was suddenly very still, smiling. "Nothing, of course. With all of the craziness with Cadenda, I was afraid something may have happened to you both. I can't tell you how relieved I am to find you here, and safe. But Great Muses, you look a fright! Both of you — begging your pardon, your Majesty."

Dorramon laughed. "No need to worry, Tralice. I know what I look like. We've both agreed a bath and a nap are the best course of action at this point. There's just one more thing I have to do, and I'll be out of your hair."

"One more thing?" Tralice looked curious, though Alannys was pretty sure she never would have admitted it. "What would that be?"

"Just this." He leaned forward and scooped the engagement ring off the table. "I know that was no way to treat a royal relic, but Tralice was under strict orders not to touch a single thing in this room until you returned. Call me superstitious...but it made me feel better." He lifted her left hand, and slipped the ring back on. "There, now. See that it stays put until the big day this time. We still have a wedding to plan."

"Yes," Alannys said, smiling at him, "we do."

"Indeed. We barely got started before all this trouble broke out. Tomorrow we should — "

Tralice loudly cleared her throat, interrupting him. They both looked at her in shock.

"I did say one thing, didn't I?" Dorramon said, trying to keep the mood light. "Very well, I'll — "

"No, your Majesty," Tralice said, interrupting again, stopping him as he moved for the door, "that's not my concern. I just...forgive me, your Highness, but it sounded as though you intend to move forward with this wedding, right away."

"I do. We do." Dorramon's conciliatory smile faded, and the frown that replaced it looked considerably less friendly. "I take it you have a problem with that?"

"No. No, not at all. I just...I'm not sure right now is the best time for a wedding. The country's in an uproar. We've just come out of a civil war — not just the threat of one, actual battles were fought. People died. The Great Palace itself is still repairing the damage. And then this whole mess with Cadenda...from the threat of war to this plot to take over the throne...a plot that very nearly succeeded, mind you...and there is battle at sea as well..."

Dorramon folded his arms. "I never thought I would say this, but you worry too much. I'm the king — still, somehow — shouldn't you let me worry about things like that?"

Tralice couldn't quite seem to look at him. She fidgeted instead. "Of course I know that you do, your Highness. And yet...and yet I wonder if you might not push those concerns aside, right now, even though it would be wiser not to."

"I don't think that's really a good thing to say to the king," Alannys said, frowning between them.

"I'm trying to say these things as respectfully as possible, but honestly I think you have the same problem, my Lady. You're both biased, and it's clouding your judgment. This is about the worst time imaginable for a royal wedding — but especially for *this* royal wedding. You are the two people everybody in the country blames for all of the things I just mentioned. If you got married right now...I can't even imagine the backlash you would face. Can you?"

Alannys remembered the battle-wrecked, blood-smeared Great Hall, and she thought maybe she could imagine, at least on some level. She looked at Dorramon, and it seemed to her that the hollows in his cheeks and the lines around his eyes said he could imagine too. She sighed — she knew everything Tralice said to be true, but it still didn't feel very nice to hear it said out loud.

"But I'm still inclined to say to the Seven Hells with the

naysayers," Dorramon said. "I'm King of Ravanmark, Alannys is Redeemer — it doesn't mean Ravanmark owns either of us. I know you understand, Alannys — exactly how much of myself am I expected to give up for my country?"

"I don't know. There's no easy answer to that question. If I had everything my way, I would be selfish and keep you all to myself, and then it wouldn't be an issue." Alannys's remark got a laugh, but it was sharp, harsh laughter. She understood — the conversation was painful for both of them. "But I don't get to have everything my way, and it's better that I don't. They need you, Dorramon. There's no one better to do what you do. There's no one who cares about this country more. So I guess what we have to figure out is how to fix it so you get Ravanmark and me."

"What do you think I've been trying to do the last three months?" He reached over and pushed her hair behind her ear, studying her face. "I can't say things have gotten much better, though."

"That's not your fault. How could you have predicted Rathmar's treachery? If there's one thing Rathmar was good at, even more than scheming, it was manipulating public opinion. And public opinion isn't very high right now, of either of us."

"Now that's the first sensible thing I've heard you say," Tralice said approvingly. "You see it too, don't you, your Highness? I don't think you have any choice."

"She's right," Alannys said, but she sounded glum, even to her own ears. "We're going to have to postpone the wedding. Don't these things take a long time to prepare, anyway?"

"They do." Dorramon looked away. "Still, those preparations can continue. But when you say postpone the wedding...postpone until *when?* I'd love to know what you think we can do to improve this, because I'm not seeing it."

"I can tell you that," Tralice said, "but you aren't going to like it. There is one thing that is guaranteed to boost your support, one thing that will single-handedly make Lady Alannys more respected than she's ever been."

"No." Dorramon stared at Tralice in horror, or something very much like it. "No, you can't be serious."

"I told you that you wouldn't like it," Tralice said, and turned to Alannys. "But you, my Lady—you can't afford to dismiss this out of hand. You must do this. You haven't proven yourself worthy of a king, and until you do, you're going to be stuck here, like this."

"Prove myself worthy," Alannys echoed, and she could feel the answer clicking into place. "The acts. It's time for the acts of the Redeemer."

Tralice nodded, her manner very solemn. "You must have known this was coming for a while now."

"Wait," Dorramon said. "Just wait. The acts of the Redeemer? Already? Doesn't that seem a bit...sudden?" His face was pale and strained; Alannys had to admire his restraint.

"It's time. If we're ever going to be able to face the people together, I have to come out of your shadow, Dorramon. I have to prove that I'm worthy of you, of your kingdom. I have to have some importance of my own."

His frown did not bode well. "Assuming I agree with any of that, what makes you think you don't already have importance of your own? You're the Redeemer—I don't think it gets much more important. Ravanmark has had other kings, and will have more. But there's only one Redeemer."

"True, and why does anybody think it's me? Because you said so. Because you took the risk of publicly endorsing me, because you had an investiture ceremony and gave me Songstrike. Let's face it, without you, my claim is no more valid than Kiarin's, or anyone else I met while I traveled. Any importance I have, I have because of you." She could see his protest coming, and waved it off.

"I know what you believe, but in the eyes of the people, my only legitimacy comes from you. How can I change that? How else, but through the acts of the Redeemer, can I prove that I am who you say I am?"

"You can't. I know that—it's the only way to definitively settle the question. But Alannys, it's dangerous." This time he held up a hand to forestall her protest. "I know you've done dangerous things before. Your whole life since coming to Ravanmark has been danger, and I understand that. But this...this is dangerous on a level that dwarfs anything you have done before. This is a kind of magic, a level of magic, that hasn't existed in this world for centuries. It's capable of things we can't even imagine. How can we know what might happen when you sing those songs? How can we know what it might do to the world? How can we know what it might do to *you?*"

"I don't know," she said. "We can't know, until the thing is done. But it doesn't really matter—I don't really have any choice. I stood in the Great Hall of this very palace and swore to the world that I would perform the acts of the Redeemer, or die trying."

"And that's it, isn't it?" His voice was barely audible, but she didn't really need to hear the words—pain was etched into every line of his face, and she could see the agony in the clouded blue eyes that looked deep into hers. She stared into those deep pools of blue, and the rest of the world might have ceased to exist. "That's the part that terrifies me."

He pulled her into a bone-crushing embrace, and all she could do was wrap her arms around him and hug him back with everything she had. There was nothing she could say to him that would make any of this easier.

The truth was, it terrified her, too.

Chapter Three

TRAVEL AND TREACHERY

*T*he royal dining room was just the same as Alannys remembered. The scenic tapestries in the flickering torchlight looked soft, and their familiarity soothed her. The big polished table and the shiny silver tableware gleamed, and two Royal Guards stood watch at the door. She sat in her velvet-upholstered chair, with Dorramon beside her and Raman across from her with Kalyn beside him, and she thought everything was so much the same, she could almost forget that everything had changed.

"What?" Raman said, staring at them over a forkful of food that wasn't moving—his arm might have been frozen, by the looks of it. "Have you both lost your minds?"

Well, maybe *everything* hadn't changed.

"Now, be reasonable," Dorramon said. "It was actually Tralice who suggested postponing the wedding, but Alannys and I think it makes a lot of sense."

"Of course it does! After everything that just happened, things need to settle down first. You'll get no argument from me on that."

"For once," Dorramon said under his breath, and Alannys put her napkin to her mouth to hide a smile.

"But," Raman barreled on, "you are going to have to do some serious tap-dancing to get from there to what you just said. There is no way this makes sense. There just isn't."

"I disagree." Dorramon sounded completely calm; Alannys figured after so many years he had to be pretty well used to Raman's blunt, forthright attitude.

Raman shook his head and turned to her, pointing his fork in her direction. "And that's not even to mention you! I know well enough where all of this started—with you and your cursed songs. Tell me, my Lady, what makes you think these acts must be performed *now?*"

"What?" She blinked at him, taken off guard by his sudden switch. Evidently she was not nearly as accustomed to Raman as Dorramon was. "Why shouldn't they be done now?"

"Muses, I should have expected as much." Raman turned his fork back on his meal. "After the way you obsessed over finding the songs, I should have known you would be in a fever to go out and use them."

"That's not fair. The acts of the Redeemer are my job. Putting off a job rarely comes to anything good. What would we gain if I waited?"

"Stability." The word was sharp and sour, and Raman's brown eyes were uncharacteristically hard. "You know well enough what this country just went through. It wouldn't hurt to let people settle down, let things get back to normal."

"Stability is exactly what we hope to gain by moving now!" Alannys sat back and forced herself to calm down. She was aware of Kalyn watching them, her head turning back and forth like she was watching a tennis match, but she couldn't just let this drop. It was too important. "Look, Raman...answer me this. Have things been normal since I came to Ravanmark?"

He looked away.

"That's what I figured. I could sit waiting here at the Great Palace for the rest of my life—things may never be normal again, not while I'm here. You know what it's like out there. You know how they see me, what they say about me. For every person who likes me, there's one who would like to see me dead. I've nearly been stoned as a false Redeemer, more than once. There's only one way to put that kind of thing to rest, and the sooner the better.

You can't argue that."

"I damn sure can. Things have changed, for both of you. Dorramon is king of the most powerful nation on the planet, and you are his formal betrothed, and it is not suiting for either of you to go gallivanting off any more."

"That's bullshit, Raman," Alannys shot back. "I'm sorry, but it is. I was officially the Redeemer way before I was officially engaged—who are you to say which role takes precedence? This mission has been mine since I got here—it's who I am. How can you expect me to stop being me, just because I've agreed to marry? It comes down to this—I have to do what I have to do. And I have to do the acts."

Dorramon reached under the table and took her hand in his. "I understand that this is hardly usual. But I'm going with her. These are extraordinary times, Raman; we must all be prepared to act accordingly. I just got her back —I don't intend to let her go again."

"That's the kind of maudlin sentimentality a king can't afford," Raman said. "You're both adults. She's got her responsibility, as she keeps reminding me, and you've got yours. You should be able to handle that."

"Don't give me that." Dorramon's voice was suddenly hard, and she could feel the strain in his hand on hers. "We've been toeing that plank for three months. I'm not doing it any more."

"But you're the king," Raman insisted. "Your people need you here, in the palace."

"Is that so? I have to say, my people didn't seem so keen on having me in the palace a few hours ago."

"Dorramon…" Raman sighed and looked away.

"Listen, Raman, I know this feels like a risk. But it doesn't matter if I go or stay, not if you really look at it."

"Doesn't matter..?"

"No. It doesn't. Honestly, if something happens to Alannys, if she...fails, how long do you think I'm going to last? I can't count the number of times you've said I have thrown my lot in with hers. If she falls out there, we fall together. There's no point in pretending otherwise."

Alannys swallowed hard. She had certainly never realized, all those months ago when she stood in the Great Hall with Dorramon at her investiture ceremony, the magnitude of what he was doing for her, the risk he was taking for her. It was humbling, and she didn't know what to say to it now.

Raman looked pained. "Be that as it may, I don't think you should leave the palace right now. Things are going to be...busy."

"Is *that* what this is about? You don't want to be confined to the palace right now? Really, Raman, you've made such a good start, in such a short time...things are going so well, I can't imagine that Archford will suffer if you stay here to cover for me while I'm gone. You can still supervise, and you can carry on traveling there by painting when it's necessary. In the long run it won't make much difference."

"Archford?" Alannys said. "What's this about, then?"

"It's nothing." Raman cleared his throat and looked at her, then looked away, fidgeting with his goblet. "Just a personal project of mine."

"A personal project?" She didn't know what to make of his attitude—was it possible...could Raman actually be *embarrassed?* She didn't think she could even imagine such a thing. "Archford?"

"He's restoring Archford Estate," Kalyn said, practically bubbling over with excitement. "Archford Holding is going to be reinstated, and we'll be officially invested as the duke and duchess. Isn't it wonderful?"

"It is," Alannys said, hoping she didn't look as gobsmacked as she felt. It did make sense of Dorramon's remarks in the Great Hall before the bomb attack— *you're going to have to get used to being in charge at some point.* He must have had plans for this even then. "Restoring Archford Estate. I didn't know you had any plans for that,

Raman."

"I didn't," he said, "not until recently. I just...I don't know, I spent so many years fighting against King Caleb and Queen Farrine, fighting and losing...I had pretty well decided any kind of real change was impossible. I'd been held here in the palace for so long I guess I had given up on ever having a life I didn't hate. But it's actually happening now — I've been using paintings to supervise the work and keep in touch with my crews. We've just gotten started, but you can already see the difference."

"Wow. That's amazing, Raman. I'm really happy for you."

He smiled then, and it was the most genuine smile she had seen from him in a while. "Thank you, Alannys. I'm happy too. You must come see it when it's finished...it's my hope that you won't even recognize the place."

Alannys shivered. If she ever set foot again in the place she had come to think of as Archford Prison, she dearly hoped she wouldn't recognize it too. Hoped it fervently, from the bottom of her soul.

Dorramon stood up from the table suddenly, as though he sensed her discomfort, and she hurried to stand with him. "It has been a pleasure," he said. "I'm going to escort Lady Alannys to her room — we should all get in early tonight. Enjoy the rest of your evening."

His tone was a bit too formal — a match for the stiff half-bow he dropped in Raman and Kalyn's direction. Alannys figured he must have been trying to leave no opening for Raman to bring up more objections. She took his arm, and together they left the dining room.

"I had no idea there was reconstruction work at Archford," she said. "When did he start on that?"

"Immediately after the Dark Alliance was defeated," Dorramon said. "It's amazing, really, how much he's accomplished in such a short time."

"Amazing," she echoed. "And after so many years believing there was nothing he could do. What happened?

Why did he finally decide to take action?"

He glanced at her sidelong. "Don't you see? He was inspired."

"In—inspired?"

"Certainly. We've all been inspired, you could say, all over Ravanmark...doing things that would normally not even be considered. Allowing music in our towns, suffering Talented people to live among us without persecution, looking upon the Singari as people—why, there are even rumors the King of Ravanmark himself plans to run away on a fantastic journey by sea, at a most inopportune time. Don't you see?" He laced his fingers between hers and drew her hand to his lips. "There is one thing—one wonderful, incredible thing—responsible for the massive changes happening all around us; one amazing thing responsible for making Raman believe that dreams are worth chasing, even when they seem impossible and out of reach.

"Alannys, it's *you*."

♫

Alannys could tell she wasn't alone long before she woke up, could hear someone muttering around her rooms before she was even conscious enough to open her eyes. Still, she couldn't quite believe it when she sat up in her bed and saw Tralice, bustling around the room packing clothes, shoes, and toiletries into a trunk.

"Tralice?" She glanced over at the window—not the faintest ray of sunshine broke the blackness outside. "What are you doing here this early?"

Tralice looked at her a bit sharply. Her wild curly hair was pulled back into a severe-looking bun, and she wore a long, brown coat, still buttoned up. Evidently she had not paused even long enough to put her coat away. "Unless I am much mistaken, my Lady and my Lord King are departing today?"

"Well, yes, but..." She darted another glance at the window, doing her best to smother a yawn. "I don't think we'll be leaving quite this early. Besides, I packed last night." She nodded towards the table out in the sitting room, where a beat-up leather travel bag rested, holding a few changes of clothes and the songs she had recovered at Castle Glennayre. She remembered vividly and with great fondness her previous journeys on horseback with Dorramon, and she knew she would not be needing much from her chambers.

"I saw." Tralice turned away to hide her expression, but Alannys could hear the dismissive sniff in her tone. "I am sure my Lady meant well, but I fear the effort may have been insufficient. My Lady knows very little of proper travel. Don't worry, I'll make sure you are well prepared. I put your breakfast on the table by your...luggage. You should probably eat while I finish up here. When you are done, I'll help you dress."

Alannys didn't know what to say to that, so she dragged herself out of bed and into the sitting room, where she found poached eggs and fried potatoes on a platter. She worked her way through the meal, contemplating her apparently insufficient luggage. It was true, she had packed on the light side, but she didn't want to be weighed down with unnecessary possessions.

Truth be told, she was really looking forward to it. Just Dorramon and her, away from all the drama and the rigmarole of the court, traveling like the old days. Oilcloth tents, dried food in waxed paper packets, evenings spent around a flickering, crackling campfire...it made her feel unexpectedly nostalgic, and she couldn't wait.

When she finished breakfast, she found Tralice waiting for her, holding a sunny yellow gown with lace ruffles at the collar and hem, and a wide sash at the waist. It looked like something she might wear to take tea in the courtyard.

"Are you sure about this, Tralice?" Alannys cast a dubious eye over the gown, and its matching yellow slippers. "I can't imagine riding a horse in that."

"A horse! I should say not!" Tralice struggled to help

her out of her nightgown in the throes of a fit of outrage. "You're traveling to the harbor as the betrothed of the King of Ravanmark, my Lady—you sure as anything won't be riding a horse! You must try to remember your station. A horse, indeed. It wouldn't be proper."

"Proper. I see." She thought sadly of Quicksilver and tried her best not to look out-of-sorts, staring into the mirror. Tralice was fixing her hair—quite a challenge, really, given how little of it there was these days, but the maid was doing her best, pinning it back and braiding sections on either side of her face. It made her think of Lord Arik and Mirendasith Hall, and she smiled at her reflection.

"I'm pleased to see you open to the concept," Tralice said, looking into the eyes of Alannys's reflection. "You're set to be our next queen, see? Everything you do now has to be done with that in mind. I'm here to keep you out of trouble, but I can't do that without a little help from you. I know you are aware of the unrest that has plagued the palace lately—it is important that you do your part, by your behavior, to squelch it. The people expect propriety."

It was an odd speech, surely—even odder coming from Tralice, who was one of the least proper people Alannys had ever met. And yet she couldn't deny it was true, regardless of the source. So she said nothing, but she had to admit her gown, her hair—everything Tralice was doing—made more sense in light of her words. Even as she headed out on a journey to undertake the acts of the Redeemer, people would be watching and weighing what they saw, judging her against their ideas about the next queen—or worse, judging her against the standard of the Cadendan candidate they had just lost.

It was enough to make her want to go back to bed.

Instead she stood up from her stool, and turned to thank Tralice with a smile she hoped looked more genuine than it felt. Tralice was packing Songstrike and her dagger away in the trunk, and the sight gave Alannys a pang, even though she could imagine the response she would get if she tried to leave the palace wearing either one. She grabbed the Seeing Stone and settled it around her neck before it could meet a similar fate. "I'll try to keep that in mind. Really."

"Thank you, my Lady." Tralice turned away, and came back holding the golden royal bracelet, clasping it around Alannys's wrist in a brisk motion. "You won't want to leave this behind again, I think." She threw a quick glance at the dark window. "We should be going." Tralice turned and grabbed hold of the big wooden trunk.

"Wait!" Alannys said in sudden alarm. "You can't carry that by yourself — let me help you."

Tralice waved her off. "Didn't you just say you would be mindful of your station? This is not a job for royalty."

"I said I would *try*. I'm not royalty yet. Besides, even if I was — you can't pick that up alone. Why won't you let me help you?"

For just a moment, it looked like Tralice would answer her. She stood there, fists balled, staring at Alannys, almost quivering with the force of what she wanted to say.

Then a knock sounded from the door, and the moment was broken. Tralice was just a busy maid once more, bustling and impatient, as she hurried off to answer it. Alannys took the opportunity while her back was turned to stuff her beat-up knapsack into the trunk.

Then she trailed behind her maid. What had just happened in there? What was behind this new attitude of hers, this darkness and hostility that seemed to permeate every interaction with her? What was she hiding?

And what would it cost them all, when it finally came to light?

♫

The commotion from the sitting room finally distracted Alannys from her dismal thoughts. She couldn't even guess what was going on out there — nothing had ever happened in her chambers that should have caused the flurry of outraged squawking assaulting her ears now.

She stopped dead in the archway, staring at Tralice in confusion that was probably ill-disguised. "Tralice...what are you doing?"

Alannys didn't hold her breath waiting for an answer —she knew Tralice probably hadn't even heard the question. The maid leaned back against the door, pushing with all her might, digging her heels into the stone floor. She was shouting so fast the words were a blur — the only words Alannys actually understood were the last two: "*not appropriate!*"

"Tralice!" Alannys's angry shout cut cleanly though the maid's incoherent tirade. "Open that door."

Tralice's face knotted up sullenly. "No. Someone must have a care for your reputation, my Lady — if you won't do it yourself, then I'll do it for you!"

Alannys shook her head, listening to the furious pounding from the other side of the door. "I propose an alternate plan, Tralice — forget about my reputation and open that damned door. Or I will do it for you. And then I will talk to Dorramon about assigning me a new maid."

"You wouldn't dare!"

"Watch me." She took a single, threatening step toward the door.

"Fine. Fine! On your own head be it!" Tralice stepped away from the door, fixing Alannys with a mutinous glare.

The door flew open and Chen stomped in, shouldering past Tralice without even looking at her, his eyes locked on Alannys. "You weren't even going to tell me, were you?" His dark eyes were accusing, his face flushed and angry, and Alannys found herself taking a reflexive step backwards.

"Tell you..?"

"You're *leaving!* Headed out to do the acts of the Redeemer, to sing the songs everyone knows no normal person can sing. You're going on a journey that could —

that could be your last, and you weren't even going to tell me?"

Her gaze slid away from his, and her face burned with sudden heat. He was right, and she couldn't deny it. "I'm...I'm sorry, Chen. It's just been busy, and crazy, and...I wasn't trying to hurt your feelings. Honestly. I just don't know how to stand in front of my friends and say goodbye, knowing that I might not be coming back."

"That's horse shit, Alannys." He crossed his arms, glaring at her uncompromisingly. "You don't get to beg off of basic human decency because it's *uncomfortable* for you."

"Chen! I'm sorry—I've already said I'm sorry. But there isn't much else I can do at this point."

"I disagree." He sighed, glancing back at the belligerent maid staring daggers into him. "Look, we've been through a lot together. I think it's understood, no matter the situation, that we care about each other. And this is not how you treat someone you care about."

"Okay. Okay, I give you that—you're right. But what do you want me to do about it?"

"Take me along," he said, clapping a hand to her shoulder. The gesture was rougher than she expected, and when she looked up she was surprised to see his eyes looked as moist as hers felt. "Let me come with you."

"Chen, I..." Her shoulders slumped under his hand. "I don't know. Singari don't travel by sea, remember?"

"This is different."

"It's going to be really dangerous."

"And how is *that* different from anything else I've followed you into?"

"I don't know." She sighed. "It just doesn't feel right, letting anybody else risk themselves for this."

"The king is going, isn't he?"

"Not by my choice! I still think he should stay here, where it's halfway safe. But I can't really tell him no. He is the king, after all, and his stake in this is nearly as big as mine."

"And mine isn't? Alannys, this isn't fair. At least let me go as far as the harbor with you. You don't have to tell me goodbye. Just let me see you wave from the ship. You can't know what this is like, getting left behind this way."

She turned away, biting her lip. "We'll have to talk to Dorramon about it. But I wouldn't hold my breath, Chen. I think he's planning on this journey being just us, alone."

"Alannys..." Chen's face said clearly he wasn't going to let it drop, and she braced herself for the onslaught.

"I do beg your pardon," said a rich, cynical voice from her open doorway, startling them all into silence, "have I picked a bad time?"

Alannys felt her stomach drop, and turned slowly around, knowing what she would find there. Her wide-eyed gaze met the knowing leer of Prince Cardoth, leaning against the frame of her open door as if he owned the place. A shiver skittered down her back—that look said he *did* own the place, and he would soon enough own her, too.

♫

Tralice regained her senses first, grabbing hold of the door and swinging it round, attempting to slam it on Cardoth. "No, no, no!"

Prince Cardoth adjusted his posture slightly, pushing his boot between the door and the jamb. "Lady Alannys," he said, wedged uncomfortably in the slight opening of the door, and yet incredibly ignoring Tralice so completely she might not even have existed, "might I beg a moment of your time?"

"My Lady," Tralice said, her tone a warning, "I must protest. Not just one unmarried man in your private rooms, but two? It's absolutely unthinkable!"

What she said was true, Alannys knew that. But still...she looked from Cardoth's crooked grin to Chen, looking on suspiciously, and she thought that if the Prince of Cadenda was determined to talk to her, it would be just as well to have that conversation with others around. Being alone with him had never taken her anywhere she wanted to go.

Alannys did her best to smile at him as though none of that had just crossed her mind. "Prince Cardoth — of course. Please come in." She was glad, suddenly, that her dagger was in that gigantic trunk and not on her leg.

Tralice abandoned the door, brushing past Alannys with a hard look in her eyes. "I trust my Lady will try harder in the future to remember that such scandalous behavior reflects not only upon herself."

Alannys could feel the color climbing high in her cheeks. She knew — again — that Tralice's point was valid, but she still figured a little scandalous behavior was probably preferable to facing Cardoth on his own.

Cardoth shoved the door back open with his toe, and pushed himself off the door frame, approaching her with a swagger that reminded her exactly why she wanted her friends with her. "Good morning, Lady Alannys."

She crossed her arms defensively over her chest. "Is it?"

For just a second, that seemed to throw him, pausing the swagger while his eyebrows climbed up his forehead. Then he was moving again, his expression carefully smoothed over. "Why, naturally, my Lady — any morning that involves your smiling face is good."

"That's not what I meant." She threw a dark glance at the blackness outside her window. "Are you sure it's *morning?*"

Cardoth laughed out loud. "A fine jest means a fine mood. It seems I picked a good time after all."

"Picked a good time for what, exactly?" Chen demanded, appearing to quite accidentally stand in Cardoth's way. "You have no business here. Have you somehow forgotten you kidnapped her? Treason doesn't earn you unfettered access to the keep."

"Stand down, Singari. It's hardly treason; she isn't

queen yet." He drew his sword and used the flat of the blade to nudge Chen to the side. "And have *you* forgotten the part where I brought her home and fought my own father for her?"

Outrage burned white-hot through her, consuming the polite deference she would usually have shown for a head of state—especially a head of state that Ravanmark dearly needed as an ally. "Put that blade away—where do you think you are? It's plain you've come here to ask me for something, and I don't know what you think you're going to gain by that sort of behavior. I don't tolerate racism either, Cardoth; anyone would think you might know that by now."

"Racism?" Cardoth's eyebrows shot straight up to his hairline. "It's racism now to acknowledge someone's race?"

"Gee, I don't know—you tell me. How about I just start calling you Cadendan?"

The prince glowered like a royal thundercloud. "I don't believe that would be at all appropriate."

"Exactly my point. Chen has a name. I advise you to start using it. Now if you wouldn't mind being on your way, we have a lot to do this morning."

"Yes, I have heard that you intend to leave," Cardoth said musingly, continuing to saunter her direction as though their previous prickly exchange hadn't even happened. "That's actually what I came to talk to you about."

"I don't see what it has to do with you," Alannys said in sudden alarm. "You can't stop me, if that's what you came for."

"Now why would you jump to a conclusion like that? Nothing could be further from the truth."

Alannys grunted noncommittally, preferring not to elaborate on the multitude of reasons for her distrust. She had become adept at recognizing when Cardoth was angling for something, and it didn't make her feel any better to know it was happening now.

"Muses forbid I should disrupt your plans—farthest thing from my mind, I assure you. Quite the opposite, in fact."

"Opposite?" Alannys said, dread growing in her tone as she began to understand what he was getting at. "Surely you can't mean…"

"Indeed." Prince Cardoth inclined his head with practiced grace. "I wish to accompany you."

"No," Alannys said reflexively. "I don't see any way that would be appropriate. How can you even ask that after what just happened?"

"Water under the bridge," Cardoth said smoothly, with a magnanimous wave of his hand.

"Alannys." Chen moved back to her side, glaring unabashedly at Cardoth. "That's not right. That's not *fair*. You can't take him and tell me no. You just can't."

"I believe she can, actually," Cardoth said, holding his nose a bit higher in the air than before, "and it is my belief that she should. It's only logical."

"Logical?" Alannys echoed, as though she had never heard the word. "I don't think I follow."

Cardoth sighed. "No, I don't suppose you do. It's simple—my sister and I need to get to the harbor to get home. You have to get to the harbor to embark on your next noble mission or whatever you're calling it now. It only makes sense, then, that we should go together."

"It only makes sense," Chen snorted, shaking his head. "What color is the sky in Cadenda, where things like that can be true? You kidnapped her. Period. In no way does it make sense for her to have anything to do with you."

"Pshaw. Always so simple-minded, you Singari. Bygones are better left as bygones. Alannys understands that heads of state cannot afford to take things personally, and that preserving friendly relations between nations is far more important than any personal slight. Wouldn't you agree, Alannys?"

In theory, of course Alannys agreed. In practice, standing there and telling Prince Cardoth that he could accompany them to the harbor, ignoring every horrible thing that had happened between them...it was hard. Much harder than she expected, and even though she knew what the right answer was—she knew what she had to say—she just couldn't seem to force the words out. She took a defensive step backward, and another, and found the royal tapestry looming behind her, the entire royal family of Ravanmark seeming to lend her their support as they regarded Cardoth over her head.

If only, she thought.

"While I am certain that Lady Alannys does indeed grasp the concepts you present, Prince Cardoth, it seems to me that a man wishing to negotiate on his position as a head of state would be wise to plead his case to another head of state. Don't you think?"

The congenial voice from the doorway caught them all by surprise, and they turned as one to see King Dorramon standing in the open doorway with his arms folded, regarding them all with a crooked smile.

For just a moment, Cardoth's face became a perfect picture of ugly, undisguised shock. He smoothed it over with a practiced smile. "As you say. But then, if one seeks results, one should always push where it gives."

"I see." Dorramon's tone cooled as he stepped farther into the room. "A practical philosophy, I suppose, but one that will gather you little favor when what you are pushing against is my betrothed." He let the silence hang for a beat, allowing his words to settle. "But you are right —it does make sense that we should travel together. You and your sister are welcome to ride with us."

"Excellent. I shall convey the good news and have our things prepared at once." Cardoth clapped his hands together in evident excitement, and strode from the room. Dorramon frowned after him.

And Chen frowned at Dorramon. "Well, and what was

that all about?"

Dorramon turned reluctantly back to the rest of them. "I wish I knew. I didn't hear everything, but I heard enough." His gaze traveled over Tralice and Chen, and his eyes looked distant to Alannys somehow, guarded. "Tralice, it's good to finally see you again. You're dressed for traveling, it seems."

Alannys looked at her maid in sudden surprise. How had she not gotten that—Tralice hadn't forgotten to put her coat away at all.

"Aye, my Lord King. You can't possibly intend to go without me. A lady needs her maid, especially a fine lady like Lady Alannys, and most especially when she needs to be mindful of her position. And that's to say nothing of you, your Highness." Tralice squared her shoulders, buckling down to press her case, and drew breath to speak again.

"That's fine," Dorramon said. A half-smile played around his lips, as if he might have found her fervid argument amusing, but Alannys thought he still looked as though his mind was elsewhere. "You, too, Chen—you should come along as well. At least as far as the harbor."

"Finally," Chen said, with real satisfaction in his voice, "someone willing to talk sense."

"Pardon me, my Lord King." Tralice sounded a good deal less satisfied, and she looked as though she had just bitten into something that disagreed with her. "I don't think that's appropriate."

"Try not to worry too much, Tralice, you'll make yourself old before your time. Everyone here is welcome to come along. We'll make a regular party of it. Now why don't you run and fetch a handcart for that trunk. Don't worry, we won't sneak off without you. But try to be quick —we haven't much time."

Tralice dropped a perfunctory curtsy and disappeared out the door, her brisk, business-like footsteps fading down the corridor.

"Perhaps we should go ahead outside," Dorramon said. There was something pensive about his frown, something restless in the way his gaze never seemed to fully land on anything it touched. "I find the palace feels...close, and confining, after everything that has happened recently. I'm quite ready to be gone, I think."

Alannys understood — she couldn't blame him at all — and yet she couldn't help frowning back at him. She felt the same discontent herself, and it didn't exactly feel like a positive omen. So she watched, and chewed on her lip, but said nothing.

"Ah!" Dorramon finally seemed fully focused on something, smiling the first real smile she had seen from him that morning. "I heard the grand chancellor raised quite a fuss about that."

She followed his gaze to the handfasting ribbon, tied around the vase of primroses. "Tralice mentioned that."

"Don't worry — I told him to stand down. It will be right here when you return, safe and sound. It rather looks as though it's keeping your flowers safe too, doesn't it? Something certainly seems to be agreeing with them."

Alannys followed him out of the room, craning her head back around to look at her flowers. He had a point — she hadn't had them very long, of course, but not a single petal had dropped, not a single blossom had wilted or browned. Even the water in the vase sparkled crystal clear and beautiful.

Even then, she thought it was strange.

♫

Alannys walked with Dorramon out into the inner ward, her sunny yellow dress cutting a strange contrast to the overcast sky, where the light of morning was just beginning to make some headway against the gloomy darkness. Chen followed behind them, lugging that ridiculous trunk.

"So," she finally said, "Cardoth and Chen — and even Tralice. You agreed to all of that easier than I would have expected."

"Did I?" His clear blue eyes looked directly into hers, but she thought they still seemed veiled somehow. "I admit I hadn't planned on bringing anyone along, much less a whole crowd."

"Why did you?" Chen said, setting the trunk on the ground in front of him. "If you don't mind my asking."

Dorramon looked at him, then glanced back at the keep. "I don't mind, no. I would prefer that this was not mentioned in front of Tralice, though. All servants enjoy their gossip, and Tralice is no exception. And I'm going on little more than a gut feeling...I think it would be best if we kept it among ourselves. But something isn't right here. I'm surprised Cardoth wants to travel with us at all, given everything that's happened—and there's no way it makes sense to approach Alannys about it. I don't know. I can't put my finger on it, but something isn't right. Something about the way he acted, the way he spoke...he's up to something. I don't know what, but something here isn't what it seems, and I wouldn't mind throwing the numbers a bit more in our favor. In sheer numbers, we would have been evenly matched before. Of course, I don't think Princess Varilyn is a threat to much of anyone. I'd be surprised if she even knows how to hold a sword. But Cardoth..." He shook his head. "You and I together could probably best him, Alannys. But I would just as soon not rely on that. The man's a demon in a battle. The more people we have with us, the better."

Alannys dug her dagger out of the trunk and strapped it to her leg. She might have been inclined to discuss the matter further—nothing they had said made her feel at all better about any of this. But it didn't matter—she didn't have time. An explosion of people and activity was headed their way. Alannys could hear nervous, agitated voices firing off question after question, shouting for the king, and she realized they weren't going to get away from here as quietly as she had hoped.

Dorramon moved to stand in front of her, scanning the crowd with an ominous frown, latching on to one familiar face and addressing him as though the rest weren't even there. "Good morning, Ebrad."

The grand chancellor pushed importantly to the front of the jostling, squabbling crowd. "Is it, your Majesty? Is it really?"

"It seemed so, from where I'm standing, right up until you showed up." He folded his arms and cast a glance over the knot of fretful dignitaries, courtiers, and administrators. "What's all this, then—a squawking lot of frightened ninnies?"

"Your Majesty, that hardly seems—"

"I shouldn't have to remind you that this is certainly not the first time the king has left the Great Palace—the royal family has often toured Ravanmark. Somehow you've all managed to survive before."

"Certainly, your Majesty," Ebrad said peevishly, "but the comparison hardly seems fair. You must admit this is the first time the king has left the palace under circumstances like these."

"Well, naturally." Dorramon didn't sound like he thought he had to admit anything—he sounded grumpy and impatient. "But what did you expect? Whatever happens out there, it's going to have an enormous impact on Ravanmark. On the world. It would be a foolish king indeed to sit at home with his head in the sand while things like that happened around him."

"Out of here, the lot of you!" Arch-Prince Raman came storming from the barracks of the Royal Guard, with Captain Grayble right behind him. "I will be here and I've got this well in hand, so you can all stop clucking about like a bunch of old hens. Don't bother the king any more with your nonsense."

Grumbling reluctantly, the crowd dispersed.

"Useless, the lot of them," Grayble said. "Can't see past the end of their own noses."

"Then it's a good thing you'll be here to keep them in line," Dorramon said mildly.

Something like pain crossed Grayble's craggy face. "Your Highness...I'll go with you. You know that."

"I do. But I am afraid, honestly, to leave the Royal Guard here without you in charge of it. If our friends from Cadenda have shown us nothing else, they have proved that the treachery in the guard runs deeper than we ever imagined. Besides, what good would guards do, where we're going?"

Grayble nodded stiffly. "I still don't like it, my Lord King. The King of Ravanmark should not be going anywhere with no protection, and the palace in such a state. If you and Lady Alannys are leaving...the arch-prince and I should be going with you. Nothing else feels right."

"I know," Dorramon said. "But we'll be fine. See that things here are fine as well."

"Yes, your Highness." Captain Grayble crossed one arm over his chest and bowed.

"Left behind while Alannys goes off to do the fun stuff *again*," Raman complained. "Are you sure about this, Dorr? Ebrad could keep things in hand here."

"I'm not so sure," Dorramon said. "Not this time. As much as I hate to admit it, this really isn't the same as a royal tour. Where we're going, what we're doing...it's going to cause fear, and unrest. I can't even say how long we'll be gone. We need someone here with more authority than Ebrad, with a stronger constitution, someone who can put down anything that might start. Whatever is going on in the Royal Guard...I don't think it's isolated, and this might be an opportunity for it to break out. Someone has to make sure it doesn't."

"And the lucky bastard is me. So be it, then. Just...be careful, both of you. Be safe."

Dorramon inclined his head, and Alannys managed a shaky smile. Grayble and Raman walked away, and she watched them go, wondering when she might see them again.

Tralice hurried up, dragging a handcart, carrying a white cloak that she threw over Alannys's shoulders, muttering about the wet air and how ladies might catch their death in it. It was a long, hooded cloak of white velvet—beautiful, but she had to wonder how long it would survive this journey. It certainly looked suitable for the next queen, though, and it settled around her with a weight that seemed to remind her of her new responsibilities. She pulled it tighter around her against the damp chill of the morning air, looking around the inner ward, for the last time for a long time. The morning felt heavy and sad, and Alannys wondered if the others felt it too. She wondered why exactly Cardoth had come to her with his request. She wondered what exactly the prince was planning.

But most of all she wondered why, when she remembered his dark, menacing eyes regarding her over a black scarf, the idea of increased numbers gave her no comfort at all.

♫

So they walked out into the outer ward, toward the royal stables, in a quiet, downcast little group. Dorramon led them, Alannys's arm through his own, his blue riding cloak fluttering out behind his long, determined strides. He held his head high, looking very regal that morning, seeming unaware of the sidelong glances and furious whispers that littered his wake. Alannys peeked over at his stately profile and wondered how much of his apparent confidence was a deliberate act, one last gesture to soothe the people he lived for, even as he left them.

Chen trailed along behind them, pulling the handcart that carried Alannys's trunk. Nobody had questioned its size or its necessity—indeed, nobody seemed to give it a second thought at all—but Alannys found its great bulky presence shaming, especially compared against the simple leather satchel Tralice carried for the king. A servant *and* a trunk big enough to live out of for several weeks? Every person they passed must have thought Alannys to be the most spoiled woman in the realm.

And none of it was even her choice.

"How will we be going to the harbor?" Alannys asked, eager to get her mind off of her thoughts, off of the agitated people gawping around them. "The royal carriage was destroyed in Lord Malrec's bomb attack. It can't possibly have been repaired yet, can it?"

Dorramon looked at her in surprise. "No. No, it hasn't. But even if it had, we wouldn't be taking that to the harbor. It's more...ceremonial."

"It is? It's very beautiful."

"Well, yes." His mood must have been better than hers —he sounded as though he might have laughed, under other circumstances. "Almost too beautiful, really. It wouldn't hold up for hard use. It's meant for state use, around the Great Palace. And for that, it works very well. But it wouldn't be suitable for anything more demanding than that."

Alannys realized he was right—just the blue silk upholstery she had so admired should have been proof of that. It was far too fragile for extended use. Dorramon had mentioned royal tours—how could the entire royal family have traveled the country in that? There wasn't even room for all of them to sit comfortably. The royal carriage was a gorgeous, romantic means of transport, but not very practical.

What waited for them in front of the royal stables would have been called neither gorgeous nor romantic, but it was quite practical. The large, dark, polished wood body was almost boxy, with only the slightest curve to its sides. Glass windows were covered from the inside with black, heavy curtains, and brass rails around the top seemed to indicate an area for luggage. Six horses waited patiently in the harnesses. The driver sat up on the bench seat on top, away from the passenger compartment, and as they approached, the footman hopped from his perch on the back and ran toward them—or more accurately, ran toward her.

"My Lady!" he gasped, giving her a practiced bow, and with a start of surprise, Alannys recognized the same footman who had ridden with them on the royal carriage on the day of the explosion.

"How lovely to see you again!" she exclaimed. "Oh, I'm so glad Dorramon didn't replace you after all."

"What?" The footman looked at her keenly, suddenly pale.

"Nothing! Nothing, don't mind me. So this is the royal coach—it's very impressive."

"Indeed," the footman said, nodding meaningfully, "and my Lady may sit anywhere she wishes inside. *Anywhere.*"

Alannys knew the others were watching, and the way Dorramon cleared his throat next to her made her suspect he was reconsidering keeping the footman after all. She scrambled for some other direction to steer the conversation. "Yes, very nice. And six horses!"

Dorramon flicked a smile in her direction. "Speed is a bit of a necessity. And the royal coach is quite a bit heavier than the carriage."

"Yes," Chen said, "especially with this trunk on it." The footman hurried over to help him load it up, and Alannys felt her face flush—again.

Alannys peeked inside the coach, and was surprised to find that the interior was actually very nice. The long bench seats across the front and back were upholstered with a heavy black leather, and all of the hardware was polished brass. There was plenty of head room and leg room, and the highly figured wood interior was soothing to look at.

If she had to travel halfway across the country in a horse-drawn coach, this was definitely the one she would have picked. And yet, Tralice's repeated lectures about the gravity of her position aside, she couldn't really feel like she belonged in there; she couldn't really feel like something like this was meant for *her*.

So it was that she stood awkwardly back, looking surreptitiously at Chen and at Tralice, who both stood watching her, all of them waiting for some clue as to what they should do.

Dorramon cast a glance over all of them and laughed, stepping back from the coach. "I'm afraid this isn't going to be much fun if you all keep that attitude. We're leaving the Great Palace—let's leave the formalities of the court with it. After you, Alannys."

She couldn't have said why, but it felt momentous, taking his hand and stepping up into that regal coach. It felt like the beginning of something big, something whose outcome she couldn't even begin at this point to guess.

Fitting, really, because that was exactly what it was.

She sat down in the middle of the surprisingly comfortable seat, and Dorramon and Chen followed her in, settling in on either side of her. Tralice stepped inside the coach and stopped, facing them over crossed arms with that stern look Alannys was already growing to dread. "Now there's a pretty picture, and no mistake." Her tone was sharp and cutting. "Hardly fitting for any of you. And you, my Lady—riding halfway across the country wedged between the king and a Singari—if the people could see you now! This is wildly inappropriate."

Dorramon leaned forward, making room to snake his arm around Alannys's shoulders. "I'm sorry, Tralice, but this time I'm going to have to override your complaints, as well-meant as I'm sure they are. These seats are all we have, and we're going to have to work with it, unless you would like Alannys to ride outside with the driver?"

Tralice's face darkened. "I'm serious, my Lord King!"

"And so am I. This journey may not be comfortable for any of us, but we will be bringing two guests along. And as these are guests who have very recently demonstrated some hostility toward Alannys, I'm keeping her right here, safely between two people she can trust till the songs of the Muses run dry."

The words affected Tralice like a physical slap. Her eyes widened, the color drained from her face, and she turned without a word to sink down on the other bench seat, pulling the curtains back to stare morosely out the window. She ignored the rest of them entirely.

What was that about? Dorramon looked to Alannys, raising his eyebrows, but all she could do was shrug. Tralice had stopped making sense to her a long time ago.

They all stewed in the uncomfortable silence as the driver called to the horses with a flick of the reins and the coach lurched into motion, everyone carefully avoiding everyone else's eyes. The entire morning had felt awkward and off somehow, and all Alannys could hope for was that the mood would improve soon. Two days of this might kill her.

She pushed the thought aside, leaning into Dorramon beside her, savoring the warmth of his arm around her. It felt like it had been forever since she had been close to him.

And yet she couldn't help sneaking a glance in Tralice's direction, watching her impassive face look out the window, wondering again what was really behind this attitude of hers.

♫

The Raven's Nest was a tall, sprawling, ramshackle building of native stone, staggering up and out in more directions than had originally been planned, by the look of it. It leaned against the curtain wall to the inner ward as if it might tumble without the support, but it had a generous yard around it and tall iron fences, with uniformed guards at the gate. They stood in stiff salute as the royal coach rumbled past, coming to a smooth stop under the red and white striped awning stretching out over the front entryway. Alannys knew the Raven's Nest was the favorite of visiting nobility, but even so, it far outclassed any of the inns she had seen on her travels. Chen shifted uncomfortably on the seat beside her, and she guessed he was probably feeling the same way.

Prince Cardoth and Princess Varilyn waited out in front of the inn under the awning, next to a visibly unnerved innkeeper holding their bags. Varilyn stood completely unmoving, her hands folded in front of her, her eyes closed and her face tipped down. The slight rise and fall of her chest was the only outward indication that she wasn't a graceful, perfectly sculpted statue, with her carefully braided and bound hair, and her flowing blue gown. Cardoth, in sharp contrast, fidgeted with barely concealed impatience, pacing and fussing with the cuffs of his shirt. The innkeeper had their bags loaded on the coach almost before it had completely stopped, and dropped a quick, perfunctory bow before hurrying back inside.

Cardoth charged into the coach with all the subtlety of a bull entering the fighting ring, bringing a heavy, tense air with him. He regarded them all with exaggerated surprise, hardly seeming to notice as his sister came in behind him and settled herself next to Tralice with her usual grace and economy of motion. "Well, now, this is quite the coterie you've got here, Dorramon. I thought it was just to be the four of us."

If Alannys hadn't known Dorramon so well, she might have missed the faint trace of a frown that flickered across his face. "The surest plans of mortal men—you know how it goes. We've got a couple of guests making the journey with us. It'll be quite cozy, but I think we shall all survive, don't you?"

Cardoth cocked an eyebrow at him, obviously unconvinced. "I suppose I can't begrudge a lady her maid —although you'll forgive me if I do say I'm not entirely satisfied that the need is genuine. This particular lady just finished a three-month tour of the country, after all, alone and on horseback—and leading a group of itinerant people behind her. The idea that she requires a personal servant now...well, *laughable* might be too strong a word, but not by much."

Alannys did her best to hold her head high, to ignore the burning in her cheeks that said he had a point. Dorramon's arm tightened around her shoulders, and she drew courage from the gesture. Her dagger was warming against her leg, and she tried hard not to squirm.

"So you do begrudge a lady her maid after all," Dorramon said mildly. "Didn't you have servants of your own to worry about? I seem to recall quite a retinue the day you came to court."

"No, no." Cardoth gave a dismissive wave of his hand. "They scattered to the four winds the day my father fell. But the maid doesn't bother me. I do understand, after all —Alannys's situation has changed. If she were formally engaged to me, I shouldn't allow her to continue gallivanting around like that either. It's encouraging, one might say, to see that she's taking her newfound status seriously. No, the maid is of no consequence, and entirely fitting."

"Well, I'm glad to hear that you approve," Dorramon said, with just the faintest touch of sarcasm. "Now that we have that sorted, perhaps you would care to take a seat?"

"I would hardly say we're sorted. The maid is entirely fitting. But on the other hand, the *Singari*..."

The air in the coach seemed to frost over. Alannys felt herself go stiff, and she had to force her hands to remain still in her lap, had to force herself not to look at Chen, to do nothing that might be seen as defensive. Chen, for his part, watched the exchange with the same bland expression he'd worn all those weeks ago at Danningham Manor, listening to Alannys and Duke Morryn discuss his people as though he wasn't even there. It got her back up, and she had to force herself to keep quiet and let Dorramon handle it.

"The Singari," Dorramon said evenly, "has a name. And I'm fairly certain that you know it, Cardoth."

Cardoth snorted. "It hardly matters, does it? He doesn't belong here. Some might call it offensive, expecting royalty to travel with Singari."

"Might they? I'm royalty as well, in case you hadn't noticed, and I can't say I feel particularly offended. Not by Chen, at least. As far as I can see, Chen earned his right to be here when he rescued Alannys from a hay cart bent on sneaking her out of the country."

Cardoth had the good grace to look uncomfortable at that, clearing his throat and shifting his stance. "Now see here, I don't think I like what you're implying. Is he here as some sort of bodyguard? Do you think she needs *protection,* when she travels with me?"

"Chen is here as a friend," Dorramon said, "nothing more, and nothing less."

"I don't know if I believe that," Cardoth said.

For a long, long moment, nobody spoke. The silence was thick and tense, and heavy enough it felt crushing.

"You are being ridiculous," Varilyn said suddenly, with surprising sharpness. "Now will you please sit down, and stop delaying everybody with your silly posturing?"

Cardoth grumbled and complained under his breath, but he flopped down on the seat next to Varilyn without any further outbursts. The coach lumbered into motion a moment later, its rumbling and creaking the only sound inside.

Alannys knew she should have felt relieved, but she couldn't quite manage to do it. She didn't think it was any coincidence that Prince Cardoth had zeroed in on the only other armed man in the coach. Whatever else the exchange had done, it had proven to her that Dorramon's suspicions were well-founded.

And that didn't make her feel any better at all.

♫

Alannys had spent some time poring over Lord Arik's

parchment map before she packed her things—it was riding along with them, actually; she had seen Tralice stow it in that enormous trunk. She knew that Mount Mouseion, which held the ruins of the Spire of Glory, was pretty much a straight shot east from the Great Palace— maybe a six or seven day ride, if you could travel the ocean on horseback. She had expected, then, that they would set out east from the palace, and take to the sea at a harbor somewhere on the coast of Glennayre Holding.

Glennayre Holding! The last bastion of the Dark Alliance, synonymous in Alannys's mind with her personal nemesis, Lord Malrec. The man's recent death did little to quell the cold fear she felt at the idea of returning there—Glennayre Holding had been groomed for years for the failed rebellion, and she could only imagine the resentment that must linger there still. Riding through the towns of Glennayre Holding to reach the port sounded like running her own personal gauntlet. She imagined Dorramon must feel much the same, and she envied the calm control that allowed him to sit next to her and look so completely placid.

So she was quite surprised, looking out the window as they left the palace anteyard behind, to find that they never turned east at all, but instead stayed on the main road.

"We're going...south?" The silence in the royal coach had been heavy and oppressive—it should have been a relief to break it. And it might have been, except for the way everyone immediately looked at her. Their sudden, silent attention felt somehow critical to her, and she shrank back against the leather seat back without really meaning to.

"Yes." She heard the smile in the single word, and turned to find Dorramon watching her without any of the negativity she sensed from the other bench seat. "Is that a problem?"

"No. No, I mean I—just expected that we would be

going east, I guess. Wouldn't that be fastest?"

"Oh, absolutely, if we traveled like peasants." Cardoth's tone was sharp enough to cut. "For a commoner, any floating rat-trap is good enough. But there is only one royal ship. When you travel with the royal family, you depart from the royal port. To ask anything else is offensive."

"Now, that's hardly called for," Chen said.

"I would hold my tongue, Singari, if I were you," Cardoth said, with the same ice in his voice. "You have no place butting into a conversation among your betters."

"Betters!" Alannys sputtered. "Now that really is uncalled for. Chen is here as a guest of the King of Ravanmark, just like you, and he has as much right to speak to anyone in this carriage as you do."

"There's decency for you," Cardoth said. "Does anybody in this rig have any propriety at all?"

"Everyone but you, it seems," Dorramon said. He sounded impossibly cheerful.

Tralice looked from Dorramon to Alannys and back in gaping disbelief, then shook her head and turned back to her dismal contemplation of the landscape passing by her window.

"Tralice…" Alannys was upset by her disapproval for some reason she couldn't articulate. "I'm sorry. I know you think I don't consider my position enough. But I meant what I said."

"Of course you did, my Lady." Her voice was flat, and she didn't turn from the window. "But that doesn't make it right."

"I think it is right." The words came out sharper than she intended. "We're all here together. Why should anything else matter?"

Tralice did look at her then, and the darkness in her eyes was unsettling. "Why, indeed. This is a civilized society, Lady Alannys, or at least it claims to be. And in a civilized society there are *rules*, rules for how you treat people, rules for how people treat you."

"So it's a rule now, is it?" said Alannys, going from conciliatory to outraged in less than a second. "I always thought these backward attitudes were the unfortunate result of ignorance and bias, but you're saying it's actual malice? The same rules that say we should use titles of courtesy to address King Dorramon, or Prince Cardoth— those same rules say it's all right to address Chen not by name, but by race, like he's an *object?*"

Tralice shook her head. "Don't cloud the issue with emotion. This is important. The rules are there for a reason. Class distinctions, no matter how determined you seem to be to ignore them, also exist for a reason. You are in a different class now, and you've got to act like it!"

"So that's what this is about." Alannys sat back and folded her arms. "No wonder you told me not to cloud the issue—you don't care how badly Cardoth treats Chen. You don't think I treat him badly *enough.*"

"Lady Alannys, this has nothing to do with Chen! I am talking only about you. *You* crossed a boundary that should not have been crossed. Class boundaries exist for a *reason.*"

"And what reason is that?" Alannys demanded, in a fit of high frustration. "Quit tiptoeing around it and just spit it out! What fundamental law of the universe have I broken, by daring to love a king?"

Tralice floundered, looking uncomfortably around the coach and seeming quite unable, now that it came to it, to put her reasons into words.

"Perhaps I can be of some help here." The voice was so completely devoid of its usual arrogance and cutting sarcasm that it took Alannys a moment to realize Cardoth had spoken. "The upper classes are brought up to perspectives, values, and concerns that the lower classes don't share, and wouldn't understand."

"Yes," Tralice said, "and the lower classes don't magically gain those perspectives, just because they manage to finagle themselves a way up." She nodded vigorously at Prince Cardoth.

"Well said." Cardoth offered Tralice his polished smile, and looked into her face until she blushed. "And yet…"

Tralice's pleased smile abruptly wilted.

"I have to admit that Lady Alannys's arguments have a certain appeal. A base appeal, no doubt, and yet I confess I am curious to see where her changes might lead…what a society might look like, with her in power." This time Cardoth's glowing smile shone on Alannys, and to her dismay it made her blush, too.

"I see," Tralice sniffed. "Perhaps there was some truth to King Rathmar's wild stories after all. Any clear-minded person would tell you it's crazy to think you can upset the entire social order on a whim."

Alannys heaved a long-suffering sigh. "I'm not—"

"You are," Tralice insisted. "You're telling us to ignore all of the rules, just because you said so. Just another example, I suppose, of Talented people thinking they can do whatever they want, without ever giving a thought to the consequences. My Lady."

Tralice turned back to the window without another word or glance at any of them. The unexpected bitterness in her words shocked Alannys, who couldn't quite seem to muster up a response. The very air in the carriage felt colder. How could someone who once ruined her voice seeking Talent herself speak so hatefully of it now?

Dorramon squeezed her shoulders in silent support, but it seemed he didn't have any answer either. They all sat there in the ringing silence after Tralice's outburst, none of them quite able to look at any of the others, none of them quite sure what to say.

♫

It was midday when Alannys felt the relentless pace of the carriage finally slow, felt the clattering bump of cobblestone under the wheels, and looked out to find they were traveling the streets of a town. The carriage wasn't exactly inconspicuous, and even at a glance it was obvious how much attention they were drawing. It made her uncomfortable, even though she knew there wasn't much chance anybody could see inside the carriage very well — they were moving slowly through the streets of the little town, but they were still moving.

"We're stopping?" She tried to sound disinterested, but she couldn't quite keep her surprise from her tone.

"Yes." Dorramon flashed her a look she couldn't decipher. "Would you rather we didn't?"

"No — no, of course not. I just thought we were in a hurry...I assumed we would be skipping lunch."

"Lunch?" Prince Cardoth said. "You think we're stopping to *eat?*" He shook his head. "I don't know what you're thinking, Dorramon — she really isn't suitable to marry you at all. She doesn't know the first thing about anything, do you realize that?"

"Cardoth..." Dorramon's tone held a warning, as did the hard look he leveled in the prince's direction, before he turned back to Alannys. "We aren't stopping for us, Alannys — it's the horses. We can't keep this pace up all day with the same horses, we'd kill them. We're stopping to switch out for fresh horses."

"You can do that?" She knew her bald ignorance was doing nothing to impress Prince Cardoth, but then, she didn't really feel like impressing Prince Cardoth was her job. "You have royal stables here in...what is this little town, anyway?"

"Duxol," Dorramon said. He sounded amused. She could see he was trying his level best to keep his expression even, but a small, treacherous smile played around the corners of his mouth. "No, we don't. The only royal stable is at the Great Palace. We do maintain stabling agreements, though — almost every town of any size anywhere in Ravanmark has a stable in it somewhere that has a stabling agreement with the Great Palace. Part of that agreement allows anyone bearing a royal medallion to trade their horses, any time."

"That's convenient." Even as she watched, a large stable came into sight, with a big packed-dirt arena out front that looked very well-used.

"It's not just convenient, it's a necessity," Dorramon said. "Can you imagine how much longer any journey would be, if we had to make the entire trip with the same horses we started with?"

"Oddly enough, I can." This time it was her turn to be amused. "I just traveled Ravanmark for three months on the same horse. And I don't believe the Singari had stabling agreements in any of the towns we visited."

Chen suddenly covered his mouth with his hand. He played it off as a coughing fit, but Alannys recognized a man hiding a laugh when she saw one.

"Be that as it may," Dorramon said, in a manner that made her think he saw through Chen's ruse as well, "when you're traveling on business of the Crown, you have to move faster than that. A royal tour wouldn't be possible, if we had to do it that way. We wouldn't spend money maintaining these agreements if we didn't need them."

"Of course not," she said, patting his arm. "I didn't mean to imply otherwise. It is a clever solution to the problem."

"Clever," Cardoth snorted, shaking his head. "What a bumpkin."

Alannys ignored him. He'd had a bad attitude all day, almost daring the lot of them to argue with him. She didn't understand it, but she knew she didn't want to encourage him, and she didn't want to engage him. So she did the next best thing and pretended he wasn't there at all. It was easier than she expected—the carriage was already lurching to a stop in the dusty arena. She could feel it jostling around her as the footman dismounted from his seat and came around to open the door for them. They all piled out, squinting in the light after so many hours inside. Regardless of the reason for their stop, Alannys had to admit it felt good to stand tall and stretch her legs and back. "What do we do now?"

"Still after a meal?" Cardoth said.

"Did I say anything about eating?" Her tone was sharper than she had intended, and it elicited a nasty chuckle in response. She took a deep, calming breath. "I'm just not sure what we're supposed to do while they're taking care of the horses."

"It's a valid question," Dorramon said mildly. "I'm afraid we'll just be in the way here."

Alannys's stomach picked just that moment to issue a loud, unladylike growl. Her face flushed bright, glowing red, and she tried her best not to notice the sharp look Cardoth sent her way.

"A meal it is, then," Dorramon laughed.

"I'm sorry." Alannys tried to ignore the way her ears were burning, but she wasn't exactly successful. "We can't really do that, though, can we? I mean...we can't just walk into a tavern...there isn't much chance people would miss a king."

"Two kings," Cardoth said sourly. "I obviously haven't had my coronation yet, but I will as soon as I return. In point of law, I'm King of Cadenda."

"Lucky Cadenda," Alannys muttered under her breath. "Of course," she said out loud, "two kings. And a princess. That makes it worse, doesn't it? We'll draw attention wherever we go. You won't be able to eat a bite, you'll be so swamped with people."

"It's true," Dorramon said grudgingly, kneading the ball of his thumb with his teeth, surveying the lot of them standing there in an uneasy knot. "It isn't really a good idea for us to go to a tavern—or any public place, really—especially with no guards. But it appears we have precious little choice at this point, unless we wish to stay in this dusty, dirty stable until they are finished."

"I most emphatically do not wish to stay," Cardoth

said. "This may be fine for the lot of you, but my sister's health can be delicate. She must not remain in such a place." He took Varilyn's arm solicitously.

"So says the man who dragged me halfway across the country in the back of a hay wagon," Varilyn said. "My brother has as little desire to remain here as any of you, but of course he would never admit that himself. Shall we see what alternatives we can find?"

"Begging your Grace's pardon, but I really wouldna recommend that." The sudden, unexpected voice startled Alannys, and she turned to find the stablemaster standing there; a big, blond man twisting a bandana in his hands as though every aspect of this interaction was stressful. She could see Prince Cardoth's posture stiffen and hoped that for once he would just keep his mouth shut—the address wasn't really appropriate for any of them, and he probably took it as an insult. Obviously the man had no bad intentions, but Cardoth could be counted on not to care about that or cut him any slack for it.

"I'm afraid I don't understand." Dorramon spoke up before Cardoth could, sounding confused but not hostile. "What do you mean—you don't recommend that we eat in Duxol?"

"No indeed, your Grace, but more—I wouldna recommend going out into Duxol at all, if you can help it. It's a small town, aye, but perhaps a bit odd. Got its share of characters, to be sure."

"Characters," Dorramon echoed, with a hint of skepticism, and Alannys wondered if, like her, he was reflecting back on some of the characters they'd had at the Great Palace. Surely nobody here could top that. "I see. Thank you."

"Don't mention it, your Grace," the stablemaster said, turning back to attend to the horses.

"Your Grace," Cardoth muttered under his breath. "What a backwater town. Look, Dorramon, we can't stay in this stable—it's absolutely out of the question. You can't let some backwater clodhopper tell us what to do."

"I am certain no one in Duxol would presume to do anything of the sort," Dorramon said smoothly. "As much as I hate to disregard a well-meant warning, I don't relish the idea of staying here either, and we do need something to eat. What do you think, Alannys?"

Alannys cast a glance around, taking in the dry, dusty, dirt floor, and the dirty, sweaty men working on unharnessing their dirty, sweaty horses. She couldn't have felt more ridiculous, standing in the middle of all that in a ruffled yellow dress with a snowy white velvet cloak. She held it fastidiously up off of the ground, trying not to soil it. It would feel like soiling her new position, like failing before she had even begun. "I'm with you. Let's go find something to eat. What have we got to lose?"

And so they set out as a group, leaving the stable behind and walking along the cobblestone street, hoping to find a meal without too much attention. It didn't seem promising—Alannys was already uncomfortably aware of the glances and whispers they were attracting. It was hard to remember a time she had felt more conspicuous. That, she thought, probably didn't bode too well.

Because it was even harder to remember a time when feeling conspicuous had led her to anything good.

♫

"Duxol," Alannys said, walking down the street between Dorramon and Chen, looking around them with interest. She had visited so many towns all across Ravanmark, and yet nothing she saw was ever the same. "I've never been here. Have you, Chen?"

It was a simple enough question, and she thought it was reasonable given how widely the Singari traveled, but it seemed to make him uncomfortable. "Well," he said, glancing around, "I've been near here. Unmarrieds don't usually go into town."

"You went with me." She sounded a little stung, perhaps by the implication that she didn't already know that. She was becoming an outsider...at least that's what it felt like, and she hated it.

"Yes, well, I said *usually*. There was nothing usual about your situation, or mine."

He looked even more uncomfortable now. Was it just her imagination, or were his ears red? She sneaked a sidelong glance at him, hoping to figure out what he was thinking without embarrassing him, only to find him sneaking a sidelong glance at her.

There were any number of reasonable reactions she might have had to this. She could have cleared her throat awkwardly and looked away. She could have burst out laughing, and made a joke out of it. She could even have called him out directly and made an uncomfortable situation downright miserable.

Instead, she stopped stone-still in the middle of the street, staring wide-eyed at something no one else could see. Her friends, the cobblestone street, the entire town around her just abruptly disappeared, and she found herself propped uncomfortably in a straight-backed wooden chair, with her arms bound behind her back. She didn't know where she was or what was going on around her, but she knew enough to recognize a Second Sight fueled vision when she found herself in one. The insulated silence of the mossy, stone-walled room she found herself in filled her ears as fully as any sound, and the damp, musty smell that assaulted her olfactory senses made her wish that her hands were free, if for no other reason than to allow her to cover her nose.

She felt a tugging at the ropes binding her wrists, and realized with a sudden start that there was someone behind her.

"You have a choice to make, Alannys," said an unfamiliar voice behind her, cold and almost metallic with dislike. To her disoriented ears, it sounded unsettlingly like Lord Malrec. "Your life, or the king's."

♫

"Alannys? Alannys, are you all right?" The voice was Chen's, and she saw him there before her, waving his hand in front of her eyes.

"It's the Second Sight," Dorramon said grimly. "She's had a vision."

"Second Sight?" Prince Cardoth sounded unnerved. "She can do that?"

"How wonderful!" Princess Varilyn sounded significantly less unnerved, and significantly more like someone who had just received an unexpected gift. "I've never even heard of anyone who could do that! But is she all right? Because she doesn't look like she's all right."

The little cobblestone main street of Duxol swam back into focus around her, and she found all of the rest of her friends standing nearby, watching her with varying levels of concern.

"I'm fine," she said. The tremor in her voice made her sound anything but fine. She swallowed hard. "But...but something bad is going to happen here."

"I don't like the sound of that," Dorramon said. "Maybe we should go back to the stables."

"That might be a little hasty," Chen said, frowning at her, at the whole street. "Trying to run from prophecy is often how you end up running right into it. Where is this bad thing supposed to happen? What is it?"

"I don't know," Alannys admitted, feeling more foolish by the second. "I didn't recognize the place at all. I couldn't tell much about it...I think it was underground."

"Underground," Cardoth echoed. "Lovely. Maybe we shouldn't pay any attention to this at all. How bad is this bad thing? What kind of danger are we talking here?"

"For most of you, I don't know. But for Dorramon and me...mortal danger. That much was clear."

They stood staring at her in shock, while she stood staring at her feet and wishing she was anywhere else. None of them were paying any attention to anything else around them.

So it was that a stranger plowed right into Alannys, bowling her over onto her backside, and she never even saw him coming. Privately she thought he must have been moving awfully fast, because she had been standing stone still, and he had still managed somehow to run into her.

But she couldn't deny she hadn't been paying any mind at all to her surroundings.

Dorramon was at her side almost before she hit the ground, helping her back onto her feet and dusting her off. "Up you go, then. No harm done?"

"Not to me, anyway," she said. It was true—she was unhurt, but the white velvet cloak she was wearing had not fared so well. Mud splattered its fine surface, and street grime was caked into the pile of the heavy fabric. If she hadn't known better, she would never have recognized it as the same pristine garment Tralice had put over her shoulders that same morning. It felt like forever ago...the cloak seemed to weigh on her. Alannys had done her best to take proper care of it on the journey, regarding its frankly unnecessary luxury as a symbol of her new position and responsibilities. And now...it was ruined. She regarded the sullied material morosely, thinking of the implications of that, aware of Tralice's disapproving gaze on her back.

"Now, now," Dorramon said, lifting the dirty cloak from her shoulders and tossing it to Tralice, "that's a small loss. You are all right—that's the important thing. Let's go rescue Chen, shall we?"

Alannys had no idea what he was talking about. She looked around, trying to regain her bearings, and found Chen standing a few feet away, the unwilling recipient of an unfamiliar young man's fervent apologies. The stranger looked about twenty, and fair, with hair so light it glimmered in the sun, and pale blue eyes that seemed a bit too large for his face, giving him a fragile aspect that was hard to distrust. His features were delicate and refined, his clothes finely tailored and elegantly constructed.

Dorramon took her arm and they joined Chen, just in time to hear him trying to put the young man off.

"No, no, I couldn't hear of it!" the fellow insisted, clutching at Chen's arm, the ruffled cuff of his sleeve draping stylishly over the back of his hand. "It was unforgivably offensive of me, just unforgivable!"

"Look," Chen said bluntly, irritated past courtesy, "I'm Singari. I don't get offended. You don't need to apologize to me."

"Ach!" the stranger cried, his face suddenly blanching as he caught sight of Dorramon and Alannys. "And now I find you are traveling with the King of Ravanmark himself! I am so, so sorry, your Majesty! Please, you must forgive me—I beg of you!"

"There's nothing to forgive, it was an accident." Dorramon didn't laugh, but his tone indicated he might have wanted to. "But if you are so intent on receiving absolution, I suggest you petition Lady Alannys. She is, after all, the one you ran into."

"Lady...Alannys?" The pale eyes traveled up and down her figure, and widened in horror. "The lady I've so grievously injured...is our very own Redeemer of the Realm?" He dropped to one knee in an exaggerated posture of abject penitence, his head dipped so low his forehead nearly touched the cobblestone. "A thousand apologies, my Lady—ten thousand! I had no idea I was in the presence of such an important personage. Nothing in your manner of dress or comportment gave me to know your status—I crave your pardon!"

"That's—that's really not necessary," Alannys stammered, flustered. She looked over at Dorramon, but he seemed as surprised as she was. For the first time she thought maybe Tralice was right after all; maybe the maid had a point if this fellow had no idea she was of any account. It was true; her yellow dress, as much as she resented it, was nowhere near as fancy as even the shirt this young man wore—the material was higher quality, the fit was finer, even the ruffles at his cuffs were more ornate than hers. She flushed, wondering what people had thought of her all the time she had been in Ravanmark, dressing, apparently, completely inappropriately most of the time. "Really, I'm fine. It was just an accident—I was standing in the middle of the street. I should apologize to you!"

"*No*, my Lady!" He looked up then, and he looked honestly shocked. "The fault is all mine, I fear. I could never apologize to you enough." There was something burning in his eyes just then—something that seemed entirely sincere, though his words were completely out of proportion with the situation. She didn't know what to make of it, and so she looked uncomfortably away.

"I assure you," he said, scrambling to his feet and dropping a low bow, "all of you, I meant no offense. You must let me make reparations to you."

"Reparations..?" Dorramon said. "Honestly, that is not necessary. There is nothing to repay. We won't keep you longer." He took Alannys's arm in his, moving to lead her away.

"No, your Majesty, *please!*" The young man's frantic, desperate tone stopped them both; they turned back to see him extending a pleading hand in their direction. "Please, you must allow me to make reparations! It must never be said that Sir Athniss, Baronet of Duxol, does not honor his debts!"

A frown crossed Dorramon's face, as though the young man had said something rude. His expression smoothed over almost immediately, but Alannys wondered what could have prompted it to begin with. "Indeed, Sir Athniss," he said, "I would not have it said that I placed a man in such a position. But we were on our way to eat— we have a limited time before our carriage is ready to proceed again. And as I keep telling you, there is no debt here."

"Eat?" Athniss echoed. "Here in Duxol? Ach, my Lord

King, I would not wish that upon you! You'll find no peace here—and nothing to suit a royal palate. Please, allow me to entertain you and your companions at Agapios Periousia."

"Agapios Periousia?" Dorramon sounded lost.

"My estate. Please, my Lord King. You would have a much better meal, and enjoy it out of the public eye. And I would make amends for my offense."

Dorramon heaved a long-suffering sigh, and Alannys could practically hear him explaining, once again, that there was no offense. But he said nothing—aloud. *I suppose he has a point about avoiding unwanted attention. And after your vision—perhaps it would be best if we accepted?*

Perhaps, she said, casting a nervous glance up and down the little street. *I have to admit, after that...being here makes me uncomfortable.*

Me, too. Dorramon cleared his throat and turned his attention back to Athniss. "We would be honored to accept your hospitality, Sir Athniss. But please don't put yourself to any trouble for us. We can stay but briefly."

"Oh, thank you, my Lord King! You've made my whole week. Maybe my whole life. Please, follow me. I left my carriage at the edge of town—I'm afraid my driver is not accustomed to the busy streets." He bustled off briskly ahead of them, back towards the stable they had left behind.

"What an odd man," Dorramon murmured.

"I quite agree," Prince Cardoth said from behind him, and Dorramon and Alannys both turned in surprise. She hadn't realized he was so close. "Are you sure this is wise, Dorramon? I got the impression he wasn't prepared to take no for an answer—it makes me wonder why. Do you really think his wounded honor was behind that display? We don't really know anything about this Athniss."

"No," Dorramon said, watching the baronet's back recede. "We really don't. He's right about one thing, though—we would cause quite a stir here in town, no matter what we did. And if he does value his honor that highly, far be it from me to soil it."

"Someone values their honor highly enough to apologize to a Singari?" Chen shook his head. "That's news to me. He seems decent enough, though, I suppose."

"Apologizing makes him more decent, Chen, not less," Alannys said. "Besides, we're probably going to be fine. Agapios means love, after all."

They all laughed stiff, half-hearted laughs, falling into step to follow Sir Athniss out of town.

All except Prince Cardoth. He was watching them grimly, not laughing at all. "Gallows humor," he muttered, and Alannys shivered.

Because now that he mentioned it, it did have the ring of gallows humor, after all. And she had to wonder, where exactly were the gallows?

And who exactly were they for?

♫

Just past the stables, they found Sir Athniss waiting for them, next to a light, rounded eight-person coach with a single horse. The driver stood stiffly at attention, his thin dark hair combed neatly and severely off to the side, his black uniform crisp and fastidiously clean. His flinty eyes passed over all of them, then snapped back to stare expressionlessly straight ahead. He never moved or said a word, but Alannys was left with the impression of intense dislike.

"Rodriset," Athniss said mildly, "these are our guests. They will be traveling back to the estate with me."

Rodriset nodded sharply and reached for the door to the coach. He stood holding it open, and as they all climbed in Alannys noticed how stiff the suspension was, how the fine velvet upholstery had not yet had its pile crushed or its surface rubbed from use.

"Wow," Prince Cardoth said, breathing deep of the scents of wood varnish and paint. "It has that new carriage smell."

Sir Athniss's face flushed a deep scarlet. "Indeed. You are very observant, my Lord Prince."

"And quite outspoken," Dorramon said, with a sharp glance in Cardoth's direction, an unspoken reminder to play nice. "It's quite nice, Sir Athniss. I can see why you wouldn't want an inexperienced driver taking it into town."

"Is the driver new too?" Cardoth asked, just a bit too innocently, with a smile that was just a bit too sharp.

Athniss held his head high, but he couldn't stop his face from reddening further — if he blushed any deeper, he was going to be purple. "Only as a driver, my Lord Prince. Rodriset has served my family well in other capacities since before I was born. I would trust him with my life."

"Or indeed the lives of us all," Cardoth muttered, turning to the window. "It's curious, isn't it? A family with the money for an eight-man coach, but only one underfed nag to pull it. And a nice starched uniform for a man who has never driven before. One might wonder about the state of the nobility in Duxol — something doesn't seem quite up to snuff."

"You are being rude, Cardoth," Dorramon said. "I'll thank you not to offend our host."

Strangely, though, Athniss did not look offended, watching their exchange with a grin that was almost too intense, almost feral. "Don't worry, your Highness — you will find me quite difficult to offend. Years of practice, you know, in taking abuse."

In the wake of that curious comment, nobody seemed to know quite what to say. They sat in awkward, stifling silence, watching the landscape pass by the windows, none of them making eye contact with the others.

Alannys sat next to Dorramon, her hand in his, pressed back into the cushions as though she wished to hide inside them. Across from her, Sir Athniss watched them all avidly, but his gaze always came back to land on Dorramon — or more specifically, on his hand wrapped around hers, resting on the seat cushions between them. She supposed it really shouldn't bother her — their engagement, while not a secret, was still very new, and it must have been weird to see the king so casually familiar with someone so soon after going to war over his previous betrothal. And yet it did bother her, for some reason she couldn't quite put her finger on, to watch him watching them like that.

He caught her looking, and broke out into that feral grin...the one that made her wonder if he didn't sharpen his teeth when no one was looking. "It is nice to see you both so happy. But so soon after all that...unpleasantness, do you really think it is wise?"

"It's not related," Dorramon said shortly. "We had agreed to marry before the delegation from Cadenda ever arrived at the palace." He didn't even look at Athniss; he was focused closely on Alannys's face. *How are you feeling? Any more visions?*

No — no, I'm fine. She glanced back over at Athniss; her engagement ring was gleaming in the sunlight, and he was watching it sharply, tilting his head, like a crow contemplating a shiny trinket.

"So you are formally engaged," he said musingly, as if he was talking to himself. "I did not realize that."

"Don't feel bad," Alannys said. "I imagine most people don't know yet."

"Mmm." The sound was noncommittal. He fingered the silk ruffle at his wrist as if it bothered him. "This might complicate things."

"I don't see how," Alannys said. "Everything with Cadenda is settled. We're all good."

"All good." Athniss's smile broadened. "Indeed we are."

Alannys didn't know what to make of his strange attitude. She turned to look out of the window with the others, trying to put it out of her mind.

It didn't help; watching the scenery pass by didn't do

much to relieve her agitation. Every yard of dirt road they traveled only deepened her misgivings—how far was Sir Athniss planning to take them? Didn't he realize they didn't have much time? She had heard Dorramon explain to him that they were waiting for their carriage, and she didn't like traveling this far from it, especially in someone else's transportation.

Or maybe one too many bad experiences was making her jumpy. Either way, she seemed to feel worse about this trip all the time.

And Athniss was still brooding over her hand in Dorramon's. She didn't see what concern it could be of his, and she couldn't say why his preoccupation with their relationship should bother her more than anything else about all of this.

But there was no denying that it did.

♫

Alannys couldn't quite conceal the rush of relief she felt when the carriage finally approached a sprawling stone building, with a high front gable supported by a row of towering columns. It was a big rectangle, with those columns all around, like an ancient Greek temple. It should have been impressive.

But something about this place really did make her feel like she was looking at ancient ruins. A sadness permeated the place, a sense of fallen majesty. Gray stone, chipped and weathered, had only a few stubborn bits of whitewash left clinging to its pitted surface, and the trees and plants looked ragged and overgrown. It was a haunted place, a place that had once been overwhelming, but was now filled only with memories and ghosts. Alannys watched it solemnly as the coach pulled up in front of it, suddenly a lot less eager to arrive.

Athniss hopped out of the carriage almost before the wheels had stopped moving, not even waiting for his driver to open the door. "Welcome," he said, bowing to them with a showy flourish, "to Agapios Periousia."

They scrambled out of the carriage behind him, all eyes fixed on the impressive facade before them. It seemed ominous somehow, looming over them, tall and dark in the midday sun. Its sharp lines were jagged and uneven, missing stone where it had broken away in places that had not been patched. It gave Alannys a shiver to think about what it must have looked like, ages ago, when it was newer and better kept. It might have been an allegory for all of Ravanmark, and that bothered her more than she could express.

Rodriset dismounted stiffly from the driver's bench, paused to speak quietly to Sir Athniss, and then stood at attention holding open the tall, narrow front door, staring woodenly off into the distance as though the rest of them didn't exist.

"If you will all kindly follow me," Athniss said, turning toward the door, "I will show you to your rooms."

"Rooms?" Dorramon said. "We just came for lunch."

"Ah, but my Lord King, Rodriset will require some time to prepare the meal. We should be ready in an hour or so — in the meantime, I assume you would enjoy a chance to rest. Travel is so tiring, after all."

"Your driver is also your cook?" Cardoth either couldn't quite conceal the disdain in his tone, or didn't really try. "What kind of staff is this?"

"The best, in some ways," Athniss said shortly. He led them without another word down a long, empty corridor, around a corner, and through another corridor, finally to a hallway lined with polished doors. It seemed a long path to travel so short a distance. They passed many dark wood pedestals — so many Alannys lost count — pedestal after pedestal, up and down the long corridors, all of them dust-covered and completely empty. Whatever precious objects had once decorated the estate — and there had clearly been many — were gone now, and the emptiness they left behind imparted a peculiar melancholy to the halls.

"You'll find the guest chambers here," Sir Athniss said, breaking a silence that was beginning to seriously grate on them all. "My Lord King, this first room is for you." He bowed low towards the door, reaching out with both arms in a gesture that was probably meant to encourage Dorramon to enter.

Dorramon raised an eyebrow. "Thank you." He took Alannys's arm and pulled her toward the door with him.

Quick as the strike of a snake, Athniss grabbed her other arm, and pulled her back. She knew the shock on Dorramon's face had to be a match for the shock on her own, but Athniss regarded them both with a broad smile and a pleasant laugh. "I'm afraid this room is for our noble king—not our fair Redeemer."

Dorramon looked from the pale, long-fingered hand grasping her arm to the translucent eyes smiling into his face, and he glowered like a thundercloud. Alannys had only ever seen two people make that particular expression: Dorramon, and his mother, and in either case it made you want to do what you were told, and quickly. "And what is that supposed to mean?" he demanded, in a tone that matched his expression. "You must be aware that we are formally engaged."

"Ah, but your Highness, formally engaged is not married. Until you are one in the eyes of the Muses, it would not do for you to be one under the roof of Agapios Periousia. My family has always placed the highest importance on tradition, on propriety. I know it may seem old-fashioned but I beg your indulgence for this—what remains of my family's honor depends upon it."

Dorramon regarded him with raised eyebrows. "I thought we were only waiting an hour for lunch? Do you think us such animals that we can't sit alone for an hour without damaging your spotless honor?"

Athniss rolled his eyes dramatically skyward. "I do not speculate, your Highness—I simply ask that proper decorum be observed."

Dorramon did not look convinced. "Where exactly do you intend to keep her, then?"

Athniss gestured magnanimously at the row of doors lining the corridor. "I beg you not to worry yourself, my Lord King. As you can see, Agapios Periousia has plenty of room for everyone."

"I don't like this," Dorramon grumbled.

"Begging your pardon, your Majesty," Tralice said hesitantly, "but I think it would be a good idea, in this instance, to humor Sir Athniss. Too much propriety never hurt anyone."

"Speak for yourself," Dorramon said, but he looked from the door to Athniss, and he seemed to be considering it. "I suppose it is only for a short time." *What do you think, Alannys?*

I think it's probably not a big deal. Athniss is strange, and a bit off-putting, but he does seem to be trying to help us. Out loud, she said, "I think you're right—it is only for a little while. I wouldn't want to damage his family's honor."

"Indeed." Dorramon tipped a nod in her direction, and disappeared into the room.

Athniss's smile widened. "Now then, with that settled, Prince Cardoth, Princess Varilyn, I think the next two rooms will suit you nicely. Tralice, you may use the next room—I encourage you not to think of yourself as a servant while you are here. Let us take care of you for a change."

Tralice curtsied and disappeared into the indicated room, as the doors closed behind Cardoth and Varilyn. Everyone must have been more tired than they let on— Alannys had forgotten how travel could wear a person out.

"And Chen, my friend, the last door is for you. I know it isn't your accustomed style, but please try to make yourself comfortable here."

Chen glowered in a fine impression of Dorramon, first at the door, then at Sir Athniss. "Quartering a Singari in your home? Your generosity knows no bounds. But tell me this—there are only five rooms here, and six people. Where do you intend to keep Lady Alannys? You promised the king she would be here with the rest of us."

"Ah, my friend, your distrust, it burns! What have I done to deserve such suspicion? Did you imagine I had forgotten Lady Alannys? Never you fear, my fine Singari friend, never you worry—our dear Redeemer shall be quite well looked after." Something about the baronet's ingratiating smile seemed in that moment quite chilling to Alannys. She swallowed the feeling, trying her best to remain rational in this gloomy, fallen place that seemed to push her toward emotional, magical thinking.

Chen's eyes cut to her, and she guessed that he felt much the same. "I'm going to hold you to that, Sir Athniss. She has many friends, most much more important than me. I'll be the least of your problems, if you fail to keep your word—but I *will* be a problem."

"Now, now—you wound me!" Athniss waved his hands in front of himself, laughing. "I assure you, you have nothing to worry about. Do I look so mad as to plan mischief against the king's betrothed?"

Chen's expression did not change. He studied Sir Athniss a long moment, but the baronet's smile only broadened. "For your sake, Sir Athniss, I hope you are telling the truth."

Chen turned and went into his room, but before he closed the door he gave Alannys a long look that seemed to say *watch yourself.* She knew it was good advice and she agreed, but at the same time it bothered her.

However smoothly Sir Athniss brushed it aside, it did seem pretty clear that he had been disingenuous with Dorramon. That was dangerous, no matter who you were or what your reason was. Why would Athniss take that risk? What was his reason?

How could she watch herself against a threat she couldn't even identify?

♫

Sir Athniss turned to Alannys as soon as Chen's door clicked shut. "Now then, my Lady, we had better get you to your room. We mustn't worry your friends any further."

She didn't know what to say to that, so she said nothing, falling into step behind Sir Athniss as he led her on past Chen's door, and around another corner. She had never been anywhere with so many long hallways— Agapios Periousia, while basically rectangular, sprawled over far more land than she had initially realized.

They turned another corner, and still Athniss showed no signs of slowing. The estate was quiet and still, so much so that Alannys began to think Rodriset really was the only staff here. Walking those corridors, mere shadows of their former selves, made her anxious to leave...there was something about being in this crumbling remnant of past majesty that made her feel like crumbling too. It was like being trapped in a great mausoleum, with no choice but to molder there with it.

Finally they stopped, in front of another row of doors on the complete opposite side of the estate from the rooms he had given Dorramon and the others. "Here we are," he said pleasantly.

"Here?" She looked around doubtfully, but saw nothing to bolster her confidence. "Isn't this a little far from the others?"

"Ah, but Agapios Periousia doesn't have rooms for this many guests...I'm afraid the estate was not designed with this kind of gathering in mind."

"What are you playing at? You just assured Dorramon that you had plenty of room for everyone."

"Ah, engaged couples, aren't they precious—the liberties they take!" Athniss folded his hands and rolled his eyes heavenward. "Already on a first name basis! Charming—but not appropriate for public, my dear lady, I'm sure you know that."

345

"Sir Athniss…"

He waved aside her protest. "Now, now, there's nothing to get upset about. What I told our noble king was entirely true—there is plenty of room for everyone…just not actual guest rooms. The only rooms I have left, I fear, are the servant's quarters."

"Servant's quarters." Alannys folded her arms and studied him, trying to decide whether it was just chance that she had been the one to end up so far from the rest. She was probably just being paranoid, the place was just getting to her, but… "And why am I the one being placed in these quarters? We do have an actual servant with us, you know."

"Ah!" Athniss's sharp burst of laughter felt mocking. "I did not expect such elitism from you, my Lady! She's your servant, not mine—I will not permit her to lift a finger here. I thought you would appreciate the consideration. Do you think you aren't being treated in a manner that suits your station?"

Her face burned at the accusation, but she waved a hand, as if she could simply wave the words aside. "You aren't going to distract me into a silly argument, Sir Athniss. If you know half as much about me as you pretend to, you already know I don't care about station. At some point you had to make a decision—you had to choose me for this room. All I'm asking for are your reasons for that choice."

The baronet's laughing face suddenly became serious. "Ah, my Lady, you do insist on asking the hard questions, don't you? Well, between you and me…" He cast a conspiratorial glance up and down the deserted hall. "I can tell you this much. My rationale for this is your safety."

"My safety." She didn't mean to sound to skeptical. "All of my traveling companions are my friends. Why in the world would you be making vague arguments about my safety?"

"Not your safety — your lack of it. I don't feel you are safe with that group. Certainly, most of them are devoted and trustworthy — even in my brief experience of them I can see that — but honestly, I feel that certain members of your party are not. I have watched you all closely — I know you have noticed. I have seen the look and the tone of your interactions with each of them, and I feel you may be subject to threats you do not yet perceive. Do you see? I want you to have some time away from them to consider these things and later, you can go back with fresh eyes."

Alannys raised an eyebrow. "Sir Athniss, I —"

"Please!" he cut her off, waving his hands in front of himself frantically. "Say nothing of this to the others. It's better for my conscience if they don't know where to find you. I would be distraught — utterly distraught — if any harm came to you at Agapios Periousia."

"Who, then?" she demanded. "If you think my friends are dangerous, tell me which ones. Name names."

Sir Athniss smiled ingratiatingly. "My Lady, if there is one thing my sad family history has taught me, it is not to get involved in the disputes of nobles. I beg you, take this time to relax, compose your thoughts, and when you go among your companions again, watch them. Watch them very carefully. This is the only help I can offer you for now, but it may prove life-saving in the end." He gestured at the door, bowing theatrically, as he had done for Dorramon. "I hope that you will rest well, I hope that you will feel safe here at the estate. I have heard some stories, after all — we all have. You don't need to worry here. Rodriset and I will do our best to take care of you."

She didn't know what to say to that. She couldn't doubt his sincerity — his pale blue eyes, wide and clear, seemed to look at her with such complete openness that she couldn't imagine them concealing anything. She let her gaze slip away, to the door in front of her, and sighed. "Thank you, I suppose. You'll let me know when it's time to eat?"

"Rely on it."

Alannys turned away and went inside the room, closing the door behind her, aware of those pale blue eyes still on her back.

♪

There was nothing much to do in the servant's room Alannys had been given, and not much space to do it in. The room was narrow and short—the entire thing could have fit easily inside her closet at the Great Palace. A hay mattress was pushed up against one wall—really just a flattened pile of hay with some rough wool blankets thrown on top. A trunk with no latch held a tallow candle she had no intention of lighting; tallow candles smelled awful. A straight-backed chair completed the room's sparse furnishings. There was barely room to stand.

Alannys turned the chair to face to dirty, small window and stared outside. Unfortunately, there wasn't much to look at outside, either—just an overgrown field of dead and dying trees that looked as if it had once been an orchard. She watched the sun crawl across the sky, beginning its downward descent towards evening, and wrestled with the urge to stomp out right then and demand to get back on the road. They had only planned to stop to change horses—this delay wasn't helping any of them at all. But she had to be honest; that wasn't her only reason for wanting to leave, or even her biggest reason. Agapios Periousia gave her a trapped, uncomfortable feeling that she knew wasn't rational. It made her want nothing more than to leave, and yet she didn't feel like she could justify making a scene without a better reason than that. So she sat and stared out the window, stewing in her own frustration.

The position of the sun told her it was at least two and a half hours later when a brisk rap sounded at her door. She smothered a curse and pulled it open, to find Rodriset standing there, his salt-and-pepper hair combed back from his face, his steel-gray eyes regarding her without a flicker of warmth or humor.

"Dinner," he said stiffly, "is served."

"Thank you," she said, attempting to hide her irritation —after all, they had come for lunch, not dinner—but he didn't acknowledge the remark, or indeed even seem to hear. He turned away and started down the corridor at such a pace that she decided she had better follow and quickly, or she would be left behind. She didn't fancy wandering lost through Agapios Periousia, so she hurried to get behind him.

"We really appreciate all that you're doing for us," she said, hoping to crack his stony exterior.

No response at all. She may as well have spoken to the walls or the empty pedestals. She sighed, but said nothing further.

Either the dining room was farther from her room than the others, or Rodriset had taken her the long way around, because everyone else was already there when she arrived. It was tempting to think that Athniss and his manservant didn't want her to know her way around, but she knew that was just her hard-earned paranoia talking.

It looked to Alannys as though all of the space the builders of the estate had saved by scrimping on the servant's quarters must have gone right into the dining room—it was enormous. The walls were lined with more dusty, long-empty pedestals, and the room was dominated by an elaborately carved, polished round table. It looked like something King Arthur and his famous knights might have sat around; it was that impressive. The ceiling was domed and the color of a clear summer sky. At one time, this room had been the crown jewel of the estate.

But it was obvious she was not the only one ill at ease there. Her friends milled uncomfortably around the room, none of them getting very close to the massive table. Rodriset disappeared immediately out of an archway in the back of the room, presumably to the kitchen. Dorramon hurried to Alannys's side and swept her into a hug.

"There you are," he said. "I was beginning to worry— Chen told us they didn't put you in a room with ours. Where were you?"

"In the servant's quarters," she told him, "on the other side of the estate." She knew she was clinging to him longer than was strictly necessary, but the feel of his familiar velvet doublet against her face was comforting. For the first time, she really resented Athniss for forcing her into a separate room.

"The other side of the estate," Dorramon echoed. "That is not how he made it sound when I asked him about it. Why would he do that?"

"I don't know. I asked him, and he talked a lot about being concerned for my safety."

"Your safety? I would be rather more concerned for your safety, having you so far away. Do you think he was telling the truth?"

"I think so. It's awfully hard to tell with him. But if he had any other reasons, I couldn't tell. He's strange, no doubt, and off-putting. But he seems to really want to help...even though he keeps *not* doing what we ask."

Dorramon frowned, considering it. "Odd, that. Still, I suppose it doesn't matter. We aren't staying. We've been here too long already."

"I completely agree."

She saw his mouth twitch in a smile—apparently the words hadn't been as neutral as she had hoped. Before either of them could say any more, however, Sir Athniss came back in through the archway, pushing a heavy serving cart laden with covered trays and steaming tureens. Rodriset followed behind him, carrying even more food on platters. The scents wafted over all of them, heavy and mouth-watering, and Alannys was suddenly acutely aware of every hour that had passed since breakfast. It had been a good many hours, and they were all ravenous.

"Sir Athniss." Dorramon strode over to the baronet as if he was completely immune to the bewitching smells of the food spread on the table. "I thank you for your hospitality, but we must leave."

"Now?" Athniss stared at him, frozen in the act of placing a tray of sliced, roasted beef on the dining table. "That would be a bit of a waste, wouldn't it—you came all this way to have dinner with us."

"We came all this way to have *lunch* with you," Dorramon said. "Unfortunately the time for that has quite passed, and we are still in a hurry. We must get back to Duxol with all haste, and get our coach back on the road at once. We are due at the harbor tomorrow."

"But...but my Lord King, you simply must stay and enjoy the meal. You must see that this is far too lavish for Rodriset and I—this was prepared expressly for you and your companions. It would wound us if you were to refuse this, wound us ever so deeply."

Alannys figured if the baronet had a superpower, that was it—that uncanny ability he had to make a person feel obligated to humor him, as though the only decent thing to do was to go along with whatever he asked. He had a positive gift for making people feel guilty.

Dorramon frowned, surveying the table in front of them, obviously struggling with some of that guilt himself as he regarded the cream soups, brown breads, steaming meats, and buttered vegetables. "I do understand. And I have no wish to see your efforts wasted. But..." He glanced out of the big leaded glass window, gauging the position of the sinking sun, and his frown deepened. "But we must depart immediately after the meal. It grows late, and we have not traveled nearly far enough." He nodded at the others, and they all began to find seats around the table.

It was large and round, so there was no head and no foot. Alannys wound up sitting rather uncomfortably between Dorramon and Sir Athniss, shrinking against the back of her chair and wishing she had never heard of the town of Duxol, or Agapios Periousia.

"I do hope," Sir Athniss said, flipping open a stiff linen napkin with a flourish and spreading it across his lap, "that you will consider staying the night here. We have planned entertainment for your enjoyment this evening, after dinner."

Prince Cardoth was already shaking his head before Athniss even finished speaking, his face twisted into an expression of clear disapproval. "I know I just heard the king tell you 'immediately after the meal.' And he's explained our situation to you before, several times. Are you deaf, or just stupid?"

Athniss's face flushed, but he didn't engage Cardoth. Instead, to Alannys's immense horror, he turned directly to her. "You must make them see reason, my Lady! Surely you can see that entertainment, lavish meals...these things are costly, and not the usual fashion for a baronet with a single manservant. Your king would have us bankrupt ourselves preparing for his visit, only to leave without bothering to enjoy all that we have worked so hard for, and at such expense? You know my only concern is your safety — with the setting sun come wolves and thieves around Duxol. You simply must stay."

Alannys felt cornered by the man's earnestness — and his bluntness. These were not things discussed in polite society, even she knew that. And why was he addressing his plea to *her*? She squirmed in her chair, trying to arrange some response that wasn't unspeakably rude.

"I find it curious," Dorramon said from her other side, "how a man can bankrupt himself preparing for a royal visit that was quite unplanned. Wasn't this all due to a run-in you had with us on the street — a run-in that you claimed was entirely accidental?"

Now it was the baronet's turn to squirm, and he did, visibly. "Well, my Lord King, you must see...that is, surely you can understand..." He took a deep breath and sat up straighter. "You've found me out, I admit that. It's true I knew of your coming and I tarried in town, hoping I might chance to meet you and convince you to pay me a visit."

"*Manipulate* me into a visit, more accurately," Dorramon said. "I don't like being manipulated, and I like it even less when I can't discern the purpose. What could you have hoped to gain by this?"

"Ah, my Lord King, food does not sit well on a frown like that. Such a disposition will sour your supper. Look, here is Rodriset to serve us our meal. Thank you, Rodriset — please see to our king first. It's only fitting."

Alannys could practically feel Dorramon stewing next to her, but he didn't press the issue. They all sat in a silence that felt hostile and charged as Rodriset moved slowly around the table, laboriously filling each plate from the steaming dishes before them. It all looked wonderful, and it smelled wonderful, and it probably tasted wonderful too — Alannys couldn't have said. Everything sat like sawdust in her mouth; she didn't see how any of them could enjoy a meal in that atmosphere.

Athniss was giving his best impression, however, eating with a hearty gusto that had to be forced, as Rodriset returned to the serving cart by the wall. "Isn't this divine!" he exclaimed. "Rodriset's carrot soup can't be bested, really it can't. See if you don't agree."

"Athniss, you cannot avoid this," Dorramon said. "I won't let you dodge my question. You've been dishonest with us, and that's not a wise thing to be with a king. I demand an explanation. *Now.*"

Athniss sighed, carefully dabbing his napkin at his mouth without looking at any of them. "Your Highness, I am always careful to use the proper honorifics when I address you. I might expect that you would do the same for me. But Ravanmark's royalty lives, it seems, only to fail in the simplest expectations. My title, humble though it may be, is every bit as valid as yours."

"Is it, now?" Contrary to Alannys's every expectation,

Dorramon didn't sound absolutely furious. She sneaked a glance at him and found him rubbing his chin, staring thoughtfully into the distance, as if Athniss's words had revealed more than she got from them.

"Naturally. I already knew you didn't value us the way you value the other lords. But I confess myself surprised — I honestly never realized that you had forgotten us completely. And yet you ask why I would resort to deception to get your attention — what else is a baronet to do?" Athniss placed his fork on the side of his plate; Alannys couldn't help noticing as he did so that his hands were shaking. "We are discriminated against, and most unfairly. Attending court is the right — the *duty* — of every nobleman. They follow a set rotation, attending court on schedule, and when it is their turn they are brought to court, fed and quartered in the Raven's Nest, enjoy personal audiences with the king — all at the palace's expense. But not a baronet. Not me. I must *petition* for the *privilege* of attending court, like any commoner, a petition which is usually rejected out of hand. But if by some miracle my plea should be granted, I must get myself to the Great Palace, and arrange my own room and board at my expense, and I am never granted a private audience. How else, then, am I to have a moment of my king's time, unless that moment is gained by subterfuge? I ask only for those things which my family's honor demands. My circumstances may be reduced, but my honor remains, even when it is tarnished." He stood suddenly in the shocked silence of the dining room, pressing a pale hand to his waxy forehead. "But I must apologize. I never brought you here to tell you such things, and in such a manner. I am not feeling well, your Highness — you must excuse me. Please, I beg of you, enjoy the remainder of your meal. Rodriset will have liquor and cakes waiting after, and then we shall see to your entertainment."

Athniss turned and swept out of the room, still holding his head, leaving behind a silence that felt cold and threatening.

♫

"Well, now." Prince Cardoth's face, when Alannys looked across the table at him, appeared much as his voice sounded—smug. "It's nice to see that Cadenda isn't the only country with embittered, entitled nobles ready to air dirty laundry at the drop of a hat."

Alannys frowned at him, and cut her eyes to Rodriset, waiting silently beside the serving cart at the back of Agapios Periousia's large dining room. He looked utterly bored, which she would have bet meant that he was paying very close attention to every word that was spoken.

Cardoth followed her gaze, and his expression stiffened. The nod he sent in her direction was barely perceptible, but he turned his attention back to his meal without another word, and offered no further comment on their situation or their host.

They finished their dinner in that strangling, heavy silence, broken only by the clinks of silverware and the slight shuffling sounds of people shifting uncomfortably in their seats. The food looked wonderful, and Alannys didn't doubt it tasted as good as it looked—but she couldn't have said what it was, even as she was eating it...she didn't even make a conscious decision to eat, she just went though the motions mechanically, like everyone around her. Athniss's unanticipated hostility changed everything, she knew that, even if she couldn't quite figure out how. They had been tricked into coming here, and Alannys felt sure that Athniss's overtly displayed friendliness was as false as the pretenses that had brought them all to this place. But what could they do about it now? They were here, and the means that had brought them were closed to them now, until Athniss chose to have them taken back to town. And soon it would be dark, with the thieves and the wolves and who-knew-what-else. It seemed they really did have no choice.

When they had all finished, they stood and turned toward the door, headed with one mind back to the guest rooms, where they could converse without other ears listening in.

But Rodriset stood there in their way, his prim form somehow an immovable bulk filling the doorway. His gaze was hard and uncompromising. "Allow me to show you to the drawing room, where my Lord has ordered after-dinner refreshments for you."

"*Refreshments.*" Cardoth's voice dripped with disdain. He stomped up to Rodriset, his hand on the hilt of his sword. "You know what would be refreshing? If you quit playing games and let us out of here, right now. We are in a hurry."

Rodriset stood completely unmoved, looking down his nose at Cardoth as though the threat of physical violence didn't affect him at all. "Certainly, sir. If you would prefer slaughter along the road to accepting my Lord's hospitality, then you are of course welcome to wander off into the night and meet your unhappy fate. But as neither he nor I have any wish to see you all dead, I would much prefer it if you would simply adjourn to the drawing room for refreshments like civilized human beings."

"I am prepared to gut you and any thugs who care to show themselves on the way back to town," Cardoth shot back. "How's that for civilized? I—"

Dorramon held up a hand, cutting off Cardoth's rant. He inspected Rodriset's stony expression carefully, and Rodriset regarded him evenly, the hard lines of his face offering no sign of weakness.

Alannys stood there, one hand on Dorramon's arm, not sure what she should do. She could feel his tension, his muscles tight under her hand with the same apprehension that gripped them all. They hung there, all of them waiting for some sign from the king as to how they should react.

I think, his voice rang in her mind, *that we shall be retiring to the drawing room.*

What? Why?

Look at him, Alannys. Utterly unshaken. He should have reacted, however slightly, to the idea that we are ready to cross all boundaries and physically harm him. But he didn't...and that worries me.

It's almost like he was prepared for it, Alannys mused.

Exactly. Why? Why are they so confident? We need those answers, and we need them before this escalates any further. This whole thing feels like a trap. But if we resist too much, we may spring it early. I don't want that, either.

You're right, she told him, realizing the truth of it. *We have to go along with him. I don't like it, but there isn't much we can do about it.*

Dorramon gave her a barely perceptible nod. Rodriset looked on with polite interest.

"The ladies are tired after our long journey," Dorramon said. She didn't need to look at him to know he was watching Rodriset as closely as she was, probing his facade for any weak points. "I'm sure they would much rather rest than eat, after the day we've had."

"I think your Highness underestimates the women who travel with him," Rodriset said smoothly, his expression never flickering. "Sir Athniss has provided ample relaxation this afternoon, I should think. It would not do to refuse my Lord's generous hospitality, especially not for reasons such as these."

"I'm getting awfully tired of that line," Dorramon muttered under his breath, but to Rodriset he simply nodded.

The butler nodded back once, smartly, then turned on his heel and led them out of the dining room, to a door farther on down the hall. The wood of the door was deeply carved, and gilded with gold. But the gold was worn and thin, with dark wood showing through in places, and heavy dust was caked into the crevices.

The drawing room might have felt elegant and cozy under other circumstances, but as it was Alannys found it uncomfortable and strangely threatening. The ceiling was low and polished, looming over them like a hard, gleaming sky that couldn't quite be trusted not to fall on them. Heavy green velvet drapes trimmed in gold silk fringe completely covered the room's only window, and carved wood chairs upholstered in matching green velvet peppered the room, with delicate end tables at their sides. A dark, heavy sideboard sat along the far wall, its top covered with silver platters bearing cakes and cookies, tarts and pies. Like everything else she had seen since coming to the estate, it was overkill, and it left Alannys feeling pressured. It *was* too much for one man and his servant, and she had to wonder what they wanted in return. This whole crazy charade had to have a point. What was it?

And would they have the time or the means to avert it, once they found out?

♫

If Alannys had harbored any hopes that Rodriset, having accomplished his goal, would make himself scarce and give them some privacy in the drawing room, he dashed those hopes almost immediately, opening the doors of the sideboard and withdrawing a bottle of wine and several glasses. As she watched, he calmly began to pour, and she realized he had no plans to leave them at all.

"Strawberry tarts," Dorramon said suddenly from beside her, and she looked at him in surprise to find him holding a tart out to her. "These are my favorite."

"So I've heard," she said. She reached out to accept the tart, surprised to see the way her hand was shaking. "Sorry—I'm not really at ease, I guess."

He patted her shoulder. "I would worry about you if you were, I think. Our gracious host has been quite careful to keep us in the dark." His gaze was on Rodriset as he spoke, and his eyes were hard, belying his mild tone.

Alannys understood. She felt the same way. But there was nothing she could say out loud while Rodriset lingered among them, all too ready to overhear their discussions and report them to his master. She chewed her way through her strawberry tart, watching the man make his rounds of the room, ostensibly dusting off the furniture and serving the guests. She felt uncharitable about her thoughts, but she was sure he was actually just spying and eavesdropping.

As if he could sense her thoughts, Rodriset glanced at her—rather sharply, she thought, though she had done nothing she could imagine would offend him. He lifted a wine glass in each hand from the sideboard, and offered one to her and one to Dorramon. "A very fine wine," he said stiffly, as though making conversation was a skill completely foreign to him. "Well over one hundred years old, brought in clear from Mirendasith Holding. It would please my Lord immensely if it met with your favor."

"Thank you," Dorramon said, "but you shouldn't have gone to such trouble. It wasn't necessary, not for us."

"That is where my Lord King is mistaken. The baronet would spare no effort, no expense, to please his king. My Lord does not have much, but he would give it all for you. You must not doubt this." Rodriset pushed the glasses forward again, silently urging Dorramon and Alannys to accept.

Dorramon did, so Alannys did too. She swirled the glass under her nose, wafting the rich, earthy scent of the wine toward her face. She remembered all too well the last time she had taken wine from a man with suspicious motives, and she was not inclined to go down that road again. It smelled strong, and she thought that even after such a big meal, it probably wouldn't be a very good idea to drink too much of it. She didn't like this place, and she didn't trust these people, and the last thing she wanted was to lose any alertness while she was here. She sniffed the wine again, and took a cautious sip. Stout, and very dry. She would have to be careful.

"I don't doubt it," Dorramon said, sipping at his own

wine, "not really. You must see, though, that it would be much easier to believe in your eagerness to please if you simply let us be on our way. We are, as we have said several times, in a hurry."

"Ah, yes," Rodriset said, his flinty eyes cutting briefly to Alannys. "She has great deeds to attempt, as I've heard it."

"Attempt, nothing," Dorramon bristled. "She will succeed. I won't hear any other sort of speculation, and I suggest you refrain from it."

"Of course, of course." Rodriset waved his hands placatingly in front of himself. "I meant no offense, your Highness — you must see that. I simply intended to convey my respect for her bravery. It takes a tremendous amount of courage to set out as she is doing, knowing the risks involved."

"There are no risks." Dorramon ground the words through gritted teeth. "Not for her." Alannys put her hand on his arm, painfully aware of the reasons for his obstinate avoidance of this particular truth. Why was Rodriset twisting the knife this way?

"Naturally, naturally," Rodriset said. "I didn't mean to upset you, my Lord King. Allow me to congratulate you on your betrothed — rarely have I seen a woman of such grace and kindness."

"Finally," Dorramon said, winking at Alannys, "something we can agree on."

"Indeed. I'm quite impressed. I've never seen a woman quite like Princess Varilyn before...I am certain she will be a fine match for your Majesty."

Alannys did her best to sip her wine with a neutral expression, uncomfortably aware of how Chen must have felt all those times he'd had to pretend he felt no offense.

Dorramon watched Rodriset silently a moment, his blue eyes harder and colder than she had ever seen them. "If it is your intent to insult Lady Alannys, I will warn you right now that you are taking a very unwise course of action. I know that we explained to Sir Athniss that we are engaged; my agreement with Cadenda has been dissolved."

Rodriset's surprise was too perfect to be genuine. "Is that so, my Lord King? I do apologize—my Lord must have been too busy to pass that along. I do offer my congratulations to you both; I'm sure you know best. And yet, I can't help but wonder...does my Lord King really think it wise, to do as you are doing?"

"What in the world are you talking about?" Dorramon slugged back more wine than she would have dared.

"I certainly don't intend to question your judgment, please understand. But it seems...perhaps...ill-advised, don't you think?"

"Rodriset," the king sighed, "*out* with it already, before I lose my patience entirely. What are you trying to say?"

"Traveling with the servant of Soth," Rodriset hissed, lowering his voice and darting a glance around them. "Is that really prudent, given Lady Alannys's unfortunate relation to Soth? It would seem a better choice to distance yourself from anything to do with him—a better choice for both of you, if you'll forgive my saying so."

Dorramon stared at Rodriset as if he hadn't the faintest idea what the man was talking about—and he probably didn't, Alannys realized. But as for her—she had heard the stories, hadn't she? She had seen before the prejudice that underpinned attitudes like this, seen it more times than she could count. But to find it here, now...she felt like her head might explode. "Excuse me," she said sharply, her voice rising in shrill outrage, "are you talking about *Chen?* I don't know what you've heard and I don't care what you think—I thought you had better sense than to stand in front of me and spout bigoted nonsense like that!"

Tingling, electric silence blanketed the room in the wake of her furious outburst. She could hear her pulse thumping in her ears, gradually slowing. No one moved, no one spoke—every person in the room stood stone still, staring at Rodriset and at her.

Alannys knew that provoking their hosts—captors?—was not on Dorramon's agenda, and she knew she was endangering his speak-softly policy. She wasn't happy about that, but she knew she wouldn't be able to do any better as long as Rodriset stood there taking potshots at her friends.

She had only one option, then: completely disengage. "I'm sorry," she said under her breath to Dorramon, then turned her back on Rodriset and stomped away.

She flopped down in one of the velvet-upholstered chairs and occupied herself with a silent, morose contemplation of the wall.

Almost immediately, Chen sauntered over and parked himself in the chair next to hers, doing his best to look casual, as though he had just happened to pick that seat and that moment.

"Did you come to lecture me?" she said dryly, not fooled by his studied nonchalance.

Chen glanced at her in surprise, then joined her in wall-watching. "No—of course not. How could I? You were defending me, after all, and nobody ever does that."

"Mmm." She gave a non-committal grunt, still focused on the wall. "But you are going to lecture me anyway."

"No!" Chen looked away and sighed. "I just...I just want to ask you to watch yourself. That's all. They are goading you on purpose, you know."

"You think so? Why, I wonder?"

"I wish I knew. I don't know exactly what's going on here, but they are setting you up for something."

"For what?" she said. "A conniption fit? I don't deny that they are really aggravating me—both of them—but they are hardly the first people to do that, are they?"

Chen shook his head. "I'm serious, Alannys. I think—"

He cut himself off as a shadow fell over their chairs. "We're looking cozy over here. Enjoying ourselves?"

Alannys tensed up as soon as she heard that voice, and

slowly twisted around in her chair to face the speaker.

It was Sir Athniss.

♫

Sir Athniss stood behind the chairs, a worn-looking cloak hanging down from his shoulders and his gaze fixed on Chen. In that first split second of startled recognition, Athniss didn't look surprised, or even curious — he looked angry, glaring at Chen as though he knew exactly what was going on here and didn't approve.

Which, Alannys had to admit, was better than she was doing — she was still trying to figure out what *was* going on.

Then Athniss shifted his gaze to her, and the smile he gave her didn't seem angry at all. She wouldn't have called it friendly, though — to be honest, she could only think of one word for the look on his face, and that was smug. It made her wish even more that she understood what was happening around her.

"My Lady, please allow me to apologize for any offense my manservant has given. I assure you this was not his intent, nor mine. We wish only to serve and assist you." Athniss spoke in honeyed tones, placing a solicitous hand on her shoulder.

"Then I would suggest that attacking my friends with prejudiced stereotypes is a poor way to achieve that," she said, but she couldn't put any real sting in the words, not while his pale blue eyes locked onto hers, practically glowing with sincerity.

"Indeed," Dorramon said, approaching them with an air of distinct displeasure. "Perhaps the best way to demonstrate your good will would be to simply get out of our way, *now*. As much as we appreciate your thoughtfulness in preparing a meal and providing entertainment, we —"

"Ah!" Athniss exclaimed, as though he had only just remembered. "The entertainment! I am so glad you reminded me, your Highness. In my anxiety over my

Lady's unhappiness, I completely forgot the reason I came in the first place. Lady Alannys, I must beg a favor of you. Would you come with me for a moment? I need to discuss tonight's entertainment with you."

"And you can't do it here?" Dorramon demanded.

Athniss smiled a thin, pained smile. "Oh, your Highness, you must understand...some things are meant to be surprises. Such surprise would be difficult to maintain if these talks were held here in front of everybody."

Dorramon glowered, clearly unsatisfied with this response. Alannys realized that his diplomatic strategy was about to be violated again, and not by her this time. She spoke quickly, hoping to intervene. "All right. I'll go with you."

"Excellent." Athniss moved toward the door, keeping his hand on her arm as though he thought she might make a run for it. He might have been on to something, too—she had a bad feeling about this vague entertainment he kept going on about, and she figured there was probably a good reason he didn't want Dorramon around when he talked about it. If Dorramon wasn't likely to approve, it couldn't be good for her. "And Chen, my friend, would you very much mind coming with us?"

"Not at all," Chen muttered. He exchanged a grim glance with Dorramon, nodded, and fell into step behind them.

Sir Athniss led them out into a hallway, and then out through a heavy iron-framed glass door on the opposite side of the corridor from every other door. It took them outside, and there they found an enormous garden like nothing Alannys had ever seen. Dense, tall, hedges framed the space, filled with stone walkways that passed under arched trellises covered with climbing roses and winding grapevines. The center of the garden was a brick-paved square, surrounded by small flowers with a strong scent. Each corner of the main garden opened into smaller, specialized gardens with water features and carefully selected, color-coordinated plants and flowers. It was easily the best thing she had seen at Agapios Periousia, and it made her want to reconsider her opinion of the entire estate.

It still wasn't enough to make up for the people who lived there, though.

And it made her wonder. The rest of the estate showed obvious signs of neglect; it had been falling into disrepair for a long time, and the evidence was all around them. Yet this garden had been recently, carefully tended — not a single weed or blade of grass peeked out between the bricks, and the plants and bushes were lush and thick, drooping with heavy blooms. A lot of time and effort had been poured into this garden — why? What on earth would make a garden important enough to merit that kind of attention, while your house fell into ruin around you?

Sir Athniss walked out into the middle of the brick square, then turned suddenly to face them, his pale blue eyes wide in a sincere expression that Alannys was certain did not bode well. "My friends," he said, "I fear I must ask for your assistance with tonight's entertainment."

"We aren't singing for you," Chen said shortly.

Alannys looked at him in surprise, wondering how he could have deduced so quickly the direction this conversation was taking — surely, that was just a wild guess. She couldn't imagine even Athniss would make such an outrageous request as that.

And yet, the baronet did not look surprised, as she might have expected — only strained and uncomfortable to hear his request denied before he had even made it. "Please, you must! As much as I regret saying it, what I said at dinner was true — my station does not provide me the opportunities other noblemen take for granted. This is the first time I have ever seen our king in person, and it is likely to be the last. That's what I'm fighting against, don't you see? It isn't fair, and it isn't right — no nobleman should be treated this way. My family has never been treated equally with other noble families — the Crown has been perfectly content to take money from us, over the years, watching us sink into destitution to help support them, and yet never according us the rights and the respect that should be ours! I ask you, does this seem fair? Does this seem right? How many other baronets are out there, suffering these same circumstances, who will never have this opportunity? How many other families has the Crown bankrupted, without ever even acknowledging them? You have a reputation of fighting against what you believe to be wrong, Lady Alannys. Is this wrong something you wish to allow to stand?"

"Alannys…" The skepticism in Chen's tone was easy to understand. She had been all over Ravanmark, and she couldn't say she had ever heard of a single baronet before this one — let alone silent multitudes of them, suffering under the yoke of royal oppression.

But still…something had laid this once-great family low, she couldn't deny that. The whole estate spoke to her of years of neglect, of not enough people and not enough money to maintain it properly. And Dorramon certainly had not denied any of the baronet's complaints. It was plain that there was something amiss here, even if she didn't understand perfectly what it was. Knowing that, how could she justify turning her back? How could she leave without even hearing him out, not even knowing what he wanted, or if it was something she could do?

Alannys sighed, defeated by her own overactive conscience. "What do you want me to sing?"

Sir Athniss's face lit up with hope. "Oh, thank you, my Lady!"

"Don't thank me yet," she crabbed. "I haven't said I'll do it."

"Perhaps not, but you're willing to consider it, and that alone is a great favor." He reached into his cloak, and withdrew two rolled scrolls, offering one to each of them.

"I'll need your help too, Chen, if you won't mind."

"That's rich, considering everything Rodriset just said about him," Alannys said. "I understand why you figured you could guilt me into helping you, but you must have one hell of a nerve to ask him. Why, I've half a mind to—"

"Alannys." Chen cut her off quietly, reaching out to squeeze her arm with a surprisingly firm grasp. He turned back to Athniss. "If she'll do it, I will too."

"I confess I suspected as much." Athniss sounded smug, or perhaps Alannys was imagining it. Either way, it made her want to punch him in the nose.

Instead she distracted herself by turning her attention to the yellowing, ancient scroll in her hands. She unrolled it carefully, scanning the written music scrawled across it, and frowned. The names Orpheus and Eurydice jumped out at her, stopping her brain and making it hard to process anything else. She'd had no idea that particular legend existed in Ravanmark. "Sir Athniss, what is this?"

His gaze roamed the garden around them, as though he couldn't quite look at her. "You would never know it now, but back hundreds of years ago there was a time when great pageants would be performed, to entertain the people. Back then it was common for nobles to hold pageants when the royal family visited on tour, or to mark special occasions. This song is from one of those pageants. I thought it would be a fitting tribute to our king...one that even I could put on, with my limited means—and your help."

"It is an interesting notion," Chen said, frowning at his scroll, held open in his hands, "but don't you think it would be more appropriate for the king himself to sing?"

Even in the faint light of dusk, Alannys could see Athniss's face color. "In terms of subject matter alone, you have a point, I'll grant you that. But this is a performance for his pleasure, to commemorate his visit—it would be unseemly to ask him to sing! Please, I beseech you both. I'll be in a terrible bind if you won't help me. Royal visits are enormously important events; they must be honored with festivities of a certain caliber. I have no other way to meet my obligations—I beg you to understand."

Alannys looked over the lyrics closely, but she couldn't see any danger in the song, any way that it would threaten their audience. "All right," she sighed. "We'll do it."

"Oh, bless you, my Lady, bless you! And you too, Chen. Thank you so much. I'm going to have Rodriset light the torches and bring out the chairs—you two wait right here. This is going to be fantastic!" Still talking excitedly to himself, with a bounce in his step that Alannys had never seen there, Athniss hurried back into the estate.

"I wonder if this is a good idea," Alannys muttered, rolling up the scroll in her hand with more force than was strictly necessary.

"To tell the truth, I wonder the same thing," Chen said, glancing toward the house to make sure Athniss was gone. "He's good at making people feel obligated...but I'm starting to think if he's asking for it, it can't be good."

""Then why did you stop me? I was ready to really give him a piece of my mind."

"I know. I just...I stand by what I said inside, Alannys, I don't think you should make them mad. You are being set up."

"I don't think so."

"No?" He sounded like he thought she might be teasing him, or being deliberately dense.

"No. I think they're setting up Dorramon—anything they do to me is just a distraction to keep him upset and off-balance."

"You really believe that?"

"I do. He seems to have a pretty big axe to grind with the Crown. That's probably the purpose of this 'entertainment' too, one way or another."

"I disagree," Chen said. "But I suppose it doesn't matter—there's no way he can hurt anyone with this. The only ones who decide what effect this song has are us."

"I agree, and I don't have any intention of projecting anything at all," Alannys said. "We'll just perform the song, try to entertain everyone, and get this all over with as quickly as possible. The sooner we are out of here, the better I'll like it." She looked at Chen for a moment, watching him examine the music in his hand, and a sudden thought occurred to her. "Chen, can you read sheet music?"

"No," he said, frowning again. "At least, that's what I would have told you if you had asked me that five minutes ago. But now..." He shook his head and glanced up at her, then back at the music. "Is this how it works for you?"

"How? How what works?"

Chen was still shaking his head. "I don't know how to explain it, I...when I look at this music...it's like I can *hear* it. In my head. I know what this song sounds like, Alannys, and I've never heard it in my life. And I have no idea what these symbols mean—but I can hear them. Isn't that insane?"

Alannys had to admit it was—and it was disturbing, too. Every time she started to feel comfortable in Ravanmark, every time she felt like she had a handle on how things worked here, some crazy thing came out of left field to remind her that she didn't know everything; she wasn't safe here yet.

She kneaded the ball of her thumb with her teeth, watching Chen stare into the music as though he would have liked to look away, but couldn't tear himself from it. She wondered what he heard when he looked at it. She wondered why she didn't hear it too, and what else music might be capable of. She wondered how she could protect her friends and herself from forces she didn't fully understand, using forces she didn't fully understand. Finally she realized the hard truth of the matter.

No matter what she did, no matter where she went, no

matter how much she thought she knew...she might never be safe here.

Maybe none of them would be safe here, ever again.

♫

Dorramon had never seen Sir Athniss look quite so smug and self-satisfied as he did when he summoned them all out to the garden with a low, sweeping bow. The dining room chairs had been dragged out, and torches cast a soft light across the bricked square in the center of the garden. Their traveling companions sat around him, regarding Chen and Alannys with expressions that ran the gamut from amused (Prince Cardoth) to horrified (Tralice).

"It pleases me greatly," Sir Athniss said, in his own peculiar style, "to be able to welcome all of you, my honored guests, to Agapios Periousia's garden this fine night. A visit from the king himself is a very special occasion, and it deserves to be marked in a very special manner. Toward that end, with the gracious assistance of Lady Alannys and Chen, I am pleased to present a selection from *The Miracles of Orpheus the Mighty*."

There was a smattering of confused applause. Dorramon did his best to keep his reservations to himself, biting his tongue to silence himself, holding the mindlink steadfastly shut. There wasn't a thing about this he liked — as much as Sir Athniss tried in his oily manner to spin this as a tribute, it felt more like a trap. The fact that he couldn't see the teeth didn't make him worry any less about wandering into its jaws.

He was beginning to wonder, though, if this trap was for *him* at all, or if it ever had been. The situation felt too slippery to get a good grip on, and that worried him as much as anything.

There wasn't much he could do about it now, though, short of stomping off and forbidding the whole thing. He didn't want to do that without a very good reason. He was familiar with *The Miracles of Orpheus the Mighty* — there was nothing in there that anybody could call dangerous, not even someone who was looking for an excuse.

So he sat in silence, a grim expression on his face, while Athniss smiled, one arm around Alannys's shoulders, and the other around Chen's, as though the three of them were the best of friends. Athniss gave them each a final squeeze and walked out of the brick-square-cum-stage, moving to stand behind the line of chairs. Chen and Alannys gave weak, half-hearted bows in response to the weak, half-hearted round of applause that greeted them. A short, uncomfortable moment later, they unrolled the scrolls they were holding, turned stiffly to face each other, and Chen began to sing:

"The sun that brightened my life,
once warm, was extinguished,
leaving me in the darkness
and the cold."

"Most impressive," Sir Athniss murmured. Sometime after the song began, he had moved behind Dorramon's chair. "I'd heard about the natural Talents of the Singari, but I certainly never imagined it was all true."

"Shush," Dorramon admonished in a fierce whisper. Something about the knowing edge on the baronet's tone brought to mind the unpleasant innuendos Rathmar and Cardoth had used to run Alannys out of the royal dinner. It felt like forever ago now, but that didn't soften the bitter outrage the memory brought. He felt his back stiffen, but forced himself to say nothing further. This particular duet between Orpheus and Eurydice, at the moment when they first saw each other after her untimely death, was particularly beautiful, and he didn't want to disrupt it any more than they already had. He turned his attention back to the performance as Alannys began to sing.

"Cold, and alone

waiting in the darkness
for you.
Can words describe my loneliness?
Can words describe my happiness now
to see you standing there,
to feel you near me once again?"

This time no one spoke, no sound broke the small, perfect silence that hung between her lines and Chen's next verse.

"The light in my life
once I thought gone for good,
now shines again bright
and warm in my heart."

"I believe it," Athniss said. He sounded even closer now—Dorramon could practically feel him looming over the back of the chair. "You can feel it, even without the music. Look at how they look at each other. I had heard the rumors about them, but I never imagined...you can see the truth of it, shining in his eyes, can't you? And Lady Alannys...I know she promised to marry you, but they are fabulous together..." He trailed off meaningfully. "Well, they are both gifted performers, I suppose."

"That's enough." Dorramon's last thread of patience snapped, and he stood up out of his chair in sudden, blinding fury. The singing had surrendered to blistering silence, and every person in the garden stared at him in undisguised shock. He knew all that, but on some level, he didn't care. "I don't know what you think you're doing, Athniss, but it ends *right now.*"

Athniss watched him with eyes as wide as tea saucers, all the color gone from his face. "But...but your Majesty...the performance..."

"This *performance,*" Dorramon shot back, "is over."

He turned his back without another word, and

stomped off through one of the arch-shaped trellises, neither knowing nor caring what he would find on the other side.

♫

"I'm sorry," Chen said immediately, under his breath, to Alannys. "I should never have gone along with this. I should have guessed something like this might happen."

Alannys shook her head, watching Rodriset hurriedly gather chairs and haul them back inside. "It's isn't your fault." Prince Cardoth and Princess Varilyn walked back inside, their heads close together as they talked, and she guessed they were probably expressing very similar opinions to Chen's—this should never have been allowed to happen. Tralice trailed solicitously along behind them, but she paused near the door to turn and level a withering stare at Alannys, clearly expecting her to follow. Alannys turned away. "It isn't Dorramon's fault, either. This would usually not have happened, no matter what we sang. Athniss was baiting him."

"Was he?" Chen sounded surprised. "I didn't hear anything."

"You wouldn't have. I was watching him, standing behind Dorramon's chair and muttering. What do you suppose he was saying, that he didn't want anyone else to overhear? He set us up for this—all that talk about honoring the king was nonsense. He intended this from the start. Like I said before, this was all about striking out at Dorramon."

"I'm sorry you feel that way." They both spun to find Athniss standing behind them, regarding them over folded arms with uncharacteristic hardness in his pale eyes. "I assure you my only intention here was to offer an entertaining evening for my honored guests. If the king is upset, perhaps you should look to your own egregious behavior before blaming others. The Baronet of Duxol does not easily forgive such slights." He turned and stalked off back inside the manor, with Rodriset following close behind.

Chen shook his head. "A well-spoken line of horse manure, I'm afraid. I don't think he really meant a word of that."

"I'm beginning to wonder if he really meant a single word he said to any of us. He's certainly bold," Alannys mused, watching the baronet's retreating back. "I wonder what he's actually up to here."

"I don't know. And that worries me, because there's no way this is just about taking an opportunity to get in the king's good graces. He never would have risked that little display if it was. I have no idea what he's trying to accomplish. But it almost makes me want to say we would all be better off if we just walked out of this estate right now, and kept walking until we got back to Duxol ourselves, no matter how long it took or what we ran into on the way."

"That may be a bit extreme," Alannys said, "but I know what you mean." She glanced around the empty garden that suddenly seemed quite eerie in the darkness left by the extinguished torches sending tendrils of smoke toward the sky, and heaved a sigh. "I'm going to go talk to Dorramon. Watch yourself, Chen."

"You too, Alannys. I don't know what's going on here, but he didn't put us on the spot by accident." He ruffled her hair, then turned and headed back inside, cutting a stark and somehow lonely figure against the light spilling out from the estate.

♫

Alannys watched the door to the estate after Chen disappeared inside, wondering what any of them were supposed to do now. The whole situation felt...wrong, but she didn't know how to salvage it at this point. And standing alone in a dark, creepy garden wasn't bringing her any epiphanies.

So she went through the same arched, vine-covered tunnel Dorramon had disappeared into. At the end she found another, smaller garden, completely devoted to roses. An enormous stone birdbath stood in the center, nearly as big around as a dinner table.

And standing at the edge of the birdbath, staring morosely into the dark water, was Dorramon.

"I'm sorry," he said, before she could utter a word. "That was an unseemly display on my part. I should not have reacted so badly."

"That's funny, I was just about to apologize to you." She moved behind him and put her arms around him, resting her cheek on his back. "I should never have let Athniss guilt me into that performance. I know there have been rumors about me and Chen—I can't even imagine what people must have said to you. I should have known better than to sing with him, especially a song like that."

He leaned away from her, then turned around and wrapped her in a warm embrace. "You shouldn't worry about what people say, you know that. The song was beautiful. It's Athniss that's the problem. I don't think anything about this was just coincidence—not even his choice of song."

"I think you're right. What was that song, Dorramon? Athniss just said it was from a pageant that used to be performed for state occasions."

"Well, that's accurate, I suppose, as far as it goes. It just entirely omits the reasons why he chose it in the first place, I'm sure."

"I see. I know who Orpheus was where I come from...but like so much that's similar between our worlds, I fear my knowledge may be incomplete, or misleading. Who is Orpheus here?"

Dorramon's expression abruptly sobered. "It's not important."

"I think it is." She had no wish to upset him, but... "Like you said, the choice was no coincidence. I would like to understand why he picked that song."

"I think it's obvious," Dorramon said, a little shortly.

"He wanted to upset me, to make me lose my temper. And he succeeded."

"Indeed," she said. "But is that *all* he was after? Can we be sure? Nothing he's done here has been for the reasons that are immediately apparent. Why should this be any different?"

"Alannys…"

"Okay. Never mind. If you don't want to tell me, that's fine. Let's talk about something else."

"What? What are you up to?"

"Nothing," she said, a little too innocently. "Push where it gives, isn't that what Prince Cardoth says?"

"Prince Cardoth is a terrible role model. I would hate for you to start living by his example."

"You have a point. But in this case, so does he. Chen seems to think Sir Athniss is setting me up, too. If he's right, then something about that song was a message for me, too. If that's the case, I imagine all I have to do is ask him about it, and he'll be more than happy to tell me."

"That has got to be the worst idea you've ever had. I don't want you anywhere near that man."

Alannys brightened. "Then you'll tell me?"

Dorramon sighed and ran his fingers through her hair. "I don't suppose you leave me a lot of choice." He leaned back against the birdbath. "Orpheus lived hundreds of years ago, after the Sothwar. He was a Crown Prince of Ravanmark."

Something in his tone made her shiver, and then she realized — he had said Orpheus was a crown prince — not a king. That was probably not a good sign.

"Orpheus was Talented, perhaps the most Talented musician the world had ever seen, or has seen since. It was said that his singing could move the very rocks to tears. Orpheus was betrothed to a woman he'd loved since they were children, a woman named—"

"Eurydice," Alannys said grimly. This was all sounding sadly familiar, even with the details being so different.

"Yes. Eurydice fell deathly ill, with a fast-spreading, deadly plague that was tormenting large parts of Ravanmark at the time. The king and queen hid her illness from him as long as they were able, and when he finally found out, they forbade him to visit her. It was all an effort to protect the heir to the throne, but you can imagine how Orpheus felt about it. He considered it a betrayal. But there was worse to come."

Alannys had figured as much—so far, this story bore more than a passing resemblance to the Greek myth she had learned in middle school. And even in that myth... "Eurydice died."

Dorramon nodded. He released her and turned to face the birdbath again, and she could see the reflection of the moonlight on the water, and in his eyes. He wrapped his fingers around the edge of the stone basin, gripping it as though he needed the support. It was Alannys's first indication of how *much* he really didn't want to tell this story to her, and she had to wonder why. "Yes. Eurydice died, and once again the king and queen hid the truth. Orpheus didn't find out until after the funeral, when she had already been laid to rest in her family's tomb.

"You can imagine how Orpheus must have felt then. Maybe you can even imagine it better than me—all I can ever seem to think of is the emptiness, the horrible despair —and I don't doubt that he felt that way. But more than that, Orpheus was angry, blisteringly angry. He was half-mad with anger when he took up his sword against the Royal Guards sworn to protect him, fought his way out of the Great Palace, and journeyed to Eurydice's tomb. I don't think he ever stopped to consider the risks of what he was doing, or the impossibility of what he planned—he entered the tomb and wrested her back from the very jaws of death using nothing but the sheer power of song."

"Back from death?" Alannys felt like the whole world had taken a sudden step sideways without her. "That's not possible. It would have killed him before he ever revived her."

"It *should* have killed him. But he survived, and so did she. Don't ask me why, because I can't explain it. Everyone agreed that Soth was the most powerful musician who ever lived. But even he never brought back the dead. It was too much, it couldn't be hidden. Eurydice's entire family — the entire town she lived in — knew her to be dead. They had been to the funeral; they had seen her laid to rest in the tomb. And now she was back, and there was no concealing how it came to be. Throughout the kingdom, Orpheus was known now as a musician."

"Lucky him," Alannys said, perhaps a little sourly, remembering some of her own experiences around Ravanmark with people who had known of her Talent.

Dorramon quirked a smile at her. "Well, he did have one advantage — given the magnitude of what he had done, and the undeniably heroic nature of the deed, he was pretty well unanimously hailed as the Redeemer. Now as you know, that can bring its own set of problems, but at least he didn't have anybody trying to stone him at the palace gates. He did have one hell of a case of Muse's Fever, though — for two months he suffered, burning and delirious."

Alannys shivered — even after turning back a tidal wave, probably the biggest thing she'd ever done, she had never suffered a two-month-long Muse's Fever. She couldn't even imagine it.

"He woke up to an investiture ceremony. He took Songstrike and the songs of the Redeemer and set out that same day to perform the acts."

Dorramon fell silent, and Alannys tried to imagine it — someone else taking the vows she had taken, someone else carrying Songstrike. Had the blade turned blue when he was in trouble, and if it had, had Orpheus known what it meant? Or had it boggled him, as it had boggled her? Had

Songstrike sung its songs to him, the same way it sang to her?

She didn't even want to think about it. It felt weird — wrong, somehow, like a kind of betrayal.

It took her a moment to realize that her mind had been wandering for several minutes now, but Dorramon had made no attempt to continue his story. He stood unmoving, staring into the dark water, almost as if he'd forgotten she was there.

She moved to stand next to him, placing her hands on the edge of the birdbath next to his. "So what happened?"

Dorramon started — it looked like he really *had* forgotten she was there. "I'm sorry, what?"

"What happened to him? Orpheus?"

Dorramon sighed, reaching out to cover her hand with his own. "You can probably guess. He failed." The anguish in his eyes made it clear to her why he brushed aside all discussion of her own attempt at the acts. "He died at the Spire of Glory. I don't think he even made it through the first line. They brought back his body, home to the catacombs, and Songstrike, which went back into the vaults of the Palace Chapel. Somewhere on the journey back, the songs of the Redeemer were lost, and never seen again — until now."

Alannys stood there unmoving, her hand suddenly cold under his. "He...failed? Even with all that power, he failed?" She swallowed hard, struggling against sudden, disorienting vertigo. "Dorramon, I could never do what he did. Not on my best day. I can't even imagine that much power — and he still failed? I haven't got a hope, have I? At the end of the day, is that what I'll be? Another failed Redeemer?"

His hand clenched convulsively around hers. "No. Don't you start thinking that way, Alannys, because that's exactly what Athniss wants. That's why he picked a song from that pageant — he had to know you would find out the story behind it, eventually. He's trying to torment you with it." He wasn't looking at her, he was still staring grimly out at the water, but suffering was plain in the tense muscles of his face.

"He's trying to torment *us* with it." Seeing the look on his face just then, she couldn't doubt the truth of it. "Whether I ever found out about the story or not, he knew that you would already know it. The song was a message for you, at least as much as for me."

"In more ways than one," Dorramon muttered.

"What?"

"Nothing." He turned to face her suddenly, his eyes dark in the moonlight. "What you must remember is this: being the Redeemer of the Realm is not about brute strength. It's not even about having the most Talent. It requires something more, something not many people have, Talented or not. Something I don't think even Orpheus had, at least not enough."

"What?" The word was little more than a ragged whisper. She couldn't tear her eyes away from his face— she wanted very desperately to believe that what he was telling her was true, that there was some way that she could still survive what she had set out to do.

"Put simply, a sense of self-sacrifice."

"Self-sacrifice? Is that a joke? He went into a tomb to sing a woman back from the dead—he had to think he was going to die."

"Certainly. But that isn't what I'm talking about. Anybody could be expected to sacrifice for someone they love. But would Orpheus have offered the same for a king who had shown him nothing but distrust and hostility, and then offered again, months later, for a different king who had worked only to destroy him? How many people would have risked their own death for a little girl they didn't even know, or a town full of uniformly unfriendly people?"

Alannys frowned, thinking about it.

"It's different in those circumstances, it's a kind of

service, and service is a kind of love. Being the Redeemer requires that kind of love. It requires a willingness to put yourself in harm's way for others, sometimes for others you have never met, will never meet, and have no reason to risk yourself for. You've shown that willingness over and over since you came to Ravanmark, Alannys — for me, for Raman, and for countless others. You fought to save people who were your friends, people you'd only just met, and entire towns and tribes. No one else who ever called themselves the Redeemer could claim that, and I think it matters more than strength or Talent. Because what are the acts of the Redeemer about, really, except sacrificing yourself for the welfare of other people?"

♫

Alannys swallowed hard, considering this new revelation. "You're right — of course you're right. I mean, everything you're saying is right, and it makes sense. I just...I just wish there was some way I could be sure. It scares me, to tell you the truth. It scares me more than anything I've ever done."

"Me, too." His voice sounded as rough as she felt. "I can hardly sleep at night for thinking of you, of the risk you're going to take that I can do nothing to mitigate. I'm the King of Ravanmark. Most people would say I'm the most powerful man on the planet. But I wonder, what good is it to be king when I can do nothing to protect the woman I love? What good is all that power, if it can do nothing to save you?"

"Dorramon..." She reached out to touch his face. The feel of his skin against hers grounded her; the gentle electricity that played between them seemed to reinforce that the connection between them would not be easy to break. "I wish there was something I could say to make it better. But I know there isn't, because I understand how you feel. If there's one good thing about all of this, it's that you don't have to do it. I don't think I could bear to stand back and watch you risk your life that way. You're very strong, Dorramon. I don't think I could manage as well, in your place."

"Strong," Dorramon snorted. "I think you mean helpless. It's hardly strength to do nothing about something you can't control."

Alannys shook her head, pulling her hand back. "That kind of cynicism isn't like you, Dorramon. I think the Baronet of Duxol has gotten under your skin."

"Don't say that." He turned back to the birdbath.

"Don't say what? That he's annoyed you? It seems pretty obvious to me—I imagine everyone else who was in the garden tonight would think so, too."

"No, not that. Baronet of Duxol. Don't say that, it isn't proper."

"Isn't...proper?" Alannys cast a glance around the garden. It remained still and quiet, empty except for the two of them, moonlight reflecting off the water and giving the rose blossoms a gentle, glowing, fuzzy sort of halo effect. "Why not? It's what he calls himself, isn't it?"

"It is," Dorramon said grimly, "but that doesn't make it right."

"Hold on, I'm confused. Is Athniss a baronet, or is he not?"

Dorramon sighed. "He is. But it doesn't mean what he thinks it means, or what you seem to think it means."

She just stared at him. She got the very strong feeling that he didn't really want to talk about this, but it had to happen, from what she could see. What he was saying didn't make sense, and it felt like this business with his title was the root of all Athniss's hostility toward the Crown.

"Look, Alannys, you've probably noticed that the system of nobility in Ravanmark is not exactly simple. Lords, barons, earls, dukes—there are many ranks with different privileges and responsibilities...and levels of respect...afforded to each. There are so many noble houses of so many stations, who have intermarried and merged

Sandra Miller

over the decades—I couldn't tell you how many lords
there are in Ravanmark, or how many barons. But what I
can tell you with absolute certainty is that there is not, nor
has there ever been, a noble rank of baronet."

"But—but—are you saying Athniss just...just *made his
title up,* out of thin air, and everyone just goes along with
it?"

"No. No, he does have the title of baronet, and his
family has had it for a very long time. So long...we actually
weren't even aware there were any families left claiming
that title. It looks like he's the last of this one...maybe the
last, period."

"I don't understand." She didn't even bother trying to
ask any of her myriad questions—there were so many, she
had no idea where to even start.

"You've heard a bit about the Sothwar, about how the
country of Ravanmark was born from its ashes. I'm sure
you can imagine that in the aftermath of that great war,
things were not all roses and rainbows here. Everyone
with any power or money was jockeying for position, and
quite a few other countries decided at different times that
what Ravanmark really needed was a hostile invasion, to
be taken in as part of somewhere else. Even a well-
established monarchy has trouble dealing with those types
of threats—I guess you've seen that well enough for
yourself. But what they had back then, back in the early
days of Ravanmark—and for longer than I would
probably like to admit—was nothing like a well-
established monarchy. It was a brand-new, shaky, weak
monarchy that even the general population had yet to
fully accept, let alone the rich and powerful. The
monarchy was trying to establish itself in a country with
no infrastructure, no existing power structure...at least
none worth keeping...and no public money. There was no
royal treasury to fall back on, and the new government
had to be defended against encroachers, both foreign and
domestic. The newly-invested nobles contributed as much

as they were able, but there was still a lot of money untapped in families that were not noble, but were wealthy."

"So the title of baronet came from...a need for money?" It felt indecent somehow...money was a matter most noble families wouldn't even deign to discuss. Buying a title...she couldn't even imagine how they would think about something like that.

"Exactly. It wasn't our proudest moment, and I wouldn't say it was the wisest thing the monarchy has ever done, but it was a case of desperate times. In exchange for money — a set amount over a set time — a wealthy family received the title of baronet."

"He *bought* his title." Alannys couldn't quite keep the shock from her tone — the whole thing seemed to run against everything she imagined Ravanmark's system of government to stand for.

"Indeed. He doesn't seem to know that, though — doubtless his forefathers didn't see fit to pass down that particular detail. Let's be absolutely clear on this, Alannys: in no way is baronet a truly noble title. He doesn't have the right to summon the lords of the holdings, he doesn't even have the right to attend court. It isn't a landed title."

"Landed title?"

"Right...he doesn't have the right to call himself baronet *of* anything. He has a title, but he's still common."

Alannys turned around and leaned heavily against the edge of the birdbath. "So all these slights he perceives against himself and his family — all of this 'discrimination' he keeps talking about — none of it is real. It's all just him misunderstanding what his title means, what it even is."

"It is."

"Well, shouldn't we tell him? I mean, shouldn't we explain?"

Dorramon folded his arms and regarded her solemnly. "I can't imagine it would do any good. Do you really think he's going to believe me, over the family history that's been passed down all these generations?"

She sighed, deflated. "No. Honestly, Dorramon, he seems to bear the Crown quite a bit of ill will. I think anything you could tell him, he would only regard as you trying to get out of your obligations, trying to cover up the wrongs he perceives."

"I think so too. Regardless of all his talk about impressing me, I don't think there's anything I could say that would make him less bitter." He sighed, looking up at the night sky. "It's getting awfully late, and tomorrow's going to be another long day. We had better get to bed."

"You're right." She pushed herself off the birdbath, heading back for the archway where they came in. "Watch yourself, Dorramon. I think he carries quite the grudge against you."

"Me? I'm not convinced it's me you need to worry about, Alannys. It's not me he's got back in the servant's quarters away from everyone else."

She stopped cold, and turned around to look at him. He didn't look like he was teasing; his face, pale and somber in the moonlight, regarded her seriously. "You think he's got a problem with me?"

"I do. Look at it, Alannys, every thing he has done since we got here has been aimed at isolating you, cutting you off from the rest of us. He physically separated you by the room he put you in, but that clumsy, rude question of Rodriset's was aimed at pushing you away from Chen. And the comments about Varilyn, and that song...he was trying to drive a wedge between us."

"I can't argue that...I get the feeling he's been trying to upset us all since we got here. But I don't think I'm his target. I think I'm the only one so far away because I'm the only one you can call for help without saying a word, no matter what."

"You think he knows about the mindlink?" Dorramon looked startled. "I hadn't even considered that."

Alannys shrugged. "I don't think it's a real secret—

people like to gossip."

"It doesn't matter." Dorramon waved the issue away, shaking his head as though trying to get his thoughts back on track. "He is driving wedges. And I can't help but wonder why he would try so hard to turn us all against each other."

In the moonlight, his eyes were inscrutable, as dark and deep as the night itself. It made his solemn expression look even more grim, and she shivered. "I don't know. I don't have an answer for that. What should we do?"

His troubled gaze slid away from hers. "I don't know. I don't think there is much we *can* do, unfortunately. We're well out from town...far too much distance to cover on our own, on foot in the middle of the night. All we can do, I suppose, is try to get some rest so that we're alert tomorrow, ready for whatever it is he's planning to spring on us."

She nodded. "I understand. But I still don't like it."

"Me either. Just be careful. Be very, very careful, and let me know the instant anything out of the ordinary happens."

"I will." She took two big steps and threw her arms around him. "You too. And promise me, no matter what he says, you won't let him drive any wedges between us."

"Never." His voice was hoarse, and his embrace so tight it almost hurt. "You know me better than that." He took her arm, and together they went back inside. Dorramon led her down the deserted corridor, in the direction of the guest rooms. "Given everything that's happened, I think it would be wise if you stayed with me tonight."

"I'm sorry, your Highness," said a voice behind them, "but I've already explained I can't let her do that."

They stopped short, and turned to face the frowning figure of Sir Athniss. It took everything Alannys had not to groan out loud.

"Not this again," Dorramon said, in a tone that implied

he felt much the same.

"I am deeply sorry my family's traditions are such an inconvenience to you," Athniss said, his tone biting. "But I will not allow you to smear our honor in this way."

"Smear your honor," Dorramon echoed. "You must see that this is ridiculous."

"I know that you think it is — the Crown would never treat any family it respected the way mine has been treated."

"That isn't what I meant. We've had a rocky time of it, and I'm not letting her out of my sight."

"I say that you *are*," Athniss countered, suddenly sounding genuinely angry. "It is said that a man's home is his castle. In this one I am king, and I say that while you are here, you *will* observe propriety!"

Dorramon's face turned dark, angry red, and he opened his mouth to respond.

Alannys grabbed his arm to stop him. "Dorramon, I think he may be right."

Athniss smiled at her ingratiatingly. Dorramon turned and stared at her as though she had suddenly sprouted a second head. "What?"

She looked away, not making eye contact with either of them. "Tralice has been telling me the same thing — that I must be proper, that I must have a care for my position. Maybe this is the kind of thing she meant. If people would view us rooming together as improper...then I'll go back to my own room."

"Alannys...you shouldn't worry about things like that. You know that. Just be yourself."

"I'm afraid 'myself' isn't noble, and is prone to do things wrong. I don't want to drag you down with me." She squeezed his arm. "It's okay. Just don't forget what you promised."

"Of course."

Sir Athniss, now in a considerably improved mood, bowed low to her. "My Lady, it would be my honor to escort you to your room."

"That's not necessary."

"Please, I insist." He started off, and she fell into step behind him. Tralice would be pleased that her lessons were sinking in. She knew that from most perspectives, she had made the right choice.

But she could feel Dorramon's frown on her back the whole way. He was not pleased, not at all.

♫

True to his word, Sir Athniss walked Alannys all the way back to her room. She dragged herself along behind him, wishing she was anywhere else. In the dark, the estate with its long corridors and rundown, once-was-nice elegance was creepy and depressing. She was relieved to see her door, thinking of flopping down on the bed and staring outside. Maybe it would help her escape the awful tension the place seemed to inspire in her.

Sir Athniss lurked behind her in the hall, watching her push open the door as though he thought she might suddenly turn and try to escape.

That didn't sound like such a bad idea, really.

Alannys had to stifle a groan when the door swung open and she could see into her little room. The smelly tallow candle was already burning, and standing in the center of the room with crossed arms and a severe expression, was Tralice.

"Good evening," Alannys said uncertainly, wondering what had brought the maid to her room, and what kind of reception she could expect now that she was here.

"I suppose you must think so, as long as you've been out." Tralice reached around her and pushed the door shut. "Good *night* is more like it, I should think. Do you really think that's appropriate for the king or his consort?"

Alannys bristled. "I think I am getting awfully tired of people telling me what I should and shouldn't do. I think Dorramon and I are both grown adults capable of making our own decisions. Besides, there's nobody here to see or to judge."

Tralice sighed. "You may not think so, my Lady, but I think that is just because you are—as usual—quite unaware of how much attention you command. This baronet, he imagines himself an influential man. The currency of influence is insider information, I can tell you that from experience. Don't doubt for a moment that he is closely watching both of you, ready to spread what he sees around as much of the kingdom as he is able. You should never have allowed him to put you in this wretched part of the manor...all by yourself...it's disgraceful."

"He didn't give me much choice," Alannys said sourly. "It doesn't matter anyway. I don't doubt Sir Athniss is watching all of us very carefully, but I don't think he's doing it so he can spread rumors. I don't think those sorts of things have nearly the power out here that they do in the Great Palace. I don't know what his true intentions are, but I think they're a fair bit worse than idle gossip."

Tralice's eyes widened, and she looked away. "Oh, I can't imagine anyone wishing you harm, my Lady, or King Dorramon."

Alannys grunted. "I can, easily enough. Seems like there's been plenty of it going around." The sarcastic comment seemed to cast a dark pall over the room, and Alannys was abruptly tired of the conversation. "Tralice, why are you here?"

"Simply to talk to you, my Lady." Tralice sounded miffed. "Simply to beg you to watch what you do, what you say, very carefully—especially when you are with the king."

Alannys crossed her arms and stifled a yawn. "I see. Have you spoken with the king about this?"

"I can't! He doesn't listen to a thing I say—he hasn't since before we left the palace!"

"I see. Well, maybe the best thing to do is just trust him to handle this. It seems to me—"

"No, my Lady, I beg you to hear me out!" Tralice

paused and took a deep breath. "I know you dislike Sir Athniss — and I fully agree, what manner of person expects royalty to sleep in their clothes like the meanest of peasants? — but I fear that you aren't taking him seriously. I have worked for the royal family for many years. Do you realize how rare it is for his Majesty to lose his temper like that, in front of others? I have seen him face far more dangerous adversaries, with far more aplomb. A man who could provoke such a reaction from his Majesty, in such a short time...if what you are saying is true, my Lady, and he harbors ill intentions, he could prove to be a formidable opponent. A formidable opponent indeed."

♫

The silence in the little room after Tralice left felt deep and depressing. Alannys envied her maid the freedom to walk away from it. She wished she could do that too. The room's single, small window didn't open, but for a moment she fantasized about breaking the glass out with the chair, hurling herself headfirst through the opening, and running screaming off into the abandoned orchard.

Instead she blew out the smelly candle and stretched out on the bed. It was as uncomfortable as only a hay mattress could be. She was alone and miserable, and it occurred to her that if Dorramon was right, and Sir Athniss was trying to isolate her...he was succeeding. She lifted the Seeing Stone into her hands, gripping the stone like a talisman against the loneliness that threatened to consume her. She fervently wished, just then, that her room was closer to her friends.

She rolled over and stared out the window, willing the hours to pass.

The hours stubbornly refused to cooperate.

Finally, the swaying, undulating trees in the breeze outside put her in a sort of trance, and she began to drift off to sleep.

She was floating there, somewhere between consciousness and dreams, thoughts wandering through her mind with no coherence, when the voice crashed into her mind, frantic and panicked. *Alannys!*

She shot bolt upright in the bed, her chest gripped with a sudden fear so sharp and intense it was painful. *Dorramon! Dorramon, what happened?*

No time. Need help. He sounded strange — rough, somehow — like a bad imitation of himself.

There was no time to worry about that, though, no time for questions or hesitation. She had been *right,* Athniss was trying to keep her away from Dorramon, and he needed her help *now.* She barreled out of the bed, reaching for the doorknob as she responded. *Where are you?*

Corridor, came the short reply.

She frowned, ignoring the cold sweat that broke out on her forehead. It wasn't like Dorramon to be so curt — whatever had happened must have been really bad. She flung the door open and ran out into the hallway.

The hall was dimly lit by the moonlight from the window at the end. A man's silhouette stood in front of the window, his features completely lost in the white backlight. "Dorramon!" She veered toward him, wondering what on earth was going on.

She was halfway there before she realized that the figure in the window was most certainly not Dorramon. She recognized the stiff, unfriendly form of Rodriset in the same moment that a sudden dark shape lunged toward her from the shadows of the hallway. A sharp, bright pain exploded in her head, and everything went dark.

♪

It felt like waking up in slow motion. Alannys's brain felt fuzzy, and her thoughts were sluggish — but at the same time, it seemed like she couldn't get a good grip on any one of them before it flittered off, only to be replaced by another vague, half-formed impression, completely unrelated to the first. It felt like struggling to consciousness through layers of mud, like waking up with a terrific hangover. Only she was pretty sure she hadn't been drinking.

At least, as sure as she was of anything, which right at that moment wasn't very sure at all. The air around her smelled dank and musty, and she was pretty certain that wasn't right, either. And the mindlink was gone, that familiar opening in her mind closed as completely as if it had never been. Could the dank, musty place where she found herself now have been Talent-proofed?

She creaked her eyes open, ignoring the dull pounding in her head, hoping that with some visuals things would start to make some sense. Her right eye didn't want to open—only after she managed to pry it open anyway did she realize it had been matted shut. That whole side of her face was stiff and strange-feeling; nothing moved or felt like it should, it was all covered in dried...blood?

What had happened to her? She searched her memory but couldn't find anything to explain what her scattered senses were telling her.

She was slumped uncomfortably in a wooden chair, with a back and seat that were ramrod straight, without the slightest bit of give. Her wrists were tied together behind the chair, and her ankles were bound to its legs. She ached in more places than she could count. And in from of her, arms folded, staring down at her with undisguised hostility, was the baronet.

"Athniss." She knew the lack of title would aggravate him, and she knew it probably was not wise to be aggravating him in her current position, but she couldn't help it. She'd be *damned* if she would say 'sir' to someone who had done this, and she didn't see anyone else around to blame. "What's going on? Where is Dorramon?"

"How charming." Athniss's peal of merry laughter sounded honestly amused. "She still hasn't figured it out. The king is in his room, sleeping soundly. He's quite safe —for now."

"What?" She struggled against her bonds, trying to sit up straighter in her chair, ignoring the way it made her head pound. "What do you mean, for now?"

"Well, now, that all depends on you. So many things are temporary, fleeting...sometimes we can hold on to those things. Sometimes they slip through our fingers like grains of sand. In this particular case, well, it's all up to you, my Lady."

"I don't understand. He said he needed help..."

"My, you really are slow tonight. What you heard was not King Dorramon at all, Alannys."

"Not..?"

"It was me."

She stared at him, feeling the room dance oddly around her addled brain. It was a good thing she had the chair holding her up, because she couldn't have managed to stay upright on her own just then. "That's not possible. How could you..."

He laughed again. "Dear me. You have carried that little trinket for months, but you really don't have any idea how it works, do you?"

She followed his gaze down from her face to the Seeing Stone hanging around her neck. She frowned into its fiery, gold-streaked depths for a moment, failing to see his point.

With slow, exaggerated motions, Athniss pulled back his ragged cloak, reached into his pocket and withdrew...

...the Seeing Stone.

♫

Of course Sir Athniss couldn't have the Seeing Stone, not really. How could he? The Seeing Stone hung around her neck right now, and it felt just as solid and heavy as ever, reassuring in its familiarity. What she was seeing didn't make any sense. Why would anyone make a copy of the Seeing Stone? Why would anyone *want* a copy of the Seeing Stone?

"It isn't a copy," Athniss said, and she jerked her gaze back to him, wondering if her thoughts were that plain in her expression. "I assure you, Alannys, my Seeing Stone is every bit as authentic as yours — and every bit as powerful. By the Sacred Song, you really had no idea, did you?"

She slowly shook her head. The only thing that seemed clear about this situation was her utter helplessness — he had every advantage here. All she had was a bunch of questions she couldn't even articulate clearly, let alone puzzle out answers for.

"Well, then." Athniss sounded smug — clearly he was enjoying his game. "Let me tell you a few things that you may find enlightening. Have you ever heard of a group called the Lord's Retainers?"

"No. Should I have?"

"Well, not necessarily, I suppose. But I can tell you they have certainly heard of you. And they regard you, if you don't mind me saying so, with a very great deal of animosity." He seemed to relish what he was telling her.

"Me? Why?"

"Something about an insult you dealt them. Hanged if I know. Hanged if I *care*, to tell you the truth. To be perfectly frank, money is what I care about. Restoring a noble family's lost honor doesn't come cheap, and these people have more than enough to help me do that. And there's only one thing they require of me."

"What's — what's that?"

"What, haven't you guessed?" Athniss laughed, a shrill, derisive sound that made her skin crawl. "What they want me to do, Lady Alannys, is dispose of you. *Permanently.*"

♫

Alannys sat there staring at Athniss for a long, silent moment, feeling like she had missed a shift somewhere. These people whose name she didn't even recognize were willing to pay this man she hardly knew — to kill her? "Why?"

"Well, not that it matters much to me personally, you understand, but I asked that very same question. It seems these people have been waiting an awfully long time for someone—someone they thought was you. You proved them wrong, evidently. The Redeemer they expected isn't the one they got, so they tell me there's only one thing to do about it—get rid of you so they can try again."

"Get rid of..." Alannys was still fighting her post-concussive trauma hangover, but even her befuddled brain was beginning to understand. The room around her was small and uneven, with walls of lumpy, badly cut stone, with moss growing on the rocks and the mortar between them. The musty, mildewed smell probably meant they were underground—the insufficient light from the single tallow candle made it hard to be sure. And here she was tied to a chair, stuck here, while Athniss spoke so casually of disposing of her, his eyes glittering malevolently in the low light.

"Help!" Alannys shouted at the top of her lungs. "Somebody help me!" She threw herself to the side, then to the other side, testing her restraints with her entire body weight. She had the little chair rocking, but her restraints held.

"By all means, scream if it makes you feel better. But allow me to point out that down here, absolutely no one can hear you. Except me." He smiled a broad, self-satisfied smile. "And you may have already guessed that I will do nothing to help you."

She stared at him balefully, panting, feeling her pulse slow and trying to come to terms with her situation. Her only way out of this, it seemed, was through him. For now, she was going to have to play his game. At least Dorramon was safe.

For now.

She tried to focus on the things he had told her, her befuddled brain struggling to make sense out of what he was saying. The wrong Redeemer...waiting for a long time...

She had a fleeting, vivid memory of a young man's eyes, narrowed in anger and hate. She clearly remembered his words: "You must know this will not be forgotten." Garrant. The Inn of the Abandoned Lord...and the Soth-worshiping crowd. The name itself took a moment to float up from the recesses of her mind...

"Corran," she whispered. "Soth worshipers? These Lord's Retainers—they are Soth worshipers?"

"Seems that way." Athniss shrugged, as though the matter was utterly inconsequential. "They have a great many relics and papers of Soth. Along with this stone, they had several letters Soth wrote to Ravan. The stones, you see, were a matched pair, meant to work together. In his letters Soth beseeched Ravan never to let her stone out of her sight, because used properly, it would allow anyone to encroach on the mindlink. Along with the money to finance everything you've seen and done here, they left this stone. It has been most helpful, wouldn't you say?"

Alannys ignored him. "Athniss, you have to let me go. You must know you can't possibly get away with this."

"*Sir* Athniss!" he roared. "You must see this kind of casual, ingrained disrespect is exactly why I *can't* let you go! No nobleman should be treated this way. The things Rodriset and I have had to do, simply to scrape by another day...with the money the Retainers have promised me, no one will ever ignore my rightful title again!"

Alannys shifted around in her chair, trying to relieve some of the burning ache in her shoulders and her knees. She needed a way out—this man was insane, and not just a little—how had she not seen it sooner? She figured she had better humor him by using his title, out of concern for her own safety if not out of respect. "You're wrong. Baronet isn't a noble title—you must know that, Sir Athniss. Your family bought that title, and you're right, I should use it—but nobody's disrespecting you by denying you the privileges of nobility. You aren't noble!"

"Lies!" Athniss shouted back at her. "You and your precious king will do anything to bury the mistakes you've made!" He stopped suddenly, rubbing at his temples until the flush in his cheeks faded. "But we are getting off course. The Retainers don't matter, my Lady, and you don't need to worry about my title."

All at once he stopped talking, which worried her more than anything he had said. He moved around behind her chair, and she squirmed again, twice as nervous as she had been with him in front of her. "Put simply, it comes down to this," he said. She felt a tugging at the ropes binding her wrists, and realized he was untying her. Even that felt ominous — he had kept her restrained all this time; what made him suddenly confident enough to release her?

"You have a choice to make, my Lady — your life or the king's."

♫

The shock of recognition hit her like a slap. Alannys realized that Chen's words had been as prophetic as her Second Sight — in trying to flee from the vision, they had run right to it. Despair and helplessness rose up around her like a choking fog...if their best efforts had only led them right to where they would have wound up anyway, did that mean they really had no choice but to dance to the tune of fate, in the end? Did their will — did her will — count for nothing after all?

No. No, she refused to believe that. All that was too close to Tryn's philosophies of doom and grief. Tryn had already been proven wrong once, and Alannys wasn't ready to concede defeat now. So they had wound up here...it wasn't what any of them had wanted, but it didn't mean all was lost, and she would never stop fighting.

Her resolution made, and her courage found, she finally swallowed hard and spoke. "A choice...I don't understand."

Athniss's bark of laughter was sharp and cruel. "No, I rather suspected you wouldn't." The rope fell from her wrists and he came back around to her front, kneeling and untying the ropes around her ankles.

Alannys stretched and flexed her sore muscles, and

leaned over to rub her aching ankles. While he stood over her, watching on with a sadistic sneer over crossed arms, she slipped her hand up under the hem of her yellow dress and palmed the handle of her dagger, thanking whatever impulse had prompted her to put it on back at the palace, what felt like forever ago.

"Well, now," Athniss said, "if you've recovered your wits, perhaps we can proceed. I don't think there is any mystery about what must happen here. I intend to fulfill the task set to me by the Retainers." He seemed very much like a monster to her in that moment, saying such horrible things with such perfect equanimity. He reached out for her with one hand, and in her eyes his fingers looked like horrid talons.

Alannys didn't think, didn't question—she saw him put his hand out toward her and she lashed out with her dagger. The blade dug into his palm and he jerked his hand back, cradling it against his chest. She could already see the blood spreading across his dingy, frilly shirt.

Before she even had time to register his intent, he struck out with his other hand, knocking the dagger from her hand and sending it spinning across the uneven stone floor.

Alannys launched herself out of the chair. She could see her dagger, its blue jewels glittering in the low light as it spun, and she could see her own fingers, scrabbling against the stone in a desperate attempt to reach it.

The next thing she saw was Athniss's leather boot moving in her peripheral vision, before it crashed like a bludgeon into the side of her head, sending her sprawling onto the floor, hopelessly far away from her only weapon.

Her head reeled, her vision swam, but her body lay limp and useless on the floor while Athniss stomped over and grabbed her arm. He dragged her to her feet, and it occurred to her dazed mind that for all his dandified manners, right down to his manner of dress, the baronet was actually quite strong underneath.

That didn't do much to make her feel better about her chances of surviving this encounter.

Athniss gave her a vicious shake and pushed her back down into the chair. "I don't advise you to try that again. Even with an injured hand, I am more than a match for you, Alannys. I detest violence—I prefer to do this with as little damage as possible. But I am more than willing to forego my preference, if that is your choice."

"Damage?" Alannys said. The word sounded so ridiculous just then that she was sure she must have misheard. "As little *damage as possible?* You just said you intended to dispose of me. Surely you didn't think I would just go along with that?"

"Actually, that's just what I thought. And I assure you, in the end, you will." He clenched his hand into a fist, but it did little to staunch the bleeding. He frowned at it, then put it to his side and ignored it. "Contrary to what you seem to believe, I have no intention of attacking you. I merely offered my hand to help you up."

"Help me...up? You aren't making sense."

"Never confuse a lack of understanding on your part with a lack of coherence on mine. I said the Retainers want you dead, before you can perform the acts of the Redeemer. That doesn't mean I need to strike you, or," he grimaced at his hand again, "stab you. I simply need you to walk into that alcove, right there."

He stepped back from her, gesturing with a flourish to a shallow, arched alcove in the mossy stone wall behind him. She could see moisture clinging to the surface even from where she sat, and a pair of rusty iron manacles on chains, bolted high on the wall.

"No," she said immediately. "You're crazy. I would never voluntarily walk into that. Where is this place?"

"The dungeon," Athniss said shortly. "I am afraid that Agapios Periousia rather predates what you might call a civilized Ravanmark. This particular facility doesn't see much use anymore—even the entrance is well hidden.

And as you have probably already guessed, it has been Talent-proofed. If you are looking for help, it will not find you here. If your bones are ever discovered here, it will be long after the world outside has forgotten you ever lived."

She just stared at him. She didn't even know what to say to him. As far as she could see, the only thing stopping her from walking out of that dungeon right then was him, and her own swimming senses. If only he hadn't kicked her head quite so hard...

"Now, I'm going to encourage you to just drop that line of thought right there," Athniss said, removing his Seeing Stone and laying it carefully down on a table. At least, at first glance Alannys assumed it to be a table. A second glance revealed it to be rather oddly made for a table, with cuffs at the head and foot to hold a person fast, a split across the middle, and a winching device to pull the two halves apart. She shuddered and looked away. "There are a few things you don't know, which might change your view of this situation. First of all I should tell you that the dinner served to you and your friends this evening contained a rather powerful poison. I'm not well-versed in such things myself—I'm a peaceful man, I've never sought to hurt anyone—but as in so many other matters, the Retainers are experts, and they are more than willing to share what they know with those who serve them well. I daresay you and your friends never suspected while you were eating, just as the Retainers assured me."

She could feel her eyes widen.

"Now, now, don't panic. All is not lost. This particular poison has a very effective antidote. You can take as proof of this the fact that you are here right now, in full possession of your faculties and not in any particular pain. Rodriset placed the antidote in the wine he gave you earlier. Fast-acting, undetectable—again, all as the Retainers promised. You are perfectly restored. Your friends, though, and your precious king..." He shook his head mournfully. "I am afraid that they have not been so fortunate. Even now, they are suffering, already their grasps on this world begin to slip. And yet all is not lost, even now—their salvation is still possible. Rodriset has prepared the antidote, and at this moment is waiting to administer it to your friends. Whether or not they will ever receive it...well, that depends entirely upon you."

"What do I have to do?" Her voice sounded hoarse and strained—much the way she felt right then. Was he lying to her? She thought he was—she felt he had to be. Why go to the trouble of such an elaborate scheme, when he could just tell her that he had, and the result would be the same? It made sense. And yet, cold fear gripped her stomach, for how could she be sure? And could she risk the consequences, if what he said was true?

"That's more like it. Just walk into the alcove, my Lady —I'll close it up and that will be that."

"This is insane. You can't ask me to do this."

"I'm not asking you—I'm telling you. You are going to walk into that alcove, or everyone you care about is going to die. Are you prepared to live with that?"

"No." She leaned forward in the chair, feeling her muscles shake and wondering it if was from physical exertion or fear. The iron manacles hung there in front of her, a few feet away, mocking her. She swallowed hard. "Why do you insist I walk in there? Why didn't you just put me in there while I was unconscious? I could have just woken up chained."

"Believe me, I considered it. But our friends with the Retainers have assured me that they would not be happy if anything was done to you against your will."

"What? They want you to kill me, and they want me to *approve* of that?"

Athniss shrugged. "In a manner of speaking. You don't have to like it, Alannys. You just have to choose it. You have to walk into that alcove of your own free will, fully understanding what it means. They say it's important— something about you willfully stepping aside for Soth. I don't know. I don't care, really — the lot of them sound half crazy to me. But they have the money I need, and this is what they want, so this is what they'll get. You have a choice to make, Alannys, and it's a simple one. Your life or the king's."

"I — this is inhumane, Athniss! How can you do something like this, in a place named for love?"

"It makes perfect sense from where I'm standing. It's all a question of perspective, my Lady — that is, who or what one loves. Much like the question facing you now, actually. Which will it be, then? Your life, or his?"

♪

Alannys swallowed hard. What could she do? In the end, she knew there was every possibility Athniss was lying to her — she couldn't even use the mindlink to check, and he knew that as well as she did. "Why should I believe you will actually honor your word? How do I know that if I do go in there, you will spare my friends?"

His laugh was harsher now. "Because," he said, "it's the only hope any of you have now. You're already dead, Alannys. I will never let you leave this place alive. But your friends — do nothing and they will die, too. Do you understand that? Dorramon will *die*. Only if you walk willingly into that cell does he have a chance. Anything else is certain death for him. Do you want to die with that on your conscience? Do you want to go to your Muses knowing that you took him with you, to buy yourself a few more minutes?"

Of course she didn't want that. She wasn't willing to gamble with other people's lives. She wasn't willing to gamble with *Dorramon's* life, not under any circumstances, not ever. And yet she couldn't help resisting the idea, couldn't help thinking there had to be some way out of this. It couldn't be as bad as it seemed.

But she wasn't in any condition for a fight — she knew she couldn't win. Her head still felt woozy and her balance was shot. Her breath came hard and fast after the kick he had dealt her, and without the chair holding her up, she probably would have been on the floor. She couldn't use her Talent, and none of her friends knew where she was — or that she was even gone to begin with.

She couldn't fight her way out, she couldn't sing her way out, and nobody was coming to help her. As much as it burned to admit it, it looked like Athniss was right — she wasn't getting out of there alive. If she was doomed anyway, and by her death had the chance to save Dorramon...well, there wasn't really much to think about, was there?

Alannys pushed herself up out of the chair. She swallowed hard and stumbled on her shaky legs into the alcove, trying not to feel the lump in her throat, or the hot tears already beginning to trickle down her cheeks.

"Tsk, tsk, my Lady — don't ruin the moment with tears." Athniss pulled her arms up and snapped the manacles around her wrists with quick, biting motions. He grinned maliciously at her. "As usual, the Retainers get their way in the end. They certainly have you figured out, Alannys, or at least your weakness — you would do anything to save your friends. You just can't resist an opportunity to be noble. And this is a very noble thing, you know, maybe the most noble thing you've ever done. If it makes you feel any better, I'm dead certain the king would do the same thing for you."

Somehow that didn't make her feel any better at all. She slumped against the stone wall, wishing she could block her senses, turn off her brain — but she was painfully aware of the cold, rough iron biting into her wrists, of the dark red smear of Athniss's blood on her arm where he'd grabbed her, of the damp stone seeping wetness into the fabric of her gown behind her, of the moldy, foul air filling her nostrils with every breath. It would have been a welcome relief to believe, even for a moment, that this was just a dream that wasn't really happening to her.

"Sir Athniss." Alannys put everything she had left into her voice, trying to sound braver than she felt, trying to sound like she wasn't pleading with him, even though she clearly was. "Look, this isn't necessary. I know you can see that. You seem like a good man, the kind of man who knows right from wrong. Simple circumstance can't change a good man into a bad man. You don't have to do this. I can see that you're desperate, but I can help you. We can help you."

He stood silent and unmoving, regarding her in the heavy darkness of the dungeon. Hope pulsed through her veins like a drug — had she gotten through to him at last? Was there still a chance that they could all leave here alive after all?

Athniss laughed in her face. "Have you learned nothing from all you've seen here? My family begged the Crown for help for years...decades...before things passed the point of no return for us. For you to offer that help now, after everything...it just adds insult to injury. You won't help us to save *us,* but you'll help us to save *yourself.* Don't you see that? I need nothing from the Crown. I *hate* the Crown."

"But I'm not the Crown!"

"You're as good as! You can't honestly think any differently. You can't publicly ally yourself with them, officially promise to marry yourself into the family, and then claim it's all nothing to do with you. I would rather die than accept help from you or your king." His eyes flared in the low light, making him look committed, unwavering, and utterly insane.

"That's fine for you to say," Alannys said, "but you aren't the one who's dying. Why on earth should I have to die for your principles?"

Athniss gave her a feral grin. "Why, that's what makes it so perfect, don't you see? Your king may not be the one who personally caused my family's disgrace, but his ancestors did. And dear Dorramon has certainly shown no inclination during his short reign of rectifying their mistakes. To be quite honest, I wouldn't mind seeing him suffer. The death of his precious betrothed, the woman he went to war for, ought to do nicely, don't you think?"

She jerked her wrists against the manacles in frustration, rattling the chains and bruising her skin. "Then why not just kill me outright? Why stick me in this horrible dungeon and leave me to suffocate or starve?"

Athniss's smile broadened, and he leaned right into her face. "I'm a bit squeamish about it, really...I don't have any reason personally to harm you. But to tell you the total truth, I wouldn't mind seeing you suffer, either."

Athniss lifted her Seeing Stone over her head and backed out of the alcove. She didn't pay too much attention to what he was doing—what could it possibly matter to her now?—until she realized he was fitting a mortared stone panel across the opening of the alcove. She didn't know where he'd gotten it from or when he'd made it, but even from where she was standing it was obvious it had been constructed specifically to match the walls around her. It fit snugly, too. When he pushed it up into place, the alcove was dark, only a few pinpricks of light coming in at the edges of the wall.

She heard the thick, slopping sounds of mortar being applied around the edge of the panel, being worked in to seal every crevice. The pinpricks of light disappeared.

"And now," Athniss said, his voice raised to carry through the stone, "I must bid you farewell. Think of all the good you've done with your noble sacrifice. Good travels, Redeemer!"

His footsteps receded, and Alannys was left alone in the dark and the cold, with only as much time left in her life as the oxygen in the little alcove would allow her.

♫

Time lost all meaning in that tiny, moldering tomb. Alannys had no idea how long she had been walled up in there—it could have been minutes, it could have been hours. It was even possible it could have been days...the way her mind lurched unsteadily from one brief idea to another made it very hard to tell. She lingered long over inane thoughts that could have no real meaning, and rushed right past important matters without even slowing down. Time became formless and fluid. Trapped in that odd, stale stasis, she no longer seemed subject to its unbending march — the fleeting whims of her own fevered mind ruled all.

The darkness danced and dipped around her, and her own labored gasps filled her ears. It had to be all in her head — surely one panicked person couldn't burn through that much oxygen that fast. She told herself that, firmly and repeatedly, but the alcove continued to spin and she continued to pant. Little sparkles pinpricked the blackness around her.

She didn't know which was worse — being left in this wretched, dark hole to die, or knowing it was the Soth worshipers who had schemed and paid to put her there. She wished that she really *had* said everything she was thinking when she left the Inn of the Abandoned Lord. She'd tried hard to stay civil, to play straight with them, and this was how they repaid that effort? Murder? And all in the name of bringing back Soth the Demented. She was no expert on Soth, but she had heard enough to know no sane, rational person would want someone like that walking the planet.

If only she could have made it to Mount Mouseion without ever running into that bastard Athniss. Would that even have been enough? Or had the Retainers set snares like this at every likely stop on the way to the harbor?

She sighed, puffed her cheeks out with moldy air. It didn't matter now. It sounded like the only thing that would get the Retainers off of her back now was the acts of the Redeemer.

Not that she had much chance of performing them,

chained to a wall in a sealed-off alcove where no one could ever find her. She was a complete failure, utterly disappointing every single person who had believed in her. She would never attempt the acts, let alone heal the world. And what would happen to her stewards then, when she disappeared and the world labeled her false? She would even let Dorramon down, in the end—even that simple promise would be more than she could keep.

Alannys hung from the rusty chains, her back pressed against the mossy stone wall, and she cried. Thick, choking sobs racked her throat, for more reasons than she could count. She cried for the friends and the strangers she had let down, for the king who'd had the ill luck to throw in his lot with someone doomed to fail him in the end.

But most of all she cried for herself, for the million precious, ordinary things she always took for granted and now would never experience again. The warmth of the golden sun on her skin, the fresh smell of a dewy spring morning. The light in Dorramon's clear blue eyes when he looked at her, the passion in his lips pressed against hers, the tender electric tingle of his palm, gentle against her cheek. She could remember his voice, that beautiful ringing tenor that resonated in her very soul, so vividly she could almost hear it there with her in her horrible little tomb.

"Alannys!"

She raised her head, catching her shuddering breath and holding it. She really *was* hearing his voice, and there was no way that could be good. Was she going mad, was the lack oxygen telling on her? She didn't know—almost didn't care, she was so grateful to be hearing that voice in what were surely her last moments. If this was a hallucination, she would take it.

"Alannys! Alannys, are you in here?"

She could hear panic rising in that familiar, beloved voice, could hear it straining to the breaking point. That didn't seem right. Why would her fading mind offer her comfort—only to torment her with it? Could it be...was it even possible that she wasn't imagining that voice—that it was real, that he had somehow managed to find her?

"Seven Hells, Cardoth, there's nothing here, he's taken her with him. I swear if he harms her, I'll—"

"Dorramon!" That was Prince Cardoth's voice, as sharp as a slap. "She's been here. Look."

Alannys bit her lip through a heavy silence, wondering what they were looking at.

"It's her dagger." Chen sounded choked, like he was on the verge of tears. "She wore it everywhere."

"Indeed," Cardoth said. "And it's bloody."

This drove Dorramon right over the edge, right past the limit of whatever fragile control he had held on to that far. "Alannys!" he howled. "Alannys, where are you?"

"Dorramon?" She felt stupid, deep inside, for responding to her own fevered imaginings, but she couldn't ignore his pain, even if she told herself it wasn't real. Her voice sounded faint in her ears, rusty with disuse. She would have to try harder, if her hallucinated friends were to have a chance of hearing her. "Dorramon, I'm here!"

"Alannys!" His voice caught in his throat. She could hear him getting closer to her tomb. "Chen, Cardoth, she's over here! She must be—I can hear her, but I can't find her..."

"Forget about that!" she snapped. "Dorramon, you've got to get out of here—you and the others—you need to find Rodriset and make him give you the antidote."

"Antidote?" Dorramon sounded confused. "What are you talking about?"

"He should have given it to you already! I did what they asked. You've got to make him give you the cure for the poison, while there is still time!"

"What poison? Alannys, we're fine. It's you we need to worry about. Where are you?"

She couldn't even answer. She slumped against her

chains, wilting under the heavy knowledge that she had done it all for nothing. Of course, she'd known that was a possibility, but to hear it confirmed, to know for certain how adeptly Athniss had played her for a fool...

"Right here." She heard Cardoth's rich voice, closer than the others. He sounded right in front of her, like she could have reached out and touched him if she hadn't been chained to a wet, mossy wall. "This mortar here, see? It's darker than the rest—and look, it's still soft. All of this right here was recently set."

"Seven Hells." That sounded like Chen. "How are we going to get her out of there? Athniss really did this up right."

"He did." Cardoth sounded sour. "But we're going to move this thing, and we're going to get her out. I tried for three months to kill her. I'm not going to let some no-account baronet succeed where I failed."

She could hear scratching sounds at the wall in front of her, and little by little the mortar began to fall away. Pinpricks of light began to shine through into her cell again, and she began to think that maybe she would survive this after all. And none too soon, really. Was it her imagination, or was the air getting seriously thin?

It felt like a long time later when she heard the heavy scraping of the rock panel sliding on the ground, and slowly, inch by painful inch, it was shoved out of the way. Cardoth, Chen, and Dorramon stood on the other side, dusty and disheveled, staring at her with almost identical expressions of disbelief.

"You can't imagine," she said with feeling, "how wonderful it is to see you again."

"You'd be surprised," Dorramon said gruffly. He stepped into the alcove and wrapped his arms around her, ignoring for the moment the manacles on her wrists and the blood on her face. "Thank the Muses," he whispered, right next to her ear. "I was so *worried*...I thought I might go mad."

Alannys didn't have any words. She craned her head around and pressed her lips against his dirty cheek, hoping that might say it all for her.

"I hate to intrude," Chen said, from somewhere behind Dorramon, "but maybe we should consider releasing her?"

Dorramon turned, and Alannys could clearly see what Chen handed him—a rusty, over-sized, executioner's axe. Her eyes widened and she immediately averted her gaze —looking at that axe made her very much want to look at something else. Anything else.

"You may want to close your eyes," Dorramon said, turning back to her. She did, but the image of him with that horrible axe was already burned into her retinas, like an after-image of the sun.

She squeezed her eyes shut even more tightly and ducked down, leaving her arms stretched above her, visions of severed hands filling her imagination. Two powerful, ear-splitting blows later, the manacles hung broken above her, gaping open like jagged, toothy jaws.

Dorramon dropped the axe, and she threw her arms around him. "What happened?" she demanded, desperate for something to make her feel less foolish. "Did Rodriset already give you the antidote?"

"Antidote?" Dorramon still sounded confused, but there was something more than that—concern, clouding his blue eyes as he frowned at her. Did he doubt her sanity —did he think she had snapped? "What in the world are you talking about?"

She sighed heavily. "That's what I was afraid of. There never was any poison. It would have been so much simpler to just make up that story—given my situation, how could it matter?"

"Alannys?" Chen sounded easily as worried as Dorramon. Maybe she really was cracking up. "Are you all right?"

"I am now." She decided it was easier—and probably

better—just not to explain. "Did you find Athniss?"

Prince Cardoth shook his head grimly. "Afraid not. We only found you because he's apparently bleeding. I found the trail—one direction led away from the estate, the other led here. We had a choice—we could chase him, or we could come after you. You can guess which one we chose."

"And I'm very grateful you did. But...do you think we have any chance of catching him?"

"Catching him?" Cardoth looked at her like she had just asked to nip back to the Great Palace because she'd forgotten her favorite hair clip. "I would say that's probably pretty impossible, given our current lack of means and his substantial head start. Why in the world would we even want to do that?"

She sighed. "I don't really expect you to understand. It's just..." She grabbed Dorramon's arm and pulled him away from the others, into a dark corner of the dungeon, and lowered her voice, glancing hurriedly back. "Dorramon, how did you find me? I mean, why were you even looking for me? How did you know anything had happened?"

"You disappeared," he said simply, with none of Cardoth's impatience. "It's this Talent-proofed room, I suppose...as soon as you came in here, the mindlink disappeared. There was no way I could miss it, even when I was asleep."

"Of course. I had forgotten that. There are so many things about the mindlink I take for granted, Dorramon...so many things we both do. I think we're going to have to be more careful about that. Athniss isn't working alone. Everything that happened here happened at the direction of the Lord's Retainers. They haven't forgiven me for not being Soth, and they intend to get rid of me before I can finish my work here. Maybe they figure the next Redeemer will suit them better."

"That's awful," Dorramon breathed.

"It is, and it isn't the worst of it. The Retainers have a

relic — they gave it to Athniss, or loaned it to him, I suspect, since I don't see it here now. It's a Seeing Stone."

"What?" Dorramon sounded like he'd had the wind knocked out of him. "That's...that's not possible."

"Unfortunately it is. As I understand it, they were originally a pair, and Soth and Ravan each had one. But that isn't the worst part. The worst part is that it allows him — or whoever has it, apparently — to access the mindlink."

"To *what?* That can't be true!" Dorramon had gone beyond shock; he looked physically unwell.

Alannys tightened her hold on his arm. She understood — she had felt much the same way herself, when she found out...she still felt the same way now, talking about it. "I thought so too, but I can tell you pretty definitively that it works. How do you think he tricked me out of my room, managed to knock me out without you ever knowing anything was amiss? He's running back to the Retainers now, and he's got their Seeing Stone — and mine, too."

He just stared at her for a long, long moment. He looked completely shell-shocked. "I swear that is the most terrifying thing I've ever heard. And I've heard some pretty terrifying things, since you came to Ravanmark. What are we going to do?"

"If you didn't like that, you're going to hate this. But I don't think there is anything we can do. Prince Cardoth already said we can't catch him. Either he or the Retainers will have the stones, and there isn't really anything we can do at this point to stop them."

Dorramon blew out his cheeks. "You're right. I do hate that. It's bad, really bad. These people aren't just going to give up."

She nodded, but didn't say anything. What was there to say? He was right, but that wasn't the worst part. The worst part was what she wasn't telling him, what she couldn't tell him, what she didn't think she would ever be able to say aloud to another living soul.

Now that they had both stones, Dorramon was in danger, too.

♫

"I don't think we should hang around here," Chen fretted, glancing around into the shadows of the dark dungeon. "I don't know where Athniss went, but how do we know that butler of his won't wake up and come check his handiwork?"

"You're right," Dorramon said, leading Alannys from the corner where they had been conferring. "We don't. We should go."

For some reason they all turned to look at her, as though there was a single chance she would disagree. "The sooner we're out of here, the better I'll like it," she said, scooping up her dagger and wiping it clean on the hem of her dress. She felt bad about it, but then, that dress was ruined anyway. She slipped it back into its concealed sheath. "I've no desire to see Athniss ever again."

"Very well, then." Dorramon took her hand. "We need to do some looking—we know Athniss has a carriage and a horse around here somewhere."

She picked her way carefully along beside him in the dim light, holding fast to his hand. The stone floor was uneven, sloping at odd angles as though it had been hand carved out of the bedrock. At the far end of the room she found a wide case of lumpy, shallow stone stairs, curving away up into the light above them. The staircase was wide enough she and Dorramon could walk up it side by side, but at the top a small square of thin, early-morning sunlight crept in under a heavy stone slab, just big enough for one person to crawl through at a time.

So she let go of Dorramon, got down on the slick, mossy stone ground in her dirty, rumpled gown, and scooted under the stone on her belly.

She had barely pushed her head out into the breaking light of the dawn outside when something rushed past her face with a whoosh she could feel on her skin, and suddenly the point of a short sword was buried in the grass in front of her nose.

"Hang it all," muttered a familiar stiff, proper voice, and when she followed the blade up to the handle, the hands she found wrapped around the grip belonged to...

"Rodriset!" she gasped. He yanked the sword free and took a step back, swinging around to try again.

She scooted faster, pushing herself through the opening with her elbows and knees, head down and concentrating only on speed. If she was too slow, if Rodriset landed his second strike before she was free...she never wanted to know.

She was clear of the hole from her knees up, so she rolled onto her side, pulling her legs up to her chest and pushing herself sideways, away from Rodriset. She heard the blade rush back behind her, and rolled back over onto her stomach again, pushing herself to her feet, yanking her dagger from its sheath as she stood to face him again.

"I knew that was you in the hallway. You're both insane, do you realize that?" She had the dagger out defensively in front of her, but it was all for show — she knew that she'd be gored on the end of that sword long before she touched him with the dagger.

"You'll forgive me," Rodriset grunted, "if I really couldn't care less what you think. You have but one purpose to serve here, and that is to die." He swung with the sword, and she skittered backwards, pressing her back up against the ivy-covered stone behind her. This particular part of the garden had several of these massive, flat-faced rocks, placed around the edges like obelisks. She had just crawled out from under one, and now she was cowering against another. It didn't make things look very good for her.

But even she could see that Rodriset's strike went very wide, and dragged him along with it. He wasn't prepared for the weight or the momentum of the moving weapon, and she realized he hadn't had much experience with blades. If only she'd had Songstrike, she could have defended herself easily.

Unfortunately, Songstrike was back in her trunk, in that dusty stable in Duxol. It may as well have been on the moon.

"Rodriset!" The angry roar came from behind the butler. She darted a glance that direction and saw Dorramon scrambling to his feet, drawing his own sword with a savage motion that bespoke a fair bit more experience than Rodriset could claim. "How in the Seven Hells are you back on your feet so fast?"

"It takes more than a slap from a girl to keep me down," Rodriset sneered, but he staggered when he said it, the sword wavering in his grasp as though he found its weight too great to handle. "The master has given me a purpose here, and I intend to achieve it."

"How noble," Alannys said bitingly. "Look, your master also said that my death would count for nothing if it wasn't met willingly, that the Retainers wouldn't pay him otherwise. What about that? Aren't you kind of wrecking that for him right now?"

"We did our best," Rodriset said shortly. "What possible difference could it make? If I gut you and stuff your body back into the alcove, they never have to know it happened this way, don't you agree?"

Chen rolled out of the hole, popped to his feet, and ran to stand stubbornly in front of Alannys. "You really need to learn how to talk to ladies, *sharo*." He turned his head to address her over his shoulder. "Princess Varilyn laid him out with a chair to the back of the head — he came after us before, when we were trying to find you. I don't know how he got back up so quickly."

Alannys couldn't even imagine Varilyn doing such a thing, not in her wildest dreams. "I'm sorry I missed it," she said, "for several reasons."

"Don't sweat it," Chen said. "The day we run out of people who want you dead is the day I start seriously worrying that the end of the world is upon us."

She laughed, but she kept her eyes on Rodriset. The butler wasn't giving up—he had hefted his borrowed sword into something approximating a steady stance, and he was dragging himself closer to Dorramon as she watched.

Dorramon met him halfway, taking two great strides forward and bringing his sword around in a wide, fast arc that looked set to sever the butler's hands from his body.

Instead, the flat of the blade smacked soundly into his wrist. The sword fell from his grasp and slid a few feet away on the slick, dewy garden grass. Rodriset wrapped his other hand around his injured wrist, backing up against the stone behind him, but glaring fiercely at Dorramon nonetheless. "You should not have interfered, your Majesty. None of this had to concern you."

"Didn't have to *concern* me? You people are even crazier than I realized. Look, Rodriset, it's over. What you've done is treasonous, and I should kill you where you stand. But I'm not fond of killing people who don't have to be killed. I want your word that you and your master will drop this. Don't hunt her any farther—leave both of us alone."

Rodriset slowly relaxed his grip on his left wrist, and stepped forward, extending his right hand as though for a handshake…

…and a viciously curved blade whipped out between them, a glittering blur in the morning sun. Alannys barely had time to blink before Rodriset was sprawled in a graceless heap at the foot of the stone, disemboweled.

♪

The entire garden froze in horror and shock for a long, silent moment. Even the birds in the trees stopped their chirping; even the restless breeze stood outraged and still. All eyes turned at once to the hands holding the sword, the hands of Prince Cardoth. Already he had pulled back his sword, and he busied himself with wiping it clean on the grass, ignoring all of them.

Finally he stood, and cast a sharp glance around the garden. "Why are the lot of you standing there staring at me like that? Haven't any of you got eyes in your heads? Look at him!"

Reluctantly, Alannys did—she had been studiously avoiding the pile of gore that had once been Rodriset. His right arm sprawled out in front of him, and slipping between his limp fingers was the tell-tale gleam of a knife.

Alannys stared at it in dumb horror. She'd had no idea Rodriset was hiding it—given the impossibility of his predicament, she really had expected him to surrender. The slight twinkle of the blade in the early morning sunlight seemed to mock her, reminding her how little she understood about the opponents she was facing now...reminding her that no matter what, they would never give up.

And Cardoth—she looked over at him again. He inspected the tip of his sword before he jammed it back into the sheath, seeming completely oblivious to her attention. She had seen him kill before, of course, but never so thoughtlessly, almost instinctively—never in quite such cold blood. It made her think of all the months he had alluded to earlier, all the time he had spent hunting her like an animal across the country, all the times he'd very nearly dispatched of her as well. And she wondered about this newly-formed alliance of theirs. She wondered how strong his loyalty was after all, to her and to Dorramon.

And she wondered if she might find herself on the business end of that sword again, one day.

♬

It didn't take Alannys and her friends very long to locate Athniss's coach and horse. The entire estate had fallen so far into disuse and disrepair that signs of recent activity stood out wherever they occurred; the stables were no exception to this. The enormous building held more stalls than Alannys could count at a glance, but only a single one was clean and currently in use. Cardoth's observations about the animal, while tactless, had certainly been accurate—the poor creature was in such bad shape Alannys felt bad asking him to pull. The Retainers's generosity clearly hadn't extended to proper food and care for the horse—just what was needed to propagate their ruse and no more.

While Dorramon and Chen did what they could to care for Athniss's unfortunate horse, Cardoth leaned back against the wall and watched, shaking his head and muttering about lost causes. Alannys went with Varilyn and Tralice to raid the kitchen for food they could take with them. The princess busied herself sorting through it all and wrapping it in waxed paper, something Alannys would not have expected her to be good at.

Tralice pulled Alannys outside and attempted to beat the grime off of her yellow dress, a pursuit which brought vividly to Alannys's mind Cardoth's words about lost causes. This one was a dandy—she wasn't sure that dress would ever be presentable again, but if it was possible, it was going to require more than a beating, she was dead certain of that. Still Tralice persisted in her efforts, thumping and brushing away what she could, and she raked her fingers through Alannys's hair in an effort to tame it that was probably doomed to failure.

With such preparations as they could make completed, they were ready to depart for Duxol before the sun had marked another hour in the sky.

Dorramon volunteered to drive the coach. It wasn't really his place, as Tralice was quick to remind him, but in the end it wasn't really appropriate for any of them, and most of them had no idea how to drive a coach.

So Dorramon sat up on the driver's bench, and Alannys sat next to him, and they bumped and jostled their way back toward town, chewing on dried fruit and salted meat from the packets Varilyn made. The driver's bench was nowhere near as comfortable as the seats inside, but the ride was much nicer anyway, sitting in the open morning air, free from the expectations and condemnation of her travel companions.

The whole thing felt miraculous. She'd had hours that felt like days to accept her own death, locked in that alcove, hours to come to terms with the end of her own existence. And yet here she was, bouncing along a badly-maintained dirt road next to the man she loved, on her way to a town she had never heard of a couple of days before...it was a miracle, there was just no other word for it. The morning sun warming her face, the deep, uninterrupted blue of the sky, the steady clip-clop of the horse's hooves, even the smell of her own dirty, sweaty clothes...these things felt like gifts to her now, precious and wonderful in a way they never had been before. She beamed at all of it, caught up in the sheer joy of existing, and then she turned to beam at the one who made it all so special for her.

"It's a beautiful morning, isn't it?" she said brightly.

Dorramon said nothing, holding the reins steady and grimly contemplating the swaybacked horse in front of him.

"All days are beautiful on some level, I suppose," she rattled on, pausing momentarily to appreciate the sensation of the breeze in her hair. "But it's different, somehow, when you thought you wouldn't be here to see it."

Silence.

"We're just lucky, I guess, that we all made it out to see this perfect day. Don't you think so?"

Dorramon slumped down in his seat, his mouth set in a stubborn, tight line, his gaze never wavering from the path ahead.

"Dorramon? Are you mad at me?"

"Mad at you. You could say that, yes." He made as if to flick the reins, then took pity on the poor beast in the rigging and checked the motion. "While you sit here thinking about how happy you are to live another day, *I'm* sitting over *here* thinking about how close you came to *not* living another day, how close we all came to losing you! And I'm trying to come to terms with the knowledge that you did that to yourself."

"To...myself?" His anger hit her like a dash of cold water, and in the shock of it she had a hard time making sense of what he had actually said.

"Indeed. I heard what you said to Rodriset, Alannys — that your death counted for nothing if it wasn't willingly met. I'm not stupid. I know what that means."

"Well, no — of course you aren't, but — "

"I cannot believe you would do such a thing. I just can't accept that you would make a decision you knew full well would lead to your own demise."

"Dorramon..." She didn't think she had ever seen him so angry — so far beyond angry. She couldn't have imagined it, and she wasn't sure how to handle having all that blistering rage directed at her.

"You have to know that isn't what I meant!" He was also beyond listening. "I didn't talk to you about sacrifice so you could go throw yourself at the first opportunity to die that came your way!"

"I know that!" Her hands were balled into angry, defensive fists; she took a deep breath and forced herself to relax. "Dorramon, honestly, that didn't happen the way you think it did."

"No?" The single word question was clipped and short. "Then explain it to me, if you please, and teach me this new definition of 'willingly,' because it seems pretty clear to me."

"I was going to die anyway. I need you to understand that — I woke up tied to a chair in that dungeon, with nothing except my dagger to fight with, and he disarmed me pretty quickly when I tried. The Retainers hired him to kill me, and that's what he was going to do, one way or another. He told me dinner was poisoned — they had already given me the antidote, but they wouldn't give it to you unless I walked into that alcove on my own, so he could fill the letter of the Retainers's request without lying to them. I thought he might be lying to *me*, but...for all I knew, you were going to die."

"That doesn't make me feel any better." Dorramon's jaw was clenched; it sounded like he spoke through gritted teeth. "You think I want you to die to save *me*? You think I'm going to say it's all right in that case — well done?"

"I am trying to tell you it wasn't like that!" She was doing her best, but she was starting to sound frustrated. "It wasn't a choice between dying or not — I was dead either way. My only choice, the only decision I had to make, was whether to take you with me. If there was a better decision I could have made with what I had, I didn't see it. I still don't."

The silence around them felt charged, like lightning ready to strike. It felt like minutes passed before Dorramon sighed, and his posture relaxed. "I'm sorry. You must think I'm crazy. I just...I had that long talk with you about self-sacrifice — *you*, probably the last person in the world who need to hear that — and then what you said earlier...I felt like you were out looking for opportunities to fall on your sword, so to speak, and all because I told you that was what the Redeemer needed to do."

"I'm not. Really I'm not — I never have. I only do what I feel is necessary."

He nodded, but said nothing. His jaw was clenched tight, his eyes focused straight ahead.

She scooted over closer to him, and placed a tentative hand on his arm. "Are you all right?"

"Me? I'm just fine. But I'm not the one you need to be worried about. I can't help wondering when we'll run into Athniss again."

Alannys shivered, listening to the way he said *when*,

not *if*. "The good news is that it sounded as though the Retainers wanted this done before I could perform the acts of the Redeemer. And we're headed out to do that now — when the acts are done, maybe that will stop them."

"Maybe." Dorramon didn't sound optimistic. "But there's more going on than just them, I think. Nothing that happened here seems to bear any similarity to the problems we saw at the palace — none of that 'winds of change' rhetoric we've encountered everywhere from Lord Malrec's apprentice to Lord Diabon, to the Royal Guard. It makes me think they aren't related. One has relics of Soth capable of getting inside your head, the other can spirit people out of our own dungeon under our very noses. Both have tried to kill you. Which is worse? I don't like fighting wars on two fronts."

"I know what you mean." She sat in silence a moment, listening to the rhythmic thumps of the horse's hooves on the packed dirt and the creaking of the coach, feeling the warmth of the morning sun on her face. It all felt so far removed from the grim things they discussed. "I'm afraid I don't have any answers. It looks like I'm just doomed to cause strife wherever I go."

Dorramon shifted the reins to his right hand, reaching out with his free hand to cover hers on his arm. "And I'll be here, doing everything I can to make sure you can keep causing strife as long as I live. I have to wonder, though, if ever a king has felt quite so powerless. You have many friends, Alannys. But I don't know if we can protect you from the threats you're facing now."

The warm morning sun suddenly felt cold and harsh. He was right, she knew — nobody could really protect her from whatever was going on out there. Nobody knew for certain what *was* going on out there, not even her. If she even made it to Mount Mouseion, if she even survived what she had to do there...she still had to come back and face whatever this thing was, brewing in the shadows of Ravanmark. She knew she couldn't quit, couldn't back down. The only way out was through. But it didn't make her feel any better. She tried not to sigh, but did anyway, thinking of all that still lay before her.

"Indeed." Dorramon's tone was wry, and then he was silent for a long moment. "I know who the Lord's Retainers are, Alannys. But I didn't know they were after you."

"Me either. I've only run into them once before, in Garrant. It was entirely accidental; I asked a baker to direct me to an inn when I rode into town, and he sent me to one of theirs. As soon as I figured out what was going on, I left. I refused to sneak out; I checked out with the same person who checked me in, and I told him exactly why I was leaving. I'm afraid he didn't take it very well."

"It seems not," Dorramon said. "Is that really what started all of this?"

"I think so. I really do. Up until that moment, they all seemed to really believe that I was Soth born again. When I told them they were wrong and left...I think that's when they started thinking along these lines. I never realized how determined they were to see Soth return."

"Do you think it would work? From what you said, it sounded like they believe that if you willingly sacrifice yourself, he would return. Is that true?"

She shook her head. "You're asking the wrong person. I have no idea. It all sounds crazy to me, but I guess that doesn't matter — they obviously believe it, and that's enough to make it dangerous for us. I'm inclined to say it's nonsense, because I spent most of my life in a place where such things are utterly impossible. But then, most of the things I've done since coming here would have been utterly impossible there. So maybe my instincts aren't something we can rely on, not about things like this. What about you, Dorramon? What do *you* think?"

He didn't answer right away, which seemed like a bad sign. For a long, long time the silence stretched out between them, and the air around Alannys seemed to grow colder and colder.

"If you had asked me that six months ago," he said, slowly, "I would have laughed out loud. Such a possibility is not even hinted at in anything I know of Talent or religion. And I was very comfortable then with my understanding of both. But since you came to Ravanmark, I have learned that you could fill the royal vaults with things I don't know about either one. The Retainers have already proven that they know more about magic than we do. And now…"

She waited for his final verdict, dread blossoming in her chest like a terrible dark flower.

"I can't say for certain that such a thing is possible, Alannys. But I can't say for certain that it isn't. And that is enough to give me nightmares."

♫

It seemed a violation of natural law that Alannys and her friends found the stable in Duxol looking just the same as they had left it, after everything that had happened. The royal coach, the driver, and the footman all waited right where they had left them the day before, with varying degrees of impatience.

"Your Majesty!" The footman ran out to meet them as they piled out of their borrowed carriage, gasping for breath and nearly beside himself. "We've been so *worried!* A few people in town saw you leave with some minor nobleman — we thought everything was all right — but then you didn't come back. And the stablemaster told us the man is *odd!* I can't tell you how relieved we are to see you safe! No one could even tell us where this fellow lives so we could follow you!"

"Don't feel bad," Prince Cardoth said dryly, watching the footman wring Dorramon's hand in enthusiastic greeting. "You didn't miss much."

Dorramon's sudden bark of laughter must have startled the footman — he stepped back next to the driver and looked them all over closely. "Are — *are* you all right, your Majesty? Lady Alannys?"

"Of course," she said, stifling a laugh of her own. "We're fine. I think we would all very much like to get back underway." There were noises of assent all around her.

"I see. I see! Very well!" The footman snapped to attention, holding the coach door open for them with one hand, and the other crossed over his chest in stiff salute. The driver climbed up on top, and in a matter of moments they were pulling away from the stable, leaving Duxol and Agapios Periousia receding into the distance behind them.

Alannys thought she might never have been quite so happy to leave a place—and she had left behind some doozies. Athniss's poor ghost of a horse seemed to love the stables—especially his stall with all the oat mash he could eat—but Alannys was supremely glad just to see it all disappearing behind them. As stifling and uncomfortable as the royal coach had seemed when they left the Great Palace, it was a great relief to be back in it now, with familiar faces around her that she could be pretty sure weren't about to kill her.

At least not with so many witnesses. Even her dagger was quiet and cool, apparently tuned now to Athniss, and Cardoth's presence didn't cause her any burning discomfort against her leg.

The driver seemed to feel some need to make up for their lost time—watching out the window, Alannys could tell they were moving faster than they had the day before. Under normal circumstances, the harbor was a two-day ride from the palace—the coach was heavy, but with the number of horses they had pulling, and the way they changed them during the day, they would only have had to find lodging for one night, and the next day they'd have arrived at the harbor. With the half day they had wasted with Sir Athniss, though, they were well behind—Alannys couldn't imagine they could still make it to the harbor that day. When they stopped just before noon to change horses, though, she began to realize that the driver seriously intended to try.

None of them left the coach this time. The footman dashed out while the driver handled the business with the horses, and returned with hot beef sandwiches on thick brown bread for all of them. They were back on the road in under half an hour—record time, Dorramon assured her, for trading horses.

They stopped again four or five hours later, trading horses one more time. The pace the driver was keeping wore them out quickly—Alannys saw the way the stablemaster shook his head, leading the spent horses back to the stalls. "This isn't necessary," she whispered under her breath to Dorramon. "We aren't in this much of a hurry."

"Aren't we?" Dorramon sounded mild, but he looked at her evenly, as though he was prepared to argue the point. "I think we should be. The Lord's Retainers must have a massive, organized operation, maybe even with contacts inside the Great Palace. It's the only way they could have pulled off what they did. After everything that's happened, I don't think it would be wise to tarry any longer than we absolutely have to."

"I'm not suggesting we tarry," she said, "just that we don't have to go at such a breakneck pace."

"In a situation like this, anything less than best possible speed is just the same as tarrying." He sat back against the cushions, tilted his head back, and threw his arm across his eyes, as though he intended to nap.

It was as good a way as any to indicate the subject was closed, she supposed. She sighed, watching the driver and the stableboys rig up their replacement horses, and silently prayed that they didn't have too much farther to go.

The coach bounced suddenly, and the door flung open. Dorramon sat up in surprise, and Alannys twisted quickly around to find a familiar man leaning in the opening. Strong and compact, with a serviceable linen shirt and an undecorated, business-like short sword, Duke Morryn of Danningham looked very much the same as the last time she had seen him—only the angry scowl on his face was different. "So, you thought you could just ride into Newstark and ride back out again without a word, did you?"

"So," Dorramon shot back, "you thought you could just barge in and disrupt the king's sleep with no care for consequence, did you?"

The two men glared at each other with all the mock hostility they could muster, while Alannys snickered behind her hand. They didn't last five seconds before both burst into laughter. Cardoth and Varilyn looked back and forth between them as though the entire world had stopped making sense.

"Morryn, it's good to see you." Dorramon leaned forward and shook the duke's hand.

"Your Highness, it's always a pleasure. But it seems as though every time I see you or your beautiful betrothed lately," he nodded a greeting to Alannys, "it's under less than ideal circumstances."

The joking atmosphere abruptly vanished. "What has happened?" Dorramon said.

"Nothing so terrible as you must be imagining," Duke Morryn said, "yet I would be very much obliged if you and Lady Alannys could join me for a walk."

"Of course." Dorramon took Alannys's hand and helped her out of the coach. No sooner had her dirty, scuffed yellow slippers hit the ground, though, than she heard Prince Cardoth's cutting voice behind her.

"Surely you don't intend to run off and leave my sister and myself here in this coach. That seems a poor way to treat guests, doesn't it?"

Dorramon turned back to the coach with a smile that did not reach his eyes. "You must understand, these are matters of state. No slight is intended."

"Matters of state?" Cardoth echoed. "I know a smoke

screen when I see one. Come on, Dorramon—Varilyn and I are in all of this up to our eyeballs anyway. Your 'matters of state' are exceedingly likely to affect us as well." The prince started to rise from his seat, gesturing to Princess Varilyn to follow.

Dorramon held up a forbidding hand, making the gesture forceful enough it stopped Cardoth in his tracks. "I assure you I would not neglect to tell you anything that concerned you or your sister, but you are not privy to every state secret Ravanmark possesses, and you are both going to have to wait right here in the coach."

Cardoth opened his mouth to speak again, and his face made it apparent he wasn't planning to express his agreement.

"Oh, for pity's sake," Varilyn snapped. "You know you aren't being reasonable, Cardoth. Sit down and stop sticking your nose where you are perfectly aware it does not belong. Go ahead, your Majesty—we will all wait for you here."

Alannys turned from the coach with Duke Morryn's chuckle in her ears. "A bit of a spitfire, isn't she?" he said.

"Not usually," Dorramon replied. "But even she can be pushed too far, and if there exists an expert at pushing people past their limits, it surely must be Prince Cardoth."

"I did get that impression." Duke Morryn led them through the stablehouse, his pace unhurried. The smells of horses, of leather and hay, reminded Alannys as always of Larric, and she felt a twinge, remembering the letter she had received last time she was in Newstark. It was one of life's bitter ironies, how certain people could be so influential in your life, and you only saw it clearly after they were gone. She hoped that wherever Larric was now, he knew how grateful she was for his influence in her life.

"In a way," Morryn continued, completely unaware of Alannys's melancholy line of thought, "it's really too bad she isn't going to be marrying you, your Highness—she should stay in Ravanmark. She has a good head on her shoulders, much more sensible than Sheeana. I might be inclined to trade."

Something about Dorramon's stilted laugh brought to Alannys's mind comments Duchess Sheeana had made last time she was here—comments about having her own sights set on Dorramon—and made her wonder if the duchess's secret ambitions were not so secret as she had imagined.

They walked out of the stablehouse, through the back door into a rolling pasture of thick green grass that looked like it must have gone on forever. In the sharp light of the setting sun, the grass had an almost blue tinge to it. It brought back full force all of her earlier musings about Larric, made her feel that if she turned around suddenly, she would find him standing at her shoulder. It gave her a shiver, and it made her wonder what he would say to her, if he saw her now. Would he be pleased with how far she had come, how much she had accomplished? Would he support her in her new mission to perform the acts of the Redeemer?

Or would he tell her that she was a fool, that she would find nothing at Mount Mouseion but her own death?

♫

"Please forgive the horse pasture," Duke Morryn said, looking around without any of the morbidity which plagued Alannys. "It was the only nearby place I could think of that we would have to ourselves at this hour. The horses are all put up for the night, but all the same—I'd be careful where you step."

"Duly noted," Dorramon said wryly.

"This is beautiful, your Grace," Alannys said, making a concerted effort to remember titles, to be proper. She looked around at the large, old-growth trees dotting the pasture. Most of the trees had flowering bushes planted around their bases. She could even see the gleam of sunlight on water, off in the distance. "I don't think I've ever seen a horse pasture quite so lovely as this one."

For just a moment, Morryn looked startled, before he recovered himself. "Naturally," he said archly, tossing her a wink. "It's mine."

"Careful with the compliments, Alannys," Dorramon said. "You'll only make him more insufferable than he already is."

They all laughed, but it didn't last long. The silence that followed felt heavy, dense with expectation, as if the whole pasture around them waited to hear Duke Morryn's words.

"Things have improved," he finally said, gravely, "since your last visit, Lady Alannys."

"That's wonderful news, your Grace," she said, trying to figure out how such positive sentiments could possibly deserve the grim tone in which he delivered them. "Things have been improving in Orinthal Holding as well, I take it?"

"Indeed. Your new baron has done fine work there. I have offered such help as I have been able, and have even been out to visit him on a couple of occasions. The progress he has made is nothing short of amazing."

"But?" Dorramon prompted.

Morryn sighed heavily. "But he has seen some troubling things recently...signs of something he has not been able to eradicate. At the time I wasn't sure how much of a problem it really could be — after all, Orinthal has been in a bad way for years, and it seems unrealistic to expect to remedy that in a few weeks. This particular problem, though...Baron Trago tells me not only is it not disappearing, it's actually *spreading*."

Alannys frowned. "Spreading from Orinthal Holding." She had run into several problems in Orinthal herself, none of which she would really care to see anywhere else.

"Indeed. I have a man in my jail right now who seems to be part of just that problem — our dear friend Prubard. He's gone a bit odd, though, preoccupied all the time, like he isn't even aware he's incarcerated, really. Strange talker, always going on about the winds of change and the power of the few going to the many."

Alannys stumbled, and Dorramon reached out and steadied her with a grip like iron on her elbow. "I want to see him," he said immediately.

Duke Morryn folded his arms, frowning first at Dorramon, then at her. "So this is familiar to you. I admit I suspected as much, but why have you been keeping this from me?"

"Morryn," Dorramon said, "we don't have time for this."

It seemed to be the wrong thing to say. The duke's face closed up, knotted like a fist, and obstinacy could be read in every line. "With all due respect, your Highness, we have time if I say we do. This is my holding, my jail, and my prisoner. I've been fighting for months to hold things together, and this new movement is jeopardizing everything. I want answers, your Majesty, and I think I deserve them."

Dorramon sighed, raking his hand through his hair. "I swear, Morryn, if you were anyone else... But all right. What answers do you think you deserve?"

Duke Morryn's expression did not soften, and his posture did not relax. "What does this rhetoric mean? Why was the ex-baron rabble-rousing in my town?"

"I don't know," Dorramon said shortly.

"What? Your Highness, I must protest! You've made me fight for the right to even put forward my questions, and now you're going to sidestep them? You should have told me these things before, I should never have had to ask! What purpose can all this secrecy serve?"

"It isn't secrecy." Dorramon started briskly back toward the stable, pulling Alannys with him, leaving Duke Morryn little choice but to follow. "I don't have the answers you want. Diabon was recently captured spouting similar rhetoric. He and Prubard disappeared from the same cell in the palace dungeon. We still don't know how that trick was accomplished. Or who sent him there, or what any of this gibberish means. Now you know as much as we do."

Morryn gave him a hard look, brimming with disbelief.

"It's true, your Grace," Alannys offered. "This movement is too new, and too shadowy...I don't think anyone knows what's going on—except the people in it. And they're not telling."

A moment of silence passed. "Alannys, are you mad at me?"

"Mad at you, Duke Morryn? Of course not. Why would I be?"

He frowned, but let it go. "Well then, let us see if our old friend has any light to shed for us."

It was only a short, silent ride in Morryn's plain, unadorned buggy to Newstark's jail. Alannys sat squashed between the duke and the king in a buggy that was meant for two, watching the familiar stone building come into sight and trying not to dwell on the last time she was there. It made her feel unexpectedly nostalgic, but then, it seemed like everything she saw lately did.

Two guards in uniforms stood at the front entrance, each bearing a short sword that could have been a match for Morryn's. Something about their posture made Alannys think they knew exactly what to do with the weapons, too. She tried to remember if either of these guards had been involved with her prior unfortunate trip to the jail. It was no good; the details were too fuzzy.

The guards snapped to attention as the group from the buggy approached. Duke Morryn nodded to each of them in acknowledgement. "How is our guest today?"

"All's quiet, your Grace. No one has been in or out since you left. We have guards at all entrances to the jail and regular patrol sweeps of the area. No one will get in or out of here without our knowledge."

"Very good. Carry on." Morryn led Dorramon and Alannys between the two guards and into the jail building, lowering his voice. "I've ordered increased security, as you probably guessed. Whatever happened at the Great Palace, I would just as soon not have it happen here. I imagine you have some questions for him."

"You could say that." Dorramon hurried down the corridor, each stride sharp and purposeful.

They were almost to the cell when Alannys felt all the hair on the back of her neck abruptly stand on end. "Painting," she said, in the same instant that she saw the shock on Dorramon's face, and knew he felt it too.

"What?" Duke Morryn looked back and forth between them in confusion.

"If you have questions for your prisoner, you had better hurry," she said, "because someone is opening a painting in there, and I doubt they're just popping in to say hello...your Grace."

They broke into a run, pounding down the corridor, arms and legs pumping, skidding to a halt to find a dirty, disheveled, but visibly cheerful Prubard, complete with matted fur cloak. He tossed them a coy wave with the tips of his fat fingers as he waddled his great bulk into a shifting gray, misty blur that winked out of existence the moment he disappeared inside.

The cell stood empty, mocking them.

Dorramon pounded the side of his fist against the iron bars and swore. Alannys understood, but she said nothing.

There was nothing to say.

♫

"My Lord King, I can't tell you how sorry I am." Duke Morryn really did sound agitated, stomping down the dirt path toward the waiting buggy. He had already launched his guards on a complete search of the town, even though they all knew there would be nothing for them to find.

Dorramon waved him off. "I have told you at least a dozen times now that there is nothing for you to apologize for. Nobody saw that coming. The same thing happened at the palace—but we certainly never imagined Talent was involved."

"Maybe we should have," Alannys said. "Creft's note was full of that same rhetoric, remember? And he was certainly Talented, even if he was no great power. And he was Lord Malrec's apprentice...and we now know that Lord Diabon and Baron Prubard are involved with this somehow too. Was the entire Dark Alliance part of this? Is that what we're dealing with here—the remnants of the Dark Alliance?"

"No," Dorramon said immediately. "At least, not entirely. That cell at the palace was Talent-proofed, remember? They had to be moved somewhere else before they could be painted out, and only the Royal Guard could have done that."

"Hold on," Duke Morryn said. "The cell was Talent-proofed? You can do that—treat locations to prevent the use of Talent? Why haven't you told the rest of us? This is exactly the kind of thing I'm getting at—that's useful information we should *all* have!"

"Morryn." Dorramon sounded considerably less friendly than he had a moment before. "Now is not the time for this."

"I can hardly think of a better time!" They had arrived at the buggy, but Morryn made no move to get inside, pacing up and down in front of it. Alannys watched him with trepidation; he looked as if he might at any moment start pulling his hair out in great handfuls. "Except perhaps when you discovered it—it could have prevented this escape!"

"I don't know how to make it! Alannys sent a barrel of Talent-proofing solution to the palace—I have no idea how it is produced. *Now* are you willing to be reasonable and focus on the problem at hand?"

Duke Morryn stopped pacing and sighed heavily. "Your Highness, you won't like this, but from my perspective this *is* the problem at hand. With better information, we could have prevented this escape. With better information, maybe we could have prevented Prubard from being here altogether. This is bigger than all of us—I would bet this thing, whatever it is, this movement, has infected every holding in the kingdom by now. We're all facing it. But you aren't telling us anything."

"And the Lords of the Holdings aren't telling me anything either," Dorramon retorted. "Surely you can agree proper communication has been a bit of a challenge for everyone lately."

"Indeed, and it isn't likely to get any better, with you charging off to Mount Mouseion," Duke Morryn grumbled.

Dorramon crossed his arms. "Proper communication may be impossible, but the rumor mill is performing as well as ever."

"Some things never change," Morryn said with a shrug. "Look, we can't all keep fighting the same enemies, all of us learning the same things separately because no one is sharing their information. We can't win that way, it isn't practical."

"Of course. Arch-Prince Raman is in charge while I'm gone, and he knows that as well as you or I. I assure you, re-establishing proper order in his highest priority."

Duke Morryn finally relaxed. "That's very good to know. So...this rhetoric, what do you know about the people behind it?"

He climbed up into the buggy, and Dorramon helped Alannys in after him. "Precious little," he said. "I don't think this comes from the Dark Alliance—'the power of the few' they intend to spread to the many is Talent, and Malrec would never have advocated sharing that, ever. Even only metaphorically. Whether the others were involved, or later became involved, or not, their leader had nothing to do with it. Whatever we are up against now, it is not the Dark Alliance."

"I think he's right, your Grace," Alannys said, as Dorramon settled in next to her. "Lord Malrec would not have endorsed anything that diminished his own advantages. And that talk...I heard it in a few places around Ravanmark, from people who had nothing to do with the Dark Alliance. I'm certain Dorramon's right that they're separate—or at least they started out that way—but to be honest, I'm not sure that helps us much. We still don't have any idea who these people are, or where they're coming from, or what they want."

"What they want seems clear enough to me," Dorramon said. "Neither King nor Redeemer shall long last, remember?"

Alannys didn't know what to say to that. He was right, she couldn't argue it.

And yet she wasn't convinced—Lord Malrec had wanted to get rid of her and Dorramon, too, but she didn't think this group felt anything like that. Whatever they were up to, there was more behind it than simply avarice or lust for power. That much she was sure of.

And it didn't make her feel any better, not at all.

After a short ride in heavy, pensive silence, the buggy creaked to a halt in front of the stables where the royal coach waited. Dorramon climbed out and helped Alannys out, and Duke Morryn hopped out behind them.

The dark, looming form of the royal coach reminded Alannys of Tralice, and her many admonitions. That made her nervous—she had tried to be careful to address the duke appropriately, but who knew what niceties she had forgotten?

She turned to Duke Morryn with a big smile and a deep curtsy. "It was so wonderful to see you again, your Grace. I do hope we'll have the pleasure again soon."

For a moment, both men looked at her as if they had never seen her before.

Then Dorramon reached out to shake the duke's hand. "Thank you, Morryn."

"Indeed, your Highness. I would like to congratulate you on your engagement, but I don't like the changes I see in Alannys."

"You and me both," Dorramon muttered, while Alannys fidgeted, practicing again Chen's disinterested expression, pretending not to know her face was flaming red.

They turned away and started back towards their own coach. "I'm sorry if I embarrassed you," she said quietly.

"Never," he said. He reached out and took her hand, lacing his fingers between hers. "Duke Morryn likes you, Alannys. It's easy for him — and me — to see when you're trying to be something you're not."

Strangely enough, that didn't make her feel much better. "So Prince Cardoth is right, then. I'm really not suitable to marry you."

"What?" He shot her a sharp glance, full of surprise. "How did you get from what I said to that? I asked you — that makes you plenty suitable."

She didn't say anything.

"Look, I know Tralice has been hard on you lately. She's your friend and you value her opinion, I know that too. Just...don't try too hard, all right?"

"All right," she said, but she felt a little trapped, pinned between conflicting pieces of well-meant advice. "I'm not trying to upset anybody. I'm just trying to be better than just me."

"If you say so," Dorramon said. "Personally, I think just you is the best person anyone can be. Good enough for me, anyway."

Her face burned red again, but for a totally different reason this time.

Chapter Four

THE ATROMITOS

he sun had long since set. The first moon was high and nearly full, the second moon low in the sky and scarcely more than a crescent lighting up the thin, wispy clouds that covered it. Alannys was just beginning to seriously wish for her bed when they rode into Port Grandview, the southernmost harbor in Ravanmark, and home port of the royal ship.

Even in the dark of night, it was obviously the biggest city she had ever seen—even Garrant had nothing on this. The warm flicker of olive oil lamps lit up windows of houses and businesses—there were even a few oil street lamps. She'd had no idea street lamps even existed in Ravanmark, and their cozy glow seemed to beckon to her, to welcome her home to someplace she had never been. Farther out, behind the sprawl of the city with its neat brick houses and cobblestone streets, out past the wooden boardwalk, she could see boats and ships rocking gently with the motion of the sea, lanterns hanging from their bows and sterns. Even at this hour she could see people moving through the streets, alone and in couples and groups, could see sailors working on the decks of the big ships, and stevedores loading and unloading cargo. The light, the noise, the neverending motion...Port Grandview seemed to possess a life of its own, separate from all the individual lives within it, perhaps greater than all of them put together. It gave her a shiver, thinking about it, and she leaned into Dorramon, closer to the window, staring out at the view.

"This is Port Grandview?" Her voice was hardly more than a whisper; even to her own ears, she sounded awed.

Dorramon smiled at her, turning to look at her. His face was closer than she had realized, and something about the way his eyes met hers in the dim light made her heart race. "Indeed it is. A suiting name, don't you think?"

"Indubitably," she breathed, staring back at him. "It's the grandest view I've ever seen, and no mistake."

But she wasn't looking out the window when she said it.

Dorramon's grin broadened and he leaned closer to her, just as the sound of a throat being loudly cleared tore through the air around them.

Alannys jerked back and turned to find Tralice glaring at them over crossed arms. "I trust," the maid said, a little too loudly, "that your Majesty has made *appropriate* lodging arrangements for himself and his guests?"

Dorramon smiled, but it didn't quite reach his eyes. There was something hard in his expression, as though there was a limit to how long he would put up with this challenging attitude of hers—and perhaps she was approaching it faster than she realized. "I'm not sure what you could mean, Tralice. Surely you were aware that we are traveling to the royal ship?"

"Of course, your Majesty. But it is so late—surely we will require lodging for the night?"

Dorramon laughed. "I shouldn't think so. It's the *royal ship,* Tralice. If I arrived this late to the Great Palace, would you expect me to stay at the Raven's Nest for the night—simply because of the time?"

Tralice turned suddenly red—Alannys could even see it in the poor light inside the carriage. "No—no, of course not. I am sorry, my Lord King—apparently I understand very little about this trip."

Dorramon waved off her concern with a magnanimous gesture, but his eyes were hard, and they never left her face. "There's nothing to apologize for, Tralice—how could you be expected to know? You've never been in this situation before. All I ask is that you consider that perhaps your king is not the helpless thimbleskull you imagine him to be. And our Redeemer is certainly not. Perhaps not every action either of us take needs questioning."

Tralice dropped her gaze, but said nothing.

"Of course," Dorramon said cheerfully, finally turning away from her, "our guests from Cadenda are a different story. We will be headed in different directions from here, and you will be needing someplace to pass the night. I can recommend a couple of suitable inns that my family has used in the past."

"Actually," Prince Cardoth said, his tone studiously casual, and Alannys felt her spine stiffen as her guard went up, "my sister and I discussed it, and we rather hoped we might be permitted to accompany you."

"Accompany us...to Mount Mouseion?" Dorramon sounded about like she felt—confused, perhaps, and a bit taken aback by the sudden request.

"Just so. We are not from Ravanmark, but if she really intends to do the things you've said — it concerns the entire world, don't you think? As Cadenda's next king, I would very much appreciate the opportunity to witness what transpires out there."

Dorramon's frown deepened. "I'm not sure I understand."

"Please," Varilyn cut in. "We have been through a lot with you both. This...this is risky. Can't we be there, as your friends, while you go through this?"

Dorramon looked away from her. Alannys understood...she didn't doubt that the princess meant what she said. Cardoth, on the other hand...

She looked over at Prince Cardoth, and found him already watching her, his expression inscrutable, his dark eyes gleaming in the low light.

And she might have been crazy, but she didn't think they were gleaming with friendship and concern. She didn't doubt Princess Varilyn sincerely meant what she said, but what Prince Cardoth's motives were for following them...she couldn't have guessed.

♫

The coach rattled and bumped down through the cobblestone streets to the docks. The inside of the carriage was so deathly quiet and still, Alannys could hear every creak, every groan of each protesting part. The silence weighed on her like a physical force, but there was nothing she could do to alleviate it—what could she possibly say? What could any of them say? Dorramon had given Prince Cardoth permission to accompany them, even though she knew he didn't feel any better about it than she did. Strong relations with Cadenda were an absolute necessity—they had seen that well enough. And Cardoth had saved Dorramon's life at Agapios Periousia— that had to count for something.

The coach dropped them off right at the edge of the boardwalk. The footman wished them a hearty goodbye, and she couldn't help thinking he must be relieved to finally be clear of them—she remembered well his anxiety in Duxol when they had disappeared. At least now, he must have been thinking, if something happened to the king, it wouldn't happen on his watch.

The driver bowed low to Dorramon, tipped his hat to her, and climbed back up on the coach. They clattered away back up the winding cobblestone street, probably to find themselves someplace to stay the night before heading back to the Great Palace in the morning.

Alannys felt oddly cut adrift, watching their coach rumble off without them. It was like seeing their last tie to the palace fade away into the distance. And yet...

She turned around and looked down the pier in front of them. Docked there was the most enormous ship she had ever laid eyes on—triple-masted and square-rigged, with a long bowsprit and a row of big, square windows across the stern. It towered over them, towered over the other ships in the harbor. To Alannys's wide eyes it looked like something that had sailed right out of a pirate movie, with its flickering lamps swaying gently in the darkness, and its gleaming, polished railings. She had been with Dorramon to some pretty amazing places, but none of them were as overwhelming, none of them communicated the essence of royalty like that massive, majestic ship rocking gently on the water. She felt small and unworthy.

Sailors in linen trousers and blue and white striped shirts hustled down the pier. They took the king's leather bag and the few bags Cardoth and Varilyn had brought, and headed back up the pier, escorting them toward the ship as though this was all quite ordinary. She stared up at the tall masts, stretching up into the sky past what she could see, and tried to find anything about this that felt normal to her.

"Alannys?" Belatedly she realized the others had all gone on down the pier with the sailors—only Chen stood beside her now, next to the trunk, looking at her doubtfully. "Are you all right?"

"Fine." She looked from him to the ship, and swallowed hard. "I know we only discussed coming as far as the harbor, but..."

Chen reached out and ruffled her hair. "You think I would leave now? Not hardly, not when things are just starting to get interesting. You'll have to beat me off with a stick, if you want me gone."

She managed a smile that only felt slightly sick. "Thanks, Chen." She could hear the breakers slapping into the wooden pillars of the docks, and the big ship in front of her dipped, catching her attention again. "I've never been on anything like that before."

Chen snorted. "*You* haven't? Singari don't travel by sea, remember? If I can get on that thing and survive to tell the tale, so can you."

"All right, then." She took one of the trunk's handles, and Chen took hold of the other, and between them they hefted the thing up and started awkwardly hobbling down the pier.

They were halfway down the pier when a couple of sailors in their blue striped linen uniforms hustled out to meet them and took the trunk. Moving as if it weighed much less than she knew it did, they hurried back up the pier, to the base of the boarding ramp, where the rest of their party waited. Dorramon cast his royal glare over all of them, and Alannys was instantly on edge, wondering what had happened.

"I've never been witness to such an ignominious display in all my life," he barked, crossing his arms and glaring at the sailors, who stood there silently with their heads bowed. "This is going to be a very unpleasant journey if you insist on taking that attitude. I can promise you that snubbing Lady Alannys — or her friends — will not make your lives any easier."

"This is your fault," Tralice hissed in her ear. "How are these men supposed to know you are important, when you stand around gawping like you're nobody? You will never be accorded proper respect until you start conducting yourself as though you deserve it."

Dorramon smiled at her before she could respond. "I'm sorry," he said. "We shouldn't have left you. I wasn't paying close enough attention."

"No, it was my fault," she said immediately, feeling somehow shamed to hear the King of Ravanmark publicly apologize to her. "I'm afraid this ship completely overwhelmed me. I sort of forgot myself." She promised herself in that moment to double down on her efforts to improve — she was an embarrassment to Dorramon. Nobody had snubbed Princess Varilyn, after all; everyone tripped over themselves to help her whenever she needed it.

He turned to follow her gaze to the ship. "It is impressive, isn't it? It's the *Atromitos* — the biggest galea ever built."

"Atromitos?"

"It means intrepid," Dorramon said. "And it is. It's the finest ship ever made. It would be my honor to escort you on board." He held out his arm to her.

She glanced at him sidelong, wondering how much he guessed. She arranged her face into a smile, doing her best to play it off. "The honor," she said stiffly, taking his arm, "is all mine."

They walked together up the wide boarding ramp, and all of their companions fell in behind them. It felt like the beginning of something big, like everything she had done in Ravanmark up until now was just leading up to this.

And yet she couldn't help glancing back over her shoulder at the warm glow of Port Grandview. The solid familiarity of city streets beckoned to her, offering comfort and respite from the dangers of the unknown. She had never been out on the sea before, and she had seen firsthand how fickle and deadly it could be. For just a moment, the relative safety of Port Grandview called to her, tempting her to turn back from the peril that lay ahead.

Then she remembered standing in the Great Hall, looking into Dorramon's eyes and vowing to perform the acts or die trying. *The only way out,* she told herself, *is through.* She straightened her shoulders, tightened her grip on Dorramon's arm, and strode up the boarding ramp to the royal ship.

♫

On the deck of the *Atromitos* waited two stiff, unnatural-looking people in heavily starched uniforms. One was a weathered-looking, gray-haired man of about fifty, barrel-chested and built like a bear. Behind him fidgeted a freckle-faced teenager with a shock of unruly red hair, who watched them all with keen, wide-eyed interest. While other members of the crew showed the rest of their party to their rooms, Alannys followed Dorramon's lead and stopped in front of them.

"Your Majesty," the older man said solemnly, with gravel in his voice, "welcome aboard."

"Captain Morgain." Dorramon reached out to shake his hand. "It's a pleasure, as always."

"And for me as well." Morgain shifted his stance, puffing out his chest and pulling the teenager up to stand next to him. "I'd like to introduce you to my boy, Tassin."

"It's good to meet you, Tassin," Dorramon said, and reached to shake his hand as well. "If you take after your father at all, you'll be running this ship before long."

"Is that Alannys?" Tassin blurted, his gaze barely pausing on the king before locking on her. "The one they call the Redeemer?"

Dorramon frowned ominously.

"Hush, boy," Morgain admonished, pulling his son back. "That's Lady Alannys to you, and she's none of your business." He flashed a nervous smile at the king. "The lad's right excited. First voyage, and already he's first mate. Now then, your Highness, I trust everything meets with your approval so far? We've kept her ready to sail at the drop of a hat."

Tassin had not taken his eyes off Alannys. He gave her an odd half-smile, and she moved to stand a bit more behind Dorramon.

"Don't worry about him," Morgain told her, giving his son a shove. "He's been over the moons, knowing the two of you were coming."

Alannys smiled weakly.

"Indeed," Dorramon said. "Actually, I do have a concern to raise with you, Captain. Your crew left Alannys and Chen to lug a heavy trunk aboard themselves. That hardly seems appropriate, and I hope we will have no similar incidents moving forward."

"Chen?" Morgain rubbed his grizzled chin. "I'm sorry, your Highness—who is Chen?"

"Chen is a member of our party," Dorramon explained patiently. "A Singari."

"A *brownskin?* Now, it hardly seems fair to get all over my men—they're busy, they can't be dropping everything for just anyone. They look down the pier and see a dirty girl and a dirty brownskin, what do you expect them to do?"

"Morgain!" Dorramon's voice lashed like a whip, and it silenced the captain. "One more racial epithet and I'll have you off this ship, and I don't care who you are. Let's get one thing clear right now—I will not tolerate that attitude, from you or your men. Not toward Chen, and not toward Alannys. She is the next Queen of Ravanmark, and I encourage you to remember that. *Always.*"

Captain Morgain swallowed visibly. "Yes, your Majesty. Sorry, your Majesty. You can leave it all to me and my first mate." He threw one beefy arm around Tassin's shoulders, seeming not to notice the boy's grimace. "You'll have a voyage to remember with us, and no mistake."

The captain was utterly sincere. Alannys couldn't explain, as he and his son turned away, why his words gave her such a chill.

♫

Alannys had spent a lot of time on their ride south thinking, trying to imagine what the royal ship would be like, what it would be like to be on it. After spending a few minutes on the *Atromitos,* though, she had to admit nothing she had imagined had even been close. The ship felt even bigger than she could have dreamed, looking at it from the docks. It didn't feel like a floating house—it felt like a floating city. Dorramon walked her all across the different levels of the deck, showing her from the main deck up to the quarter deck, up again to the sterncastle deck, and finally to the stern deck itself, high on the back of the ship. The royal flag flew high at the top of the main mast, but there was also a pair of them here, on flagpoles angled off the back of the deck railing, snapping in the wind that surrounded them. Alannys reached up and held her hair back out of her face, watching the lights of Port Grandview behind them. She could hear the shouts and the bustling of the crew preparing the ship for departure, and it gave her an odd, apprehensive feeling.

"The great cabin is directly below this deck we're standing on," Dorramon told her. His tone was conversational, but he watched her carefully, and she suspected he was trying to distract her. "Far and away the best quarters on this ship—easily as big as the royal apartment at the palace."

"Mmm." She knew she should sound impressed, she *wanted* to sound impressed, but she just couldn't seem to work up any enthusiasm for it. She stepped closer to the polished wood railing, resting her free hand on it. "That sounds very nice."

Dorramon followed her, covering her hand on the railing with his own. "What's on your mind?"

"Where should I start? I have enough to worry about, that's for sure. But right now, I can't stop thinking..." She swallowed hard, looked at him, and then back out at the city. "I can't stop thinking that I'm never going to see this place again."

"You're just tired," Dorramon said immediately, nipping that line of thought in the bud. "It's been a long, rough couple of days for all of us, but especially for you."

"If you say so."

He squeezed her hand, and she could practically feel him willing her to listen. "I do. Look, you are going to feel so much better in the morning. This is all Athniss's fault, really—the middle of the night is no time to put to sea. Wait until you come out on deck in the morning—the bright sun on the waves, the salty sea breeze in your hair —everything in the world will seem better."

Alannys smiled at him. Whatever else she might be feeling, she had to appreciate the effort he was putting into cheering her up. She turned away from the railing. "It sounds wonderful. I can hardly wait."

"That's the spirit." He put his arm around her shoulders, walking with her back toward the staircase down to the sterncastle deck. "Wait until you see the great cabin. You'll love it."

Tralice waited for them on the sterncastle deck, standing next to the mizzenmast with that grimace that always made Alannys feel like she should apologize for something, even if she was never quite sure what.

Dorramon's sigh was barely audible. "Is something the matter, Tralice?"

"I should say so, your Highness. Where are you going with my charge?"

"Your charge?" His mild tone belied the frown on his face. "I believe you were assigned as her maid, not her nanny."

"One can be very much like the other," Tralice said unapologetically. "I can only assume that a lady of her station will not be put in the guest quarters with the rest of us—sleeping on rows of bunks against the walls! It would be completely inappropriate. Given the limited accommodations here, I would like to know where you'll be putting her. It's very difficult to serve someone I can't find, you know."

"Of course." Dorramon's arm tightened around Alannys's shoulders, but if this conversation was aggravating him, his tone gave no sign of it. "I confess I had not planned on having our guests from Cadenda sail with us. They are in the lesser cabin."

Tralice nodded.

"That leaves the general guest quarters, which, as you've already said, are not suitable. Alannys will be staying in the great cabin."

"Your Majesty…"

"With me."

"Your Majesty! I have to protest! You must be aware that the eyes of the entire kingdom are—"

"Are what, Tralice? Are exactly *what?*" Annoyance

boiled over into the Dorramon's tone, and the maid took a hesitant step back. "Are you suggesting that the entire kingdom has the means to watch us, even here?"

"Of...of course not, your Majesty, I—"

"Then you are questioning her judgment, is that it? Lady Alannys is not able to tell us, if she thinks the situation is unsuitable? She would let us make her uncomfortable because she simply lacks the means to express her reservations?"

"No, my Lord King, certainly not."

"Then you surely must be questioning *my* judgment. I am not capable of making such decisions, not competent enough to consider the available accommodations, the people who need to be quartered, and arrive at a reasoned conclusion? Is that what this is about?"

"My Lord King! Of course not! You should know better than that."

"I am glad to hear it—I confess, I would question the sanity of anyone who voluntarily served a man as foolish as that. But it seems to me, then, that you have no cause for protest, don't you agree?"

"Your Highness..." Tralice couldn't seem to look at him. She twisted her fingers together, as though she could wring from them an answer that would appease him. "It isn't that easy, you know it isn't. What you call 'propriety' so dismissively—it's rules, your Majesty, the rules that make civil society civil. It isn't safe to ignore them for your own convenience."

Dorramon heaved a dramatic, long-suffering sigh. "You really aren't going to let this go, are you? You must be aware that all these things you worry so much about— what people think about us, whether we're improper or shameless or something along those lines? I don't care about them. I just do not care, and I'm never going to welcome you trying to make me care. Look, Tralice, let me ask you something. Where would *you* put Alannys?"

The maid obviously hadn't been expecting that

question. She blinked at him, once, twice, her mouth working silently as she puzzled her way through the situation. "Well," she finally said, "she belongs in the lesser cabin."

"A logical assumption, if the lesser cabin were available. Where, then, do you propose to put the King Apparent of Cadenda and his sister?"

Tralice floundered again.

Dorramon shook his head. "This isn't getting us anywhere. You're so concerned about Alannys's reputation, you tell me. Does she sleep in the rows of bunks against the wall, like common guests and crew, or does she sleep in the great cabin with all the status that confers? Decide quickly, because it's late and we haven't got all night."

Tralice looked from him to Alannys with eyes the size of tea saucers, her pale face almost glowing white in the lantern light.

"I'm sorry, Tralice," Alannys said, "but he's right. I know this isn't your ideal, but it is what it is, and you're going to have to find a way to accept it. I don't care about status, you know that. I don't mind sleeping in the bunks."

"My Lady!"

Alannys held up a hand, cutting off her maid's horrified gasp. "I said I don't mind, and I don't. I would rather stay here, with Dorramon. But not if it's going to have you hanging over my shoulder harping about the impropriety of my situation. Let me tell you this though — I'm trying to go along with you, Tralice, but I keep thinking about this...about me, setting out to do something that may kill me, and I'm all alone in a strange place, and I know Dorramon is nearby but I can't see him. And I don't know if I can do that. It sounds like torture. Why is it proper to make me suffer?"

Tralice bit her lip, but said nothing.

"Forget it," Alannys said. "So which is it? What do I need to do to make you happy?"

Tralice swallowed hard, glancing quickly around them as though she feared they might be overheard. "You could share a room with Prince Cardoth, your Highness, and put Lady Alannys with Princess Varilyn."

"I have to admit I didn't consider that," Dorramon said. "But I won't do it. Do you honestly expect me to turn my back and go to sleep with Cardoth in the same room, after everything that's happened?"

"Are you saying you distrust a man who betrayed his own father to help you?" The question could have been challenging, but Tralice's tone was curious, devoid of hostility.

"Indeed he did help," Dorramon said, "after spending three months hunting Alannys across the country, and scheming to frame me for his sister's apparent murder, and kidnapping Alannys right out from under us. Drugged her, too, as I recall. Tell me, Tralice, would *you* trust him?"

Her gaze fell away from his. "I don't suppose I would at that, your Majesty. Seems there's nothing for it then—we can't have a lady in the bunks. Just...consider her position, won't you? Both of you? Honestly, I'm not trying to make anyone suffer. But Lady Alannys isn't noble-born, everyone knows that. She's going to face resistance enough without doing anything to compromise what status she has."

"Of course, Tralice," Alannys said, her voice cracking. It was difficult to stay angry at someone who insisted so doggedly on looking out for your well-being, even when it made you want to throttle them.

Tralice turned on her heel and strode away from them without a look back, evidently satisfied with the assurances she had secured from them. Dorramon watched her go, shaking his head. "She doesn't discourage easily, I'll give her that. Now, my Lady, let us away to the great cabin."

"Of course." She took his arm again, but as they turned

to go, her gaze skimmed across something that gave her a start—Prince Cardoth, leaning against the far railing with his arms folded, watching them both. His dark eyes were inscrutable in the low light.

Surely that was coincidence. Surely he wasn't deliberately watching them; surely he hadn't overheard anything they'd said.

Slowly, deliberately, he met her gaze and inclined his head.

She turned away, a cold chill gripping her insides. What had he heard, and what had he made of it? Why had he even come along in the first place? Prince Cardoth was too many question, and not enough answers.

And she couldn't shake the feeling that she might actually be better off not knowing.

♫

The big, polished double doors at the back of the sterncastle deck opened into a short, wide corridor, with doors on either side, and one at the opposite end. Dorramon told her that one of the side doors led to the guest quarters, and the other to the lesser cabin. It was the door at the end that he reached for, though, the wide door adorned with a detailed carving of the royal crest—two stags on their hind legs, their antlers locked in combat. She didn't need to ask where that door led; any person in the world would have known a door like that led only to a room for the King of Ravanmark.

And she was staying in that room, too...it made her feel apprehensive, like it represented expectations yet unmet. Alannys knew she wasn't fit to step foot in a room like that, but she also knew that Dorramon and a sizable segment of the population of Ravanmark thought she was. Wasn't that the point of this whole trip, in a way, to gain some status of her own? To give her a start at becoming someone worthy of the man she was engaged to marry?

In the meantime....

"Fake it till you make it," she muttered under her

breath, and followed Dorramon into the great cabin.

Everything he had told her about the great cabin was true — she saw that much in her first glance. She had not expected anything so big, or so luxurious, on a ship — even a royal ship. Off to her right was a bath chamber, and to her left a sitting area lined with bookshelves built into the walls. The shelves had heavy glass doors that latched shut, presumably to keep their contents from spilling all over the room in rough weather. A red velvet sofa sat near the bookshelves, facing the door, and she could even see a small dining table with a couple of chairs.

But the real attention-grabber, the thing that took her breath away, was the far side of the room. It was easily as big as her whole suite of rooms at the palace, open and inviting. A big four-poster bed sat on the right side of the room, its headboard built into the wall, its frame seeming to rise out of the floor as though it was a natural outgrowth of the wood. It was clothed in red velvet that matched the rest of the furniture, with cotton quilts neatly folded at the foot. A wardrobe dominated the left side of the room, and in the middle was a massive desk, its surface polished to a high shine.

But behind all of this loomed the back wall of the room — the top part of the stern of the ship — a massive wall of heavy square windows, taller than Alannys and stretching the width of the room. Misty starlight filtered in through that wall of glass, scattering across the room. The rich woodwork that framed the room seemed to glow in the ethereal light, panels climbing the curving walls and beams arching up over her head. Running along the wall below the windows was a long, wide bench seat.

"Wow," Alannys croaked. Her voice sounded hoarse, overwhelmed — pretty much the way she felt, looking around the cabin.

Dorramon turned to look back at her, and a smile played across his face. "Didn't I tell you? Being on this ship never gets old. You are going to love it here. Just give it some time."

She nodded. It was easier to believe that now, standing in the soft light and warm wood of the great cabin. "I couldn't have imagined anything like this. I almost...I feel like I don't deserve this, Dorramon. I'm not the kind of person who should be in a place like this. I would be better off in the guest quarters with Tralice and the others."

"Stop that kind of talk." Dorramon took both of her hands in his own and pulled her farther into the room. "You are as worthy of this as anyone. I know that royalty is hereditary, and noble titles are inherited as well. But how do you think any of us got those titles to begin with?"

She just shook her head, staring into his eyes, deep and mysterious in the darkness.

"Service, Alannys—service and character. These titles were originally earned through deeds. And if anyone has done enough to earn the benefits of a title in Ravanmark, it's you."

"I don't know," Alannys hedged. "I hear you saying that, and I know that you believe it, but...it all just feels like too much for a commoner."

"Commoner," Dorramon snorted. "I hate that word, I really do—the way it implies that everyone who isn't royal or noble is somehow the same. Tell me, Alannys, what makes a person common? Their birth? That's common, it's true...we all go through it. If there is one thing in the world you are not, it's common. You are perfectly fine just the way you are, and you shouldn't change for me or Tralice or anyone else. As special as you think this place is, it isn't half as special as you."

She wasn't convinced. But she couldn't seem to force her voice to make words, not with Dorramon's eyes burning hers, and the misty starlight lighting up his face.

He chuckled, and the low, masculine sound of it made her heart leap to her throat. "I can see you don't believe me. So let me offer this alternative—if you don't think your service suffices, there is something else that proves you belong here."

"What's that?" She couldn't look away.

Dorramon leaned down, bringing his face within inches of hers. She could feel his breath against her lips — he was so close she was afraid he would hear the way her heart was pounding. "The king," he whispered, "loves you more than you will ever know."

All at once his lips pressed against hers, hot and demanding, and his hands twisted into her hair, and the entire *Atromitos* around them might have ceased to exist. The familiar tingle of electricity between them whenever they touched flared up into a crackling current she could neither control nor ignore. The intensity of her emotion threatened to undo her, and she wobbled on her feet, leaning against his broad chest for support. "Dorramon…"

He pulled back from her, searching her face in the low light.

"I love you, too."

Dorramon groaned and crushed her against him. Her eyes fell shut, as she surrendered to another breathless kiss that made her knees weak.

A sudden, loud rap sounded at the big door. "My Lady, my Lord King, please pardon my interruption."

Dorramon froze. Alannys could feel the muscles of his back tense under her hands, but his tone was mild. "What is it, Tralice?"

No one had told her to enter, so the maid stayed on the other side of the door. "I — I've just come to help my Lady out of her gown." She sounded uncomfortable.

"She doesn't need any help with that."

"I beg your pardon, your Majesty?"

"Nothing." Dorramon winked at Alannys. "We're fine — I'm afraid we won't require any help tonight. Good night, Tralice."

"As you say. Good night, your Majesty."

They could hear her footsteps recede, and the slight

creaking of the door to the guest quarters.

"Thank the Muses," Dorramon breathed against her skin. "I thought she'd never leave."

"What? But she was only here for a moment."

"Are you sure?" He nuzzled his face into her neck, covering it with warm kisses that made it hard for her to pay attention to the conversation. "It felt like forever. Sometimes I think she does it on purpose, I swear."

"She does have...particularly bad timing," Alannys said, holding onto him, trying to keep her balance. It didn't work, and she stumbled.

Dorramon caught her, with a low laugh. "Careful, there. Whatever could be the matter?"

"I'm sure I don't know." Her cheeks burned, giving away the lie. "I suppose I'm just tired."

"Tired, are you?" he said, and before she knew what was about to happen, he swung her up off of the floor and into his arms. "Only one place for you, then."

The bed felt decadently soft under her back, a world away from the moldy hay pile she had slept in the night before. The only thing that felt better was the heat of Dorramon's hands as they tracked down her rumpled gown, tracing the lines of her body through the fabric. She looked up into his eyes, deep and dark in the low light, and shivered. Her hands reached up as if of their own accord, and she tangled her fingers into his thick black hair.

"What's wrong?" he said, studying her face.

"Nothing. Nothing at all. I just...sometimes I can't quite believe I'm really here with you, that I don't have to be away from you anymore."

He turned his head suddenly, kissing the inside of her wrist. "I'm sorry. I wish I could have gone with you, all that time...I would understand, you know, if you chose to stay with the Singari tribe...with Chen. He has all the freedom I don't. You might be happier there. You're letting yourself in for a lifetime of stress and anxiety, chained to the Great Palace all the time...chained to the king."

"Stop that kind of talk. The Singari are great, but I could never stay with them, not forever. For all the fun and freedom, there's one thing the Singari just don't have."

"What's that?" He sounded honestly curious, and the doubt in his face tugged at her heart.

"You." She wrapped her arms around his neck and pulled him down, her lips meeting his with an urgency neither of them could deny. His hands moved to the laces of her gown, and hers to the buttons of his shirt, and in a matter of moments her bare chest pressed against his, electricity rippling between them, taking everything each of them felt and magnifying it, intensifying it, until they both burned with it, unaware of anything and anyone else in the world.

Alannys.

She froze, gasping, her body suddenly rigid with fear. The voice ripped through her mind, harsh and unexpected.

And it hadn't come from Dorramon.

♫

Alannys fought against the sudden, violent intrusion in her mind, squeezing her eyes shut, trying with everything she had to force the mindlink closed as well. She could feel her attacker on the other end, forcing it open.

I'm coming for you, Alannys, Athniss hissed inside her mind. *You can run, but you can't hide, not from me. The doom I carry is yours, and you will not escape it.*

"No!" She hadn't meant to shout out loud, but the word hung on the air around her, mocking her. She gritted her teeth, pushed with everything she had, and forced the mindlink shut.

He didn't try to open it again, which was good. The fight had exhausted her, and she didn't know how long she could have held it closed.

"Alannys?"

Her eyes popped open—Dorramon sat next to her, regarding her with worry written in his blue eyes. His rumpled clothes and disheveled hair might have been amusing, under other circumstances.

Her heart sank. What could she tell him? His fuse had been noticeably shorter since Sir Athniss had come into their lives—she didn't think she could bear to add to his burdens with her own. "I'm sorry." She was panting, and she didn't know if it was because of their intensity together, or her terror at Athniss's sudden mental attack.

His forehead creased into a frown. "I'm not interested in apologies. What happened?"

Her gaze slid away from his, and she pulled her gown awkwardly up over herself, suddenly feeling very exposed—in more ways than one. Covering her body did nothing to help close the gaping hole she sensed in her psyche. "I—I don't know."

"Don't know? You seemed terrified."

"I know." She bit her lip, clenching her fingers around the fabric of her gown to hide the way her hands were shaking. She didn't know what to do, couldn't think of what to say—she didn't think she had it in her to lie to him, but she knew she couldn't tell him the truth. This was her burden to bear, and she'd be damned if she would saddle him with it. "I just...I just..."

To her horror, her eyes brimmed up, and tears rolled down her face. Dorramon looked stricken, watching her. "Why are you crying?"

"I don't know." That, at least, was the honest truth. "So much has happened, and I...I don't know what to do."

He scooped her up, gathering her against his chest in a warm embrace, as if he meant to block out everything she feared. "Then don't do anything." He sounded unutterably sad, but his arms tightened around her, and he kissed the top of her head. "I'm sorry—I'm always pushing you, asking too much of you." Still holding onto her, he leaned back into the pillows. She ended up stretched out on the bed, cradled up against Dorramon, surrounded by his warmth and the softness of cotton quilts.

"No," she said, "that's not—"

"Shh." He placed one warm finger across her lips, and stroked her tangled hair back from her face. "No more talk. Just sleep. It's all going to work out, you'll see."

She wanted to argue with him, to make him understand that what had happened had nothing to do with him—but she didn't know how to do that without telling him what *had* happened, and she was afraid that would upset him even more.

She lay there in the misty half-light of the starlit great cabin, feeling the gentle rolling of the big ship, listening to the steady cadence of Dorramon's heartbeat beside her, her mind spinning in anxious circles, looking for a way out of her quandary, a way she seemed completely unable to find.

♫

When Alannys woke up, the gentle warmth that had surrounded her was gone. The cotton quilts lay cool and soft around her, but the big bed was empty.

Dorramon was gone.

"Dorramon?" She sat up, clutching her gown to her chest, scanning the dark room in sudden, irrational fear. He couldn't have gone far—she could still sense his presence in her mind, close by.

She saw him, sitting across the room on the big bench seat, staring out of the windows. Relief washed over her—she couldn't have said exactly what she'd been afraid of, but the fear had been real. She slipped her arms back through the sleeves of her gown, then slid out of bed and went to sit beside him.

He didn't even seem to notice. He didn't move, didn't look at her, gave no indication at all that he even knew she was there. She reached up and laid her hand tentatively on his shoulder, and felt him jump.

"Alannys! I'm sorry, I didn't hear you get up."

"I gathered that much." The words were wry, but she watched him with growing worry; she had never seen him brood like this before. "What's wrong?"

"Nothing." He turned back to look out the window, contemplating the roiling wake behind them, and the whitecaps lit up by the high moons.

Alannys pulled her hand back. She regarded it, lying limp in her lap, a tangible symbol of her helplessness just then. She knew she had no right to feel upset or shut out— this was her fault, she couldn't deny that. But she couldn't leave it like this, either. What could she do? "Not to argue with you," she said carefully, "but it seems pretty clear *something* is bothering you, doesn't it?"

He looked at her in surprise.

"I didn't mean to upset you earlier, or hurt your feelings. You must know that."

For a moment he didn't speak, and she wondered if he doubted her.

"*That's* what you're worried about?" He reached for her hand, drew it to his face and kissed it. "I don't know what to say to that." He turned back to the window, but still held her hand tightly in his lap. "You've done so much here...you see so much that I miss...but sometimes, Alannys, it's like you're way off in a different world entirely. I promise you I have not been sitting here nursing my injured ego."

"What have you been doing?"

"Thinking," he said simply. "Trying to figure out how I can protect you now."

"Protect me..?" She wasn't the only one who seemed to be somewhere else entirely.

"Yes. Didn't you think you could trust me enough to tell me that Athniss is tormenting you again?"

She felt herself tense up, instantly defensive. She knew he had to be able to feel it in her hand, but she couldn't stop it. "You...you knew?"

He nodded. Just a short, simple gesture, but for her it changed everything. She saw everything that had happened—what he'd said, the sadness in his face—differently now. "The mindlink feels...different somehow, when he does that. *Wrong*. I can't explain."

"I'm sorry." She couldn't look at him, knowing how greatly she had failed him. "It wasn't an issue of trust, surely you know that."

"Wasn't it, though? I wouldn't say you lied to me, Alannys. But you came awfully close, and what you did say certainly wasn't the truth. Why else would you do that, why would you go to so much trouble to avoid telling me, unless you couldn't trust me with it?"

His calm, quiet words felt like accusations, and they burned. She clenched her hand around his and jerked him around to face her. "I wasn't trying to lie to you, Dorramon, I was trying to *protect* you! Don't you think I knew how much this would upset you? There's nothing I can do about it, and there's nothing you can do about it, and there's no reason on earth you should have to carry that burden!"

He stared at her for a long moment. She listened to the gradual slowing of her pounding heart, wondering if she had finally gone too far. She wasn't intimately familiar with Ravanmark's laws, but she would have bet money it was treasonous, jerking on the king and shouting at him like that. She dropped her gaze and pulled her hands back, wringing them in her lap. How many more ways could she hurt him, before he tossed her overboard?

And all she had been trying to do was look out for him.

Dorramon caught her up in a crushing hug, then held her back and looked seriously into her face. "Alannys, I love you more than anything, you know that. But I swear I'm going to strangle you if you don't stop treating me like something made of glass, like something to be coddled and protected."

"But—"

"It's shutting me out, that's what it is. And I won't stand for it. Any threat to you is a threat to me, don't you see that? You can't keep that from me. It hurts that you would even try."

"I'm sorry." She wrapped her arms around him, burying her face into his chest. "I'm sorry, I never meant to upset you. It's just...it's hard to talk about something that scares me so much, you know? And even harder, knowing that it's going to scare you, too. He's crazy, and he's desperate. He terrifies me, Dorramon, and there's nothing we can do about it."

His arms went around her back. "I know." His voice sounded strained, and yet the rumble of it in his chest under her ear was soothing. "I'm not asking anything of you, Alannys, except that you talk to me. You're playing right into his hands when you keep everything bottled up. Don't shut me out, don't try to be strong all on your own. I can't take it." He scooped her up and carried her to the bed, pulling the quilts over her and tucking them around her as if she was a small child. She watched him solemnly, unable to shake the feeling she had done something wrong. How could anything that made him look that way *not* be wrong?

He climbed into bed next to her, and she pushed herself up against him, clinging to him as though she was afraid he might disappear. He stroked her hair, and hummed quiet, soothing melodies to her, and against her every expectation, she slept.

♫

Alannys woke up alone, with a striking sense of deja vu. She sat up in the rumpled bed, pushing her messy hair out of her face. Everything stood as she remembered it, only brighter, as the morning sunlight began to streak its way across the room—the wardrobe, the bookshelves, the big desk, all as they should be.

But except for her, the room was empty.

She sighed, shoulders slumping, feeling somehow abandoned. She didn't know why she should expect anything different — not after what she had put Dorramon through the night before.

She pushed herself out of bed and went to the wooden wardrobe, hoping to find something she could wear, something more presentable than the crumpled, filthy gown she had slept in. To her surprise, everything she'd had in the big trunk had been put neatly inside — she supposed they must have taken care of it while she had been on the stern deck with Dorramon the night before.

Whenever they had done it, she was grateful. She pulled out her familiar work shirt and leather pants, happy for once to be able to dress herself. Tralice probably had never realized she had stuffed her knapsack into the trunk. It had felt spiteful at the time, but she couldn't help but be thankful now. A quick trip to the bath chamber and she left the great cabin behind, heading out to the sterncastle deck.

It was like walking into a different world from the one she had been in the night before. Dorramon had been right — the morning sun lit up the full sails a bright, happy white, and the brilliant blue sea around them reflected that light back at them, scattered it like jewels. All around her sailors worked in their blue-striped shirts and linen trousers, adjusting sails, cleaning and polishing, keeping a lookout from the crow's nest and manning the ship's great wheel. Cheerful chatter surrounded her, some of which she would have been embarrassed to repeat.

"Well, now, you're looking chipper this morning." The voice was familiar, but she had to turn around and see him before she recognized Tassin, the captain's son — freckles, unruly red hair, and all. He carried a roll of heavy twine over his shoulder.

She covered up her surprise with a big smile, doing her best to actually appear chipper.

"Still not very much like royalty, though," he said,

eyeing her critically. "Or even like you belong on a ship, really."

Her smile curdled. Always blunt, that seemed to be the way of this kid. She thought she could say the same for him — the deep, peeling sunburn across his nose and cheeks didn't seem very much like someone who presumably spent most of his life at sea. But she remembered herself and took the high road. "Ah, well, leopards can't change their spots, can they? Tell me, Tassin, have you seen the king this morning?"

"Aye," Tassin replied, gesturing with a jerk of his head toward the stern deck behind them. "Up there he is, with the captain."

"Thank you."

"Don't mention it, Lady Alannys. I think you'll surprise us all yet. Leopards are great and all, but I ain't never seen a cat that had anything on you."

Alannys stood there a bit baffled, trying to work out whether she had just been complimented or insulted. In the end it didn't matter; Tassin was already gone. She could see him, hustling across the main deck with his rope, calling cheerfully to the other sailors.

She shook her head and hurried up the stairs to the stern deck. She could see Dorramon up there, just as Tassin had said, in an animated conversation with Captain Morgain. The wind carried bits of their conversation to her, and she tried to get a feel for what was going on before she got there.

"...and I'm telling you, your Majesty, there just ain't nothing I can do for you."

"Captain, I don't think you understand the urgency of the situation." Frustration made Dorramon's words short, but his tone was carefully neutral. "As I've explained —"

"Begging your pardon, your Majesty, but as *I've* explained, the urgency of the situation don't matter. Best speed is best speed — it's in the Muses's hands, not mine." Captain Morgain saw her approaching and dipped his head to her, touching his fingers to the brim of his hat.

Dorramon turned to follow the gesture. For just a moment she could see his aggravation in the taut lines of his face, but as his eyes met hers all of that smoothed away in a welcoming smile. "Good morning, Alannys. You're up early."

"Not as early as you, it seems."

"Ah, yes. That's true. Old habits, I suppose. I had to shoo off Tralice so she would let you sleep. Besides, I wanted to have a talk with Captain Morgain this morning."

"Aye." The word was flat, as though perhaps this conversation was not the high point of Morgain's morning.

"I see. I'm sorry to intrude, then." She studied Dorramon's face carefully, and Morgain's grizzled visage, but they might have been wearing masks for all she could tell from them.

"Nothing to apologize for," the captain said, turning away to look out over the railing at the sea. "We was pretty much done anyway, wouldn't you say, your Highness?"

"Captain..." Dorramon's tone sounded warning.

"I'm sorry, your Highness. I wish there was something I could do. But we're already at ship's best speed, and that's where we'll stay. Patience, that's the key. You're safe on my ship—enjoy the ride."

Captain Morgain turned and headed down the stairs, leaving them alone on the stern deck, not looking back or giving the king any opening to argue.

Dorramon swore under his breath, and turned to the railing himself, gripping it in both hands as though he would have liked to crush it. Tendons stood out on the backs of his hands, tense and knotted.

Alannys moved to stand next to him, leaning her elbows on the railing as though she had nothing more on her mind than contemplating the view. The wind whipped her hair around her face, and billowed the fabric of her shirt around her, but she made no move to correct any of it. It felt good—refreshing, in a way, as though the wind was blowing away something she had grown tired of carrying. "Anything I can help with?"

"No," he said immediately, with a sharp edge, as though he feared she would do just that. "Like I said, just a little talk with the captain."

"It didn't really seem to go well. Mind if I ask what it was about?"

"I think you already did." His tone was dry, but the words carried no sting. "It's no secret. I was simply encouraging Captain Morgain to get us to Mount Mouseion as quickly as possible."

"Ship's best speed," she mused. "So that's what he meant."

"Indeed. *Atromitos* is exclusively wind-powered. Doesn't look like we even have any capacity for rowers."

"Rowers?" She craned her head around to look at him. He was staring grimly out over the water, but he looked like he didn't even see it. "You would put men to oars, to get us there faster? Would that even work?"

"I don't know. Probably not—the wind's good, I don't know how much we could really add. But at least we would be trying, not sitting here doing nothing while your enemies plot against you."

"Dorramon." She stood up, pulling him away from the railing, and turned him to face out over the body of the ship. From where they stood, they could see the entire deck—clear over to the forecastle deck on the other end of the great ship. "Look at these men. Nobody on this ship is doing nothing."

"Nobody," he said sourly, "except me. I'm sorry, Alannys. I'd better go."

He stomped off toward the sterncastle deck without another word.

♫

For a long time Alannys stood alone on the stern deck, leaning on the railing and staring out at the water, watching the sunlight skitter across its undulating surface, shattering the light into bright, piercing reflections that scattered in every direction. It felt peaceful somehow, mind-numbing. The salty breeze played through her hair, and the gentle swaying of the big ship felt soothing.

It didn't help, though—as calming as her surroundings were, they couldn't quite touch the anxiety that coursed through her when she thought about Dorramon, about the grim set of his jaw when he had stomped away, about the way his gentle hands had clenched into fists as he left her.

She knew it wasn't her fault, not really; she knew he wasn't angry with her or anything she had done. And yet she couldn't help *feeling* responsible—she had failed to reach him, there was no denying that. If only she had spoken more eloquently, if only she had chosen her words with more care. She wasn't exactly sure what she could do now, but she knew there had to be something. She had to try. She couldn't stand seeing him like this.

She was halfway down the stairs to the sterncastle deck when she realized she was not alone. The voices were tense but faint—far too quiet for her to understand what they were talking about, or even who they belonged to. But just the fact of their presence prompted her to look up from her dismal contemplation of her own leather boots, and down on the deck she saw Prince Cardoth and Princess Varilyn, between the mizzenmast and the stairs. They were arguing; she could tell that without words from their strained expressions and sharp gesticulations, but their voices were so quiet she couldn't hear them from just a few feet away—probably because of the crewman on the other side of the mast, manning the ship's big wheel.

There was probably a worse place on the ship to have a private conversation, but offhand she couldn't imagine where it would be.

She froze, her hand on the polished rail, her foot

hanging in the air halfway between steps. What in the world was she supposed to do now? Clearly this was a scene she should not have witnessed. She could hardly just waltz blithely on by at this point. But neither could she just stand there gaping at them, and she couldn't turn and slink back up the stairs either—what could they assume then, but that she intended to eavesdrop some more?

Cardoth settled the issue, before she'd had time to do more than register her predicament, before anyone had even realized she was there. "I'm sorry," he said, loudly enough for her to hear, each word short and clipped. "I disagree. And there's really no point in discussing this further. It isn't your concern."

And he turned and stomped off—right up the stairs Alannys was standing on.

He stopped cold on the bottom step, staring up at her in outraged disbelief. "How long have you been standing there spying?"

"Cardoth!" Varilyn's gasp sounded shocked, but she looked as surprised as he did to find Alannys standing there.

"Well?" Cardoth prompted impatiently. "Nothing to say for yourself?"

"I—I'm sorry," Alannys stammered. "I was looking for Dorramon."

Cardoth quirked a doubtful eyebrow at her.

Her face burned, right up to her ears. That probably didn't help her case any. "I've been on the stern deck all morning. Dorramon left a few minutes ago—I was hoping to catch him."

"Ballocks," Cardoth snorted. "Nobody left a few minutes ago; we would have seen it. Do you have any idea what would happen to you if you were caught doing that in Cadenda?" He waved a dismissive hand in her direction, and turned his back on her. "It doesn't matter—why am I even bothering with this? You want to spy on me, have at it. It's no difference to me. You all have made it clear where I stand."

"Wait!" Alannys said, holding up a hand, stopping him before he could stomp off in the other direction. He stopped, but he didn't turn around, and she had to content herself with talking to his back. "I really am sorry, Cardoth. I'm sorry for interrupting, but I also want to apologize for what you overheard last night. I know Dorramon would never have said it if he had known you could hear. We're all your friends here, Cardoth."

"You're raving." He never turned back, but she could see Varilyn's face looking at his, and what she saw reflected there wasn't good. "I'm from Cadenda. I don't have friends."

This time he did stomp off, and neither Alannys nor Varilyn made a move to stop him.

♫

"Try not to feel bad," Varilyn told Alannys. Her words were soothing, but her smile was shaky. "I'm afraid his mood was ruined before you ever showed up."

"I did get that impression." Alannys finally came down the rest of the stairs, and went to stand near Varilyn, pretending not to notice the crewman at the wheel, who pretended not to notice them. In spite of the heat of the day, and in spite of the fact that they were onboard a ship, the princess looked as put-together as she had at the palace, sporting a candy pink gown with a full skirt over petticoats, and her dark hair pulled up into an elegant twist. Alannys felt quite plain and graceless by comparison, even though she was well aware her hair wasn't long enough for a twist like that, and the only thing she hated more than a gown she couldn't put on alone was a petticoat. "I want to apologize to you too, Varilyn—I meant what I told him. I've been on the stern deck all morning; I had no idea you two were down here. I thought it hadn't been that long since Dorramon left...I guess I lost track of time."

"You don't need to apologize to me. You don't really need to apologize to him, either — any fool could see you're telling the truth, except maybe that one. I can't imagine that he really believes you set out to spy on him." Varilyn sighed. It made her sound much older, and very tired. "But I guess I can't claim to understand much of anything he thinks right now."

Alannys watched the princess's face, torn between sympathy and a desire not to pry. "What happened, if you don't mind my asking?"

Varilyn shook her head. "It's no secret. You've probably already guessed. In some ways, I suppose it was the same thing you just talked to him about."

"What, Dorramon's remark?"

"That too. Everything, really. I don't know what to do for him — and it's pretty plain he doesn't really want my help. He doesn't want to hear anything I have to say."

"That does make him hard to talk to." Privately Alannys thought that was an understatement, but she was trying to be civil, not stir things up. "I don't think I've seen him quite this caustic in a while. What happened to him?"

"Hmm." Varilyn stared out over the railing at the puffy, white clouds. Her eyes seemed to lose focus; her gaze looked so distant it seemed she must actually be staring at something *beyond* the clouds, something so far away Alannys couldn't even conceive of it. "Let me ask you a question. Why did you apologize to my brother?"

"For what Dorramon said?" Alannys frowned. "That seems obvious — I was afraid we had hurt his feelings."

"Obvious...I suppose. Let me ask you another question, then. Doesn't that seem strange to you? Think back to Cardoth when you first met him — not as the man seeking to assassinate you, but as the Prince of Cadenda. Think about all the time you spent with him at the Great Palace, and in that hay cart traveling though the countryside. The things he did, the plans he'd made — plans he was actively carrying out.

"Now try to imagine that man having his feelings hurt by anything you could say or do."

Alannys blinked at her in sudden surprise.

"Do you see what I'm getting at? You can't even imagine it, can you? Cardoth is a very reasonable man — a very practical man. He knows which way the water runs, Alannys, he knows it isn't reasonable to expect he would be fully trusted already, after everything he's done. And yet...Cadenda isn't Ravanmark — it's different in ways so fundamental, I'm not sure you could even imagine it. There's so much fear there, and so much secrecy...the state controls everything. It even seeks to control things that just *can't* be controlled, like the thoughts and the feelings of its people. I've seen some of Ravanmark over the years. I've seen festivals, and funerals, and I've seen the people here rally to support their king."

"Don't those things happen in Cadenda?" Alannys asked.

"Well, they do — of course they do — but it's different. There's no real joy or sorrow in any of it, just fearful people pretending. There's no *choice* in any of it. People don't celebrate state occasions because they want to, they celebrate because it's compulsory. Everyone is carefully watched; those who don't comply are treated as enemies of the state. And where the state has no eyes, the eyes of neighbors and family members take over. A man's own child might turn him in, if he said the wrong thing behind closed doors, or failed to make the proper observances. Such betrayal is considered heroism, in Cadenda."

"Wow."

"Indeed," Varilyn said. "I've spent a lot of time in Ravanmark, Alannys, since I was pretty young. And the differences were hard even for me to accept. Being here...changed me in ways that really made me unsuitable to ever live in Cadenda again. And even for me, even for someone who never really fit in there to begin with...that was hard for me to accept. At some point I had to look at what was happening to me and make a choice, make a deliberate decision to allow it. A deliberate decision to cut all real ties with the land that raised me."

"That must have been hard for you," Alannys said.

Varilyn inclined her head, acknowledging the comment without addressing it. "But think of Cardoth. He had none of my advantages, if you can call them that—he wholeheartedly embraced the society that raised him. He never even considered any other way to govern, to live. He fit in, he made his parents proud. And he had never had any experience of Ravanmark at all before he came over here on his mission to murder you. He was entirely out of his element."

Alannys thought about it. "He was a lot different then. He used to talk a lot about duty, about the necessity of doing things that weren't pleasant, things that went against your conscience, if duty required it."

"Of course. In Cadenda, there is no other way. But these last weeks...the changes in him have been very strong. You must have noticed as well. I have never seen my brother speak openly to so many people, have never seen him joke and laugh the way he has recently. And at Agapios Periousia, something happened that was so profound, he actually spoke to me about it. I understand that in the garden, after your rescue, he attacked Rodriset to save the king."

"He did," Alannys said, remembering. "I really think Rodriset might have killed him otherwise—none of us saw it coming. Except Cardoth."

"That's one advantage of growing up in Cadenda. Maybe the only advantage. If there is an opportunity for treachery, Cardoth will see it. But this time...he acted so quickly, it was almost without thought. And he did it entirely for someone else, with no thought to his own benefit."

"It was a noble thing," Alannys said, although she couldn't shake the memory of how quickly, how mercilessly, he had struck, and how it had chilled her to see it.

"It was," Varilyn agreed. "But it was more than that, don't you see? As a royal from Cadenda, he's never in his life had what you would call a real friend—someone who liked him for what he was, not what he could do for them. Someone who supported him because they cared about him, not because they thought he could advance them. He never would have wanted anything like that—in Cadenda's royal family, that kind of softness can get you killed, and they would say you deserved it. But now, he has spent time here, and he's seen you with Dorramon, and he's seen something there he never saw between his own parents. He's seen you interact with so many people —from the arch-prince, to the Captain of the Guard, even that nice Singari fellow—and he's sensed something there he never saw back home. He told me he couldn't think of one single interaction he'd ever had in his whole life that had that *thing* in it, and all of the sudden that felt like a hole—a hole that he wanted to fill. And with Rodriset...it was the first time Cardoth had ever acted on someone else's behalf, the first time he ever acted without thinking of the risks or the rewards for himself. It was such a big thing, even he had to notice it. Even he couldn't pretend anymore that he wasn't changing, that Ravanmark wasn't having an effect on him. It worried him, but mostly he was happy. Because he thought he was one of you, you see? He thought he was beginning to fill that hole."

"Oh, no," Alannys groaned. "Then he heard Dorramon say he couldn't be trusted, and it threw ice water all over his warm new feelings."

Slowly, Varilyn began to nod. "It isn't Dorramon's fault —what he said was entirely reasonable. Like I said, Cardoth and I are both well aware of what he has done. We both know there's no way a rational person in your position would trust him at this point—how could you? But he was just starting to be vulnerable, and this cut him down. And now...I think he may be turning his back on change altogether. He doesn't want to talk to me about it, he doesn't want to hear reason—and he certainly doesn't want to hear about friends. He says the whole thing is a weakness, and he's got to cut that weakness out of himself."

"Oh, Varilyn." Alannys shook her head, paced off a short, frustrated length, and shook her head again. "I feel just awful. I wish there was something I could do."

"I'm afraid anything you could do now would be unwelcome at best. It might actually push him farther away. I think we must give him time, Alannys. He likes you, all of you, whether he will admit it or not. That's going to win out."

"Are you sure?" Alannys couldn't help fretting. Cardoth was a formidable opponent—she knew that better than most—and she didn't want him fighting her again.

"I'm positive," Varilyn said, and she smiled.

But it was still a shaky smile.

♫

Alannys frowned but said nothing, watching the princess head back towards the cabin she and her brother shared. She couldn't fault Varilyn's lack of confidence— the whole thing worried her, too, more than she could express. But what could she do? Cardoth wouldn't want to hear about it from her, and as Varilyn kept pointing out, it wasn't even really her fault.

But you know better, don't you? hissed a voice in her mind, completely unwelcome.

Alannys staggered and reached for the railing, doing her best not to gasp out loud. Instinctively she tried to close the mindlink, but Athniss seemed to be holding it open. She hadn't even known the Seeing Stone could give someone that kind of advantage, but it was awfully hard to fight against it. She didn't know if Athniss could tell that she was fighting to close the connection, either.

But she could hear his low laugh in her mind, reedy

and unpleasant. *Don't fight the truth, Alannys. It has already started, even you must see that. Your friends don't stand a chance, in the end. You'll tear them apart, one by one — peel each from the others, and destroy them.*

No! She hadn't intended to say the word aloud — in fact she was fairly certain she *hadn't* spoken aloud, but the crewman at the wheel turned to toss a worried glance in her direction, and she couldn't think of any other explanation for it.

She tried to offer him a reassuring smile, and managed a sort of bared-tooth grimace. It was the best she could do — this forced mindlink exchange was nothing like a regular mindlink conversation. It was stressful, painful, more like a violation than a conversation...it made it very hard to fight against it at all. She didn't seem to have complete control of her mind or her body, but she did the best she could to rally herself against her attacker. *That will never happen, Athniss. I know what you and the Retainers believe about me, but you're wrong. Soth destroyed his friends. I won't make that same mistake.*

Won't you, though? Another laugh clawed its way through her mind, making her brain itch. *You are wrong about so many things, Alannys. It seems to me that the Retainers are putting themselves to all of this trouble specifically because they believe you're not Soth. Silly, really.*

She gripped the railing until her fingers ached and her hands shook, struggling to close the mindlink. It didn't work. *Silly, is it?* she snapped back, more to hide how hard she was working than to continue the conversation.

Indeed. Or at the least, premature. A little thought would put them straight soon enough. Soth didn't light upon the land fully formed, after all, wreaking havoc from his first breath, now did he?

Stop this. Her legs were beginning to shake; she didn't know how much longer she could endure this. And what would happen then, when the strain of this encounter proved too much for her and her mind gave way? She prayed she wouldn't have to find out. *Leave me alone. I am not Soth. I will <u>never</u> be Soth!*

Not yet, dear lady, not yet. You can't seriously mean to go, not before you've heard my reasoning. You're just getting started, don't you see? Soth himself started just as you have – saving people, helping people, doing the Muses's good work here in Ravanmark. Everything you've done...you're just following in his footsteps, don't you see? All you need is a little more time, and the Retainers themselves will wonder why they ever doubted you.

No, she grunted. It felt like forcing the word out through clenched teeth. The suggestion that she really was Soth, that she might yet destroy everyone and everything she cared about...it was her deepest, darkest fear, the fear she never admitted even to herself. Hearing Athniss describe it was a kind of torture. She couldn't tolerate it. *You're wrong!*

Am I? Athniss, on the other hand, sounded as though he was having a wonderful time. It made Alannys want to strangle him, and as soon as she had that thought, he laughed even louder, as though he found her ire amusing. *You're already heading that way, Alannys. Prince Cardoth is only the first. Last to become your friend, first to succumb to your unholy powers of destruction. But don't worry, you'll take them all down – in time. Watch it happen, Alannys, watch the total destruction of everyone you hold dear, and realize that Soth did the very same thing. And remember – I told you it would happen. You are Soth born again, whether you want to see it or not, and you will drag all of your friends – and all of Ravanmark – into the Seven Hells with you before you are finished.*

"NO!" This time she did shout out loud, screamed from the bottom of her soul. Her fingers clawed into the railing, her face contorted painfully and her back arched, as she poured everything she had, everything she was, into forcing the mindlink closed.

It closed. She couldn't have said whether she was

finally successful, or Athniss had simply tired of his game, but the mindlink snapped shut. With its closing she felt herself regain full control once more over her body and her mind — only to find them both completely exhausted, every resource she possessed expended in her confrontation with Sir Athniss.

"Thank the Muses," she sighed, and as if she meant to do it, as if she had practiced and planned, she crumpled to the deck, floating gracefully into the blackness at the bottom of her mind.

♫

"Alannys." She could hear the voice dimly, sounding as though it came to her from someplace very distant. It was easy to ignore, so she did.

"Alannys!" The voice, though distant, was persistent, and tinged with anxiety. It made her feel anxious too, just hearing it. She didn't like that. She pushed the voice aside and carried on doing exactly what she had been doing before the voice disturbed her, which as far as she could tell, was nothing.

Alannys. Finally the voice came after her where she couldn't ignore it, couldn't push it aside and pretend not to hear. Dorramon was worried — she could feel it, looming like a thundercloud behind the single word — but his voice through the mindlink was gentle and soft, barely brushing against her own mind.

And yet, it hurt, it *burned,* as though the mindlink itself was sore. How was that possible? What was Athniss *doing* when he forced his way into the mindlink like that? Was the Seeing Stone even meant to be used that way? How much more of this could she stand?

She didn't have any answers, and they seemed unlikely to come find her in the darkness. She pushed the questions aside and pried her eyes open, surprised to find the clear blue sky there, the noon sun from its high perch gazing back down at her.

She squinted against the glare and tried to sit up. Every

single muscle in her body ached, and her head pounded dully with the movement. She fell back against the deck again. "What happened?" Her voice sounded about like she felt—rough and completely used up.

"Careful, there." The voice was Dorramon's. With more effort than the simple action should have required, she turned her head and found him there, kneeling beside her, his brow knit with the same concern she heard in his voice. He took her arm, encouraging her to stay put. "You fainted. You don't remember?"

"I guess...I guess I do."

"You gave us a right scare, and no mistake." The brash voice from her other side startled her, and she turned that way to find Tassin grinning at her. "Glad to see you doing better."

"I wouldn't say she's doing better yet," Dorramon said. "She's still flat on her back in the sun."

"Well, and that's her own fault, ain't it? Don't see no one holding her down."

Alannys looked away from them, embarrassed, and noticed the complete emptiness of the desk around them. "Where is everybody? I know there was at least one person here, at the wheel..."

"They're gone." Dorramon sounded apologetic. "I'm afraid they all probably cleared out of here before you hit the ground. I got here as fast as I could...I could feel something wasn't right..."

"It isn't your fault." She stared at the big wooden wheel, standing there eerily unmanned. It gave her a disconcerting feeling, like being on a ghost ship. "Is that safe, though, for a big ship like this to be full sail with no one at the wheel?"

"No. No, of course it isn't. Under other circumstances I think Captain Morgain would toss them all overboard himself. But this..." He looked away and shook his head. "Mindlinks, music...it's all magic, and none of them want any truck with it. I'm sorry."

Alannys let her gaze wander the abandoned deck. It saddened her — she had been making an effort, after all, to do better lately, to be conscious of her position and her behavior, and still everybody ran away when she was in trouble. "If Princess Varilyn had collapsed on deck...they would all have helped her, wouldn't they?"

Dorramon frowned.

"Oh, absolutely," Tassin said cheerfully. "The princess is a great lady. Half the crew's devoted to her — the other half ain't met her yet."

"But Varilyn isn't Talented," Dorramon said immediately. "That changes everything. You need to stop trying so hard to live up to other people's standards, Alannys, and start making your own. Varilyn is not the only great lady on this ship."

Alannys braced her hands against the deck, ready to push herself up. Dorramon looked at her in sharp surprise. "What do you think you are doing? Do you really think you're in any condition to get up?"

"Maybe not, but I don't think I have a lot of choice. Unless you intend to steer this ship?"

"Under other circumstances, certainly. But right now..." He sighed in defeat. "I'm afraid I couldn't pay proper attention to it, not with you like this. But I still don't think you need to be moving around just yet."

"So we're just going to let the ship drift? I'm not willing to let that happen, just because I fainted."

He focused on her sharply; she could see his blue eyes narrow. "You didn't just faint, Alannys — you know that. I don't know what exactly this is that Athniss does, but it's rough and intrusive and it isn't right. You don't know what it might be doing to you, and you're clearly exhausted. This isn't a normal fainting spell, and you need to rest. Just wait here, all right? I'll get Captain Morgain to bring a stretcher, and help me move you."

"No!" She redoubled her efforts to sit up. "The only thing more humiliating than lying here passed out because of something that only happened in my head, would be having you and the captain haul me off like an invalid because of something that only happened in my head. I would rather crawl."

"Alannys…"

Tassin laughed suddenly, taking her arm and helping her sit up. "You picked a good one, your Majesty. She's got fire. Wouldn't do to put it out, would it?"

Dorramon heaved a long-suffering sigh, raking a hand through his hair. "I want you to know I am doing this against my better judgment." Moving quickly, like he wanted to get it over with before he thought better of it, he caught her hand in his and hauled her to her feet.

Immediately she stumbled, clinging to his hand for support and swaying on her feet anyway. Dorramon's ominous frown did not escape her, but he just put his other arm around her waist to steady her. "The things you put yourself through for other people," he muttered.

She pretended not to hear that, staggering along between him and Tassin toward the great cabin. There was nothing she could say to that, after all. Maybe a remark about the pot and the kettle?

As they approached the door with its daunting insignia, Tassin suddenly stopped. "This is as far as I go. It wouldn't be proper for me to go inside."

Dorramon looked over at him in surprise. "Don't worry about that. It's perfectly fine."

"Ah, your Majesty is too generous. It's more than my job's worth to go in there—a man's got to know his place. The great cabin ain't no place for ordinary folk." He gave Alannys a hard look as he released her arm, and dropped a nod in her direction as he turned to leave. He never said another word, but she heard the rebuke loud and clear. It stung, coming from someone who had just seemed to be getting around to liking her.

"What a strange, stubborn young man," Dorramon muttered. "Come on, we had better get you inside."

The big bed in the cabin had been neatly made, the great room freshly dusted. She had no idea what passed for a housekeeping staff on the ship — was this considered part of the crew's duties? — but she was grateful for it. She landed on the bed with a bit more force than she had intended, doing her best not to show how winded she was. This really *wasn't* any normal fainting spell, as much as it irked her to admit it.

Dorramon watched her, a frown on her face and worry clouding his eyes. "Are you all right?"

"I'm fine." She perched herself on the edge of the bed, gripping it harder than was probably necessary. "Just...maybe let me rest a moment — it feels like the room is moving." The way he stood leaning against the slightly curved wall made her feel dizzy, but he folded his arms casually, as though it didn't bother him.

"The room is moving," Dorramon said dryly. "You're on a ship."

She could feel her face flush bright red. "Well, more than usual. I just need a minute to clear my head."

He pushed himself away from the wall and came to stand in front of her. "You need more than that, I think."

"Oh?" Her tone was light and teasing, an attempt to lighten his mood. "What do I need?"

"A nap, to start with." He bit his lip, regarding her seriously — apparently her attempt at humor had not reached him at all. "You look like you're about two steps this side of the Valley of the Muses."

"No, I just —"

"Really," he cut her off, as though he hadn't even noticed she was speaking, "you shouldn't get out of that bed for the rest of the day."

"What? But I...I..."

"You what?"

"I can't do that, Dorramon. I don't have time to be just lying around like that."

"No?" He grabbed her boots around the ankles and

swung her feet up onto the bed. "What, exactly, is it that you have to do? Because from where I'm standing, it looks like you're on a ship that's being run perfectly well without you, and you really have nothing you need to do until it gets you where you're going."

She bit her lip, but said nothing. She didn't like the characterization—she certainly didn't *feel* like someone with nothing to do, but she didn't have a good argument against it, either.

"And do you know what else seems pretty clear from where I'm standing? What you have to do when you get where you're going is something that requires a lot of strength. It's going to be harder than anything you've ever done before, harder even than the tidal wave at Garrant. You're going to need all of your energy for it—it seems to me you had better rest while you can. Honestly, if you keep going the way you are...I don't see how you're even going to have the strength to fight off Athniss and this *thing* he does, let alone perform the acts of the Redeemer."

"Maybe that's the whole point," she said, realizing it for the first time. "It's pretty clear the Retainers don't want me performing the acts. This could be one way to stop me, even if he can't physically reach me—just wear me out before I get there."

"Well, see, that's just another reason you can't let him win. This can't be easy on him—using the Seeing Stone the way he is must be hard work. You can bet he's recuperating every chance he gets. If you don't do the same, you're going to be at a disadvantage."

"I know. But..."

"But what?" He went around to the other side of the bed and stretched out next to her, lying back against the pillows and stroking her hair, staring up at the ceiling.

It occurred to her that if he was trying to distract her from her concerns, he was doing an uncommonly good job.

"It's easier to say than do."

She heard his low chuckle, right near her ear. "Many things in life are."

Alannys didn't answer that. She lay limp against the pillows for a moment, enjoying the quiet and the rhythmic movements of Dorramon's hand in her hair, spreading tingling sensations across her scalp. "Dorramon," she said finally, "do you think there's any chance I really am Soth reborn?"

His hand froze. "No. No, of course not." He started stroking her hair again, and it was a relief to feel it—more of a relief than it should have been, really. The feeling made it obvious how much the question had been eating at her, which frustrated her because she knew that had been Athniss's precise intent. "Is that what he's been saying to you?"

"It's kind of hard to just deny it out of hand, though, isn't it? I mean, sure, *I* don't think I'm evil...but if you had asked Soth himself that, he would have answered the same. And for many years, everyone around him would have, too."

"Alannys..."

"It wasn't obvious right away. The changes would have been small at first, easy to miss. And even when you could see them...I don't imagine the people close to him did, not for a while. It would have been too painful...they probably did everything they could *not* to see."

His hand had stopped again. "Alannys, please..."

"And what about Ravan? How could she ever admit what had become of the man she loved? How long did it take *her* to face it, do you suppose?"

"That's it. I forbid you to say another word." His tone was surprisingly firm, and she looked over at him with wide eyes. "Is this the kind of stuff he's been torturing you with? Or are you torturing yourself? You can't give a single thought to anything that comes out of that man's mouth. Not one. All he's trying to do is trip you up, fill you with doubt...distract you from your goal."

"I know, but—"

"Not another word, remember? You can't keep him out of the mindlink, but you can keep him out of your head. Don't reflect any further on anything he says, now or in the future. You don't need to worry about ridiculous things like that." At some point, his voice had taken on the familiar lilting of speak-singing, and she could feel it now, pushing her towards sleep. "What you need is rest."

It was true, she knew that, but it didn't lessen her worries. She peered at him through eyes suddenly blurry, fuzzy with her almost physical need to sleep. 'Ridiculous,' he'd said, but was it really? Soth the Blessed, they had called him once, Soth the Great. And then...

"*Sleep,*" she heard him say, and her thoughts lost coherence in the dreamless depths.

♫

When Alannys woke up there was still daylight streaming in through the massive windows. It meant it wasn't too late; she hadn't wasted the *whole* day, and she regarded it gratefully before swinging her feet to the floor.

Dorramon was nowhere to be seen. She had no idea where he had gone, and on some level it didn't matter — with a flash of guilt, she thought that if he wasn't there, it made it that much easier for her to leave. Testing her strength and apparent freedom, she took a step toward the door, then another.

"Sorry," said a voice from the sitting area, "can't let you do that."

"Chen?" She turned toward the velvet-upholstered sofa just in time to see him push himself out of it and come her direction. "What are you doing here?"

"Honoring a request from the king," he said. He didn't quite meet her eyes; he sounded uncomfortable. "He had to step out, and he asked me to sit with you."

She stuck her hip out to one side and crossed her arms, trying her best not to look as shaky as she felt. Dorramon had been right after all — she needed more than just an afternoon nap. No way would she admit that, though, not to either of them. "Sit with me?"

"That's right. And I seem to remember something about you not leaving the room. 'Not under any circumstances,' I believe he said."

"I see." She watched him a moment, weighing her obstinance against his. In her condition, it didn't look good. She sighed, defeated, and abandoned her defensive posture, heading back to flop down on the edge of the bed. "I suppose it's a good thing. He must really trust you."

Chen laughed, but he sounded even more uncomfortable now. "I don't know," he said, scratching the back of his head awkwardly. "I think it's you he trusts."

"If he trusted me," she retorted, "you wouldn't need to be here."

"You do have a point there. I guess it depends on the situation. He trusts you not to get into anything inappropriate with me. He just trusts me to henpeck you."

He said this lightly, like a joke, but she couldn't seem to laugh. "And some people," she said darkly, "he just doesn't trust at all."

Chen looked at her in surprise. "What?"

She shook her head. "It's nothing, really — I probably shouldn't have said anything."

"Oh, it's too late to say that now." He pulled one of the chairs away from the dining table, and flipped it around to face the bed. "Whatever's going on, it's obvious it bothers you. Talk to me. Maybe I can help."

"I doubt it," she said, but she took a deep breath and told him all the same. She told him about Tralice's argument with Dorramon, what Prince Cardoth had heard and how he had reacted. She told him about running into Cardoth earlier, what he had said and how Princess Varilyn explained it. "I would have followed him, tried to explain — tried to apologize," she finished. "I still think I should. But Varilyn thinks that would only make things worse, drive him farther away. She says I have to give him time."

"I see." Chen sat back in his chair, seeming to mull it over.

"Tell me she's wrong. I mean, she has to be wrong, right? What kind of friend does that?"

"Slow down, Alannys. I see what you're saying, but...do you think it's possible Princess Varilyn understands this better than you?"

She pressed her lips into a tight line, forcing herself not to say something snappy. She had asked for his opinion, after all—she could at least hear it out before disagreeing with it.

"Neither of us have ever been to Cadenda. It's hard to imagine what it must be like over there, even with everything she said. And Prince Cardoth...he's a stubborn man. A strong man, with some semblance of a conscience these days, but still...stubborn. If he thinks you're trying to push him, or change him, he's going to dig in."

Alannys bit the inside of her lips. *Let him finish...*

"The advice seems good to me," he said. "I think she's right, Alannys."

"But—but how can I just ignore him, when I know that he misunderstood?"

"I don't think he misunderstood anything. It sounds to me like the king was pretty clear. I know you're worried that he got his feelings hurt, but..." He hesitated for a moment, searching her face. "To tell you the truth, it reminds me of another situation, with another stubborn man, where you decided to ignore advice to keep quiet."

For a moment, she could only stare at him, completely lost, and then it finally clicked. "You're talking about Trago."

"I am." He didn't quite meet her gaze. "And it seems to me a lot of suffering could have been avoided, if you'd only left well enough alone."

She could feel her face burning. "Maybe. Maybe it

would have happened anyway."

He shrugged, still looking somewhere over her left shoulder. "Maybe. I can't tell you that. What I can tell you is that you stubbornly insisted on visiting the *prathamol* every single day — and he never recovered until you were tied up taking care of me and couldn't visit him anymore. I know it goes against your nature, Alannys, but sometimes people really do just need to be left alone."

"I...I see." It hurt to hear it, to be reminded of that time, but she couldn't deny that the story was true as he told it. "It just doesn't feel right, you know?"

"I know. But sometimes what feels right and what is right aren't the same thing. Maybe this is one of those times, that's all I'm saying. Princess Varilyn probably knows what she's talking about."

"You're right." She didn't like to admit that, either. She just couldn't get past the feeling that she should be *doing* something about this. "Maybe all of the world's problems aren't mine to solve."

It was a joke, but the humor was bitter. Chen didn't laugh. "It's about time you realized that, don't you think?"

He threw a quick glance around the room. "I need to go tell the king you're up. Can I trust you to stay here?"

Alannys sighed. "I suppose so. It sounds like I have some thinking to do. Besides, I'm not sure I feel up to wandering around just yet."

"Finally," Chen said. "That's been obvious ever since you woke up, but I didn't think you would ever admit it."

"What?"

"It's something you and Prince Cardoth have in common, actually. You're pretty stubborn, you know? Just like those snooty nobles you're always copying."

He ruffled her hair, and left the room.

She stared at the door. That was probably the first time she had ever been compared to royalty, and it wasn't even a compliment. It made her think — whatever Tralice might say on the subject, 'those snooty nobles' weren't exactly paragons of excellence themselves. Was that really what she wanted to turn herself into?

Did she have any choice? Or was it too late to even ask the question?

♫

Alannys really did feel rough — like something big had wrung her out and tossed her aside. She managed to pick herself up off the bed and drag herself over to the bench seat by the window, but she couldn't imagine going much farther than that. It was a good thing Chen had been there after all — if she had actually gone wandering around the ship, it would have caught up to her almost immediately. She might not even have been able to get back to the cabin under her own steam, and that was embarrassing just to *think* about. The crew already feared and mistrusted her. No sense making them contempt her, too.

She was staring out at the foaming water in the ship's tumultuous wake, thinking unhappy thoughts along those lines, when the cabin door swung open and Dorramon edged in sideways, carrying a covered tray.

"That took a while," she said. "Did Chen make a full report?"

He looked at her, then immediately looked away. His blue eyes looked a little wide. "No, no, nothing like that. I was waiting on the chef — I figured you would be hungry. It's past dinnertime."

"You brought me food?" She watched him slide the tray onto the dining table, then pushed herself off the bench and wobbled over that direction.

"What, was I wrong?" He caught her arm and walked her over to the table.

"No, it's not that, it's just...I don't know what to say. It's disconcerting, being waited on by a king. You could have had Tralice do that, you know."

"I know." He sounded amused. "But Tralice has been a bit of a handful lately. I wasn't sure you would feel up to dealing with her. Besides, I wanted to do this. There isn't much I can do for you right now...and there will be even less when we get to Mount Mouseion. Just let me take care of you for now, however I can."

"I—I suppose." She knew that wasn't the ringing endorsement he had hoped for, but she honestly had no idea how she was supposed to answer a request like that when it came from a king. She couldn't really refuse, but she couldn't really accept, either, and so what came out was a sort of half-hearted mumble that was not totally either one.

She settled herself into a chair, and Dorramon lifted the cover from the tray, revealing a bowl of hot, chunky vegetable soup and a mug of berry juice. She hadn't expected it to smell so good, and it surprised her to find that she was hungry, after all.

"Don't get too used to that," Dorramon said, pulling the chair Chen had used back over to the table, and seating himself across from her. "Fresh vegetables don't last long at sea. I'm afraid we won't be seeing soup like that for a while."

"That's too bad. It's delicious."

He smiled but said nothing, watching her eat for a moment in silence. When he did finally speak, he sounded almost excessively casual. "So do you feel better after your nap? Nothing bothering you?"

She froze, her soup spoon halfway between the bowl and her mouth. "What? What's this all of the sudden?"

Dorramon glanced at her face, then made a show of settling back in his chair, as though they weren't discussing anything of any importance. "I don't know, I just get the feeling you have something on your mind. Did Athniss say anything else to you? Prince Cardoth?"

Alannys dropped her spoon back into the bowl, frowning. "So he *did* report everything to you!"

"Alannys..."

"I always knew he was a bit of a mother hen, but I never realized he just likes to gossip. I suppose I should just expect all of my conversations to be public knowledge then, and save us all some discomfort?"

"Now calm down. I can see you've got the wrong idea about this."

"Do I?" She knew it probably wasn't wise to challenge him, but his complete composure agitated her. She wanted to push him, to see that faultless exterior crack.

And she knew that was a small, petty desire, and that bothered her even more.

"Yes, you do." Dorramon refused to crack, much to her chagrin. "Chen doesn't make a habit of reporting everything you say to him, Alannys. And I never ordered him to tell me about that one. I never even asked him. I trust you, you know that."

"I know." She did know, but she still sounded disgruntled. "I just…"

Dorramon watched her struggle for words and finally smiled, taking pity on her. "You just hate knowing people are talking about you, even though you're the most famous person in Ravanmark, maybe in the world."

She grunted a non-committal response, and picked up her spoon again.

"It's an odd sort of modesty, that. I'm afraid you're just going to have to get used to it. You're setting out to change the world here…I don't think people are going to ignore that. But in this case, I can assure you nothing nefarious was going on. As I said, Chen doesn't usually pass along your conversations. He talked to me this time because he was concerned that you might put yourself in danger."

"Danger?" She had to admit, she hadn't seen that coming. It was hard to imagine danger here, out on the open ocean on the king's ship, with a crew loyal to the Crown.

"That's what he said. He seemed to think you were out to pick a fight with Cardoth."

"He's got the wrong end of the stick," she said. "I only wanted to apologize to Prince Cardoth. I hardly think an apology constitutes a dangerous undertaking."

"If Prince Cardoth is involved, any undertaking can be dangerous. It wasn't so long ago that he was out to kill you." He waved aside her protest. "Why don't you tell me what you think you have to apologize for?"

"You," she said shortly. "He overheard what you said last night."

"Last night?" Dorramon looked thoroughly confused. "What did I say that could have mattered to him?"

"You said you didn't trust him. After everything that's happened, after all the risks he's taken...I think it really hurt his feelings to hear that from you."

"Hurt his..." Dorramon stared at her a moment, while she tried to carry on eating as though she wasn't aware of his scrutiny. "I said I didn't trust him, Alannys, and it's true as far as it goes. Would you trust him?"

She didn't want to give him that—part of her wanted to insist just to be contrary. But she couldn't honestly deny it, and Dorramon would immediately pick up on a lie. "Not completely," she hedged. "But I've traveled halfway across the country with him, and that's something I would never have believed a month ago. He's changed, you have to give him credit for that."

"He has changed," Dorramon said grudgingly, "but perhaps not as much as you seem to imply. It's going to take a lot more before I feel as though I can really trust him, and I imagine it's the same for you. He knows that— he has to. Cardoth isn't exactly the world's most trusting man either."

"No, but..." She paused, looking for a way out of the corner he had backed her into. Finding none, she sighed and barreled on. "He's still human. It had to hurt to hear his friends talk about him that way."

"If Cardoth even considers us his friends," Dorramon mused. "Look, either way, Prince Cardoth is not a delicate flower. I don't think he will go out of his way to look for offense where none was intended. But I also think an apology is not likely to go over well with him. You might want an apology in his shoes...but you and Cardoth are very different people. I think it would be a mistake to judge this situation by what you would want—Cardoth might find that insulting. You may actually wind up offending him more by apologizing than just leaving well enough alone."

"That seems to be the general consensus," she muttered.

Dorramon smiled. "Try not to worry too much about Cardoth. He'll work things out on his own."

She didn't like that answer. But every single person she had spoken to had given her the same advice—at some point, she had to admit that only a fool would ignore that. It certainly wouldn't be the first time she was totally wrong about something. She knew that, but it didn't make her feel any better.

Alannys gave up and ate her soup, trying to push from her mind the darkness she had seen in Prince Cardoth's eyes.

♫

Whatever Chen had said to Dorramon must have worried him more than he let on. He spent the rest of the evening sitting in the great cabin with Alannys, stepping out only long enough to handle brief conversations with Captain Morgain, before returning wearing a smile so placid she couldn't help but think it had to be false.

Alannys never minded spending time with Dorramon. After the three months they had been separated while she traveled the country, she was all too keenly aware of just what that treasure was worth. And yet, this...this felt like he was forcing himself to be there, like he was hanging around because he didn't trust her to stay put if he left. And that wasn't any fun at all—that made her feel as though she almost would have been happier by herself. She tried to keep herself busy, to keep her mind distracted from the restless sort of vibe that exuded from him, but there wasn't much to do in the great cabin. It made it hard to feel at ease.

She ended up on the big bench again, staring out at the reflections cast by the setting sun on the water, and trying not to think about how sad it was that she was directing her attention out there, when Dorramon was in here.

She jumped when his hand landed suddenly on her shoulder — she'd had no idea he was so close. Last time she had looked back, he had been absorbed in one of the massive, ancient books in the sitting area, turning the yellowed pages with the most serious frown she had ever seen on someone reading.

"Are you all right?" He looked at her, real concern welling up in his blue eyes, and she had no idea why.

"Yes, of course." She searched his face, trying to find some clue, some reason, for the worry she saw in his expression. She scooted over on the bench, grabbing his hand on her shoulder and pulling him down next to her. "You don't look so good, though. Bad book?"

"What?"

"You were reading, weren't you? And now you seem upset. Am I wrong? Was it something I said?"

Dorramon tried to laugh, but it came out sounding more like a sob. "I'm turning this ship around, Alannys. We'll ride straight back to the Great Palace, and get married, and spend the rest of our lives pretending we never heard of the acts of the Redeemer. How does that sound?"

She would have laughed if he hadn't looked so earnestly, honestly serious — there was no joking in his eyes, only the bright light of desperation. "I don't know, Dorramon." She spoke carefully, frowning, trying to figure out where this sudden reversal had come from. "I think it sounds great — all except, you know, the part where they drag me to the palace gates and stone me as a false Redeemer."

"Let them try." He balled his hands into fierce, white-knuckled fists.

"Dorramon..."

"At least I have a chance of protecting you from that," he muttered, letting his gaze slip from hers and turning to stare out the big windows.

"Dorramon, why don't you just tell me what's got you so upset? What kind of book were you reading?"

His gaze wandered away again and he sighed, like maybe he had been hoping to avoid that question. "An early, lesser known work of Phosos the Learned. *The Redeemer of the Realm Through the Ages: A Study of Beliefs and Misconceptions.*"

"Wow." She sat in silence a moment, parsing through that whopper of a title. She had not heard one like that since her college days—it reminded her of dusty libraries and stale research papers. "I didn't know books like that existed. Books about the Redeemer."

"There aren't very many," Dorramon said. "In fact, this may be the only one still around today, and I wouldn't be surprised if the only remaining copy is the one on this ship. Phosos is very well known, very highly regarded— even today—but this particular volume was written early in his career, long before he had any sort of reputation. I never had any idea this book was onboard until yesterday. It seemed like a prudent thing to read, given our situation."

Alannys sat quietly and watched him, saying nothing. It was obvious he had found something in the old book he didn't like; she could read that in the lines and hollows of his face, just as clearly as he had read the text on the yellowed pages of the tome she had seen him with. But she wasn't going to push him—that never made anybody feel better.

Besides, there was a very good chance that whatever had him so upset wasn't going to make her day, either.

"Phosos talks about the Song of Joining," he finally said. His eyes found hers, then shied away again, and something about the glance alarmed her. She could feel her heart start to pound double-time, and she wondered what he could have read that could make him look quite that way. "It's funny, really—all this time I've been worrying about the Song of Raising. All that land mass to move, all that *energy*...I never really worried about the Song of Joining. That seemed like the easy part.

"That was a mistake."

"What do you mean?" The calm sound of her own voice surprised her. How could anyone sound so normal, when they were so shaky and cold inside? Maybe it was Dorramon's influence, but she had always considered the songs the same way. "The purpose of the Song of Joining is to bring the Muses back to Ravanmark, right? How can that be harder than raising a continent from the sea floor?"

Dorramon said nothing, staring out of the window behind them and working his hands in his lap as though he could wring from them an answer to the problems he was facing.

"Dorramon? That is the purpose of the song, isn't it?"

He gave a long, shuddering sigh. "I always thought so. But to be honest, Alannys, I can't even tell you for certain where I got that particular belief. I haven't had any formal religious training—I'm not a keeper, after all—and most of what I learned, I learned in childhood...learned so long ago I can't even remember when or how. Phosos the Learned doesn't think that's the purpose of the song at all —he never even mentions it as a possibility. Phosos thinks the purpose of the Song of Joining is to...to *make the singer one with the Muses.*"

A sudden, violent shiver wracked Alannys, and she leaned into the bench seat's back, running her hands through her hair, trying to hide it. She knew a euphemism for death when she heard one. No wonder Dorramon was so rattled! "That's...not great. I know how it sounds. But you said this book was old, Dorramon. Maybe that phrase doesn't mean what we think it means."

"I think it does." He sounded inexpressibly tense, like a rope that had been stretched so tight individual strands were beginning to snap. "I think it has to. Phosos...he specifically cautions that the Redeemer must not be permitted to make the ascent up the Spire of Glory alone. Someone must be there to..." He paused for a moment, his hands clawing each other in his lap, his throat visibly working to force the words out. "To bring them back down afterwards."

Alannys swallowed hard. That did sound grim. She didn't like the idea of Dorramon carrying her mortal remains back down the Spire of Glory any more than he did. But she hated even more to see him suffering like this, and to know that it was because of her. "That just can't be right. I can't really die. I'm supposed to sing the Song of Raising, remember? How can one person sing two songs, if the first one kills them?"

Dorramon was shaking his head before she even finished talking, his mouth set into a tight, thin line. "According to Phosos, the idea of the Redeemer as a single person is a common misconception. *Misconception.* He says it's rooted in a mistranslation of some ancient letter...I forget all the details."

"Misconception?" Alannys felt the firm ground of her understanding begin to rumble beneath her. "How can that be a misconception? If the Redeemer isn't a single person, then..." She couldn't bring herself to finish that sentence. The inevitable conclusion yawned there before her, as dark and foreboding as an abyss, and she feared that all she would find at the bottom was insanity. She had always known that this was dangerous, that she might not survive. But this was the first time she had heard that she might not be *meant* to survive, and it made her memories of the lights of Port Grandview seem suddenly ten times more appealing.

No wonder Dorramon wanted to turn the ship around.

He took a deep breath. He probably meant it to be

steadying for himself, and it might have been for her too, except for the jerking, uneven way it shuddered as he drew it. "The Redeemer of the Realm, according to Phosos, was never intended to be a single person. It is a role fulfilled by a group of people, each committed to a different aspect of the work to be done. Over time the various aspects have come to be amalgamated into the common perception of a single person, but he doesn't believe that's how it actually works. He says there's no way a single person could do all of that." He glanced up from his somber contemplation of his hands, which appeared to be locked in a battle to the death, and smiled wanly at her. "Of course, he never met you."

It hurt, seeing him force that sickly-looking expression on his face for her benefit, but she appreciated what he was trying to do. "That's right," she said, making her tone deliberately bright. "Phosos probably never imagined someone could be brought in from another world to be the Redeemer." She reached out and took one of his hands in hers, prying it from the deathgrip of the other. "I don't think you should worry too much about what this scholar says. It's all just speculation in the end—it's never been done before. Unless the Muses themselves came down and told him exactly how it all should work, he can't really have known much more than we do. Maybe even less—if Phosos wasn't a musician himself, it would have been hard for him to imagine what might or might not have been possible."

"You're right," he said. He didn't sound exactly convinced, but Alannys could tell he was making a concerted effort to be more positive—or at least to sound more positive.

"Of course I am. Have you ever known me to be wrong when it really mattered? Since we met, Dorramon, I've managed to do so many things that I would have sworn were impossible before...this will be the same, you'll see. You won't get rid of me this easily."

"I'll give you that much," he said, with a dry laugh. "You have the luck of the very devil. If it were anyone else, I would say you haven't got a chance. But you...damn me, but I think you might actually be able to do this. I don't know what makes me crazier—believing you can do this, or risking losing you so that you can try."

"Neither," she said, struggling to maintain her bravado in the face of his sudden honesty, honesty that made her feel somehow exposed. "There's crazy enough to go around, but none of it is coming from you. I don't think you see how brave you are, and how brave it makes me, knowing that I have you beside me." Her face burned with embarrassment just saying such things out loud, but it was worth it if it helped make him feel better.

Alannys didn't have to suffer her shame for long— before the burn in her cheeks had even begun to fade, she felt Dorramon's hand tighten on hers and he pulled her into an embrace, cradling her head against his chest. "Brave." The single word was a derisive snort. His voice cracked. "I used to think I was. That was ages ago, a lifetime ago, before I met you and saw everything you have put yourself through in the last half a year. Now I think I never even knew the meaning of the word."

She tipped her face up to his and kissed him, savoring the familiar tingle of electricity playing between their lips. She couldn't argue with an ancient scholar, not really— there was no doubt that Phosos the Learned, whoever he was, knew more about what she had to do and what it would cost her than she did. But for the moment, she thought she had eased some of Dorramon's anxiety, and she thought that was enough. Whatever was to come would come in the end, no matter how hard she fought to stop it. The irony was bitter and unavoidable—she had come to Ravanmark as an escape, when she had nowhere else to go, not really understanding what she would find there or what Tryn expected her to do. She had been at rock bottom, and she hadn't had anything invested in her success — or her failure. It was just a second chance, and one she wasn't even sure she deserved. If she had died then, she probably would have met her own demise with one great big shrug. But now...now she had found the love of her life here, had met people who mattered to her — the whole *world* mattered to her — and now that she had things to fight for, now that she really *cared...now* she found out she had always been meant to die, all along? It was like a giant kick in the teeth from fate.

But until that kick came, however long or short that time might be, she was going to spend it with Dorramon.

♫

The flaming orange light of evening flared and faded to the cool blue of night, and the gentle ocean waves outside reflected only starlight. Alannys couldn't have said exactly how long she and Dorramon had been there on the bench seat in the great cabin, trading blistering kisses and tangling their fingers into each other's hair, but the room had grown dark and cool around them. The stress and fear they had both been carrying, fighting, and suppressing, worked its way to the surface and found vent in the little explosions of electricity every time they touched. Their emotions wound tighter and tighter, until the very air around them seemed to hum with everything they felt but could not adequately express. Alannys could feel it crackling there around them, waiting for release — together they stood swaying on the edge of some precipice she couldn't even see, and she could not imagine what they would find there, should they fall.

She didn't even know whether she *wanted* to fall. Her pulse pounded in her ears, and her breathing came fast and shallow, and she wasn't even really sure which way was up anymore.

Something in the darkness around them seemed to shift; some change that Alannys could feel but not understand raced through her bones, and suddenly the hands on her shoulders dug in like claws, the lips on hers were rough and demanding, pushing her back into the bench, not even allowing her to breathe. She turned her face into the leather upholstery, seeking escape, wondering what could have happened to make him like this. He didn't even feel familiar to her anymore—she almost felt as though she was sprawled on the bench seat with a stranger. That thought made her feel suddenly cold, and she pushed her hands against his chest, trying to gain herself some space. "Dorramon...wait."

He didn't answer.

What on earth was the matter? Alannys looked up into his face...and screamed.

The eyes looking back at her were Athniss's. The face leering at her was Athniss's. The fingers digging like talons into her shoulders belonged to Sir Athniss. He wore his usual ruffled shirt and ragged cloak—the person next to her, whose body was even now pressing against her, was unmistakably Sir Athniss.

This couldn't be real. There was no possible way this was actually happening—*this couldn't be real.* She buried her face into her hands, shrinking away from him. "Stop." Her voice sounded weak and pleading, on the verge of tears. "Please stop this."

The cold hands that wrapped around hers and pulled them away from her face certainly felt real. He ran his index finger down her cheek, and that felt real—disturbingly real. She shuddered, pulling away from the unpleasant touch. It felt like a skeleton brushing against her face, and she smothered the urge to scream again. It wouldn't do her any good anyway—she was pretty sure no one could even hear her.

Except Athniss.

He laughed, a nasty, unpleasant sound that burrowed its way into her ears and made her brain itch. She would get no sympathy here, and there was no reasoning with this man.

Alannys pulled suddenly away, springing to her feet

and running for the door. There had to be some way out of this, there had to be some way to get away from him.

She was two steps away from the door and freedom, reaching out with clawing fingers for the handle, when a crushing grip closed around her other arm and jerked her backwards, spinning her around and slamming her up against the wall. Her head bounced against its polished surface, rattling her teeth and blurring her vision. She blinked and shook her head, trying to clear it, and Sir Athniss leaned over her, pushing his face right up in front of hers.

"Now, now, Alannys." She could hear his voice in her ears, but also in her brain, scratching across the surface of her mind like fingernails. It made her want to cry, to scream. Instead she pressed her hands over her ears and pushed herself against the wall behind her as if she hoped to disappear into it. "You can't escape from me. You can't run; you can't hide. The sooner you accept this, the sooner you feel the truth of it in your bones, the better."

"Better for who?" she said, trying her best to sound strong. "You or me?"

Again the creepy, scratchy laugh. "I'm surprised at you. Better for you, of course. You seemed to suffer earlier. Tell me, Alannys, is it exhausting, fighting me through your precious mindlink? Is it draining? Does it...hurt?" His face, mere inches from her own, stretched into a leering, awful smile. "I would be ever so pleased if it did."

Alannys shoved her hands flat against the wall behind her to hide their trembling, and did her best to meet his gaze levelly. She'd be damned if she would give him the satisfaction of an answer. She had a hunch he could tell well enough what these forced intrusions did to her.

"There's no need to answer," he said, cupping her cheek in his hand, resisting her attempts to shake it off. "I can see the truth of it in your eyes. So you may assume it to be your own best interests we are discussing here. You can't keep this up. It's too demanding. You will injure yourself. Your mind will crack. Can you deny it?"

She glared at him, balling her hands into angry fists against the wall. The hell of it was, she *couldn't* deny it, and she suspected he knew that as well as she did. She also suspected this was no picnic on his side, either, though he would never admit that. The only question, then, was who would crack first.

And she intended to do everything in her power to make sure it wasn't her.

"Still you resist." He laughed lightly, as though it was of no consequence, patted her cheek condescendingly, and pulled his hand away from her face. "I suppose you are telling yourself right about now that this isn't real, that it doesn't count." Casually, almost as though he wasn't even paying attention, he dealt her a slap across the face.

Alannys could feel that slap—could feel the sting of it on her cheek, could feel the curious numb heat spread across her face immediately after. The sharpness of it brought burning tears to her eyes.

"This is real, my dear lady, and I don't advise you to forget it. You cannot stop me."

She hated him, *hated* him! She wanted him out of her face, out of her mind, but she couldn't seem to marshal up enough strength to force him out, not after fighting him so hard earlier that same day. Her fingers curved into white-tendoned talons and she launched them at his face, intent on tearing his flesh from his skull with her bare hands, if that was what it took to get away from him.

Athniss caught one of her wrists in each of his hands and held her there, her arms outstretched, her hands too far away from him to cause damage. He made it look effortless, too, as though he could perceive her intentions before she even moved. She gritted her teeth in useless anger, panting from the exertion of fighting this far. "What...do you want?"

"Finally!" His laugh sounded pleased, and it made her hate him even more. "I have no interest in you personally,

Alannys, you must see that. I don't like you. You don't like me. No matter the circumstances of our meeting, that would never have changed. My only interest in you, is in your destruction."

"But you aren't here to do that now." It wasn't a question.

"No. No! That would be too easy, you see? Destroying you is only part of my intent. You took everything from me. I intend to take everything from you, destroy everything you hold dear. Then, and only then, will I finish you."

"Destroy everything..." She stared at his twisted face in unseeing horror, trying to figure out exactly what he had just threatened.

"Just so. You may have thought when you met me that I could not be destroyed any further — that I was already so low there was nothing left for me to lose. And at the time, I probably would have agreed with you. Before the Retainers came, we didn't even have enough food to keep both of us alive. We had already sold everything of value in the estate. We never knew where our next meal was coming from. We didn't have any clothes that were more than rags. We scratched along from one day to the next, holding each other up, doing our best just to continue existing. I would have laughed at a threat. What did I have left to lose?

"I was wrong." His fingers clawed into the backs of her hands, digging down in between the bones. She tried to wrestle free, but it was no good — he thumped her back against the wall and held her there. "You took everything from me, Alannys, everything I didn't realize I still had. The Retainers turned on me after you escaped — they hunt me now, like a dog, seeking vengeance for my failure. You took my estate from me, where their men wait even now for me to return, wait to slaughter me because you yet live. You took Rodriset."

Suddenly her hands were free, and his fingers locked

in a death grip around her throat. "You took *Rodriset,* the only friend I had left, the only person in this whole world who mattered to me, and you gutted him like an animal and left him for dead."

She couldn't argue, couldn't defend herself, couldn't even breathe. Strange, sparkling lights filled her peripheral vision, and her throat burned with fire under his fingers. "So don't worry, I'm not here to kill you. Not *yet.*" He leaned forward, rasping right in her ear, and she still had to struggle to hear him over the roaring sound that filled her brain. "You still have your dear king, Alannys. The closest person in the world to you still draws breath. First I will kill him, gut him as you gutted Rodriset. I will destroy him completely, and you will watch me do it."

Each word he said burned a line like fire across her brain, sending blistering pain deep into her being. But she could do nothing but hang there against the wall as he drew back and smiled at her, a grotesque combination of bared teeth and narrowly slitted eyes that inspired no confidence at all. "Then," he said, as casually as if they were discussing the weather, "I will kill you and clear my name. You may take that as a promise."

Athniss stepped back and released her. She tried to pull a gasping breath past the burning in her throat, but it didn't seem to work. The last thing she saw was Athniss standing over her, smiling viciously as she crumpled into a heap at the base of the wall.

♬

"Alannys?"

She turned her face away from the familiar voice, not even willing to open her eyes. The blackness behind her eyelids matched the blackness in her brain and right then, it suited her. She didn't remember why, but she knew she preferred the darkness and the silence to whatever had come before.

"Alannys! Come on now, wake up!"

Her head was resting on someone's arm; she became

aware of that as they shifted her around. The motion hurt her neck, and she remembered.

Sir Athniss! She had collapsed — he was still in the room!

Her eyes popped open and her body flew into motion as though somebody else had control of it, her legs scrambling for purchase to push her upright, her arms flailing. The angle of the room wasn't right; she was looking straight across at the spot where she fell — had Athniss moved her? Why?

"Alannys! Calm down!" Strong hands caught her arms and held them, bringing back vivid memories of Athniss doing the same thing, just before he choked her. She buckled down to fight harder, to free herself no matter what she had to do, when she finally saw the purple velvet cloak next to her, the worried blue eyes frowning at her, and realized with a rush of relief that she was not fighting the baronet. She was still on the bench in the back of the great cabin with Dorramon.

Athniss was nowhere to be seen.

Alannys stared around in muddled disbelief. Had the whole thing just been some kind of dream? And if it had, why could she still *feel* it? "What happened?" Her voice sounded rough. She *felt* rough. She put a hand to her head, hoping to quell the dull pounding.

"I had rather hoped to ask you the same thing."

His tone was wry, and she suspected he already knew. She looked away. "I fainted."

"Believe it or not, I had already figured out that much. Why? What happened?"

Alannys bit her lip. His hands still gripped her arms, warm and gentle, not at all like the iron grip she remembered. She knew she owed him answers, she knew he had to be worried, and yet...she didn't want to talk about it. She just didn't want to talk about it at all, and she knew how unfair that was, and she almost didn't care. Talking about what had just happened would be acknowledging it...making it real. And she preferred to keep everything the way it was right now, where she could still pretend she had just randomly passed out and had some sort of weird dream. Anything else...like admitting that Athniss and his horrible intentions were real...she just wasn't sure she could handle that. So she bit into her lip until she tasted blood, but she said nothing.

"*Alannys*. You can't hide this, and I don't think you should try. I can't stop him—I wish I could tell you how much I hate saying that. I've had my fill of standing by helpless while bad things happen to you, I've had enough to last me a lifetime. I can't stop it, but I would at least like to be here for you. I can't even do that if you won't talk to me. I know he was using the mindlink. But this fainting is new...on deck, and now...what did he do?"

She sighed, defeated. "I don't know how to explain it. I've always just heard him through the mindlink before, which was bad enough. But this time, I could *see* him."

"See him? I don't understand. Do you mean like a vision, or a dream?"

"No. No, this felt real—not like a dream at all. I can't even say exactly when it happened. It isn't like he just walked in the door, Dorramon, he...he took your place. I didn't even know it was him at first. He was sitting right here, holding me, he even—" She cut herself off, averting her eyes. "I tried to run. He grabbed me." She touched her neck, and the pain that shot under her fingers reinforced her memories. "It all felt real. Very, very real."

"I'm sorry." He reached out and brushed his fingers against her face, and she realized for the first time that there were warm tears tracking down her cheeks. "I wish there was some way I could make this stop, some way I could shield you from it. He has the other stone, my stone. Why does he only ever do this to you? Why doesn't he use mine?"

Alannys shook her head. What could she tell him, that Athniss wanted to deliver this threat first? That he wanted to make sure, when he tormented Dorramon, that she would know it was all her fault? "I hope he never does," she said, and she could hear the desperation in her own voice. "I hope he never does."

She threw herself into his arms, wanting nothing more in the world in that moment than to make sure that Athniss never got to Dorramon. It was a fool's hope, but it was all she had.

So she clung to it, just as desperately as she clung to him.

♫

Sometime in the middle of the night, Alannys woke up. This was peculiar, because she had been completely wiped out by Athniss's most recent attack, and she was so dead tired she could hardly haul her eyes open. She was pretty sure, at this point, that she could have slept through the Rending of the World.

So why was she awake?

She was pondering this question, staring up at the rippled, watery reflections the moonlight on the sea cast onto the ceiling, when the realization finally made its way into her befuddled brain that the mindlink felt weird.

She was instantly alert, every nerve ending tingling with sharp, crackling fear. Had Athniss come back? Was he here to torture her some more? She scanned the room, peering hard into the deep shadows that piled like spiders in the corners, looking for even the tiniest movement.

"Alannys..."

She heard Dorramon's hoarse, tormented moan beside her, and knew with a rush of cold nausea that it wasn't her Athniss sought to torture this time.

"Oh, no. No, no, no, no..." She rolled over and found Dorramon as still as death, a sheen of sweat across his forehead, his skin so pale it seemed to glow in the moonlight. She reached out to touch his arm—every muscle was knotted and bunched under her fingers, tensed as though he fought some thing she couldn't see.

And she was afraid she knew just what — or who — that thing was.

There had to be some way she could stop this. There had to be something she could do. There *had* to be. Clinging to that one thought, she squeezed her eyes shut and reached out for the mindlink.

It was occupied, she could tell that; it felt electric, almost glowing with the energy that pulsed through it. Energy that was not meant for her — she could feel that, too. It almost hummed, low and constant, like a droning busy signal in her mind, impossible to ignore.

She didn't care. She imagined that busy mindlink as a cable, and grabbed onto it with both hands, determined to force her way inside. Once she was inside, she figured she could help force Athniss out.

She learned two things almost immediately. One was that grabbing onto that cable felt like grabbing a live wire, and the power of it coursed through her like electricity, painful and uncontrollable. The only way clear of it would be to let go — and she wondered with sudden fear if she would even be *able* to let go, or if she would find, now that she had put her hands to it, that the mindlink was holding *her*.

In the next second she learned that forcing her way into that occupied mindlink felt very much like trying to force her way through a brick wall, and she had just about the same chance of success.

She refused to give up. She gripped tighter, flexing her fingers around that imaginary cable that burned and twitched in her hands. She squeezed her eyes shut so tightly they hurt, and threw her entire mind at that wall, *willing* herself to break through.

It was no use. She collapsed against the pillows, her chest heaving as she panted for air, opening her eyes and abandoning the cable and the wall. It didn't matter how long she worked at it, or how hard she tried — she would never break through that.

But neither could she sit idly by, safe and useless, while Dorramon suffered. She pushed herself up on her elbows and turned to face him, tears of anger and frustration burning the backs of her eyes. He still lay unmoving, stiff and tense, strung so tightly he practically quivered, fighting against Athniss with everything he had. She brushed his damp hair back from his face and took his hand in hers. It was stiff and cool, his fingers splayed and curved into claws, but she lifted it to her lips, brushing away her tears where they landed on his skin.

"Come on, Dorramon," she said. She knew he couldn't hear her wherever he was — not consciously, anyway — but she hoped that somehow her words might reach him anyway, help him stay strong through an experience that she knew was hellish. "Hang in there."

She scrubbed at her eyes with her free hand, angry at her stupid tears, and at the helplessness that drove them. How did Dorramon *stand* this? She had spent so much time these last few months feeling sorry for herself, never realizing how completely awful Dorramon's situation was.

And it was awful, there could be no doubt of that. She spent the next twenty minutes becoming intimately acquainted with just *how* awful, watching Dorramon moan and strain, fighting against a threat she couldn't even see, let alone help with. All she could do for him was whisper encouragement and push his hair out of his face, which seemed about as close to 'nothing at all' as she could imagine right then. She sang songs to give him strength, but the hijacking of the mindlink even seemed to interfere with that — the usual rushing channel of magic was little more than a strangled trickle, and she couldn't imagine it helped him at all.

Twenty minutes, under the right circumstances, could feel like a lifetime.

♫

Dorramon's eyes finally dragged open, misty and bloodshot, and he spoke in a voice that was little more than a croak. "Alannys?"

He looked awful, and he sounded awful, but in that moment she was so relieved to see him awake and alert again, she almost didn't care. She buried her face in his chest, trying to hide her tears. "I'm here, Dorramon. Are you all right?"

"I think so," he said, "now." He reached up to slowly stroke her hair, and his hand felt so weak it scared her. She could feel his whole arm trembling with fatigue. "I'm sorry I frightened you."

"Don't you dare apologize. I know what this is like. I'm just glad you're back. What did he say to you?"

His eyes met hers, then skittered away. "Not much. I don't really think it's important, Alannys—I would rather not talk about it."

"Oh, no you don't. Wasn't it you telling me just a few hours ago that you couldn't be there for me if I wouldn't talk to you? And now you're going to clam up? That hardly seems fair, does it?"

"No, I suppose not. I just…" He paused, and the silence stretched out so long it seemed maybe he had fallen asleep. Finally he sighed. It was a heavy, defeated sound, and it made her wonder just exactly what he was trying so hard to avoid. "You mentioned before that Athniss said something about you becoming Soth."

"Yes," she said, confused.

"I think he's still hoping to upset you with that. Me too, I suppose—he doesn't seem to understand how ridiculous I think that idea is. It's something to laugh at, not something to fear. But he's trying hard to convince us both that it's a real possibility."

His tone was strange…he talked about that almost as if he was making her an offering of the information. A peace offering, she supposed, and she knew that this couldn't be what had upset him so profoundly. He had said it himself, hadn't he, that the idea was ridiculous?

She waited another moment, but he didn't say

anything else. He stared up at the ceiling in the dark as though he was pretending to be alone, though she was certain he was aware of her watching him expectantly. The rippled light reflected off of his face, highlighting his unnaturally pale skin, and she remembered with a flash of guilt what he had just been through. She felt bad, pushing him when he was so obviously shaken, but on the other hand...Athniss had told her flatly that he meant to destroy Dorramon. She was desperate to prevent that—she would do anything to stop that from happening—but she had no earthly idea what Athniss planned to do. Her only possible source of clues was this conversation. She couldn't afford to go easy.

Not on either of them.

"What else?" she finally prompted, resorting to false brightness to keep her misgivings out of her tone. It sounded strange, like they were discussing an upcoming party instead of a brutal psychological attack, and she cringed at the sound of her own words.

He shook his head, but he didn't look at her. "No. That was it."

"Dorramon..." This felt like badgering, and she hated to do it. "Are you sure? That seems like a lot of trouble for him to just repeat something he already said before."

His gaze flicked across her face for just a moment, then he frowned back up at the ceiling again. "You seem very interested in what Athniss had to say. I thought we had agreed it was best not to think too much on it."

"This is different. I need to know what he said to you, Dorramon, it's important."

"Important. The man is a raving lunatic, Alannys—how could anything he says be important?"

It occurred to her that, however interested she was in what Athniss said, Dorramon was at least as interested in not talking about it. She understood, to a certain extent, but this seemed excessive. It made her worry even more—what could Athniss have possibly said that Dorramon would want to hide from her this badly? "It's important because he threatened you! He told me he intends to kill you, and I can't let that happen. Anything he said might have had some clue in it. I have to know!"

He hadn't expected that answer, that much was obvious. He sat suddenly up in bed, staring at her in surprise. For just a fraction of a second, his eyes met hers. Then he looked away, pushing himself out of the bed, raking his hands through his hair. "No. I'm sorry, Alannys, I understand where you're coming from, but I don't want to discuss this. I don't think you'll find any clues here anyway."

But it was too late. As his gaze had slipped from hers, in that tiny split second she had gotten something though the mindlink. A clear, sharp, moving image — like something out of a high definition video she might have watched back before she came to Ravanmark. It was a dark, dim image of the silhouette of the Spire of Glory, in sharp relief against a muddy red sunset.

And her body fell lifeless from the top of it, her leather riding cloak flapping around her like the broken wings of some dark bird.

♫

Alannys couldn't catch her breath. She had only seen the image for a brief moment, but it was etched into her brain in fine detail, and there was no mistaking what it depicted. And she knew, knew with absolute certainty, that this was what Dorramon wanted so badly to keep from her.

"Alannys?" Concern filled Dorramon's tone — she had sat silent too long, when he had expected protest. He frowned at her, seeing the frozen look of shock on her face. "Are you all right?"

She just stared at him. Because, the content of the image aside, an even bigger question had occurred to her — how, through a mindlink conversation with Athniss, had Dorramon even come to possess such a clear moving image? This wasn't like a vague imagining; this was even more vivid and detailed than an actual memory would have been. It shouldn't have been possible. What was she missing?

"Alannys?" He waved his hand in front of her face. "What's the matter?"

"You," she croaked. "That...image, of me falling from the Spire of Glory. Where did that come from? Nothing Athniss could have said to you could have created that."

Dorramon's eyes widened, and he swore under his breath. "The mindlink. I'm sorry, Alannys, I never meant for you to have to see that. I'm more tired than I realized...I slipped."

"Dorramon, you aren't dodging this question. What's going on here? Didn't Athniss attack you through the mindlink, like he's been doing to me?"

He hesitated, and she peered up into his face. He was frowning, his blue eyes clouded with something unpleasant. "No," he said finally. "I don't think this was the same. At least, I hope not. Has Athniss...has he ever come after you in your sleep?"

"In my sleep?" she echoed dumbly, her mind utterly refusing to make sense of the words. "No. I've always been awake."

He blew out a puff of air, a heavy sigh that seemed to come from his very bones. "Well, I know that's no fun, but perhaps it's a mercy after all."

"What? Dorramon, what are you talking about?"

The look on his face just then...Alannys couldn't tell how much of it was sympathy, and how much was fear. "Athniss can apparently use the stone...or the mindlink...to invade our dreams. And once he's in there...Alannys, he can *control* them."

♫

The morning sun crept upward in its slow ascent of the sky, casting its bright, blue-tinged light over Ravanmark and the sea that surrounded it.

But from where Alannys sat at the dining table in the great cabin, staring out through the big wall of windows on the stern of the *Atromitos,* she couldn't see it. The ship's enormous shadow shrouded their churning wake in gloomy darkness. Watching it disquieted her. It felt like an ill omen.

Dorramon sat across from her at the polished table, as he had sat all night, slumped into his chair, dark circles under his eyes that probably matched the ones she had under hers. Half-empty goblets of room-temperature berry juice sat ignored on the table...somehow, following Dorramon's revelation, neither of them had felt much like eating or drinking.

Neither of them had felt much like sleeping, either. They were both bone-tired, their brains fuzzy with exhaustion, their eyes gritty in the manner that only a night of no sleep could produce. And yet neither of them had made a move toward the bed, and now at daybreak, they both kept *not* making that move, despite the screaming, grumpy protest of their bodies. They didn't talk about it. They didn't have to.

"It's like a cage," Dorramon said out of the blue, pushing his goblet around the table with no apparent intention of actually drinking from it.

Alannys looked up at him in surprise, startled at the sudden breaking of the long silence. "What's like a cage?"

He kept shoving the goblet around, watching morosely as the liquid sloshed up the sides. "This room. This ship. All of it—we're trapped here. Sitting ducks, easy for him to attack whenever he wants. And no way for us to retaliate."

"Yes." She watched him a moment, idly wondering if he was going to end up sloshing berry juice all over the table. She couldn't seem to care much about it—all of her senses and all of her emotions felt dulled after the long night. "I wish there was some way we could stop him."

He glanced over to find her watching him, and sighed,

abandoning the goblet. He tried to smile reassuringly at her, but it came off wan and shaky. "I don't think there is. It's...it's hard to describe. Have you ever had one of those dreams that just keeps getting worse and worse, and you can't wake up, even when you try, like it won't *let* you wake up?"

Alannys nodded. She felt numb all over, like her system had decided it couldn't handle any more shocks and had shut down in self-defense. She couldn't even say that would have been a bad approach—she certainly didn't have any better ideas for self-defense right then.

"This is like that. Sort of. It's like he's holding you there, no matter how hard you try to escape. He's there, controlling everything that you see and everything that happens, forcing you to stay there and suffer through it. And it's a dream...so it seems fuzzy at first, and you don't expect it to make sense, and you don't even realize, for a long time, that you *can* fight back." He sighed again and gave his goblet another push, staring at the rocking berry juice as though it might hold some kind of answer for him.

"You're right," Alannys said finally. "There really isn't any way to fight back against that. I can barely manage to fend him off, when I'm awake and not exhausted. In a dream..." She shook her head. "The best solution I can see is just not to sleep."

He flicked a glance at her. "So here we are. How's that working out for us?"

The words carried a sting, even though she knew he wasn't irritated at her. "I don't know. I'll answer that as soon as I can think clearly again."

His laugh was dry and humorless. "That may not happen for a while, if we're boycotting sleep."

"That's true." She looked back out at the water, but found nothing there to make her feel better. "I don't know what else to do, though. Sleep is an opening for him, an opening I'm not going to give him if I don't have to."

"I agree," Dorramon said, but he sounded as

indifferent as she felt. "I'm just not sure how long we'll be able to keep it up."

She didn't say anything to that. What could she say? He was right and they both knew it. She already felt half-zombified. How many more nights like that could she take? How many more nights like that could either of them take?

She didn't want to think about it. Any thinking at all seemed like hard work right then, but thinking of a way to change the subject felt like less work than worrying, so she did that instead, picking up her own goblet and swigging unpleasantly warm berry juice to gain some time. "What do we do in the meantime?"

The question seemed to surprise him. "We stay right here. Right here, in this room."

"What, until we reach Mount Mouseion? Isn't that still days away?"

"It is, but I don't see how that changes anything. You know how this works, Alannys. We aren't safe anywhere, but I think we are only in more danger if we go out on the decks right now. The crew is already afraid of you — either of us suffering one of these attacks in front of them would be a very bad thing. We don't need a riot on the ship."

She couldn't argue with that, so she slugged back more of her juice. It didn't taste any better this time.

"I say we hunker down in here until we arrive. Tralice can bring us meals and anything else we need, and we can just stay out of sight."

"Sure." She sighed. "I'm sorry, Dorramon."

"Why in the world are you apologizing?"

"Athniss is after me, in the end. He's doing all of this to get to me. You've probably never had a sea voyage as awful as this one, and I feel like it's all my fault."

"Oddly enough, I feel like it's all Athniss's fault." She thought he might be teasing her, but he didn't sound much like joking. "Don't be so quick to call this awful, Alannys. Days — more than one! — with nothing to do but spend time with you? Granted, the circumstances could be better, but still, when was the last time we had time like that?"

Alannys wished she could share his enthusiasm. She appreciated his attempt to find a bright side, but to her, this just felt like trading a big cage for a small one.

And she couldn't imagine a smaller cage leading to anything good for the people trapped inside it.

The door flew open without even a perfunctory knock, and Alannys and Dorramon both jumped in their seats, twisting around to see the door. Captain Morgain stood there, uncharacteristically ruffled, his graying hair loose and flapping around his damp, red face. "Your Highness!"

"Captain." Dorramon frowned, but Alannys felt like it was more from concern than irritation. "What's wrong?"

"Forgive me, your Highness, but you have to come with me. Right now. Someone fell overboard."

Dorramon's hand twitched on the table, as though he was itching to jump from his chair. He reached for his goblet again, perhaps to hide the motion. "I am sorry to hear it. But why…"

"Please, your Highness! You have to come now! It's Princess Varilyn!"

DEATH AT SEA

*T*he room felt small, airless. Dorramon's face blanched, suddenly white and translucent, like the alabaster vases between the books on the big mahogany shelves. His eyes cut to hers, and she knew he was thinking about the promise they had just made not to leave this room.

"You have to go," she said. "I don't think Princess Varilyn even knows how to swim. Whatever happens, you have to be there."

He nodded once, shortly, and stood to leave. He turned immediately back around when Alannys moved to follow him. "But you don't." He squeezed her shoulder, probably trying to soften his words, but it didn't work. She still felt the rebuff clearly. "I'm sorry, Alannys, but I think you should stay here. I'll tell you what happens."

"What? No! Dorramon..." She saw Morgain staring at her, no doubt appalled by the tears welling up in her eyes, but she couldn't do anything about it. She was way beyond exhausted, and her control was suffering as a result. "She's my friend, too. Please, you have to let me help."

"I'm sorry." Dorramon looked at her with understanding in his eyes, but he wasn't changing his mind. "I know she's your friend, and that's actually part of the reason I think you should stay here. The crew is afraid of you, remember? I wouldn't want your presence to distract them...they need to focus on getting her back safe and sound. I know you wouldn't want to risk her."

What could she say? She knew she wasn't necessary, she knew there was nothing she could contribute to the rescue effort, but still...it was hard to stomach staying behind, sitting in safety while a friend was in danger. She sank back into her chair, eyes locked on her own boots, afraid to say anything that might come out bitter.

Captain Morgain headed for the door, waving at Dorramon to follow. The king took two big, fast steps in that direction, then turned back to face Alannys again. "I'm serious, Alannys. Don't leave this room, not for any reason. No matter what."

"No matter what," she echoed dully, twisting her hands in her lap. "Got it."

He watched her a split second longer. She could feel the weight of his frowning gaze on her, inspecting her, looking presumably for any evidence that she intended to make a run for it as soon as he was out of sight. "I'm sorry," he said finally, and ran out the door after Morgain.

Alannys slumped into her chair, feeling deflated. What was happening out there? How had Varilyn ended up in the water anyway? Did they have her back on the ship yet? Not knowing what was happening was maddening. She would far rather face danger herself than know that her friends were.

It didn't help to know that this particular sentiment was probably exactly why Dorramon was so eager to leave her here. She glared at the open doorway, willing him to come back, to tell her everything that had happened.

And almost immediately a shadow approached, raising her hopes. She sat up in her chair, expectantly.

But it wasn't Dorramon who came to stand in the doorway; it wasn't Dorramon who greeted her with a mock-salute and a dip of his red head. "Morning, ma'am," Tassin said, standing just at the entry, bringing to mind his earlier comments about the cabin. "I wonder if I might trouble you for your help."

Alannys frowned—his speech seemed more elevated than any other time she had spoken with him, and for some reason that put her guard up. "I'm sorry," she said, hoping she sounded sorrier than she felt. "Dorramon just

Sandra Miller

told me I'm not to leave this room, not for any reason."

"Oh!" Tassin took a step back. "I see. That's that, then — sorry to bother you. Mind telling me where the king is right now?"

"On deck, I think," she said, "someone fell overboard. Why do you need him?"

"Oh, well, I reckon maybe he could help me instead. After all, he knows Chen nearly as well as you do, right?" Tassin was already on his way to the deck, tossing this remark over his shoulder as he turned.

"What? Wait!" Alannys didn't remember getting out of her chair, but she was standing suddenly, reaching toward the door with a desperate outstretched hand. Tassin stopped and turned back to her, eyebrows raised. "What is it? What's happened to Chen?"

Tassin bit his lip, apparently considering whether he should tell her. "I know I shouldn't have said that name — I'm sorry. A slip of the tongue."

"Tassin!"

"All right, all right! He's asking for you, Lady Alannys. He's got himself into some trouble — he needs your help!"

♫

Alannys never made a conscious decision to move — she was headed toward the door before her brain caught up. "What's wrong with Chen? What happened?"

Tassin held his hands up in front of himself, like he was trying to hold her in the room. "Oh, no. No, no, no. Sorry, miss, but that's as far as you go. I never should've said that to you at all — forget you heard it."

"Tassin!"

He shook his head. "Uh-uh. The king made it right clear how he wants you treated, ma'am — if he said stay, stay it is."

"You keep telling yourself that." She grabbed his arm and dragged him with her, out of the doorway and into the little corridor. "Where do we go?"

"Lady Alannys..." Tassin fretted, biting his lower lip.

"If the king said—"

"I need you to stop wasting time. *Take me to Chen!*"

A scant moment longer he hesitated. Then he grabbed her hand and they were running, through the corridor out into the dazzling sunlight of the sterncastle deck, across the quarterdeck and down to the main desk. Before her eyes had even begun to adjust to the light and colors assaulting them, Tassin dragged her through an unfamiliar door, into the dank darkness of a part of the ship she had never seen before. The smell hit her nose the way the light had hit her eyes—stale seawater, mildew, sweat, and things she didn't even dare guess at combined to make a powerful reek that was far removed from anything she had experienced in the royal part of the ship.

She skidded to a reflexive halt, yanking her hand away from Tassin and pushing her face into the crook of her elbow, breathing through the fabric of her sleeve. After days spent at sea, she didn't smell great, but she wasn't anything like as bad as what hung there in the air around her. "What is this? Where are you taking me?"

Tassin turned to face her. He was barely more than a silhouette in the dark room, but the red hair sticking out from under his bandana in all directions gave him a wild and threatening aspect, and Alannys had to fight not to take a step backwards. "Does it matter?" His tone startled her—was he angry with her? Did he really think Dorramon would hold *him* responsible for this? "Your friend's in trouble. If you want to save him, you'll follow me, and you won't waste time asking stupid questions."

He turned and headed farther into the rank darkness without another word. He didn't seem to notice or care about the horrific smell, and for the first time Alannys thought about the difference between what she had seen and the real *Atromitos* – what kind of conditions did the crew endure? She would have wagered there was nothing to match the royal cabin anywhere else on the ship—not even the captain himself traveled so well. Could that be what this was about? Some kind of jealousy?

She didn't think so. Tassin gave off lots of vibes, to be sure, but jealousy was nowhere among them. The one thing she was certain about was that this setup stank as badly as the stale air surrounding her — if she was smart, she would turn around and run back above deck as fast as her legs could carry her...perhaps Tassin had good reason to fear the king's retribution after all.

But she already knew she couldn't do that. Tassin had said Chen was in trouble, and that trouble sounded even worse after his last remark. Could she save herself at the risk of dooming Chen?

No. No, of course she couldn't. And she suspected that Tassin knew that every bit as well as she did, given the confident way he swaggered away from her without even a look back to see if she would follow.

Against her better judgment, she did. And she promised herself that from now on, she was wearing Songstrike and her dagger every waking moment of her life, no matter who was around or who might take offense. She could have faced any danger without blinking if Songstrike had been with her, humming its soothing melodies in her mind.

But Songstrike was back in her trunk in the royal cabin, and Alannys was doing her best to follow Tassin across the uneven decking on feet that wobbled too much for comfort. The ceiling was low and the giant bracing timbers cut directly through her line of sight on their way to the walls, waiting for her to dash her brains out against one of them in a careless moment. Giant, hulking forms lined the wall with regular intervals between them, each neatly concealed under its own oilcloth cover. Stout racks hung on the walls in the gaps, each holding — were those steel bolts? With sharpened heads? Were those covered machines *ballistas?* Her uncertain steps slowed as she took in the sheer amount of firepower surrounding her. It shouldn't have surprised her — where there was sea trade, there was piracy, and what could present a more attractive target than a royal ship? Still, it gave her stomach an unpleasant turn to see those big war machines lined up along the wall, facing the closed hatches they would fire through, if they needed to. She tore her eyes away and forced herself to pick up her step, following Tassin's rapidly receding form.

Narrow shafts of sunlight cut in through tiny gaps around the hatches and angled across the room, highlighting the splintered floor and the dust motes hovering above it. Alannys picked her way across the deck, thinking about the smell and the weapons and the dark and wondering, what on earth would Chen be doing here? Not for the first time, she had a really bad feeling about the whole thing.

"Tassin?" she called uncertainly into the dusty darkness. It felt like she had walked a mile, and she didn't seem to be any closer to him, or for that matter, to Chen.

"Almost there, ma'am." Was he deliberately taunting her, or was that just an effect of the echoes in the big room? "Just a little further."

"Alannys?" The voice from the darkness was Chen's, and it sounded frantic. Her heart kicked into overdrive and she moved even faster across the badly-lit deck, ducking under timbers and around ballistas. "Alannys, no, don't come any closer! You've got to go back! Get out of here — *now!*"

♫

Alannys froze, Chen's warning ringing in her ears. What should she do? Her frazzled brain tried to decide, but it was already too late for that. She could see Tassin's shadowy form ahead, hauling on a rope, and one of the big firing hatches in the side of the ship creaked open. Alannys threw her hands up in front of her face, shielding her eyes from the sudden, painful light, and gasped. In the glare she could see Chen, against the side wall on the other side of the open hatch from her.

And his arms were tied behind him, his legs bound together.

Alannys turned to Tassin in blistering fury, her hands clenching into involuntary fists. "What is the meaning of this?"

Tassin held his hands up, but he didn't look particularly concerned. "Just what I told you. This is your chance to save your friend. You and your twice-blessed king love to play hero, don't you? Now will you do as I say, or will I toss this trussed-up brownskin out the hatch?"

Alannys's mouth felt suddenly dry, her throat tight with fear. If only she could tell this kid how much she despised playing hero... "What must I do?"

"Alannys, no!" Chen struggled against his bonds, to no avail.

Tassin paid him no mind. He took a step closer to her, warming to his game, and gestured to the opening yawning in the hull of the ship. "Simple enough. One of you is going out that hatch. I can toss your lapdog here out, ropes and all, and we can find out how well brownskins breathe underwater. Or you can jump yourself."

"Myself..." She looked from the gaping hatch to the broad grin stretching Tassin's face. "Why do you want to kill me?"

"Now, now," Tassin protested. He sounded amused. "I ain't killing anyone. I'm only asking—nicely—that you get yourself off this here ship, through that there firing hatch. Now."

"Quibbling over semantics, are we?" Alannys frowned. What possible difference could any of this make to him? "What do you suppose will happen to me after I toss myself out of the hatch? Just because I'm not tied up doesn't mean I can survive indefinitely in the ocean."

"I don't doubt it. You'll meet your death out there, one way or another, that much is fact. What's important is that you go to meet it yourself."

All at once it clicked in her mind, with a sound she could almost hear, and she understood exactly why this mattered to him. "Are you working for the Lord's Retainers?" She took a reflexive step back away from him.

"I don't work for them." Tassin's grin widened, broadened, sharpened into something predatory and threatening. "I am one of them. And I'm here to finish what we started in Duxol."

Alannys felt like she had spent every waking moment since boarding the *Atromitos* worrying—and most of the sleeping ones, too. But this was one scenario even her compulsively fretting imagination had never dreamed up. She had no idea what to do and so she did the only thing that seemed to make sense right then: she stalled for time. "Someone is going out the firing hatch, you say. What makes you think it has to be Chen or me?"

"Ah, yes, they told me you had gravel. I'm not too worried, though—I think I can take a woman in a fight, don't you?"

Damn him, he still sounded as though all of this was just one big joke contrived specifically for his amusement. Anger burned in her chest and her cheeks, and she clenched her hands into impotent fists, trying to rein in her temper. "Maybe you've forgotten that I don't have to touch you to fight you."

"Oh, sure. The singing." The casual, confident way he threw out the words gave her pause. What had the Retainers told him? Why didn't he seem to fear her *at all*, in stark contrast to just about every other human being she had met in Ravanmark? "That might matter," he continued smugly, "if I wasn't dead set on seeing you and that king of yours destroyed, no matter what it takes. Do you really think your will can overpower mine that easily?"

"I think," she said stiffly, "you will find my will to be surprisingly capable."

"And I think you think too much of yourself. You're a palace fixture, not a fighter. You're used to a soft life being pampered. I spend half my life up in the rigging. You might have the sword of prophecy, but unless I'm flat wrong, you ain't carrying it now. I, at least, am armed." He jerked his chin toward his leg, flaunting a black leather sheath strapped to his boot, holding a wicked-looking dagger.

She stared at it, then at him, trying her best to figure some way out of this fix.

"And to take a page from your book, I don't have to touch you to fight you, either." He grabbed Chen's face in his hand, pinching his cheeks and shaking his head roughly. "After all, you wouldn't want to see anything happen to your pet brownskin, would you?"

"Stop calling him that," she muttered.

Chen faced her evenly, with no hint of fear in his dark eyes. "Alannys, you can't do this. You know what they're trying to do. You can't let them win."

"Now, now," Tassin mocked. "She could hardly just watch you die, could she? Lady Alannys of Gale, preaching to us all about equality. Who is she to say the Redeemer is worth more than a brownskin dog?"

"Stop calling him that!" Alannys's temper finally got the better of her, and even Tassin jumped at the edge on her tone. "Get away from him. I'll do what you're asking. Just leave him alone."

"Whatever you say," Tassin said, and stepped away from Chen, holding his hands up in an exaggerated gesture.

"Alannys…" Chen sounded desperate.

"Shut up, Chen. This isn't up for debate." What else could she do, after all? What kind of Redeemer would let her friends die to save her own skin? What kind of *person* could do that? Alannys didn't want to die. But neither did she want to be that person. "Tell Dorramon I love him. Tell him I'm sorry."

"Soth's eye," Chen muttered. "Why don't you tell him yourself?"

She knew what he was asking. She tried to smile, but it didn't feel like it worked, so she just shook her head. "If I use the mindlink right now, he's going to come storming in here, you know that. And then you and I will both be in the drink. I can't swim well enough for both of us."

"You don't have to." His voice caught in the back of his throat.

"Hush, Chen." Her voice sounded about the same as his. "The Singari need their steward. And who else could be an ambassador between the *zhotha* and the Great Palace?"

"Hang the *zhotha*," he grumbled. "This is insanity."

"Probably," she said, picking her way up to the hatch. "But you've always said I was crazy." The ballista that had once sat at this hatch had already been pushed out into the room's main walkway. Alannys wondered how long Tassin had planned this, how long this place had stood ready, waiting for this moment. Then she wondered why on earth she would care, and what it said about her that she would be thinking about a thing like that at a time like this.

It didn't matter, really. Thinking about any of it was better than thinking about what lay ahead of her right now.

Alannys glanced back. Her eyes slid over Chen without stopping—she couldn't bear to examine his expression too closely just then. Tassin watched her with a broad smile, not even bothering to try to conceal his satisfaction. She hated him. She hated that a group of people she had never met knew her so well, could play her as well as she played her violin. She wished she could turn off her weaknesses to spite them, but then, what kind of person would that make her? Like one of them? No, she knew what she had to do, even if it made her the fool they all believed she was. After all, it made her a good Redeemer.

She sighed. She understood it. But she didn't have to like it.

She stepped up on the low wall covering the bottom half of the hatch, balancing herself on the narrow lip that ran across the top, her arms spread wide to brace herself against the sides. The wind rushed in around her, pushing against her.

"Alannys, please..." She could hear Chen's pained voice behind her, but she didn't dare turn around. If she did, she would lose her nerve. Every minute she waited was a minute Tassin might lose his patience, and then Chen would be in a good deal more trouble than she could get him out of. One of them was leaving this ship, now...that much was clear.

Her job was to make sure it was only one of them.

"Not smart to wait." Tassin's words were short but he sounded disinterested. She could almost see him, in her mind's eye, using the tip of that dagger to idly clean his fingernails. "I might get bored over here, and that wouldn't be good for your brownskin lapdog, right?"

She wanted to lash out at him, but she didn't dare. The sharp remark burning on her tongue died unspoken—she was relying on whatever goodwill Tassin possessed to keep him to his end of this bargain. She knew that.

It didn't make it any easier.

"Enough stalling," she muttered. She tensed against the frame of the firing hatch around her, and launched herself from it with everything she could muster—the last thing she wanted to do was slap into the side of the big ship, or get caught in its tumultuous wake. She couldn't survive out here in the open ocean; she was as good as dead as soon as she left the ship. She knew that. But she still intended to try. She would not surrender to death as easily as that—she would not go down without a fight.

She had just finished telling herself that when she

splashed down into the icy, bottomless water, and sank below the choppy waves.

♫

Alannys burst gasping through the surface of the sea, shaking her head to fling the water from her hair and her eyes, relishing the feel of fresh salty air in her lungs again. She couldn't have been underwater more than a few seconds, but it felt like a lifetime.

The *Atromitos* loomed there before her, swaying carelessly on its way, cutting a deep, foam-trimmed furrow through the sea. She could hear the giant timbers groaning, could hear the creaking of the masts and the ropes. The whoosh of the water foaming past seemed loud in her ears.

But she could hear something else too — she could hear Chen raising a mighty fuss from the other side of the firing hatch, yelling like the devil.

"Alannys! Alannys, you can't do this! You'll die out there!"

She puffed out her cheeks, treading water as best as she could in her heavy clothes. What on earth did he hope to accomplish? She couldn't even imagine — he had to know it was too late, now, for turning back. He didn't seem to care, though, bellowing for all he was worth. She could hear him clearly, even from outside. Tassin snapped at him, evidently trying to shut him up, but it only made him louder. It was funny, in a way. Chen never had the sense to give up. Even now.

She was well aware that he would say the same thing about her, and that made it seem even funnier.

That was about the only funny thing about her situation, though. She pulled her attention away from the ship and turned a slow circle in the water, scanning the ocean in every direction for another boat, land, debris — anything she might swim toward, anything that might help her stay afloat a little while longer.

No, Chen was definitely not the only one here who

lacked the sense to give up.

Unfortunately it looked as if she wouldn't have any choice. There was nothing — no island, not even a rock broke the surface of the glittering water for as far as she could see.

And she was already losing this fight, she could tell that much. Water drenched all of her heavy work clothes, weighing her down. Her leather pants pulled on her, dragging her toward the briny bottom. Already she was struggling to keep her face above the water — waves washed over her and she spluttered and gasped for breath. She couldn't even sing her way out of this — even if she could keep clear of the water long enough, anything that could save her now risked the ship and all of the people on it.

And she was so *cold*. The water seemed to suck the warmth right out of her — already she couldn't quite feel her hands, paddling numbly around her in an effort to keep her afloat that was probably futile.

She could still hear Chen, over it all, still yelling like the very devil. It made her want to laugh and cry at the same time, made her wish she could grab him by the shoulders and shake him till his teeth fell out.

Apparently she wasn't the only one. Before she could quite accept the reality of what she was seeing, a figure splashed down into the water yards ahead of her — a figure with his hands and feet still bound. Tassin's patience or his goodwill — or both — had run out, and he had condemned Chen to death every bit as certainly as Alannys, only faster.

♫

Alannys stared at Chen, bound and flapping helplessly in the water, fighting a doomed battle to stay afloat. She couldn't believe, *just could not believe* Tassin had thrown him out there like that. Not for the first time, she cursed his red head, and all of the rest of him too.

Then she cut out swimming across the water, fighting

numbness and fatigue, her heavy clothes and the rolling sea itself to reach him before it was too late.

"F—fancy meeting you here," Chen stammered, spluttering salty water all over his face and hers. He was kicking with both legs together but unable to move his arms at all, and he couldn't quite keep his face out of the water. She didn't see how he had managed to stay afloat this long, honestly. "I'm starting to see why Singari hate the ocean."

"This is no time for wisecracks," Alannys snapped, grabbing the arm closest to her and hauling him up. It wasn't easy; pulling him up seemed to push her even farther down. Treading water for both of them was no mean feat. "Are you insane? Why can't you ever just be quiet?"

"What difference does it make? If you drown, we're all in a lot more trouble than this. Besides, he doesn't have a hostage now—he can't force you or anyone else to do anything for my sake. And even my big mouth may turn out useful, in the end."

She wanted to ask him what on earth he was talking about; not a single thing he had just said made any sense at all. But she couldn't open her mouth without water pouring in; she couldn't keep her face above water any longer at all. Her clothes pulled her, dragged on her like an anchor. Sea water flooded her eyes, and everything she could see was amorphous and tinged with blue. She could hear Chen's frantic shouts, but they sounded strange in her ears—distant, somehow, and muffled. She heard a splash, but that didn't sound right, either, and she wondered fleetingly if she could trust her own perceptions anymore. Was this what drowning felt like, this curious disassociation from her own senses? She tightened her grip on Chen, gave him one last, desperate push toward the surface, and finally surrendered.

The last thing she saw as her heavy clothes dragged her inexorably toward the fathomless depths was an outstretched hand, grasping frantically, uselessly, beneath the water — a hand that she could never reach.

♫

Consciousness returned slowly to Alannys, which surprised her — she had never expected it to return at all. It was a miracle, really, and she didn't know what to make of it. She could feel cool grass under her face, could hear water splashing, and birds singing somewhere in the distance.

But the last thing she expected to see when she opened her eyes was the peaceful garden in the courtyard of the keep.

Alannys pushed herself to sit up. The dirt squished under her hands, and the grass poked up between her fingers. It all felt so real.

But it couldn't be, could it? Not a thing she saw matched up with anything in her recent memory. This was the palace courtyard, no doubt about it — she was on the ground near the water garden, just outside the circle of benches. Everything was just as it had been the last time she had been at the palace — she even recognized the white and blue dress she was wearing. She remembered clearly the day Tralice had brought it to her, right after she had escaped the ruins of Archford Estate, with her short, ragged hair. "You're cute as a ceramic poppet," Tralice had said, and Alannys could still hear the words clearly.

But that had been ages ago, before Tralice became so...different. That dress had been destroyed in Lord Malrec's bomb attack on the Great Palace.

And she remembered all of that, but nothing about it explained how she could have gotten here from the bottom of the sea.

"Am I...am I *dead?*" It made a strange sort of sense. It was about the only explanation she could imagine for what her senses were telling her. And if she got to pick a place to spend her afterlife, she couldn't think of anywhere she would rather be than the Great Palace. Especially if her friends were there.

But the only person in the palace right now seemed to be her.

Alannys stood up on legs that wobbled, like they hadn't been used in a long time. She turned a long, slow circle, breathing deep and taking in everything. Not a detail was out of place. Every smell, every sound, every sensation was perfect. Maybe this was what being dead was like. Maybe this was what *heaven* was like.

She could think of worse ways to spend eternity.

She probably could have gone anywhere she wanted just then; out to the inner ward, maybe, to see the Great Hall, or to admire the gleaming white figure of the keep against the sky. But she turned instead and headed for her own room.

She couldn't have said why. If she was looking for people, outside was definitely the way to go. Perhaps that was why she *didn't* go outside — perhaps she wanted to cling to the illusion of some kind of normalcy for as long as she could. An empty inner ward...a Great Hall with no Captain Grayble, no Raman, no Dorramon...that would not be pleasant. She would avoid those things as long as she could.

Her door swung open on a sitting room that was exactly as she remembered it. Precisely. It was starting to feel eerie, how perfectly identical everything was to her memory. If she hoped to preserve the idea that she was home and nothing strange was going on, this wasn't helping. People should have been moving through here in her absence, time would have passed, things would have changed. But nothing had — the sofa and the chair sat in her room just exactly as she remembered them, with not so much as a layer of dust on the coffee table to mark any passage of time at all.

Even the palace housekeeping staff wasn't that good.

She shivered, looking around the perfect, empty room. It felt like being in a ghost town, or visiting the home of someone who had recently passed away. She couldn't explain those impressions, but she was pretty sure they were warnings. And whatever they were warning her about wasn't anything good.

She pushed all of that aside and turned for the archway that led into her bedroom. If this was to be her tomb, she had better start getting used to it.

Then she caught sight of her big, familiar bed—and the foppishly dressed man reclined against her pillows, his dirty boots leaving smudges on the white linens, his watery, pale blue eyes narrowed in a smile that didn't feel friendly at all.

And she knew that if this was her afterlife, she hadn't gone to heaven after all.

"Why, if it isn't my dear Lady Alannys!" Athniss said, standing up from her bed, arms outstretched as though he might have expected her to hug him. "How nice of you to finally join me. It isn't polite, you know, to keep your visitor waiting."

"Visitor?" she echoed, with no understanding at all. She wanted to turn around and run headlong from the room. Instead she took a tiny step backward.

Athniss's smile sharpened. "Naturally, dear lady. These are your rooms, are they not? You surely can't imagine that you have come here to visit me!"

"No. I mean, I—I don't imagine I'm in much state to visit anyone, not anymore. As best as I can figure, I should be at the bottom of the sea right now."

"Ah, yes, I see." He sounded quite satisfied, but he didn't say anything more about it, just turned suddenly away from her and began wandering her room, inspecting each thing he saw. "This is a very nice place, Alannys. I can see that our hopes to impress you with Agapios Periousia were misplaced, to say the least of it. I've never entered the Great Palace before in my life. I had no idea what to expect. It doesn't make me feel any better, you know, about the situation your king has put my family into."

"Nobody put your family in any situation," she said, aware that she was probably wasting her breath. It was too late for her, but if she could ease his wrath towards Dorramon, even a little, she had to try. "Your family bought a title they couldn't afford; baronet isn't even a noble title. You can't keep blaming the Crown for your situation. You've misunderstood."

"I've misunderstood *nothing!*" he exploded, rounding on her in sudden fury. "Royals will say anything, twist anything, rewrite history itself to exonerate themselves. You are a fool if you listen to them, Alannys, and I advise you very seriously not to say another word against my family or my estate. I might forget my own intentions and kill you where you stand, and that would not please either of us, in the end."

He seemed irate. He certainly *looked* irate, his anger putting color into his face that had been lacking only moments before. And yet it couldn't seem to reach her; none of this felt real. She stared over his shoulder, at the dust motes floating in the sunbeams angling through the window. They seemed to move in a lazy sort of slow motion that only reinforced her feelings. "You can't kill me," she said dully. "I'm already dead."

He laughed out loud, a barking, unpleasant sound that set her teeth on edge. "You aren't dead. At least, not yet."

"What?" She stared at him in complete confusion. "How can I not be dead? The last thing I remember was sinking under the water, hundreds of miles from here. There's no possible way I can be here."

"You *are* dull-witted, aren't you?" He swept past her into the sitting room, and sprawled himself out on her sofa, propping his dirty boots on the gleaming coffee table. "You aren't really here, Alannys, at least not physically. This place, these rooms..." He glanced around and shrugged. "They are all from your memories. It is a nice change of pace, isn't it? But this is all the mindlink. I assure you it would not work if you were dead."

"The mindlink?" She looked around her sitting room, so familiar and so strange all at once, and abruptly it made sense. "I'm not dead—I'm asleep! I *survived!*"

"Indeed. And a most joyous thing it is, too." His tone was flat, as if he couldn't have cared less, but he was watching her closely. "I would be most unhappy if anyone else were to kill you now."

Alannys went to stand in front of the massive tapestry on her wall. She could bear to look at it now, now that she knew she would see Dorramon again, and all she had to do was wake up. "Why?" She sounded about as interested as Athniss had. "What possible difference can it make to you? Dead is dead, right?"

"Certainly. Dead is dead, as you so charmingly put it. Dying, though—that's different. There's dying, and then there's *dying.*"

Something in his tone chilled her, crawled up her back like an insect. She spun to face him, surprised by the intensity in his expression.

"The difference," he continued, watching her evenly as he spoke, "is in the suffering, you see. The dead can't suffer, but the *dying…*"

He looked demented, he sounded demented, and he had never scared Alannys as much as he did in that moment. Her eyes cut to the door, gauging her chances of escape, and Athniss smiled.

"Do you understand? I'm not after your death, Alannys. I'm after revenge. Death isn't revenge. Suffering is revenge. Dying can be revenge." He stood up, and she sidled for the door, unnerved by the way his pale eyes seemed to glow when he spoke of her death. "I'm going to meet you at Mount Mouseion, Alannys. I'll be waiting for you there. And then," he paused and graced her with a smile that was positively unholy, "you are going to *die.*"

♫

Alannys bolted for the door to her chambers, exploding

from stillness into flight with an alacrity that she hoped might give her an edge, might give her a chance to outrun Athniss. She heard his chilling laugh behind her, heard him chasing after her and she ran even faster, her only thought of getting to the door and closing it behind her. What would happen if she died here, if Athniss really did kill her in one of these odd, hallucinogenic dreams? She didn't know. And she bloody well wasn't going to wait around to find out.

Unfortunately this was a dream, and Athniss seemed to have all the control. The door was only a few feet away from her, but no matter how far or how fast she ran, it stayed just out of her reach. Athniss hadn't caught her, so she had to be moving—but somehow she wasn't reaching the door. It was the kind of reality-defying paradox that could only occur in a dream, and she hated it.

She risked a glance over her shoulder to find him behind her, his pale face twisted into a grotesque mask of hatred. He reached for her with fingers curved into talons, and she launched herself toward the door with everything she had. His fingers scraped down her back like claws— but her hand landed on the handle of the door. With the solid feel of cool brass under her fingers, everything else around her seemed to lose solidity, to fade around her, and she realized she had done it—she was waking.

But even as the world around her disintegrated, even as she felt the softness of a bed she hadn't known she was in, she could hear Athniss's low, throaty laugh in her ears. And she knew then that he had let her go. He was toying with her, like a cat playing with a mouse. It was a game for him.

And he was enjoying it.

♪

Alannys pried her eyes open, her heart pounding in her chest, too angry and upset to even feel relieved.

Dorramon leaned over her, frowning into her face and filling her field of vision. She knew what bursting free of that dream had felt like to her, but she couldn't imagine what it must have seemed like to him. She cleared her throat and squirmed awkwardly against the pillows, embarrassed.

"You're awake," Dorramon said, and relief filled his tone, telling her exactly how bad it had been for him. His dark hair shone with water, dripping down into his face, but he didn't even seem to notice. "Thank the Muses. Are you all right?"

"Yes," she said, quickly in her embarrassment—maybe too quickly, given the way Dorramon's frown deepened. "What happened?"

"Your Prince Charming rescued you." The voice was dry, a bit sarcastic, and unmistakably Chen. She craned her head around and saw him, in one of the chairs in the sitting room, sopping wet.

"Chen! You're alive!"

He inclined his head. "They fished me out too. See, I told you my big mouth would come in handy."

She tried to smile, but it felt shaky. She looked up into Dorramon's eyes, touched his damp hair, and it got even shakier. "You jumped into the sea...for me? You shouldn't have done that, it was too dangerous. But thank you. I—I didn't expect to see this room again."

Dorramon's mouth twitched convulsively, as though there were things he would have liked to say. "No, I'd wager you didn't." He looked as if he had more to say—a lot more to say, and most of it things she would probably prefer not to hear—but the door to the room suddenly crashed open, cutting him off with a bang.

"Your Highness! What is the meaning of this?" Captain Morgain barged into the room, looking worse than she had ever seen him, even worse than when he'd run in that morning in a disheveled heap to tell them Princess Varilyn had fallen overboard. He sounded like he couldn't quite catch his breath. "Why is my son in the brig?"

Tassin was in the brig. Alannys hadn't been lying there

worrying that he was going to burst in and force her overboard again, but she couldn't deny a certain relief at hearing those words. And judging by the way Dorramon's eyes cut to her before he answered, he knew it.

"I know you've been busy — three rescues in a morning is hardly typical." He spoke evenly, with a lack of anger that Alannys found admirable, given how Morgain had just addressed him, but there was an iron edge to his tone that she didn't think boded well for any of them. "But even so, I would expect that you have heard by now."

"There's nothing to hear," Morgain shot back, "nothing but rumor! The woman ain't even woke up yet!"

Alannys blinked at him in surprise. His eyes touched her face and then slid away, leaving her with the impression of something desperate and not altogether friendly.

"I should think it would be obvious you are wrong there," Dorramon said dryly. "But even putting that aside, you must also realize that Alannys wasn't the only witness to Tassin's villainy. We've already had the whole story from Chen."

"Chen?" The old captain's glance darted to the sitting area, where Chen leaned back in his chair, watching the whole conversation with nothing but mild interest visible on his face. Morgain's eyes widened with surprise — and something more. "You'd take the word of a dirty, lying brownskin over my son? Over me?"

Dorramon drew himself up to his full height and crossed his arms, regarding the captain with a stern gaze and a hardened jaw. Even with his dripping hair, he cut a grim figure, the low gleam of purple velvet around his shoulders reminding them all how necessarily foolish it was to court his displeasure. "I have already warned you about the racial slurs, Morgain. If you wish to join your son in the brig, keep going." He studied Morgain's obstinate glare. "Are you sure you want to put yourself on the line to vouch for your son? I would think very carefully before I made such a statement, if I were you."

"Tassin said some pretty racist things earlier," Alannys said. She wasn't sure whether it was wise for her to enter this conversation, but she felt she had to. She knew that passive look on Chen's face well enough—it was the way he always looked when he was deliberately letting other people's censure slide. It was a look that she hated, and she hated that it was still necessary, even here, on the royal ship. "I guess I can see well enough now where those attitudes come from. I can't say it makes me happy, though."

"No, nor me," Dorramon said. "It's sad to see someone clinging so vigorously to their backward attitudes, when the rest of the country is making such strides toward change."

A dainty sneeze distracted them all. Alannys followed the sound to the sitting area and found Varilyn in the chair across from Chen, bundled up in a blanket. Her hair was damp and she looked thoroughly chilled. "Chen is no liar," she said. Alannys had never heard her gentle voice sound quite so firm—or quite so offended. "I have heard the story he tells, and I don't doubt it. Everything he says is consistent with what I know of him, and Alannys...and unfortunately, of Tassin as well. It was unquestionably Tassin who pushed me overboard." She leveled a challenging glare at the captain. "Will you question my word to my face as well?"

♫

Morgain's face darkened, going straight past red to purple. But even in his state, he apparently could see the danger in what the princess was suggesting. "Of course not." His voice sounded strained, like he was forcing the words out. "If your Highness says it, I must of course take it as truth. I do wonder, though, why it is the lot of you have it out for my son."

"Have it out for your son? Sun's light, man, are you blind? Or just daft?" The cutting, sarcastic voice was undoubtedly Prince Cardoth's, which startled Alannys more than it should have because she'd had no idea he was even in the room. Only when he spoke, as sharp and cutting as the curved blade he carried, did she see him, standing leaning against the wall beside the big bookcases.

"I—I don't like your tone, my Lord Prince." The captain had clearly not known Cardoth was there, either.

"Tough for you," Cardoth said bluntly. "I don't have a dog in this fight. Not my ship, not my captain. I couldn't care less for your delicate sensibilities, Morgain. I am only here to find out who attempted to assassinate my sister, and what is being done about it. We have our answer to the first question, it seems, for those not too stubborn to hear it."

Morgain's face had lost its purple color, drained to the color of unbaked pastry dough. "I don't...I can't..." He cleared his throat and tried again. "For four generations my family's served the Crown. Why could my son want to throw that proud heritage away? Nothing I have heard today answers that simple question, and until I have that answer, none of your grand conclusions are worth spit to me."

Cardoth's sigh painted a vivid picture of exasperation for them all. "Do you still not understand? You've raised your son to be a Soth worshiper! You put someone like that on a boat with the alleged Redeemer, what do you *think* is going to happen?"

Captain Morgain gasped out loud, a wrenching, painful sound. He seemed to stumble, to fold in on himself right where he stood. Alannys knew he hadn't changed, and yet, he seemed shorter and slighter than he had only a moment before. "My....my son...he's a...are you sure?"

Dorramon raised an eyebrow, watching him thoughtfully. "You did not know this? How is that possible?"

"I—I may have given you the wrong impression, your Majesty, about me and my son." Morgain reached out with a shaking hand to lean on the entryway wall beside him. "Tassin was an orphan. I mean, that is...his mother died giving him life."

"I am sorry to hear it," Dorramon said. "You have my condolences. But an orphan is a child who has lost both parents. Are you not his father?"

"I am! That is...I am now, I suppose. But years ago, when he was born...I wasn't in no shape to be anyone's father then. It was his mother, you see — she was all I lived for. And then she was just *gone*...and I didn't know what to do, didn't know how to deal with the helpless, noisy thing she left behind."

No one moved, no one spoke. They stared as one at Captain Morgain, waiting for him to continue.

"What could I do? The only thing I was any good at was sailing, and that ain't no kind of life for a kid. I found a family back in Port Grandview, with a couple of kids of their own, and they took him in. I sent them money for his care, and he had a normal life. Well, until maybe a week ago, when he showed up at the docks begging to work on the *Atromitos*. How could I say no? I was proud he wanted to follow after me, right proud."

"Normal," Dorramon echoed. "Until a week ago. So your son is a stranger to you?"

"No! No, of course not. Not really. I used to visit him, you know, once or twice a year. I sent him some birthday presents. He even wrote me letters, after he learned how to write."

Alannys frowned. This entire story was rubbing her the wrong way, and changing her opinions of both Tassin and Morgain. "He wrote you letters? Did you ever write him back?"

His eyes slipped away from hers. "Well no, not really. Mostly all he wrote was how he wanted me to come visit him. How was I going to answer that?"

Nobody seemed to want to touch that question.

"So," Dorramon finally said, "this family. Were they

Soth-worshipers?"

"No! Well, that is, how would I know? That ain't exactly the sort of thing you just ask a body, you know?"

"It might be," Dorramon said, "if you were considering allowing them to raise your son. So he's been brought up in the Lord's Retainers. And you never knew it. And they sent him here to do just what he did. And this deep devotion to the Crown you told us about...it would be unlikely, don't you think, in a child of such circumstances?"

Morgain's face crumpled. "Honestly, your Highness, I hoped he could learn that here. Tassin, he maybe holds something of a grudge. To him the Crown is the thing that's kept me from him all these years...he blames it all on my duty, not on my own weaknesses."

"Well there you have it," Cardoth said shortly. "Tassin did this thing, and you know he did it, and now you know why. The only question left is how we make sure nothing like this happens again. I don't fancy my sister facing any more danger." He said this with a hard look at Dorramon, with a darkness in his eyes that Alannys found ominous.

"I don't think you have to worry about that," Dorramon said, waving a hand as if to wave aside Cardoth's concerns. "Tassin is in the brig. He can't very well attack any of us from there."

"That's it?" Cardoth said. "That's your answer? Just put him in the brig and everything's as good as sunlight again? You are aware that he nearly killed the Princess of Cadenda, aren't you? Wars have been started for less."

Dorramon frowned, casting a quick glance around a room suddenly blanketed in a heavy silence. Alannys knew he couldn't have missed the peculiar way the prince leaned on his last words, the heavy threat he was bringing to bear.

"Cardoth, please don't overreact." That was Varilyn, trying hard to sound firm and reasonable, but her tone couldn't quite conceal her worry. "I am perfectly fine. You know that boy wasn't targeting me at all—I was just a distraction, so he could get to Alannys. It's silly to take offense at such a thing. It could have been any of us."

"It's not silly. Any injury to you is an injury to all of Cadenda, you know that. And I am supremely uninterested in the circumstances of that injury. If Ravanmark wishes to preserve any sort of relationship at all, they would also do well to take such things seriously." He took Varilyn by the hand and hauled her from the chair, fairly dragging her out of the room without another word.

Morgain stepped out of their way, shrinking against the wall to avoid bringing any of Prince Cardoth's barely concealed fury down on himself. Only when the sounds of their footsteps had faded completely behind them did he finally speak. "My Lord King...my son..."

"Your son will stay right where he is, Morgain."

"But your Highness!"

"Not another word, Captain!" Dorramon's words were sharp, and they cut the old man off as effectively as a slap. "There will be no leniency here, and you must not ask for it. Your son is lucky he is still alive, do you understand that? He could easily be put to death for any one of the things he has done."

Tears brimmed in the captain's eyes. He wiped a gnarled hand across his grizzled face, blinking fast. "This's my fault," he muttered, "all of it. If only I'd been there, if only I'd done more..." He turned away and tottered out the door, almost as if he didn't see any of them any more. "Tassin, my son, my boy, what can I do for you now?"

The door fell shut behind him with a thunk that sounded ominously final.

♪

Dorramon frowned at the closed door, kneading his thumb against his teeth. He didn't say a word, and Alannys wondered with sudden worry what he could be thinking about, with a look as dark as that.

"That was...uncomfortable," Chen said, looking from the king's face to hers.

Dorramon didn't even seem to hear him—Chen's words certainly didn't appear to interrupt his grim contemplation of the door.

Chen looked at Alannys and shrugged.

She shrugged back. She didn't know what to make of it either.

"You aren't safe here." Dorramon whirled to face her, examining her face solemnly, as if there was any conceivable way she didn't already know that.

"It isn't that bad," she said haltingly. "He's in the brig. You can't really imagine anybody else on the ship would try a crazy thing like that."

He didn't seem to hear her, any more than he had heard Chen a few moments before. "What did he say to you?"

She blinked at him, confused by the abrupt change of subject. "Tassin? I don't think it matters, really—you know how those people think. I—"

"No, not *Tassin*." He sounded impatient, like he thought she was deliberately misunderstanding. "Athniss. What did Athniss say to you? He used the mindlink, didn't he?"

"Wait, wait," Chen interrupted, sitting up in his chair. "Athniss? Using the mindlink? Alannys, what is he talking about? I thought this mindlink thing was just between you two."

"It's—it's supposed to be." She frowned between the two of them, displeased with the position she found herself in, and not completely understanding how she had gotten there. It wasn't like Dorramon to speak so casually of the mindlink in front of others...and it certainly wasn't like him to talk about Athniss hijacking it in front of anyone, not even Chen. And even now he seemed totally oblivious to Chen's presence, utterly ignoring both the question and Alannys's scattered attempt to pull together an answer for it. She wasn't exactly keen on talking about it either, but she couldn't very well avoid it now. "Athniss has my Seeing Stone...and another one...and he can use them to kind of force his way in. It's...extremely unpleasant."

"Wait, wait." Chen waved his hands in front of himself, flopping back against the chair. "This is too much. Hold on. That stone — that same stone you've been wearing ever since the day I met you — it can be used like a weapon, to attack you? To attack the mindlink?"

"Yes. I'm sorry, Chen. I know it's a lot to take in, and I don't even understand it that well myself. I don't even know if this is how these relics are supposed to work, or if Athniss is twisting them somehow. But apparently there are two of them; like the mindlink, they are meant to work in a pair. With both of them, Athniss can get to either of us, any time he wants. And he's found some pretty ingenious ways to torture us."

Chen rubbed his forehead, making a show of thinking it over. "I can hardly believe it. I never imagined anything like this was possible. What has he been doing to you?"

"Don't make me go there, Chen. It's...it's not pretty. He's found out he can talk to us, of course, whether we want him to or not, but he can also bring on really vivid hallucinations, ones you can't tell from reality. And he can get inside our dreams, and control them. Don't make me tell you what he says, what he does — you can imagine."

"Yes. Yes, unfortunately I can." His voice sounded rough, but he looked absolutely furious. Alannys didn't think she had ever seen him so angry. "And this has been going on how long — ever since we left the harbor?"

She couldn't imagine anything good coming from answering that. She let her gaze slip away but said nothing.

"Damn it, Alannys! When were you planning on telling me about this? Or *were* you planning on telling me about this? Here was I, shocked to discover you aren't safe on this ship—but you haven't been safe anywhere, ever since we left Duxol! Are you ever going to stop trying to take on everything in the world by yourself?"

Her first instinct was to lash back at him. She smothered it, closing her eyes and counting a slow ten, trying her best not to escalate this. It seemed to her there had been enough confrontation today.

But when she opened her eyes, she found herself facing the purple expanse of Dorramon's cloak—he stood glowering in front of her, staring Chen down in a matter that did not promise to dampen the conflagration. "I don't think I appreciate your tone. Alannys has done nothing wrong. This is a matter that does not concern you."

"Doesn't concern me? Doesn't *concern* me? If it concerns Alannys, it bloody well concerns me too; I would figure you'd know that by now! Why do you think I'm even *here?*"

"I confess to entertaining that question on occasion myself."

Chen threw his hands up and turned away. Alannys was used to exaggerated displays of temper from him, but this—this seemed far too genuine for her to be comfortable with. She had never anticipated a reaction like this, and she wished again that the subject had never been brought up in front of him. "Damn it, she's supposed to be *safe!* I can't keep her safe—we've all seen that over and over again. But you—you're the king! You were supposed to be better than me. I've been doing my best to be so bloody noble, stepping aside because it's what Alannys wanted, trying my damnedest to honor her wishes over my own. And now she's in danger again, constant, horrible danger that I can't do anything about, and it's all because of her relationship with you, the relationship I've been trying to be so damned respectful of!"

"That's not fair!" Alannys tried to step around Dorramon, but he held an arm out to stop her. "This affects the mindlink; he's not safe either!"

"Alannys." Dorramon's voice was flat; he didn't even look at her. "Chen and I need to settle this matter between ourselves, I think."

She didn't particularly like being told to butt out, but she could see nothing she said would make any difference here. Chen hadn't even glanced her direction; she might as well not have spoken at all. So she bit her tongue as Dorramon took a step forward, his royal purple cloak billowing out to conceal her once again from whatever swirled in the air between the two men. It chilled her — she didn't think either of them were acting very much like themselves, and she wondered how much more time they could take on this floating prison before they were all at each other's throats like a pack of hungry wild dogs.

"I can't believe I *sent* her to you," Chen muttered, raking a hand through his disheveled hair. "What was I thinking? She'll never be safe with you, ever."

"Alannys isn't safe anywhere." Dorramon didn't exactly snap, but his words were clipped and sharp, a world removed from the gentle voice Alannys loved. "She knows that. I would have expected you to know that, too — or have the Singari forgotten, over the years, what it means to be the Redeemer?"

Alannys checked herself mid-motion, catching her hand halfway to Dorramon's arm and forcing it back to her side. She knew he wouldn't welcome her interference — he had made that pretty clear — but the way he was acting *wasn't right*. It wasn't like him to take shots at Chen, and she didn't see how any of this could lead to anywhere good.

"Of course I *know*, your Majesty." Chen's words absolutely dripped with sarcasm. She had never heard him so derisive and cutting, not even in his worst arguments with her. "Forgive me if I expected a king to protect her from that better than a lowly, itinerant brownskin! What exactly is all that power good for, if this is the best you can do?"

What happened then happened so fast Alannys's eyes didn't seem to process it at all—one minute Dorramon was standing protectively right in front of her, then a blur crossed her vision and in the next minute he was all the way over at the far wall, holding Chen pinned against it by the throat. "Do you think I haven't asked myself that?" His voice was a low, dangerous growl that she never would have recognized as his. "Do you really think I haven't asked myself that question *every single day?*"

"Dorramon!" Her shocked gasp sounded like it came from someone else. She flew across the room on feet that felt like they belonged to someone else, and latched on to his arm. "Let go of him!"

"Sit *down,* Alannys!" Dorramon's voice was cold, almost metallic, and frightening in its utter unfamiliarity. "I told you I will settle this!"

"How?" she demanded, hauling on his arm. She slipped and skidded on the wood floor, but her efforts didn't seem to make any difference at all. "By killing him? Great Muses, Dorramon, look at what you're doing!"

For a long, long moment it seemed he would pay her exactly as much mind as he had before—precisely none. Nobody moved, nobody even breathed, and then all at once Dorramon took a stumbling step backward, jerking his hand away from Chen as though he had only just awakened to find himself doing something unspeakable.

"I'm—I'm sorry. I don't know what came over me." He sank into Varilyn's recently vacated chair without looking either of them in the eye.

He *sounded* sorry, Alannys thought. But more than that, he sounded upset. She couldn't be sure, but she guessed he was more upset at his own actions than the argument the two men had just had. She felt like she should say something to him, but she hesitated, wondering if he was really back to normal just yet.

Chen pushed himself away from the wall and returned to his own chair, moving gingerly, watching Dorramon as though he might be wondering the same thing. His expression smoldered, and she knew then that if she let him say anything, they would be right back into it again.

"This is ridiculous," she said sharply, shattering the silence before either of them could do it. "None of us are in the wrong here. None of us are to blame. There is only one person responsible for this, and he is miles away, watching us try to destroy each other. That's what he wants, don't you get it? When you two attack each other like animals, you're giving him what he wants. You have to stop. You have to."

They stared at her, their faces twin portraits of stubborn anger. She turned away, smothering a defeated sigh—it was painfully obvious nothing she could say stood a chance of getting through to them. Their situation hit too many sore spots. It was the only reason she could imagine why they would react the way they had, and nothing she could say would touch it.

"You're right." The voice was even and reasonable, and Alannys spun back around to find Dorramon facing her calmly from his chair, looking exactly as though the last ten minutes had never happened. "You're right, and I'm sorry I made it necessary for you to say that. Nothing that has happened here today is going to help us get through this."

"I'm sorry too," Chen piped up immediately, not to be outdone. "You told me something important, and I reacted badly. I'm sorry. I just...I just wasn't ready for this. I'm still not sure I'm ready."

"None of us are ready, Chen," she said dryly. "None of us would have chosen this. But none of us can stop it, either. So the only thing to do is soldier on the best we can, and do what we can to support and protect each other. We'll never make it through this otherwise."

"Of course." Chen did not look quite as eerily composed as Dorramon; he ran his hands through his damp hair as if he sought to tame it. "I should thank you, really, for finally telling me. It's not as if everyone on the ship couldn't tell something's going on—you two have both looked awfully rough lately."

"You're no work of art yourself, Chen."

His bark of laughter sounded almost normal, almost entirely concealing how deeply disturbing the whole incident had been.

"Yes, yes," Dorramon said impatiently. "But with all of that out of the way, you still haven't answered my question, Alannys. I know you saw Athniss, before you woke up. What did he say to you?"

"Nothing." The word was flat, decisive. Anyone else would have believed her. But she knew she couldn't fool Dorramon, and she couldn't look him in the face.

"Damn it, Alannys." In two strides Dorramon was in front of her, his hands gripping her shoulders and his eyes boring into hers. "You can't lie to me. I can't believe you would even try."

"I'm not lying," she lied. "It's just..." She looked desperately around for some excuse, some thing that would get her out of this.

Dorramon gave her a shake. "Just what? I don't want excuses, Alannys, I want answers."

"I don't want to give you answers! Have you somehow missed everything that just happened in here? I can't take a chance on upsetting you, Dorramon—I haven't got any idea what you're capable of right now!"

Dorramon flinched as if she had struck him. Then he stepped back, lifting his hands from her in an exaggerated motion. "I suppose I deserved that. I was out of line. I don't deny that. I lost my temper, and I've apologized. Do I seem out of control to you now, Alannys?"

"Well, no," she hedged, "but this doesn't seem like something we should just brush aside. That was...that was more unlike you than anything I have ever seen you do before, Dorramon. You are not a violent man. And whatever drove you to it—I'm not sure it's going to be that easy to get away from."

"I see." He folded his arms, regarding her with wry humor, seeming a world away from the man she had seen a few minutes before. It tore at her heart; she wanted, in the worst, most visceral way possible, to believe the face he presented her now, the one that said that everything was normal and she had no reason to doubt him. "So you're the type that holds a grudge, then."

Chen's sudden snort of laughter felt mean-spirited to Alannys. She threw him a dirty look, and turned back to Dorramon. "No. But I am worried."

"And I'm telling you that you don't need to be. Is that enough? Do you trust me, or will you require a signed statement from the royal healers? Shall I confine myself to the brig with Tassin?"

She sighed and sank down onto the edge of the bed. "Of course I trust you. This has just...it's been hard on us all, I suppose."

"Don't I know it," Dorramon said. "What did Athniss say to you?"

"Not much we didn't already know." Her voice sounded flat, defeated, even to her own ears. "He intends to kill me, but he wants me to suffer first. He said he'll be waiting for me at Mount Mouseion."

"Mount Mouseion." Dorramon ground the words out, the muscles of his jaw standing out in taut, stark anger, as though something about the place had offended him personally. "He knows that's where we are going, and he is going there too. Now."

"Yes." She didn't know what else to say.

"He will be in a smaller boat," Dorramon said, "taking a more direct route that would be unsafe for a ship this size, and he won't be delayed by rescues and assassination attempts. The bastard could very well beat us there."

"Yes."

Dorramon didn't say anything else. She watched him a moment, frowning at the way his face twitched, wondering what he was thinking.

He turned from her and stomped out of the room, slamming the door shut behind him.

♫

"You want to watch that one." Chen's voice was grim, so low that Alannys almost couldn't make out the words, but it still startled her. She had forgotten, for the moment, that he was even still in the room with her.

"What? He said he was sorry, Chen. Are *you* the type that holds a grudge?"

He didn't rise to the bait. He stood up out of the chair, rubbing thoughtfully at the back of his neck, not quite meeting her gaze. "There are things a person can apologize for, Alannys, and there are things that go deeper than that. Things where saying you're sorry doesn't mean you won't do it again — or do something even worse, when it comes to it. Which do you think this is?"

"Don't be dramatic." She waved a hand, trying to brush the whole thing aside, not even really looking at him. "I can't excuse what he did. But I couldn't excuse what Trago did, either, and he never did anything like that again. He's a fine man now, and a good baron."

"Yes, and how long in the *prathamol* did it take for him to become that way?" Chen wasn't backing down. "If you ask me, that's where *he* belongs, too!"

"No!" Something inside Alannys seemed to snap then, and she wasn't ready for it. "Stop saying things like that. You aren't being rational."

"I'm not being rational?" He crossed his arms and looked at her in plain disbelief. "You know this isn't right. You *know* it. Why are you covering for him?"

Alannys flopped herself down of the edge of the bed, scrubbing at her eyes with the heels of her hands. "I need him, Chen."

"Alannys…"

"No, you don't understand. I rely on him, he's my anchor. I couldn't do half of what I'm doing without him beside me."

Chen sighed. "You can't keep hiding from this. Even I can see he's not acting like himself. And it's getting worse." He finally looked her in the face. The bleakness she could see in his eyes startled her — it matched the bleakness she felt in her soul just then, realizing at last that the person she loved most in the world was headed for some kind of mental breakdown, and there wasn't a thing she could do to stop it. "It's eating him alive, Alannys. I should never have thrown that in his face. I had no idea it had driven him this far."

She just sat there, burying her face into her hands. She refused to acknowledge that, but she couldn't deny it — what she had seen here was so far removed from the Dorramon she knew, she wouldn't have believed it if she hadn't seen it with her own eyes.

"The acts of the Redeemer, this thing with Athniss...there's only so much of that kind of helplessness he can take. And I think he's about to hit his limit."

"What then?" The words were barely more than a hoarse whisper — how could so much horror be contained in a sound so *quiet*?

Chen shook his head. "I can't say, Alannys. But I wish I knew. Because I've had experience with this, firsthand, remember? And the one thing I can tell you for sure is that he's going to snap. And when that happens, whatever he does..." His eyes rose slowly to meet hers, filled with a dread she had not seen there in a long time. The air in the room felt thick; it took a concerted effort for her to keep breathing under the weight of it. "It's not going to be good for any of us. Not good at all."

♫

Alannys didn't speak another word to anyone that day. The crew — and Prince Cardoth — avoided her as if they thought her ill luck might be contagious. She never saw Princess Varilyn or Chen at all. And Dorramon seemed more than ever to be off in his own world, miles removed from anything and anyone on the ship around him. They ate dinner, prepared for bed, and retired, all in a heavy, ominous silence that felt almost electric to Alannys, tingling with the dreadful anticipation of things yet to come. Something was going to happen, Chen was certainly right about that. All she had to do was look at Dorramon's brooding, preoccupied face and she could feel that much in her bones.

But she had no idea what he might do, or how she might stop him, or if stopping him might only make everything worse.

So she did the only thing there was for her to do just then; she climbed into bed and clung to Dorramon like a lifeline, like she thought he might disappear in the night. He seemed completely lost in thoughts she couldn't even guess at, but his hand stroked rhythmically through her hair. Any other time, she would have found it comforting.

As it was, she lay there staring into the darkness, burning with a sense of urgency she could do nothing to cool, clutching a man who almost didn't even seem to know she was there, and praying.

"Oh Muses, what strength I have, if I have any at all, please give it to him. I don't know what's coming, but I know he's going to need more than just me to get through it. Help him, Muses, watch over him, I beg you..."

Sometime in the middle of her anguished pleas, Alannys fell asleep. She woke up in a disoriented panic, like she had overslept for something important, but couldn't quite remember what it was.

The bed was empty.

All at once her panic wasn't so vague, and she scrambled out of the bed, throwing on her clothes as fast as she could manage with fingers that felt suddenly numb. She knew she could well be overreacting. She had woken up alone so many times on this ship, it should have felt old hat...and yet, she couldn't shake a cold, hollow anxiety, gnawing at the edges of her awareness like a rat.

This was different. It wasn't *right*. She could feel it, even if she couldn't articulate exactly why.

And that bothered her; that scared her more than she could say.

Alannys slung her swordbelt around her, and fumbled with the fastener. She was so spooked her hands were shaking, and the buckle on her belt seemed to be an obstacle too great for her to conquer. She didn't even have a logical reason for it — a quick glance through the wall of windows showed her a perfect, peaceful morning. The sight didn't make her feel any better, though. The horrible tension in her middle just kept ratcheting higher.

She finally got the belt fastened and hurried for the door. It felt almost like wasting time — what was Dorramon going to do that a sword would protect her from? — but she had promised herself, in the aftermath of yesterday's attack, that she would wear the blade everywhere from then on, no matter what. So Songstrike went with her, humming tunes that couldn't quite reach her, as she ran out into the mid-morning sun — or at least what should have been the sun. She had seen it just a few moments before, dappling the floor of the great cabin with a bright cheer she could not share. But now, as she burst out onto the sterncastle deck, black clouds boiled up in the sky around her. Lightning flashed and crackled, sizzling through the sky uncomfortably close to the ship, and the strong, shifting wind whipped her hair around in every direction. The ship lurched perilously under her and she staggered, trying to get her head around what was undeniably happening, but should have been impossible. How did the weather change that drastically — that *fast?*

Then she heard the sound of singing, faint over the rising wind, the unmistakable ringing tenor of a voice she would know anywhere, a voice that spoke directly to her soul, sounding as if it came from a great distance away. The sterncastle desk seemed crowded, with every sailor on board running in different directions, but there was no sign of Dorramon anywhere. His voice seemed to issue from everywhere at once, carried on the buffeting winds, teasing her like a fleeting spirit she could never catch.

♫

Alannys turned and ran for the stairs to the stern deck, stumbling over her own feet in her clumsy haste to reach higher ground. She had to see Dorramon, had to find him, had to stop him. Why was he singing in the first place, summoning this great storm? Was this what Chen had warned her about? Even the mindlink was closed tight, giving no answers. *Where was Dorramon?*

Someone grabbed her by the arm, pulling her to a sudden stop halfway up the stairs. She spun around and would probably have fallen back down to the deck below if that same someone hadn't caught her other arm and steadied her.

It was Chen, and the look he was giving her wasn't pleasant, his face hard and his dark eyes boring into hers as though he thought she might be responsible for the chaos around them. "What's going on here, Alannys? What does he think he's doing?"

Alannys shook her head. "How should I know?" She had to shout to be heard over the rising wind, even though he was standing right in front of her. "I just got out here. It's not like he discussed this with me. I'm sure he only intends to help, though. Where is he?"

Chen turned and pointed up at the top of the great main mast. She followed the gesture and there, up in the crow's nest with his arms spread wide and his face tipped up towards the darkening sky, was Dorramon. He had his back pressed against the mast, but the tempestuous wind still whipped his purple cloak around his legs so fiercely she couldn't imagine how he ignored it so completely. "Alannys, that doesn't look like helping. The entire crew is in a panic. It sounds like he's trying to summon a wind, but...he's got to be stopped. Look around—he'll kill us all!"

Alannys was looking, and she couldn't argue with the assessment. All around her were frantic men, desperately trying to combat the growing storm, to keep the great ship afloat. "I'll go," she said immediately, shouldering Chen aside, heading back down the stairs.

But Chen caught her by the arm again. "No. No way are you going up there—it's too dangerous." He glanced up at the crow's nest again, swearing under his breath. "I'll go. You just...stay right here. Keep out of trouble." He turned and bounded down the stairs, leaving Alannys alone halfway between decks, as he headed for the single most dangerous spot on the whole ship. She knew that, and she knew he was doing it in her stead.

And none of that made her feel any better at all.

♫

Alannys stood there on the steps, racked with indecision, watching Chen weave his way between the sailors down on the main deck. Her eyes followed the narrow, precarious rope ladder up the mast to the crow's nest, where the king still sang to the sky, oblivious to the panic he was causing. She bit her lip. She couldn't bear to see either of them in danger, but both of them were, and there didn't seem to be much of anything she could do about it. Singing, trying to stop a singer—neither were safe pursuits, especially when they were undertaken in the crow's nest of a ship in the kind of weather they were suffering now.

From what she could hear, Chen was right—it *did* sound like Dorramon was summoning a wind. Only...from the way it pushed against her like giant hands from all directions, from the way the big sails puffed in and out as frantic sailors tried to furl them...it was pretty clear he was actually getting more than one wind, and Dorramon wasn't really in control. She couldn't imagine what had driven him up there, but it was plain that the intensity of that emotion, whatever it was, was completely overwhelming what he meant to project in his song. His emotions were divided, his song was divided, and this deadly squall was the result—a sea divided, fiercely battling itself. Against that, what chance did they really have? What could any of them do?

Well, she couldn't speak for any of the others, but there was always something she could do. She ran up the stairs to the stern deck, moving away from the frenetic chaos of the lower decks, preparing herself to sing.

Not to stop the storm, of course. That would only pit her will against Dorramon's, and intensify what was already the worst squall any of them had ever seen. That wouldn't end well for any of them. But she could try her best to help him, sing for things like safety and strength, because it was obvious to her that whatever he had left of both were waning.

So up alone on the stern deck, with the damp, salty wind whipping through her hair, Alannys threw together a few appropriate words and began singing a song of her own, beseeching the Muses to bolster Dorramon and help him gain control over this nightmare he had conjured.

It wasn't the most powerful or effective song she had ever sung; her mind was too scattered, and she was too worried about too many other things...but it *was* working. She could feel the channel opening, the magic beginning to flow, and she sang louder, digging even deeper. With this song, she could help turn this around. It was possible they might survive after all.

No sooner had that thought crossed her mind than she heard a shout; it sounded like Captain Morgain himself. "They're trying to sink my ship! Stop that woman! This singing will be the death of us all!"

To her horror, two crewman bounded up the stairs toward her. She backed away, her song falling into fearful silence, abandoning Dorramon to wage battle against the weather—and himself—on his own. "No, stop...you don't understand. I have to help him!"

This answer did not seem to please the sailors, whose frowns only deepened. "Help him what, lassie? Sink our ship?" one of them sneered. "I don't reckon so. You're coming with us."

"No." Her voice was unexpectedly strong; the sound of it surprised even her. She drew Songstrike; even its defensive blue glow seemed to her to exude not the fear she usually associated with it, but determination. "I am not going anywhere and I advise you not to try to make me. Your king is up there, do you understand? Without help, he will die!"

"And if you sing with him, we're all going to die." To her consternation, the sailors seemed just as stubborn as her, and they both drew cutlasses.

Could she really take on two of these guys, both armed? She was competent with a blade, but she was no expert, and she didn't like these odds. But she wasn't giving up. Dorramon needed her help, and she didn't have time for this.

He didn't have time for this.

She swallowed hard and adjusted her grip on Songstrike. It rubbed her the wrong way, fighting men who were supposed to be servants of the Crown, but she knew she had very little choice at this point. She hesitated, trying to decide which of them to engage first, and how she might end this quickly without killing anyone.

The men advanced on her, chuckling, evidently taking her hesitation for fear. Alannys decided on a charging middle attack on the sailor to her left, and pulled Songstrike back and to her side, leveled and ready to thrust.

But before she could launch her attack, someone was there, right in front of her, facing down the sailors with a wickedly curved blade and a lot less hesitance: Prince Cardoth.

♫

Alannys's attackers looked as surprised as she felt.

"Are you mad, man?" one of them demanded, incredulously. "You can't really mean to help these...these *musicians!*" He spat the word with the same disgust he might have used to utter a curse.

"I certainly don't intend to let you lot skewer either of them, you disrespectful louts. I'm here at their pleasure, after all. If you dispose of them, where does that leave me, and my sister that you've already tried to murder once?"

"This's nothing to do with you," the sailor said, but he sounded uncertain, and both of them were shuffling backwards as they spoke, evidently a good deal less confident taking on Cardoth than Alannys.

"Cardoth?" She didn't sound too terribly confident herself, just then. "What are you doing?"

"Saving your skin, apparently," he said dryly, not looking at her. "Believe me, I don't much fancy it either. But I spent three months trying to kill you and failed...I'm certainly not going to let these thimbleskull sailors succeed." He snorted disdainfully and charged down the stairs after her attackers.

Left on her own once more, Alannys turned her back to the confusion of the rest of the ship, looking out at the vast expanse of churning sea and thundering sky behind them, trying to draw some sort of calm from it for herself. She felt a desperate, urgent need to know what was going on in the crow's nest, but she knew that kind of distraction would only sap the strength of her song, and so she did her best to put it all out of her mind. She held tightly onto Songstrike, drawing courage from its steady blue glow and quiet humming in her mind, and started her song anew.

She never heard the heavy footsteps charging up the stairs behind her. She was concentrating so intensely on the song that she did not realize anything was amiss until something slammed into her like a wrecking ball, sending her sprawling on the deck and Songstrike skittering from her grasp. She lurched halfway to her feet, pushing herself after it, but someone caught her by the arm and hauled her back.

"How dare you raise a blade to my men!" Captain Morgain had grabbed her, apparently, and he sounded beside himself with rage.

She didn't have time for this, not while Songstrike spun toward the edge of the deck. She jerked her arm, trying to pull it loose, but Morgain only held on tighter. He gave her a shake, like her lack of attention infuriated him. "My son is in the brig because of you! How much farther will you go to destroy my ship? What have you done to turn his Highness against us?" He shook her again. "Mindlinks, singing...I've had my fill of magic and I'm putting a stop to it right now!"

Alannys didn't answer him; she didn't even really hear a word he said. Her attention was focused on Songstrike, on watching in a kind of awful slow-motion as the ship took a sudden dip sideways and all of the water on the stern deck washed under the railing, over the side of the ship and into the sea...taking her sword with it. Her sword was gone.

Songstrike...was gone.

♫

Songstrike was gone.

The dreadful refrain seemed to echo through her being like her heartbeat, implacable, unchangeable.

Songstrike was gone. She could feel it growing distant, as its soothing melodies slowly faded from her mind.

Alannys was screaming—howling, like a grievously wounded animal—but no one seemed to hear it but her. It surprised her to find it was only in her head; she couldn't seem to actually make a sound, even when she tried. One thought consumed her entire being: she had to get Songstrike back. She had to get it *back!* She pulled again on her arm, but whatever was holding her didn't seem ready to let go just yet.

A man stomped up the stairs toward her, swarthy and

muscular, a curved blade in one hand and anger radiating from his dark eyes in waves she could almost feel rolling over her. She knew this man...she knew him, but she could not seem to put a name to him. It was as though part of her brain was simply offline. And the worst part was, she couldn't even seem to care much about it—all she knew was that remembering this fellow's name would in no way help her get Songstrike back.

"Morgain," the familiar, nameless man growled, "if you would like to keep your hand attached to your arm, you had better remove it from her immediately."

He did, but he didn't look too happy about it. "Prince Cardoth, your Highness, you don't understand. She—"

She stopped listening. Cardoth, of course. She remembered now. And she had been right; it hadn't helped her get Songstrike back at all. She probably should have thanked him, but she didn't even acknowledge him. As soon as the captain released her, she stumbled over to the railing, on feet that felt numb and useless—much like the rest of her, without Songstrike. Even her brain felt numb and useless. She stood there, at the very spot where she had seen Songstrike go over. Leaning over, she could still see the blue glow under the surface—Songstrike, lighting up the dark, stormy water as it sank.

She didn't think, didn't plan. She just grabbed the railing and swung her leg up over it. Songstrike was down there, so she had to go down there, too. That was all.

Strong arms wrapped around her middle and hauled her back from the railing. "Are you daft?" Cardoth's voice growled right in her ear, sounding almost as angry as when he had shouted at the captain. "There's enough to worry about right now just keeping this ship afloat without having to fish for you in this storm."

"Let me go!" Alannys flailed her arms, kicked her legs, and even bit at any part of Cardoth she could reach. He swore, but hung onto her. They fought as hard now as any time they had fought with swords. "Let me go!"

"What, so you can toss yourself overboard again? Do you think the king will thank me for that?"

"Cardoth, you don't understand! Songstrike, it...it..."

"Yes, your sword is gone." The flat declaration of it dug painfully into her, but Cardoth didn't appear to notice. He managed to pin her arms to her sides. "Swords can be replaced, Alannys, even the best of them."

"Not this one!" she protested hotly, shocked to feel the stinging of tears at the backs of her eyes.

"Right—precious blade of prophecy and all that." He sounded thoughtful, just for a moment. "I don't care. You can get another sword. We can't get another Redeemer. We're all going out here to see what this 'acts of the Redeemer' business is about, and that can't happen unless you are here. I don't know yet what all this is supposed to do or whether there's any truth to any of it or not—and unless we finish this, I never will. So you are by the sun's light staying here, and that's that."

She couldn't make him listen to her, and she couldn't break free. All she could do was stand there helplessly at the railing and howl at the tempestuous sky, watching as Songstrike's familiar blue light slowly faded from sight beneath the dark, choppy waves.

♫

Alannys was disoriented even before she woke up, swirling in a haze of feelings and disjointed impressions that she somehow knew were not her own. She saw herself falling, over and over, from the Spire of Glory, her cloak flapping around her like dark, broken wings. She watched Dorramon sobbing, carrying her limp, lifeless body down an endless flight of cracked stone stairs. And she knew that didn't make any sense; both of those things couldn't happen together, but she didn't have any control over what was happening.

She finally broke free and found herself, sleep-addled and befuddled, sprawled out on the big bed in the great cabin, and so she thought perhaps her confused recollections were of some dream.

But the frenzy of thoughts and memories poured into her mind unabated, and she realized this was no dream. This was Muse's Fever—Dorramon's Muse's Fever, after singing that whopper of a storm.

For just a moment, relief overwhelmed her, and she felt like melting into the bed under her. Dorramon was alive!

Then she realized it *hadn't* been a dream—none of it had. It wasn't one of Sir Athniss's hallucinations. That left her just one possibility: it had all really happened. The crew had turned against her. Songstrike had...Songstrike was at the bottom of the sea. Realizing it was like losing her bladed sidekick all over again, like a blow to the stomach when she wasn't expecting it. The enormity of it washed over her in waves until she wanted to scream in howling grief. It had happened; she had watched Songstrike sink beneath the waves, and done nothing.

She pushed herself upright in the bed, one hand pressed to her forehead—she had a blistering headache. Whether it was from Dorramon's Muse's Fever or from her sudden separation from Songstrike, she couldn't have said, but it was worse than any natural headache she had ever had, nauseating in its intensity. She tried to function past the miserable pounding, tried to look for Dorramon.

He was on the other side of the bed, next to her. Her relief at this discovery was immediately replaced by fear— he was bound and gagged, his ankles lashed together and his wrists tied behind his back with heavy twine. And he was face-down on the soft quilts, as if someone had dumped him there and he hadn't moved since. He was breathing, and that was the only thing about the situation that quelled her rising sense of panic at all. But she didn't see *how* he was breathing, unconscious and unable to move, burning with fever with his face buried in heavy quilts and a gag in his mouth.

Alannys darted a glance into the sitting area, afraid to call attention to herself—it felt like the very air around her crackled with hostility.

She had woken up in the middle of something, that much was clear. She didn't know exactly what just yet, but she could tell it wasn't friendly.

Captain Morgain sat in one of the chairs at the dining room table, across from Prince Cardoth. Her swordbelt with its empty scabbard hung from the back of the prince's chair, mocking her. Chen sprawled out on the sofa facing them, spread out as though he was trying to discourage anyone from sitting next to him. They conversed quietly but intently, and they all had grim scowls on their faces—even Chen.

Definitely not friendly.

She turned back to Dorramon. He still hadn't moved, which wasn't surprising, but it was concerning. "Dorramon..." She said it as softly as she could, hoping not to catch herself any unwanted attention. The mindlink was out of the question—he would never hear her over his Muse's-Fever-fueled visions. She reached out and tentatively jogged his arm; it had exactly as much effect as her words, which was to say, none. Dorramon didn't speak, didn't sit up, didn't even twitch. And he was still burning up.

And they had left him there in all of his heavy clothes —even his boots and cloak! She couldn't imagine how uncomfortable that had to be, with the high fever he was running. And his airflow was obstructed. The lack of consideration it bespoke struck her as ominous—what kind of person treated the king they supposedly served with such utter disregard for his well-being?—but she didn't have time to worry about it just then, not with Dorramon suffering in front of her. She pushed her annoyance with the crew aside and reached for the knot on the back of his head, reminding herself that it was always more important to fix the problem than to cast blame, reciting it like a mantra to keep her simmering anger in check.

She had barely begun to loosen the gag when large, calloused hands suddenly closed around hers, stopping her cold. She looked up into the hard eyes of Captain Morgain; she had been so focused she hadn't even noticed his approach. Again. "You'll be stopping right there, missy. Don't go waking him just yet."

"What?" She blinked at him, completely flummoxed, but he just stared at her, stubbornly refusing to offer any sort of explanation. "I'm not even trying to wake him. Frankly, I don't think I could if I did try. I'm just trying to get this gag off of him—he can't breathe like this. He's going to suffocate!"

"Let him," Morgain said shortly, squeezing her wrists until the bones ground painfully together. "He nearly destroyed my ship, and every man jack on it. He don't need breath, not if he's going to use it to try to kill us."

Alannys jerked her hands back from him and rubbed her wrists, running his words through her memory and considering what she should do now. "This is the king's ship," she said carefully, each word distinct and precise. "It is deeply concerning to hear you say otherwise. And this other talk...that sounds downright treasonous. I didn't have you pegged as a traitor, Morgain, not after your proud speech about your generations of noble service."

Morgain's face darkened. She could see Chen over his shoulder, watching her with wide eyes, shaking his head in a slight warning gesture no one else was meant to see. But it was too late—the captain was already speaking, sounding as though he was barely keeping his own temper in check. "The Crown owns this ship, that's true enough. But any ship has only one captain, and for this ship, that's me. And a captain's first duty is the well-being of his ship and his crew. That man just threatened both, and I don't care if he's a king or a scullery maid, I can't overlook that. And I'll take on anyone who wants to stand against me on that point. *Anyone.*"

♬

They all stood there for a beat of silence in the great cabin, shocked at Captain Morgain's outright treason.

"Now, now." Chen placed a hand on Morgain's shoulder, suddenly a whole lot closer behind the captain than he had been a moment before. "I don't think there's any need for threats, or for accusations of treason. We're all friends here. Alannys just woke up. Maybe we should give her a chance to find her bearings before we start taking sides against her."

"You have to let me help him," Alannys said brokenly. "How can he breathe, with that awful gag? If I could just sing for him...he isn't going to wake up for days if I don't."

"This is insane," the captain muttered. "Why are we even listening to this?"

"I think she's right," Chen said. "It wouldn't hurt to get that gag off of him, at the least. No singing, though — it's too dangerous. He summoned a storm — he isn't going to be waking up for quite a while. Weather is very dangerous to deal with, and very draining. Or at least, that's what Alannys has told me before."

"Whatever you say." Morgain shrugged off Chen's hand and stomped back to the table like the whole thing disgusted him.

Alannys supposed she could forgive him for that. She was feeling pretty queasy herself just then.

Prince Cardoth didn't even acknowledge Chen, except to wave a disinterested hand in their direction. Alannys decided that was as close to a positive response as she was likely to get, and went back to work on the knot. Chen stood there watching, either to prevent the others from interfering again, or to make sure she didn't do anything crazy, like sing. She really couldn't tell which, and she wasn't sure, at this point, that she wanted to guess.

Finally she got the gag unfastened, and Chen helped her roll Dorramon over and pull off his velvet cloak. "So," she said under her breath, "who put you in charge?"

Chen laughed, but it was uncomfortable. "Nobody,

really. I sure don't feel like I'm in charge. It's more like...they see me as an objective outsider."

"Objective?" Her single word came out more like a snort.

"I should think you would be glad of that, right now," Chen sniffed. "I shouldn't need to tell you that your situation isn't very good. A friendly face would be welcome—I would think."

"That isn't what I meant. Don't they know you can sing?"

"Hush your mouth!" Chen darted a look over his shoulder to make sure the others weren't paying attention. "Of course they don't. And if they find out, your friend on the inside will be gone, so if I were you, I wouldn't go around announcing it."

"I see." She loosened Dorramon's shirt around him, stalling for time while she thought it over. "Let me ask you this, Chen...Dorramon is the king. And you say you are my friend, and his. Why is this even happening?"

Chen took a step back. "Muses, Alannys, that stings. Maybe turn off that overprotective instinct of yours for a minute, and I think it will make more sense to you. What do you think happened here today?"

She averted her gaze. "Look, I'm not excusing his bad judgment in this instance—"

"Bad judgment? Bad *judgment*? I wonder if we're even talking about the same thing here—this goes way beyond bad judgment. There's no rational explanation for what he did. You've got to see that."

"No, there is." She didn't like the way Chen eyed her when she said that, like maybe he was sizing up her sanity, but she couldn't stand back and let them demonize Dorramon that way. "I honestly believe he was trying to help."

"You said that before, too. It isn't making any more sense now, Alannys. I still think you're blinded by your own feelings. No part of that was helpful."

"I didn't say it was. I said it was supposed to be."

She had piqued his interest now. He folded his arms and frowned at her. "All right, I'll bite. How exactly did he imagine that conjuring up a killer squall would help us?"

She shook her head. Cardoth and Morgain were listening attentively now, not even bothering to pretend they couldn't hear. She tried to choose her words carefully, aware of the damage she could do if this came out wrong. "Your assumptions are wrong, don't you see? You are assuming that Dorramon meant to summon a storm. You're also assuming that he meant to help all of you."

"Whoa, whoa, whoa," Chen said, waving his hands in the air in front of him. "What is that supposed to mean? That he meant to harm us?"

"That's pretty much what he did," Morgain muttered sourly, swigging something from the tankard in front of him.

Alannys shot a mean-spirited glare at the oblivious captain. She knew his son's betrayal had been a blow to him, but still...it was becoming very hard to like the man anymore. "Of course that wasn't his intent. Don't be stupid. Why would he try to sink a ship with himself on it? It doesn't make sense."

"Men do many things that don't make sense, when they snap," Cardoth said matter-of-factly. "What's your point?"

"He's not insane, if that's what you're implying," Alannys said sharply. "Just...conflicted. And I think that's the root of the whole problem, really. Don't you get it? He was trying to help me."

She looked to Chen, hoping to see some understanding on his face, some sign that he had put the pieces together, but he just frowned at her, gnawing on the ball of his thumb and saying nothing.

"That's the best you've got?" Cardoth demanded. "He was trying to help you? By killing us all?"

"Stop doing that!" Alannys shook her head, trying to regain her composure, aware that she wasn't going to convince anyone of anything by shouting at them. "You're still assuming the result he got was the result he intended. With music, it doesn't always work like that."

"She's right," Chen said suddenly. He sounded surprised, but she didn't know if that meant he had figured anything out or not. "I've...I've seen it happen. It's all about intent."

"This is a waste of time," Morgain said. "Intent, indeed. That just means that he meant for this to happen. You're talking in circles."

"Damn it, it's not that simple!" There she went again, forgetting her resolution not to yell at these people. "It is all about intent—about what you truly want, not what you say you want or what you pretend you want or what is acceptable to others. And I'm telling you that what Dorramon truly wanted, what he's wanted ever since we boarded this ship, if not before, is to help me. Here's the question, though, how could he do that?"

"Get us there faster," Captain Morgain said immediately. "That's all he's been asking for since we set sail. Better time, faster sailing. That's why he sang for wind, I suppose. Nothing else would make a difference."

"Being on this ship *has* been hard on both of you," Chen said slowly. She could sense the care he was taking with his words, the deliberate effort to leave any mention of Sir Athniss out of what he was trying to say. "But would he really be helping you by getting you there faster, knowing what's going to be there waiting for you?"

"That's it, that's it exactly," Alannys said, holding hand out in his direction, trying to encourage everyone in the room to pay attention. "That's what I've been trying to say. I think that is exactly the problem. The...things that will happen at Mount Mouseion are difficult and dangerous, and I think on one hand Dorramon must feel like I would be better off not going there at all. But on the other hand it can't be avoided; there's too much at stake. There can be no lasting peace in Ravanmark until the acts are performed, and the Lord's Retainers will certainly never give up until then."

"So he was torn," Prince Cardoth said shortly. "Always so many words with you, to say things that are so simple. He knew we needed to keep pushing forward—and quickly—but he also wanted to go back."

"And he sang," Chen said, "in that state, and without enough sleep...he never had a chance of controlling it."

Alannys nodded at both of them. "Just so. He ended up calling up winds in opposing directions...it all turned into a real corker of a storm. And it's no surprise, when you look at what he's been feeling."

"Why are you all nodding?" Morgain demanded, glaring around at each of them in turn. "You all look pretty satisfied, like you've sorted some great mystery. But it don't change anything!"

"It changes everything!" Alannys protested hotly. "You've all been holed up in here trying to sit in judgment of a king, and you claim it's all right because he acted with malicious intent. But I've just shown you he didn't. Now let me sing for him!"

Morgain shoved his chair back from the table, sending it flipping over backwards behind him, and stood up, red-faced, leveling one big, meaty finger at her. "None o' that changes what he did to my ship! I'll have no one singing here—he can get better by himself or not at all!"

Prince Cardoth cut him off, taking him by the arm. His manner was casual, but the tendons standing out white against his hand made her think that grip must have been like iron. "Perhaps you should come out on the deck with me, Captain."

"The deck?" Morgain sounded confused, but he was still staring daggers into Alannys. "What for?"

"I think it's probably time you make an announcement," Cardoth said. "You need to tell your crew that the king lives and that he is recovering."

"What? But—"

"You also need to tell them that this was just a passing illness, and there's nothing more to worry about, and he will be awake soon."

"Soon? But she just said—"

Prince Cardoth let go of the captain, and folded his arms. "What do you care about more, the truth, or stopping a riot?"

For a moment longer Morgain glared at him, then he sighed and waved a hand. "'Spose so. Ain't much to be accomplished here, seems like."

Cardoth pulled the captain toward the door, turning back to toss a nod in Alannys's direction. "Do what you can for the king, my Lady. We shall hope to hear of his speedy recovery." He dropped a discreet wink at her.

Alannys watched the two men leave the room, trying to hide the realization that was belatedly dawning on her —Cardoth was manufacturing excuses, deliberately taking Morgain away just to give her a chance to sing. He still cared, on some level, for her and for Dorramon.

At least, she hoped he did.

♫

Chen watched Alannys watching the door, with a frown that probably matched the one she figured she was wearing right then. She gestured weakly at the door. "Why didn't you go with them? You must realize I'm about to disobey Captain Morgain's direct order to abandon Dorramon."

Chen shook his head. "I don't have any interest in punishing him, Alannys. That isn't why I was here."

"Then why didn't you stand up for him?" Anger flared in her chest and then fizzled out—she was too tired to sustain it and her words came out sounding merely annoyed. "They are taking this way too far. Why didn't you stop them?"

His gaze slid from hers and he cast about for

something else to look at. "You aren't going to like this, but I don't think they're wrong. Not completely, anyway. They may have misunderstood what he did and why, but there's no question he endangered us all."

"Chen! Dorramon would never hurt us, any of us. You know that as well as I do—how can you throw him under the bus like this?"

"How can I...what?"

"Never mind. My point is that he's been a friend to you, Chen. And so have I." She glared at him, her eyes hard and accusing. "How can you turn on us like this?"

"Turn on—Alannys, what do you want me to do? We need someone on your side who can talk to both sides, someone that they think is at least a little bit objective. Why do you think I hid my Talent from them?"

"To cozy up to the enemy," she shot back, "so that you wouldn't get treated the way we did."

"No." Chen sighed and rolled his eyes. "No, of course not. If they know I can sing, they're going to assume I'm biased. The king needs a friend on the inside, remember?"

"Well, why can't that be me?"

Chen tried to squelch a laugh, and ended up snorting. "Are you joking? If anybody had any doubts about your biases, you showed them off for everybody when you took on the whole room. You're not capable of a measured approach, not where he's concerned."

She looked away, turning to Dorramon and stroking his damp hair back from his face.

"Just so." Chen sighed. "I don't enjoy this, Alannys, whatever you may think. But it's obvious to me that neither of you have been yourselves since...well, since Duxol. And it's only getting worse. You must see that."

She stared at him, stricken.

"I told you before I thought he had almost hit his limit. It's pretty clear now that he has. What I didn't tell you is that I think you're getting awfully close to yours as well." He glanced at Dorramon's unconscious form on the bed and quickly looked away, his gaze barely touching her before landing on the door. He turned in that direction, raking his hands through his hair. "I think you should do everything you can for him. And when he wakes up, I don't think you should tell those two, or anybody else. I think you should talk all of this over with him, and stay here. He shouldn't set foot out of this room, and neither should you. Because he is a danger to us all, and he isn't the only one.

"You are, too."

♫

Alannys sat stone still, the heavy silence ringing in her ears, staring numbly at the door Chen had just closed behind himself. She had dearly wanted to argue with him, wanted with every fiber of her being to hotly insist that neither she nor Dorramon presented any danger to anyone —they were the *good* guys, after all—but she couldn't do it. It galled her to admit it, even to herself, but the fact was that Chen had a point. Dorramon hadn't been himself for days, and to be perfectly honest, neither had she. Athniss wasn't likely to start taking it easy on them, and none of the problems they faced were going to suddenly get simpler. Both of them were only likely to become more irrational. Much as she hated it, the truth was that either of them could become a threat to the people around them, just as Dorramon had a few hours ago.

And there didn't seem to be a damn thing she could do about it.

She shook her head, doing her best to clear that unpleasant train of thought. Right now the uncertain future wasn't her problem—her problem was the king, lying unconscious in the same position she and Chen had left him earlier, burning with fever. Removing the heavy velvet cloak and the gag had been a help, of course, but it wasn't a cure. Nothing was a cure for Muse's Fever, nothing could really hasten its departure. Muse's tea helped, but she had neither the recipe nor the ingredients.

There was nothing she could do.

Well, nothing *except...*

She pulled a chair up next to the bedside and settled herself into it, taking his hand in hers, pushing aside the rush of unrestrained thoughts and impressions from the mindlink, pushing aside her own pounding headache, and began to sing.

She woke up still in the chair, leaned over with her face down on the mattress, both of her arms reached out over her head to grip Dorramon's hand. She had no idea how long she had sung, or how long she had slept after. The first thing she realized, before she even opened her eyes, was that the mindlink was no longer flooding her brain like a tidal wave. The second thing she realized was that her head was still pounding like a jackhammer.

She dragged her aching head off the bed, opened her gritty eyes, and found that Dorramon was awake. And he was watching her.

"I—I'm sorry," she said, in a voice that sounded about like her eyes felt. "How long have I been out?"

"I haven't the faintest idea," Dorramon said, grinning at her. His smile was warm and there was a twinkle in his blue eyes that she hadn't seen for quite a while, and it was only now, seeing it again, that she realized how very much she had missed it. "It was so nice seeing you sleep peacefully for once, I've just been sitting here enjoying it."

She understood the sentiment; it *was* unusual, for either of them—in fast she was rather inclined to just sit and enjoy it some more herself. But that wasn't practical. A world waited on the other side of the cabin door, and it was growing less friendly by the minute. "I'm glad to see you are well," she hedged, unsure how to broach everything that was on her mind.

Dorramon frowned. Inwardly she flinched; she should have expected that. Nothing got past him—no lie, no half-truth, and apparently not even minor dodges. He always seemed to know if there was something she was trying not to say. "Alannys, you may as well be straight with me. I don't remember everything, but I remember enough. How bad is it?"

"Bad." She couldn't look at his face. "I'm afraid they don't trust us...either of us...at this point."

"Who?" Strain tightened his voice; he sounded the way a clenched fist looks. "The crew? Captain Morgain?"

"Everyone." Now that she was paying attention, she didn't sound so good, either. "I think Morgain wants us locked up, or worse. Cardoth was here...he already had his issues with us, but now...even Chen was with them. He isn't as rabid as the others, but even he...even he..." She shook her head and swallowed hard. "I tried to explain what happened, but most of them still really seem to believe that you set out intending to sink this ship."

Dorramon scrubbed at his face with the heels of his hands. "I'm sorry, Alannys. I just...I just wasn't thinking clearly, I suppose."

"You don't need to apologize." She sat back in the chair, sighing. "I don't mind admitting, though, I have no idea what we are going to do now."

"It can't be that bad," Dorramon said. She couldn't tell, from his tone, whether he was trying to convince her or himself. "I had...some trouble earlier, that's true. I wasn't myself. I can't deny that. But they can't think...they can't honestly believe..."

The door to the great cabin flew open before he could finish, slamming against the wall with a loud crack that cut him off completely. Both of them stared in startled silence as Prince Cardoth swept into the room, with Captain Morgain close behind him. "See, see?" Morgain said, pointing toward them with a grizzled hand. "I told you this is how you'd find things. A few days if nothing was done, that's what she said, right in this room, and we all heard her. And now here he is bright-eyed and bushy-tailed after just a few hours. She's been singing, it's plain. I'm captain of this ship, and if that woman can't follow my orders I can have *her* put in the brig!" His voice broke oddly; it sounded almost like a sob.

Prince Cardoth glowered ominously, a dark expression that seemed to cast a dour pall across the entire room. "Calm yourself, Captain. I know your feelings upon this matter, but hasty judgments are no help to any of us. Lady Alannys, did you choose to disobey Captain Morgain, and sing on board this vessel?"

She struggled to hold her chin high under the weight of his evident disapproval. Cardoth had no right to judge her, but it was difficult not to feel like a misbehaving child under that chastising tone, even though she was sure he had covertly schemed to allow her to do what she had done. "I did."

"Then surely you won't mind if I ask you why?"

"Because Lady Alannys does not answer to Captain Morgain." Dorramon's words were short and clipped, each one conveying uncommonly well the irritation of the man who spoke them. "She is not obligated to follow his instructions, or yours."

Prince Cardoth's jaw hardened. "I don't know how much you understand about the current situation—"

"I understand next to nothing about the current situation. And yet I seem to understand the one thing you all are dangerously close to forgetting: whatever has happened, whatever I may or may not have done, I am still the King of Ravanmark. The lack of respect I'm sensing in these dealings is astonishing."

An uneasy silence fell over the room like a shadow, weighing on each of them as they considered the threat implicit in Dorramon's words. Captain Morgain squirmed, as if he might have liked to simply melt into the wood paneling on the wall behind him. Even Prince Cardoth had the good grace to look uncomfortable. He cleared his throat loudly before he spoke, turning back to the captain with something that looked an awful lot like relief. "I think you should go find Chen and bring him here.

Honestly, he seems to be the only one of us able to keep a level head about all of this, and I think we could really use that right about now."

"Amen," Alannys muttered unpleasantly under her breath, but when Cardoth turned to shoot a questioning glance in her direction, she only smiled.

♫

The moment Morgain disappeared, Cardoth charged farther into the great cabin, fists balled, talking fast. "You can't speak freely in front of them. You *can't*. I understand your concerns, your Highness, and I understand the necessity of proper deference. But I want to encourage you to change the way you're thinking, and change it fast. What happened today was awful, and it was unprecedented, and something is going to have to be done. Some recognition of this is going to have to take place, if this ship is going to keep sailing."

"Recognition," Alannys echoed. "Is that your euphemism for the house arrest you all tried to put us under earlier?"

She had hoped that calling him out directly might embarrass him into a less confrontational attitude, but he faced her defiantly, tipping a barely respectful nod in her direction. "Call it whatever you like," he said. "But a threat was made apparent today, and it imperils every person on this ship. If some action is not taken to contain that threat, we are going to have a mutiny on our hands. And regardless of your royal status or mine, we are outnumbered here. This is fact."

"Mutiny," Dorramon said softly. His gaze was distant, as though he was looking as things the rest of them couldn't see — Alannys could practically see the thoughts swirling in his head, and they were dark. "Am I really perceived that badly? I don't clearly remember everything that happened this morning. Was it really that bad?"

"Your Majesty, it was worse." The honest, earnest voice coming from the door was not Cardoth's; Alannys turned in time to see Chen walk into the room, behind Captain Morgain. "Prince Cardoth is too tight-lipped to tell you the truth; Alannys is too kind. But it was bad, very bad."

"It was," Alannys interjected, trying to forestall any recounting of the details. She didn't know all of those details herself, but she couldn't imagine that hearing them would help Dorramon at all. "But let me just ask you straight out, Chen—do you think we should be incarcerated?"

"Wait, we?" Dorramon said. "Why we? You didn't do anything."

Alannys shook her head, not quite looking him in the eye. "I sang to help you. You were losing it up there, Dorramon, so I sang...in front of everyone. Music is the threat they perceive here, and we both used it. And they all know that."

"I see." Dorramon's tone was grave, and she got the impression that for him, this changed everything. He turned to Chen, suddenly seeming interested in an exchange that hadn't concerned him a moment before. "In that case, Chen, what *do* you think?"

Chen hesitated, looking at Alannys with an expression that begged for forgiveness. "I think...yes. You two need to be restrained, and not just as a show to reassure the crew. I think there really is a danger here. We were lucky this time. Next time we might not be."

"I...I see." Dorramon was struggling to hide his surprise, but he couldn't quite conceal the shock in his words. "Look, what happened earlier was out of line. I know that. I accept that. It isn't going to happen again. Isn't the vow of a king enough for you?"

"I'm sorry." Chen was shaking his head, and Alannys finally understood how serious he was, how serious all of them were about this. "I know you mean well, I do. But...well, I've told the others about some of the things going on right now."

"You ratted us out?" Alannys hadn't even meant to

speak, but the angry words couldn't be held back. "Can I trust you with anything anymore?"

"Hold on, I think they needed to know." Chen held up his hands defensively. "Neither of you are sleeping properly, you're trapped here, and you're both being tortured inside your own heads. It's no wonder, really, that something like this happened. What's surprising is that either of you would think you can guarantee this or something like it won't happen again. And we can't have anything like this happen again. We just can't. Our sails are shredded; the crew is working on that right now. Sailors were injured. Tassin was killed."

"Tassin...killed?" Alannys gasped, her anger abruptly deflating. This was the first she had heard of that!

Chen nodded, not quite looking at any of them. "In all the pitching around, it seems he hit his head, hard enough to break his neck."

Alannys darted a glance at Captain Morgain. His face was unnaturally placid, almost lifeless, except for his bloodshot eyes that burned like coals. His antagonistic, hateful attitude made sense to her now, and she couldn't summon any anger for him.

Dorramon buried his face in his hands. "I killed him."

"No," Chen said at once. "No one is saying that. But we can't risk anything like this happening again."

"You're right," Alannys sighed. "What did you have in mind? You have to know that just trapping us in here won't stop us from causing destruction, not if one of us decides to sing."

"No." Chen turned away, rubbing at his temples; Alannys couldn't help but think he found this conversation as grim and unsettling as she did. Even in the worst of his mother hen days, he had never had to do anything like this. "Of course you're right; locking you up isn't enough. We have to be sure you can't sing. I'd thought...I had thought about drugging you." He turned back around, and his eyes in that moment were as bleak as she had ever seen them. However much she hated hearing this—and she hated it a lot—it was plain that he hated saying it even more. "Laudanum, or the like, so you sleep. You can't sing if you're sleeping."

"No." Alannys spoke before she formed any conscious intention of doing so. The visceral horror boiling in her stomach poured out in her tone; she pressed herself into the back of her chair as though she could hide in it, and her hands balled into white-knuckled fists. "Not that. You're throwing us on Athniss's mercy and abandoning us there. Force us to sleep, and not *let* us wake up? That's as close to hell as anything I can imagine, Chen. You can't do that to us. I'll jump ship first. Anything but that."

"She's right," Dorramon said. His frown looked merely concerned, but through the mindlink she could feel some of his terror—the same terror the idea inspired in her. "It's hard enough to fight him off when you're awake. Asleep, we have almost no defense at all."

"It's the mindlink that's the problem," Alannys said. "If we had some way to shut it down, we could sleep forever with no problem. But I only know of one drug that does that, and I don't have any."

"And what drug is that?" Cardoth inquired, with a sudden, bright interest that didn't feel entirely healthy to her.

"Belladonna," she said sourly, remembering her involuntary experience with it. It took her a moment to recognize the blankness in the expressions of everyone else in the room with her. "Oh, right—sorry. Deadly nightshade."

"Deadly nightshade stops the mindlink?" Chen sounded surprised. "I never knew that."

"I doubt it's something that would be used very often," Alannys said, "given how rare mindlinks are. But it's true; you can't use the mindlink at all until it starts to wear off. And even then, it gives you an excruciating headache. It's only safe and painless to use the mindlink again after it completely wears off. And that takes a long time."

"I can't say I much care for the excruciating headache part," Dorramon said, "but it does sound like it would make it safe for us to sleep. Too bad we don't have any onboard."

Alannys couldn't help but notice that he didn't actually sound very regretful at all.

"Actually," Cardoth said, with a smile that gave her the shivers, "I believe I may be able to help with that."

He turned and swept out of the room without another word, leaving the rest of them glancing nervously around at each other.

"Just out of curiosity," Chen said, sounding anything but curious, "where did you run into deadly nightshade before? When you found out it could keep you from using the mindlink?"

"Cardoth." She wanted the single word to be flat, devoid of any emotion at all, but it came out sharp and bitter, like she had a mouthful of old vinegar when she said it. "He drugged me with it the night he kidnapped me from the Great Palace. It's why I wasn't able to defend myself; I couldn't even tell Dorramon what was happening."

Dorramon swore under his breath. Nobody else seemed to have anything to add.

Not even two minutes later, Cardoth strode back into the cabin. He carried a corked glass vial, nearly full of an inky liquid. Something about the way it sloshed in the vial made Alannys want to toss the whole thing overboard, though she supposed it was possible she was biased. "There should be enough deadly nightshade here to keep both of you asleep for the rest of the voyage. It's from the berries, so it doesn't taste too bad, but I would still recommend taking it in wine or something similar. I think you'll find the alcohol aids in the effect."

Dorramon's glare could have cut stone. "If you don't mind my asking, why exactly did you bring that onboard?"

Cardoth chuckled. "Nothing like what you're imagining, I assure you. We were packing to leave Ravanmark, after all. Clearly I had this in my possession at the palace."

"Clearly," Alannys grumbled. "But why did you think you needed it here? Why not just leave it behind?"

"You seem to forget that I didn't plan on coming here." Prince Cardoth's smile didn't fool anyone; neither did his excuse. "I thought at the time I was going home. Deadly nightshade can be tricky to obtain, and costly. So naturally I brought it with me. It seems to me that you should be thanking me. It sounds like the alternative is...less than pleasant."

"That's true." Dorramon sounded as begrudging as Alannys felt. "I suppose it is well for us that you had this after all." Alannys watched the dark liquid in the vial, and she couldn't help but think that Dorramon didn't sound like he felt very thankful at all.

But then again, neither did she.

♫

Dorramon and Alannys sat facing each other across the dining table in the great cabin, grimly watching as Prince Cardoth counted drops of inky juice into two goblets of wine. Everyone else had left; the time was near at hand, and when it came to it, nobody wanted to be there when it happened.

Except Cardoth.

"Dosing this stuff can be tricky," he said conversationally. "You have to consider a person's size, of course, but when you mix it with wine there's also alcohol tolerance to consider. It amplifies the deadly nightshade, so too much of either is dangerous. And some people just have a bad reaction to it no matter how little you give them; any amount could be fatal."

"So you could have killed me that night." Alannys imagined him out behind the Singari camp, dripping poison into her drink just as he was right now, and she wondered if anyone else in the room was as creeped out by this conversation as she was.

"For all you know, I could be killing you now." Cardoth stepped back from the table and tossed her an insouciant smile, corking the vial. "I guess you won't really know until you wake up. *If* you wake up."

Dorramon frowned at the goblets, then at Prince Cardoth. "Remind me again why we are trusting you."

Cardoth's grin widened.

"At the moment," Alannys said, "it would appear we have little choice. Besides, he's saved us both before."

"He also spent three months trying to kill you."

"Ancient history," Prince Cardoth said helpfully.

Dorramon glanced at him sidelong, and started drumming his fingers on the tabletop. "He also abducted you, and assisted in an attempt to steal the throne of Ravanmark."

"Water under the bridge," Cardoth said. "If it makes you feel any better, you have very little to worry about. I have more experience in administering deadly nightshade than probably anyone else on the planet. I very rarely make mistakes."

"Somehow, that fails to reassure me at all." Dorramon sighed heavily. "How much time do we have after we drink this?"

Alannys cast her mind back, trying to recall the details of an experience that was still quite hazy in her memory. "It's pretty quick, but not immediate. You won't pass out on the table, if that's what you're worried about. You'll have plenty of time to get to bed and make yourself comfortable. But...I'm afraid it isn't going to be pleasant. I got really loopy after I drank that. I couldn't really walk or even stand...I guess you remember. Nothing seemed to make much sense...and I saw, heard, even felt things that weren't there." She shook her head, trying to shake away the memories. She could still feel those sensations, and they were still unpleasant, even now.

"And yet you still figured out who I was, even in that state," Cardoth mused. "It's remarkable."

"It was luck," she said flatly. "One of those awful hallucinations—which were terrifying, by the way, I want to sincerely thank you for them—happened to highlight some clues. I could not have figured my way out of a paper bag right then." She turned back to Dorramon. "I'm serious. There's really no telling what might happen...what we might think is happening."

Dorramon sighed and shook his head. "This all sounds riskier the more I hear about it. I hate that it's even necessary."

"*Is* it necessary?" Alannys said quietly, staring into her goblet of wine and thinking morbid thoughts about it that she could only imagine must have matched the ones it harbored about her. "I mean, Dorramon is right. This is an awfully big risk to take with the king. Maybe it's an unacceptably big risk."

"Alannys..." Cardoth's tone held a warning.

She chose to ignore it. "Hear me out," she said, pressing a hand to her forehead. How long was this miserable headache going to last? "Dorramon is a king, Cardoth. He can't just be drugged up and put to sleep like a common criminal, especially when he might not wake up. Would *you* submit to that?"

Cardoth frowned at her. "Now see here, I'm not the problem here. I—"

"Don't listen to her," Dorramon interrupted, waving their argument aside. "She isn't thinking clearly. You really don't need to do this to her; she hasn't done anything to anybody. You can tell the crew whatever you need to, and just let her stay in the great cabin until we arrive. There's no need to subject her to this."

Cardoth snorted. "Look at you two, throwing yourselves in front of each other like a pair of star-crossed teenagers. It's sickening. You both already know the answer to his. One person has already died—who can say who among us would be next? And you, Alannys...you certainly seemed broken up earlier. How many more priceless relics can you stand to lose?"

The words cut into her, sending fingers of pain stabbing deep into her middle. She flinched, but said nothing. What was there to say? She missed Songstrike like she would miss part of her own body, but she still wasn't convinced that justified risking Dorramon's life.

"Wait a minute," Dorramon said, suddenly sitting up straight in his chair, his eyes locked on her face. "What is he talking about? Cardoth, what are you talking about?"

"She didn't tell you?" Cardoth frowned, looking between them. "In all the chaos above deck during the storm, her sword washed overboard. She nearly went after it herself—*would* have gone after it if I hadn't held her back. Literally, I had to hold her back from the railing. I don't think I've ever seen her that upset before. I can't believe she didn't tell you."

She could feel their eyes on her, feel the pressure of their combined gazes like a physical force, but she stared resolutely at the table. It was too late now, but she wished Cardoth had never brought that up, had never told Dorramon what had happened. What good could it do now? All this would accomplish was upsetting Dorramon, and aggravating a grievous wound in her soul that hadn't even begun to heal.

"Alannys?" Dorramon's voice brushed against her, soft and gentle, overflowing with sadness, impossible to ignore. "Look at me."

Completely against the screaming protest of her better judgment, she did. She didn't really have any choice, not against that tone.

"Is that true? Is Songstrike...gone?"

The words dredged up the memory, unwelcome but sharp and pristine. She could *see* it there in front of her for a single, horrible moment—Songstrike's familiar blue glow sinking inexorably beneath the water, fading from her sight.

She swallowed a sudden lump in her throat, conscientiously keeping her eyes away from the empty scabbard. "It is."

He didn't say a word, and his eyes never left hers. But his entire face changed...his expression shifted to one of such pain, such abject misery, she wasn't sure if she could bear to continue looking at it. In that one moment she knew that, contrary to how it had felt all day, she was not the only person who would grieve Songstrike's loss. She wanted to reach out to him, to say something, anything, to make things better, but she couldn't. There *was* no way to make it better.

Dorramon reached out and snatched the goblet closest to him from the table, throwing his head back and draining it in one long drink.

♫

Alannys stared at Dorramon wide-eyed, completely pole-axed. "Dorramon..."

He thumped his empty goblet back down. "I never should have hesitated. If I wake up, Cardoth, bring me more. Keep me asleep until we arrive, no matter what. There's been too much death, too much loss. I won't be the cause of any more."

Cardoth nodded solemnly, his dark eyes inscrutable.

"It isn't your fault," Alannys said. "Nobody blames you."

"*I* blame me." Dorramon looked at her levelly, not shrinking from his negative self-assessment. "I'm sorry. I have to talk to Captain Morgain as well, but it looks like that will have to wait—I'm too much of a danger to stay awake right now. I only meant to help you, Alannys, and instead I cost you something absolutely irreplaceable. I hope you can forgive me."

"Dorramon—"

"Not now," he cut her off. "Too soon. Take your time.

Think about it. But I hope, eventually, you'll be able to forgive me."

He pushed himself away from the table before she could reply, stumbled to his feet with a lurch that sent his empty goblet skittering across the table.

"Steady there," Cardoth said, catching him by the arm. He held the wobbling king upright, wearing a frown Alannys didn't much like the look of. "That was fast...much faster than I expected. Do you suppose he's sensitive to it?"

"You're the expert here." She scrambled to her feet and took Dorramon's other arm. "You tell me. Is he going to be all right?"

"I think so." The words brimmed with confidence that was probably false, judging by his deep frown. "Just let me think...oh...he hasn't eaten in nearly forever, has he?"

"Neither of us have." She tried to stay calm, but anger boiled into her voice. "You know that."

"I do, but...I didn't exactly consider it."

"What? You're the self-professed expert and you didn't take into consideration an *empty stomach?"*

"Alannys…"

"Even I know alcohol hits you faster on an empty stomach! Are you *trying* to kill him?"

"If I am, I'm trying to kill you both!" he shouted. "So how about you help me get him into bed? Because you're next. If you have anything you need to do before your long sleep, you had better do it now, because you aren't going to have as much time as we thought."

Alannys shivered; Cardoth's reference to a long sleep brought with it associations she didn't like but couldn't escape. Indeed it *would* be a long sleep, and quite possibly her last. "Just one thing." The calm sound of her own voice surprised her. She leaned over Dorramon, and pushed his hair back from his face. "I don't need to forgive you. It wasn't your fault. There's nothing to forgive. The only irreplaceable thing in my life is you." She kissed him on the forehead.

"Of course," Dorramon said. He sounded completely composed, but his eyes wandered; he probably hadn't even heard her. She wondered what he was seeing, whether he would even remember this when they woke up. It didn't matter; she couldn't go to sleep without telling him.

The door behind her burst open, and Tralice charged into the room, looking around frantically. "Am I too late? Tell me she isn't asleep yet!"

"Not yet," Prince Cardoth said, sounding considerably less ruffled than Alannys felt. "But if you have something to say, you'd better hurry. She isn't going to last much longer."

Any other time, Alannys would have resented being talked about as though she wasn't even in the room. Right now, though, she really was feeling off, and she didn't have the energy for anger. She just looked at Tralice expectantly, wondering what she was there for. Was there some rule she was breaking, was Tralice here to chastise her for taking belladonna, to tell her it wasn't proper?

Possibly, considering the expression on her face.

"Where is Chen?" Cardoth asked, frowning. Alannys couldn't imagine what he was talking about, and it took her a long moment to realize he wasn't actually talking to her. "I thought he said he was coming, too."

"Chen?" Tralice managed to pack an awful lot of disbelief and outrage into the single word. "I'm sorry, but the great cabin is no place for Singari. The royal ship is no place for Singari—he's like a fish out of water here, haven't you noticed? More class boundaries that shouldn't have been crossed, right there. I don't know how Lady Alannys talks to him, let alone travels with him."

Alannys heard the words, and understood the words, but she was having trouble focusing on them. She rubbed at her temples and tried to concentrate—something important was bubbling around in the soup her mind had turned into, and if she didn't catch it now, it would disappear forever.

I don't know how she talks to him, Tralice had said.

He's seen you interact with so many people...the arch-prince, the Captain of the Guard, even that nice Singari fellow... Princess Varilyn's words rang in her mind as well.

Alannys frowned, trying to think. That was unusual, wasn't it, for someone to have friends in so many classes, to move so freely among those classes? Her brain was addled just then, but she couldn't think of anyone like that. Tralice thought it was bad. Princess Varilyn didn't.

What did Alannys think?

All of that must not have taken as long to go through her mind as it felt like, because Tralice was just turning her direction, preparing to speak.

"Wait," Alannys said, heading her off. "I know spending this voyage baked on belladonna is not in keeping with my position. But I'm doing it anyway, because I think it's important. I'm doing it for everyone on this ship, so that I don't endanger a single life—noble, common, or Singari. I'm sorry if you don't agree, but you won't talk me out of it."

Tralice looked at her a bit sheepishly. "Is that why you think I'm here? I'm sorry—I've come to tell you something else." She took a deep breath. "I've thought it all over...everything you said, and everything his Highness said...and I've decided that you're right. Both of you. When you wake up, my Lady, I'll try not to harp on you so much. I promise."

Alannys sighed with relief. "That's wonderful, Tralice, but is that all?"

For the tiniest fraction of a second, Tralice looked alarmed. "I'm sorry, my Lady, I don't know what you could mean."

"Come on," Alannys said. "Yes, you do. You're so different lately, so serious. Aren't you going to tell me what's really going on with you?"

Tralice just smiled blankly at her.

"All right," Alannys muttered, "maybe when I wake up. *If* I wake up."

"What?" Tralice looked seriously alarmed by that, and Alannys wondered fleetingly what kind of sugar-coated story had been handed out to the rest of the ship.

"Sorry," Cardoth said suddenly, taking Tralice's arm and pulling her toward the door. "I really must ask you to leave now."

Tralice protested, but she was already nearly out the door. Alannys turned away and frowned, watching Dorramon watch things that weren't really there. She remembered all too well what it felt like, not being able to trust any of her sensory input at all, never being sure what was actually real. "I don't think we should be alone until we fall asleep," she said suddenly. "It might not be safe. Someone should be here who knows what's real."

"I'll stay," Cardoth said, handing her the remaining goblet. "I'll be here until you're both completely asleep."

But she couldn't decide, as she drank the unnaturally sweet wine, watching his dark eyes glitter over the top of her goblet, whether that made her feel better or worse. She crawled into the bed, almost unbearably tired, consciously ignoring everything her senses told her. Dorramon seemed to glow, there beside her — as she settled in next to him he looked as though he had a halo. She took his hand in hers and squeezed it tight. The electricity was already beginning to fade, and even though she had expected it, it scared her.

The last thing she saw as her eyes drifted shut were Prince Cardoth's leathery black wings, unfolding from behind him and reaching toward the ceiling, reminding her of spiders. She wondered if they would still be there when she woke up.

If she woke up.

Acts of the Redeemer

Don't miss the exciting continuation of Alannys's story:

$\mathcal{L}$ake of $\mathcal{F}$ire

$\mathcal{A}$lannys and her friends have finally set out to perform the acts that will prove her--or ruin her--for all time. With Baronet Athniss hunting them, they arrive at last at Mount Mouseion. But they discover more among the ruins of the Spire of Glory than simple murder. The ancient monument conceals many secrets, some of which could change the world as they know it.

$\mathcal{U}$nanticipated consequences of the acts of the Redeemer throw Alannys and her dearest friends into mortal jeopardy. As they close in on the Lord's Retainers and those who seek to 'bring the power of the few to the many,' they discover an even bigger threat lurking in the shadows--a threat vast beyond imagining.

$\mathcal{J}$oin Alannys and her friends as they fight to save each other, Ravanmark...and the world.

www.ingramcontent.com/pod-product-compliance
Lightning Source LLC
Chambersburg PA
CBHW020820030726
47496CB00001B/20